DIVERGENT - INSURGENT

DIVERGENT - INSURGENT

VERONICA ROTH

SFBC
SCIENCE
FICTION

This is a work of fiction. All of the characters, organizations and events portrayed in this novel are either products of the author's imagination or are used fictitiously and are not to be construed as real. Any resemblance to actual events, locales, organizations, or persons, living or dead, is entirely coincidental.

DIVERGENT   Copyright © 2011 by Veronica Roth
   Publication History: Katherine Tegen Books hardcover, May 2011
INSURGENT   Copyright © 2012 by Veronica Roth
   Publication History: Katherine Tegen Books hardcover, May 2012

First Science Fiction Book Club Printing: February 2013

Selected by Rome Quezada, SFBC Senior Editor

Published by arrangement with
HarperCollins Publishers
10 East 53rd Street
New York, NY 10022

For more awesome omnibuses, visit the SFBC online at *sfbc.com*

ISBN # 978-1-62490-155-3

Printed in the United States of America.

DIVERGENT

To my mother,

who gave me the moment when Beatrice realizes how strong

her mother is and wonders how she missed it for so long

CHAPTER
ONE

THERE IS ONE mirror in my house. It is behind a sliding panel in the hallway upstairs. Our faction allows me to stand in front of it on the second day of every third month, the day my mother cuts my hair.

I sit on the stool and my mother stands behind me with the scissors, trimming. The strands fall on the floor in a dull, blond ring.

When she finishes, she pulls my hair away from my face and twists it into a knot. I note how calm she looks and how focused she is. She is well-practiced in the art of losing herself. I can't say the same of myself.

I sneak a look at my reflection when she isn't paying attention—not for the sake of vanity, but out of curiosity. A lot can happen to a person's appearance in three months. In my reflection, I see a narrow face, wide, round eyes, and a long, thin nose—I still look like a little girl, though sometime in the last few months I turned sixteen. The other factions celebrate birthdays, but we don't. It would be self-indulgent.

"There," she says when she pins the knot in place. Her eyes catch mine in the mirror. It is too late to look away, but instead of scolding me, she smiles at our reflection. I frown a little. Why doesn't she reprimand me for staring at myself?

"So today is the day," she says.

"Yes," I reply.

"Are you nervous?"

I stare into my own eyes for a moment. Today is the day of the aptitude test that will show me which of the five factions I belong in. And tomorrow, at the Choosing Ceremony, I will decide on a faction; I will decide the rest of my life; I will decide to stay with my family or abandon them.

"No," I say. "The tests don't have to change our choices."

"Right." She smiles. "Let's go eat breakfast."

"Thank you. For cutting my hair."

She kisses my cheek and slides the panel over the mirror. I think my mother could be beautiful, in a different world. Her body is thin beneath the gray robe. She has high cheekbones and long eyelashes, and when she lets her hair down at night, it hangs in waves over her shoulders. But she must hide that beauty in Abnegation.

We walk together to the kitchen. On these mornings when my brother makes breakfast, and my father's hand skims my hair as he reads the newspaper, and my mother hums as she clears the table—it is on these mornings that I feel guiltiest for wanting to leave them.

+ + +

The bus stinks of exhaust. Every time it hits a patch of uneven pavement, it jostles me from side to side, even though I'm gripping the seat to keep myself still.

My older brother, Caleb, stands in the aisle, holding a railing above his head to keep himself steady. We don't look alike. He has my father's dark hair and hooked nose and my mother's green eyes and dimpled cheeks. When he was younger, that collection of features looked strange, but now it suits him. If he wasn't Abnegation, I'm sure the girls at school would stare at him.

He also inherited my mother's talent for selflessness. He gave his seat to a surly Candor man on the bus without a second thought.

The Candor man wears a black suit with a white tie—Candor standard uniform. Their faction values honesty and sees the truth as black and white, so that is what they wear.

The gaps between the buildings narrow and the roads are smoother as we near the heart of the city. The building that was once called the Sears Tower—we call it the Hub—emerges from the fog, a black pillar in the skyline. The bus passes under the elevated tracks. I have never been on a train, though they never stop running and there are tracks everywhere. Only the Dauntless ride them.

Five years ago, volunteer construction workers from Abnegation repaved some of the roads. They started in the middle of the city and worked their way outward until they ran out of materials. The roads where I live are still cracked and patchy, and it's not safe to drive on them. We don't have a car anyway.

Caleb's expression is placid as the bus sways and jolts on the road. The gray robe falls from his arm as he clutches a pole for balance. I can tell by the constant shift of his eyes that he is watching the people around us—striving to see only them and to forget himself. Candor values honesty, but our faction, Abnegation, values selflessness.

The bus stops in front of the school and I get up, scooting past the Candor man. I grab Caleb's arm as I stumble over the man's shoes. My slacks are too long, and I've never been that graceful.

The Upper Levels building is the oldest of the three schools in the city: Lower Levels, Mid-Levels, and Upper Levels. Like all the other buildings around it, it is made of glass and steel. In front of it is a large metal sculpture that the Dauntless climb after school, daring each other to go higher and higher. Last year I watched one of them fall and break her leg. I was the one who ran to get the nurse.

"Aptitude tests today," I say. Caleb is not quite a year older than I am, so we are in the same year at school.

He nods as we pass through the front doors. My muscles tighten the second we walk in. The atmosphere feels hungry, like every sixteen-year-old is trying to devour as much as he can get of this last day. It is likely that we will not walk these halls again after the Choosing Ceremony—once we choose, our new factions will be responsible for finishing our education.

Our classes are cut in half today, so we will attend all of them before the aptitude tests, which take place after lunch. My heart rate is already elevated.

"You aren't at all worried about what they'll tell you?" I ask Caleb.

We pause at the split in the hallway where he will go one way, toward Advanced Math, and I will go the other, toward Faction History.

He raises an eyebrow at me. "Are you?"

I could tell him I've been worried for weeks about what the aptitude test will tell me—Abnegation, Candor, Erudite, Amity, or Dauntless?

Instead I smile and say, "Not really."

He smiles back. "Well . . . have a good day."

I walk toward Faction History, chewing on my lower lip. He never answered my question.

The hallways are cramped, though the light coming through the windows creates the illusion of space; they are one of the only places where the factions mix, at our age. Today the crowd has a new kind of energy, a last day mania.

A girl with long curly hair shouts "Hey!" next to my ear, waving at a distant friend. A jacket sleeve smacks me on the cheek. Then an Erudite boy in a blue sweater shoves me. I lose my balance and fall hard on the ground.

"Out of my way, Stiff," he snaps, and continues down the hallway.

My cheeks warm. I get up and dust myself off. A few people stopped when I fell, but none of them offered to help me. Their eyes follow me to the edge of the hallway. This sort of thing has been happening to others in my faction for months now—the Erudite have been releasing antagonistic reports about Abnegation, and it has begun to affect the way we relate at school. The gray clothes, the plain hairstyle, and the unassuming demeanor of my faction are supposed to make it easier for me to forget myself, and easier for everyone else to forget me too. But now they make me a target.

I pause by a window in the E Wing and wait for the Dauntless to arrive. I do this every morning. At exactly 7:25, the Dauntless prove their bravery by jumping from a moving train.

My father calls the Dauntless "hellions." They are pierced, tattooed, and black-clothed. Their primary purpose is to guard the fence that surrounds our city. From what, I don't know.

They should perplex me. I should wonder what courage—which is the virtue they most value—has to do with a metal ring through your nostril. Instead my eyes cling to them wherever they go.

The train whistle blares, the sound resonating in my chest. The light fixed to the front of the train clicks on and off as the train hurtles past the school, squealing on iron rails. And as the last few cars pass, a mass exodus of young men and women in dark clothing hurl themselves from the moving cars, some dropping and rolling, others stumbling a few steps before regaining their balance. One of the boys wraps his arm around a girl's shoulders, laughing.

Watching them is a foolish practice. I turn away from the window and press through the crowd to the Faction History classroom.

CHAPTER
TWO

THE TESTS BEGIN after lunch. We sit at the long tables in the cafeteria, and the test administrators call ten names at a time, one for each testing room. I sit next to Caleb and across from our neighbor Susan.

Susan's father travels throughout the city for his job, so he has a car and drives her to and from school every day. He offered to drive us, too, but as Caleb says, we prefer to leave later and would not want to inconvenience him.

Of course not.

The test administrators are mostly Abnegation volunteers, although there is an Erudite in one of the testing rooms and a Dauntless in another to test those of us from Abnegation, because the rules state that we can't be tested by someone from our own faction. The rules also say that we can't prepare for the test in any way, so I don't know what to expect.

My gaze drifts from Susan to the Dauntless tables across the room. They are laughing and shouting and playing cards. At another set of tables, the Erudite chatter over books and newspapers, in constant pursuit of knowledge.

A group of Amity girls in yellow and red sit in a circle on the cafeteria floor, playing some kind of hand-slapping game involving a rhyming song. Every few minutes I hear a chorus of laughter from them as someone is eliminated and has to sit in the center of the circle. At the table next to them, Candor boys make wide gestures with their hands. They appear to be arguing about something, but it must not be serious, because some of them are still smiling.

At the Abnegation table, we sit quietly and wait. Faction customs dictate even idle behavior and supersede individual preference. I doubt all the Erudite want to study all the time, or that every Candor enjoys a lively debate, but they can't defy the norms of their factions any more than I can.

Caleb's name is called in the next group. He moves confidently toward the exit. I don't need to wish him luck or assure him that he shouldn't be nervous. He knows where he belongs, and as far as I know, he always has. My earliest memory of him is from when we were four years old. He scolded me for not giving my jump rope to a little girl on the playground who didn't have anything to play with. He doesn't lecture me often anymore, but I have his look of disapproval memorized.

I have tried to explain to him that my instincts are not the same as his—it didn't even enter my mind to give my seat to the Candor man on the bus—but he doesn't understand. "Just do what you're supposed to," he always says. It is that easy for him. It should be that easy for me.

My stomach wrenches. I close my eyes and keep them closed until ten minutes later, when Caleb sits down again.

He is plaster-pale. He pushes his palms along his legs like I do when I wipe off sweat, and when he brings them back, his fingers shake. I open my mouth to ask him something, but the words don't come. I am not allowed to ask him about his results, and he is not allowed to tell me.

An Abnegation volunteer speaks the next round of names. Two from Dauntless, two from Erudite, two from Amity, two from Candor, and then: "From Abnegation: Susan Black and Beatrice Prior."

I get up because I'm supposed to, but if it were up to me, I would stay in my seat for the rest of time. I feel like there is a bubble in my chest that expands more by the second, threatening to break me apart from the inside. I follow Susan to the exit. The people I pass probably can't tell us apart. We wear the same clothes and we wear our blond hair the same way. The only difference is that Susan might not feel like she's going to throw up, and from what I can tell, her hands aren't shaking so hard she has to clutch the hem of her shirt to steady them.

Waiting for us outside the cafeteria is a row of ten rooms. They are used only for the aptitude tests, so I have never been in one before. Unlike the other rooms in the school, they are separated, not by glass, but by mirrors. I watch myself, pale and terrified, walking toward one of the doors. Susan grins nervously at me as she walks into room 5, and I walk into room 6, where a Dauntless woman waits for me.

She is not as severe-looking as the young Dauntless I have seen. She has small, dark, angular eyes and wears a black blazer—like a man's suit—and jeans. It is only when she turns to close the door that I see a tattoo on the back of her neck, a black-and-white hawk with a red eye. If I didn't feel like my heart had migrated to my throat, I would ask her what it signifies. It must signify something.

Mirrors cover the inner walls of the room. I can see my reflection from all angles: the gray fabric obscuring the shape of my back, my long neck, my knobby-knuckled hands, red with a blood blush. The ceiling glows white with light. In the center of the room is a reclined chair, like a dentist's, with a machine next to it. It looks like a place where terrible things happen.

"Don't worry," the woman says, "it doesn't hurt."

Her hair is black and straight, but in the light I see that it is streaked with gray.

"Have a seat and get comfortable," she says. "My name is Tori."

Clumsily I sit in the chair and recline, putting my head on the head-rest. The lights hurt my eyes. Tori busies herself with the machine on my right. I try to focus on her and not on the wires in her hands.

"Why the hawk?" I blurt out as she attaches an electrode to my fore-head.

"Never met a curious Abnegation before," she says, raising her eye-brows at me.

I shiver, and goose bumps appear on my arms. My curiosity is a mis-take, a betrayal of Abnegation values.

Humming a little, she presses another electrode to my forehead and explains, "In some parts of the ancient world, the hawk symbolized the sun. Back when I got this, I figured if I always had the sun on me, I wouldn't be afraid of the dark."

I try to stop myself from asking another question, but I can't help it. "You're afraid of the dark?"

"I *was* afraid of the dark," she corrects me. She presses the next elec-trode to her own forehead, and attaches a wire to it. She shrugs. "Now it reminds me of the fear I've overcome."

She stands behind me. I squeeze the armrests so tightly the redness pulls away from my knuckles. She tugs wires toward her, attaching them to me, to her, to the machine behind her. Then she passes me a vial of clear liquid.

"Drink this," she says.

"What is it?" My throat feels swollen. I swallow hard. "What's going to happen?"

"Can't tell you that. Just trust me."

I press air from my lungs and tip the contents of the vial into my mouth. My eyes close.

+ + +

When they open, an instant has passed, but I am somewhere else. I stand in the school cafeteria again, but all the long tables are empty, and I see through the glass walls that it's snowing. On the table in front of me are two baskets. In one is a hunk of cheese, and in the other, a knife the length of my forearm.

Behind me, a woman's voice says, "Choose."

"Why?" I ask.

"Choose," she repeats.

I look over my shoulder, but no one is there. I turn back to the baskets. "What will I do with them?"

"Choose!" she yells.

When she screams at me, my fear disappears and stubbornness replaces it. I scowl and cross my arms.

"Have it your way," she says.

The baskets disappear. I hear a door squeak and turn to see who it is. I see not a "who" but a "what": A dog with a pointed nose stands a few yards away from me. It crouches low and creeps toward me, its lips peeling back from its white teeth. A growl gurgles from deep in its throat, and I see why the cheese would have come in handy. Or the knife. But it's too late now.

I think about running, but the dog will be faster than me. I can't wrestle it to the ground. My head pounds. I have to make a decision. If I can jump over one of the tables and use it as a shield—no, I am too short to jump over the tables, and not strong enough to tip one over.

The dog snarls, and I can almost feel the sound vibrating in my skull.

My biology textbook said that dogs can smell fear because of a chemical secreted by human glands in a state of duress, the same chemical a dog's prey secretes. Smelling fear leads them to attack. The dog inches toward me, its nails scraping the floor.

I can't run. I can't fight. Instead I breathe in the smell of the dog's foul breath and try not to think about what it just ate. There are no whites in its eyes, just a black gleam.

What else do I know about dogs? I shouldn't look it in the eye. That's a sign of aggression. I remember asking my father for a pet dog when I was young, and now, staring at the ground in front of the dog's paws, I can't remember why. It comes closer, still growling. If staring into its eyes is a sign of aggression, what's a sign of submission?

My breaths are loud but steady. I sink to my knees. The last thing I want to do is lie down on the ground in front of the dog—making its teeth level with my face—but it's the best option I have. I stretch my legs out behind me and lean on my elbows. The dog creeps closer, and closer, until I feel its warm breath on my face. My arms are shaking.

It barks in my ear, and I clench my teeth to keep from screaming.

Something rough and wet touches my cheek. The dog's growling stops, and when I lift my head to look at it again, it is panting. It licked my face. I frown and sit on my heels. The dog props its paws up on my knees and licks my chin. I cringe, wiping the drool from my skin, and laugh.

"You're not such a vicious beast, huh?"

I get up slowly so I don't startle it, but it seems like a different animal than the one that faced me a few seconds ago. I stretch out a hand, carefully, so I can draw it back if I need to. The dog nudges my hand with its head. I am suddenly glad I didn't pick up the knife.

I blink, and when my eyes open, a child stands across the room wearing a white dress. She stretches out both hands and squeals, "Puppy!"

As she runs toward the dog at my side, I open my mouth to warn her, but I am too late. The dog turns. Instead of growling, it barks and snarls and snaps, and its muscles bunch up like coiled wire. About to pounce. I don't think, I just jump; I hurl my body on top of the dog, wrapping my arms around its thick neck.

My head hits the ground. The dog is gone, and so is the little girl. Instead I am alone—in the testing room, now empty. I turn in a slow circle and can't see myself in any of the mirrors. I push the door open and walk into the hallway, but it isn't a hallway; it's a bus, and all the seats are taken.

I stand in the aisle and hold on to a pole. Sitting near me is a man with a newspaper. I can't see his face over the top of the paper, but I can see his hands. They are scarred, like he was burned, and they clench around the paper like he wants to crumple it.

"Do you know this guy?" he asks. He taps the picture on the front page of the newspaper. The headline reads: "Brutal Murderer Finally Apprehended!" I stare at the word "murderer." It has been a long time since I last read that word, but even its shape fills me with dread.

In the picture beneath the headline is a young man with a plain face and a beard. I feel like I do know him, though I don't remember how. And at the same time, I feel like it would be a bad idea to tell the man that.

"Well?" I hear anger in his voice. "Do you?"

A bad idea—no, a very bad idea. My heart pounds and I clutch the pole to keep my hands from shaking, from giving me away. If I tell him I know the man from the article, something awful will happen to me. But I can convince him that I don't. I can clear my throat and shrug my shoulders—but that would be a lie.

I clear my throat.

"Do you?" he repeats.

I shrug my shoulders.

"Well?"

A shudder goes through me. My fear is irrational; this is just a test, it isn't real. "Nope," I say, my voice casual. "No idea who he is."

He stands, and finally I see his face. He wears dark sunglasses and his mouth is bent into a snarl. His cheek is rippled with scars, like his hands. He leans close to my face. His breath smells like cigarettes. *Not real*, I remind myself. *Not real.*

"You're lying," he says. "You're *lying!*"

"I am not."

"I can see it in your eyes."

I pull myself up straighter. "You can't."

"If you know him," he says in a low voice, "you could save me. You could *save* me!"

I narrow my eyes. "Well," I say. I set my jaw. "I don't."

CHAPTER THREE

I WAKE TO sweaty palms and a pang of guilt in my chest. I am lying in the chair in the mirrored room. When I tilt my head back, I see Tori behind me. She pinches her lips together and removes electrodes from our heads. I wait for her to say something about the test—that it's over, or that I did well, although how could I do poorly on a test like this?—but she says nothing, just pulls the wires from my forehead.

I sit forward and wipe my palms off on my slacks. I had to have done something wrong, even if it only happened in my mind. Is that strange look on Tori's face because she doesn't know how to tell me what a terrible person I am? I wish she would just come out with it.

"That," she says, "was perplexing. Excuse me, I'll be right back."

Perplexing?

I bring my knees to my chest and bury my face in them. I wish I felt like crying, because the tears might bring me a sense of release, but I don't. How can you fail a test you aren't allowed to prepare for?

As the moments pass, I get more nervous. I have to wipe off my hands every few seconds as the sweat collects—or maybe I just do it because it helps me feel calmer. What if they tell me that I'm not cut out for any faction? I would have to live on the streets, with the factionless. I can't do that. To live factionless is not just to live in poverty and discomfort; it is to live divorced from society, separated from the most important thing in life: community.

My mother told me once that we can't survive alone, but even if we could, we wouldn't want to. Without a faction, we have no purpose and no reason to live.

I shake my head. I can't think like this. I have to stay calm.

Finally the door opens, and Tori walks back in. I grip the arms of the chair.

"Sorry to worry you," Tori says. She stands by my feet with her hands in her pockets. She looks tense and pale.

"Beatrice, your results were inconclusive," she says. "Typically, each stage of the simulation eliminates one or more of the factions, but in your case, only two have been ruled out."

I stare at her. "Two?" I ask. My throat is so tight it's hard to talk.

"If you had shown an automatic distaste for the knife and selected the cheese, the simulation would have led you to a different scenario that confirmed your aptitude for Amity. That didn't happen, which is why Amity is out." Tori scratches the back of her neck. "Normally, the simulation progresses in a linear fashion, isolating one faction by ruling out the rest. The choices you made didn't even allow Candor, the next possibility, to be ruled out, so I had to alter the simulation to put you on the bus. And there your insistence upon dishonesty ruled out Candor." She half smiles. "Don't worry about that. Only the Candor tell the truth in that one."

One of the knots in my chest loosens. Maybe I'm not an awful person.

"I suppose that's not entirely true. People who tell the truth are the Candor . . . and the Abnegation," she says. "Which gives us a problem."

My mouth falls open.

"On the one hand, you threw yourself on the dog rather than let it attack the little girl, which is an Abnegation-oriented response . . . but on the other, when the man told you that the truth would save him, you still refused to tell it. Not an Abnegation-oriented response." She sighs. "Not running from the dog suggests Dauntless, but so does taking the knife, which you didn't do."

She clears her throat and continues. "Your intelligent response to the dog indicates strong alignment with the Erudite. I have no idea what to make of your indecision in stage one, but—"

"Wait," I interrupt her. "So you have no idea what my aptitude is?"

"Yes and no. My conclusion," she explains, "is that you display equal aptitude for Abnegation, Dauntless, and Erudite. People who get this kind of result are . . ." She looks over her shoulder like she expects someone to appear behind her. ". . . are called . . . *Divergent.*" She says the last word so quietly that I almost don't hear it, and her tense, worried look returns. She walks around the side of the chair and leans in close to me.

"Beatrice," she says, "under no circumstances should you share that information with anyone. This is very important."

"We aren't supposed to share our results." I nod. "I know that."

"No." Tori kneels next to the chair now and places her arms on the armrest. Our faces are inches apart. "This is different. I don't mean you shouldn't share them now; I mean you should never share them with anyone, *ever*, no matter what happens. Divergence is extremely dangerous. You understand?"

I don't understand—how could inconclusive test results be dangerous?—but I still nod. I don't want to share my test results with anyone anyway.

"Okay." I peel my hands from the arms of the chair and stand. I feel unsteady.

"I suggest," Tori says, "that you go home. You have a lot of thinking to do, and waiting with the others may not benefit you."

"I have to tell my brother where I'm going."

"I'll let him know."

I touch my forehead and stare at the floor as I walk out of the room. I can't bear to look her in the eye. I can't bear to think about the Choosing Ceremony tomorrow.

It's my choice now, no matter what the test says.

Abnegation. Dauntless. Erudite.

Divergent.

+ + +

I decide not to take the bus. If I get home early, my father will notice when he checks the house log at the end of the day, and I'll have to explain what happened. Instead I walk. I'll have to intercept Caleb before he mentions anything to our parents, but Caleb can keep a secret.

I walk in the middle of the road. The buses tend to hug the curb, so it's safer here. Sometimes, on the streets near my house, I can see places where the yellow lines used to be. We have no use for them now that there are so few cars. We don't need stoplights, either, but in some places they dangle precariously over the road like they might crash down any minute.

Renovation moves slowly through the city, which is a patchwork of new, clean buildings and old, crumbling ones. Most of the new buildings are next to the marsh, which used to be a lake a long time ago. The Abnegation volunteer agency my mother works for is responsible for most of those renovations.

When I look at the Abnegation lifestyle as an outsider, I think it's beautiful. When I watch my family move in harmony; when we go to dinner parties and everyone cleans together afterward without having to be asked; when I see Caleb help strangers carry their groceries, I fall in love with this life all over again. It's only when I try to live it myself that I have trouble. It never feels genuine.

But choosing a different faction means I forsake my family. Permanently.

Just past the Abnegation sector of the city is the stretch of building skeletons and broken sidewalks that I now walk through. There are places where the road has completely collapsed, revealing sewer systems and empty subways that I have to be careful to avoid, and places that stink so powerfully of sewage and trash that I have to plug my nose.

This is where the factionless live. Because they failed to complete initiation into whatever faction they chose, they live in poverty, doing the work no one else wants to do. They are janitors and construction workers and garbage collectors; they make fabric and operate trains and drive buses. In return for their work they get food and clothing, but, as my mother says, not enough of either.

I see a factionless man standing on the corner up ahead. He wears ragged brown clothing and skin sags from his jaw. He stares at me, and I stare back at him, unable to look away.

"Excuse me," he says. His voice is raspy. "Do you have something I can eat?"

I feel a lump in my throat. A stern voice in my head says, *Duck your head and keep walking.*

No. I shake my head. I should not be afraid of this man. He needs help and I am supposed to help him.

"Um . . . yes," I say. I reach into my bag. My father tells me to keep food in my bag at all times for exactly this reason. I offer the man a small bag of dried apple slices.

He reaches for them, but instead of taking the bag, his hand closes around my wrist. He smiles at me. He has a gap between his front teeth.

"My, don't you have pretty eyes," he says. "It's a shame the rest of you is so plain."

My heart pounds. I tug my hand back, but his grip tightens. I smell something acrid and unpleasant on his breath.

"You look a little young to be walking around by yourself, dear," he says.

I stop tugging, and stand up straighter. I know I look young; I don't need to be reminded. "I'm older than I look," I retort. "I'm sixteen."

His lips spread wide, revealing a gray molar with a dark pit in the side. I can't tell if he's smiling or grimacing. "Then isn't today a special day for you? The day before you *choose*?"

"Let go of me," I say. I hear ringing in my ears. My voice sounds clear and stern—not what I expected to hear. I feel like it doesn't belong to me.

I am ready. I know what to do. I picture myself bringing my elbow back and hitting him. I see the bag of apples flying away from me. I hear my running footsteps. I am prepared to act.

But then he releases my wrist, takes the apples, and says, "Choose wisely, little girl."

CHAPTER FOUR

I REACH MY street five minutes before I usually do, according to my watch—which is the only adornment Abnegation allows, and only because it's practical. It has a gray band and a glass face. If I tilt it right, I can almost see my reflection over the hands.

The houses on my street are all the same size and shape. They are made of gray cement, with few windows, in economical, no-nonsense rectangles. Their lawns are crabgrass and their mailboxes are dull metal. To some the sight might be gloomy, but to me their simplicity is comforting.

The reason for the simplicity isn't disdain for uniqueness, as the other factions have sometimes interpreted it. Everything—our houses, our clothes, our hairstyles—is meant to help us forget ourselves and to protect us from vanity, greed, and envy, which are just forms of selfishness. If we have little, and want for little, and we are all equal, we envy no one.

I try to love it.

I sit on the front step and wait for Caleb to arrive. It doesn't take long. After a minute I see gray-robed forms walking down the street. I hear laughter. At school we try not to draw attention to ourselves, but once we're home, the games and jokes start. My natural tendency toward sarcasm is still not appreciated. Sarcasm is always at someone's expense. Maybe it's better that Abnegation wants me to suppress it. Maybe I don't have to leave my family. Maybe if I fight to make Abnegation work, my act will turn into reality.

"Beatrice!" Caleb says. "What happened? Are you all right?"

"I'm fine." He is with Susan and her brother, Robert, and Susan is giving me a strange look, like I am a different person than the one she knew this morning. I shrug. "When the test was over, I got sick. Must have been that liquid they gave us. I feel better now, though."

I try to smile convincingly. I seem to have persuaded Susan and Robert, who no longer look concerned for my mental stability, but Caleb narrows his eyes at me, the way he does when he suspects someone of duplicity.

"Did you two take the bus today?" I ask. I don't care how Susan and Robert got home from school, but I need to change the subject.

"Our father had to work late," Susan says, "and he told us we should spend some time thinking before the ceremony tomorrow."

My heart pounds at the mention of the ceremony.

"You're welcome to come over later, if you'd like," Caleb says politely.

"Thank you." Susan smiles at Caleb.

Robert raises an eyebrow at me. He and I have been exchanging looks for the past year as Susan and Caleb flirt in the tentative way known only to the Abnegation. Caleb's eyes follow Susan down the walk. I have to grab his arm to startle him from his daze. I lead him into the house and close the door behind us.

He turns to me. His dark, straight eyebrows draw together so that a crease appears between them. When he frowns, he looks more like my mother than my father. In an instant I can see him living the same kind of life my father did: staying in Abnegation, learning a trade, marrying Susan, and having a family. It will be wonderful.

I may not see it.

"Are you going to tell me the truth now?" he asks softly.

"The truth is," I say, "I'm not supposed to discuss it. And you're not supposed to ask."

"All those rules you bend, and you can't bend this one? Not even for something this important?" His eyebrows tug together, and he bites the corner of his lip. Though his words are accusatory, it sounds like he is probing me for information—like he actually wants my answer.

I narrow my eyes. "Will you? What happened in *your* test, Caleb?"

Our eyes meet. I hear a train horn, so faint it could easily be wind whistling through an alleyway. But I know it when I hear it. It sounds like the Dauntless, calling me to them.

"Just . . . don't tell our parents what happened, okay?" I say.

His eyes stay on mine for a few seconds, and then he nods.

I want to go upstairs and lie down. The test, the walk, and my encounter with the factionless man exhausted me. But my brother made breakfast this morning, and my mother prepared our lunches, and my father made dinner last night, so it's my turn to cook. I breathe deeply and walk into the kitchen to start cooking.

A minute later, Caleb joins me. I grit my teeth. He helps with everything. What irritates me most about him is his natural goodness, his
inborn selflessness.

Caleb and I work together without speaking. I cook peas on the stove.
He defrosts four pieces of chicken. Most of what we eat is frozen or
canned, because farms these days are far away. My mother told me once
that, a long time ago, there were people who wouldn't buy genetically en-
gineered produce because they viewed it as unnatural. Now we have no
other option.

By the time my parents get home, dinner is ready and the table is set.
My father drops his bag at the door and kisses my head. Other people see
him as an opinionated man—too opinionated, maybe—but he's also loving. I try to see only the good in him; I try.

"How did the test go?" he asks me. I pour the peas into a serving bowl.

"Fine," I say. I couldn't be Candor. I lie too easily.

"I heard there was some kind of upset with one of the tests," my
mother says. Like my father, she works for the government, but she man-
ages city improvement projects. She recruited volunteers to administer
the aptitude tests. Most of the time, though, she organizes workers to
help the factionless with food and shelter and job opportunities.

"Really?" says my father. A problem with the aptitude tests is rare.

"I don't know much about it, but my friend Erin told me that something went wrong with one of the tests, so the results had to be reported
verbally." My mother places a napkin next to each plate on the table. "Apparently the student got sick and was sent home early." My mother shrugs.
"I hope they're all right. Did you two hear about that?"

"No," Caleb says. He smiles at my mother.

My brother couldn't be Candor either.

We sit at the table. We always pass food to the right, and no one eats
until everyone is served. My father extends his hands to my mother and
my brother, and they extend their hands to him and me, and my father
gives thanks to God for food and work and friends and family. Not every
Abnegation family is religious, but my father says we should try not to
see those differences because they will only divide us. I am not sure what
to make of that.

"So," my mother says to my father. "Tell me."

She takes my father's hand and moves her thumb in a small circle
over his knuckles. I stare at their joined hands. My parents love each
other, but they rarely show affection like this in front of us. They taught
us that physical contact is powerful, so I have been wary of it since I was
young.

"Tell me what's bothering you," she adds.

I stare at my plate. My mother's acute senses sometimes surprise me, but now they chide me. Why was I so focused on myself that I didn't notice his deep frown and his sagging posture?

"I had a difficult day at work," he says. "Well, really, it was Marcus who had the difficult day. I shouldn't lay claim to it."

Marcus is my father's coworker; they are both political leaders. The city is ruled by a council of fifty people, composed entirely of representatives from Abnegation, because our faction is regarded as incorruptible, due to our commitment to selflessness. Our leaders are selected by their peers for their impeccable character, moral fortitude, and leadership skills. Representatives from each of the other factions can speak in the meetings on behalf of a particular issue, but ultimately, the decision is the council's. And while the council technically makes decisions together, Marcus is particularly influential.

It has been this way since the beginning of the great peace, when the factions were formed. I think the system persists because we're afraid of what might happen if it didn't: war.

"Is this about that report Jeanine Matthews released?" my mother says. Jeanine Matthews is Erudite's sole representative, selected based on her IQ score. My father complains about her often.

I look up. "A report?"

Caleb gives me a warning look. We aren't supposed to speak at the dinner table unless our parents ask us a direct question, and they usually don't. Our listening ears are a gift to them, my father says. They give us their listening ears after dinner, in the family room.

"Yes," my father says. His eyes narrow. "Those arrogant, self-righteous—" He stops and clears his throat. "Sorry. But she released a report attacking Marcus's character."

I raise my eyebrows.

"What did it say?" I ask.

"Beatrice," Caleb says quietly.

I duck my head, turning my fork over and over and over until the warmth leaves my cheeks. I don't like to be chastised. Especially by my brother.

"It said," my father says, "that Marcus's violence and cruelty toward his son is the reason his son chose Dauntless instead of Abnegation."

Few people who are born into Abnegation choose to leave it. When they do, we remember. Two years ago, Marcus's son, Tobias, left us for the Dauntless, and Marcus was devastated. Tobias was his only child—and his only family, since his wife died giving birth to their second child. The infant died minutes later.

I never met Tobias. He rarely attended community events and never joined his father at our house for dinner. My father often remarked that it was strange, but now it doesn't matter.

"Cruel? Marcus?" My mother shakes her head. "That poor man. As if he needs to be reminded of his loss."

"Of his son's betrayal, you mean?" my father says coldly. "I shouldn't be surprised at this point. The Erudite have been attacking us with these reports for months. And this isn't the end. There will be more, I guarantee it."

I shouldn't speak again, but I can't help myself. I blurt out, "Why are they doing this?"

"Why don't you take this opportunity to listen to your father, Beatrice?" my mother says gently. It is phrased like a suggestion, not a command. I look across the table at Caleb, who has that look of disapproval in his eyes.

I stare at my peas. I am not sure I can live this life of obligation any longer. I am not good enough.

"You know why," my father says. "Because we have something they want. Valuing knowledge above all else results in a lust for power, and that leads men into dark and empty places. We should be thankful that we know better."

I nod. I know I will not choose Erudite, even though my test results suggested that I could. I am my father's daughter.

My parents clean up after dinner. They don't even let Caleb help them, because we're supposed to keep to ourselves tonight instead of gathering in the family room, so we can think about our results.

My family might be able to help me choose, if I could talk about my results. But I can't. Tori's warning whispers in my memory every time my resolve to keep my mouth shut falters.

Caleb and I climb the stairs and, at the top, when we divide to go to our separate bedrooms, he stops me with a hand on my shoulder.

"Beatrice," he says, looking sternly into my eyes. "We should think of our family." There is an edge to his voice. "But. But we must also think of ourselves."

For a moment I stare at him. I have never seen him think of himself, never heard him insist on anything but selflessness.

I am so startled by his comment that I just say what I am supposed to say: "The tests don't have to change our choices."

He smiles a little. "Don't they, though?"

He squeezes my shoulder and walks into his bedroom. I peer into his room and see an unmade bed and a stack of books on his desk. He closes the door. I wish I could tell him that we're going through the same thing. I wish I could speak to him like I want to instead of like I'm supposed to.

But the idea of admitting that I need help is too much to bear, so I turn away.

I walk into my room, and when I close my door behind me, I realize that the decision might be simple. It will require a great act of selflessness to choose Abnegation, or a great act of courage to choose Dauntless, and maybe just choosing one over the other will prove that I belong. Tomorrow, those two qualities will struggle within me, and only one can win.

CHAPTER FIVE

THE BUS WE take to get to the Choosing Ceremony is full of people in gray shirts and gray slacks. A pale ring of sunlight burns into the clouds like the end of a lit cigarette. I will never smoke one myself—they are closely tied to vanity—but a crowd of Candor smokes them in front of the building when we get off the bus.

I have to tilt my head back to see the top of the Hub, and even then, part of it disappears into the clouds. It is the tallest building in the city. I can see the lights on the two prongs on its roof from my bedroom window.

I follow my parents off the bus. Caleb seems calm, but so would I, if I knew what I was going to do. Instead I get the distinct impression that my heart will burst out of my chest any minute now, and I grab his arm to steady myself as I walk up the front steps.

The elevator is crowded, so my father volunteers to give a cluster of Amity our place. We climb the stairs instead, following him unquestioningly. We set an example for our fellow faction members, and soon the three of us are engulfed in the mass of gray fabric ascending cement stairs in the half light. I settle into their pace. The uniform pounding of feet in my ears and the homogeneity of the people around me makes me believe that I could choose this. I could be subsumed into Abnegation's hive mind, projecting always outward.

But then my legs get sore, and I struggle to breathe, and I am again distracted by myself. We have to climb twenty flights of stairs to get to the Choosing Ceremony.

My father holds the door open on the twentieth floor and stands like a sentry as every Abnegation walks past him. I would wait for him, but the crowd presses me forward, out of the stairwell and into the room where I will decide the rest of my life.

The room is arranged in concentric circles. On the edges stand the sixteen-year-olds of every faction. We are not called members yet; our decisions today will make us initiates, and we will become members if we complete initiation.

We arrange ourselves in alphabetical order, according to the last names we may leave behind today. I stand between Caleb and Danielle Pohler, an Amity girl with rosy cheeks and a yellow dress.

Rows of chairs for our families make up the next circle. They are arranged in five sections, according to faction. Not everyone in each faction comes to the Choosing Ceremony, but enough of them come that the crowd looks huge.

The responsibility to conduct the ceremony rotates from faction to faction each year, and this year is Abnegation's. Marcus will give the opening address and read the names in reverse alphabetical order. Caleb will choose before me.

In the last circle are five metal bowls so large they could hold my entire body, if I curled up. Each one contains a substance that represents each faction: gray stones for Abnegation, water for Erudite, earth for Amity, lit coals for Dauntless, and glass for Candor.

When Marcus calls my name, I will walk to the center of the three circles. I will not speak. He will offer me a knife. I will cut into my hand and sprinkle my blood into the bowl of the faction I choose.

My blood on the stones. My blood sizzling on the coals.

Before my parents sit down, they stand in front of Caleb and me. My father kisses my forehead and claps Caleb on the shoulder, grinning.

"See you soon," he says. Without a trace of doubt.

My mother hugs me, and what little resolve I have left almost breaks. I clench my jaw and stare up at the ceiling, where globe lanterns hang and fill the room with blue light. She holds me for what feels like a long time, even after I let my hands fall. Before she pulls away, she turns her head and whispers in my ear, "I love you. No matter what."

I frown at her back as she walks away. She knows what I might do. She must know, or she wouldn't feel the need to say that.

Caleb grabs my hand, squeezing my palm so tightly it hurts, but I don't let go. The last time we held hands was at my uncle's funeral, as my father cried. We need each other's strength now, just as we did then.

The room slowly comes to order. I should be observing the Dauntless; I should be taking in as much information as I can, but I can only stare at the lanterns across the room. I try to lose myself in the blue glow.

Marcus stands at the podium between the Erudite and the Dauntless and clears his throat into the microphone. "Welcome," he says. "Welcome to the Choosing Ceremony. Welcome to the day we honor the democratic philosophy of our ancestors, which tells us that every man has the right to choose his own way in this world."

Or, it occurs to me, one of five predetermined ways. I squeeze Caleb's fingers as hard as he is squeezing mine.

"Our dependents are now sixteen. They stand on the precipice of adulthood, and it is now up to them to decide what kind of people they will be." Marcus's voice is solemn and gives equal weight to each word. "Decades ago our ancestors realized that it is not political ideology, religious belief, race, or nationalism that is to blame for a warring world. Rather, they determined that it was the fault of human personality—of humankind's inclination toward evil, in whatever form that is. They divided into factions that sought to eradicate those qualities they believed responsible for the world's disarray."

My eyes shift to the bowls in the center of the room. What do I believe? I do not know; I do not know; I do not know.

"Those who blamed aggression formed Amity."

The Amity exchange smiles. They are dressed comfortably, in red or yellow. Every time I see them, they seem kind, loving, free. But joining them has never been an option for me.

"Those who blamed ignorance became the Erudite."

Ruling out Erudite was the only part of my choice that was easy.

"Those who blamed duplicity created Candor."

I have never liked Candor.

"Those who blamed selfishness made Abnegation."

I blame selfishness; I do.

"And those who blamed cowardice were the Dauntless."

But I am not selfless enough. Sixteen years of trying and I am not enough.

My legs go numb, like all the life has gone out of them, and I wonder how I will walk when my name is called.

"Working together, these five factions have lived in peace for many years, each contributing to a different sector of society. Abnegation has fulfilled our need for selfless leaders in government; Candor has provided us with trustworthy and sound leaders in law; Erudite has supplied us with intelligent teachers and researchers; Amity has given us understanding counselors and caretakers; and Dauntless provides us with protection from threats both within and without. But the reach of each faction is not limited to these areas. We give one another far more than can be adequately summarized. In our factions, we find meaning, we find purpose, we find life."

I think of the motto I read in my Faction History textbook: *Faction before blood.* More than family, our factions are where we belong. Can that possibly be right?

Marcus adds, "Apart from them, we would not survive."

The silence that follows his words is heavier than other silences. It is heavy with our worst fear, greater even than the fear of death: to be factionless.

Marcus continues, "Therefore this day marks a happy occasion—the day on which we receive our new initiates, who will work with us toward a better society and a better world."

A round of applause. It sounds muffled. I try to stand completely still, because if my knees are locked and my body is stiff, I don't shake. Marcus reads the first names, but I can't tell one syllable from the other. How will I know when he calls my name?

One by one, each sixteen-year-old steps out of line and walks to the middle of the room. The first girl to choose decides on Amity, the same faction from which she came. I watch her blood droplets fall on soil, and she stands behind their seats alone.

The room is constantly moving, a new name and a new person choosing, a new knife and a new choice. I recognize most of them, but I doubt they know me.

"James Tucker," Marcus says.

James Tucker of the Dauntless is the first person to stumble on his way to the bowls. He throws his arms out and regains his balance before hitting the floor. His face turns red and he walks fast to the middle of the room. When he stands in the center, he looks from the Dauntless bowl to the Candor bowl—the orange flames that rise higher each moment, and the glass reflecting blue light.

Marcus offers him the knife. He breathes deeply—I watch his chest rise—and, as he exhales, accepts the knife. Then he drags it across his palm with a jerk and holds his arm out to the side. His blood falls onto glass, and he is the first of us to switch factions. The first faction transfer. A mutter rises from the Dauntless section, and I stare at the floor.

They will see him as a traitor from now on. His Dauntless family will have the option of visiting him in his new faction, a week and a half from now on Visiting Day, but they won't, because he left them. His absence will haunt their hallways, and he will be a space they can't fill. And then time will pass, and the hole will be gone, like when an organ is removed and the body's fluids flow into the space it leaves. Humans can't tolerate emptiness for long.

"Caleb Prior," says Marcus.

Caleb squeezes my hand one last time, and as he walks away, casts a long look at me over his shoulder. I watch his feet move to the center of the room, and his hands, steady as they accept the knife from Marcus, are deft as one presses the knife into the other. Then he stands with blood pooling in his palm, and his lip snags on his teeth.

He breathes out. And then in. And then he holds his hand over the Erudite bowl, and his blood drips into the water, turning it a deeper shade of red.

I hear mutters that lift into outraged cries. I can barely think straight. My brother, my selfless brother, a faction transfer? My brother, born for Abnegation, *Erudite*?

When I close my eyes, I see the stack of books on Caleb's desk, and his shaking hands sliding along his legs after the aptitude test. Why didn't I realize that when he told me to think of myself yesterday, he was also giving that advice to himself?

I scan the crowd of the Erudite—they wear smug smiles and nudge each other. The Abnegation, normally so placid, speak to one another in tense whispers and glare across the room at the faction that has become our enemy.

"Excuse me," says Marcus, but the crowd doesn't hear him. He shouts, "Quiet, please!"

The room goes silent. Except for a ringing sound.

I hear my name and a shudder propels me forward. Halfway to the bowls, I am sure that I will choose Abnegation. I can see it now. I watch myself grow into a woman in Abnegation robes, marrying Susan's brother, Robert, volunteering on the weekends, the peace of routine, the quiet nights spent in front of the fireplace, the certainty that I will be safe, and if not good enough, better than I am now.

The ringing, I realize, is in my ears.

I look at Caleb, who now stands behind the Erudite. He stares back at me and nods a little, like he knows what I'm thinking, and agrees. My footsteps falter. If Caleb wasn't fit for Abnegation, how can I be? But what choice do I have, now that he left us and I'm the only one who remains? He left me no other option.

I set my jaw. I will be the child that stays; I have to do this for my parents. I have to.

Marcus offers me my knife. I look into his eyes—they are dark blue, a strange color—and take it. He nods, and I turn toward the bowls. Dauntless fire and Abnegation stones are both on my left, one in front of my shoulder and one behind. I hold the knife in my right hand and touch the blade to my palm. Gritting my teeth, I drag the blade down. It stings, but I barely notice. I hold both hands to my chest, and my next breath shudders on the way out.

I open my eyes and thrust my arm out. My blood drips onto the carpet between the two bowls. Then, with a gasp I can't contain, I shift my hand forward, and my blood sizzles on the coals.

I am selfish. I am brave.

CHAPTER
SIX

I TRAIN MY eyes on the floor and stand behind the Dauntless-born initiates who chose to return to their own faction. They are all taller than I
am, so even when I lift my head, I see only black-clothed shoulders.
When the last girl makes her choice—Amity—it's time to leave. The
Dauntless exit first. I walk past the gray-clothed men and women who
were my faction, staring determinedly at the back of someone's head.

But I have to see my parents one more time. I look over my shoulder
at the last second before I pass them, and immediately wish I hadn't. My
father's eyes burn into mine with a look of accusation. At first, when I feel
the heat behind my eyes, I think he's found a way to set me on fire, to
punish me for what I've done, but no—I'm about to cry.

Beside him, my mother is smiling.

The people behind me press me forward, away from my family, who
will be the last ones to leave. They may even stay to stack the chairs and
clean the bowls. I twist my head around to find Caleb in the crowd of Erudite behind me. He stands among the other initiates, shaking hands
with a faction transfer, a boy who was Candor. The easy smile he wears is
an act of betrayal. My stomach wrenches and I turn away. If it's so easy for
him, maybe it should be easy for me, too.

I glance at the boy to my left, who was Erudite and now looks as pale
and nervous as I should feel. I spent all my time worrying about which
faction I would choose and never considered what would happen if I
chose Dauntless. What waits for me at Dauntless headquarters?

The crowd of Dauntless leading us go to the stairs instead of the elevators. I thought only the Abnegation used the stairs.

Then everyone starts running. I hear whoops and shouts and laughter all around me, and dozens of thundering feet moving at different

rhythms. It is not a selfless act for the Dauntless to take the stairs; it is a wild act.

"What the hell is going on?" the boy next to me shouts.

I just shake my head and keep running. I am breathless when we reach the first floor, and the Dauntless burst through the exit. Outside, the air is crisp and cold and the sky is orange from the setting sun. It reflects off the black glass of the Hub.

The Dauntless sprawl across the street, blocking the path of a bus, and I sprint to catch up to the back of the crowd. My confusion dissipates as I run. I have not run anywhere in a long time. Abnegation discourages anything done strictly for my own enjoyment, and that is what this is: my lungs burning, my muscles aching, the fierce pleasure of a flat-out sprint. I follow the Dauntless down the street and around the corner and hear a familiar sound: the train horn.

"Oh no," mumbles the Erudite boy. "Are we supposed to hop on that thing?"

"Yes," I say, breathless.

It is good that I spent so much time watching the Dauntless arrive at school. The crowd spreads out in a long line. The train glides toward us on steel rails, its light flashing, its horn blaring. The door of each car is open, waiting for the Dauntless to pile in, and they do, group by group, until only the new initiates are left. The Dauntless-born initiates are used to doing this by now, so in a second it's just faction transfers left.

I step forward with a few others and start jogging. We run with the car for a few steps and then throw ourselves sideways. I'm not as tall or as strong as some of them, so I can't pull myself into the car. I cling to a handle next to the doorway, my shoulder slamming into the car. My arms shake, and finally a Candor girl grabs me and pulls me in. Gasping, I thank her.

I hear a shout and look over my shoulder. A short Erudite boy with red hair pumps his arms as he tries to catch up to the train. An Erudite girl by the door reaches out to grab the boy's hand, straining, but he is too far behind. He falls to his knees next to the tracks as we sail away, and puts his head in his hands.

I feel uneasy. He just failed Dauntless initiation. He is factionless now. It could happen at any moment.

"You all right?" the Candor girl who helped me asks briskly. She is tall, with dark brown skin and short hair. Pretty.

I nod.

"I'm Christina," she says, offering me her hand.

I haven't shaken a hand in a long time either. The Abnegation greeted one another by bowing heads, a sign of respect. I take her hand, uncertainly, and shake it twice, hoping I didn't squeeze too hard or not hard enough.

"Beatrice," I say.

"Do you know where we're going?" She has to shout over the wind, which blows harder through the open doors by the second. The train is picking up speed. I sit down. It will be easier to keep my balance if I'm low to the ground. She raises an eyebrow at me.

"A fast train means wind," I say. "Wind means falling out. Get down."

Christina sits next to me, inching back to lean against the wall.

"I guess we're going to Dauntless headquarters," I say, "but I don't know where that is."

"Does anyone?" She shakes her head, grinning. "It's like they just popped out of a hole in the ground or something."

Then the wind rushes through the car, and the other faction transfers, hit with bursts of air, fall on top of one another. I watch Christina laugh without hearing her and manage a smile.

Over my left shoulder, orange light from the setting sun reflects off the glass buildings, and I can faintly see the rows of gray houses that used to be my home.

It's Caleb's turn to make dinner tonight. Who will take his place—my mother or my father? And when they clear out his room, what will they discover? I imagine books jammed between the dresser and the wall, books under his mattress. The Erudite thirst for knowledge filling all the hidden places in his room. Did he always know that he would choose Erudite? And if he did, how did I not notice?

What a good actor he was. The thought makes me sick to my stomach, because even though I left them too, at least I was no good at pretending. At least they all knew that I wasn't selfless.

I close my eyes and picture my mother and father sitting at the dinner table in silence. Is it a lingering hint of selflessness that makes my throat tighten at the thought of them, or is it selfishness, because I know I will never be their daughter again?

+ + +

"They're jumping off!"

I lift my head. My neck aches. I have been curled up with my back against the wall for at least a half hour, listening to the roaring wind and watching the city smear past us. I sit forward. The train has slowed down in the past few minutes, and I see that the boy who shouted is right: The Dauntless in the cars ahead of us are jumping out as the train passes a rooftop. The tracks are seven stories up.

The idea of leaping out of a moving train onto a rooftop, knowing there is a gap between the edge of the roof and the edge of the track, makes me want to throw up. I push myself up and stumble to the opposite side of the car, where the other faction transfers stand in a line.

"We have to jump off too, then," a Candor girl says. She has a large nose and crooked teeth.

"Great," a Candor boy replies, "because that makes perfect sense, Molly. Leap off a train onto a roof."

"This is kind of what we signed up for, Peter," the girl points out.

"Well, I'm not doing it," says an Amity boy behind me. He has olive skin and wears a brown shirt—he is the *only* transfer from Amity. His cheeks shine with tears.

"You've got to," Christina says, "or you fail. Come on, it'll be all right."

"No, it won't! I'd rather be factionless than dead!" The Amity boy shakes his head. He sounds panicky. He keeps shaking his head and staring at the rooftop, which is getting closer by the second.

I don't agree with him. I would rather be dead than empty, like the factionless.

"You can't force him," I say, glancing at Christina. Her brown eyes are wide, and she presses her lips together so hard they change color. She offers me her hand.

"Here," she says. I raise an eyebrow at her hand, about to say that I don't need help, but she adds, "I just . . . can't do it unless someone drags me."

I take her hand and we stand at the edge of the car. As it passes the roof, I count, "One . . . two . . . *three!*"

On three we launch off the train car. A weightless moment, and then my feet slam into solid ground and pain prickles through my shins. The jarring landing sends me sprawling on the rooftop, gravel under my cheek. I release Christina's hand. She's laughing.

"That was fun," she says.

Christina will fit in with Dauntless thrill seekers. I brush grains of rock from my cheek. All the initiates except the Amity boy made it onto the roof, with varying levels of success. The Candor girl with crooked teeth, Molly, holds her ankle, wincing, and Peter, the Candor boy with shiny hair, grins proudly—he must have landed on his feet.

Then I hear a wail. I turn my head, searching for the source of the sound. A Dauntless girl stands at the edge of the roof, staring at the ground below, screaming. Behind her a Dauntless boy holds her at the waist to keep her from falling off.

"Rita," he says. "Rita, calm down. Rita—"

I stand and look over the edge. There is a body on the pavement below us; a girl, her arms and legs bent at awkward angles, her hair spread in a fan around her head. My stomach sinks and I stare at the railroad tracks. Not everyone made it. And even the Dauntless aren't safe.

Rita sinks to her knees, sobbing. I turn away. The longer I watch her, the more likely I am to cry, and I can't cry in front of these people.

I tell myself, as sternly as possible, *that is how things work here.* We do dangerous things and people die. People die, and we move on to the next dangerous thing. The sooner that lesson sinks in, the better chance I have at surviving initiation.

I'm no longer sure that I will survive initiation.

I tell myself I will count to three, and when I'm done, I will move on. *One.* I picture the girl's body on the pavement, and a shudder goes through me. *Two.* I hear Rita's sobs and the murmured reassurance of the boy behind her. *Three.*

My lips pursed, I walk away from Rita and the roof's edge.

My elbow stings. I pull my sleeve up to examine it, my hand shaking. Some of the skin is peeling off, but it isn't bleeding.

"Ooh. *Scandalous!* A Stiff's flashing some skin!"

I lift my head. "Stiff" is slang for Abnegation, and I'm the only one here. Peter points at me, smirking. I hear laughter. My cheeks heat up, and I let my sleeve fall.

"Listen up! My name is Max! I am one of the leaders of your new faction!" shouts a man at the other end of the roof. He is older than the others, with deep creases in his dark skin and gray hair at his temples, and he stands on the ledge like it's a sidewalk. Like someone didn't just fall to her death from it. "Several stories below us is the members' entrance to our compound. If you can't muster the will to jump off, you don't belong here. Our initiates have the privilege of going first."

"You want us to jump off a *ledge*?" asks an Erudite girl. She is a few inches taller than I am, with mousy brown hair and big lips. Her mouth hangs open.

I don't know why it shocks her.

"Yes," Max says. He looks amused.

"Is there water at the bottom or something?"

"Who knows?" He raises his eyebrows.

The crowd in front of the initiates splits in half, making a wide path for us. I look around. No one looks eager to leap off the building—their eyes are everywhere but on Max. Some of them nurse minor wounds or brush gravel from their clothes. I glance at Peter. He is picking at one of his cuticles. Trying to act casual.

I am proud. It will get me into trouble someday, but today it makes me brave. I walk toward the ledge and hear snickers behind me.

Max steps aside, leaving my way clear. I walk up to the edge and look down. Wind whips through my clothes, making the fabric snap. The building I'm on forms one side of a square with three other buildings. In the center of the square is a huge hole in the concrete. I can't see what's at the bottom of it.

This is a scare tactic. I will land safely at the bottom. That knowledge is the only thing that helps me step onto the ledge. My teeth chatter. I can't back down now. Not with all the people betting I'll fail behind me. My hands fumble along the collar of my shirt and find the button that secures it shut. After a few tries, I undo the hooks from collar to hem, and pull it off my shoulders.

Beneath it, I wear a gray T-shirt. It is tighter than any other clothes I own, and no one has ever seen me in it before. I ball up my outer shirt and look over my shoulder, at Peter. I throw the ball of fabric at him as hard as I can, my jaw clenched. It hits him in the chest. He stares at me. I hear catcalls and shouts behind me.

I look at the hole again. Goose bumps rise on my pale arms, and my stomach lurches. If I don't do it now, I won't be able to do it at all. I swallow hard.

I don't think. I just bend my knees and jump.

The air howls in my ears as the ground surges toward me, growing and expanding, or I surge toward the ground, my heart pounding so fast it hurts, every muscle in my body tensing as the falling sensation drags at my stomach. The hole surrounds me and I drop into darkness.

I hit something hard. It gives way beneath me and cradles my body. The impact knocks the wind out of me and I wheeze, struggling to breathe again. My arms and legs sting.

A net. There is a net at the bottom of the hole. I look up at the building and laugh, half relieved and half hysterical. My body shakes and I cover my face with my hands. I just jumped off a roof.

I have to stand on solid ground again. I see a few hands stretching out to me at the edge of the net, so I grab the first one I can reach and pull myself across. I roll off, and I would have fallen face-first onto a wood floor if he had not caught me.

"He" is the young man attached to the hand I grabbed. He has a spare upper lip and a full lower lip. His eyes are so deep-set that his eyelashes touch the skin under his eyebrows, and they are dark blue, a dreaming, sleeping, waiting color.

His hands grip my arms, but he releases me a moment after I stand upright again.

"Thank you," I say.

We stand on a platform ten feet above the ground. Around us is an open cavern.

"Can't believe it," a voice says from behind him. It belongs to a dark-haired girl with three silver rings through her right eyebrow. She smirks at me. "A Stiff, the first to jump? Unheard of."

"There's a reason why she left them, Lauren," he says. His voice is deep, and it rumbles. "What's your name?"

"Um . . ." I don't know why I hesitate. But "Beatrice" just doesn't sound right anymore.

"Think about it," he says, a faint smile curling his lips. "You don't get to pick again."

A new place, a new name. I can be remade here.

"Tris," I say firmly.

"Tris," Lauren repeats, grinning. "Make the announcement, Four."

The boy—Four—looks over his shoulder and shouts, "First jumper—Tris!"

A crowd materializes from the darkness as my eyes adjust. They cheer and pump their fists, and then another person drops into the net. Her screams follow her down. Christina. Everyone laughs, but they follow their laughter with more cheering.

Four sets his hand on my back and says, "Welcome to Dauntless."

CHAPTER
SEVEN

WHEN ALL THE initiates stand on solid ground again, Lauren and Four
lead us down a narrow tunnel. The walls are made of stone, and the ceiling slopes, so I feel like I am descending deep into the heart of the earth.
The tunnel is lit at long intervals, so in the dark space between each dim
lamp, I fear that I am lost until a shoulder bumps mine. In the circles of
light I am safe again.

The Erudite boy in front of me stops abruptly, and I smack into him,
hitting my nose on his shoulder. I stumble back and rub my nose as I
recover my senses. The whole crowd has stopped, and our three leaders
stand in front of us, arms folded.

"This is where we divide," Lauren says. "The Dauntless-born initiates are with me. I assume *you* don't need a tour of the place."

She smiles and beckons toward the Dauntless-born initiates. They
break away from the group and dissolve into the shadows. I watch the last
heel pass out of the light and look at those of us who are left. Most of the
initiates were from Dauntless, so only nine people remain. Of those, I
am the only Abnegation transfer, and there are no Amity transfers. The
rest are from Erudite and, surprisingly, Candor. It must require bravery
to be honest all the time. I wouldn't know.

Four addresses us next. "Most of the time I work in the control room,
but for the next few weeks, I am your instructor," he says. "My name is
Four."

Christina asks, "Four? Like the number?"

"Yes," Four says. "Is there a problem?"

"No."

"Good. We're about to go into the Pit, which you will someday learn to
love. It—"

Christina snickers. "The Pit? Clever name."

Four walks up to Christina and leans his face close to hers. His eyes narrow, and for a second he just stares at her.

"What's your name?" he asks quietly.

"Christina," she squeaks.

"Well, Christina, if I wanted to put up with Candor smart-mouths, I would have joined their faction," he hisses. "The first lesson you will learn from me is to keep your mouth shut. Got that?"

She nods.

Four starts toward the shadow at the end of the tunnel. The crowd of initiates moves on in silence.

"What a jerk," she mumbles.

"I guess he doesn't like to be laughed at," I reply.

It would probably be wise to be careful around Four, I realize. He seemed placid to me on the platform, but something about that stillness makes me wary now.

Four pushes a set of double doors open, and we walk into the place he called "the Pit."

"Oh," whispers Christina. "I get it."

"Pit" is the best word for it. It is an underground cavern so huge I can't see the other end of it from where I stand, at the bottom. Uneven rock walls rise several stories above my head. Built into the stone walls are places for food, clothing, supplies, leisure activities. Narrow paths and steps carved from rock connect them. There are no barriers to keep people from falling over the side.

A slant of orange light stretches across one of the rock walls. Forming the roof of the Pit are panes of glass and, above them, a building that lets in sunlight. It must have looked like just another city building when we passed it on the train.

Blue lanterns dangle at random intervals above the stone paths, similar to the ones that lit the Choosing room. They grow brighter as the sunlight dies.

People are everywhere, all dressed in black, all shouting and talking, expressive, gesturing. I don't see any elderly people in the crowd. Are there any old Dauntless? Do they not last that long, or are they just sent away when they can't jump off moving trains anymore?

A group of children run down a narrow path with no railing, so fast my heart pounds, and I want to scream at them to slow down before they get hurt. A memory of the orderly Abnegation streets appears in my mind: a line of people on the right passing a line of people on the left, small smiles and inclined heads and silence. My stomach squeezes. But there is something wonderful about Dauntless chaos.

"If you follow me," says Four, "I'll show you the chasm."

He waves us forward. Four's appearance seems tame from the front, by Dauntless standards, but when he turns around, I see a tattoo peeking out from the collar of his T-shirt. He leads us to the right side of the Pit, which is conspicuously dark. I squint and see that the floor I stand on now ends at an iron barrier. As we approach the railing, I hear a roar—water, fast-moving water, crashing against rocks.

I look over the side. The floor drops off at a sharp angle, and several stories below us is a river. Gushing water strikes the wall beneath me and sprays upward. To my left, the water is calmer, but to my right, it is white, battling with rock.

"The chasm reminds us that there is a fine line between bravery and idiocy!" Four shouts. "A daredevil jump off this ledge will end your life. It has happened before and it will happen again. You've been warned."

"This is incredible," says Christina, as we all move away from the railing.

"Incredible is the word," I say, nodding.

Four leads the group of initiates across the Pit toward a gaping hole in the wall. The room beyond is well-lit enough that I can see where we're going: a dining hall full of people and clattering silverware. When we walk in, the Dauntless inside stand. They applaud. They stamp their feet. They shout. The noise surrounds me and fills me. Christina smiles, and a second later, so do I.

We look for empty seats. Christina and I discover a mostly empty table at the side of the room, and I find myself sitting between her and Four. In the center of the table is a platter of food I don't recognize: circular pieces of meat wedged between round bread slices. I pinch one between my fingers, unsure what to make of it.

Four nudges me with his elbow.

"It's beef," he says. "Put this on it." He passes me a small bowl full of red sauce.

"You've never had a hamburger before?" asks Christina, her eyes wide.

"No," I say. "Is that what it's called?"

"Stiffs eat plain food," Four says, nodding at Christina.

"Why?" she asks.

I shrug. "Extravagance is considered self-indulgent and unnecessary."

She smirks. "No wonder you left."

"Yeah," I say, rolling my eyes. "It was just because of the food."

The corner of Four's mouth twitches.

The doors to the cafeteria open, and a hush falls over the room. I look over my shoulder. A young man walks in, and it is quiet enough that I can hear his footsteps. His face is pierced in so many places I lose count, and his hair is long, dark, and greasy. But that isn't what makes him look menacing. It is the coldness of his eyes as they sweep across the room.

"Who's that?" hisses Christina.

"His name is Eric," says Four. "He's a Dauntless leader."

"Seriously? But he's so young."

Four gives her a grave look. "Age doesn't matter here."

I can tell she's about to ask what I want to ask: *Then what does matter?* But Eric's eyes stop scanning the room, and he starts toward a table. He starts toward *our* table and drops into the seat next to Four. He offers no greeting, so neither do we.

"Well, aren't you going to introduce me?" he asks, nodding to Christina and me.

Four says, "This is Tris and Christina."

"Ooh, a Stiff," says Eric, smirking at me. His smile pulls at the piercings in his lips, making the holes they occupy wider, and I wince. "We'll see how long you last."

I mean to say something—to assure him that I *will* last, maybe—but words fail me. I don't understand why, but I don't want Eric to look at me any longer than he already has. I don't want him to look at me ever again.

He taps his fingers against the table. His knuckles are scabbed over, right where they would split if he punched something too hard.

"What have you been doing lately, Four?" he asks.

Four lifts a shoulder. "Nothing, really," he says.

Are they friends? My eyes flick between Eric and Four. Everything Eric did—sitting here, asking about Four—suggests that they are, but the way Four sits, tense as pulled wire, suggests they are something else. Rivals, maybe, but how could that be, if Eric is a leader and Four is not?

"Max tells me he keeps trying to meet with you, and you don't show up," Eric says. "He requested that I find out what's going on with you."

Four looks at Eric for a few seconds before saying, "Tell him that I am satisfied with the position I currently hold."

"So he wants to give you a job."

The rings in Eric's eyebrow catch the light. Maybe Eric perceives Four as a potential threat to his position. My father says that those who want power and get it live in terror of losing it. That's why we have to give power to those who do not want it.

"So it would seem," Four says.

"And you aren't interested."

"I haven't been interested for two years."

"Well," says Eric. "Let's hope he gets the point, then."

He claps Four on the shoulder, a little too hard, and gets up. When he walks away, I slouch immediately. I had not realized that I was so tense.

"Are you two . . . friends?" I say, unable to contain my curiosity.

"We were in the same initiate class," he says. "He transferred from Erudite."

All thoughts of being careful around Four leave me. "Were you a transfer too?"

"I thought I would only have trouble with the Candor asking too many questions," he says coldly. "Now I've got Stiffs, too?"

"It must be because you're so approachable," I say flatly. "You know. Like a bed of nails."

He stares at me, and I don't look away. He isn't a dog, but the same rules apply. Looking away is submissive. Looking him in the eye is a challenge. It's my choice.

Heat rushes into my cheeks. What will happen when this tension breaks?

But he just says, "Careful, Tris."

My stomach drops like I just swallowed a stone. A Dauntless member at another table calls out Four's name, and I turn to Christina. She raises both eyebrows.

"What?" I ask.

"I'm developing a theory."

"And it is?"

She picks up her hamburger, grins, and says, "That you have a death wish."

+ + +

After dinner, Four disappears without a word. Eric leads us down a series of hallways without telling us where we're going. I don't know why a Dauntless leader would be responsible for a group of initiates, but maybe it is just for tonight.

At the end of each hallway is a blue lamp, but between them it's dark, and I have to be careful not to stumble over uneven ground. Christina walks beside me in silence. No one told us to be quiet, but none of us speak.

Eric stops in front of a wooden door and folds his arms. We gather around him.

"For those of you who don't know, my name is Eric," he says. "I am one of five leaders of the Dauntless. We take the initiation process very seriously here, so I volunteered to oversee most of your training."

The thought makes me nauseous. The idea that a Dauntless leader will oversee our initiation is bad enough, but the fact that it's Eric makes it seem even worse.

"Some ground rules," he says. "You have to be in the training room by eight o'clock every day. Training takes place every day from eight to six, with a break for lunch. You are free to do whatever you like after six. You will also get some time off between each stage of initiation."

The phrase "do whatever you like" sticks in my mind. At home, I could never do what I wanted, not even for an evening. I had to think of other people's needs first. I don't even know what I like to do.

"You are only permitted to leave the compound when accompanied by a Dauntless," Eric adds. "Behind this door is the room where you will be sleeping for the next few weeks. You will notice that there are ten beds and only nine of you. We anticipated that a higher proportion of you would make it this far."

"But we started with twelve," protests Christina. I close my eyes and wait for the reprimand. She needs to learn to stay quiet.

"There is always at least one transfer who doesn't make it to the compound," says Eric, picking at his cuticles. He shrugs. "Anyway, in the first stage of initiation, we keep transfers and Dauntless-born initiates separate, but that doesn't mean you are evaluated separately. At the end of initiation, your rankings will be determined in comparison with the Dauntless-born initiates. And they are better than you are already. So I expect—"

"*Rankings?*" asks the mousy-haired Erudite girl to my right. "Why are we ranked?"

Eric smiles, and in the blue light, his smile looks wicked, like it was cut into his face with a knife.

"Your ranking serves two purposes," he says. "The first is that it determines the order in which you will select a job after initiation. There are only a few *desirable* positions available."

My stomach tightens. I know by looking at his smile, like I knew the second I entered the aptitude test room, that something bad is about to happen.

"The second purpose," he says, "is that only the top ten initiates are made members."

Pain stabs my stomach. We all stand still as statues. And then Christina says, "*What?*"

"There are eleven Dauntless-borns, and nine of you," Eric continues. "Four initiates will be cut at the end of stage one. The remainder will be cut after the final test."

That means that even if we make it through each stage of initiation, six initiates will not be members. I see Christina look at me from the corner of my eye, but I can't look back at her. My eyes are fixed on Eric and will not move.

My odds, as the smallest initiate, as the only Abnegation transfer, are not good.

"What do we do if we're cut?" Peter says.

"You leave the Dauntless compound," says Eric indifferently, "and live factionless."

The mousy-haired girl clamps her hand over her mouth and stifles a sob. I remember the factionless man with the gray teeth, snatching the bag of apples from my hands. His dull, staring eyes. But instead of crying, like the Erudite girl, I feel colder. Harder.

I will be a member. I will.

"But that's . . . not fair!" the broad-shouldered Candor girl, Molly, says. Even though she sounds angry, she looks terrified. "If we had *known*—"

"Are you saying that if you had known this before the Choosing Ceremony, you wouldn't have chosen Dauntless?" Eric snaps. "Because if that's the case, you should get out now. If you are really one of us, it won't matter to you that you might fail. And if it does, you are a coward."

Eric pushes the door to the dormitory open.

"You chose us," he says. "Now we have to choose you."

+ + +

I lie in bed and listen to nine people breathing.

I have never slept in the same room as a boy before, but here I have no other option, unless I want to sleep in the hallway. Everyone else changed into the clothes the Dauntless provided for us, but I sleep in my Abnegation clothes, which still smell like soap and fresh air, like home.

I used to have my own room. I could see the front lawn from the window, and beyond it, the foggy skyline. I am used to sleeping in silence.

Heat swells behind my eyes as I think of home, and when I blink, a tear slips out. I cover my mouth to stifle a sob.

I can't cry, not here. I have to calm down.

It will be all right here. I can look at my reflection whenever I want. I can befriend Christina, and cut my hair short, and let other people clean up their own messes.

My hands shake and the tears come faster now, blurring my vision.

It doesn't matter that the next time I see my parents, on Visiting Day, they will barely recognize me—if they come at all. It doesn't matter that I ache at even a split-second memory of their faces. Even Caleb's, despite how much his secrets hurt me. I match my inhales to the inhales of the other initiates, and my exhales to their exhales. It doesn't matter.

A strangled sound interrupts the breathing, followed by a heavy sob. Bed springs squeal as a large body turns, and a pillow muffles the sobs, but not enough. They come from the bunk next to mine—they belong to a Candor boy, Al, the largest and broadest of all the initiates. He is the last person I expected to break down.

His feet are just inches from my head. I should comfort him—I should *want* to comfort him, because I was raised that way. Instead I feel disgust. Someone who looks so strong shouldn't act so weak. Why can't he just keep his crying quiet like the rest of us?

I swallow hard.

If my mother knew what I was thinking, I know what look she would give me. The corners of her mouth turned down. Her eyebrows set low over her eyes—not scowling, almost tired. I drag the heel of my hand over my cheeks.

Al sobs again. I almost feel the sound grate in my own throat. He is just inches away from me—I should touch him.

No. I put my hand down and roll onto my side, facing the wall. No one has to know that I don't want to help him. I can keep that secret buried. My eyes shut and I feel the pull of sleep, but every time I come close, I hear Al again.

Maybe my problem isn't that I can't go home. I will miss my mother and father and Caleb and evening firelight and the clack of my mother's knitting needles, but that is not the only reason for this hollow feeling in my stomach.

My problem might be that even if I did go home, I wouldn't belong there, among people who give without thinking and care without trying.

The thought makes me grit my teeth. I gather the pillow around my ears to block out Al's crying, and fall asleep with a circle of moisture pressed to my cheek.

CHAPTER
EIGHT

"THE FIRST THING you will learn today is how to shoot a gun. The second thing is how to win a fight." Four presses a gun into my palm without looking at me and keeps walking. "Thankfully, if you are here, you already know how to get on and off a moving train, so I don't need to teach you that."

I shouldn't be surprised that the Dauntless expect us to hit the ground running, but I anticipated more than six hours of rest before the running began. My body is still heavy from sleep.

"Initiation is divided into three stages. We will measure your progress and rank you according to your performance in each stage. The stages are not weighed equally in determining your final rank, so it is possible, though difficult, to drastically improve your rank over time."

I stare at the weapon in my hand. Never in my life did I expect to hold a gun, let alone fire one. It feels dangerous to me, as if just by touching it, I could hurt someone.

"We believe that preparation eradicates cowardice, which we define as the failure to act in the midst of fear," says Four. "Therefore each stage of initiation is intended to prepare you in a different way. The first stage is primarily physical; the second, primarily emotional; the third, primarily mental."

"But what . . ." Peter yawns through his words. "What does firing a gun have to do with . . . bravery?"

Four flips the gun in his hand, presses the barrel to Peter's forehead, and clicks a bullet into place. Peter freezes with his lips parted, the yawn dead in his mouth.

"Wake. Up," Four snaps. "You are holding a loaded gun, you idiot. Act like it."

He lowers the gun. Once the immediate threat is gone, Peter's green eyes harden. I'm surprised he can stop himself from responding, after speaking his mind all his life in Candor, but he does, his cheeks red.

"And to answer your question . . . you are far less likely to soil your pants and cry for your mother if you're prepared to defend yourself." Four stops walking at the end of the row and turns on his heel. "This is also information you may need later in stage one. So, watch me."

He faces the wall with the targets on it—one square of plywood with three red circles on it for each of us. He stands with his feet apart, holds the gun in both hands, and fires. The bang is so loud it hurts my ears. I crane my neck to look at the target. The bullet went through the middle circle.

I turn to my own target. My family would never approve of me firing a gun. They would say that guns are used for self-defense, if not violence, and therefore they are self-serving.

I push my family from my mind, set my feet shoulder-width apart, and delicately wrap both hands around the handle of the gun. It's heavy and hard to lift away from my body, but I want it to be as far from my face as possible. I squeeze the trigger, hesitantly at first and then harder, cringing away from the gun. The sound hurts my ears and the recoil sends my hands back, toward my nose. I stumble, pressing my hand to the wall behind me for balance. I don't know where my bullet went, but I know it's not near the target.

I fire again and again and again, and none of the bullets come close.

"Statistically speaking," the Erudite boy next to me—his name is Will—says, grinning at me, "you should have hit the target at least *once* by now, even by accident." He is blond, with shaggy hair and a crease between his eyebrows.

"Is that so," I say without inflection.

"Yeah," he says. "I think you're actually defying nature."

I grit my teeth and turn toward the target, resolving to at least stand still. If I can't master the first task they give us, how will I ever make it through stage one?

I squeeze the trigger, hard, and this time I'm ready for the recoil. It makes my hands jump back, but my feet stay planted. A bullet hole appears at the edge of the target, and I raise an eyebrow at Will.

"So you see, I'm right. The stats don't lie," he says.

I smile a little.

It takes me five rounds to hit the middle of the target, and when I do, a rush of energy goes through me. I am awake, my eyes wide open, my hands warm. I lower the gun. There is power in controlling something that can do so much damage—in controlling something, period.

Maybe I do belong here.

+ + +

By the time we break for lunch, my arms throb from holding up the gun and my fingers are hard to straighten. I massage them on my way to the dining hall. Christina invites Al to sit with us. Every time I look at him, I hear his sobs again, so I try not to look at him.

I move my peas around with my fork, and my thoughts drift back to the aptitude tests. When Tori warned me that being Divergent was dangerous, I felt like it was branded on my face, and if I so much as turned the wrong way, someone would see it. So far it hasn't been a problem, but that doesn't make me feel safe. What if I let my guard down and something terrible happens?

"Oh, come on. You don't remember me?" Christina asks Al as she makes a sandwich. "We were in Math together just a few *days* ago. And I am *not* a quiet person."

"I slept through Math most of the time," Al replies. "It was first hour!"

What if the danger doesn't come soon—what if it strikes years from now and I never see it coming?

"Tris," says Christina. She snaps her fingers in front of my face. "You in there?"

"What? What is it?"

"I asked if you remember ever taking a class with me," she says. "I mean, no offense, but I probably wouldn't remember if you did. All the Abnegation looked the same to me. I mean, they still do, but now you're not one of them."

I stare at her. As if I need her to remind me.

"Sorry, am I being rude?" she asks. "I'm used to just saying whatever is on my mind. Mom used to say that politeness is deception in pretty packaging."

"I think that's why our factions don't usually associate with each other," I say, with a short laugh. Candor and Abnegation don't hate each other the way Erudite and Abnegation do, but they avoid each other. Candor's real problem is with Amity. Those who seek peace above all else, they say, will always deceive to keep the water calm.

"Can I sit here?" says Will, tapping the table with his finger.

"What, you don't want to hang out with your Erudite buddies?" says Christina.

"They aren't my buddies," says Will, setting his plate down. "Just because we were in the same faction doesn't mean we get along. Plus, Edward and Myra are dating, and I would rather not be the third wheel."

Edward and Myra, the other Erudite transfers, sit two tables away, so close they bump elbows as they cut their food. Myra pauses to kiss Edward. I watch them carefully. I've only seen a few kisses in my life.

Edward turns his head and presses his lips to Myra's. Air hisses between my teeth, and I look away. Part of me waits for them to be scolded. Another part wonders, with a touch of desperation, what it would feel like to have someone's lips against mine.

"Do they have to be so *public*?" I say.

"She just kissed him." Al frowns at me. When he frowns, his thick eyebrows touch his eyelashes. "It's not like they're stripping naked."

"A kiss is not something you do in public."

Al, Will, and Christina all give me the same knowing smile.

"What?" I say.

"Your Abnegation is showing," says Christina. "The rest of us are all right with a little affection in public."

"Oh." I shrug. "Well . . . I guess I'll have to get over it, then."

"Or you can stay frigid," says Will, his green eyes glinting with mischief. "You know. If you want."

Christina throws a roll at him. He catches it and bites it.

"Don't be mean to her," she says. "Frigidity is in her nature. Sort of like being a know-it-all is in yours."

"I am not *frigid*!" I exclaim.

"Don't worry about it," says Will. "It's endearing. Look, you're all red."

The comment only makes my face hotter. Everyone else chuckles. I force a laugh and, after a few seconds, it comes naturally.

It feels good to laugh again.

+ + +

After lunch, Four leads us to a new room. It's huge, with a wood floor that is cracked and creaky and has a large circle painted in the middle. On the left wall is a green board—a chalkboard. My Lower Levels teacher used one, but I haven't seen one since then. Maybe it has something to do with Dauntless priorities: training comes first, technology comes second.

Our names are written on the board in alphabetical order. Hanging at three-foot intervals along one end of the room are faded black punching bags.

We line up behind them and Four stands in the middle, where we can all see him.

"As I said this morning," says Four, "next you will learn how to fight. The purpose of this is to prepare you to act; to prepare your body to respond to threats and challenges—which you will need, if you intend to survive life as a Dauntless."

I can't even think of life as a Dauntless. All I can think about is making it through initiation.

"We will go over technique today, and tomorrow you will start to fight each other," says Four. "So I recommend that you pay attention. Those who don't learn fast will get hurt."

Four names a few different punches, demonstrating each one as he does, first against the air and then against the punching bag.

I catch on as we practice. Like with the gun, I need a few tries to figure out how to hold myself and how to move my body to make it look like his. The kicks are more difficult, though he only teaches us the basics. The punching bag stings my hands and feet, turning my skin red, and barely moves no matter how hard I hit it. All around me is the sound of skin hitting tough fabric.

Four wanders through the crowd of initiates, watching us as we go through the movements again. When he stops in front of me, my insides twist like someone's stirring them with a fork. He stares at me, his eyes following my body from my head to my feet, not lingering anywhere—a practical, scientific gaze.

"You don't have much muscle," he says, "which means you're better off using your knees and elbows. You can put more power behind them."

Suddenly he presses a hand to my stomach. His fingers are so long that, though the heel of his hand touches one side of my rib cage, his fingertips still touch the other side. My heart pounds so hard my chest hurts, and I stare at him, wide-eyed.

"Never forget to keep tension here," he says in a quiet voice.

Four lifts his hand and keeps walking. I feel the pressure of his palm even after he's gone. It's strange, but I have to stop and breathe for a few seconds before I can keep practicing again.

When Four dismisses us for dinner, Christina nudges me with her elbow.

"I'm surprised he didn't break you in half," she says. She wrinkles her nose. "He scares the hell out of me. It's that quiet voice he uses."

"Yeah. He's . . ." I look over my shoulder at him. He is quiet, and remarkably self-possessed. But I wasn't afraid that he would hurt me. ". . . definitely intimidating," I finally say.

Al, who was in front of us, turns around once we reach the Pit and announces, "I want to get a tattoo."

From behind us, Will asks, "A tattoo of what?"

"I don't know." Al laughs. "I just want to feel like I've actually left the old faction. Stop crying about it." When we don't respond, he adds, "I know you've heard me."

"Yeah, learn to quiet down, will you?" Christina pokes Al's thick arm. "I think you're right. We're half in, half out right now. If we want all the way in, we should look the part."

She gives me a look.

"No. I will not cut my hair," I say, "or dye it a strange color. Or pierce my face."

"How about your bellybutton?" she says.

"Or your nipple?" Will says with a snort.

I groan.

Now that training is done for the day, we can do whatever we want until it's time to sleep. The idea makes me feel almost giddy, although that might be from fatigue.

The Pit is swarming with people. Christina announces that she and I will meet Al and Will at the tattoo parlor and drags me toward the clothing place. We stumble up the path, climbing higher above the Pit floor, scattering stones with our shoes.

"What is wrong with my clothes?" I say. "I'm not wearing gray anymore."

"They're ugly and gigantic." She sighs. "Will you just let me help you? If you don't like what I put you in, you never have to wear it again, I promise."

Ten minutes later I stand in front of a mirror in the clothing place wearing a knee-length black dress. The skirt isn't full, but it isn't stuck to my thighs, either—unlike the first one she picked out, which I refused. Goose bumps appear on my bare arms. She slips the tie from my hair and I shake it out of its braid so it hangs wavy over my shoulders.

Then she holds up a black pencil.

"Eyeliner," she says.

"You aren't going to be able to make me pretty, you know." I close my eyes and hold still. She runs the tip of the pencil along the line of my eyelashes. I imagine standing before my family in these clothes, and my stomach twists like I might be sick.

"Who cares about pretty? I'm going for noticeable."

I open my eyes and for the first time stare openly at my own reflection. My heart rate picks up as I do, like I am breaking the rules and will be scolded for it. It will be difficult to break the habits of thinking Abnegation instilled in me, like tugging a single thread from a complex work of embroidery. But I will find new habits, new thoughts, new rules. I will become something else.

My eyes were blue before, but a dull, grayish blue—the eyeliner makes them piercing. With my hair framing my face, my features look softer and fuller. I am not pretty—my eyes are too big and my nose is too long—but I can see that Christina is right. My face is noticeable.

Looking at myself now isn't like seeing myself for the first time; it's like seeing someone else for the first time. Beatrice was a girl I saw in stolen moments at the mirror, who kept quiet at the dinner table. This is someone whose eyes claim mine and don't release me; this is Tris.

"See?" she says. "You're . . . striking."

Under the circumstances, it's the best compliment she could have given me. I smile at her in the mirror.

"You like it?" she says.

"Yeah." I nod. "I look like . . . a different person."

She laughs. "That a good thing or a bad thing?"

I look at myself head-on again. For the first time, the idea of leaving my Abnegation identity behind doesn't make me nervous; it gives me hope.

"A good thing." I shake my head. "Sorry, I've just never been allowed to stare at my reflection for this long."

"Really?" Christina shakes her head. "Abnegation is a strange faction, I have to tell you."

"Let's go watch Al get tattooed," I say. Despite the fact that I have left my old faction behind, I don't want to criticize it yet.

At home, my mother and I picked up nearly identical stacks of clothing every six months or so. It's easy to allocate resources when everyone gets the same thing, but everything is more varied at the Dauntless compound. Every Dauntless gets a certain amount of points to spend per month, and the dress costs one of them.

Christina and I race down the narrow path to the tattoo place. When we get there, Al is sitting in the chair already, and a small, narrow man with more ink than bare skin is drawing a spider on his arm.

Will and Christina flip through books of pictures, elbowing each other when they find a good one. When they sit next to each other, I notice how opposite they are, Christina dark and lean, Will pale and solid, but alike in their easy smiles.

I wander around the room, looking at the artwork on the walls. These days, the only artists are in Amity. Abnegation sees art as impractical, and its appreciation as time that could be spent serving others, so though I have seen works of art in textbooks, I have never been in a decorated room before. It makes the air feel close and warm, and I could get lost here for hours without noticing. I skim the wall with my fingertips. A picture of a hawk on one wall reminds me of Tori's tattoo. Beneath it is a sketch of a bird in flight.

"It's a raven," a voice behind me says. "Pretty, right?"

I turn to see Tori standing there. I feel like I am back in the aptitude test room, with the mirrors all around me and the wires connected to my forehead. I didn't expect to see her again.

"Well, hello there." She smiles. "Never thought I would see you again. Beatrice, is it?"

"Tris, actually," I say. "Do you work here?"

"I do. I just took a break to administer the tests. Most of the time I'm here." She taps her chin. "I recognize that name. You were the first jumper, weren't you?"

"Yes, I was."

"Well done."

"Thanks." I touch the sketch of the bird. "Listen—I need to talk to you about . . ." I glance over at Will and Christina. I can't corner Tori now; they'll ask questions. ". . . something. Sometime."

"I am not sure that would be wise," she says quietly. "I helped you as much as I could, and now you will have to go it alone."

I purse my lips. She has answers; I know she does. If she won't give them to me now, I will have to find a way to make her tell me some other time.

"Want a tattoo?" she says.

The bird sketch holds my attention. I never intended to get pierced or tattooed when I came here. I know that if I do, it will place another wedge between me and my family that I can never remove. And if my life here continues as it has been, it may soon be the least of the wedges between us.

But I understand now what Tori said about her tattoo representing a fear she overcame—a reminder of where she was, as well as a reminder of where she is now. Maybe there is a way to honor my old life as I embrace my new one.

"Yes," I say. "Three of these flying birds."

I touch my collarbone, marking the path of their flight—toward my heart. One for each member of the family I left behind.

CHAPTER NINE

"SINCE THERE ARE an odd number of you, one of you won't be fighting to-day," says Four, stepping away from the board in the training room. He gives me a look. The space next to my name is blank.

The knot in my stomach unravels. A reprieve.

"This isn't good," says Christina, nudging me with her elbow. Her elbow prods one of my sore muscles—I have more sore muscles than not-sore muscles, this morning—and I wince.

"Ow."

"Sorry," she says. "But look. I'm up against the Tank."

Christina and I sat together at breakfast, and earlier she shielded me from the rest of the dormitory as I changed. I haven't had a friend like her before. Susan was better friends with Caleb than with me, and Robert only went where Susan went.

I guess I haven't really had a friend, period. It's impossible to have real friendship when no one feels like they can accept help or even talk about themselves. That won't happen here. I already know more about Christina than I ever knew about Susan, and it's only been two days.

"The Tank?" I find Christina's name on the board. Written next to it is "Molly."

"Yeah, Peter's slightly more feminine-looking minion," she says, nodding toward the cluster of people on the other side of the room. Molly is tall like Christina, but that's where the similarities end. She has broad shoulders, bronze skin, and a bulbous nose.

"Those three"—Christina points at Peter, Drew, and Molly in turn—"have been inseparable since they crawled out of the womb, practically. I hate them."

Will and Al stand across from each other in the arena. They put their hands up by their faces to protect themselves, as Four taught us, and shuffle in a circle around each other. Al is half a foot taller than Will, and twice as broad. As I stare at him, I realize that even his facial features are big—big nose, big lips, big eyes. This fight won't last long.

I glance at Peter and his friends. Drew is shorter than both Peter and Molly, but he's built like a boulder, and his shoulders are always hunched. His hair is orange-red, the color of an old carrot.

"What's wrong with them?" I say.

"Peter is pure evil. When we were kids, he would pick fights with people from other factions and then, when an adult came to break it up, he'd cry and make up some story about how the other kid started it. And of course, they believed him, because we were Candor and we couldn't lie. Ha ha."

Christina wrinkles her nose and adds, "Drew is just his sidekick. I doubt he has an independent thought in his brain. And Molly . . . she's the kind of person who fries ants with a magnifying glass just to watch them flail around."

In the arena, Al punches Will hard in the jaw. I wince. Across the room, Eric smirks at Al, and turns one of the rings in his eyebrow.

Will stumbles to the side, one hand pressed to his face, and blocks Al's next punch with his free hand. Judging by his grimace, blocking the punch is as painful as a blow would have been. Al is slow, but powerful.

Peter, Drew, and Molly cast furtive looks in our direction and then pull their heads together, whispering.

"I think they know we're talking about them," I say.

"So? They already know I hate them."

"They do? How?"

Christina fakes a smile at them and waves. I look down, my cheeks warm. I shouldn't be gossiping anyway. Gossiping is self-indulgent.

Will hooks a foot around one of Al's legs and yanks back, knocking Al to the ground. Al scrambles to his feet.

"Because I've told them," she says, through the gritted teeth of her smile. Her teeth are straight on top and crooked on the bottom. She looks at me. "We try to be pretty honest about our feelings in Candor. Plenty of people have told me that they don't like me. And plenty of people haven't. Who cares?"

"We just . . . weren't supposed to hurt people," I say.

"I like to think I'm helping them by hating them," she says. "I'm re-minding them that they aren't God's gift to humankind."

I laugh a little at that and focus on the arena again. Will and Al face each other for a few more seconds, more hesitant than they were before. Will flicks his pale hair from his eyes. They glance at Four like they're waiting for him to call the fight off, but he stands with his arms folded, giving no response. A few feet away from him, Eric checks his watch.

After a few seconds of circling, Eric shouts, "Do you think this is a leisure activity? Should we break for naptime? Fight each other!"

"But . . ." Al straightens, letting his hands down, and says, "Is it scored or something? When does the fight end?"

"It ends when one of you is unable to continue," says Eric.

"According to Dauntless rules," Four says, "one of you could also concede."

Eric narrows his eyes at Four. "According to the *old* rules," he says. "In the *new* rules, no one concedes."

"A brave man acknowledges the strength of others," Four replies.

"A brave man never surrenders."

Four and Eric stare at each other for a few seconds. I feel like I am looking at two different kinds of Dauntless—the honorable kind, and the ruthless kind. But even I know that in this room, it's Eric, the youngest leader of the Dauntless, who has the authority.

Beads of sweat dot Al's forehead; he wipes them with the back of his hand.

"This is ridiculous," Al says, shaking his head. "What's the point of beating him up? We're in the same faction!"

"Oh, you think it's going to be that easy?" Will asks, grinning. "Go on. Try to hit me, slowpoke."

Will puts his hands up again. I see determination in Will's eyes that wasn't there before. Does he really believe he can win? One hard shot to the head and Al will knock him out cold.

That is, if he can actually hit Will. Al tries a punch, and Will ducks, the back of his neck shining with sweat. He dodges another punch, slipping around Al and kicking him hard in the back. Al lurches forward and turns.

When I was younger, I read a book about grizzly bears. There was a picture of one standing on its hind legs with its paws outstretched, roaring. That is how Al looks now. He charges at Will, grabbing his arm so he can't slip away, and punches him hard in the jaw.

I watch the light leave Will's eyes, which are pale green, like celery. They roll back into his head, and all the tension falls from his body. He slips from Al's grasp, dead weight, and crumples to the floor. Cold rushes down my back and fills my chest.

Al's eyes widen, and he crouches next to Will, tapping his cheek with one hand. The room falls silent as we wait for Will to respond. For a few seconds, he doesn't, just lies on the ground with an arm bent beneath him. Then he blinks, clearly dazed.

"Get him up," Eric says. He stares with greedy eyes at Will's fallen body, like the sight is a meal and he hasn't eaten in weeks. The curl of his lip is cruel.

Four turns to the chalkboard and circles Al's name. Victory.

"Next up—Molly and Christina!" shouts Eric. Al pulls Will's arm across his shoulders and drags him out of the arena.

Christina cracks her knuckles. I would wish her luck, but I don't know what good that would do. Christina isn't weak, but she's much narrower than Molly. Hopefully her height will help her.

Across the room, Four supports Will from the waist and leads him out. Al stands for a moment by the door, watching them go.

Four leaving makes me nervous. Leaving us with Eric is like hiring a babysitter who spends his time sharpening knives.

Christina tucks her hair behind her ears. It is chin-length, black, and pinned back with silver clips. She cracks another knuckle. She looks nervous, and no wonder—who wouldn't be nervous after watching Will collapse like a rag doll?

If conflict in Dauntless ends with only one person standing, I am unsure of what this part of initiation will do to me. Will I be Al, standing over a man's body, knowing I'm the one who put him on the ground, or will I be Will, lying in a helpless heap? And is it selfish of me to crave victory, or is it brave? I wipe my sweaty palms on my pants.

I snap to attention when Christina kicks Molly in the side. Molly gasps and grits her teeth like she's about to growl through them. A lock of stringy black hair falls across her face, but she doesn't brush it away.

Al stands next to me, but I'm too focused on the new fight to look at him, or congratulate him on winning, assuming that's what he wants. I am not sure.

Molly smirks at Christina, and without warning, dives, hands outstretched, at Christina's midsection. She hits her hard, knocking her down, and pins her to the ground. Christina thrashes, but Molly is heavy and doesn't budge.

She punches, and Christina moves her head out of the way, but Molly just punches again, and again, until her fist hits Christina's jaw, her nose, her mouth. Without thinking, I grab Al's arm and squeeze it as tightly as I can. I just need something to hold on to. Blood runs down the side of Christina's face and splatters on the ground next to her cheek. This is the first time I have ever prayed for someone to fall unconscious.

But she doesn't. Christina screams and drags one of her arms free. She punches Molly in the ear, knocking her off-balance, and wriggles free. She comes to her knees, holding her face with one hand. The blood streaming from her nose is thick and dark and covers her fingers in seconds. She screams again and crawls away from Molly. I can tell by the heaving of her shoulders that she's sobbing, but I can barely hear her over the throbbing in my ears.

Please go unconscious.

Molly kicks Christina's side, sending her sprawling on her back. Al frees his hand and pulls me tight to his side. I clench my teeth to keep from crying out. I had no sympathy for Al the first night, but I am not cruel yet; the sight of Christina clutching her rib cage makes me want to stand between her and Molly.

"Stop!" wails Christina as Molly pulls her foot back to kick again. She holds out a hand. "Stop! I'm . . ." She coughs. "I'm done."

Molly smiles, and I sigh with relief. Al sighs too, his rib cage lifting and falling against my shoulder.

Eric walks toward the center of the arena, his movements slow, and stands over Christina with his arms folded. He says quietly, "I'm sorry, what did you say? You're done?"

Christina pushes herself to her knees. When she takes her hand from the ground, it leaves a red handprint behind. She pinches her nose to stop the bleeding and nods.

"Get up," he says. If he had yelled, I might not have felt like everything inside my stomach was about to come out of it. If he had yelled, I would have known that the yelling was the worst he planned to do. But his voice is quiet and his words precise. He grabs Christina's arm, yanks her to her feet, and drags her out the door.

"Follow me," he says to the rest of us.

And we do.

+ + +

I feel the roar of the river in my chest.

We stand near the railing. The Pit is almost empty; it is the middle of the afternoon, though it feels like it's been night for days.

If there were people around, I doubt any of them would help Christina. We are with Eric, for one thing, and for another, the Dauntless have different rules—rules that brutality does not violate.

Eric shoves Christina against the railing.

"Climb over it," he says.

"What?" She says it like she expects him to relent, but her wide eyes and ashen face suggest otherwise. Eric will not back down.

"Climb over the railing," says Eric again, pronouncing each word slowly. "If you can hang over the chasm for five minutes, I will forget your cowardice. If you can't, I will not allow you to continue initiation."

The railing is narrow and made of metal. The spray from the river coats it, making it slippery and cold. Even if Christina is brave enough to hang from the railing for five minutes, she may not be able to hold on. Either she decides to be factionless, or she risks death.

When I close my eyes, I imagine her falling onto the jagged rocks below and shudder.

"Fine," she says, her voice shaking.

She is tall enough to swing her leg over the railing. Her foot shakes. She puts her toe on the ledge as she lifts her other leg over. Facing us, she wipes her hands on her pants and holds on to the railing so hard her knuckles turn white. Then she takes one foot off the ledge. And the other. I see her face between the bars of the barrier, determined, her lips pressed together.

Next to me, Al sets his watch.

For the first minute and a half, Christina is fine. Her hands stay firm around the railing and her arms don't shake. I start to think she might make it and show Eric how foolish he was to doubt her.

But then the river hits the wall, and white water sprays against Christina's back. Her face strikes the barrier, and she cries out. Her hands slip so she's just holding on by her fingertips. She tries to get a better grip, but now her hands are wet.

If I help her, Eric would make my fate the same as hers. Will I let her fall to her death, or will I resign myself to being factionless? What's worse: to be idle while someone dies, or to be exiled and empty-handed?

My parents would have no problem answering that question.

But I am not my parents.

As far as I know, Christina hasn't cried since we got here, but now her face crumples and she lets out a sob that is louder than the river. Another wave hits the wall and the spray coats her body. One of the droplets hits my cheek. Her hands slip again, and this time, one of them falls from the railing, so she's hanging by four fingertips.

"Come on, Christina," says Al, his low voice surprisingly loud. She looks at him. He claps. "Come on, grab it again. You can do it. Grab it."

Would I even be strong enough to hold on to her? Would it be worth my effort to try to help her if I know I'm too weak to do any good?

I know what those questions are: excuses. *Human reason can excuse any evil; that is why it's so important that we don't rely on it.* My father's words.

Christina swings her arm, fumbling for the railing. No one else cheers her on, but Al brings his big hands together and shouts, his eyes holding hers. I wish I could; I wish I could move, but I just stare at her and wonder how long I have been this disgustingly selfish.

I stare at Al's watch. Four minutes have passed. He elbows me hard in the shoulder.

"Come on," I say. My voice is a whisper. I clear my throat. "One minute left," I say, louder this time. Christina's other hand finds the railing again. Her arms shake so hard I wonder if the earth is quaking beneath me, jiggling my vision, and I just didn't notice.

"Come on, Christina," Al and I say, and as our voices join, I believe I might be strong enough to help her.

I will help her. If she slips again, I will.

Another wave of water splashes against Christina's back, and she shrieks as both her hands slip off the railing. A scream launches from my mouth. It sounds like it belongs to someone else.

But she doesn't fall. She grabs the bars of the barrier. Her fingers slide down the metal until I can't see her head anymore; they are all I see.

Al's watch reads 5:00.

"Five minutes are up," he says, almost spitting the words at Eric.

Eric checks his own watch. Taking his time, tilting his wrist, all while my stomach twists and I can't breathe. When I blink, I see Rita's sister on the pavement below the train tracks, limbs bent at strange angles; I see Rita screaming and sobbing; I see myself turning away.

"Fine," Eric says. "You can come up, Christina."

Al walks toward the railing.

"No," Eric says. "She has to do it on her own."

"No, she doesn't," Al growls. "She did what you said. She's not a coward. She did what you said."

Eric doesn't respond. Al reaches over the railing, and he's so tall that he can reach Christina's wrist. She grabs his forearm. Al pulls her up, his face red with frustration, and I run forward to help. I'm too short to do much good, as I suspected, but I grip Christina under the shoulder once she's high enough, and Al and I haul her over the barrier. She drops to the ground, her face still blood-smeared from the fight, her back soaking wet, her body quivering.

I kneel next to her. Her eyes lift to mine, then shift to Al, and we all catch our breath together.

CHAPTER
TEN

THAT NIGHT I dream that Christina hangs from the railing again, by her toes this time, and someone shouts that only someone who is Divergent can help her. So I run forward to pull her up, but someone shoves me over the edge, and I wake before I hit the rocks.

Sweat-soaked and shaky from the dream, I walk to the girls' bathroom to shower and change. When I come back, the word "Stiff" is spray-painted across my mattress in red. The word is written smaller along the bed frame, and again on my pillow. I look around, my heart pounding with anger.

Peter stands behind me, whistling as he fluffs his pillow. It's hard to believe I could hate someone who looks so kind—his eyebrows turn upward naturally, and he has a wide, white smile.

"Nice decorations," he says.

"Did I do something to you that I'm unaware of?" I demand. I grab the corner of a sheet and yank it away from the mattress. "I don't know if you've noticed, but we are in the same faction now."

"I don't know what you're referring to," he says lightly. Then he glances at me. "And you and I will *never* be in the same faction."

I shake my head as I remove my pillowcase from the pillow. *Don't get angry.* He wants to get a rise out of me; he won't. But every time he fluffs his pillow, I think about punching him in the gut.

Al walks in, and I don't even have to ask him to help me; he just walks over and strips bedding with me. I will have to scrub the bed frame later. Al carries the stack of sheets to the trash can and together we walk toward the training room.

"Ignore him," Al says. "He's an idiot, and if you don't get angry, he'll stop eventually."

"Yeah." I touch my cheeks. They are still warm with an angry blush. I try to distract myself. "Did you talk to Will?" I ask quietly. "After . . . you know."

"Yeah. He's fine. He isn't angry." Al sighs. "Now I'll always be remembered as the first guy who knocked someone out cold."

"There are worse ways to be remembered. At least they won't antagonize you."

"There are better ways too." He nudges me with his elbow, smiling. "First jumper."

Maybe I was the first jumper, but I suspect that's where my Dauntless fame begins and ends.

I clear my throat. "One of you had to get knocked out, you know. If it hadn't been him, it would have been you."

"Still, I don't want to do it again." Al shakes his head, too many times, too fast. He sniffs. "I really don't."

We reach the door to the training room and I say, "But you have to." He has a kind face. Maybe he is too kind for Dauntless.

I look at the chalkboard when I walk in. I didn't have to fight yesterday, but today I definitely will. When I see my name, I stop in the middle of the step.

My opponent is Peter.

"Oh no," says Christina, who shuffles in behind us. Her face is bruised, and she looks like she is trying not to limp. When she sees the board, she crumples the muffin wrapper she is holding into her fist. "Are they serious? They're really going to make *you* fight *him*?"

Peter is almost a foot taller than I am, and yesterday, he beat Drew in less than five minutes. Today Drew's face is more black-and-blue than flesh-toned.

"Maybe you can just take a few hits and pretend to go unconscious," suggests Al. "No one would blame you."

"Yeah," I say. "Maybe."

I stare at my name on the board. My cheeks feel hot. Al and Christina are just trying to help, but the fact that they don't believe, not even in a tiny corner of their minds, that I have a chance against Peter bothers me.

I stand at the side of the room, half listening to Al and Christina's chatter, and watch Molly fight Edward. He's much faster than she is, so I'm sure Molly will not win today.

As the fight goes on and my irritation fades, I start to get nervous. Four told us yesterday to exploit our opponent's weaknesses, and aside from his utter lack of likable qualities, Peter doesn't have any. He's tall enough to be strong but not so big that he's slow; he has an eye for other people's soft spots; he's vicious and won't show me any mercy. I would like to say that he underestimates me, but that would be a lie. I am as un-skilled as he suspects.

Maybe Al is right, and I should just take a few hits and pretend to be unconscious.

But I can't afford not to try. I can't be ranked last.

By the time Molly peels herself off the ground, looking only half-conscious thanks to Edward, my heart is pounding so hard I can feel it in my fingertips. I can't remember how to stand. I can't remember how to punch. I walk to the center of the arena and my guts writhe as Peter comes toward me, taller than I remembered, arm muscles standing at attention. He smiles at me. I wonder if throwing up on him will do me any good.

I doubt it.

"You okay there, Stiff?" he says. "You look like you're about to cry. I might go easy on you if you cry."

Over Peter's shoulder, I see Four standing by the door with his arms folded. His mouth is puckered, like he just swallowed something sour. Next to him is Eric, who taps his foot faster than my heartbeat.

One second Peter and I are standing there, staring at each other, and the next Peter's hands are up by his face, his elbows bent. His knees are bent too, like he's ready to spring.

"Come on, Stiff," he says, his eyes glinting. "Just one little tear. Maybe some begging."

The thought of begging Peter for mercy makes me taste bile, and on an impulse, I kick him in the side. Or I would have kicked him in the side, if he hadn't caught my foot and yanked it forward, knocking me off-balance. My back smacks into the floor, and I pull my foot free, scrambling to my feet.

I have to stay on my feet so he can't kick me in the head. That's the only thing I can think about.

"Stop playing with her," snaps Eric. "I don't have all day."

Peter's mischievous look disappears. His arm twitches and pain stabs my jaw and spreads across my face, making my vision go black at the edges and my ears ring. I blink and lurch to the side as the room dips and sways. I don't remember his fist coming at me.

I am too off-balance to do anything but move away from him, as far as the arena will allow. He darts in front of me and kicks me hard in the stomach. His foot forces the air from my lungs and it hurts, hurts so badly I can't breathe, or maybe that's because of the kick, I don't know, I just fall.

On your feet is the only thought in my mind. I push myself up, but Peter is already there. He grabs my hair with one hand and punches me in the nose with the other. This pain is different, less like a stab and more like a crackle, crackling in my brain, spotting my vision with different colors, blue, green, red. I try to shove him off, my hands slapping at his arms, and he punches me again, this time in the ribs. My face is wet. Bloody nose. More red, I guess, but I'm too dizzy to look down.

He shoves me and I fall again, scraping my hands on the ground, blinking, sluggish and slow and hot. I cough and drag myself to my feet. I really should be lying down if the room is spinning this fast. And Peter spins around me; I am the center of a spinning planet, the only thing staying still. Something hits me from the side and I almost fall over again.

On my feet on my feet. I see a solid mass in front of me, a body. I punch as hard as I can, and my fist hits something soft. Peter barely groans, and smacks my ear with the flat of his palm, laughing under his breath. I hear ringing and try to blink some of the black patches out of my eyes; how did something get in my eye?

Out of my peripheral vision, I see Four shove the door open and walk out. Apparently this fight isn't interesting enough for him. Or maybe he's going to find out why everything's spinning like a top, and I don't blame him; I want to know the answer too.

My knees give out and the floor is cool against my cheek. Something slams into my side and I scream for the first time, a high screech that belongs to someone else and not me, and it slams into my side again, and I can't see anything at all, not even whatever is right in front of my face, the lights out. Someone shouts, "Enough!" and I think *too much* and *nothing at all.*

+ + +

When I wake up, I don't feel much, but the inside of my head is fuzzy, like it's packed with cotton balls.

I know that I lost, and the only thing keeping the pain at bay is what is making it difficult to think straight.

"Is her eye already black?" someone asks.

I open one eye—the other stays shut like it's glued that way. Sitting to my right are Will and Al; Christina sits on the bed to my left with an ice pack on her jaw.

"What happened to your face?" I say. My lips feel clumsy and too large.

She laughs. "Look who's talking. Should we get you an eye patch?"

"Well, I already know what happened to *my* face," I say. "I was there. Sort of."

"Did you just make a *joke*, Tris?" Will says, grinning. "We should get you on painkillers more often if you're going to start cracking jokes. Oh, and to answer your question—I beat her up."

"I can't believe you couldn't beat Will," Al says, shaking his head.

"What? He's *good*," she says, shrugging. "Plus, I think I've finally learned how to stop losing. I just need to stop people from punching me in the jaw."

"You know, you'd think you would have figured that out already." Will winks at her. "Now I know why you aren't Erudite. Not too bright, are you?"

"You feeling okay, Tris?" Al says. His eyes are dark brown, almost the same color as Christina's skin. His cheek looks rough, like if he didn't shave it, he would have a thick beard. Hard to believe he's only sixteen.

"Yeah," I say. "Just wish I could stay here forever so I never have to see Peter again."

But I don't know where "here" is. I am in a large, narrow room with a row of beds on either side. Some of the beds have curtains between them. On the right side of the room is a nurse's station. This must be where the Dauntless go when they're sick or hurt. The woman there looks at us over a clipboard. I've never seen a nurse with so many piercings in her ear before. Some Dauntless must volunteer to do jobs that traditionally belong to other factions. After all, it wouldn't make sense for the Dauntless to make the trek to the city hospital every time they get hurt.

The first time I went to the hospital, I was six years old. My mother fell on the sidewalk in front of our house and broke her arm. Hearing her scream made me burst into tears, but Caleb just ran for my father without saying a word. At the hospital, an Amity woman in a yellow shirt with clean fingernails took my mother's blood pressure and set her bone with a smile.

I remember Caleb telling her that it would only take a month to mend, because it was a hairline fracture. I thought he was reassuring her, because that's what selfless people do, but now I wonder if he was repeating something he had studied; if all his Abnegation tendencies were just Erudite traits in disguise.

"Don't worry about Peter," says Will. "He'll at least get beat up by Edward, who has been studying hand-to-hand combat since we were ten years old. For fun."

"Good," says Christina. She checks her watch. "I think we're missing dinner. Do you want us to stay here, Tris?"

I shake my head. "I'm fine."

Christina and Will get up, but Al waves them ahead. He has a distinct smell—sweet and fresh, like sage and lemongrass. When he tosses and turns at night, I get a whiff of it and I know he's having a nightmare.

"I just wanted to tell you that you missed Eric's announcement. We're going on a field trip tomorrow, to the fence, to learn about Dauntless jobs," he says. "We have to be at the train by eight fifteen."

"Good," I say. "Thanks."

"And don't pay attention to Christina. Your face doesn't look that bad." He smiles a little. "I mean, it looks good. It always looks good. I mean—you look brave. Dauntless."

His eyes skirt mine, and he scratches the back of his head. The silence seems to grow between us. It was a nice thing to say, but he acts like it meant more than just the words. I hope I am wrong. I could not be attracted to Al—I could not be attracted to anyone that fragile. I smile as much as my bruised cheek will allow, hoping that will diffuse the tension.

"I should let you rest," he says. He gets up to leave, but before he can go, I grab his wrist.

"Al, are you okay?" I say. He stares blankly at me, and I add, "I mean, is it getting any easier?"

"Uh . . ." He shrugs. "A little."

He pulls his hand free and shoves it in his pocket. The question must have embarrassed him, because I've never seen him so red before. If I spent my nights sobbing into my pillow, I would be a little embarrassed too. At least when I cry, I know how to hide it.

"I lost to Drew. After your fight with Peter." He looks at me. "I took a few hits, fell down, and stayed there. Even though I didn't have to. I figure . . . I figure that since I beat Will, if I lose all the rest, I won't be ranked last, but I won't have to hurt anyone anymore."

"Is that really what you want?"

He looks down. "I just can't do it. Maybe that means I'm a coward."

"You're not a coward just because you don't want to hurt people," I say, because I know it's the right thing to say, even if I'm not sure I mean it.

For a moment we are both still, looking at each other. Maybe I do mean it. If he is a coward, it isn't because he doesn't enjoy pain. It is because he refuses to act.

He gives me a pained look and says, "You think our families will visit us? They say transfer families never come on Visiting Day."

"I don't know," I say. "I don't know if it would be good or bad if they did."

"I think bad." He nods. "Yeah, it's already hard enough." He nods again, as if confirming what he just said, and walks away.

In less than a week, the Abnegation initiates will be able to visit their families for the first time since the Choosing Ceremony. They will go home and sit in their living rooms and interact with their parents for the first time as adults.

I used to look forward to that day. I used to think about what I would say to my mother and father when I was allowed to ask them questions at the dinner table.

In less than a week, the Dauntless-born initiates will find their families on the Pit floor, or in the glass building above the compound, and do whatever it is the Dauntless do when they reunite. Maybe they take turns throwing knives at each other's heads—it wouldn't surprise me.

And the transfer initiates with forgiving parents will be able to see them again too. I suspect mine will not be among them. Not after my father's cry of outrage at the ceremony. Not after both their children left them.

Maybe if I could have told them I was Divergent, and I was confused about what to choose, they would have understood. Maybe they would have helped me figure out what Divergent is, and what it means, and why it's dangerous. But I didn't trust them with that secret, so I will never know.

I clench my teeth as the tears come. I am fed up. I am fed up with tears and weakness. But there isn't much I can do to stop them.

Maybe I drift off to sleep, and maybe I don't. Later that night, though, I slip out of the room and go back to the dormitory. The only thing worse than letting Peter put me in the hospital would be letting him put me there overnight.

CHAPTER ELEVEN

THE NEXT MORNING, I don't hear the alarm, shuffling feet, or conversations as the other initiates get ready. I wake to Christina shaking my shoulder with one hand and tapping my cheek with the other. She already wears a black jacket zipped up to her throat. If she has bruises from yesterday's fight, her dark skin makes them difficult to see.

"Come on," she says. "Up and at 'em."

I dreamt that Peter tied me to a chair and asked me if I was Divergent. I answered no, and he punched me until I said yes. I woke up with wet cheeks.

I mean to say something, but all I can do is groan. My body aches so badly it hurts to breathe. It doesn't help that last night's bout of crying made my eyes swell. Christina offers me her hand.

The clock reads eight. We're supposed to be at the tracks by eight fifteen.

"I'll run and get us some breakfast. You just . . . get ready. Looks like it might take you a while," she says.

I grunt. Trying not to bend at the waist, I fumble in the drawer under my bed for a clean shirt. Luckily Peter isn't here to see me struggle. Once Christina leaves, the dormitory is empty.

I unbutton my shirt and stare at my bare side, which is patched with bruises. For a second the colors mesmerize me, bright green and deep blue and brown. I change as fast as I can and let my hair hang loose because I can't lift my arms to tie it back.

I look at my reflection in the small mirror on the back wall and see a stranger. She is blond like me, with a narrow face like mine, but that's where the similarities stop. *I* do not have a black eye, and a split lip, and a bruised jaw. *I* am not as pale as a sheet. She can't possibly be me, though she moves when I move.

By the time Christina comes back, a muffin in each hand, I'm sitting on the edge of my bed, staring at my untied shoes. I will have to bend over to tie them. It will hurt when I bend over.

But Christina just passes me a muffin and crouches in front of me to tie my shoes. Gratitude surges in my chest, warm and a little like an ache. Maybe there is some Abnegation in everyone, even if they don't know it.

Well, in everyone but Peter.

"Thank you," I say.

"Well, we would never get there on time if you had to tie them yourself," she says. "Come on. You can eat and walk at the same time, right?"

We walk fast toward the Pit. The muffin is banana-flavored, with walnuts. My mother baked bread like this once to give to the factionless, but I never got to try it. I was too old for coddling at that point. I ignore the pinch in my stomach that comes every time I think of my mother and half walk, half jog after Christina, who forgets that her legs are longer than mine.

We climb the steps from the Pit to the glass building above it and run to the exit. Every thump of my feet sends pain through my ribs, but I ignore it. We make it to the tracks just as the train arrives, its horn blaring.

"What took you so long?" Will shouts over the horn.

"Stumpy Legs over here turned into an old lady overnight," says Christina.

"Oh, shut up." I'm only half kidding.

Four stands at the front of the pack, so close to the tracks that if he shifted even an inch forward, the train would take his nose with it. He steps back to let some of the others get on first. Will hoists himself into the car with some difficulty, landing first on his stomach and then dragging his legs in behind him. Four grabs the handle on the side of the car and pulls himself in smoothly, like he doesn't have more than six feet of body to work with.

I jog next to the car, wincing, then grit my teeth and grab the handle on the side. This is going to hurt.

Al grabs me under each arm and lifts me easily into the car. Pain shoots through my side, but it only lasts for a second. I see Peter behind him, and my cheeks get warm. Al was trying to be nice, so I smile at him, but I wish people didn't want to be so nice. As if Peter didn't have enough ammunition already.

"Feeling okay there?" Peter says, giving me a look of mock sympathy—his lips turned down, his arched eyebrows pulled in. "Or are you a little . . . *Stiff*?"

He bursts into laughter at his joke, and Molly and Drew join in. Molly has an ugly laugh, all snorting and shaking shoulders, and Drew's is silent, so it almost looks like he's in pain.

"We are all awed by your incredible wit," says Will.

"Yeah, are you sure you don't belong with the Erudite, Peter?" Christina adds. "I hear they don't object to sissies."

Four, standing in the doorway, speaks before Peter can retort. "Am I going to have to listen to your bickering all the way to the fence?"

Everyone gets quiet, and Four turns back to the car's opening. He holds the handles on either side, his arms stretching wide, and leans forward so his body is mostly outside the car, though his feet stay planted inside. The wind presses his shirt to his chest. I try to look past him at what we're passing—a sea of crumbling, abandoned buildings that get smaller as we go.

Every few seconds, though, my eyes shift back to Four. I don't know what I expect to see, or what I want to see, if anything. But I do it without thinking.

I ask Christina, "What do you think is out there?" I nod to the doorway. "I mean, beyond the fence."

She shrugs. "A bunch of farms, I guess."

"Yeah, but I mean . . . past the farms. What are we guarding the city from?"

She wiggles her fingers at me. "Monsters!"

I roll my eyes.

"We didn't even have guards near the fence until five years ago," says Will. "Don't you remember when Dauntless police used to patrol the factionless sector?"

"Yes," I say. I also remember that my father was one of the people who voted to get the Dauntless out of the factionless sector of the city. He said the poor didn't need policing; they needed help, and we could give it to them. But I would rather not mention that now, or here. It's one of the many things Erudite gives as evidence of Abnegation's incompetence.

"Oh, right," he says. "I bet you saw them all the time."

"Why do you say that?" I ask, a little too sharply. I don't want to be associated too closely with the factionless.

"Because you had to pass the factionless sector to get to school, right?"

"What did you do, memorize a map of the city for fun?" says Christina.

"Yes," says Will, looking puzzled. "Didn't you?"

The train's brakes squeal, and we all lurch forward as the car slows. I am grateful for the movement; it makes standing easier. The dilapidated buildings are gone, replaced by yellow fields and train tracks. The train stops under an awning. I lower myself to the grass, holding the handle to keep me steady.

In front of me is a chain-link fence with barbed wire strung along the top. When I walk forward, I notice that it continues farther than I can see, perpendicular to the horizon. Past the fence is a cluster of trees, most of them dead, some green. Milling around on the other side of the fence are Dauntless guards carrying guns.

"Follow me," says Four. I stay close to Christina. I don't want to admit it, not even to myself, but I feel calmer when I'm near her. If Peter tries to taunt me, she will defend me.

Silently I scold myself for being such a coward. Peter's insults shouldn't bother me, and I should focus on getting better at combat, not on how badly I did yesterday. And I should be willing, if not able, to defend myself instead of relying on other people to do it for me.

Four leads us toward the gate, which is as wide as a house and opens up to the cracked road that leads to the city. When I came here with my family as a child, we rode in a bus on that road and beyond, to Amity's farms, where we spent the day picking tomatoes and sweating through our shirts.

Another pinch in my stomach.

"If you don't rank in the top five at the end of initiation, you will probably end up here," says Four as he reaches the gate. "Once you are a fence guard, there is some potential for advancement, but not much. You may be able to go on patrols beyond Amity's farms, but—"

"Patrols for what purpose?" asks Will.

Four lifts a shoulder. "I suppose you'll discover that if you find yourself among them. As I was saying. For the most part, those who guard the fence when they are young continue to guard the fence. If it comforts you, some of them insist that it isn't as bad as it seems."

"Yeah. At least we won't be driving buses or cleaning up other people's messes like the factionless," Christina whispers in my ear.

"What rank were you?" Peter asks Four.

I don't expect Four to answer, but he looks levelly at Peter and says, "I was first."

"And you chose to do *this*?" Peter's eyes are wide and round and dark green. They would look innocent to me if I didn't know what a terrible person he is. "Why didn't you get a government job?"

"I didn't want one," Four says flatly. I remember what he said on the first day, about working in the control room, where the Dauntless monitor the city's security. It is difficult for me to imagine him there, surrounded by computers. To me he belongs in the training room.

We learned about faction jobs in school. The Dauntless have limited options. We can guard the fence or work for the security of our city. We can work in the Dauntless compound, drawing tattoos or making weapons or even fighting each other for entertainment. Or we can work for the Dauntless leaders. That sounds like my best option.

The only problem is that my rank is terrible. And I might be factionless by the end of stage one.

We stop next to the gate. A few Dauntless guards glance in our direction but not many. They are too busy pulling the doors—which are twice as tall as they are and several times wider—open to admit a truck.

The man driving wears a hat, a beard, and a smile. He stops just inside the gate and gets out. The back of the truck is open, and a few other Amity sit among the stacks of crates. I peer at the crates—they hold apples.

"Beatrice?" an Amity boy says.

My head jerks at the sound of my name. One of the Amity in the back of the truck stands. He has curly blond hair and a familiar nose, wide at the tip and narrow at the bridge. Robert. I try to remember him at the Choosing Ceremony and nothing comes to mind but the sound of my heart in my ears. Who else transferred? Did Susan? Are there any Abnegation initiates this year? If Abnegation is fizzling, it's our fault—Robert's and Caleb's and mine. Mine. I push the thought from my mind.

Robert hops down from the truck. He wears a gray T-shirt and a pair of blue jeans. After a second's hesitation, he moves toward me and folds me in his arms. I stiffen. Only in Amity do people hug each other in greeting. I don't move a muscle until he releases me.

His own smile fades when he looks at me again. "Beatrice, what happened to you? What happened to your face?"

"Nothing," I say. "Just training. Nothing."

"*Beatrice?*" demands a nasal voice next to me. Molly folds her arms and laughs. "Is that your real name, Stiff?"

I glance at her. "What did you *think* Tris was short for?"

"Oh, I don't know . . . weakling?" She touches her chin. If her chin was bigger, it might balance out her nose, but it is weak and almost recedes into her neck. "Oh wait, *that* doesn't start with Tris. My mistake."

"There's no need to antagonize her," Robert says softly. "I'm Robert, and you are?"

"Someone who doesn't care what your name is," she says. "Why don't you get back in your truck? We're not supposed to fraternize with other faction members."

"Why don't you get away from us?" I snap.

"Right. Wouldn't want to get between you and your boyfriend," she says. She walks away smiling.

Robert gives me a sad look. "They don't seem like nice people."

"Some of them aren't."

"You could go home, you know. I'm sure Abnegation would make an exception for you."

"What makes you think I want to go home?" I ask, my cheeks hot. "You think I can't handle this or something?"

"It's not that." He shakes his head. "It's not that you can't, it's that you shouldn't have to. You should be happy."

"This is what I chose. This is it." I look over Robert's shoulder. The Dauntless guards seem to have finished examining the truck. The bearded man gets back into the driver's seat and closes the door behind him. "Besides, Robert. The goal of my life isn't just . . . to be happy."

"Wouldn't it be easier if it was, though?" he says.

Before I can answer, he touches my shoulder and turns toward the truck. A girl in the back has a banjo on her lap. She starts to strum it as Robert hoists himself inside, and the truck starts forward, carrying the banjo sounds and her warbling voice away from us.

Robert waves to me, and again I see another possible life in my mind's eye. I see myself in the back of the truck, singing with the girl, though I've never sung before, laughing when I am off-key, climbing trees to pick the apples, always peaceful and always safe.

The Dauntless guards close the gate and lock it behind them. The lock is on the outside. I bite my lip. Why would they lock the gate from the outside and not the inside? It almost seems like they don't want to keep something out; they want to keep us in.

I push the thought out of my head. That makes no sense.

Four steps away from the fence, where he was talking to a female Dauntless guard with a gun balanced on her shoulder a moment before. "I am worried that you have a knack for making unwise decisions," he says when he's a foot away from me.

I cross my arms. "It was a two-minute conversation."

"I don't think a smaller time frame makes it any less unwise." He furrows his eyebrows and touches the corner of my bruised eye with his fingertips. My head jerks back, but he doesn't take his hand away. Instead he tilts his head and sighs. "You know, if you could just learn to attack first, you might do better."

"Attack first?" I say. "How will that help?"

"You're fast. If you can get a few good hits in before they know what's going on, you could win." He shrugs, and his hand falls.

"I'm surprised you know that," I say quietly, "since you left halfway through my one and only fight."

"It wasn't something I wanted to watch," he says.

What's that supposed to mean?

He clears his throat. "Looks like the next train is here. Time to go, Tris."

CHAPTER
TWELVE

I CRAWL ACROSS my mattress and heave a sigh. It has been two days since my fight with Peter, and my bruises are turning purple-blue. I have gotten used to aching every time I move, so now I move better, but I am still far from healed.

Even though I am still injured, I had to fight again today. Luckily this time, I was paired against Myra, who couldn't throw a good punch if someone was controlling her arm for her. I got a good hit in during the first two minutes. She fell down and was too dizzy to get back up. I should feel triumphant, but there is no triumph in punching a girl like Myra.

The second I touch my head to the pillow, the door to the dormitory opens, and people stream into the room with flashlights. I sit up, almost hitting my head on the bed frame above me, and squint through the dark to see what's going on.

"Everybody up!" someone roars. A flashlight shines behind his head, making the rings in his ears glint. Eric. Surrounding him are other Dauntless, some of whom I have seen in the Pit, some of whom I have never seen before. Four stands among them.

His eyes shift to mine and stay there. I stare back and forget that all around me the transfers are getting out of bed.

"Did you go deaf, Stiff?" demands Eric. I snap out of my daze and slide out from beneath the blankets. I am glad I sleep fully clothed, because Christina stands next to our bunk wearing only a T-shirt, her long legs bare. She folds her arms and stares at Eric. I wish, suddenly, that I could stare so boldly at someone with hardly any clothes on, but I would never be able to do that.

"You have five minutes to get dressed and meet us by the tracks," says Eric. "We're going on another field trip."

I shove my feet into shoes and sprint, wincing, behind Christina on the way to the train. A drop of sweat rolls down the back of my neck as we run up the paths along the walls of the Pit, pushing past members on our way up. They don't seem surprised to see us. I wonder how many frantic, running people they see on a weekly basis.

We make it to the tracks just behind the Dauntless-born initiates. Next to the tracks is a black pile. I make out a cluster of long gun barrels and trigger guards.

"Are we going to *shoot* something?" Christina hisses in my ear.

Next to the pile are boxes of what looks like ammunition. I inch closer to read one of the boxes. Written on it is "PAINTBALLS."

I've never heard of them before, but the name is self-explanatory. I laugh.

"Everyone grab a gun!" shouts Eric.

We rush toward the pile. I am the closest to it, so I snatch the first gun I can find, which is heavy, but not too heavy for me to lift, and grab a box of paintballs. I shove the box in my pocket and sling the gun across my back so the strap crosses my chest.

"Time estimate?" Eric asks Four.

Four checks his watch. "Any minute now. How long is it going to take you to memorize the train schedule?"

"Why should I, when I have you to remind me of it?" says Eric, shoving Four's shoulder.

A circle of light appears on my left, far away. It grows larger as it comes closer, shining against the side of Four's face, creating a shadow in the faint hollow beneath his cheekbone.

He is the first to get on the train, and I run after him, not waiting for Christina or Will or Al to follow me. Four turns around as I fall into stride next to the car and holds out a hand. I grab his arm, and he pulls me in. Even the muscles in his forearm are taut, defined.

I let go quickly, without looking at him, and sit down on the other side of the car.

Once everyone is in, Four speaks up.

"We'll be dividing into two teams to play capture the flag. Each team will have an even mix of members, Dauntless-born initiates, and transfers. One team will get off first and find a place to hide their flag. Then the second team will get off and do the same." The car sways, and Four grabs the side of the doorway for balance. "This is a Dauntless tradition, so I suggest you take it seriously."

"What do we get if we win?" someone shouts.

"Sounds like the kind of question someone not from Dauntless would ask," says Four, raising an eyebrow. "You get to win, of course."

"Four and I will be your team captains," says Eric. He looks at Four. "Let's divide up transfers first, shall we?"

I tilt my head back. If they're picking us, I will be chosen last; I can feel it.

"You go first," Four says.

Eric shrugs. "Edward."

Four leans against the door frame and nods. The moonlight makes his eyes bright. He scans the group of transfer initiates briefly, without calculation, and says, "I want the Stiff."

A faint undercurrent of laughter fills the car. Heat rushes into my cheeks. I don't know whether to be angry at the people laughing at me or flattered by the fact that he chose me first.

"Got something to prove?" asks Eric, with his trademark smirk. "Or are you just picking the weak ones so that if you lose, you'll have someone to blame it on?"

Four shrugs. "Something like that."

Angry. I should definitely be angry. I scowl at my hands. Whatever Four's strategy is, it's based on the idea that I am weaker than the other initiates. And it gives me a bitter taste in my mouth. I have to prove him wrong—I *have* to.

"Your turn," says Four.

"Peter."

"Christina."

That throws a wrench in his strategy. Christina is not one of the weak ones. What exactly is he doing?

"Molly."

"Will," says Four, biting his thumbnail.

"Al."

"Drew."

"Last one left is Myra. So she's with me," says Eric. "Dauntless-born initiates next."

I stop listening once they're finished with us. If Four isn't trying to prove something by choosing the weak, what is he doing? I look at each person he chooses. What do we have in common?

Once they're halfway through the Dauntless-born initiates, I have an idea of what it is. With the exception of Will and a couple of the others, we all share the same body type: narrow shoulders, small frames. All the people on Eric's team are broad and strong. Just yesterday, Four told me I was fast. We will all be faster than Eric's team, which will probably be good for capture the flag—I haven't played before, but I know it's a game of speed rather than brute force. I cover a smile with my hand. Eric is more ruthless than Four, but Four is smarter.

They finish choosing teams, and Eric smirks at Four.

"Your team can get off second," says Eric.

"Don't do me any favors," Four replies. He smiles a little. "You know I don't need them to win."

"No, I know that you'll lose no matter when you get off," says Eric, biting down briefly on one of the rings in his lip. "Take your scrawny team and get off first, then."

We all stand up. Al gives me a forlorn look, and I smile back in what I hope is a reassuring way. If any of the four of us had to end up on the same team as Eric, Peter, and Molly, at least it was him. They usually leave him alone.

The train is about to dip to the ground. I am determined to land on my feet.

Just before I jump, someone shoves my shoulder, and I almost topple out of the train car. I don't look back to see who it is—Molly, Drew, or Peter, it doesn't matter which one. Before they can try it again, I jump. This time I am ready for the momentum the train gives me, and I run a few steps to diffuse it but keep my balance. Fierce pleasure courses through me and I smile. It's a small accomplishment, but it makes me feel Dauntless.

One of the Dauntless-born initiates touches Four's shoulder and asks, "When your team won, where did you put the flag?"

"Telling you wouldn't really be in the spirit of the exercise, Marlene," he says coolly.

"Come on, Four," she whines. She gives him a flirtatious smile. He brushes her hand off his arm, and for some reason, I find myself grinning.

"Navy Pier," another Dauntless-born initiate calls out. He is tall, with brown skin and dark eyes. Handsome. "My brother was on the winning team. They kept the flag at the carousel."

"Let's go there, then," suggests Will.

No one objects, so we walk east, toward the marsh that was once a lake. When I was young, I tried to imagine what it would look like as a lake, with no fence built into the mud to keep the city safe. But it is difficult to imagine that much water in one place.

"We're close to Erudite headquarters, right?" asks Christina, bumping Will's shoulder with her own.

"Yeah. It's south of here," he says. He looks over his shoulder, and for a second his expression is full of longing. Then it's gone.

I am less than a mile away from my brother. It has been a week since we were that close together. I shake my head a little to get the thought out of my mind. I can't think about him today, when I have to focus on making it through stage one. I can't think about him any day.

We walk across the bridge. We still need the bridges because the mud beneath them is too wet to walk on. I wonder how long it's been since the river dried up.

Once we cross the bridge, the city changes. Behind us, most of the buildings were in use, and even if they weren't, they looked well-tended. In front of us is a sea of crumbling concrete and broken glass. The silence of this part of the city is eerie; it feels like a nightmare. It's hard to see where I'm going, because it's after midnight and all the city lights are off.

Marlene takes out a flashlight and shines it at the street in front of us.

"Scared of the dark, Mar?" the dark-eyed Dauntless-born initiate teases.

"If you want to step on broken glass, Uriah, be my guest," she snaps. But she turns it off anyway.

I have realized that part of being Dauntless is being willing to make things more difficult for yourself in order to be self-sufficient. There's nothing especially brave about wandering dark streets with no flashlight, but we are not supposed to need help, even from light. We are supposed to be capable of anything.

I like that. Because there might come a day when there is no flashlight, there is no gun, there is no guiding hand. And I want to be ready for it.

The buildings end just before the marsh. A strip of land juts out into the marsh, and rising from it is a giant white wheel with dozens of red passenger cars dangling from it at regular intervals. The Ferris wheel.

"Think about it. People used to ride that thing. For *fun*," says Will, shaking his head.

"They must have been Dauntless," I say.

"Yeah, but a lame version of Dauntless." Christina laughs. "A Dauntless Ferris wheel wouldn't have cars. You would just hang on tight with your hands, and good luck to you."

We walk down the side of the pier. All the buildings on my left are empty, their signs torn down and their windows closed, but it is a clean kind of emptiness. Whoever left these places left them by choice and at their leisure. Some places in the city are not like that.

"Dare you to jump into the marsh," says Christina to Will.

"You first."

We reach the carousel. Some of the horses are scratched and weathered, their tails broken off or their saddles chipped. Four takes the flag out of his pocket.

"In ten minutes, the other team will pick their location," he says. "I suggest you take this time to formulate a strategy. We may not be Erudite,

but mental preparedness is one aspect of your Dauntless training. Argu-
ably, it is the most important aspect."

He is right about that. What good is a prepared body if you have a
scattered mind?

Will takes the flag from Four.

"Some people should stay here and guard, and some people should
go out and scout the other team's location," Will says.

"Yeah? You think?" Marlene plucks the flag from Will's fingers. "Who
put you in charge, transfer?"

"No one," says Will. "But someone's got to do it."

"Maybe we should develop a more defensive strategy. Wait for them
to come to us, then take them out," suggests Christina.

"That's the sissy way out," Uriah says. "I vote we go all out. Hide the
flag well enough that they can't find it."

Everyone bursts into the conversation at once, their voices louder
with each passing second. Christina defends Will's plan; the Dauntless-
born initiates vote for offense; everyone argues about who should make
the decision. Four sits down on the edge of the carousel, leaning against
a plastic horse's foot. His eyes lift to the sky, where there are no stars,
only a round moon peeking through a thin layer of clouds. The muscles
in his arms are relaxed; his hand rests on the back of his neck. He looks
almost comfortable, holding that gun to his shoulder.

I close my eyes briefly. Why does he distract me so easily? I need to
focus.

What would I say if I could shout above the sniping behind me? We
can't act until we know where the other team is. They could be anywhere
within a two-mile radius, although I can rule out the empty marsh as an
option. The best way to find them is not to argue about how to search for
them, or how many to send out in a search party.

It's to climb as high as possible.

I look over my shoulder to make sure no one is watching. None of
them look at me, so I walk toward the Ferris wheel with light, quiet footsteps, pressing my gun to my back with one hand to keep it from making
noise.

When I stare up at the Ferris wheel from the ground, my throat feels
tighter. It is taller than I thought, so tall I can barely see the cars swinging at the top. The only good thing about its height is that it is built to
support weight. If I climb it, it won't collapse beneath me.

My heart pumps faster. Will I really risk my life for this—to win a
game the Dauntless like to play?

It's so dark I can barely see them, but when I stare at the huge, rusted
supports holding the wheel in place, I see the rungs of a ladder. Each

support is only as wide as my shoulders, and there are no railings to hold me in, but climbing a ladder is better than climbing the spokes of the wheel.

I grab a rung. It's rusty and thin and feels like it might crumble in my hands. I put my weight on the lowest rung to test it and jump to make sure it will hold me up. The movement hurts my ribs, and I wince.

"Tris," a low voice says behind me. I don't know why it doesn't startle me. Maybe because I am becoming Dauntless, and mental readiness is something I am supposed to develop. Maybe because his voice is low and smooth and almost soothing. Whatever the reason, I look over my shoulder. Four stands behind me with his gun slung across his back, just like mine.

"Yes?" I say.

"I came to find out what you think you're doing."

"I'm seeking higher ground," I say. "I don't *think* I'm doing anything."

I see his smile in the dark. "All right. I'm coming."

I pause a second. He doesn't look at me the way Will, Christina, and Al sometimes do—like I am too small and too weak to be of any use, and they pity me for it. But if he insists on coming with me, it is probably because he doubts me.

"I'll be fine," I say.

"Undoubtedly," he replies. I don't hear the sarcasm, but I know it's there. It has to be.

I climb, and when I'm a few feet off the ground, he comes after me. He moves faster than I do, and soon his hands find the rungs that my feet leave.

"So tell me . . . ," he says quietly as we climb. He sounds breathless. "What do you think the purpose of this exercise is? The game, I mean, not the climbing."

I stare down at the pavement. It seems far away now, but I'm not even a third of the way up. Above me is a platform, just below the center of the wheel. That's my destination. I don't even think about how I will climb back down. The breeze that brushed my cheeks earlier now presses against my side. The higher we go, the stronger it will get. I need to be ready.

"Learning about strategy," I say. "Teamwork, maybe."

"Teamwork," he repeats. A laugh hitches in his throat. It sounds like a panicked breath.

"Maybe not," I say. "Teamwork doesn't seem to be a Dauntless priority."

The wind is stronger now. I press closer to the white support so I don't fall, but that makes it hard to climb. Below me the carousel looks small. I can barely see my team under the awning. Some of them are missing—a search party must have left.

Four says, "It's supposed to be a priority. It used to be."

But I'm not really listening, because the height is dizzying. My hands ache from holding the rungs, and my legs are shaking, but I'm not sure why. It isn't the height that scares me—the height makes me feel alive with energy, every organ and vessel and muscle in my body singing at the same pitch.

Then I realize what it is. It's him. Something about him makes me feel like I am about to fall. Or turn to liquid. Or burst into flames.

My hand almost misses the next rung.

"Now tell me . . . ," he says through a bursting breath, "what do you think learning strategy has to do with . . . bravery?"

The question reminds me that he is my instructor, and I am supposed to learn something from this. A cloud passes over the moon, and the light shifts across my hands.

"It . . . it prepares you to act," I say finally. "You learn strategy so you can use it." I hear him breathing behind me, loud and fast. "Are you all right, Four?"

"Are you *human*, Tris? Being up this high . . ." He gulps for air. "It doesn't scare you at all?"

I look over my shoulder at the ground. If I fall now, I will die. But I don't think I will fall.

A gust of air presses against my left side, throwing my body weight to the right. I gasp and cling to the rungs, my balance shifting. Four's cold hand clamps around one of my hips, one of his fingers finding a strip of bare skin just under the hem of my T-shirt. He squeezes, steadying me and pushing me gently to the left, restoring my balance.

Now *I* can't breathe. I pause, staring at my hands, my mouth dry. I feel the ghost of where his hand was, his fingers long and narrow.

"You okay?" he asks quietly.

"Yes," I say, my voice strained.

I keep climbing, silently, until I reach the platform. Judging by the blunted ends of metal rods, it used to have railings, but it doesn't anymore. I sit down and scoot to the end of it so Four has somewhere to sit. Without thinking, I put my legs over the side. Four, however, crouches and presses his back to the metal support, breathing heavily.

"You're afraid of heights," I say. "How do you survive in the Dauntless compound?"

"I ignore my fear," he says. "When I make decisions, I pretend it doesn't exist."

I stare at him for a second. I can't help it. To me there's a difference between not being afraid and acting in spite of fear, as he does.

I have been staring at him too long.

"What?" he says quietly.

"Nothing."

I look away from him and toward the city. I have to focus. I climbed up here for a reason.

The city is pitch-black, but even if it wasn't, I wouldn't be able to see very far. A building stands in my way.

"We're not high enough," I say. I look up. Above me is a tangle of white bars, the wheel's scaffolding. If I climb carefully, I can wedge my feet between the supports and the crossbars and stay secure. Or as secure as possible.

"I'm going to climb," I say, standing up. I grab one of the bars above my head and pull myself up. Shooting pains go through my bruised sides, but I ignore them.

"For God's sake, Stiff," he says.

"You don't have to follow me," I say, staring at the maze of bars above me. I shove my foot onto the place where two bars cross and push myself up, grabbing another bar in the process. I sway for a second, my heart beating so hard I can't feel anything else. Every thought I have condenses into that heartbeat, moving at the same rhythm.

"Yes, I do," he says.

This is crazy, and I know it. A fraction of an inch of mistake, half a second of hesitation, and my life is over. Heat tears through my chest, and I smile as I grab the next bar. I pull myself up, my arms shaking, and force my leg under me so I'm standing on another bar. When I feel steady, I look down at Four. But instead of seeing him, I see straight to the ground.

I can't breathe.

I imagine my body plummeting, smacking into the bars as it falls down, and my limbs at broken angles on the pavement, just like Rita's sister when she didn't make it onto the roof. Four grabs a bar with each hand and pulls himself up, easy, like he's sitting up in bed. But he is not comfortable or natural here—every muscle in his arm stands out. It is a stupid thing for me to think when I am one hundred feet off the ground.

I grab another bar, find another place to wedge my foot. When I look at the city again, the building isn't in my way. I'm high enough to see the skyline. Most of the buildings are black against a navy sky, but the red lights at the top of the Hub are lit up. They blink half as fast as my heartbeat.

Beneath the buildings, the streets look like tunnels. For a few seconds I see only a dark blanket over the land in front of me, just faint differences between building and sky and street and ground. Then I see a tiny pulsing light on the ground.

"See that?" I say, pointing.

Four stops climbing when he's right behind me and looks over my shoulder, his chin next to my head. His breaths flutter against my ear, and I feel shaky again, like I did when I was climbing the ladder.

"Yeah," he says. A smile spreads over his face.

"It's coming from the park at the end of the pier," he says. "Figures. It's surrounded by open space, but the trees provide some camouflage. Obviously not enough."

"Okay," I say. I look over my shoulder at him. We are so close I forget where I am; instead I notice that the corners of his mouth turn down naturally, just like mine, and that he has a scar on his chin.

"Um," I say. I clear my throat. "Start climbing down. I'll follow you."

Four nods and steps down. His leg is so long that he finds a place for his foot easily and guides his body between the bars. Even in darkness, I see that his hands are bright red and shaking.

I step down with one foot, pressing my weight into one of the crossbars. The bar creaks beneath me and comes loose, clattering against half a dozen bars on the way down and bouncing on the pavement. I'm dangling from the scaffolding with my toes swinging in midair. A strangled gasp escapes me.

"Four!"

I try to find another place to put my foot, but the nearest foothold is a few feet away, farther than I can stretch. My hands are sweaty. I remember wiping them on my slacks before the Choosing Ceremony, before the aptitude test, before every important moment, and suppress a scream. I will slip. I will slip.

"Hold on!" he shouts. "Just hold on, I have an idea."

He keeps climbing down. He's moving in the wrong direction; he should be coming toward me, not going away from me. I stare at my hands, which are wrapped around the narrow bar so tightly my knuckles are white. My fingers are dark red, almost purple. They won't last long.

I won't last long.

I squeeze my eyes shut. Better not to look. Better to pretend that none of this exists. I hear Four's sneakers squeak against metal and rapid footsteps on ladder rungs.

"Four!" I yell. Maybe he left. Maybe he abandoned me. Maybe this is a test of my strength, of my bravery. I breathe in my nose and out my mouth. I count my breaths to calm down. One, two. In, out. *Come on, Four* is all I can think. *Come on, do something.*

Then I hear something wheeze and creak. The bar I'm holding shudders, and I scream through my clenched teeth as I fight to keep my grip.

The wheel is moving.

Air wraps around my ankles and wrists as the wind gushes up, like a geyser. I open my eyes. I'm moving—toward the ground. I laugh, giddy with hysteria as the ground comes closer and closer. But I'm picking up speed. If I don't drop at the right time, the moving cars and metal scaffolding will drag at my body and carry me with them, and then I will really die.

Every muscle in my body tenses as I hurtle toward the ground. When I can see the cracks in the sidewalk, I drop, and my body slams into the ground, feet first. My legs collapse beneath me and I pull my arms in, rolling as fast as I can to the side. The cement scrapes my face, and I turn just in time to see a car bearing down on me, like a giant shoe about to crush me. I roll again, and the bottom of the car skims my shoulder.

I'm safe.

I press my palms to my face. I don't try to get up. If I did, I'm sure I would just fall back down. I hear footsteps, and Four's hands wrap around my wrists. I let him pry my hands from my eyes.

He encloses one of my hands perfectly between two of his. The warmth of his skin overwhelms the ache in my fingers from holding the bars.

"You all right?" he asks, pressing our hands together.

"Yeah."

He starts to laugh.

After a second, I laugh too. With my free hand, I push myself to a sitting position. I am aware of how little space there is between us—six inches at most. That space feels charged with electricity. I feel like it should be smaller.

He stands, pulling me up with him. The wheel is still moving, creating a wind that tosses my hair back.

"You could have told me that the Ferris wheel still worked," I say. I try to sound casual. "We wouldn't have had to climb in the first place."

"I would have, if I had known," he says. "Couldn't just let you hang there, so I took a risk. Come on, time to get their flag."

Four hesitates for a moment and then takes my arm, his fingertips pressing to the inside of my elbow. In other factions, he would give me time to recover, but he is Dauntless, so he smiles at me and starts toward the carousel, where our team members guard our flag. And I half run,

half limp beside him. I still feel weak, but my mind is awake, especially
with his hand on me.

Christina is perched on one of the horses, her long legs crossed and
her hand around the pole holding the plastic animal upright. Our flag is
behind her, a glowing triangle in the dark. Three Dauntless-born initiates stand among the other worn and dirty animals. One of them has his
hand on a horse's head, and a scratched horse eye stares at me between
his fingers. Sitting on the edge of the carousel is an older Dauntless,
scratching her quadruple-pierced eyebrow with her thumb.

"Where'd the others go?" asks Four.

He looks as excited as I feel, his eyes wide with energy.

"Did you guys turn on the wheel?" the older girl says. "What the hell
are you thinking? You might as well have just shouted 'Here we are! Come
and get us!' " She shakes her head. "If I lose again this year, the shame
will be unbearable. Three years in a row?"

"The wheel doesn't matter," says Four. "We know where they are."

"We?" says Christina, looking from Four to me.

"Yes, while the rest of you were twiddling your thumbs, Tris climbed
the Ferris wheel to look for the other team," he says.

"What do we do now, then?" asks one of the Dauntless-born initiates
through a yawn.

Four looks at me. Slowly the eyes of the other initiates, including
Christina, migrate from him to me. I tense my shoulders, about to shrug
and say I don't know, and then an image of the pier stretching out beneath me comes into my mind. I have an idea.

"Split in half," I say. "Four of us go to the right side of the pier, three
to the left. The other team is in the park at the end of the pier, so the
group of four will charge as the group of three sneaks behind the other
team to get the flag."

Christina looks at me like she no longer recognizes me. I don't
blame her.

"Sounds good," says the older girl, clapping her hands together. "Let's
get this night over with, shall we?"

Christina joins me in the group going to the right, along with Uriah,
whose smile looks white against his skin's bronze. I didn't notice before,
but he has a tattoo of a snake behind his ear. I stare at its tail curling
around his earlobe for a moment, but then Christina starts running and
I have to follow her.

I have to run twice as fast to match my short strides to her long ones.
As I run, I realize that only one of us will get to touch the flag, and it won't
matter that it was my plan and my information that got us to it if I'm not
the one who grabs it. Though I can hardly breathe as it is, I run faster,

and I'm on Christina's heels. I pull my gun around my body, holding my finger over the trigger.

We reach the end of the pier, and I clamp my mouth shut to keep my loud breaths in. We slow down so our footsteps aren't as loud, and I look for the blinking light again. Now that I'm on the ground, it's bigger and easier to see. I point, and Christina nods, leading the way toward it.

Then I hear a chorus of yells, so loud they make me jump. I hear puffs of air as paintballs go flying and splats as they find their targets. Our team has charged, the other team runs to meet us, and the flag is almost unguarded. Uriah takes aim and shoots the last guard in the thigh. The guard, a short girl with purple hair, throws her gun to the ground in a tantrum.

I sprint to catch up to Christina. The flag hangs from a tree branch, high above my head. I reach for it, and so does Christina.

"Come on, Tris," she says. "You're already the hero of the day. And you know you can't reach it anyway."

She gives me a patronizing look, the way people sometimes look at children when they act too adult, and snatches the flag from the branch. Without looking at me, she turns and gives a whoop of victory. Uriah's voice joins hers and then I hear a chorus of yells in the distance.

Uriah claps my shoulder, and I try to forget about the look Christina gave me. Maybe she's right; I've already proved myself today. I do not want to be greedy; I do not want to be like Eric, terrified of other people's strength.

The shouts of triumph become infectious, and I lift my voice to join in, running toward my teammates. Christina holds the flag up high, and everyone clusters around her, grabbing her arm to lift the flag even higher. I can't reach her, so I stand off to the side, grinning.

A hand touches my shoulder.

"Well done," Four says quietly.

+ + +

"I can't believe I missed it!" Will says again, shaking his head. Wind coming through the doorway of the train car blows his hair in every direction.

"You were performing the very important job of staying out of our way," says Christina, beaming.

Al groans. "Why did I have to be on the other team?"

"Because life's not fair, Albert. And the world is conspiring against you," says Will. "Hey, can I see the flag again?"

Peter, Molly, and Drew sit across from the members in the corner. Their chests and backs are splattered with blue and pink paint, and they look dejected. They speak quietly, sneaking looks at the rest of us, especially Christina. That is the benefit of not holding the flag right now—I am no one's target. Or at least, no more than usual.

"So you climbed the Ferris wheel, huh," says Uriah. He stumbles across the car and sits next to me. Marlene, the girl with the flirty smile, follows him.

"Yes," I say.

"Pretty smart of you. Like . . . Erudite smart," Marlene says. "I'm Marlene."

"Tris," I say. At home, being compared to an Erudite would be an insult, but she says it like a compliment.

"Yeah, I know who you are," she says. "The first jumper tends to stick in your head."

It has been years since I jumped off a building in my Abnegation uniform; it has been decades.

Uriah takes one of the paintballs from his gun and squeezes it between his thumb and index finger. The train lurches to the left, and Uriah falls against me, his fingers pinching the paintball until a stream of pink, foul-smelling paint sprays on my face.

Marlene collapses in giggles. I wipe some of the paint from my face, slowly, and then smear it on his cheek. The scent of fish oil wafts through the train car.

"Ew!" He squeezes the ball at me again, but the opening is at the wrong angle, and the paint sprays into his mouth instead. He coughs and makes exaggerated gagging sounds.

I wipe my face with my sleeve, laughing so hard my stomach hurts.

If my entire life is like this, loud laughter and bold action and the kind of exhaustion you feel after a hard but satisfying day, I will be content. As Uriah scrapes his tongue with his fingertips, I realize that all I have to do is get through initiation, and that life will be mine.

CHAPTER THIRTEEN

THE NEXT MORNING, when I trudge into the training room, yawning, a large target stands at one end of the room, and next to the door is a table with knives strewn across it. Target practice again. At least it won't hurt.

Eric stands in the middle of the room, his posture so rigid it looks like someone replaced his spine with a metal rod. The sight of him makes me feel like all the air in the room is heavier, bearing down on me. At least when he was slouched against a wall, I could pretend he wasn't here. Today I can't pretend.

"Tomorrow will be the last day of stage one," Eric says. "You will resume fighting then. Today, you'll be learning how to aim. Everyone pick up three knives." His voice is deeper than usual. "And pay attention while Four demonstrates the correct technique for throwing them."

At first no one moves.

"Now!"

We scramble for daggers. They aren't as heavy as guns, but they still feel strange in my hands, like I am not allowed to hold them.

"He's in a bad mood today," mumbles Christina.

"Is he ever in a good mood?" I murmur back.

But I know what she means. Judging by the poisonous look Eric gives Four when he isn't paying attention, last night's loss must have bothered Eric more than he let on. Winning capture the flag is a matter of pride, and pride is important to the Dauntless. More important than reason or sense.

I watch Four's arm as he throws a knife. The next time he throws, I watch his stance. He hits the target each time, exhaling as he releases the knife.

Eric orders, "Line up!"

Haste, I think, *will not help*. My mother told me that when I was learning how to knit. I have to think of this as a mental exercise, not a physical exercise. So I spend the first few minutes practicing without a knife, finding the right stance, learning the right arm motion.

Eric paces too quickly behind us.

"I think the Stiff's taken too many hits to the head!" remarks Peter, a few people down. "Hey, Stiff! Remember what a *knife* is?"

Ignoring him, I practice the throw again with a knife in hand but don't release it. I shut out Eric's pacing, and Peter's jeering, and the nagging feeling that Four is staring at me, and throw the knife. It spins end over end, slamming into the board. The blade doesn't stick, but I'm the first person to hit the target.

I smirk as Peter misses again. I can't help myself.

"Hey, Peter," I say. "Remember what a *target* is?"

Next to me, Christina snorts, and her next knife hits the target.

A half hour later, Al is the only initiate who hasn't hit the target yet. His knives clatter to the floor, or bounce off the wall. While the rest of us approach the board to collect our weapons, he hunts the floor for his.

The next time he tries and misses, Eric marches toward him and demands, "How slow *are* you, Candor? Do you need glasses? Should I move the target closer to you?"

Al's face turns red. He throws another knife, and this one sails a few feet to the right of the target. It spins and hits the wall.

"What was that, initiate?" says Eric quietly, leaning closer to Al.

I bite my lip. This isn't good.

"It—it slipped," says Al.

"Well, I think you should go get it," Eric says. He scans the other initiates' faces—everyone has stopped throwing again—and says, "Did I tell you to stop?"

Knives start to hit the board. We have all seen Eric angry before, but this is different. The look in his eyes is almost rabid.

"Go get it?" Al's eyes are wide. "But everyone's still throwing."

"And?"

"And I don't want to get hit."

"I think you can trust your fellow initiates to aim better than you." Eric smiles a little, but his eyes stay cruel. "Go get your knife."

Al doesn't usually object to anything the Dauntless tell us to do. I don't think he's afraid to; he just knows that objecting is useless. This time Al sets his wide jaw. He's reached the limits of his compliance.

"No," he says.

"Why not?" Eric's beady eyes fix on Al's face. "Are you afraid?"

"Of getting stabbed by an airborne knife?" says Al. "Yes, I am!"

Honesty is his mistake. Not his refusal, which Eric might have accepted.

"Everyone stop!" Eric shouts.

The knives stop, and so does all conversation. I hold my small dagger tightly.

"Clear out of the ring." Eric looks at Al. "All except you."

I drop the dagger and it hits the dusty floor with a thud. I follow the other initiates to the edge of the room, and they inch in front of me, eager to see what makes my stomach turn: Al, facing Eric's wrath.

"Stand in front of the target," says Eric.

Al's big hands shake. He walks back to the target.

"Hey, Four." Eric looks over his shoulder. "Give me a hand here, huh?"

Four scratches one of his eyebrows with a knife point and approaches Eric. He has dark circles under his eyes and a tense set to his mouth—he's as tired as we are.

"You're going to stand there as he throws those knives," Eric says to Al, "until you learn not to flinch."

"Is this really necessary?" says Four. He sounds bored, but he doesn't look bored. His face and body are tense, alert.

I squeeze my hands into fists. No matter how casual Four sounds, the question is a challenge. And Four doesn't often challenge Eric directly.

At first Eric stares at Four in silence. Four stares back. Seconds pass and my fingernails bite my palms.

"I have the authority here, remember?" Eric says, so quietly I can barely hear him. "Here, and everywhere else."

Color rushes into Four's face, though his expression does not change. His grip on the knives tightens and his knuckles turn white as he turns to face Al.

I look from Al's wide, dark eyes to his shaking hands to the determined set of Four's jaw. Anger bubbles in my chest, and bursts from my mouth: "*Stop* it."

Four turns the knife in his hand, his fingers moving painstakingly over the metal edge. He gives me such a hard look that I feel like he's turning me to stone. I know why. I am stupid for speaking up while Eric is here; I am stupid for speaking up at all.

"Any idiot can stand in front of a target," I say. "It doesn't prove anything except that you're bullying us. Which, as I recall, is a sign of *cowardice.*"

"Then it should be easy for you," Eric says. "If you're willing to take his place."

The last thing I want to do is stand in front of that target, but I can't back down now. I didn't leave myself the option. I weave through the crowd of initiates, and someone shoves my shoulder.

"There goes your pretty face," hisses Peter. "Oh, wait. You don't have one."

I recover my balance and walk toward Al. He nods at me. I try to smile encouragingly, but I can't manage it. I stand in front of the board, and my head doesn't even reach the center of the target, but it doesn't matter. I look at Four's knives: one in his right hand, two in his left hand.

My throat is dry. I try to swallow, and then look at Four. He is never sloppy. He won't hit me. I'll be fine.

I tip my chin up. I will not flinch. If I flinch, I prove to Eric that this is not as easy as I said it was; I prove that I'm a coward.

"If you flinch," Four says, slowly, carefully, "Al takes your place. Understand?"

I nod.

Four's eyes are still on mine when he lifts his hand, pulls his elbow back, and throws the knife. It is just a flash in the air, and then I hear a thud. The knife is buried in the board, half a foot away from my cheek. I close my eyes. Thank God.

"You about done, Stiff?" asks Four.

I remember Al's wide eyes and his quiet sobs at night and shake my head. "No."

"Eyes open, then." He taps the spot between his eyebrows.

I stare at him, pressing my hands to my sides so no one can see them shake. He passes a knife from his left hand to his right hand, and I see nothing but his eyes as the second knife hits the target above my head. This one is closer than the last one—I feel it hovering over my skull.

"Come on, Stiff," he says. "Let someone else stand there and take it."

Why is he trying to goad me into giving up? Does he want me to fail?

"Shut *up*, Four!"

I hold my breath as he turns the last knife in his hand. I see a glint in his eyes as he pulls his arm back and lets the knife fly. It comes straight at me, spinning, blade over handle. My body goes rigid. This time, when it hits the board, my ear stings, and blood tickles my skin. I touch my ear. He nicked it.

And judging by the look he gives me, he did it on purpose.

"I would love to stay and see if the rest of you are as daring as she is," says Eric, his voice smooth, "but I think that's enough for today."

He squeezes my shoulder. His fingers feel dry and cold, and the look he gives me claims me, like he's taking ownership of what I did. I don't return Eric's smile. What I did had nothing to do with him.

"I should keep my eye on you," he adds.

Fear prickles inside me, in my chest and in my head and in my hands. I feel like the word "DIVERGENT" is branded on my forehead, and if he looks at me long enough, he'll be able to read it. But he just lifts his hand from my shoulder and keeps walking.

Four and I stay behind. I wait until the room is empty and the door is shut before looking at him again. He walks toward me.

"Is your—" he begins.

"You did that on *purpose*!" I shout.

"Yes, I did," he says quietly. "And you should thank me for helping you."

I grit my teeth. "*Thank* you? You almost stabbed my ear, and you spent the entire time taunting me. Why should I thank you?"

"You know, I'm getting a little tired of waiting for you to catch on!"

He glares at me, and even when he glares, his eyes look thoughtful. Their shade of blue is peculiar, so dark it is almost black, with a small patch of lighter blue on the left iris, right next to the corner of his eye.

"Catch on? Catch on to what? That you wanted to prove to Eric how tough you are? That you're sadistic, just like he is?"

"I am not sadistic." He doesn't yell. I wish he would yell. It would scare me less. He leans his face close to mine, which reminds me of lying inches away from the attack dog's fangs in the aptitude test, and says, "If I wanted to hurt you, don't you think I would have already?"

He crosses the room and slams the point of a knife so hard into the table that it sticks there, handle toward the ceiling.

"I—" I start to shout, but he's already gone. I scream, frustrated, and wipe some of the blood from my ear.

CHAPTER
FOURTEEN

TODAY IS THE day before Visiting Day. I think of Visiting Day like I think of the world ending: Nothing after it matters. Everything I do builds up to it. I might see my parents again. I might not. Which is worse? I don't know.

I try to pull a pant leg over my thigh and it sticks just above my knee. Frowning, I stare at my leg. A bulge of muscle is stopping the fabric. I let the pant leg fall and look over my shoulder at the back of my thigh. Another muscle stands out there.

I step to the side so I stand in front of the mirror. I see muscles that I couldn't see before in my arms, legs, and stomach. I pinch my side, where a layer of fat used to hint at curves to come. Nothing. Dauntless initiation has stolen whatever softness my body had. Is that good, or bad?

At least I am stronger than I was. I wrap my towel around me again and leave the girls' bathroom. I hope no one is in the dormitory to see me walking in my towel, but I can't wear those pants.

When I open the dormitory door, a weight drops into my stomach. Peter, Molly, Drew, and some of the other initiates stand in the back corner, laughing. They look up when I walk in and start snickering. Molly's snort-laugh is louder than everyone else's.

I walk to my bunk, trying to pretend like they aren't there, and fumble in the drawer under my bed for the dress Christina made me get. One hand clamped around the towel and one holding the dress, I stand up, and right behind me is Peter.

I jump back, almost hitting my head on Christina's bunk. I try to slip past him, but he slams his hand against Christina's bed frame, blocking my path. I should have known he wouldn't let me get away that easily.

"Didn't realize you were so skinny, Stiff."

"Get away from me." My voice is somehow steady.

"This isn't the Hub, you know. No one has to follow a Stiff's orders here." His eyes travel down my body, not in the greedy way that a man looks at a woman, but cruelly, scrutinizing every flaw. I hear my heartbeat in my ears as the others inch closer, forming a pack behind Peter.

This will be bad.

I have to get out of here.

Out of the corner of my eye, I see a clear path to the door. If I can duck under Peter's arm and sprint toward it, I might be able to make it.

"Look at her," says Molly, crossing her arms. She smirks at me. "She's practically a child."

"Oh, I don't know," says Drew. "She could be hiding something under that towel. Why don't we look and see?"

Now. I duck under Peter's arm and dart toward the door. Something pinches and pulls at my towel as I walk away and then yanks sharply— Peter's hand, gathering the fabric into his fist. The towel slips from my hand and the air is cold on my naked body, making the hair on the back of my neck stand on end.

Laughter erupts, and I run as fast as I can toward the door, holding the dress against my body to hide it. I sprint down the hallway and into the bathroom and lean against the door, breathing hard. I close my eyes.

It doesn't matter. I don't care.

A sob bursts from my mouth, and I slap my hand over my lips to contain it. It doesn't matter what they saw. I shake my head like the motion is supposed to make it true.

With shaking hands, I get dressed. The dress is plain black, with a V-neck that shows the tattoos on my collarbone, and goes down to my knees.

Once I'm dressed and the urge to cry is gone, I feel something hot and violent writhing in my stomach. I want to hurt them.

I stare at my eyes in the mirror. I want to, so I will.

+ + +

I can't fight in a dress, so I get myself some new clothes from the Pit before I walk to the training room for my last fight. I hope it's with Peter.

"Hey, where were you this morning?" Christina asks when I walk in. I squint to see the blackboard across the room. The space next to my name is blank—I haven't gotten an opponent yet.

"I got held up," I say.

Four stands in front of the board and writes a name next to mine. *Please let it be Peter, please, please. . . .*

"You okay, Tris? You look a little . . . ," says Al.

"A little what?"

Four moves away from the board. The name written next to mine is Molly. Not Peter, but good enough.

"On edge," says Al.

My fight is last on the list, which means I have to wait through three matches before I face her. Edward and Peter fight second to last—good. Edward is the only one who can beat Peter. Christina will fight Al, which means that Al will lose quickly, like he's been doing all week.

"Go easy on me, okay?" Al asks Christina.

"I make no promises," she replies.

The first pair—Will and Myra—stand across from each other in the arena. For a second they both shuffle back and forth, one jerking an arm forward and then retracting it, the other kicking and missing. Across the room, Four leans against the wall and yawns.

I stare at the board and try to predict the outcome of each match. It doesn't take long. Then I bite my fingernails and think about Molly. Christina lost to her, which means she's good. She has a powerful punch, but she doesn't move her feet. If she can't hit me, she can't hurt me.

As expected, the next fight between Christina and Al is quick and painless. Al falls after a few hard hits to the face and doesn't get back up, which makes Eric shake his head.

Edward and Peter take longer. Though they are the two best fighters, the disparity between them is noticeable. Edward's fist slams into Peter's jaw, and I remember what Will said about him—that he has been studying combat since he was ten. It's obvious. He is faster and smarter than even Peter.

By the time the three matches are done, my nails are bitten to the beds and I'm hungry for lunch. I walk to the arena without looking at anyone or anything but the center of the room. Some of my anger has faded, but it isn't hard to call back. All I have to do is think about how cold the air was and how loud the laughter was. *Look at her. She's a child.*

Molly stands across from me.

"Was that a birthmark I saw on your left butt cheek?" she says, smirking. "God, you're pale, Stiff."

She'll make the first move. She always does.

Molly starts toward me and throws her weight into a punch. As her body shifts forward, I duck and drive my fist into her stomach, right over her bellybutton. Before she can get her hands on me, I slip past her, my hands up, ready for her next attempt.

She's not smirking anymore. She runs at me like she's about to tackle me, and I dart out of the way. I hear Four's voice in my head, telling me that the most powerful weapon at my disposal is my elbow. I just have to find a way to use it.

I block her next punch with my forearm. The blow stings, but I barely notice it. She grits her teeth and lets out a frustrated groan, more animal-sounding than human. She tries a sloppy kick at my side, which I dodge, and while her balance is off, I rush forward and force my elbow up at her face. She pulls her head back just in time, and my elbow grazes her chin.

She punches me in the ribs and I stumble to the side, recovering my breath. There's something she's not protecting, I know it. I want to hit her face, but maybe that's not a smart move. I watch her for a few seconds. Her hands are too high; they guard her nose and cheeks, leaving her stomach and ribs exposed. Molly and I have the same flaw in combat.

Our eyes meet for just a second.

I aim an uppercut low, below her bellybutton. My fist sinks into her flesh, forcing a heavy breath from her mouth that I feel against my ear. As she gasps, I sweep-kick her legs out from under her, and she falls hard on the ground, sending dust into the air. I pull my foot back and kick as hard as I can at her ribs.

My mother and father would not approve of my kicking someone when she's down.

I don't care.

She curls into a ball to protect her side, and I kick again, this time hitting her in the stomach. *Like a child.* I kick again, this time hitting her in the face. Blood springs from her nose and spreads over her face. *Look at her.* Another kick hits her in the chest.

I pull my foot back again, but Four's hands clamp around my arms, and he pulls me away from her with irresistible force. I breathe through gritted teeth, staring at Molly's blood-covered face, the color deep and rich and beautiful, in a way.

She groans, and I hear a gurgling in her throat, watch blood trickle from her lips.

"You won," Four mutters. "Stop."

I wipe the sweat from my forehead. He stares at me. His eyes are too wide; they look alarmed.

"I think you should leave," he says. "Take a walk."

"I'm fine," I say. "I'm fine now," I say again, this time for myself.

I wish I could say I felt guilty for what I did.

I don't.

CHAPTER
FIFTEEN

VISITING DAY. The second I open my eyes, I remember. My heart leaps and then plummets when I see Molly hobble across the dormitory, her nose purple between strips of medical tape. Once I see her leave, I check for Peter and Drew. Neither of them is in the dormitory, so I change quickly. As long as they aren't here, I don't care who sees me in my underwear, not anymore.

Everyone else dresses in silence. Not even Christina smiles. We all know that we might go to the Pit floor and search every face and never find one that belongs to us.

I make my bed with the tight corners like my father taught me. As I pinch a stray hair from my pillow, Eric walks in.

"Attention!" he announces, flicking a lock of dark hair from his eyes. "I want to give you some advice about today. If by some miracle your families do come to visit you . . ." He scans our faces and smirks. ". . . which I doubt, it is best not to seem too attached. That will make it easier for you, and easier for them. We also take the phrase 'faction before blood' very seriously here. Attachment to your family suggests you aren't entirely pleased with your faction, which would be *shameful*. Understand?"

I understand. I hear the threat in Eric's sharp voice. The only part of that speech that Eric meant was the last part: We are Dauntless, and we need to act accordingly.

On my way out of the dormitory, Eric stops me.

"I may have underestimated you, Stiff," he says. "You did well yesterday."

I stare up at him. For the first time since I beat Molly, guilt pinches my gut.

If Eric thinks I did something right, I must have done it wrong.

"Thank you," I say. I slip out of the dormitory.

Once my eyes adjust to the dim hallway light, I see Christina and Will ahead of me, Will laughing, probably at a joke Christina made. I don't try to catch up. For some reason, I feel like it would be a mistake to interrupt them.

Al is missing. I didn't see him in the dormitory, and he's not walking toward the Pit now. Maybe he's already there.

I run my fingers through my hair and smooth it into a bun. I check my clothes—am I covered up? My pants are tight and my collarbone is showing. They won't approve.

Who cares if they approve? I set my jaw. This is my faction now. These are the clothes my faction wears. I stop just before the hallway ends.

Clusters of families stand on the Pit floor, most of them Dauntless families with Dauntless initiates. They still look strange to me—a mother with a pierced eyebrow, a father with a tattooed arm, an initiate with purple hair, a wholesome family unit. I spot Drew and Molly standing alone at one end of the room and suppress a smile. At least their families didn't come.

But Peter's did. He stands next to a tall man with bushy eyebrows and a short, meek-looking woman with red hair. Neither of his parents looks like him. They both wear black pants and white shirts, typical Candor outfits, and his father speaks so loudly I can almost hear him from where I stand. Do they know what kind of person their son is?

Then again . . . what kind of person am I?

Across the room, Will stands with a woman in a blue dress. She doesn't look old enough to be his mother, but she has the same crease between her eyebrows as he does, and the same golden hair. He talked about having a sister once; maybe that's her.

Next to him, Christina hugs a dark-skinned woman in Candor black and white. Standing behind Christina is a young girl, also a Candor. Her younger sister.

Should I even bother scanning the crowd for my parents? I could turn around and go back to the dormitory.

Then I see her. My mother stands alone near the railing with her hands clasped in front of her. She has never looked more out of place, with her gray slacks and gray jacket buttoned at the throat, her hair in its simple twist and her face placid. I start toward her, tears jumping into my eyes. She came. She came for me.

I walk faster. She sees me, and for a second her expression is blank, like she doesn't know who I am. Then her eyes light up, and she opens her arms. She smells like soap and laundry detergent.

"Beatrice," she whispers. She runs her hand over my hair.

Don't cry, I tell myself. I hold her until I can blink the moisture from my eyes, and then pull back to look at her again. I smile with closed lips, just like she does. She touches my cheek.

"Well, look at you," she says. "You've filled out." She puts her arm across my shoulders. "Tell me how you are."

"You first." The old habits are back. I should let her speak first. I shouldn't let the conversation stay focused on me for too long. I should make sure she doesn't need anything.

"Today is a special occasion," she says. "I came to see you, so let's talk mostly about you. It is my gift to you."

My selfless mother. She should not be giving me gifts, not after I left her and my father. I walk with her toward the railing that overlooks the chasm, glad to be close to her. The last week and a half has been more affectionless than I realized. At home we did not touch each other often, and the most I ever saw my parents do was hold hands at the dinner table, but it was more than this, more than here.

"Just one question." I feel my pulse in my throat. "Where's Dad? Is he visiting Caleb?"

"Ah." She shakes her head. "Your father had to be at work."

I look down. "You can tell me if he didn't want to come."

Her eyes travel over my face. "Your father has been selfish lately. That doesn't mean he doesn't love you, I promise."

I stare at her, stunned. My father—selfish? More startling than the label is the fact that she assigned it to him. I can't tell by looking at her if she's angry. I don't expect to be able to. But she must be; if she calls him *selfish*, she must be angry.

"What about Caleb?" I say. "Will you visit him later?"

"I wish I could," she says, "but the Erudite have prohibited Abnegation visitors from entering their compound. If I tried, I would be removed from the premises."

"What?" I demand. "That's terrible. Why would they do that?"

"Tensions between our factions are higher than ever," she says. "I wish it wasn't that way, but there is little I can do about it."

I think of Caleb standing among the Erudite initiates, scanning the crowd for our mother, and feel a pang in my stomach. Part of me is still angry with him for keeping so many secrets from me, but I don't want him to hurt.

"That's terrible," I repeat. I look toward the chasm.

Standing alone at the railing is Four. Though he's not an initiate anymore, most of the Dauntless use this day to come together with their families. Either his family doesn't like to come together, or he wasn't originally Dauntless. Which faction could he have come from?

"There's one of my instructors." I lean closer to her and say, "He's kind of intimidating."

"He's *handsome*," she says.

I find myself nodding without thinking. She laughs and lifts her arm from my shoulders. I want to steer her away from him, but just as I'm about to suggest that we go somewhere else, he looks over his shoulder.

His eyes widen at the sight of my mother. She offers him her hand.

"Hello. My name is Natalie," she says. "I'm Beatrice's mother."

I have never seen my mother shake hands with someone. Four eases his hand into hers, looking stiff, and shakes it twice. The gesture looks unnatural for both of them. No, Four was not originally Dauntless if he doesn't shake hands easily.

"Four," he says. "It's nice to meet you."

"Four," my mother repeats, smiling. "Is that a nickname?"

"Yes." He doesn't elaborate. What *is* his real name? "Your daughter is doing well here. I've been overseeing her training."

Since when does "overseeing" include throwing knives at me and scolding me at every opportunity?

"That's good to hear," she says. "I know a few things about Dauntless initiation, and I was worried about her."

He looks at me, and his eyes move down my face, from nose to mouth to chin. Then he says, "You shouldn't worry."

I can't keep the heat from rushing into my cheeks. I hope it isn't noticeable.

Is he just reassuring her because she's my mother, or does he really believe that I am capable? And what did that look mean?

She tilts her head. "You look familiar for some reason, Four."

"I can't imagine why," he replies, his voice suddenly cold. "I don't make a habit of associating with the Abnegation."

My mother laughs. She has a light laugh, half air and half sound. "Few people do, these days. I don't take it personally."

He seems to relax a little. "Well, I'll leave you to your reunion."

My mother and I watch him leave. The roar of the river fills my ears. Maybe Four was one of the Erudite, which explains why he hates Abnegation. Or maybe he believes the articles the Erudite release about us— *them*, I remind myself. But it was kind of him to tell her that I'm doing well when I know he doesn't believe it.

"Is he always like that?" she says.

"Worse."

"Have you made friends?" she asks.

"A few," I say. I look over my shoulder at Will and Christina and their families. When Christina catches my eye, she beckons to me, smiling, so my mother and I cross the Pit floor.

Before we can get to Will and Christina, though, a short, round woman with a black-and-white-striped shirt touches my arm. I twitch, resisting the urge to smack her hand away.

"Excuse me," she says. "Do you know my son? Albert?"

"Albert?" I repeat. "Oh—you mean Al? Yes, I know him."

"Do you know where we can find him?" she says, gesturing to a man behind her. He is tall and as thick as a boulder. Al's father, obviously.

"I'm sorry, I didn't see him this morning. Maybe you should look for him up there?" I point at the glass ceiling above us.

"Oh my," Al's mother says, fanning her face with her hand. "I would rather not attempt that climb again. I almost had a panic attack on the way down here. Why aren't there any railings along those paths? Are you all insane?"

I smile a little. A few weeks ago I might have found that question offensive, but now I spend too much time with Candor transfers to be surprised by tactlessness.

"Insane, no," I say. "Dauntless, yes. If I see him, I'll tell him you're looking for him."

My mother, I see, wears the same smile I do. She isn't reacting the way some of the other transfers' parents are—her neck bent, looking around at the Pit walls, at the Pit ceiling, at the chasm. Of course she isn't curious—she's Abnegation. Curiosity is foreign to her.

I introduce my mother to Will and Christina, and Christina introduces me to her mother and her sister. But when Will introduces me to Cara, his older sister, she gives me the kind of look that would wither a plant and does not extend her hand for me to shake. She glares at my mother.

"I can't believe that you associate with one of *them*, Will," she says.

My mother purses her lips, but of course, doesn't say anything.

"Cara," says Will, frowning, "there's no need to be *rude*."

"Oh, certainly not. Do you know what she is?" She points at my mother. "She's a council member's *wife* is what she is. She runs the 'volunteer agency' that supposedly helps the factionless. You think I don't know that you're just hoarding goods to distribute to your own faction while *we* don't get fresh food for a month, huh? Food for the factionless, my eye."

"I'm sorry," my mother says gently. "I believe you are mistaken."

"Mistaken. Ha," Cara snaps. "I'm sure you're exactly what you seem.

A faction of happy-go-lucky do-gooders without a selfish bone in their bodies. Right."

"Don't speak to my mother that way," I say, my face hot. I clench my hands into fists. "Don't say another word to her or I swear I will break your nose."

"Back off, Tris," Will says. "You're not going to punch my sister."

"Oh?" I say, raising both eyebrows. "You think so?"

"No, you're not." My mother touches my shoulder. "Come on, Beatrice. We wouldn't want to bother your friend's sister."

She sounds gentle, but her hand squeezes my arm so hard I almost cry out from the pain as she drags me away. She walks with me, fast, toward the dining hall. Just before she reaches it, though, she takes a sharp left turn and walks down one of the dark hallways I haven't explored yet.

"Mom," I say. "Mom, how do you know where you're going?"

She stops next to a locked door and stands on her tiptoes, peering at the base of the blue lamp hanging from the ceiling. A few seconds later she nods and turns to me again.

"I said no questions about me. And I meant it. How are you really doing, Beatrice? How have the fights been? How are you ranked?"

"Ranked?" I say. "You know that I've been fighting? You know that I'm ranked?"

"It isn't top-secret information, how the Dauntless initiation process works."

I don't know how easy it is to find out what another faction does during initiation, but I suspect it's not *that* easy. Slowly, I say, "I'm close to the bottom, Mom."

"Good." She nods. "No one looks too closely at the bottom. Now, this is very important, Beatrice: What were your aptitude test results?"

Tori's warning pulses in my head. *Don't tell anyone.* I should tell her that my result was Abnegation, because that's what Tori recorded in the system.

I look into my mother's eyes, which are pale green and framed by a dark smudge of eyelashes. She has lines around her mouth, but other than that, she doesn't look her age. Those lines get deeper when she hums. She used to hum as she washed the dishes.

This is my mother.

I can trust her.

"They were inconclusive," I say softly.

"I thought as much." She sighs. "Many children who are raised Abnegation receive that kind of result. We don't know why. But you have to be very careful during the next stage of initiation, Beatrice. Stay in the middle of the pack, no matter what you do. Don't draw attention to yourself. Do you understand?"

"Mom, what's going on?"

"I don't care what faction you chose," she says, touching her hands to my cheeks. "I am your mother and I want to keep you safe."

"Is this because I'm a—" I start to say, but she presses her hand to my mouth.

"Don't say that word," she hisses. "Ever."

So Tori was right. Divergent is a dangerous thing to be. I just don't know why, or even what it really means, still.

"Why?"

She shakes her head. "I can't say."

She looks over her shoulder, where the light from the Pit floor is barely visible. I hear shouts and conversations, laughter and shuffling footsteps. The smell from the dining hall floats over my nose, sweet and yeasty: baking bread. When she turns toward me, her jaw is set.

"There's something I want you to do," she says. "I can't go visit your brother, but you can, when initiation is over. So I want you to go find him and tell him to research the simulation serum. Okay? Can you do that for me?"

"Not unless you *explain* some of this to me, Mom!" I cross my arms. "You want me to go hang out at the Erudite compound for the day, you had better give me a reason!"

"I can't. I'm sorry." She kisses my cheek and brushes a lock of hair that fell from my bun behind my ear. "I should leave. It will make you look better if you and I don't seem attached to each other."

"I don't care how I look to them," I say.

"You should," she says. "I suspect they are already monitoring you."

She walks away, and I am too stunned to follow her. At the end of the hallway she turns and says, "Have a piece of cake for me, all right? The chocolate. It's delicious." She smiles a strange, twisted smile, and adds, "I love you, you know."

And then she's gone.

I stand alone in the blue light coming from the lamp above me, and I understand:

She has been to the compound before. She remembered this hallway. She knows about the initiation process.

My mother was Dauntless.

CHAPTER
SIXTEEN

THAT AFTERNOON, I go back to the dormitory while everyone else spends time with their families and find Al sitting on his bed, staring at the space on the wall where the chalkboard usually is. Four took it down yesterday so he could calculate our stage one rankings.

"There you are!" I say. "Your parents were looking for you. Did they find you?"

He shakes his head.

I sit down next to him on the bed. My leg is barely half the width of his, even now that it's more muscular than it was. He wears black shorts. His knee is purple-blue with a bruise and crossed with a scar.

"You didn't want to see them?" I say.

"Didn't want them to ask how I was doing," he says. "I'd have to tell them, and they would know if I was lying."

"Well . . ." I struggle to come up with something to say. "What's wrong with how you're doing?"

Al laughs harshly. "I've lost every fight since the one with Will. I'm not doing well."

"By choice, though. Couldn't you tell them that, too?"

He shakes his head. "Dad always wanted me to come here. I mean, they said they wanted me to stay in Candor, but that's only because that's what they're supposed to say. They've always admired the Dauntless, both of them. They wouldn't understand if I tried to explain it to them."

"Oh." I tap my fingers against my knee. Then I look at him. "Is that why you chose Dauntless? Because of your parents?"

Al shakes his head. "No. I guess it was because . . . I think it's important to protect people. To stand up for people. Like you did for me." He smiles at me. "That's what the Dauntless are supposed to do, right? That's what courage is. Not . . . hurting people for no reason."

I remember what Four told me, that teamwork used to be a Dauntless priority. What were the Dauntless like when it was? What would I have learned if I had been here when my mother was Dauntless? Maybe I wouldn't have broken Molly's nose. Or threatened Will's sister.

I feel a pang of guilt. "Maybe it will be better once initiation is over."

"Too bad I might come in last," Al says. "I guess we'll see tonight."

We sit side-by-side for a while. It's better to be here, in silence, than in the Pit, watching everyone laugh with their families.

My father used to say that sometimes, the best way to help someone is just to be near them. I feel good when I do something I know he would be proud of, like it makes up for all the things I've done that he wouldn't be proud of.

"I feel braver when I'm around you, you know," he says. "Like I could actually fit in here, the same way you do."

I am about to respond when he slides his arm across my shoulders. Suddenly I freeze, my cheeks hot.

I didn't want to be right about Al's feelings for me. But I was.

I do not lean into him. Instead I sit forward so his arm falls away. Then I squeeze my hands together in my lap.

"Tris, I . . . ," he says. His voice sounds strained. I glance at him. His face is as red as mine feels, but he's not crying—he just looks embarrassed.

"Um . . . sorry," he says. "I wasn't trying to . . . um, Sorry."

I wish I could tell him not to take it personally. I could tell him that my parents rarely held hands even in our own home, so I have trained myself to pull away from all gestures of affection, because they raised me to take them seriously. Maybe if I told him that, there wouldn't be a layer of hurt beneath his flush of embarrassment.

But of course, it is personal. He is my friend—and that is all. What is more personal than that?

I breathe in, and when I breathe out, I make myself smile. "Sorry about what?" I ask, trying to sound casual. I brush off my jeans, though there isn't anything on them, and stand up.

"I should go," I say.

He nods and doesn't look at me.

"You going to be okay?" I say. "I mean . . . because of your parents. Not because . . ." I let my voice trail off. I don't know what I would say if I didn't.

"Oh. Yeah." He nods again, a little too vigorously. "I'll see you later, Tris."

I try not to walk out of the room too fast. When the dormitory door closes behind me, I touch a hand to my forehead and grin a little. Awkwardness aside, it is nice to be liked.

+ + +

Discussing our family visits would be too painful, so our final rankings for stage one are all anyone can talk about that night. Every time someone near me brings it up, I stare at some point across the room and ignore them.

My rank can't be as bad as it used to be, especially after I beat Molly, but it might not be good enough to get me in the top ten at the end of initiation, especially when the Dauntless-born initiates are factored in.

At dinner I sit with Christina, Will, and Al at a table in the corner. We are uncomfortably close to Peter, Drew, and Molly, who are at the next table over. When conversation at our table reaches a lull, I hear every word they say. They are speculating about the ranks. What a surprise.

"You weren't allowed to have *pets*?" Christina demands, smacking the table with her palm. "Why not?"

"Because they're illogical," Will says matter-of-factly. "What is the point in providing food and shelter for an animal that just soils your furniture, makes your home smell bad, and ultimately dies?"

Al and I meet eyes, like we usually do when Will and Christina start to fight. But this time, the second our eyes meet, we both look away. I hope this awkwardness between us doesn't last long. I want my friend back.

"The *point* is . . ." Christina's voice trails off, and she tilts her head. "Well, they're fun to have. I had a bulldog named Chunker. One time we left a whole roasted chicken on the counter to cool, and while my mother went to the bathroom, he pulled it down off the counter and ate it, bones and skin and all. We laughed so hard."

"Yes, that certainly changes my mind. Of course I want to live with an animal that eats all my food and destroys my kitchen." Will shakes his head. "Why don't you just get a dog after initiation if you're feeling that nostalgic?"

"Because." Christina's smile falls, and she pokes at her potato with her fork. "Dogs are sort of ruined for me. After . . . you know, after the aptitude test."

We exchange looks. We all know that we aren't supposed to talk about the test, not even now that we have chosen, but for them that rule must not be as serious as it is for me. My heart jumps unsteadily in my chest. For me that rule is protection. It keeps me from having to lie to my friends about my results. Every time I think the word "Divergent," I hear

Tori's warning—and now my mother's warning too. *Don't tell anyone.* *Dangerous.*

"You mean . . . killing the dog, right?" asks Will.

I almost forgot. Those with an aptitude for Dauntless picked up the knife in the simulation and stabbed the dog when it attacked. No wonder Christina doesn't want a pet dog anymore. I tug my sleeves over my wrists and twist my fingers together.

"Yeah," she says. "I mean, you guys all had to do that too, right?"

She looks first at Al, and then at me. Her dark eyes narrow, and she says, "*You* didn't."

"Hmm?"

"You're hiding something," she says. "You're fidgeting."

"What?"

"In Candor," says Al, nudging me with his shoulder. There. That feels normal. "We learn to read body language so we know when someone is lying or keeping something from us."

"Oh." I scratch the back of my neck. "Well . . ."

"See, there it is again!" she says, pointing at my hand.

I feel like I'm swallowing my heartbeat. How can I lie about my results if they can tell when I'm lying? I'll have to control my body language. I drop my hand and clasp my hands in my lap. Is that what an honest person does?

I don't have to lie about the dog, at least. "No, I didn't kill the dog."

"How did you get Dauntless without using the knife?" says Will, narrowing his eyes at me.

I look him in the eye and say evenly, "I didn't. I got Abnegation."

It is half-true. Tori reported my result as Abnegation, so that is what is in the system. Anyone who has access to the scores would be able to see it. I keep my eyes on his for a few seconds. Shifting them away might be suspicious. Then I shrug and stab a piece of meat with my fork. I hope they believe me. They have to believe me.

"But you chose Dauntless anyway?" Christina says. "Why?"

"I told you," I say, smirking. "It was the food."

She laughs. "Did you guys know that Tris had never seen a hamburger before she came here?"

She launches into the story of our first day, and my body relaxes, but I still feel heavy. I should not lie to my friends. It creates barriers between us, and we already have more than I want. Christina taking the flag. Me rejecting Al.

After dinner we go back to the dormitory, and it's hard for me not to sprint, knowing that the rankings will be up when I get there. I want to get it over with. At the door to the dormitory, Drew shoves me into the wall to get past me. My shoulder scrapes on the stone, but I keep walking.

I'm too short to see over the crowd of initiates standing near the back of the room, but when I find a space between heads to look through, I see that the blackboard is on the ground, leaning against Four's legs, facing away from us. He stands with a piece of chalk in one hand.

"For those of you who just came in, I'm explaining how the ranks are determined," he says. "After the first round of fights, we ranked you according to your skill level. The number of points you earn depends on your skill level and the skill level of the person you beat. You earn more points for improving and more points for beating someone of a high skill level. I don't reward preying on the weak. That is cowardice."

I think his eyes linger on Peter at that last line, but they move on quickly enough that I'm not sure.

"If you have a high rank, you lose points for losing to a low-ranked opponent."

Molly lets out an unpleasant noise, like a snort or a grumble.

"Stage two of training is weighted more heavily than stage one, because it is more closely tied to overcoming cowardice," he says. "That said, it is extremely difficult to rank high at the end of initiation if you rank low in stage one."

I shift from one foot to the other, trying to get a good look at him. When I finally do, I look away. His eyes are already on me, probably drawn by my nervous movement.

"We will announce the cuts tomorrow," Four says. "The fact that you are transfers and the Dauntless-born initiates are not will not be taken into consideration. Four of you could be factionless and none of them. Or four of them could be factionless and none of you. Or any combination thereof. That said, here are your ranks."

He hangs the board on the hook and steps back so we can see the rankings:

1. Edward
2. Peter
3. Will
4. Christina
5. Molly
6. Tris

Sixth? I can't be sixth. Beating Molly must have boosted my rank more than I thought it would. And losing to me seems to have lowered hers. I skip to the bottom of the list.

7. Drew
8. Al
9. Myra

Al isn't dead last, but unless the Dauntless-born initiates completely failed their version of stage one of initiation, he is factionless.

I glance at Christina. She tilts her head and frowns at the board. She isn't the only one. The quiet in the room is uneasy, like it is rocking back and forth on a ledge.

Then it falls.

"What?" demands Molly. She points at Christina. "I beat her! I beat her in *minutes*, and she's ranked *above* me?"

"Yeah," says Christina, crossing her arms. She wears a smug smile. "And?"

"If you intend to secure yourself a high rank, I suggest you don't make a habit of losing to low-ranked opponents," says Four, his voice cutting through the mutters and grumbles of the other initiates. He pockets the chalk and walks past me without glancing in my direction. The words sting a little, reminding me that I am the low-ranked opponent he's referring to.

Apparently they remind Molly, too.

"You," she says, focusing her narrowed eyes on me. "*You* are going to pay for this."

I expect her to lunge at me, or hit me, but she just turns on her heel and stalks out of the dormitory, and that is worse. If she had exploded, her anger would have been spent quickly, after a punch or two. Leaving means she wants to plan something. Leaving means I have to be on my guard.

Peter didn't say anything when the rankings went up, which, given his tendency to complain about anything that doesn't go his way, is surprising. He just walks to his bunk and sits down, untying his shoelaces. That makes me feel even more uneasy. He can't possibly be satisfied with second place. Not Peter.

Will and Christina slap hands, and then Will claps me on the back with a hand bigger than my shoulder blade.

"Look at you. Number six," he says, grinning.

"Still might not have been good enough," I remind him.

"It will be, don't worry," he says. "We should celebrate."

"Well, let's go, then," says Christina, grabbing my arm with one hand and Al's arm with the other. "Come on, Al. You don't know how the Dauntless-borns did. You don't know anything for sure."

"I'm just going to go to bed," he mumbles, pulling his arm free.

In the hallway, it is easy to forget about Al and Molly's revenge and Peter's suspicious calm, and easy to pretend that what separates us as friends does not exist. But lingering at the back of my mind is the fact that Christina and Will are my competitors. If I want to fight my way to the top ten, I will have to beat them first.

I just hope I don't have to betray them in the process.

+ + +

That night I have trouble falling asleep. The dormitory used to seem loud to me, with all the breathing, but now it is too quiet. When it's quiet, I think about my family. Thank God the Dauntless compound is usually loud.

If my mother was Dauntless, why did she choose Abnegation? Did she love its peace, its routine, its goodness—all the things I miss, when I let myself think about it?

I wonder if someone here knew her when she was young and could tell me what she was like then. Even if they did, they probably wouldn't want to discuss her. Faction transfers are not really supposed to discuss their old factions once they become members. It's supposed to make it easier for them to change their allegiance from family to faction—to embrace the principle "faction before blood."

I bury my face in the pillow. She asked me to tell Caleb to research the simulation serum—why? Does it have something to do with me being Divergent, with me being in danger, or is it something else? I sigh. I have a thousand questions, and she left before I could ask any of them. Now they swirl in my head, and I doubt I'll be able to sleep until I can answer them.

I hear a scuffle across the room and lift my head from the pillow. My eyes aren't adjusted to the dark, so I stare into pure black, like the backs of my eyelids. I hear shuffling and the squeak of a shoe. A heavy thud.

And then a wail that curdles my blood and makes my hair stand on end. I throw the blankets back and stand on the stone floor with bare feet. I still can't see well enough to find the source of the scream, but I see a dark lump on the floor a few bunks down. Another scream pierces my ears.

"Turn on the lights!" someone shouts.

I walk toward the sound, slowly so I don't trip over anything. I feel like I'm in a trance. I don't want to see where the screaming is coming from. A scream like that can only mean blood and bone and pain; that scream that comes from the pit of the stomach and extends to every inch of the body.

The lights come on.

Edward lies on the floor next to his bed, clutching at his face. Surrounding his head is a halo of blood, and jutting between his clawing fingers is a silver knife handle. My heart thumping in my ears, I recognize it as a butter knife from the dining hall. The blade is stuck in Edward's eye.

Myra, who stands at Edward's feet, screams. Someone else screams too, and someone yells for help, and Edward is still on the floor, writhing and wailing. I crouch by his head, my knees pressing to the pool of blood, and put my hands on his shoulders.

"Lie still," I say. I feel calm, though I can't hear anything, like my head is submerged in water. Edward thrashes again and I say it louder, sterner. "I said, lie *still*. Breathe."

"My eye!" he screams.

I smell something foul. Someone vomited.

"Take it out!" he yells. "Get it out, get it out of me, get it out!"

I shake my head and then realize that he can't see me. A laugh bubbles in my stomach. Hysterical. I have to suppress hysteria if I'm going to help him. I have to forget myself.

"No," I say. "You have to let the doctor take it out. Hear me? Let the doctor take it out. And breathe."

"It hurts," he sobs.

"I know it does." Instead of my voice I hear my mother's voice. I see her crouching before me on the sidewalk in front of our house, brushing tears from my face after I scraped my knee. I was five at the time.

"It will be all right." I try to sound firm, like I'm not idly reassuring him, but I am. I don't know if it will be all right. I suspect that it won't.

When the nurse arrives, she tells me to step back, and I do. My hands and knees are soaked with blood. When I look around, I see that only two faces are missing.

Drew.

And Peter.

+ + +

After they take Edward away, I carry a change of clothes into the bathroom and wash my hands. Christina comes with me and stands by the door, but she doesn't say anything, and I'm glad. There isn't much to say.

I scrub at the lines in my palms and run one fingernail under my other fingernails to get the blood out. I change into the pants I brought and throw the soiled ones in the trash. I get as many paper towels as I can hold. Someone needs to clean up the mess in the dormitory, and since I doubt I'll ever be able to sleep again, it might as well be me.

As I reach for the door handle, Christina says, "You know who did that, right?"

"Yeah."

"Should we tell someone?"

"You really think the Dauntless will do anything?" I say. "After they hung you over the chasm? After they made us beat each other unconscious?"

She doesn't say anything.

For a half hour after that, I kneel alone on the floor in the dormitory and scrub at Edward's blood. Christina throws away the dirty paper towels and gets me new ones. Myra is gone; she probably followed Edward to the hospital.

No one sleeps much that night.

+ + +

"This is going to sound weird," Will says, "but I wish we didn't have a day off today."

I nod. I know what he means. Having something to do would distract me, and I could use a distraction right now.

I have not spent much time alone with Will, but Christina and Al are taking naps in the dormitory, and neither of us wanted to be in that room longer than we had to. Will didn't tell me that; I just know.

I slide one fingernail under another. I washed my hands thoroughly after cleaning up Edward's blood, but I still feel like it's on my hands. Will and I walk with no sense of purpose. There is nowhere to go.

"We could visit him," suggests Will. "But what would we say? 'I didn't know you that well, but I'm sorry you got stabbed in the eye'?"

It isn't funny. I know that as soon as he says it, but a laugh rises in my throat anyway, and I let it out because it's harder to keep it in. Will stares at me for a second, and then he laughs too. Sometimes crying or laughing are the only options left, and laughing feels better right now.

"Sorry," I say. "It's just so ridiculous."

I don't want to cry for Edward—at least not in the deep, personal way that you cry for a friend or loved one. I want to cry because something terrible happened, and I saw it, and I could not see a way to mend it. No one who would want to punish Peter has the authority to, and no one who has the authority to punish him would want to. The Dauntless have rules against attacking someone like that, but with people like Eric in charge, I suspect those rules go unenforced.

I say, more seriously, "The most ridiculous part is, in any other faction it would be brave of us to tell someone what happened. But here . . . in *Dauntless* . . . bravery won't do us any good."

"Have you ever read the faction manifestos?" says Will.

The faction manifestos were written after the factions formed. We learned about them in school, but I never read them.

"You have?" I frown at him. Then I remember that Will once memorized a map of the city for fun, and I say, "Oh. Of course *you* have. Never mind."

"One of the lines I remember from the Dauntless manifesto is, 'We believe in ordinary acts of bravery, in the courage that drives one person to stand up for another.'"

Will sighs.

He doesn't need to say anything else. I know what he means. Maybe Dauntless was formed with good intentions, with the right ideals and the right goals. But it has strayed far from them. And the same is true of Erudite, I realize. A long time ago, Erudite pursued knowledge and ingenuity for the sake of doing good. Now they pursue knowledge and ingenuity with greedy hearts. I wonder if the other factions suffer from the same problem. I have not thought about it before.

Despite the depravity I see in Dauntless, though, I could not leave it. It isn't only because the thought of living factionless, in complete isolation, sounds like a fate worse than death. It is because, in the brief moments that I have loved it here, I saw a faction worth saving. Maybe we can become brave and honorable again.

"Let's go to the cafeteria," Will says, "and eat cake."

"Okay." I smile.

As we walk toward the Pit, I repeat the line Will quoted to myself so I don't forget it.

I believe in ordinary acts of bravery, in the courage that drives one person to stand up for another.

It is a beautiful thought.

+ + +

Later, when I return to the dormitory, Edward's bunk is stripped clean and his drawers are open, empty. Across the room, Myra's bunk looks the same way.

When I ask Christina where they went, she says, "They quit."

"Even Myra?"

"She said she didn't want to be here without him. She was going to get cut anyway." She shrugs, like she can't think of anything else to do. If that's true, I know how she feels. "At least they didn't cut Al."

Al was supposed to get cut, but Edward's departure saved him. The Dauntless decided to spare him until the next stage.

"Who else got cut?" I say.

Christina shrugs again. "Two of the Dauntless-born. I don't remember their names."

I nod and look at the blackboard. Someone drew a line through Edward and Myra's names, and changed the numbers next to everyone else's names. Now Peter is first. Will is second. I am fifth. We started stage one with nine initiates.

Now we have seven.

CHAPTER
SEVENTEEN

IT'S NOON. LUNCHTIME.

I sit in a hallway I don't recognize. I walked here because I needed to get away from the dormitory. Maybe if I bring my bedding here, I will never have to go to the dormitory again. It may be my imagination, but it still smells like blood in there, even though I scrubbed the floor until my hands were sore, and someone poured bleach on it this morning.

I pinch the bridge of my nose. Scrubbing the floor when no one else wanted to was something that my mother would have done. If I can't be with her, the least I can do is act like her sometimes.

I hear people approaching, their footsteps echoing on the stone floor, and I look down at my shoes. I switched from gray sneakers to black sneakers a week ago, but the gray shoes are buried in one of my drawers. I can't bear to throw them away, even though I know it's foolish to be attached to sneakers, like they can bring me home.

"Tris?"

I look up. Uriah stops in front of me. He waves along the Dauntless-born initiates he walks with. They exchange looks but keep moving.

"You okay?" he says.

"I had a difficult night."

"Yeah, I heard about that guy Edward." Uriah looks down the hallway. The Dauntless-born initiates disappear around a corner. Then he grins a little. "Want to get out of here?"

"What?" I ask. "Where are you going?"

"To a little initiation ritual," he says. "Come on. We have to hurry."

I briefly consider my options. I can sit here. Or I can leave the Dauntless compound.

I push myself to my feet and jog next to Uriah to catch up to the Dauntless-born initiates.

"The only initiates they usually let come are ones with older siblings in Dauntless," he says. "But they might not even notice. Just act like you belong."

"What exactly are we doing?"

"Something dangerous," he says. A look I can only describe as Dauntless mania enters his eyes, but rather than recoil from it, as I might have a few weeks ago, I catch it, like it's contagious. Excitement replaces the leaden feeling inside me. We slow when we reach the Dauntless-born initiates.

"What's the *Stiff* doing here?" asks a boy with a metal ring between his nostrils.

"She just saw that guy get stabbed in the eye, Gabe," says Uriah. "Give her a break, okay?"

Gabe shrugs and turns away. No one else says anything, though a few of them give me sidelong glances like they're sizing me up. The Dauntless-born initiates are like a pack of dogs. If I act the wrong way, they won't let me run with them. But for now, I am safe.

We turn another corner, and a group of members stands at the end of the next hallway. There are too many of them to all be related to a Dauntless-born initiate, but I see some similarities among the faces.

"Let's go," one of the members says. He turns and plunges through a dark doorway. The other members follow him, and we follow them. I stay close behind Uriah as I pass into darkness and my toe hits a step. I catch myself before falling forward and start to climb.

"Back staircase," Uriah says, almost mumbling. "Usually locked."

I nod, though he can't see me, and climb until all the steps are gone. By then, a door at the top of the staircase is open, letting in daylight. We emerge from the ground a few hundred yards from the glass building above the Pit, close to the train tracks.

I feel like I have done this a thousand times before. I hear the train horn. I feel the vibrations in the ground. I see the light attached to the head car. I crack my knuckles and bounce once on my toes.

We jog in a single pack next to the car, and in waves, members and initiates alike pile into the car. Uriah gets in before me, and people press behind me. I can't make any mistakes; I throw myself sideways, grabbing the handle on the side of the car, and hoist myself into the car. Uriah grabs my arm to steady me.

The train picks up its speed. Uriah and I sit against one of the walls.

I shout over the wind, "Where are we going?"

Uriah shrugs. "Zeke never told me."

"Zeke?"

"My older brother," he says. He points across the room at a boy sitting in the doorway with his legs dangling out of the car. He is slight and short and looks nothing like Uriah, apart from his coloring.

"You don't get to know. That ruins the surprise!" the girl on my left shouts. She extends her hand. "I'm Shauna."

I shake her hand, but I don't grip hard enough and I let go too quickly. I doubt I will ever improve my handshake. It feels unnatural to grasp hands with strangers.

"I'm—" I start to say.

"I know who you are," she says. "You're the Stiff. Four told me about you."

I pray the heat in my cheeks is not visible. "Oh? What did he say?"

She smirks at me. "He said you were a Stiff. Why do you ask?"

"If my instructor is talking about me," I say, as firmly as I can, "I want to know what he's saying." I hope I tell a convincing lie. "He isn't coming, is he?"

"No. He never comes to this," she says. "It's probably lost its appeal. Not much scares him, you know."

He isn't coming. Something in me deflates like an untied balloon. I ignore it and nod. I do know that Four is not a coward. But I also know that at least one thing does scare him: heights. Whatever we're doing, it must involve being high up for him to avoid it. She must not know that if she speaks of him with such reverence in her voice.

"Do you know him well?" I ask. I am too curious; I always have been.

"Everyone knows Four," she says. "We were initiates together. I was bad at fighting, so he taught me every night after everyone was asleep." She scratches the back of her neck, her expression suddenly serious. "Nice of him."

She gets up and stands behind the members sitting in the doorway. In a second, her serious expression is gone, but I still feel rattled by what she said, half confused by the idea of Four being "nice" and half wanting to punch her for no apparent reason.

"Here we go!" shouts Shauna. The train doesn't slow down, but she throws herself out of the car. The other members follow her, a stream of black-clothed, pierced people not much older than I am. I stand in the doorway next to Uriah. The train is going much faster than it has every other time I've jumped, but I can't lose my nerve now, in front of all these members. So I jump, hitting the ground hard and stumbling forward a few steps before I regain my balance.

Uriah and I jog to catch up to the members, along with the other initiates, who barely look in my direction.

I look around as I walk. The Hub is behind us, black against the clouds, but the buildings around me are dark and silent. That means we must be north of the bridge, where the city is abandoned.

We turn a corner and spread out as we walk down Michigan Avenue. South of the bridge, Michigan Avenue is a busy street, crawling with people, but here it is bare.

As soon as I lift my eyes to scan the buildings, I know where we're going: the empty Hancock building, a black pillar with crisscrossed girders, the tallest building north of the bridge.

But what are we going to do? Climb it?

As we get closer, the members start to run, and Uriah and I sprint to catch them. Jostling one another with their elbows, they push through a set of doors at the building's base. The glass in one of them is broken, so it is just a frame. I step through it instead of opening it and follow the members through an eerie, dark entryway, crunching broken glass beneath my feet.

I expect us to go up the stairs, but we stop at the elevator bank.

"Do the elevators work?" I ask Uriah, as quietly as I can.

"Sure they do," says Zeke, rolling his eyes. "You think I'm stupid enough not to come here early and turn on the emergency generator?"

"Yeah," says Uriah. "I kinda do."

Zeke glares at his brother, then puts him in a headlock and rubs his knuckles into Uriah's skull. Zeke may be smaller than Uriah, but he must be stronger. Or at least faster. Uriah smacks him in the side, and he lets go.

I grin at the sight of Uriah's disheveled hair, and the elevator doors open. We pile in, members in one and initiates in the other. A girl with a shaved head stomps on my toes on the way in and doesn't apologize. I grab my foot, wincing, and consider kicking her in the shins. Uriah stares at his reflection in the elevator doors and pats his hair down.

"What floor?" the girl with the shaved head says.

"One hundred," I say.

"How would *you* know that?"

"Lynn, come on," says Uriah. "Be nice."

"We're in a one-hundred-story abandoned building with some Dauntless," I retort. "Why don't *you* know that?"

She doesn't respond. She just jams her thumb into the right button.

The elevator zooms upward so fast my stomach sinks and my ears pop. I grab a railing at the side of the elevator, watching the numbers climb. We pass twenty, and thirty, and Uriah's hair is finally smooth. Fifty, sixty, and my toes are done throbbing. Ninety-eight, ninety-nine, and the elevator comes to a stop at one hundred. I'm glad we didn't take the stairs.

"I wonder how we'll get to the roof from . . ." Uriah's voice trails off.

A strong wind hits me, pushing my hair across my face. There is a gaping hole in the ceiling of the hundredth floor. Zeke props an aluminum ladder against its edge and starts to climb. The ladder creaks and sways beneath his feet, but he keeps climbing, whistling as he does. When he reaches the roof, he turns around and holds the top of the ladder for the next person.

Part of me wonders if this is a suicide mission disguised as a game.

It isn't the first time I've wondered that since the Choosing Ceremony.

I climb the ladder after Uriah. It reminds me of climbing the rungs on the Ferris wheel with Four close at my heels. I remember his fingers on my hip again, how they kept me from falling, and I almost miss a step on the ladder. *Stupid.*

Biting my lip, I make it to the top and stand on the roof of the Hancock building.

The wind is so powerful I hear and feel nothing else. I have to lean against Uriah to keep from falling over. At first, all I see is the marsh, wide and brown and everywhere, touching the horizon, devoid of life. In the other direction is the city, and in many ways it is the same, lifeless and with limits I do not know.

Uriah points to something. Attached to one of the poles on top of the tower is a steel cable as thick as my wrist. On the ground is a pile of black slings made of tough fabric, large enough to hold a human being. Zeke grabs one and attaches it to a pulley that hangs from the steel cable.

I follow the cable down, over the cluster of buildings and along Lake Shore Drive. I don't know where it ends. One thing is clear, though: If I go through with this, I'll find out.

We're going to slide down a steel cable in a black sling from one thousand feet up.

"Oh my God," says Uriah.

All I can do is nod.

Shauna is the first person to get in the sling. She wriggles forward on her stomach until most of her body is supported by black fabric. Then Zeke pulls a strap across her shoulders, the small of her back, and the top of her thighs. He pulls her, in the sling, to the edge of the building and counts down from five. Shauna gives a thumbs-up as he shoves her forward, into nothingness.

Lynn gasps as Shauna hurtles toward the ground at a steep incline, headfirst. I push past her to see better. Shauna stays secure in the sling for as long as I can see her, and then she's too far away, just a black speck over Lake Shore Drive.

The members whoop and pump their fists and form a line, sometimes shoving one another out of the way to get a better place. Somehow I am the first initiate in line, right in front of Uriah. Only seven people stand between me and the zip line.

Still, there is a part of me that groans, *I have to wait for* seven *people?* It is a strange blend of terror and eagerness, unfamiliar until now.

The next member, a young-looking boy with hair down to his shoulders, jumps into the sling on his back instead of his stomach. He stretches his arms wide as Zeke shoves him down the steel cable.

None of the members seem at all afraid. They act like they have done this a thousand times before, and maybe they have. But when I look over my shoulder, I see that most of the initiates look pale or worried, even if they talk excitedly to one another. What happens between initiation and membership that transforms panic into delight? Or do people just get better at hiding their fear?

Three people in front of me. Another sling; a member gets in feetfirst and crosses her arms over her chest. Two people. A tall, thick boy jumps up and down like a child before climbing into the sling and lets out a high screech as he disappears, making the girl in front of me laugh. One person.

She hops into the sling face-first and keeps her hands in front of her as Zeke tightens her straps. And then it's my turn.

I shudder as Zeke hangs my sling from the cable. I try to climb in, but I have trouble; my hands are shaking too badly.

"Don't worry," Zeke says right next to my ear. He takes my arm and helps me get in, facedown.

The straps tighten around my midsection, and Zeke slides me forward, to the edge of the roof. I stare down the building's steel girders and black windows, all the way to the cracked sidewalk. I am a fool for doing this. And a fool for enjoying the feeling of my heart slamming against my sternum and sweat gathering in the lines of my palms.

"Ready, Stiff?" Zeke smirks down at me. "I have to say, I'm impressed that you aren't screaming and crying right now."

"I told you," Uriah says. "She's Dauntless through and through. Now get on with it."

"Careful, brother, or I might not tighten your straps enough," Zeke says. He smacks his knee. "And then, *splat!*"

"Yeah, yeah," Uriah says. "And then our mother would boil you alive."

Hearing him talk about his mother, about his intact family, makes my chest hurt for a second, like someone pierced it with a needle.

"Only if she found out." Zeke tugs on the pulley attached to the steel cable. It holds, which is fortunate, because if it breaks, my death will be swift and certain. He looks down at me and says, "Ready, set, g—"

Before he can finish the word "go," he releases the sling and I forget him, I forget Uriah, and family, and all the things that could malfunction and lead to my death. I hear metal sliding against metal and feel wind so intense it forces tears into my eyes as I hurtle toward the ground.

I feel like I am without substance, without weight. Ahead of me the marsh looks huge, its patches of brown spreading farther than I can see, even up this high. The air is so cold and so fast that it hurts my face. I pick up speed and a shout of exhilaration rises within me, stopped only by the wind that fills my mouth the second my lips part.

Held secure by the straps, I throw my arms out to the side and imagine that I am flying. I plunge toward the street, which is cracked and patchy and follows perfectly the curve of the marsh. I can imagine, up here, how the marsh looked when it was full of water, like liquid steel as it reflected the color of the sky.

My heart beats so hard it hurts, and I can't scream and I can't breathe, but I also feel everything, every vein and every fiber, every bone and every nerve, all awake and buzzing in my body as if charged with electricity. I am pure adrenaline.

The ground grows and bulges beneath me, and I can see the tiny people standing on the pavement below. I should scream, like any rational human being would, but when I open my mouth again, I just crow with joy. I yell louder, and the figures on the ground pump their fists and yell back, but they are so far away I can barely hear them.

I look down and the ground smears beneath me, all gray and white and black, glass and pavement and steel. Tendrils of wind, soft as hair, wrap around my fingers and push my arms back. I try to pull my arms to my chest again, but I am not strong enough. The ground grows bigger and bigger.

I don't slow down for another minute at least but sail parallel to the ground, like a bird.

When I slow down, I run my fingers over my hair. The wind teased it into knots. I hang about twenty feet above the ground, but that height seems like nothing now. I reach behind me and work to undo the straps holding me in. My fingers shake, but I still manage to loosen them. A crowd of members stands below. They grasp one another's arms, forming a net of limbs beneath me.

In order to get down, I have to trust them to catch me. I have to accept that these people are mine, and I am theirs. It is a braver act than sliding down the zip line.

I wriggle forward and fall. I hit their arms hard. Wrist bones and forearms press into my back, and then palms wrap around my arms and pull me to my feet. I don't know which hands hold me and which hands don't; I see grins and hear laughter.

"What'd you think?" Shauna says, clapping me on the shoulder.

"Um . . ." All the members stare at me. They look as windblown as I feel, the frenzy of adrenaline in their eyes and their hair askew. I know why my father said the Dauntless were a pack of madmen. He didn't—couldn't—understand the kind of camaraderie that forms only after you've all risked your lives together.

"When can I go again?" I say. My smile stretches wide enough to show teeth, and when they laugh, I laugh. I think of climbing the stairs with the Abnegation, our feet finding the same rhythm, all of us the same. This isn't like that. We are not the same. But we are, somehow, one.

I look toward the Hancock building, which is so far from where I stand that I can't see the people on its roof.

"Look! There he is!" someone says, pointing over my shoulder. I follow the pointed finger toward a small dark shape sliding down the steel wire. A few seconds later I hear a bloodcurdling scream.

"I bet he'll cry."

"Zeke's brother, cry? No way. He would get punched so hard."

"His arms are flailing!"

"He sounds like a strangled cat," I say. Everyone laughs again. I feel a twinge of guilt for teasing Uriah when he can't hear me, but I would have said the same thing if he were standing here. I hope.

When Uriah finally comes to a stop, I follow the members to meet him. We line up beneath him and thrust our arms into the space between us. Shauna clamps a hand around my elbow. I grab another arm—I'm not sure who it belongs to, there are too many tangled hands—and look up at her.

"Pretty sure we can't call you 'Stiff' anymore," Shauna says. She nods. "Tris."

+ + +

I still smell like wind when I walk into the cafeteria that evening. For the second after I walk in, I stand among a crowd of Dauntless, and I feel like one of them. Then Shauna waves to me and the crowd breaks apart, and I walk toward the table where Christina, Al, and Will sit, gaping at me.

I didn't think about them when I accepted Uriah's invitation. In a way, it is satisfying to see stunned looks on their faces. But I don't want them to be upset with me either.

"Where were you?" asks Christina. "What were you doing with them?"

"Uriah . . . you know, the Dauntless-born who was on our capture the flag team?" I say. "He was leaving with some of the members and he begged them to let me come along. They didn't really want me there. Some girl named Lynn stepped on me."

"They may not have wanted you there then," says Will quietly, "but they seem to like you now."

"Yeah," I say. I can't deny it. "I'm glad to be back, though."

Hopefully they can't tell I'm lying, but I suspect they can. I caught sight of myself in a window on the way into the compound, and my cheeks and eyes were both bright, my hair tangled. I look like I have experienced something powerful.

"Well, you missed Christina almost punching an Erudite," says Al. His voice sounds eager. I can count on Al to try to break the tension. "He was here asking for opinions about the Abnegation leadership, and Christina told him there were more important things for him to be doing."

"Which she was completely right about," adds Will. "And he got testy with her. Big mistake."

"Huge," I say, nodding. If I smile enough, maybe I can make them forget their jealousy, or hurt, or whatever is brewing behind Christina's eyes.

"Yeah," she says. "While you were off having fun, I was doing the dirty work of defending your old faction, eliminating interfaction conflict . . ."

"Come on, you know you enjoyed it," says Will, nudging her with his elbow. "If you're not going to tell the whole story, I will. He was standing . . ."

Will launches into his story, and I nod along like I'm listening, but all I can think about is staring down the side of the Hancock building, and the image I got of the marsh full of water, restored to its former glory. I look over Will's shoulder at the members, who are now flicking bits of food at one another with their forks.

It's the first time I have been really eager to be one of them.

Which means I have to survive the next stage of initiation.

CHAPTER
EIGHTEEN

As far as I can tell, the second stage of initiation involves sitting in a dark hallway with the other initiates, wondering what's going to happen behind a closed door.

Uriah sits across from me, with Marlene on his left and Lynn on his right. The Dauntless-born initiates and the transfers were separated during stage one, but we will be training together from now on. That's what Four told us before he disappeared behind the door.

"So," says Lynn, scuffing the floor with her shoe. "Which one of you is ranked first, huh?"

Her question is met with silence at first, and then Peter clears his throat.

"Me," he says.

"Bet I could take you." She says it casually, turning the ring in her eyebrow with her fingertips. "I'm second, but I bet any of us could take you, transfer."

I almost laugh. If I was still Abnegation, her comment would be rude and out of place, but among the Dauntless, challenges like that seem common. I am almost starting to expect them.

"I wouldn't be so sure about that, if I were you," Peter says, his eyes glittering. "Who's first?"

"Uriah," she says. "And I am sure. You know how many years we've spent preparing for this?"

If she intends to intimidate us, it works. I already feel colder.

Before Peter can respond, Four opens the door and says, "Lynn." He beckons to her, and she walks down the hallway, the blue light at the end making her bare head glow.

"So you're first," Will says to Uriah.

Uriah shrugs. "Yeah. And?"

"And you don't think it's a little unfair that you've spent your entire life getting ready for this, and we're expected to learn it all in a few weeks?" Will says, his eyes narrowing.

"Not really. Stage one was about skill, sure, but no one can prepare for stage two," he says. "At least, so I'm told."

No one responds to that. We sit in silence for twenty minutes. I count each minute on my watch. Then the door opens again, and Four calls another name.

"Peter," he says.

Each minute wears into me like a scrape of sandpaper. Gradually, our numbers begin to dwindle, and it's just me and Uriah and Drew. Drew's leg bounces, and Uriah's fingers tap against his knee, and I try to sit perfectly still. I hear only muttering from the room at the end of the hallway, and I suspect this is another part of the game they like to play with us. Terrifying us at every opportunity.

The door opens, and Four beckons to me. "Come on, Tris."

I stand, my back sore from leaning against the wall for so long, and walk past the other initiates. Drew sticks out his leg to trip me, but I hop over it at the last second.

Four touches my shoulder to guide me into the room and closes the door behind me.

When I see what's inside, I recoil immediately, my shoulders hitting his chest.

In the room is a reclining metal chair, similar to the one I sat in during the aptitude test. Beside it is a familiar machine. This room has no mirrors and barely any light. There is a computer screen on a desk in the corner.

"Sit," Four says. He squeezes my arms and pushes me forward.

"What's the simulation?" I say, trying to keep my voice from shaking. I don't succeed.

"Ever hear the phrase 'face your fears'?" he says. "We're taking that literally. The simulation will teach you to control your emotions in the midst of a frightening situation."

I touch a wavering hand to my forehead. Simulations aren't real; they pose no real threat to me, so logically, I shouldn't be afraid of them, but my reaction is visceral. It takes all the willpower I have for me to steer myself toward the chair and sit down in it again, pressing my skull into the headrest. The cold from the metal seeps through my clothes.

"Do you ever administer the aptitude tests?" I say. He seems qualified.

"No," he replies. "I avoid Stiffs as much as possible."

I don't know why someone would avoid the Abnegation. The Dauntless or the Candor, maybe, because bravery and honesty make people do strange things, but the Abnegation?

"Why?"

"Do you ask me that because you think I'll actually answer?"

"Why do you say vague things if you don't want to be asked about them?"

His fingers brush my neck. My body tenses. A tender gesture? No—he has to move my hair to the side. He taps something, and I tilt my head back to see what it is. Four holds a syringe with a long needle in one hand, his thumb against the plunger. The liquid in the syringe is tinted orange.

"An injection?" My mouth goes dry. I don't usually mind needles, but this one is huge.

"We use a more advanced version of the simulation here," he says, "a different serum, no wires or electrodes for you."

"How does it work without wires?"

"Well, I have wires, so I can see what's going on," he says. "But for you, there's a tiny transmitter in the serum that sends data to the computer."

He turns my arm over and eases the tip of the needle into the tender skin on the side of my neck. A deep ache spreads through my throat. I wince and try to focus on his calm face.

"The serum will go into effect in sixty seconds. This simulation is different from the aptitude test," he says. "In addition to containing the transmitter, the serum stimulates the amygdala, which is the part of the brain involved in processing negative emotions—like fear—and then induces a hallucination. The brain's electrical activity is then transmitted to our computer, which then translates your hallucination into a simulated image that I can see and monitor. I will then forward the recording to Dauntless administrators. You stay in the hallucination until you calm down—that is, lower your heart rate and control your breathing."

I try to follow his words, but my thoughts are going haywire. I feel the trademark symptoms of fear: sweaty palms, racing heart, tightness in my chest, dry mouth, a lump in my throat, difficulty breathing. He plants his hands on either side of my head and leans over me.

"Be brave, Tris," he whispers. "The first time is always the hardest."

His eyes are the last thing I see.

+ + +

I stand in a field of dry grass that comes up to my waist. The air smells like smoke and burns my nostrils. Above me the sky is bile-colored, and the sight of it fills me with anxiety, my body cringing away from it.

I hear fluttering, like the pages of a book blown by the wind, but there is no wind. The air is still and soundless apart from the flapping, neither hot nor cold—not like air at all, but I can still breathe. A shadow swoops overhead.

Something lands on my shoulder. I feel its weight and the prick of talons and fling my arm forward to shake it off, my hand batting at it. I feel something smooth and fragile. A feather. I bite my lip and look to the side. A black bird the size of my forearm turns its head and focuses one beady eye on me.

I grit my teeth and hit the crow again with my hand. It digs in its talons and doesn't move. I cry out, more frustrated than pained, and hit the crow with both hands, but it stays in place, resolute, one eye on me, feathers gleaming in the yellow light. Thunder rumbles and I hear the patter of rain on the ground, but no rain falls.

The sky darkens, like a cloud is passing over the sun. Still cringing away from the crow, I look up. A flock of crows storms toward me, an advancing army of outstretched talons and open beaks, each one squawking, filling the air with noise. The crows descend in a single mass, diving toward the earth, hundreds of beady black eyes shining.

I try to run, but my feet are firmly planted and refuse to move, like the crow on my shoulder. I scream as they surround me, feathers flapping in my ears, beaks pecking at my shoulders, talons clinging to my clothes. I scream until tears come from my eyes, my arms flailing. My hands hit solid bodies but do nothing; there are too many. I am alone. They nip at my fingertips and press against my body, wings sliding across the back of my neck, feet tearing at my hair.

I twist and wrench and fall to the ground, covering my head with my arms. They scream against me. I feel a wiggling in the grass, a crow forcing its way under my arm. I open my eyes and it pecks at my face, its beak hitting me in the nose. Blood drips onto the grass and I sob, hitting it with my palm, but another crow wedges under my other arm and its claws stick to the front of my shirt.

I am screaming; I am sobbing.

"Help!" I wail. "Help!"

And the crows flap harder, a roar in my ears. My body burns, and they are everywhere, and I can't think, I can't breathe. I gasp for air and my mouth fills with feathers, feathers down my throat, in my lungs, replacing my blood with dead weight.

"Help," I sob and scream, insensible, illogical. I am dying; I am dying; I am dying.

My skin sears and I am bleeding, and the squawking is so loud my ears are ringing, but I am *not* dying, and I remember that it isn't real, but it feels real, it feels so real. *Be brave.* Four's voice screams in my memory.

I cry out to him, inhaling feathers and exhaling "Help!" But there will be
no help; I am alone.

You stay in the hallucination until you can calm down, his voice continues, and I cough, and my face is wet with tears, and another crow has
wriggled under my arms, and I feel the edge of its sharp beak against my
mouth. Its beak wedges past my lips and scrapes my teeth. The crow
pushes its head into my mouth and I bite hard, tasting something foul. I
spit and clench my teeth to form a barrier, but now a fourth crow is pushing at my feet, and a fifth crow is pecking at my ribs.

Calm down. I can't, I can't. My head throbs.

Breathe. I keep my mouth closed and suck air into my nose. It has
been hours since I was alone in the field; it has been days. I push air out
of my nose. My heart pounds hard in my chest. I have to slow it down. I
breathe again, my face wet with tears.

I sob again, and force myself forward, stretching out on the grass,
which prickles against my skin. I extend my arms and breathe. Crows
push and prod at my sides, worming their way beneath me, and I let
them. I let the flapping of wings and the squawking and the pecking and
the prodding continue, relaxing one muscle at a time, resigning myself
to becoming a pecked carcass.

The pain overwhelms me.

I open my eyes, and I am sitting in the metal chair.

I scream and hit my arms and head and legs to get the birds off me,
but they are gone, though I can still feel the feathers brushing the back of
my neck and the talons in my shoulder and my burning skin. I moan and
pull my knees to my chest, burying my face in them.

A hand touches my shoulder, and I fling a fist out, hitting something
solid but soft. "Don't touch me!" I sob.

"It's over," Four says. The hand shifts awkwardly over my hair, and I
remember my father stroking my hair when he kissed me goodnight, my
mother touching my hair when she trimmed it with the scissors. I run
my palms along my arms, still brushing off feathers, though I know
there aren't any.

"Tris."

I rock back and forth in the metal chair.

"Tris, I'm going to take you back to the dorms, okay?"

"No!" I snap. I lift my head and glare at him, though I can't see him
through the blur of tears. "They can't see me . . . not like this . . ."

"Oh, calm down," he says. He rolls his eyes. "I'll take you out the
back door."

"I don't need you to . . ." I shake my head. My body is trembling and I
feel so weak I'm not sure I can stand, but I have to try. I can't be the only

one who needs to be walked back to the dorms. Even if they don't see me, they'll find out, they'll talk about me—

"Nonsense."

He grabs my arm and hauls me out of the chair. I blink the tears from my eyes, wipe my cheeks with the heel of my hand, and let him steer me toward the door behind the computer screen.

We walk down the hallway in silence. When we're a few hundred yards away from the room, I yank my arm away and stop.

"Why did you do that to me?" I say. "What was the point of that, huh? I wasn't aware that when I chose Dauntless, I was signing up for weeks of torture!"

"Did you think overcoming cowardice would be easy?" he says calmly.

"That isn't overcoming cowardice! Cowardice is how you decide to be in real life, and in real life, I am not getting pecked to death by crows, Four!" I press my palms to my face and sob into them.

He doesn't say anything, just stands there as I cry. It only takes me a few seconds to stop and wipe my face again. "I want to go home," I say weakly.

But home is not an option anymore. My choices are here or the factionless slums.

He doesn't look at me with sympathy. He just looks at me. His eyes look black in the dim corridor, and his mouth is set in a hard line.

"Learning how to think in the midst of fear," he says, "is a lesson that everyone, even your Stiff family, needs to learn. That's what we're trying to teach you. If you can't learn it, you'll need to get the hell out of here, because we won't want you."

"I'm *trying*." My lower lip trembles. "But I failed. I'm failing."

He sighs. "How long do you think you spent in that hallucination, Tris?"

"I don't know." I shake my head. "A half hour?"

"Three minutes," he replies. "You got out three times faster than the other initiates. Whatever you are, you're not a failure."

Three minutes?

He smiles a little. "Tomorrow you'll be better at this. You'll see."

"Tomorrow?"

He touches my back and guides me toward the dormitory. I feel his fingertips through my shirt. Their gentle pressure makes me forget the birds for a moment.

"What was your first hallucination?" I say, glancing at him.

"It wasn't a 'what' so much as a 'who.' " He shrugs. "It's not important."

"And are you over that fear now?"

"Not yet." We reach the door to the dormitory, and he leans against the wall, sliding his hands into his pockets. "I may never be."

"So they don't go away?"

"Sometimes they do. And sometimes new fears replace them." His thumbs hook around his belt loops. "But becoming fearless isn't the point. That's impossible. It's learning how to control your fear, and how to be free from it, *that's* the point."

I nod. I used to think the Dauntless were fearless. That is how they seemed, anyway. But maybe what I saw as fearless was actually fear under control.

"Anyway, your fears are rarely what they appear to be in the simulation," he adds.

"What do you mean?"

"Well, are you really afraid of crows?" he says, half smiling at me. The expression warms his eyes enough that I forget he's my instructor. He's just a boy, talking casually, walking me to my door. "When you see one, do you run away screaming?"

"No. I guess not." I think about stepping closer to him, not for any practical reason, but just because I want to see what it would be like to stand that close to him; just because I want to.

Foolish, a voice in my head says.

I step closer and lean against the wall too, tilting my head sideways to look at him. As I did on the Ferris wheel, I know exactly how much space there is between us. Six inches. I lean. Less than six inches. I feel warmer, like he's giving off some kind of energy that I am only now close enough to feel.

"So what am I really afraid of?" I say.

"I don't know," he says. "Only you can know."

I nod slowly. There are a dozen things it could be, but I'm not sure which one is right, or if there's even one right one.

"I didn't know becoming Dauntless would be this difficult," I say, and a second later, I am surprised that I said it; surprised that I admitted to it. I bite the inside of my cheek and watch Four carefully. Was it a mistake to tell him that?

"It wasn't always like this, I'm told," he says, lifting a shoulder. My admission doesn't appear to bother him. "Being Dauntless, I mean."

"What changed?"

"The leadership," he says. "The person who controls training sets the standard of Dauntless behavior. Six years ago Max and the other leaders changed the training methods to make them more competitive and more brutal, said it was supposed to test people's strength. And that changed the priorities of Dauntless as a whole. Bet you can't guess who the leaders' new protégé is."

The answer is obvious: Eric. They trained him to be vicious, and now he will train the rest of us to be vicious too.

I look at Four. Their training didn't work on him.

"So if you were ranked first in your initiate class," I say, "what was Eric's rank?"

"Second."

"So he was their second choice for leadership." I nod slowly. "And you were their first."

"What makes you say that?"

"The way Eric was acting at dinner the first night. Jealous, even though he has what he wants."

Four doesn't contradict me. I must be right. I want to ask why he didn't take the position the leaders offered him; why he is so resistant to leadership when he seems to be a natural leader. But I know how Four feels about personal questions.

I sniff, wipe my face one more time, and smooth down my hair.

"Do I look like I've been crying?" I say.

"Hmm." He leans in close, narrowing his eyes like he's inspecting my face. A smile tugs at the corner of his mouth. Even closer, so we would be breathing the same air—if I could remember to breathe.

"No, Tris," he says. A more serious look replaces his smile as he adds, "You look tough as nails."

CHAPTER
NINETEEN

WHEN I WALK IN, most of the other initiates—Dauntless-born and transfer alike—are crowded between the rows of bunk beds with Peter at their center. He holds a piece of paper in both hands.

"*The mass exodus of the children of Abnegation leaders cannot be ignored or attributed to coincidence,*" he reads. "*The recent transfer of Beatrice and Caleb Prior, the children of Andrew Prior, calls into question the soundness of Abnegation's values and teachings.*"

Cold creeps up my spine. Christina, standing on the edge of the crowd, looks over her shoulder and spots me. She gives me a worried look. I can't move. My father. Now the Erudite are attacking my father.

"*Why else would the children of such an important man decide that the lifestyle he has set out for them is not an admirable one?*" Peter continues. "*Molly Atwood, a fellow Dauntless transfer, suggests a disturbed and abusive upbringing might be to blame. 'I heard her talking in her sleep once,' Molly says. 'She was telling her father to stop doing something. I don't know what it was, but it gave her nightmares.'*"

So this is Molly's revenge. She must have talked to the Erudite reporter that Christina yelled at.

She smiles. Her teeth are crooked. If I knocked them out, I might be doing her a favor.

"What?" I demand. Or I try to demand, but my voice comes out strangled and scratchy, and I have to clear my throat and say it again. "*What?*"

Peter stops reading, and a few people turn around. Some, like Christina, look at me in a pitying way, their eyebrows drawn in, their mouths turned down at the corners. But most give me little smirks and eye one another suggestively. Peter turns last, with a wide smile.

"Give me that," I say, holding out my hand. My face burns.

"But I'm not done reading," he replies, laughter in his voice. His eyes scan the paper again. *"However, perhaps the answer lies not in a morally bereft man, but in the corrupted ideals of an entire faction. Perhaps the answer is that we have entrusted our city to a group of proselytizing tyrants who do not know how to lead us out of poverty and into prosperity."*

I storm up to him and try to snatch the paper from his hands, but he holds it up, high above my head so I can't reach it unless I jump, and I won't jump. Instead, I lift my heel and stomp as hard as I can where the bones in his foot connect to his toes. He grits his teeth to stifle a groan.

Then I throw myself at Molly, hoping the force of the impact will surprise her and knock her down, but before I can do any damage, cold hands close around my waist.

"That's my *father!*" I scream. "My father, you coward!"

Will pulls me away from her, lifting me off the ground. My breaths come fast, and I struggle to grab the paper before anyone can read another word of it. I have to burn it; I have to destroy it; I have to.

Will drags me out of the room and into the hallway, his fingernails digging into my skin. Once the door shuts behind him, he lets go, and I shove him as hard as I can.

"What? Did you think I couldn't defend myself against that piece of Candor trash?"

"No," says Will. He stands in front of the door. "I figured I'd stop you from starting a brawl in the dormitory. Calm down."

I laugh a little. "Calm down? Calm *down?* That's my *family* they're talking about, that's my *faction!*"

"No, it's not." There are dark circles under his eyes; he looks exhausted. "It's your old faction, and there's nothing you can do about what they say, so you might as well just ignore it."

"Were you even listening?" The heat in my cheeks is gone, and my breaths are more even now. "Your stupid ex-faction isn't just insulting Abnegation anymore. They're calling for an overthrow of the entire government."

Will laughs. "No, they're not. They're arrogant and dull, and that's why I left them, but they aren't revolutionaries. They just want more say, that's all, and they resent Abnegation for refusing to listen to them."

"They don't want people to listen, they want people to agree," I reply. "And you shouldn't bully people into agreeing with you." I touch my palms to my cheeks. "I can't believe my brother joined them."

"Hey. They're not all bad," he says sharply.

I nod, but I don't believe him. I can't imagine anyone emerging from the Erudite unscathed, though Will seems all right.

The door opens again, and Christina and Al walk out. "It's my turn to get tattooed," she says. "Want to come with us?"

I smooth my hair. I can't go back into the dormitory. Even if Will let me, I am outnumbered there. My only choice is to go with them and try to forget what's happening outside the Dauntless compound. I have enough to worry about without anxiety about my family.

+ + +

Ahead of me, Al gives Christina a piggyback ride. She shrieks as he charges through the crowd. People give him a wide berth, when they can.

My shoulder still burns. Christina persuaded me to join her in getting a tattoo of the Dauntless seal. It is a circle with a flame inside it. My mother didn't even react to the one on my collarbone, so I don't have as many reservations about getting tattoos. They are a part of life here, just as integral to my initiation as learning to fight.

Christina also persuaded me to purchase a shirt that exposes my shoulders and collarbone, and to line my eyes with black pencil again. I don't bother objecting to her makeover attempts anymore. Especially since I find myself enjoying them.

Will and I walk behind Christina and Al.

"I can't believe you got another tattoo," he says, shaking his head.

"Why?" I say. "Because I'm a Stiff?"

"No. Because you're . . . sensible." He smiles. His teeth are white and straight. "So, what was your fear today, Tris?"

"Too many crows," I reply. "You?"

He laughs. "Too much acid."

I don't ask what that means.

"It's really fascinating how it all works," he says. "It's basically a struggle between your thalamus, which is producing the fear, and your frontal lobe, which makes decisions. But the simulation is all in your head, so even though you feel like someone is doing it to you, it's just you, doing it to yourself and . . ." He trails off. "Sorry. I sound like an Erudite. Just a habit."

I shrug. "It's interesting."

Al almost drops Christina, and she slaps her hands around the first thing she can grab, which just happens to be his face. He cringes and adjusts his grip on her legs. At a glance, Al seems happy, but there is something heavy about even his smiles. I am worried about him.

I see Four standing by the chasm, a group of people around him. He laughs so hard he has to grab the railing for balance. Judging by the bottle in his hand and the brightness of his face, he's intoxicated, or on his way there. I had begun to think of Four as rigid, like a soldier, and forgot that he's also eighteen.

"Uh-oh," says Will. "Instructor alert."

"At least it's not Eric," I say. "He'd probably make us play chicken or something."

"Sure, but Four is scary. Remember when he put the gun up to Peter's head? I think Peter wet himself."

"Peter deserved it," I say firmly.

Will doesn't argue with me. He might have, a few weeks ago, but now we've all seen what Peter is capable of.

"Tris!" Four calls out. Will and I exchange a look, half surprise and half apprehension. Four pulls away from the railing and walks up to me. Ahead of us, Al and Christina stop running, and Christina slides to the ground. I don't blame them for staring. There are four of us, and Four is only talking to me.

"You look different." His words, normally crisp, are now sluggish.

"So do you," I say. And he does—he looks more relaxed, younger. "What are you doing?"

"Flirting with death," he replies with a laugh. "Drinking near the chasm. Probably not a good idea."

"No, it isn't." I'm not sure I like Four this way. There's something unsettling about it.

"Didn't know you had a tattoo," he says, looking at my collarbone.

He sips the bottle. His breath smells thick and sharp. Like the factionless man's breath.

"Right. The *crows*," he says. He glances over his shoulder at his friends, who are carrying on without him, unlike mine. He adds, "I'd ask you to hang out with us, but you're not supposed to see me this way."

I am tempted to ask him why he wants me to hang out with him, but I suspect the answer has something to do with the bottle in his hand.

"What way?" I ask. "Drunk?"

"Yeah . . . well, no." His voice softens. "Real, I guess."

"I'll pretend I didn't."

"Nice of you." He puts his lips next to my ear and says, "You look good, Tris."

His words surprise me, and my heart leaps. I wish it didn't, because judging by the way his eyes slide over mine, he has no idea what he's saying. I laugh. "Do me a favor and stay away from the chasm, okay?"

"Of course." He winks at me.

I can't help it. I smile. Will clears his throat, but I don't want to turn away from Four, even when he walks back to his friends.

Then Al rushes at me like a rolling boulder and throws me over his shoulder. I shriek, my face hot.

"Come on, little girl," he says, "I'm taking you to dinner."

I rest my elbows on Al's back and wave at Four as he carries me away.

"I thought I would rescue you," Al says as we walk away. He sets me down. "What was *that* all about?"

He is trying to sound lighthearted, but he asks the question almost sadly. He still cares too much about me.

"Yeah, I think we'd all like to know the answer to *that* question," says Christina in a singsong voice. "What did he say to you?"

"Nothing." I shake my head. "He was drunk. He didn't even know what he was saying." I clear my throat. "That's why I was grinning. It's . . . funny to see him that way."

"Right," says Will. "Couldn't possibly be because—"

I elbow Will hard in the ribs before he can finish his sentence. He was close enough to hear what Four said to me about looking good. I don't need him telling everyone about it, especially not Al. I don't want to make him feel worse.

At home I used to spend calm, pleasant nights with my family. My mother knit scarves for the neighborhood kids. My father helped Caleb with his homework. There was a fire in the fireplace and peace in my heart, as I was doing exactly what I was supposed to be doing, and everything was quiet.

I have never been carried around by a large boy, or laughed until my stomach hurt at the dinner table, or listened to the clamor of a hundred people all talking at once. Peace is restrained; this is free.

CHAPTER
TWENTY

I BREATHE THROUGH my nose. In, out. In.

"It's just a simulation, Tris," Four says quietly.

He's wrong. The last simulation bled into my life, waking and sleeping. Nightmares, not just featuring the crows but the feelings I had in the simulation—terror and helplessness, which I suspect is what I am really afraid of. Sudden fits of terror in the shower, at breakfast, on the way here. Nails bitten down so far my nail beds ache. And I am not the only one who feels this way; I can tell.

Still I nod and close my eyes.

+ + +

I am in darkness. The last thing I remember is the metal chair and the needle in my arm. This time there is no field; there are no crows. My heart pounds in anticipation. What monsters will creep from the darkness and steal my rationality? How long will I have to wait for them?

A blue orb lights up a few feet ahead of me, and then another one, filling the room with light. I am on the Pit floor, next to the chasm, and the initiates stand around me, their arms folded and their faces blank. I search for Christina and find her standing among them. None of them move. Their stillness makes my throat feel tight.

I see something in front of me—my own faint reflection. I touch it, and my fingers find glass, cool and smooth. I look up. There is a pane above me; I am in a glass box. I press above my head to see if I can force the box open. It doesn't budge. I am sealed in.

My heart beats faster. I don't want to be trapped. Someone taps on the wall in front of me. Four. He points at my feet, smirking.

A few seconds ago, my feet were dry, but now I stand in half an inch of water, and my socks are soggy. I crouch to see where the water is coming from, but it seems to be coming from nowhere, rising up from the box's glass bottom. I look up at Four, and he shrugs. He joins the crowd of initiates.

The water rises fast. It now covers my ankles. I pound against the glass with my fist.

"Hey!" I say. "Let me out of here!"

The water slides up my bare calves as it rises, cool and soft. I hit the glass harder.

"Get me out of here!"

I stare at Christina. She leans over to Peter, who stands beside her, and whispers something in his ear. They both laugh.

The water covers my thighs. I pound both fists against the glass. I'm not trying to get their attention anymore; I'm trying to break out. Frantic, I bang against the glass as hard as I can. I step back and throw my shoulder into the wall, once, twice, three times, four times. I hit the wall until my shoulder aches, screaming for help, watching the water rise to my waist, my rib cage, my chest.

"Help!" I scream. "Please! Please help!"

I slap the glass. I will die in this tank. I drag my shaking hands through my hair.

I see Will standing among the initiates, and something tickles at the back of my mind. Something he said. *Come on, think.* I stop trying to break the glass. It's hard to breathe, but I have to try. I'll need as much air as I can get in a few seconds.

My body rises, weightless in the water. I float closer to the ceiling and tilt my head back as the water covers my chin. Gasping, I press my face to the glass above me, sucking in as much air as I can. Then the water covers me, sealing me into the box.

Don't panic. It's no use—my heart pounds and my thoughts scatter. I thrash in the water, smacking the walls. I kick the glass as hard as I can, but the water slows down my foot. *The simulation is all in your head.*

I scream, and water fills my mouth. If it's in my head, I control it. The water burns my eyes. The initiates' passive faces stare back at me. They don't care.

I scream again and shove the wall with my palm. I hear something. A cracking sound. When I pull my hand away, there is a line in the glass. I slam my other hand next to the first and drive another crack through the glass, this one spreading outward from my palm in long, crooked fingers. My chest burns like I just swallowed fire. I kick the wall. My toes ache from the impact, and I hear a long, low groan.

The pane shatters, and the force of the water against my back throws me forward. There is air again.

I gasp and sit up. I'm in the chair. I gulp and shake out my hands. Four stands to my right, but instead of helping me up, he just looks at me.

"What?" I ask.

"How did you do that?"

"Do what?"

"Crack the glass."

"I don't know." Four finally offers me his hand. I swing my legs over the side of the chair, and when I stand, I feel steady. Calm.

He sighs and grabs me by the elbow, half leading and half dragging me out of the room. We walk quickly down the hallway, and then I stop, pulling my arm back. He stares at me in silence. He won't give me information without prompting.

"What?" I demand.

"You're Divergent," he replies.

I stare at him, fear pulsing through me like electricity. He knows. How does he know? I must have slipped up. Said something wrong.

I should act casual. I lean back, pressing my shoulders to the wall, and say, "What's Divergent?"

"Don't play stupid," he says. "I suspected it last time, but this time it's obvious. You manipulated the simulation; you're Divergent. I'll delete the footage, but unless you want to wind up *dead* at the bottom of the chasm, you'll figure out how to hide it during the simulations! Now, if you'll excuse me."

He walks back to the simulation room and slams the door behind him. I feel my heartbeat in my throat. I manipulated the simulation; I broke the glass. I didn't know that was an act of Divergence.

How did he?

I push myself away from the wall and start down the hallway. I need answers, and I know who has them.

+ + +

I walk straight to the tattoo place where I last saw Tori.

There aren't many people out, because it's midafternoon and most of them are at work or at school. There are three people in the tattoo place: the other tattoo artist, who is drawing a lion on another man's arm, and Tori, who is sorting through a stack of paper on the counter. She looks up when I walk in.

"Hello, Tris," she says. She glances at the other tattoo artist, who is too focused on what he's doing to notice us. "Let's go in the back."

I follow her behind the curtain that separates the two rooms. The next room contains a few chairs, spare tattoo needles, ink, pads of paper, and framed artwork. Tori draws the curtain shut and sits in one of the chairs. I sit next to her, tapping my feet to give myself something to do.

"What's going on?" she says. "How are the simulations going?"

"Really well." I nod a few times. "A little too well, I hear."

"Ah."

"Please help me understand," I say quietly. "What does it mean to be . . ." I hesitate. I should not say the word "Divergent" here. "What the hell am I? What does it have to do with the simulations?"

Tori's demeanor changes. She leans back and crosses her arms. Her expression becomes guarded.

"Among other things, you . . . you are someone who is aware, when they are in a simulation, that what they are experiencing is not real," she says. "Someone who can then manipulate the simulation or even shut it down. And also . . ." She leans forward and looks into my eyes. "Someone who, because you are also Dauntless . . . tends to die."

A weight settles on my chest, like each sentence she speaks is piling there. Tension builds inside me until I can't stand to hold it in anymore—I have to cry, or scream, or . . .

I let out a harsh little laugh that dies almost as soon as it's born and say, "So I'm going to die, then?"

"Not necessarily," she says. "The Dauntless leaders don't know about you yet. I deleted your aptitude results from the system immediately and manually logged your result as Abnegation. But make no mistake—if they discover what you are, they *will* kill you."

I stare at her in silence. She doesn't look crazy. She sounds steady, if a little urgent, and I've never suspected her of being unbalanced, but she must be. There hasn't been a murder in our city as long as I've been alive. Even if individuals are capable of it, the leaders of a faction can't possibly be.

"You're paranoid," I say. "The leaders of the Dauntless wouldn't kill me. People don't do that. Not anymore. That's the point of all this . . . all the factions."

"Oh, you think so?" She plants her hands on her knees and stares right at me, her features taut with sudden ferocity. "They got my brother, why not you, huh? What makes you special?"

"Your brother?" I say, narrowing my eyes.

"Yeah. My brother. He and I both transferred from Erudite, only his aptitude test was inconclusive. On the last day of simulations, they found his body in the chasm. Said it was a suicide. Only my brother was doing well in training, he was dating another initiate, he was *happy*." She shakes her head. "You have a brother, right? Don't you think you would know if he was suicidal?"

I try to imagine Caleb killing himself. Even the thought sounds ridiculous to me. Even if Caleb was miserable, it would not be an option.

Her sleeves are rolled up, so I can see a tattoo of a river on her right arm. Did she get it after her brother died? Was the river another fear she overcame?

She lowers her voice. "In the second stage of training, Georgie got really good, really fast. He said the simulations weren't even scary to him . . . they were like a game. So the instructors took a special interest in him. Piled into the room when he went under, instead of just letting the instructor report his results. Whispered about him all the time. The last day of simulations, one of the Dauntless leaders came in to see it himself. And the next day, Georgie was gone."

I could be good at the simulations, if I mastered whatever force helped me break the glass. I could be so good that all the instructors took notice. I could, but will I?

"Is that all it is?" I say. "Just changing the simulations?"

"I doubt it," she says, "but that's all I know."

"How many people know about this?" I say, thinking of Four. "About manipulating the simulations?"

"Two kinds of people," she says. "People who want you dead. Or people who have experienced it themselves. Firsthand. Or secondhand, like me."

Four told me he would delete the recording of me breaking the glass. He doesn't want me dead. Is he Divergent? Was a family member? A friend? A girlfriend?

I push the thought aside. I can't let him distract me.

"I don't understand," I say slowly, "why the Dauntless leaders care that I can manipulate the simulation."

"If I had it figured out, I would have told you by now." She presses her lips together. "The only thing I've come up with is that changing the simulation isn't what they care about; it's just a symptom of something else. Something they do care about."

Tori takes my hand and presses it between her palms.

"Think about this," she says. "These people taught you how to use a gun. They taught you how to fight. You think they're above hurting you? Above killing you?"

She releases my hand and stands.

"I have to go or Bud will ask questions. Be careful, Tris."

CHAPTER
TWENTY-ONE

THE DOOR TO the Pit closes behind me, and I am alone. I have not walked this tunnel since the day of the Choosing Ceremony. I remember how I walked it then, my footsteps unsteady, searching for light. I walk it sure-footed now. I don't need light anymore.

It has been four days since I spoke to Tori. Since then, Erudite has released two articles about Abnegation. The first article accuses Abnegation of withholding luxuries like cars and fresh fruit from the other factions in order to force their belief in self-denial on everyone else. When I read it, I thought of Will's sister, Cara, accusing my mother of hoarding goods.

The second article discusses the failings of choosing government officials based on their faction, asking why only people who define themselves as selfless should be in government. It promotes a return to the democratically elected political systems of the past. It makes a lot of sense, which makes me suspect it is a call for revolution wrapped in the clothing of rationality.

I reach the end of the tunnel. The net stretches across the gaping hole, just as it did when I last saw it. I climb the stairs to the wooden platform where Four pulled me to solid ground and grab the bar that the net is attached to. I would not have been able to lift my body up with just my arms when I first got here, but now I do it almost without thinking and roll into the center of the net.

Above me are the empty buildings that stand at the edge of the hole, and the sky. It is dark blue and starless. There is no moon.

The articles troubled me, but I had friends to cheer me up, and that is something. When the first one was released, Christina charmed one of the cooks in the Dauntless kitchens, and he let us try some cake batter.

After the second article, Uriah and Marlene taught me a card game, and we played for two hours in the dining hall.

Tonight, though, I want to be alone. More than that, I want to remember why I came here, and why I was so determined to stay here that I would jump off a building for it, even before I knew what being Dauntless was. I work my fingers through the holes in the net beneath me.

I wanted to be like the Dauntless I saw at school. I wanted to be loud and daring and free like them. But they were not members yet; they were just playing at being Dauntless. And so was I, when I jumped off that roof. I didn't know what fear was.

In the past four days, I faced four fears. In one I was tied to a stake and Peter set a fire beneath my feet. In another I was drowning again, this time in the middle of an ocean as the water raged around me. In the third, I watched as my family slowly bled to death. And in the fourth, I was held at gunpoint and forced to shoot them. I know what fear is now.

Wind rushes over the lip of the hole and washes over me, and I close my eyes. In my mind I stand at the edge of the roof again. I undo the buttons of my gray Abnegation shirt, exposing my arms, revealing more of my body than anyone else has ever seen. I ball the shirt up and hurl it at Peter's chest.

I open my eyes. No, I was wrong; I didn't jump off the roof because I wanted to be like the Dauntless. I jumped off because I already was like them, and I wanted to show myself to them. I wanted to acknowledge a part of myself that Abnegation demanded that I hide.

I stretch my hands over my head and hook them in the net again. I reach with my toes as far as I can, taking up as much of the net as possible. The night sky is empty and silent, and for the first time in four days, so is my mind.

+ + +

I hold my head in my hands and breathe deeply. Today the simulation was the same as yesterday: Someone held me at gunpoint and ordered me to shoot my family. When I lift my head, I see that Four is watching me.

"I know the simulation isn't real," I say.

"You don't have to explain it to me," he replies. "You love your family. You don't want to shoot them. Not the most unreasonable thing in the world."

"In the simulation is the only time I get to see them," I say. Even though he says I don't, I feel like I have to explain why this fear is so difficult for me to face. I twist my fingers together and pull them apart. My nail beds are bitten raw—I have been chewing them as I sleep. I wake to bloody hands every morning. "I miss them. You ever just . . . miss your family?"

Four looks down. "No," he says eventually. "I don't. But that's unusual."

It is unusual, so unusual it distracts me from the memory of holding a gun to Caleb's chest. What was his family like that he no longer cares about them?

I pause with my hand on the doorknob and look back at him.

Are you like me? I ask him silently. *Are you Divergent?*

Even thinking the word feels dangerous. His eyes hold mine, and as the silent seconds pass, he looks less and less stern. I hear my heartbeat. I have been looking at him too long, but then, he has been looking back, and I feel like we are both trying to say something the other can't hear, though I could be imagining it. Too long—and now, even longer, my heart even louder, his tranquil eyes swallowing me whole.

I push the door open and hurry down the hallway.

I shouldn't be so easily distracted by him. I shouldn't be able to think of anything but initiation. The simulations should disturb me more; they should break my mind, as they have been doing to most of the other initiates. Drew doesn't sleep—he just stares at the wall, curled in a ball. Al screams every night from his nightmares and cries into his pillow. My nightmares and chewed fingernails pale by comparison.

Al's screams wake me every time, and I stare at the springs above me and wonder what on earth is wrong with me, that I still feel strong when everyone else is breaking down. Is it being Divergent that makes me steady, or is it something else?

When I get back to the dormitory, I expect to find the same thing I found the day before: a few initiates lying on beds or staring at nothing. Instead they stand in a group on the other end of the room. Eric is in front of them with a chalkboard in his hands, which is facing the other way, so I can't see what's written on it. I stand next to Will.

"What's going on?" I whisper. I hope it isn't another article, because I'm not sure I can handle any more hostility directed at me.

"Rankings for stage two," he says.

"I thought there weren't any cuts after stage two," I hiss.

"There aren't. It's just a progress report, sort of."

I nod.

The sight of the board makes me feel uneasy, like something is swimming in my stomach. Eric lifts the board above his head and hangs it on the nail. When he steps aside, the room falls silent, and I crane my neck to see what it says.

My name is in the first slot.

Heads turn in my direction. I follow the list down. Christina and

Will are seventh and ninth, respectively. Peter is second, but when I look at the time listed by his name, I realize that the margin between us is conspicuously wide.

Peter's average simulation time is eight minutes. Mine is two minutes, forty-five seconds.

"Nice job, Tris," Will says quietly.

I nod, still staring at the board. I should be pleased that I am ranked first, but I know what that means. If Peter and his friends hated me before, they will despise me now. Now I am Edward. It could be my eye next. Or worse.

I search for Al's name and find it in the last slot. The crowd of initiates breaks up slowly, leaving just me, Peter, Will, and Al standing there. I want to console Al. To tell him that the only reason that I'm doing well is that there's something different about my brain.

Peter turns slowly, every limb infused with tension. A glare would have been less threatening than the look he gives me—a look of pure hatred. He walks toward his bunk, but at the last second, he whips around and shoves me against a wall, a hand on each of my shoulders.

"I will not be outranked by a Stiff," he hisses, his face so close to mine I can smell his stale breath. "How did you do it, huh? How the hell did you do it?"

He pulls me forward a few inches and then slams me against the wall again. I clench my teeth to keep from crying out, though pain from the impact went all the way down my spine. Will grabs Peter by his shirt collar and drags him away from me.

"Leave her alone," he says. "Only a coward bullies a little girl."

"A little girl?" scoffs Peter, throwing off Will's hand. "Are you blind, or just stupid? She's going to edge you out of the rankings and out of *Dauntless*, and you're going to get *nothing*, all because she knows how to manipulate people and you don't. So when you realize that she's out to ruin us all, you let me know."

Peter storms out of the dormitory. Molly and Drew follow him, looks of disgust on their faces.

"Thanks," I say, nodding to Will.

"Is he right?" Will asks quietly. "Are you trying to manipulate us?"

"How on earth would I do that?" I scowl at him. "I'm just doing the best I can, like anyone else."

"I don't know." He shrugs a little. "By acting weak so we pity you? And then acting tough to psyche us out?"

"Psyche you out?" I repeat. "I'm your *friend*. I wouldn't do that."

He doesn't say anything. I can tell he doesn't believe me—not quite.

"Don't be an idiot, Will," says Christina, hopping down from her bunk. She looks at me without sympathy and adds, "She's not acting."

Christina turns and leaves, without banging the door shut. Will follows. I am alone in the room with Al. The first and the last.

Al has never looked small before, but he does now, with his shoulders slumped and his body collapsing on itself like crumpled paper. He sits down on the edge of his bed.

"Are you all right?" I ask.

"Sure," he says.

His face is bright red. I look away. Asking him was just a formality. Anyone with eyes could see that Al is not all right.

"It's not over," I say. "You can improve your rank if you . . ."

My voice trails off when he looks up at me. I don't even know what I would say to him if I finished my sentence. There is no strategy for stage two. It reaches deep into the heart of who we are and tests whatever courage is there.

"See?" he says. "It's not that simple."

"I know it's not."

"I don't think you do," he says, shaking his head. His chin wobbles. "For you it's easy. All of this is easy."

"That's not true."

"Yeah, it is." He closes his eyes. "You aren't helping me by pretending it isn't. I don't—I'm not sure you can help me at all."

I feel like I just walked into a downpour, and all my clothes are heavy with water; like I am heavy and awkward and useless. I don't know if he means that no one can help him, or if I, specifically, can't help him, but I would not be okay with either interpretation. I want to help him. I am powerless to do so.

"I . . . ," I start to say, meaning to apologize, but for what? For being more Dauntless than he is? For not knowing what to say?

"I just . . ." The tears that have been gathering in his eyes spill over, wetting his cheeks. ". . . want to be alone."

I nod and turn away from him. Leaving him is not a good idea, but I can't stop myself. The door clicks into place behind me, and I keep walking.

I walk past the drinking fountain and through the tunnels that seemed endless the day I got here but now barely register in my mind. This is not the first time I have failed my family since I got here, but for some reason, it feels that way. Every other time I failed, I knew what to do but chose not to do it. This time, I did not know what to do. Have I lost the ability to see what people need? Have I lost part of myself?

I keep walking.

+ + +

I somehow find the hallway I sat in the day Edward left. I don't want to be alone, but I don't feel like I have much of a choice. I close my eyes and pay attention to the cold stone beneath me and breathe the musty underground air.

"Tris!" someone calls from the end of the hallway. Uriah jogs toward me. Behind him are Lynn and Marlene. Lynn is holding a muffin.

"Thought I would find you here." He crouches near my feet. "I heard you got ranked first."

"So you just wanted to congratulate me?" I smirk. "Well, thanks."

"*Someone* should," he says. "And I figured your friends might not be so congratulatory, since their ranks aren't as high. So quit moping and come with us. I'm going to shoot a muffin off Marlene's head."

The idea is so ridiculous I can't stop myself from laughing. I get up and follow Uriah to the end of the hallway, where Marlene and Lynn are waiting. Lynn narrows her eyes at me, but Marlene grins.

"Why aren't you out celebrating?" she asks. "You're practically guaranteed a top ten spot if you keep it up."

"She's too Dauntless for the other transfers," Uriah says.

"And too Abnegation to 'celebrate,' " remarks Lynn.

I ignore her. "Why are you shooting a muffin off Marlene's head?"

"She bet me I couldn't aim well enough to hit a small object from one hundred feet," Uriah explains. "I bet her she didn't have the guts to stand there as I tried. It works out well, really."

The training room where I first fired a gun is not far from my hidden hallway. We get there in under a minute, and Uriah flips on a light switch. It looks the same as the last time I was there: targets on one end of the room, a table with guns on the other.

"They just keep these lying around?" I ask.

"Yeah, but they aren't loaded." Uriah pulls up his shirt. There is a gun stuck under the waistband of his pants, right under a tattoo. I stare at the tattoo, trying to figure out what it is, but then he lets his shirt fall. "Okay," he says. "Go stand in front of a target."

Marlene walks away, a skip in her step.

"You aren't seriously going to shoot at her, are you?" I ask Uriah.

"It's not a real gun," says Lynn quietly. "It's got plastic pellets in it. The worst it'll do is sting her face, maybe give her a welt. What do you think we are, stupid?"

Marlene stands in front of one of the targets and sets the muffin on her head. Uriah squints one eye as he aims the gun.

"Wait!" calls out Marlene. She breaks off a piece of the muffin and pops it into her mouth. "Mmkay!" she shouts, the word garbled by food. She gives Uriah a thumbs-up.

"I take it your ranks were good," I say to Lynn.

She nods. "Uriah's second. I'm first. Marlene's fourth."

"You're only first by a *hair*," says Uriah as he aims. He squeezes the trigger. The muffin falls off Marlene's head. She didn't even blink.

"We both win!" she shouts.

"You miss your old faction?" Lynn asks me.

"Sometimes," I say. "It was calmer. Not as exhausting."

Marlene picks up the muffin from the ground and bites into it. Uriah shouts, "Gross!"

"Initiation's supposed to wear us down to who we really are. That's what Eric says, anyway," Lynn says. She arches an eyebrow.

"Four says it's to prepare us."

"Well, they don't agree on much."

I nod. Four told me that Eric's vision for Dauntless is not what it's supposed to be, but I wish he would tell me exactly what he thinks the right vision is. I get glimpses of it every so often—the Dauntless cheering when I jumped off the building, the net of arms that caught me after zip lining—but they are not enough. Has he read the Dauntless manifesto? Is that what he believes in—in ordinary acts of bravery?

The door to the training room opens. Shauna, Zeke, and Four walk in just as Uriah fires at another target. The plastic pellet bounces off the center of the target and rolls along the ground.

"I thought I heard something in here," says Four.

"Turns out it's my idiot brother," says Zeke. "You're not supposed to be in here after hours. Careful, or Four will tell Eric, and then you'll be as good as scalped."

Uriah wrinkles his nose at his brother and puts the pellet gun away. Marlene crosses the room, taking bites of her muffin, and Four steps away from the door to let us file out.

"You wouldn't tell Eric," says Lynn, eyeing Four suspiciously.

"No, I wouldn't," he says. As I pass him, he rests his hand on the top of my back to usher me out, his palm pressing between my shoulder blades. I shiver. I hope he can't tell.

The others walk down the hallway, Zeke and Uriah shoving each other, Marlene splitting her muffin with Shauna, Lynn marching in front. I start to follow them.

"Wait a second," Four says. I turn toward him, wondering which version of Four I'll see now—the one who scolds me, or the one who climbs Ferris wheels with me. He smiles a little, but the smile doesn't spread to his eyes, which look tense and worried.

"You belong here, you know that?" he says. "You belong with us. It'll be over soon, so just hold on, okay?"

He scratches behind his ear and looks away, like he's embarrassed by what he said.

I stare at him. I feel my heartbeat everywhere, even in my toes. I feel like doing something bold, but I could just as easily walk away. I am not sure which option is smarter, or better. I am not sure that I care.

I reach out and take his hand. His fingers slide between mine. I can't breathe.

I stare up at him, and he stares down at me. For a long moment, we stay that way. Then I pull my hand away and run after Uriah and Lynn and Marlene. Maybe now he thinks I'm stupid, or strange. Maybe it was worth it.

+ + +

I get back to the dormitory before anyone else does, and when they start to trickle in, I get into bed and pretend to be asleep. I don't need any of them, not if they're going to react this way when I do well. If I can make it through initiation, I will be Dauntless, and I won't have to see them anymore.

I don't need them—but do I want them? Every tattoo I got with them is a mark of their friendship, and almost every time I have laughed in this dark place was because of them. I don't want to lose them. But I feel like I have already.

After at least a half hour of racing thoughts, I roll onto my back and open my eyes. The dormitory is dark now—everyone has gone to bed. *Probably exhausted from resenting me so much*, I think with a wry smile. As if coming from the most hated faction wasn't enough, now I'm showing them up, too.

I get out of bed to get a drink of water. I'm not thirsty, but I need to do something. My bare feet make sticky sounds on the floor as I walk, my hand skimming the wall to keep my path straight. A bulb glows blue above the drinking fountain.

I tug my hair over one shoulder and bend over. As soon as the water touches my lips, I hear voices at the end of the hallway. I creep closer to them, trusting the dark to keep me hidden.

"So far there haven't been any signs of it." Eric's voice. Signs of what?

"Well, you wouldn't have seen much of it yet," someone replies. A female voice; cold and familiar, but familiar like a dream, not a real person. "Combat training shows you nothing. The simulations, however, reveal who the Divergent rebels are, if there are any, so we will have to examine the footage several times to be sure."

The word "Divergent" makes me go cold. I lean forward, my back pressed to the stone, to see who the familiar voice belongs to.

"Don't forget the reason I had Max appoint you," the voice says. "Your first priority is always finding them. Always."

"I won't forget."

I shift a few inches forward, hoping I am still hidden. Whoever that voice belongs to, she is pulling the strings; she is responsible for Eric's leadership position; she is the one who wants me dead. I tilt my head forward, straining to see them before they turn the corner.

Then someone grabs me from behind.

I start to scream, but a hand claps over my mouth. It smells like soap and it's big enough to cover the lower half of my face. I thrash, but the arms holding me are too strong, and I bite down on one of the fingers.

"Ow!" a rough voice cries.

"Shut up and keep her mouth covered." That voice is higher than the average male's and clearer. Peter.

A strip of dark cloth covers my eyes, and a new pair of hands ties it at the back of my head. I struggle to breathe. There are at least two hands on my arms, dragging me forward, and one on my back, shoving me in the same direction, and one on my mouth, keeping my screams in. Three people. My chest hurts. I can't resist three people on my own.

"Wonder what it sounds like when a Stiff begs for mercy," Peter says with a chuckle. "Hurry up."

I try to focus on the hand on my mouth. There must be something distinct about it that will make him easier to identify. His identity is a problem I can solve. I need to solve a problem right now, or I will panic.

The palm is sweaty and soft. I clench my teeth and breathe through my nose. The soap smell is familiar. Lemongrass and sage. The same smell surrounds Al's bunk. A weight drops into my stomach.

I hear the crash of water against rocks. We are near the chasm—we must be above it, given the volume of the sound. I press my lips together to keep from screaming. If we are above the chasm, I know what they intend to do to me.

"Lift her up, c'mon."

I thrash, and their rough skin grates against mine, but I know it's useless. I scream too, knowing that no one can hear me here.

I will survive until tomorrow. I will.

The hands push me around and up and slam my spine into something hard and cold. Judging by its width and curvature, it is a metal railing. It is *the* metal railing, the one that overlooks the chasm. My breaths wheeze and mist touches the back of my neck. The hands force my back to arch over the railing. My feet leave the ground, and my attackers are the only thing keeping me from falling into the water.

A heavy hand gropes along my chest. "You sure you're sixteen, Stiff? Doesn't feel like you're more than twelve." The other boys laugh.

Bile rises in my throat and I swallow the bitter taste.

"Wait, I think I found something!" His hand squeezes me. I bite my tongue to keep from screaming. More laughter.

Al's hand slips from my mouth. "Stop that," he snaps. I recognize his low, distinct voice.

When Al lets go of me, I thrash again and slip down to the ground. This time, I bite down as hard as I can on the first arm I find. I hear a scream and clench my jaw harder, tasting blood. Something hard strikes my face. White heat races through my head. It would have been pain if adrenaline wasn't coursing through me like acid.

The boy wrenches his trapped arm away from me and throws me to the ground. I bang my elbow against stone and bring my hands up to my head to remove the blindfold. A foot drives into my side, forcing the air from my lungs. I gasp and cough and claw at the back of my head. Someone grabs a handful of my hair and slams my head against something hard. A scream of pain bursts from my mouth, and I feel dizzy.

Clumsily, I fumble along the side of my head to find the edge of the blindfold. I drag my heavy hand up, taking the blindfold with it, and blink. The scene before me is sideways and bobs up and down. I see someone running toward us and someone running away—someone large, Al. I grab the railing next to me and haul myself to my feet.

Peter wraps a hand around my throat and lifts me up, his thumb wedged under my chin. His hair, which is usually shiny and smooth, is tousled and sticks to his forehead. His pale face is contorted and his teeth are gritted, and he holds me over the chasm as spots appear on the edges of my vision, crowding around his face, green and pink and blue. He says nothing. I try to kick him, but my legs are too short. My lungs scream for air.

I hear a shout, and he releases me.

I stretch out my arms as I fall, gasping, and my armpits slam into the railing. I hook my elbows over it and groan. Mist touches my ankles. The world dips and sways around me, and someone is on the Pit floor—Drew—screaming. I hear thumps. Kicks. Groans.

I blink a few times and focus as hard as I can on the only face I can see. It is contorted with anger. His eyes are dark blue.

"Four," I croak.

I close my eyes, and hands wrap around my arms, right where they join with the shoulder. He pulls me over the railing and against his chest, gathering me into his arms, easing an arm under my knees. I press my face into his shoulder, and there is a sudden, hollow silence.

CHAPTER
TWENTY-TWO

I OPEN MY eyes to the words "Fear God Alone" painted on a plain white wall. I hear the sound of running water again, but this time it's from a faucet and not from the chasm. Seconds go by before I see definite edges in my surroundings, the lines of door frame and countertop and ceiling.

The pain is a constant throb in my head and cheek and ribs. I shouldn't move; it will make everything worse. I see a blue patchwork quilt under my head and wince as I tilt my head to see where the water sound is coming from.

Four stands in the bathroom with his hands in the sink. Blood from his knuckles turns the sink water pink. He has a cut at the corner of his mouth, but he seems otherwise unharmed. His expression is placid as he examines his cuts, turns off the water, and dries his hands with a towel.

I have only one memory of getting here, and even that is just a single image: black ink curling around the side of a neck, the corner of a tattoo, and the gentle sway that could only mean he was carrying me.

He turns off the bathroom light and gets an ice pack from the refrigerator in the corner of the room. As he walks toward me, I consider closing my eyes and pretending to be asleep, but then our eyes meet and it's too late.

"Your hands," I croak.

"My hands are none of your concern," he replies. He rests his knee on the mattress and leans over me, slipping the ice pack under my head. Before he pulls away, I reach out to touch the cut on the side of his lip but stop when I realize what I am about to do, my hand hovering.

What do you have to lose? I ask myself. I touch my fingertips lightly to his mouth.

"Tris," he says, speaking against my fingers, "I'm all right."

"Why were you there?" I ask, letting my hand drop.

"I was coming back from the control room. I heard a scream."

"What did you do to them?" I say.

"I deposited Drew at the infirmary a half hour ago," he says. "Peter and Al ran. Drew claimed they were just trying to scare you. At least, I think that's what he was trying to say."

"He's in bad shape?"

"He'll live," he replies. He adds bitterly, "In what condition, I can't say."

It isn't right to wish pain on other people just because they hurt me first. But white-hot triumph races through me at the thought of Drew in the infirmary, and I squeeze Four's arm.

"Good," I say. My voice sounds tight and fierce. Anger builds inside me, replacing my blood with bitter water and filling me, consuming me. I want to break something, or hit something, but I am afraid to move, so I start crying instead.

Four crouches by the side of the bed, and watches me. I see no sympathy in his eyes. I would have been disappointed if I had. He pulls his wrist free and, to my surprise, rests his hand on the side of my face, his thumb skimming my cheekbone. His fingers are careful.

"I could report this," he says.

"No," I reply. "I don't want them to think I'm scared."

He nods. He moves his thumb absently over my cheekbone, back and forth. "I figured you would say that."

"You think it would be a bad idea if I sat up?"

"I'll help you."

Four grips my shoulder with one hand and holds my head steady with the other as I push myself up. Pain rushes through my body in sharp bursts, but I try to ignore it, stifling a groan.

He hands me the ice pack. "You can let yourself be in pain," he says. "It's just me here."

I bite down on my lip. There are tears on my face, but neither of us mentions or even acknowledges them.

"I suggest you rely on your transfer friends to protect you from now on," he says.

"I thought I was," I say. I feel Al's hand against my mouth again, and a sob jolts my body forward. I press my hand to my forehead and rock slowly back and forth. "But Al . . ."

"He wanted you to be the small, quiet girl from Abnegation," Four says softly. "He hurt you because your strength made him feel weak. No other reason."

I nod and try to believe him.

"The others won't be as jealous if you show some vulnerability. Even if it isn't real."

"You think I have to *pretend* to be vulnerable?" I ask, raising an eyebrow.

"Yes, I do." He takes the ice pack from me, his fingers brushing mine, and holds it against my head himself. I put my hand down, too eager to relax my arm to object. Four stands up. I stare at the hem of his T-shirt.

Sometimes I see him as just another person, and sometimes I feel the sight of him in my gut, like a deep ache.

"You're going to want to march into breakfast tomorrow and show your attackers they had no effect on you," he adds, "but you should let that bruise on your cheek show, and keep your head down."

The idea nauseates me.

"I don't think I can do that," I say hollowly. I lift my eyes to his.

"You have to."

"I don't think you *get* it." Heat rises into my face. "They touched me."

His entire body tightens at my words, his hand clenching around the ice pack. "Touched you," he repeats, his dark eyes cold.

"Not . . . in the way you're thinking." I clear my throat. I didn't realize when I said it how awkward it would be to talk about. "But . . . almost."

I look away.

He is silent and still for so long that eventually, I have to say something.

"What is it?"

"I don't want to say this," he says, "but I feel like I have to. It is more important for you to be safe than right, for the time being. Understand?"

His straight eyebrows are drawn low over his eyes. My stomach writhes, partly because I know he makes a good point but I don't want to admit it, and partly because I want something I don't know how to express; I want to press against the space between us until it disappears.

I nod.

"But please, when you see an opportunity . . ." He presses his hand to my cheek, cold and strong, and tilts my head up so I have to look at him. His eyes glint. They look almost predatory. "Ruin them."

I laugh shakily. "You're a little scary, Four."

"Do me a favor," he says, "and don't call me that."

"What should I call you, then?"

"Nothing." He takes his hand from my face. "Yet."

CHAPTER
TWENTY-THREE

I DON'T GO back to the dorms that night. Sleeping in the same room as the people who attacked me just to look brave would be stupid. Four sleeps on the floor and I sleep on his bed, on top of the quilt, breathing in the scent of his pillowcase. It smells like detergent and something heavy, sweet, and distinctly male.

The rhythm of his breaths slows, and I prop myself up to see if he is asleep. He lies on his stomach with one arm around his head. His eyes are closed, his lips parted. For the first time, he looks as young as he is, and I wonder who he really is. Who is he when he isn't Dauntless, isn't an instructor, isn't Four, isn't anything in particular?

Whoever he is, I like him. It's easier for me to admit that to myself now, in the dark, after all that just happened. He is not sweet or gentle or particularly kind. But he is smart and brave, and even though he saved me, he treated me like I was strong. That is all I need to know.

I watch the muscles in his back expand and contract until I fall asleep.

I wake to aches and pains. I cringe as I sit up, holding my ribs, and walk up to the small mirror on the opposite wall. I am almost too short to see myself in it, but when I stand on my tiptoes, I can see my face. As expected, there is a dark blue bruise on my cheek. I hate the idea of slumping into the dining hall like this, but Four's instructions have stayed with me. I have to mend my friendships. I need the protection of seeming weak.

I tie my hair in a knot at the back of my head. The door opens and Four walks in, a towel in hand and his hair glistening with shower water. I feel a thrill in my stomach when I see the line of skin that shows above his belt as he lifts his hand to dry his hair and force my eyes up to his face.

"Hi," I say. My voice sounds tight. I wish it didn't.

He touches my bruised cheek with just his fingertips. "Not bad," he says. "How's your head?"

"Fine," I say. I'm lying—my head is throbbing. I brush my fingers over the bump, and pain prickles over my scalp. It could be worse. I could be floating in the river.

Every muscle in my body tightens as his hand drops to my side, where I got kicked. He does it casually, but I can't move.

"And your side?" he asks, his voice low.

"Only hurts when I breathe."

He smiles. "Not much you can do about that."

"Peter would probably throw a party if I stopped breathing."

"Well," he says, "I would only go if there was cake."

I laugh, and then wince, covering his hand to steady my rib cage. He slides his hand back slowly, his fingertips grazing my side. When his fingers lift, I feel an ache in my chest. Once this moment ends, I have to remember what happened last night. And I want to stay here with him.

He nods a little and leads the way out.

"I'll go in first," he says when we stand outside the dining hall. "See you soon, Tris."

He walks through the doors and I am alone. Yesterday he told me he thought I would have to pretend to be weak, but he was wrong. I am weak already. I brace myself against the wall and press my forehead to my hands. It's difficult to take deep breaths, so I take short, shallow ones. I can't let this happen. They attacked me to make me feel weak. I can pretend they succeeded to protect myself, but I can't let it become true.

I pull away from the wall and walk into the dining hall without another thought. A few steps in, I remember I'm supposed to look like I'm cowering, so I slow my pace and hug the wall, keeping my head down. Uriah, at the table next to Will and Christina's, lifts his hand to wave at me. And then puts it down.

I sit next to Will.

Al isn't there—he isn't anywhere.

Uriah slides into the seat next to me, leaving his half-eaten muffin and half-finished glass of water on the other table. For a second, all three of them just stare at me.

"What happened?" Will asks, lowering his voice.

I look over his shoulder at the table behind ours. Peter sits there, eating a piece of toast and whispering something to Molly. My hand clenches around the edge of the table. I want him to hurt. But now isn't the time.

Drew is missing, which means he's still in the infirmary. Vicious pleasure courses through me at the thought.

"Peter, Drew . . . ," I say quietly. I hold my side as I reach across the table for a piece of toast. It hurts to stretch out my hand, so I let myself wince and hunch over. "And . . ." I swallow. "And Al."

"Oh God," says Christina, her eyes wide.

"Are you all right?" Uriah asks.

Peter's eyes find mine across the dining hall, and I have to force myself to look away. It brings a bitter taste to my mouth to show him that he scares me, but I have to. Four was right. I have to do everything I can to make sure I don't get attacked again.

"Not really," I say.

My eyes burn, and it's not artifice, unlike the wincing. I shrug. I believe Tori's warning now. Peter, Drew, and Al were ready to throw me into the chasm out of jealousy—what is so unbelievable about the Dauntless leaders committing murder?

I feel uncomfortable, like I'm wearing someone else's skin. If I'm not careful, I could die. I can't even trust the leaders of my faction. My new family.

"But you're just . . ." Uriah purses his lips. "It isn't fair. Three against one?"

"Yeah, and Peter is all about what's fair. That's why he grabbed Edward in his sleep and stabbed him in the eye." Christina snorts and shakes her head. "Al, though? Are you sure, Tris?"

I stare at my plate. I'm the next Edward. But unlike him, I'm not going to leave.

"Yeah," I say. "I'm sure."

"It has to be desperation," says Will. "He's been acting . . . I don't know. Like a different person. Ever since stage two started."

Then Drew shuffles into the dining hall. I drop my toast, and my mouth drifts open.

Calling him "bruised" would be an understatement. His face is swollen and purple. He has a split lip and a cut running through his eyebrow. He keeps his eyes down on the way to his table, not even lifting them to look at me. I glance across the room at Four. He wears the satisfied smile I wish I had on.

"Did *you* do that?" hisses Will.

I shake my head. "No. Someone—I never saw who—found me right before . . ." I gulp. Saying it out loud makes it worse, makes it real. ". . . I got tossed into the chasm."

"They were going to *kill* you?" says Christina in a low voice.

"Maybe. They might have been planning on dangling me over it just to scare me." I lift a shoulder. "It worked."

Christina gives me a sad look. Will just glares at the table.

"We have to do something about this," Uriah says in a low voice.

"What, like beat them up?" Christina grins. "Looks like that's been taken care of already."

"No. That's pain they can get over," replies Uriah. "We have to edge them out of the rankings. That will damage their futures. Permanently."

Four gets up and stands between the tables. Conversation abruptly ceases.

"Transfers. We're doing something different today," he says. "Follow me."

We stand, and Uriah's forehead wrinkles. "Be careful," he tells me.

"Don't worry," says Will. "We'll protect her."

+ + +

Four leads us out of the dining hall and along the paths that surround the Pit. Will is on my left, Christina is on my right.

"I never really said I was sorry," Christina says quietly. "For taking the flag when you earned it. I don't know what was wrong with me."

I'm not sure if it's smart to forgive her or not—to forgive either of them, after what they said to me when the rankings went up yesterday. But my mother would tell me that people are flawed and I should be lenient with them. And Four told me to rely on my friends.

I don't know who I should rely on more, because I'm not sure who my true friends are. Uriah and Marlene, who were on my side even when I seemed strong, or Christina and Will, who have always protected me when I seemed weak?

When her wide brown eyes meet mine, I nod. "Let's just forget about it."

I still want to be angry, but I have to let my anger go.

We climb higher than I've gone before, until Will's face goes white whenever he looks down. Most of the time I like heights, so I grab Will's arm like I need his support—but really, I'm lending him mine. He smiles gratefully at me.

Four turns around and walks backward a few steps—backward, on a narrow path with no railing. How well does he know this place?

He eyes Drew, who trudges at the back of the group, and says, "Pick up the pace, Drew!"

It's a cruel joke, but it's hard for me to fight off a smile. That is, until Four's eyes shift to my arm around Will's, and all the humor drains from them. His expression sends a chill through me. Is he . . . jealous?

We get closer and closer to the glass ceiling, and for the first time in days, I see the sun. Four walks up a flight of metal stairs leading through a hole in the ceiling. They creak under my feet, and I look down to see the Pit and the chasm below us.

We walk across the glass, which is now a floor rather than a ceiling, through a cylindrical room with glass walls. The surrounding buildings are half-collapsed and appear to be abandoned, which is probably why I never noticed the Dauntless compound before. The Abnegation sector is also far away.

The Dauntless mill around the glass room, talking in clusters. At the edge of the room, two Dauntless fight with sticks, laughing when one of them misses and hits only air. Above me, two ropes stretch across the room, one a few feet higher than the other. They probably have something to do with the daredevil stunts the Dauntless are famous for.

Four leads us through another door. Beyond it is a huge, dank space with graffitied walls and exposed pipes. The room is lit by a series of old-fashioned fluorescent tubes with plastic covers—they must be ancient.

"This," says Four, his eyes bright in pale light, "is a different kind of simulation known as the fear landscape. It has been disabled for our purposes, so this isn't what it will be like the next time you see it."

Behind him, the word "Dauntless" is spray-painted in red artistic lettering on a concrete wall.

"Through your simulations, we have stored data about your worst fears. The fear landscape accesses that data and presents you with a series of virtual obstacles. Some of the obstacles will be fears you previously faced in your simulations. Some may be new fears. The difference is that you are aware, in the fear landscape, that it is a simulation, so you will have all your wits about you as you go through it."

That means that everyone will be like Divergent in the fear landscape. I don't know if that's a relief, because I can't be detected, or a problem, because I won't have the advantage.

Four continues, "The number of fears you have in your landscape varies according to how many you have."

How many fears will I have? I think of facing the crows again and shiver, though the air is warm.

"I told you before that the third stage of initiation focuses on mental preparation," he says. I remember when he said that. On the first day. Right before he put a gun to Peter's head. I wish he had pulled the trigger.

"That is because it requires you to control both your emotions and your body—to combine the physical abilities you learned in stage one with the emotional mastery you learned in stage two. To keep a level head." One of the fluorescent tubes above Four's head twitches and flickers. Four stops scanning the crowd of initiates and focuses his stare on me.

"Next week you will go through your fear landscape as quickly as possible in front of a panel of Dauntless leaders. That will be your final test, which determines your ranking for stage three. Just as stage two of initiation is weighted more heavily than stage one, stage three is weighted heaviest of all. Understood?"

We all nod. Even Drew, who makes it look painful.

If I do well in my final test, I have a good chance of making it into the top ten and a good chance of becoming a member. Becoming Dauntless. The thought makes me almost giddy with relief.

"You can get past each obstacle in one of two ways. Either you find a way to calm down enough that the simulation registers a normal, steady heartbeat, or you find a way to face your fear, which can force the simulation to move on. One way to face a fear of drowning is to swim deeper, for example." Four shrugs. "So I suggest that you take the next week to consider your fears and develop strategies to face them."

"That doesn't sound fair," says Peter. "What if one person only has seven fears and someone else has twenty? That's not their fault."

Four stares at him for a few seconds and then laughs. "Do you really want to talk to me about what's fair?"

The crowd of initiates parts to make way for him as he walks toward Peter, folds his arms, and says, in a deadly voice, "I understand why you're worried, Peter. The events of last night certainly proved that you are a miserable coward."

Peter stares back, expressionless.

"So now we all know," says Four, quietly, "that you are afraid of a short, skinny girl from Abnegation." His mouth curls in a smile.

Will puts his arm around me. Christina's shoulders shake with suppressed laughter. And somewhere within me, I find a smile too.

+ + +

When we get back to the dorm that afternoon, Al is there.

Will stands behind me and holds my shoulders—lightly, as if to remind me that he's there. Christina edges closer to me.

Al's eyes have shadows beneath them, and his face is swollen from crying. Pain stabs my stomach when I see him. I can't move. The scent of lemongrass and sage, once pleasant, turns sour in my nose.

"Tris," says Al, his voice breaking. "Can I talk to you?"

"Are you kidding?" Will squeezes my shoulders. "You don't get to come near her ever again."

"I won't hurt you. I never wanted to . . ." Al covers his face with both hands. "I just want to say that I'm sorry, I'm so sorry, I don't . . . I don't know what's wrong with me, I . . . please forgive me, *please.* . . ."

He reaches for me like he's going to touch my shoulder, or my hand, his face wet with tears.

Somewhere inside me is a merciful, forgiving person. Somewhere there is a girl who tries to understand what people are going through, who accepts that people do evil things and that desperation leads them to darker places than they ever imagined. I swear she exists, and she hurts for the repentant boy I see in front of me.

But if I saw her, I wouldn't recognize her.

"Stay away from me," I say quietly. My body feels rigid and cold, and I am not angry, I am not hurt, I am nothing. I say, my voice low, "Never come near me again."

Our eyes meet. His are dark and glassy. I am nothing.

"If you do, I swear to God I will kill you," I say. "You coward."

CHAPTER
TWENTY-FOUR

"TRIS."

In my dream, my mother says my name. She beckons to me, and I cross the kitchen to stand beside her. She points to the pot on the stove, and I lift the lid to peek inside. The beady eye of a crow stares back at me, its wing feathers pressed to the side of the pot, its fat body covered with boiling water.

"Dinner," she says.

"Tris!" I hear again. I open my eyes. Christina stands next to my bed, her cheeks streaked with mascara-tinted tears.

"It's Al," she says. "Come on."

Some of the other initiates are awake, and some aren't. Christina grabs my hand and pulls me out of the dormitory. I run barefoot over the stone floor, blinking clouds from my eyes, my limbs still heavy with sleep. Something terrible has happened. I feel it with every thump of my heart. *It's Al.*

We run across the Pit floor, and then Christina stops. A crowd has gathered around the ledge, but everyone stands a few feet from one another, so there is enough space for me to maneuver past Christina and around a tall, middle-aged man to the front.

Two men stand next to the ledge, hoisting something up with ropes. They both grunt from the effort, heaving their weight back so the ropes slide over the railing, and then reaching forward to grab again. A huge, dark shape appears above the ledge, and a few Dauntless rush forward to help the two men haul it over.

The shape falls with a thud on the Pit floor. A pale arm, swollen with water, flops onto the stone. A body. Christina pulls herself tight to my side, clinging to my arm. She turns her head into my shoulder and sobs, but I can't look away. A few of the men turn the body over, and the head flops to the side.

The eyes are open and empty. Dark. Doll's eyes. And the nose has a high arch, a narrow bridge, a round tip. The lips are blue. The face itself is something other than human, half corpse and half creature. My lungs burn; my next breath rattles on the way in. *Al.*

"One of the initiates," says someone behind me. "What happened?"

"Same thing that happens every year," someone else replies. "He pitched himself over the ledge."

"Don't be so morbid. Could have been an accident."

"They found him in the middle of the chasm. You think he tripped over his shoelace and . . . whoopsies, just *stumbled* fifteen feet forward?"

Christina's hands get tighter and tighter around my arm. I should tell her to let go of me; it's starting to hurt. Someone kneels next to Al's face and pushes his eyelids shut. Trying to make it look like he's sleeping, maybe. Stupid. Why do people want to pretend that death is sleep? It isn't. It isn't.

Something inside me collapses. My chest is so tight, suffocating, can't breathe. I sink to the ground, dragging Christina down with me. The stone is rough under my knees. I hear something, a memory of sound. Al's sobs; his screams at night. Should have known. Still can't breathe. I press both palms to my chest and rock back and forth to free the tension in my chest.

When I blink, I see the top of Al's head as he carries me on his back to the dining hall. I feel the bounce of his footsteps. He is big and warm and clumsy. No, *was*. That is death—shifting from "is" to "was."

I wheeze. Someone has brought a large black bag to put the body in. I can tell that it will be too small. A laugh rises in my throat and flops from my mouth, strained and gurgling. Al's too big for the body bag; what a tragedy. Halfway through the laugh, I clamp my mouth shut, and it sounds more like a groan. I pull my arm free and stand, leaving Christina on the ground. I run.

+ + +

"Here you go," Tori says. She hands me a steaming mug that smells like peppermint. I hold it with both hands, my fingers prickling with warmth.

She sits down across from me. When it comes to funerals, the Dauntless don't waste any time. Tori said they want to acknowledge death as soon as it happens. There are no people in the front room of the tattoo parlor, but the Pit is crawling with people, most of them drunk. I don't know why that surprises me.

At home, a funeral is a somber occasion. Everyone gathers to support the deceased's family, and no one has idle hands, but there is no laughter, or shouting, or joking. And the Abnegation don't drink alcohol, so everyone is sober. It makes sense that funerals would be the opposite here.

"Drink it," she says. "It will make you feel better, I promise."

"I don't think tea is the solution," I say slowly. But I sip it any way. It warms my mouth and my throat and trickles into my stomach. I didn't realize how deeply cold I was until I wasn't anymore.

" 'Better' is the word I used. Not 'good.' " She smiles at me, but the corners of her eyes don't crinkle like they usually do. "I don't think 'good' will happen for a while."

I bite my lip. "How long . . ." I struggle for the right words. "How long did it take for you to be okay again, after your brother . . ."

"Don't know." She shakes her head. "Some days I feel like I'm still not okay. Some days I feel fine. Happy, even. It took me a few years to stop plotting revenge, though."

"Why did you stop?" I ask.

Her eyes go vacant as she stares at the wall behind me. She taps her fingers against her leg for a few seconds and then says, "I don't think of it as stopping. More like I'm . . . waiting for my opportunity."

She comes out of her daze and checks her watch.

"Time to go," she says.

I pour the rest of my tea down the sink. When I lift my hand from the mug, I realize that I'm shaking. Not good. My hands usually shake before I start to cry, and I can't cry in front of everyone.

I follow Tori out of the tattoo place and down the path to the Pit floor. All the people that were milling around earlier are gathered by the ledge now, and the air smells potently of alcohol. The woman in front of me lurches to the right, losing her balance, and then erupts into giggles as she falls against the man next to her. Tori grabs my arm and steers me away.

I find Uriah, Will, and Christina standing among the other initiates. Christina's eyes are swollen. Uriah is holding a silver flask. He offers it to me. I shake my head.

"Surprise, surprise," says Molly from behind me. She nudges Peter with her elbow. "Once a Stiff, always a Stiff."

I should ignore her. Her opinions shouldn't matter to me.

"I read an interesting article today," she says, leaning closer to my ear. "Something about your dad, and the *real* reason you left your old faction."

Defending myself isn't the most important thing on my mind. But it is the easiest one to address.

I twist, and my fist connects with her jaw. My knuckles sting from the impact. I don't remember deciding to punch her. I don't remember forming a fist.

She lunges at me, her hands outstretched, but she doesn't get far. Will grabs her collar and pulls her back. He looks from her to me and says, "Quit it. Both of you."

Part of me wishes that he hadn't stopped her. A fight would be a welcome distraction, especially now that Eric is climbing onto a box next to the railing. I face him, crossing my arms to keep myself steady. I wonder what he'll say.

In Abnegation no one has committed suicide in recent memory, but the faction's stance on it is clear: Suicide, to them, is an act of selfishness. Someone who is truly selfless does not think of himself often enough to desire death. No one would say that aloud, if it happened, but everyone would think it.

"Quiet down, everyone!" shouts Eric. Someone hits what sounds like a gong, and the shouts gradually stop, though the mutters don't. Eric says, "Thank you. As you know, we're here because Albert, an initiate, jumped into the chasm last night."

The mutters stop too, leaving just the rush of water in the chasm.

"We do not know why," says Eric, "and it would be easy to mourn the loss of him tonight. But we did not choose a life of ease when we became Dauntless. And the truth of it is . . ." Eric smiles. If I didn't know him, I would think that smile is genuine. But I do know him. "The truth is, Albert is now exploring an unknown, uncertain place. He leaped into vicious waters to get there. Who among us is brave enough to venture into that darkness without knowing what lies beyond it? Albert was not yet one of our members, but we can be assured that he was one of our *bravest!*"

A cry rises from the center of the crowd, and a whoop. The Dauntless cheer at varying pitches, high and low, bright and deep. Their roar mimics the roar of the water. Christina takes the flask from Uriah and drinks. Will slides his arm around her shoulders and pulls her to his side. Voices fill my ears.

"We will celebrate him now, and remember him always!" yells Eric. Someone hands him a dark bottle, and he lifts it. "To Albert the Courageous!"

"To Albert!" shouts the crowd. Arms lift all around me, and the Dauntless chant his name. "Albert! Al-bert! Al-bert!" They chant until his name no longer sounds like his name. It sounds like the primal scream of an ancient race.

I turn away from the railing. I cannot stand this any longer.

I don't know where I'm going. I suspect that I am not going anywhere at all, just away. I walk down a dark hallway. At the end is the drinking fountain, bathed in the blue glow of the light above it.

I shake my head. Courageous? Courageous would have been admitting weakness and leaving Dauntless, no matter what shame accompanied it. Pride is what killed Al, and it is the flaw in every Dauntless heart. It is in mine.

"Tris."

A jolt goes through me, and I turn around. Four stands behind me, just inside the blue circle of light. It gives him an eerie look, shading his eye sockets and casting shadows under his cheekbones.

"What are you doing here?" I ask. "Shouldn't you be paying your respects?"

I say it like it tastes bad and I have to spit it out.

"Shouldn't you?" he says. He steps toward me, and I see his eyes again. They look black in this light.

"Can't pay respect when you don't have any," I reply. I feel a twinge of guilt and shake my head. "I didn't mean that."

"Ah." Judging by the look he gives me, he doesn't believe me. I don't blame him.

"This is ridiculous," I say, heat rushing into my cheeks. "He throws himself off a ledge and Eric's calling it brave? Eric, who tried to have you throw knives at Al's head?" I taste bile. Eric's false smiles, his artificial words, his twisted ideals—they make me want to be sick. "He wasn't brave! He was depressed and a coward and he almost killed me! Is that the kind of thing we respect here?"

"What do you want them to do?" he says. "Condemn him? Al's already dead. He can't hear it and it's too late."

"It's not *about* Al," I snap. "It's about everyone watching! Everyone who now sees hurling themselves into the chasm as a viable option. I mean, why not do it if everyone calls you a hero afterward? Why not do it if everyone will remember your name? It's . . . I can't . . ."

I shake my head. My face burns and my heart pounds, and I try to keep myself under control, but I can't.

"This would *never* have happened in Abnegation!" I almost shout. "None of it! Never. This place warped him and ruined him, and I don't care if saying that makes me a Stiff, I don't care, I don't *care*!"

Four's eyes shift to the wall above the drinking fountain.

"Careful, Tris," he says, his eyes still on the wall.

"Is that all you can say?" I demand, scowling at him. "That I should be *careful*? That's *it*?"

"You're as bad as the Candor, you know that?" He grabs my arm and drags me away from the drinking fountain. His hand hurts my arm, but I'm not strong enough to pull away.

His face is so close to mine that I can see a few freckles spotting his nose. "I'm not going to say this again, so listen carefully." He sets his hands on my shoulders, his fingers pressing, squeezing. I feel small. "They are watching you. *You*, in particular."

"Let go of me," I say weakly.

His fingers spring apart, and he straightens. Some of the weight on my chest lifts now that he isn't touching me. I fear his shifting moods. They show me something unstable inside of him, and instability is dangerous.

"Are they watching you, too?" I say, so quietly he wouldn't be able to hear me if he wasn't standing so close.

He doesn't answer my question. "I keep trying to help you," he says, "but you refuse to be helped."

"Oh, right. Your *help*," I say. "Stabbing my ear with a knife and taunting me and yelling at me more than you yell at anyone else, it sure is helpful."

"Taunting you? You mean when I threw the knives? I wasn't taunting you," he snaps. "I was reminding you that if you failed, someone else would have to take your place."

I cup the back of my neck with my hand and think back to the knife incident. Every time he spoke, it was to remind me that if I gave up, Al would have to take my place in front of the target.

"Why?" I say.

"Because you're from Abnegation," he says, "and it's when you're acting selflessly that you are at your bravest."

I understand now. He wasn't persuading me to give up. He was reminding me why I couldn't—because I needed to protect Al. The thought makes me ache now. Protect Al. My friend. My attacker.

I can't hate Al as much as I want to.

I can't forgive him either.

"If I were you, I would do a better job of pretending that selfless impulse is going away," he says, "because if the wrong people discover it . . . well, it won't be good for you."

"Why? Why do they care about my intentions?"

"Intentions are the *only* thing they care about. They try to make you think they care about what you do, but they don't. They don't want you to act a certain way. They want you to *think* a certain way. So you're easy to understand. So you won't pose a threat to them." He presses a hand to the wall next to my head and leans into it. His shirt is just tight enough that I can see his collarbone and the faint depression between his shoulder muscle and his bicep.

I wish I was taller. If I was tall, my narrow build would be described as "willowy" instead of "childish," and he might not see me as a little sister he needs to protect.

I don't want him to see me as his sister.

"I don't understand," I say, "why they care what I think, as long as I'm acting how they want me to."

"You're acting how they want you to now," he says, "but what happens when your Abnegation-wired brain tells you to do something else, something they don't want?"

I don't have an answer to that, and I don't even know if he's right about me. Am I wired like the Abnegation, or the Dauntless?

Maybe the answer is neither. Maybe I am wired like the Divergent.

"I might not need you to help me. Ever think about that?" I say. "I'm not weak, you know. I can do this on my own."

He shakes his head. "You think my first instinct is to protect you. Because you're small, or a girl, or a Stiff. But you're wrong."

He leans his face close to mine and wraps his fingers around my chin. His hand smells like metal. When was the last time he held a gun, or a knife? My skin tingles at the point of contact, like he's transmitting electricity through his skin.

"My *first* instinct is to push you until you break, just to see how hard I have to press," he says, his fingers squeezing at the word "break." My body tenses at the edge in his voice, so I am coiled as tight as a spring, and I forget to breathe.

His dark eyes lifting to mine, he adds, "But I resist it."

"Why . . ." I swallow hard. "Why is that your first instinct?"

"Fear doesn't shut you down; it wakes you up. I've seen it. It's fascinating." He releases me but doesn't pull away, his hand grazing my jaw, my neck. "Sometimes I just . . . want to see it again. Want to see you awake."

I set my hands on his waist. I can't remember deciding to do that. But I also can't move away. I pull myself against his chest, wrapping my arms around him. My fingers skim the muscles of his back.

After a moment he touches the small of my back, pressing me closer, and smoothes his other hand over my hair. I feel small again, but this time, it doesn't scare me. I squeeze my eyes shut. He doesn't scare me anymore.

"Should I be crying?" I ask, my voice muffled by his shirt. "Is there something wrong with me?"

The simulations drove a crack through Al so wide he could not mend it. Why not me? Why am I not like him—and why does that thought make me feel so uneasy, like I'm teetering on a ledge myself?

"You think I know anything about tears?" he says quietly.

I close my eyes. I don't expect Four to reassure me, and he makes no effort to, but I feel better standing here than I did out there among the people who are my friends, my faction. I press my forehead to his shoulder.

"If I had forgiven him," I say, "do you think he would be alive now?"

"I don't know," he replies. He presses his hand to my cheek, and I turn my face into it, keeping my eyes closed.

"I feel like it's my fault."

"It isn't your fault," he says, touching his forehead to mine.

"But I should have. I should have forgiven him."

"Maybe. Maybe there's more we all could have done," he says, "but we just have to let the guilt remind us to do better next time."

I frown and pull back. That is a lesson that members of Abnegation learn—guilt as a tool, rather than a weapon against the self. It is a line straight from one of my father's lectures at our weekly meetings.

"What faction did you come from, Four?"

"It doesn't matter," he replies, his eyes lowered. "This is where I am now. Something you would do well to remember for yourself."

He gives me a conflicted look and touches his lips to my forehead, right between my eyebrows. I close my eyes. I don't understand this, whatever it is. But I don't want to ruin it, so I say nothing. He doesn't move; he just stays there with his mouth pressed to my skin, and I stay there with my hands on his waist, for a long time.

CHAPTER
TWENTY-FIVE

I STAND WITH Will and Christina at the railing overlooking the chasm, late at night after most of the Dauntless have gone to sleep. Both my shoulders sting from the tattoo needle. We all got new tattoos a half hour ago.

Tori was the only one in the tattoo place, so I felt safe getting the symbol of Abnegation—a pair of hands, palms up as if to help someone stand, bounded by a circle—on my right shoulder. I know it was a risk, especially after all that's happened. But that symbol is a part of my identity, and it felt important to me that I wear it on my skin.

I step up on one of the barrier's crossbars, pressing my hips to the railing to keep my balance. This is where Al stood. I look down into the chasm, at the black water, at the jagged rocks. Water hits the wall and sprays up, misting my face. Was he afraid when he stood here? Or was he so determined to jump that it was easy?

Christina hands me a stack of paper. I got a copy of every report the Erudite have released in the last six months. Throwing them into the chasm won't get rid of them forever, but it might make me feel better.

I stare at the first one. On it is a picture of Jeanine, the Erudite representative. Her sharp-but-attractive eyes stare back at me.

"Have you ever met her?" I ask Will. Christina crumples the first report into a ball and hurls it into the water.

"Jeanine? Once," he replies. He takes the next report and tears it to shreds. The pieces float into the river. He does it without Christina's malice. I get the feeling that the only reason he's participating is to prove to me that he doesn't agree with his former faction's tactics. Whether he believes what they're saying or not is unclear, and I am afraid to ask.

"Before she was a leader, she worked with my sister. They were trying to develop a longer-lasting serum for the simulations," he says. "Jeanine's so smart you can see it even before she says anything. Like . . . a walking, talking computer."

"What . . ." I fling one of the pages over the railing, pressing my lips together. I should just ask. "What do you think of what she has to say?"

He shrugs. "I don't know. Maybe it's a good idea to have more than one faction in control of the government. And maybe it would be nice if we had more cars and . . . fresh fruit and . . ."

"You do realize there's no secret warehouse where all that stuff is kept, right?" I ask, my face getting hot.

"Yes, I do," he says. "I just think that comfort and prosperity are not a priority for Abnegation, and maybe they would be if the other factions were involved in our decision making."

"Because giving an Erudite boy a car is more important than giving food to the factionless," I snap.

"Hey now," says Christina, brushing Will's shoulder with her fingers. "This is supposed to be a lighthearted session of symbolic document destruction, not a political debate."

I bite back what I was about to say and stare at the stack of paper in my hands. Will and Christina share a lot of idle touches lately. I've noticed it. Have they?

"All that stuff she said about your dad, though," he says, "makes me kind of hate her. I can't imagine what good can come of saying such terrible things."

I can. If Jeanine can make people believe that my father and all the other Abnegation leaders are corrupt and awful, she has support for whatever revolution she wants to start, if that's really her plan. But I don't want to argue again, so I just nod and throw the remaining sheets into the chasm. They drift back and forth, back and forth until they find the water. They will be filtered out at the chasm wall and discarded.

"It's bedtime," Christina says, smiling. "Ready to go back? I think I want to put Peter's hand in a bowl of warm water to make him pee tonight."

I turn away from the chasm and see movement on the right side of the Pit. A figure climbs toward the glass ceiling, and judging by the smooth way he walks, like his feet barely leave the ground, I know it is Four.

"That sounds great, but I have to talk to Four about something," I say, pointing toward the shadow ascending the path. Her eyes follow my hand.

"Are you sure you should be running around here alone at night?" she asks.

"I won't be alone. I'll be with Four." I bite my lip.

Christina is looking at Will, and he is looking back at her. Neither of them is really listening to me.

"All right," Christina says distantly. "Well, I'll see you later, then."

Christina and Will walk toward the dormitories, Christina tousling Will's hair and Will jabbing her in the ribs. For a second, I watch them. I feel like I am witnessing the beginning of something, but I'm not sure what it will be.

I jog to the path on the right side of the Pit and start to climb. I try to make my footsteps as quiet as possible. Unlike Christina, I don't find it difficult to lie. I don't intend to talk to Four—at least, not until I find out where he's going, late at night, in the glass building above us.

I run quietly, breathless when I reach the stairs, and stand at one end of the glass room while Four stands at the other. Through the windows I see the city lights, glowing now but petering out even as I look at them. They are supposed to turn off at midnight.

Across the room, Four stands at the door to the fear landscape. He holds a black box in one hand and a syringe in the other.

"Since you're here," he says, without looking over his shoulder, "you might as well go in with me."

I bite my lip. "Into your fear landscape?"

"Yes."

As I walk toward him, I ask, "I can do that?"

"The serum connects you to the program," he says, "but the program determines whose landscape you go through. And right now, it's set to put us through mine."

"You would let me see that?"

"Why else do you think I'm going in?" he asks quietly. He doesn't lift his eyes. "There are some things I want to show you."

He holds up the syringe, and I tilt my head to better expose my neck. I feel sharp pain when the needle goes in, but I am used to it now. When he's done, he offers me the black box. In it is another syringe.

"I've never done this before," I say as I take it out of the box. I don't want to hurt him.

"Right here," he says, touching a spot on his neck with his fingernail. I stand on my tiptoes and push the needle in, my hand shaking a little. He doesn't even flinch.

He keeps his eyes on me the whole time, and when I'm done, puts both syringes in the box and sets it by the door. He knew that I would follow him up here. Knew, or hoped. Either way is fine with me.

He offers me his hand, and I slide mine into it. His fingers are cold and brittle. I feel like there is something I should say, but I am too stunned and can't come up with any words. He opens the door with his free hand, and I follow him into the dark. I am now used to entering unknown places without hesitation. I keep my breaths even and hold firmly to Four's hand.

"See if you can figure out why they call me Four," he says.

The door clicks shut behind us, taking all the light with it. The air is cold in the hallway; I feel each particle enter my lungs. I inch closer to him so my arm is against his and my chin is near his shoulder.

"What's your real name?" I ask.

"See if you can figure that out too."

The simulation takes us. The ground I stand on is no longer made of cement. It creaks like metal. Light pours in from all angles, and the city unfolds around us, glass buildings and the arc of train tracks, and we are high above it. I haven't seen a blue sky in a long time, so when it spreads out above me, I feel the breath catch in my lungs and the effect is dizzying.

Then the wind starts. It blows so hard I have to lean against Four to stay on my feet. He removes his hand from mine and wraps his arm around my shoulders instead. At first I think it's to protect me—but no, he's having trouble breathing and he needs me to steady him. He forces breath in and out through an open mouth and his teeth are clenched.

The height is beautiful to me, but if it's here, it is one of his worst nightmares.

"We have to jump off, right?" I shout over the wind.

He nods.

"On three, okay?"

Another nod.

"One . . . two . . . *three!*" I pull him with me as I burst into a run. After we take the first step, the rest is easy. We both sprint off the edge of the building. We fall like two stones, fast, the air pushing back at us, the ground growing beneath us. Then the scene disappears, and I am on my hands and knees on the floor, grinning. I loved that rush the day I chose Dauntless, and I love it now.

Next to me, Four gasps and presses a hand to his chest.

I get up and help him to his feet. "What's next?"

"Its—"

Something solid hits my spine. I slam into Four, my head hitting his collarbone. Walls appear on my left and my right. The space is so narrow that Four has to pull his arms into his chest to fit. A ceiling slams onto the walls around us with a crack, and Four hunches over, groaning. The room is just big enough to accommodate his size, and no bigger.

"Confinement," I say.

He makes a guttural noise. I tilt my head and pull back enough to look at him. I can barely see his face, it's so dark, and the air is close; we share breaths. He grimaces like he's in pain.

"Hey," I say. "It's okay. Here—"

I guide his arms around my body so he has more space. He clutches at my back and puts his face next to mine, still hunched over. His body is warm, but I feel only his bones and the muscle that wraps around them; nothing yields beneath me. My cheeks get hot. Can he tell that I'm still built like a child?

"This is the first time I'm happy I'm so small." I laugh. If I joke, maybe I can calm him down. And distract myself.

"Mmhmm," he says. His voice sounds strained.

"We can't break out of here," I say. "It's easier to face the fear head on, right?" I don't wait for a response. "So what you need to do is make the space smaller. Make it worse so it gets better. Right?"

"Yes." It is a tight, tense little word.

"Okay. We'll have to crouch, then. Ready?"

I squeeze his waist to pull him down with me. I feel the hard line of his rib against my hand and hear the screech of one wood plank against another as the ceiling inches down with us. I realize that we won't fit with all this space between us, so I turn and curl into a ball, my spine against his chest. One of his knees is bent next to my head and the other is curled beneath me so I'm sitting on his ankle. We are a jumble of limbs. I feel a harsh breath against my ear.

"Ah," he says, his voice raspy. "This is worse. This is definitely . . ."

"Shh," I say. "Arms around me."

Obediently, he slips both arms around my waist. I smile at the wall. I am not enjoying this. I am not, not even a little bit, no.

"The simulation measures your fear response," I say softly. I'm just repeating what he told us, but reminding him might help him. "So if you can calm your heartbeat down, it will move on to the next one. Remember? So try to forget that we're here."

"Yeah?" I feel his lips move against my ear as he speaks, and heat courses through me. "That easy, huh?"

"You know, most boys would enjoy being trapped in close quarters with a girl." I roll my eyes.

"Not claustrophobic people, Tris!" He sounds desperate now.

"Okay, okay." I set my hand on top of his and guide it to my chest, so it's right over my heart. "Feel my heartbeat. Can you feel it?"

"Yes."

"Feel how steady it is?"

"It's fast."

"Yes, well, that has nothing to do with the box." I wince as soon as I'm done speaking. I just admitted to something. Hopefully he doesn't realize that. "Every time you feel me breathe, you breathe. Focus on that."

"Okay."

I breathe deeply, and his chest rises and falls with mine. After a few seconds of this, I say calmly, "Why don't you tell me where this fear comes from. Maybe talking about it will help us . . . somehow."

I don't know how, but it sounds right.

"Um . . . okay." He breathes with me again. "This one is from my fantastic childhood. Childhood punishments. The tiny closet upstairs."

I press my lips together. I remember being punished—sent to my room without dinner, deprived of this or that, firm scoldings. I was never shut in a closet. The cruelty smarts; my chest aches for him. I don't know what to say, so I try to keep it casual.

"My mother kept our winter coats in our closet."

"I don't . . ." He gasps. "I don't really want to talk about it anymore."

"Okay. Then . . . I can talk. Ask me something."

"Okay." He laughs shakily in my ear. "Why is your heart racing, Tris?"

I cringe and say, "Well, I . . ." I search for an excuse that doesn't involve his arms being around me. "I barely know you." *Not good enough.* "I barely know you and I'm crammed up against you in a box, Four, what do you think?"

"If we were in your fear landscape," he says, "would I be in it?"

"I'm not afraid of you."

"Of course you're not. But that's not what I meant."

He laughs again, and when he does, the walls break apart with a crack and fall away, leaving us in a circle of light. Four sighs and lifts his arms from my body. I scramble to my feet and brush myself off, though I haven't accumulated any dirt that I'm aware of. I wipe my palms on my jeans. My back feels cold from the sudden absence of him.

He stands in front of me. He's grinning, and I'm not sure I like the look in his eyes.

"Maybe you were cut out for Candor," he says, "because you're a terrible liar."

"I think my aptitude test ruled that one out pretty well."

He shakes his head. "The aptitude test tells you nothing."

I narrow my eyes. "What are you trying to tell me? Your test isn't the reason you ended up Dauntless?"

Excitement runs through me like the blood in my veins, propelled by the hope that he might confirm that he is Divergent, that he is like me, that we can figure out what it means together.

"Not exactly, no," he says. "I . . ."

He looks over his shoulder and his voice trails off. A woman stands a few yards away, pointing a gun at us. She is completely still, her features plain—if we walked away right now, I would not remember her. To my right, a table appears. On it is a gun and a single bullet. Why isn't she shooting us?

Oh, I think. The fear is unrelated to the threat to his life. It has to do with the gun on the table.

"You have to kill her," I say softly.

"Every single time."

"She isn't real."

"She looks real." He bites his lip. "It feels real."

"If she was real, she would have killed you already."

"It's okay." He nods. "I'll just . . . do it. This one's not . . . not so bad. Not as much panic involved."

Not as much panic, but far more dread. I can see it in his eyes as he picks up the gun and opens the chamber like he's done it a thousand times—and maybe he has. He clicks the bullet into the chamber and holds the gun out in front of him, both hands around it. He squeezes one eye shut and breathes slowly in.

As he exhales, he fires, and the woman's head whips back. I see a flash of red and look away. I hear her crumple to the floor.

Four's gun drops with a thump. We stare at her fallen body. What he said is true—it does feel real. *Don't be ridiculous.* I grab his arm.

"C'mon," I say. "Let's go. Keep moving."

After another tug, he comes out of his daze and follows me. As we pass the table, the woman's body disappears, except in my memory and his. What would it be like to kill someone every time I went through my landscape? Maybe I'll find out.

But something puzzles me: These are supposed to be Four's worst fears. And though he panicked in the box and on the roof, he killed the woman without much difficulty. It seems like the simulation is grasping at any fears it can find within him, and it hasn't found much.

"Here we go," he whispers.

A dark figure moves ahead of us, creeping along the edge of the circle of light, waiting for us to take another step. Who is it? Who frequents Four's nightmares?

The man who emerges is tall and slim, with hair cut close to his scalp. He holds his hands behind his back. And he wears the gray clothes of the Abnegation.

"Marcus," I whisper.

"Here's the part," Four says, his voice shaking, "where you figure out my name."

"Is he . . ." I look from Marcus, who walks slowly toward us, to Four, who inches slowly back, and everything comes together. Marcus had a son who joined Dauntless. His name was . . . "Tobias."

Marcus shows us his hands. A belt is curled around one of his fists. Slowly he unwinds it from his fingers.

"This is for your own good," he says, and his voice echoes a dozen times.

A dozen Marcuses press into the circle of light, all holding the same belt, with the same blank expression. When the Marcuses blink again, their eyes turn into empty, black pits. The belts slither along the floor, which is now white tile. A shiver crawls up my spine. The Erudite accused Marcus of cruelty. For once the Erudite were right.

I look at Four—Tobias—and he seems frozen. His posture sags. He looks years older; he looks years younger. The first Marcus yanks his arm back, the belt sailing over his shoulder as he prepares to strike. Tobias shrinks back, throwing his arms up to protect his face.

I dart in front of him and the belt cracks against my wrist, wrapping around it. A hot pain races up my arm to my elbow. I grit my teeth and pull as hard as I can. Marcus loses his grip, so I unwrap the belt and grab it by the buckle.

I swing my arm as fast as I can, my shoulder socket burning from the sudden motion, and the belt strikes Marcus's shoulder. He yells and lunges at me with outstretched hands, with fingernails that look like claws. Tobias pushes me behind him so he stands between me and Marcus. He looks angry, not afraid.

All the Marcuses vanish. The lights come on, revealing a long, narrow room with busted brick walls and a cement floor.

"That's it?" I say. "Those were your worst fears? Why do you only have four . . ." My voice trails off. Only four fears.

"Oh." I look over my shoulder at him. "That's why they call you—"

The words leave me when I see his expression. His eyes are wide and seem almost vulnerable under the room's lights. His lips are parted. If we were not here, I would describe the look as awe. But I don't understand why he would be looking at me in awe.

He wraps his hand around my elbow, his thumb pressing to the soft skin above my forearm, and tugs me toward him. The skin around my wrist still stings, like the belt was real, but it is as pale as the rest of me. His lips slowly move against my cheek, then his arms tighten around my shoulders, and he buries his face in my neck, breathing against my collarbone.

I stand stiffly for a second and then loop my arms around him and sigh.

"Hey," I say softly. "We got through it."

He lifts his head and slips his fingers through my hair, tucking it behind my ear. We stare at each other in silence. His fingers move absently over a lock of my hair.

"You got me through it," he says finally.

"Well." My throat is dry. I try to ignore the nervous electricity that pulses through me every second he touches me. "It's easy to be brave when they're not my fears."

I let my hands drop and casually wipe them on my jeans, hoping he doesn't notice.

If he does, he doesn't say so. He laces his fingers with mine.

"Come on," he says. "I have something else to show you."

CHAPTER
TWENTY-SIX

HAND IN HAND, we walk toward the Pit. I monitor the pressure of my hand carefully. One minute, I feel like I'm not gripping hard enough, and the next, I'm squeezing too hard. I never used to understand why people bothered to hold hands as they walked, but then he runs one of his fingertips down my palm, and I shiver and understand it completely.

"So . . ." I latch on to the last logical thought I remember. "Four fears."

"Four fears then; four fears now," he says, nodding. "They haven't changed, so I keep going in there, but . . . I still haven't made any progress."

"You can't be fearless, remember?" I say. "Because you still care about things. About your life."

"I know."

We walk along the edge of the Pit on a narrow path that leads to the rocks at the bottom of the chasm. I've never noticed it before—it blended in with the rock wall. But Tobias seems to know it well.

I don't want to ruin the moment, but I have to know about his aptitude test. I have to know if he's Divergent.

"You were going to tell me about your aptitude test results," I say.

"Ah." He scratches the back of his neck with his free hand. "Does it matter?"

"Yes. I want to know."

"How demanding you are." He smiles.

We reach the end of the path and stand at the bottom of the chasm, where the rocks form unsteady ground, rising up at harsh angles from the rushing water. He leads me up and down, across small gaps and over angular ridges. My shoes cling to the rough rock. The soles of my shoes mark each rock with a wet footprint.

He finds a relatively flat rock near the side, where the current isn't strong, and sits down, his feet dangling over the edge. I sit beside him. He seems comfortable here, inches above the hazardous water.

He releases my hand. I look at the jagged edge of the rock.

"These are things I don't tell people, you know. Not even my friends," he says.

I lace my fingers together and clench. This is the perfect place for him to tell me that he is Divergent, if indeed that's what he is. The roar of the chasm ensures that we won't be overheard. I don't know why the thought makes me so nervous.

"My result was as expected," he says. "Abnegation."

"Oh." Something inside me deflates. I am wrong about him.

But—I had assumed that if he was not Divergent, he must have gotten a Dauntless result. And technically, I also got an Abnegation result— according to the system. Did the same thing happen to him? And if that's true, why isn't he telling me the truth?

"But you chose Dauntless anyway?" I say.

"Out of necessity."

"Why did you have to leave?"

His eyes dart away from mine, across the space in front of him, as if searching the air for an answer. He doesn't need to give one. I still feel the ghost of a stinging belt on my wrist.

"You had to get away from your dad," I say. "Is that why you don't want to be a Dauntless leader? Because if you were, you might have to see him again?"

He lifts a shoulder. "That, and I've always felt that I don't quite belong among the Dauntless. Not the way they are now, anyway."

"But you're . . . incredible," I say. I pause and clear my throat. "I mean, by Dauntless standards. Four fears is unheard of. How could you not belong here?"

He shrugs. He doesn't seem to care about his talent, or his status among the Dauntless, and that is what I would expect from the Abnegation. I am not sure what to make of that.

He says, "I have a theory that selflessness and bravery aren't all that different. All your life you've been training to forget yourself, so when you're in danger, it becomes your first instinct. I could belong in Abnegation just as easily."

Suddenly I feel heavy. A lifetime of training wasn't enough for me. My first instinct is still self-preservation.

"Yeah, well," I say, "I left Abnegation because I wasn't selfless enough, no matter how hard I tried to be."

"That's not entirely true." He smiles at me. "That girl who let someone throw knives at her to spare a friend, who hit my dad with a belt to protect me—that selfless girl, that's not you?"

He's figured out more about me than I have. And even though it seems impossible that he could feel something for me, given all that I'm not . . . maybe it isn't. I frown at him. "You've been paying close attention, haven't you?"

"I like to observe people."

"Maybe you were cut out for Candor, Four, because you're a terrible liar."

He puts his hand on the rock next to him, his fingers lining up with mine. I look down at our hands. He has long, narrow fingers. Hands made for fine, deft movements. Not Dauntless hands, which should be thick and tough and ready to break things.

"Fine." He leans his face closer to mine, his eyes focusing on my chin, and my lips, and my nose. "I watched you because I like you." He says it plainly, boldly, and his eyes flick up to mine. "And don't call me 'Four,' okay? It's nice to hear my name again."

Just like that, he has finally declared himself, and I don't know how to respond. My cheeks warm, and all I can think to say is, "But you're older than I am . . . *Tobias.*"

He smiles at me. "Yes, that whopping two-year gap really is *insurmountable*, isn't it?"

"I'm not trying to be self-deprecating," I say, "I just don't get it. I'm younger. I'm not pretty. I—"

He laughs, a deep laugh that sounds like it came from deep inside him, and touches his lips to my temple.

"Don't pretend," I say breathily. "You know I'm not. I'm not ugly, but I am certainly not pretty."

"Fine. You're not pretty. So?" He kisses my cheek. "I like how you look. You're deadly smart. You're brave. And even though you found out about Marcus . . ." His voice softens. "You aren't giving me that look. Like I'm a kicked puppy or something."

"Well," I say. "You're not."

For a second his dark eyes are on mine, and he's quiet. Then he touches my face and leans in close, brushing my lips with his. The river roars and I feel its spray on my ankles. He grins and presses his mouth to mine.

I tense up at first, unsure of myself, so when he pulls away, I'm sure I did something wrong, or badly. But he takes my face in his hands, his fingers strong against my skin, and kisses me again, firmer this time, more certain. I wrap an arm around him, sliding my hand up his neck and into his short hair.

For a few minutes we kiss, deep in the chasm, with the roar of water all around us. And when we rise, hand in hand, I realize that if we had both chosen differently, we might have ended up doing the same thing, in a safer place, in gray clothes instead of black ones.

CHAPTER TWENTY-SEVEN

THE NEXT MORNING I am silly and light. Every time I push the smile from my face, it fights its way back. Eventually I stop suppressing it. I let my hair hang loose and abandon my uniform of loose shirts in favor of one that cuts across my shoulders, revealing my tattoos.

"What is it with you today?" says Christina on the way to breakfast. Her eyes are still swollen from sleep and her tangled hair forms a fuzzy halo around her face.

"Oh, you know," I say. "Sun shining. Birds chirping."

She raises an eyebrow at me, as if reminding me that we are in an underground tunnel.

"Let the girl be in a good mood," Will says. "You may never see it again."

I smack his arm and hurry toward the dining hall. My heart pounds because I know that at some point in the next half hour, I will see Tobias. I sit down in my usual place, next to Uriah, with Will and Christina across from us. The seat on my left stays empty. I wonder if Tobias will sit in it; if he'll grin at me over breakfast; if he'll look at me in that secret, stolen way that I imagine myself looking at him.

I grab a piece of toast from the plate in the middle of the table and start to butter it with a little too much enthusiasm. I feel myself acting like a lunatic, but I can't stop. It would be like refusing to breathe.

Then he walks in. His hair is shorter, and it looks darker this way, almost black. It's Abnegation short, I realize. I smile at him and lift my hand to wave him over, but he sits down next to Zeke without even glancing in my direction, so I let my hand drop.

I stare at my toast. It is easy not to smile now.

"Something wrong?" asks Uriah through a mouthful of toast.

I shake my head and take a bite. What did I expect? Just because we kissed doesn't mean anything changes. Maybe he changed his mind about liking me. Maybe he thinks kissing me was a mistake.

"Today's fear landscape day," says Will. "You think we'll get to see our own fear landscapes?"

"No." Uriah shakes his head. "You go through one of the instructors' landscapes. My brother told me."

"Ooh, which instructor?" says Christina, suddenly perking up.

"You know, it really isn't fair that you all get insider information and we don't," Will says, glaring at Uriah.

"Like you wouldn't use an advantage if you had one," retorts Uriah.

Christina ignores them. "I hope it's Four's landscape."

"Why?" I ask. The question comes out too incredulous. I bite my lip and wish I could take it back.

"Looks like *someone* had a mood swing." She rolls her eyes. "Like you don't want to know what his fears are. He acts so tough that he's probably afraid of marshmallows and really bright sunrises or something. Over-compensating."

I shake my head. "It won't be him."

"How would you know?"

"It's just a prediction."

I remember Tobias's father in his fear landscape. He wouldn't let everyone see that. I glance at him. For a second, his eyes shift to mine. His stare is unfeeling. Then he looks away.

+ + +

Lauren, the instructor of the Dauntless-born initiates, stands with her hands on her hips outside the fear landscape room.

"Two years ago," she says, "I was afraid of spiders, suffocation, walls that inch slowly inward and trap you between them, getting thrown out of Dauntless, uncontrollable bleeding, getting run over by a train, my father's death, public humiliation, and kidnapping by men without faces."

Everyone stares blankly at her.

"Most of you will have anywhere from ten to fifteen fears in your fear landscapes. That is the average number," she says.

"What's the lowest number someone has gotten?" asks Lynn.

"In recent years," says Lauren, "four."

I have not looked at Tobias since we were in the cafeteria, but I can't help but look at him now. He keeps his eyes trained on the floor. I knew that four was a low number, low enough to merit a nickname, but I didn't know it was less than half the average.

I glare at my feet. He's exceptional. And now he won't even look at me.

"You will not find out your number today," says Lauren. "The simulation is set to my fear landscape program, so you will experience my fears instead of your own."

I give Christina a pointed look. I was right; we won't go through Four's landscape.

"For the purposes of this exercise, though, each of you will only face *one* of my fears, to get a sense for how the simulation works."

Lauren points to us at random and assigns us each a fear. I was standing in the back, so I will go close to last. The fear that she assigned to me was kidnapping.

Because I'm not hooked up to the computer as I wait, I can't watch the simulation, only the person's reaction to it. It is the perfect way to distract myself from my preoccupation with Tobias—clenching my hands into fists as Will brushes off spiders I can't see and Uriah presses his hands against walls that are invisible to me, and smirking as Peter turns bright red during whatever he experiences in "public humiliation." Then it's my turn.

The obstacle won't be comfortable for me, but because I have been able to manipulate every simulation, not just this one, and because I have already gone through Tobias's landscape, I am not apprehensive as Lauren inserts the needle into my neck.

Then the scenery changes and the kidnapping begins. The ground turns into grass beneath my feet, and hands clamp around my arms, over my mouth. It is too dark to see.

I stand next to the chasm. I hear the roar of the water. I scream into the hand that covers my mouth and thrash to free myself, but the arms are too strong; my kidnappers are too strong. The image of myself falling into darkness flashes into my mind, the same image that I now carry with me in my nightmares. I scream again; I scream until my throat hurts and I squeeze hot tears from my eyes.

I knew they would come back for me; I knew they would try again. The first time was not enough. I scream again—not for help, because no one will help me, but because that's what you do when you're about to die and you can't stop it.

"Stop," a stern voice says.

The hands disappear, and the lights come on. I stand on cement in the fear landscape room. My body shakes, and I drop to my knees, pressing my hands to my face. I just failed. I lost all logic, I lost all sense. Lauren's fear transformed into one of my own.

And everyone saw me. Tobias saw me.

I hear footsteps. Tobias marches toward me and wrenches me to my feet.

"What the hell was that, Stiff?"

"I . . ." My breath comes in a hiccup. "I didn't—"

"Get yourself together! This is pathetic."

Something within me snaps. My tears stop. Heat races through my body, driving the weakness out of me, and I smack him so hard my knuckles burn with the impact. He stares at me, one side of his face bright with blush-blood, and I stare back.

"Shut up," I say. I yank my arm from his grasp and walk out of the room.

CHAPTER
TWENTY-EIGHT

I PULL MY jacket tight around my shoulders. I haven't been outside in a long time. The sun shines pale against my face, and I watch my breaths form in the air.

At least I accomplished one thing: I convinced Peter and his friends that I'm no longer a threat. I just have to make sure that tomorrow, when I go through my own fear landscape, I prove them wrong. Yesterday failure seemed impossible. Today I'm not sure.

I slide my hands through my hair. The impulse to cry is gone. I braid my hair and tie it with the rubber band around my wrist. I feel more like myself. That is all I need: to remember who I am. And I am someone who does not let inconsequential things like boys and near-death experiences stop her.

I laugh, shaking my head. Am I?

I hear the train horn. The train tracks loop around the Dauntless compound and then continue farther than I can see. Where do they begin? Where do they end? What is the world like beyond them? I walk toward them.

I want to go home, but I can't. Eric warned us not to appear too attached to our parents on Visiting Day, so visiting home would be betraying the Dauntless, and I can't afford to do that. Eric did not tell us we couldn't visit people in factions other than the ones we came from, though, and my mother did tell me to visit Caleb.

I know I'm not allowed to leave without supervision, but I can't stop myself. I walk faster and faster, until I'm sprinting. Pumping my arms, I run alongside the last car until I can grab the handle and swing myself in, wincing as pain darts through my sore body.

Once in the car, I lie on my back next to the door and watch the

Dauntless compound disappear behind me. I don't want to go back, but choosing to quit, to be factionless, would be the bravest thing I have ever done, and today I feel like a coward.

The air rushes over my body and twists around my fingers. I let my hand trail over the edge of the car so it presses against the wind. I can't go home, but I can find part of it. Caleb has a place in every memory of my childhood; he is part of my foundation.

The train slows as it reaches the heart of the city, and I sit up to watch the smaller buildings grow into larger buildings. The Erudite live in large stone buildings that overlook the marsh. I hold the handle and lean out just enough to see where the tracks go. They dip down to street level just before they bend to travel east. I breathe in the smell of wet pavement and marsh air.

The train dips and slows, and I jump. My legs shudder with the force of my landing, and I run a few steps to regain my balance. I walk down the middle of the street, heading south, toward the marsh. The empty land stretches as far as I can see, a brown plane colliding with the horizon.

I turn left. The Erudite buildings loom above me, dark and unfamiliar. How will I find Caleb here?

The Erudite keep records; it's in their nature. They must keep records of their initiates. Someone has access to those records; I just have to find them. I scan the buildings. Logically speaking, the central building should be the most important one. I may as well start there.

The faction members are milling around everywhere. Erudite faction norms dictate that a faction member must wear at least one blue article of clothing at a time, because blue causes the body to release calming chemicals, and "a calm mind is a clear mind." The color has also come to signify their faction. It seems impossibly bright to me now. I have grown used to dim lighting and dark clothing.

I expect to weave through the crowd, dodging elbows and muttering "excuse me" the way I always do, but there is no need. Becoming Dauntless has made me noticeable. The crowd parts for me, and their eyes cling to me as I pass. I pull the rubber band from my hair and shake it from its knot before I walk through the front doors.

I stand just inside the entrance and tilt my head back. The room is huge, silent, and smells like dust-covered pages. The wood-paneled floor creaks beneath my feet. Bookcases line the walls on either side of me, but they seem to be decorative more than anything, because computers occupy the tables in the center of the room, and no one is reading. They stare at screens with tense eyes, focused.

I should have known that the main Erudite building would be a library. A portrait on the opposite wall catches my attention. It is twice my height and four times my width and depicts an attractive woman with watery gray eyes and spectacles—Jeanine. Heat licks my throat at the sight of her. Because she is Erudite's representative, she is the one who released that report about my father. I have disliked her since my father's dinner-table rants began, but now I hate her.

Beneath her is a large plaque that reads KNOWLEDGE LEADS TO PROSPERITY. Prosperity. To me the word has a negative connotation. Abnegation uses it to describe self-indulgence.

How could Caleb have chosen to be one of these people? The things they do, the things they want, it's all wrong. But he probably thinks the same of the Dauntless.

I walk up to the desk just beneath Jeanine's portrait. The young man sitting behind it doesn't look up as he says, "How can I help you?"

"I am looking for someone," I say. "His name is Caleb. Do you know where I can find him?"

"I am not permitted to give out personal information," he replies blandly, as he jabs at the screen in front of him.

"He's my brother."

"I am not permi—"

I slam my palm on the desk in front of him, and he jerks out of his daze, staring at me over his spectacles. Heads turn in my direction.

"I said." My voice is terse. "I am looking for someone. He's an initiate. Can you at least tell me where I can find them?"

"Beatrice?" a voice behind me says.

I turn, and Caleb stands behind me, a book in hand. His hair has grown out so it flips at his ears, and he wears a blue T-shirt and a pair of rectangular glasses. Even though he looks different and I'm not allowed to love him anymore, I run at him as fast as I can and throw my arms around his shoulders.

"You have a tattoo," he says, his voice muffled.

"You have glasses," I say. I pull back and narrow my eyes. "Your vision is perfect, Caleb, what are you doing?"

"Um . . ." He glances at the tables around us. "Come on. Let's get out of here."

We exit the building and cross the street. I have to jog to keep up with him. Across from Erudite headquarters is what used to be a park. Now we just call it "Millenium," and it is a stretch of bare land and several rusted metal sculptures—one an abstract, plated mammoth, another shaped like a lima bean that dwarfs me in size.

We stop on the concrete around the metal bean, where the Erudite sit in small groups with newspapers or books. He takes off his glasses and shoves them in his pocket, then runs a hand through his hair, his eyes skipping over mine nervously. Like he's ashamed. Maybe I should be too. I'm tattooed, loose-haired, and wearing tight clothes. But I'm just not.

"What are you doing here?" he says.

"I wanted to go home," I say, "and you were the closest thing I could think of."

He presses his lips together.

"Don't look so pleased to see me," I add.

"Hey," he says, setting his hands on my shoulders. "I'm thrilled to see you, okay? It's just that this isn't allowed. There are rules."

"I don't care," I say. "I don't care, okay?"

"Maybe you should." His voice is gentle; he wears his look of disapproval. "If it were me, I wouldn't want to get in trouble with your faction."

"What's that supposed to mean?"

I know exactly what it means. He sees my faction as the cruelest of the five, and nothing more.

"I just don't want you to get hurt. You don't have to be so angry with me," he says, tilting his head. "What *happened* to you in there?"

"Nothing. Nothing happened to me." I close my eyes and rub the back of my neck with one hand. Even if I could explain everything to him, I wouldn't want to. I can't even summon the will to think about it.

"You think . . ." He looks at his shoes. "You think you made the right choice?"

"I don't think there was one," I say. "How about you?"

He looks around. People stare at us as they walk past. His eyes skip over their faces. He's still nervous, but maybe it's not because of how he looks, or because of me. Maybe it's them. I grab his arm and pull him under the arch of the metal bean. We walk beneath its hollow underbelly. I see my reflection everywhere, warped by the curve of the walls, broken by patches of rust and grime.

"What's going on?" I say, folding my arms. I didn't notice the dark circles under his eyes before. "What's wrong?"

Caleb presses a palm to the metal wall. In his reflection, his head is small and pressed in on one side, and his arm looks like it is bending backward. My reflection, however, looks small and squat.

"Something big is happening, Beatrice. Something is wrong." His eyes are wide and glassy. "I don't know what it is, but people keep rushing around, talking quietly, and Jeanine gives speeches about how corrupt Abnegation is all the time, almost every day."

"Do you believe her?"

"No. Maybe. I don't . . ." He shakes his head. "I don't know what to believe."

"Yes, you do," I say sternly. "You know who our parents are. You know who our friends are. Susan's dad, you think he's corrupt?"

"How much do I know? How much did they allow me to know? We weren't allowed to ask questions, Beatrice; we weren't allowed to know things! And here . . ." He looks up, and in the flat circle of mirror right above us, I see our tiny figures, the size of fingernails. That, I think, is our true reflection; it is as small as we actually are. He continues, "Here, information is free, it's always available."

"This isn't Candor. There are liars here, Caleb. There are people who are so smart they know how to manipulate you."

"Don't you think I would know if I was being manipulated?"

"If they're as smart as you think, then no. I don't think you would know."

"You have no idea what you're talking about," he says, shaking his head.

"Yeah. How could I *possibly* know what a corrupt faction looks like? I'm just training to be *Dauntless*, for God's sake," I say. "At least I know what I'm a part of, Caleb. *You* are choosing to ignore what we've known all our lives—these people are arrogant and greedy and they will lead you nowhere."

His voice hardens. "I think you should go, Beatrice."

"With pleasure," I say. "Oh, and not that it will matter to you, but Mom told me to tell you to research the simulation serum."

"You saw her?" He looks hurt. "Why didn't she—"

"Because," I say. "The Erudite don't let the Abnegation into their compound anymore. Wasn't that information available to you?"

I push past him, walking away from the mirror cave and the sculpture, and start down the sidewalk. I should never have left. The Dauntless compound sounds like home now—at least there, I know exactly where I stand, which is on unstable ground.

The crowd on the sidewalk thins, and I look up to see why. Standing a few yards in front of me are two Erudite men with their arms folded.

"Excuse me," one of them says. "You'll have to come with us."

+ + +

One man walks so close behind me that I feel his breath against the back of my head. The other man leads me into the library and down three hallways to an elevator. Beyond the library the floors change from wood to white tile, and the walls glow like the ceiling of the aptitude test room. The glow bounces off the silver elevator doors, and I squint so I can see.

I try to stay calm. I ask myself questions from Dauntless training. *What do you do if someone attacks you from behind?* I envision thrusting my elbow back into a stomach or a groin. I imagine running. I wish I had a gun. These are Dauntless thoughts, and they have become mine.

What do you do if you're attacked by two people at once? I follow the man down an empty, glowing corridor and into an office. The walls are made of glass—I guess I know which faction designed my school.

A woman sits behind a metal desk. I stare at her face. The same face dominates the Erudite library; it is plastered across every article Erudite releases. How long have I hated that face? I don't remember.

"Sit," Jeanine says. Her voice sounds familiar, especially when she is irritated. Her liquid gray eyes focus on mine.

"I'd rather not."

"Sit," she says again. I have definitely heard her voice before.

I heard it in the hallway, talking to Eric, before I got attacked. I heard her mention Divergents. And once before—I heard it . . .

"It was your voice in the simulation," I say. "The aptitude test, I mean."

She is the danger Tori and my mother warned me about, the danger of being Divergent. Sitting right in front of me.

"Correct. The aptitude test is by far my greatest achievement as a scientist," she replies. "I looked up your test results, Beatrice. Apparently there was a problem with your test. It was never recorded, and your results had to be reported manually. Did you know that?"

"No."

"Did you know that you're one of two people ever to get an Abnegation result and switch to Dauntless?"

"No," I say, biting back my shock. Tobias and I are the only ones? But his result was genuine and mine was a lie. So it is really just him.

My stomach twinges at the thought of him. Right now I don't care how unique he is. He called me pathetic.

"What made you choose Dauntless?" she asks.

"What does this have to do with anything?" I try to soften my voice, but it doesn't work. "Aren't you going to reprimand me for abandoning my faction and seeking out my brother? 'Faction before blood,' right?" I pause. "Come to think of it, why am I in your office in the first place? Aren't you supposed to be important or something?"

Maybe that will take her down a few pegs.

Her mouth pinches for a second. "I will leave the reprimands to the Dauntless," she says, leaning back in her chair.

I set my hands on the back of the chair I refused to sit in and clench my fingers. Behind her is a window that overlooks the city. The train takes a lazy turn in the distance.

"As to the reason for your presence here . . . a quality of my faction is curiosity," she says, "and while perusing your records, I saw that there was another error with another one of your simulations. Again, it failed to be recorded. Did you know that?"

"How did you access my records? Only the Dauntless have access to those."

"Because Erudite developed the simulations, we have an . . . *understanding* with the Dauntless, Beatrice." She tilts her head and smiles at me. "I am merely concerned for the competence of our technology. If it fails while you are around, I have to ensure that it does not continue to do so, you understand?"

I understand only one thing: She is lying to me. She doesn't care about the technology—she suspects that something is awry with my test results. Just like the Dauntless leaders, she is sniffing around for the Divergent. And if my mother wants Caleb to research the simulation serum, it is probably because Jeanine developed it.

But what is so threatening about my ability to manipulate the simulations? Why would it matter to the representative of the Erudite, of all people?

I can't answer either question. But the look she gives me reminds me of the look in the attack dog's eyes in the aptitude test—a vicious, predatory stare. She wants to rip me to pieces. I can't lie down in submission now. I have become an attack dog too.

I feel my pulse in my throat.

"I don't know how they work," I say, "but the liquid I was injected with made me sick to my stomach. Maybe my simulation administrator was distracted because he was worried I would throw up, and he forgot to record it. I got sick after the aptitude test too."

"Do you habitually have a sensitive stomach, Beatrice?" Her voice is like a razor's edge. She taps her trimmed fingernails against the glass desk.

"Ever since I was young," I reply as smoothly as I can. I release the chair back and sidestep it to sit down. I can't seem tense, even though I feel like my insides are writhing within me.

"You have been extremely successful with the simulations," she says. "To what do you attribute the ease with which you complete them?"

"I'm brave," I say, staring into her eyes. The other factions see the Dauntless a certain way. Brash, aggressive, impulsive. Cocky. I should be what she expects. I smirk at her. "I'm the best initiate they've got."

I lean forward, balancing my elbows on my knees. I will have to go further with this to make it convincing.

"You want to know why I chose Dauntless?" I ask. "It's because I was bored." Further, further. Lies require commitment. "I was tired of being a wussy little do-gooder and I wanted out."

"So you don't miss your parents?" she asks delicately.

"Do I miss getting scolded for looking in the mirror? Do I miss being told to shut up at the dinner table?" I shake my head. "No. I don't miss them. They're not my family anymore."

The lie burns my throat on the way out, or maybe that's the tears I'm fighting. I picture my mother standing behind me with a comb and a pair of scissors, faintly smiling as she trims my hair, and I want to scream rather than insult her like this.

"Can I take that to mean . . ." Jeanine purses her lips and pauses for a few seconds before finishing. ". . . that you agree with the reports that have been released about the political leaders of this city?"

The reports that label my family as corrupt, power-hungry, moralizing dictators? The reports that carry subtle threats and hint at revolution? They make me sick to my stomach. Knowing that she is the one who released them makes me want to strangle her.

I smile.

"Wholeheartedly," I say.

+ + +

One of Jeanine's lackeys, a man in a blue collared shirt and sunglasses, drives me back to the Dauntless compound in a sleek silver car, the likes of which I have never seen before. The engine is almost silent. When I ask the man about it, he tells me it's solar-powered and launches into a lengthy explanation of how the panels on the roof convert sunlight into energy. I stop listening after sixty seconds and stare out the window.

I don't know what they'll do to me when I get back. I suspect it will be bad. I imagine my feet dangling over the chasm and bite my lip.

When the driver pulls up to the glass building above the Dauntless compound, Eric is waiting for me by the door. He takes my arm and leads me into the building without thanking the driver. Eric's fingers squeeze so hard I know I'll have bruises.

He stands between me and the door that leads inside. He starts to crack his knuckles. Other than that, he is completely still.

I shudder involuntarily.

The faint *pop* of his knuckle-cracking is all I hear apart from my own breaths, which grow faster by the second. When he is finished, Eric laces his fingers together in front of him.

"Welcome back, Tris."

"Eric."

He walks toward me, carefully placing one foot in front of the other.

"What . . ." His first word is quiet. "*Exactly,*" he adds, louder this time, "were you thinking?"

"I . . ." He is so close I can see the holes his metal piercings fit into. "I don't know."

"I am tempted to call you a traitor, Tris," he says. "Have you never heard the phrase 'faction before blood'?"

I have seen Eric do terrible things. I have heard him say terrible things. But I have never seen him like this. He is not a maniac anymore; he is perfectly controlled, perfectly poised. Careful and quiet.

For the first time, I recognize Eric for what he is: an Erudite disguised as a Dauntless, a genius as well as a sadist, a hunter of the Divergent.

I want to run.

"Were you unsatisfied with the life you have found here? Do you perhaps regret your choice?" Both of Eric's metal-ridden eyebrows lift, forcing creases into his forehead. "I would like to hear an explanation for why you betrayed Dauntless, yourself, and *me* . . ." He taps his chest. ". . . by venturing into another faction's headquarters."

"I . . ." I take a deep breath. He would kill me if he knew what I was, I can feel it. His hands curl into fists. I am alone here; if something happens to me, no one will know and no one will see it.

"If you cannot explain," he says softly, "I may be forced to reconsider your rank. Or, because you seem to be so attached to your previous faction . . . perhaps I will be forced to reconsider your friends' ranks. Perhaps the little Abnegation girl inside of you would take that more seriously."

My first thought is that he couldn't do that, it wouldn't be fair. My second thought is that of course he would, he would not hesitate to do it for a second. And he is right—the thought that my reckless behavior could force someone else out of a faction makes my chest ache from fear.

I try again. "I . . ."

But it is hard to breathe.

And then the door opens. Tobias walks in.

"What are you doing?" he asks Eric.

"Leave the room," Eric says, his voice louder and not as monotone. He sounds more like the Eric I am familiar with. His expression, too, changes, becomes more mobile and animated. I stare, amazed that he can turn it on and off so easily, and wonder what the strategy behind it is.

"No," Tobias says. "She's just a foolish girl. There's no need to drag her here and interrogate her."

"Just a foolish girl." Eric snorts. "If she were just a foolish girl, she wouldn't be ranked first, now would she?"

Tobias pinches the bridge of his nose and looks at me through the spaces between his fingers. He is trying to tell me something. I think quickly. What advice has Four given me recently?

The only thing I can think of is: *pretend some vulnerability.*

It's worked for me before.

"I . . . I was just embarrassed and didn't know what to do." I put my hands in my pockets and look at the ground. Then I pinch my leg so hard that tears well up in my eyes, and I look up at Eric, sniffing. "I tried to . . . and . . ." I shake my head.

"You tried to what?" asks Eric.

"Kiss me," says Tobias. "And I rejected her, and she went running off like a five-year-old. There's really nothing to blame her for but stupidity." We both wait.

Eric looks from me to Tobias and laughs, too loudly and for too long— the sound is menacing and grates against me like sandpaper. "Isn't he a little too old for you, Tris?" he says, smiling again.

I wipe my cheek like I'm wiping a tear. "Can I go now?"

"Fine," Eric says, "but you are not allowed to leave the compound without supervision again, you hear me?" He turns toward Tobias. "And *you* . . . had better make sure none of the transfers leave this compound again. And that none of the others try to kiss you."

Tobias rolls his eyes. "Fine."

I leave the room and walk outside again, shaking my hands to get rid of the jitters. I sit down on the pavement and wrap my arms around my knees.

I don't know how long I sit there, my head down and my eyes closed, before the door opens again. It might have been twenty minutes and it might have been an hour. Tobias walks toward me.

I stand and cross my arms, waiting for the scolding to start. I slapped him and then got myself into trouble with the Dauntless—there has to be scolding.

"What?" I say.

"Are you all right?" A crease appears between his eyebrows, and he touches my cheek gently. I bat his hand away.

"Well," I say, "first I got reamed out in front of everyone, and then I had to chat with the woman who's trying to destroy my old faction, and then Eric almost tossed my friends out of Dauntless, so yeah, it's shaping up to be a pretty great day, *Four.*"

He shakes his head and looks at the dilapidated building to his right, which is made of brick and barely resembles the sleek glass spire behind me. It must be ancient. No one builds with brick anymore.

"Why do you care, anyway?" I say. "You can be either cruel instructor or concerned boyfriend." I tense up at the word "boyfriend." I didn't mean to use it so flippantly, but it's too late now. "You can't play both parts at the same time."

"I am not cruel." He scowls at me. "I was protecting you this morning. How do you think Peter and his idiot friends would have reacted if they discovered that you and I were . . ." He sighs. "You would never win. They would always call your ranking a result of my favoritism rather than your skill."

I open my mouth to object, but I can't. A few smart remarks come to mind, but I dismiss them. He's right. My cheeks warm, and I cool them with my hands.

"You didn't have to insult me to prove something to them," I say finally.

"And you didn't have to run off to your brother just because I hurt you," he says. He rubs at the back of his neck. "Besides—it worked, didn't it?"

"At my expense."

"I didn't think it would affect you this way." Then he looks down and shrugs. "Sometimes I forget that I can hurt you. That you are capable of being hurt."

I slide my hands into my pockets and rock back on my heels. A strange feeling goes through me—a sweet, aching weakness. He did what he did because he believed in my strength.

At home it was Caleb who was strong, because he could forget himself, because all the characteristics my parents valued came naturally to him. No one has ever been so convinced of my strength.

I stand on my tiptoes, lift my head, and kiss him. Only our lips touch. "You're brilliant, you know that?" I shake my head. "You always know exactly what to do."

"Only because I've been thinking about this for a long time," he says, kissing me briefly. "How I would handle it, if you and I . . ." He pulls back and smiles. "Did I hear you call me your boyfriend, Tris?"

"Not exactly." I shrug. "Why? Do you want me to?"

He slips his hands over my neck and presses his thumbs under my chin, tilting my head back so his forehead meets mine. For a moment he stands there, his eyes closed, breathing my air. I feel the pulse in his fingertips. I feel the quickness of his breath. He seems nervous.

"Yes," he finally says. Then his smile fades. "You think we convinced him you're just a silly girl?"

"I hope so," I say. "Sometimes it helps to be small. I'm not sure I convinced the Erudite, though."

The corners of his mouth tug down, and he gives me a grave look. "There's something I need to tell you."

"What is it?"

"Not now." He glances around. "Meet me back here at eleven thirty. Don't tell anyone where you're going."

I nod, and he turns away, leaving just as quickly as he came.

+ + +

"Where have you *been* all day?" Christina asks when I walk back into the dormitory. The room is empty; everyone else must be at dinner. "I looked for you outside, but I couldn't find you. Is everything okay? Did you get in trouble for hitting Four?"

I shake my head. The thought of telling her the truth about where I was makes me feel exhausted. How can I explain the impulse to hop on a train and visit my brother? Or the eerie calm in Eric's voice as he questioned me? Or the reason that I exploded and hit Tobias to begin with?

"I just had to get away. I walked around for a long time," I say. "And no, I'm not in trouble. He yelled at me, I apologized . . . that's it."

As I speak, I'm careful to keep my eyes steady on hers and my hands still at my sides.

"Good," she says. "Because I have something to tell you."

She looks over my head at the door and then stands on her tiptoes to see all the bunks—checking if they're empty, probably. Then she sets her hands on my shoulders.

"Can you be a girl for a few seconds?"

"I'm always a girl." I frown.

"You know what I mean. Like a silly, annoying girl."

I twirl my hair around my finger. " 'Kay."

She grins so wide I can see her back row of teeth. "Will kissed me."

"What?" I demand. "When? How? What happened?"

"You *can* be a girl!" She straightens, taking her hands from my shoulders. "Well, right after your little episode, we ate lunch and then we walked around near the train tracks. We were just talking about . . . I don't even remember what we were talking about. And then he just stopped, and leaned in, and . . . kissed me."

"Did you know that he liked you?" I say. "I mean, you know. Like that."

"No!" She laughs. "The best part was, that was it. We just kept walking and talking like nothing happened. Well, until *I* kissed *him.*"

"How long have you known you liked him?"

"I don't know. I guess I didn't. But then little things . . . how he put his arm around me at the funeral, how he opens doors for me like I'm a girl instead of someone who could beat the crap out of him."

I laugh. Suddenly I want to tell her about Tobias and everything that has happened between us. But the same reasons Tobias gave for pretending we aren't together hold me back. I don't want her to think that my rank has anything to do with my relationship with him.

So I just say, "I'm happy for you."

"Thanks," she says. "I'm happy too. And I thought it would be a while before I could feel that way . . . you know."

She sits down on the edge of my bed and looks around the dormitory. Some of the initiates have already packed their things. Soon we'll move into apartments on the other side of the compound. Those with government jobs will move to the glass building above the Pit. I won't have to worry about Peter attacking me in my sleep. I won't have to look at Al's empty bed.

"I can't believe it's almost over," she says. "It's like we just got here. But it's also like . . . like I haven't seen home in forever."

"You miss it?" I lean into the bed frame.

"Yeah." She shrugs. "Some things are the same, though. I mean, everyone at home is just as loud as everyone here, so that's good. But it's easier there. You always know where you stand with everyone, because they tell you. There's no . . . manipulation."

I nod. Abnegation prepared me for that aspect of Dauntless life. The Abnegation aren't manipulative, but they aren't forthright, either.

"I don't think I could have made it through Candor initiation, though." She shakes her head. "There, instead of simulations, you get lie detector tests. All day, every day. And the final test . . ." She wrinkles her nose. "They give you this stuff they call truth serum and sit you in front of everyone and ask you a load of really personal questions. The theory is that if you spill all your secrets, you'll have no desire to lie about anything, ever again. Like the worst about you is already in the open, so why not just be honest?"

I don't know when I accumulated so many secrets. Being Divergent. Fears. How I really feel about my friends, my family, Al, Tobias. Candor initiation would reach things that even the simulations can't touch; it would wreck me.

"Sounds awful," I say.

"I always knew I couldn't be Candor. I mean, I try to be honest, but some things you just don't want people to know. Plus, I like to be in control of my own mind."

Don't we all.

"Anyway," she says. She opens the cabinet to the left of our bunk beds. When she pulls the door open, a moth flutters out, its white wings carrying it toward her face. Christina shrieks so loud I almost jump out of my skin and slaps at her cheeks.

"Get it off! Get it off get it off get it off get it off!" she screams.

The moth flutters away.

"It's gone!" I say. Then I laugh. "You're afraid of . . . moths?"

"They're disgusting. Those papery wings and their stupid bug bodies . . ." She shudders.

I keep laughing. I laugh so hard I have to sit down and hold my stomach.

"It's not funny!" she snaps. "Well . . . okay, maybe it is. A little."

+ + +

When I find Tobias late that night, he doesn't say anything; he just grabs my hand and pulls me toward the train tracks.

He draws himself into a train car as it passes with bewildering ease and pulls me in after him. I fall against him, my cheek against his chest. His fingers slide down my arms, and he holds me by the elbows as the car bumps along the steel rails. I watch the glass building above the Dauntless compound shrink behind us.

"What is it you need to tell me?" I shout over the cry of the wind.

"Not yet," he says.

He sinks to the floor and pulls me down with him, so he's sitting with his back against the wall and I'm facing him, my legs trailing to the side on the dusty floor. The wind pushes strands of my hair loose and tosses them over my face. He presses his palms to my face, his index fingers sliding behind my ears, and pulls my mouth to his.

I hear the screech of the rails as the train slows, which means we must be nearing the middle of the city. The air is cold, but his lips are warm and so are his hands. He tilts his head and kisses the skin just beneath my jaw. I'm glad the air is so loud he can't hear me sigh.

The train car wobbles, throwing off my balance, and I put my hand down to steady myself. A split second later I realize that my hand is on his hip. The bone presses into my palm. I should move it, but I don't want to. He told me once to be brave, and though I have stood still while knives spun toward my face and jumped off a roof, I never thought I would need bravery in the small moments of my life. I do.

I shift, swinging a leg over him so I sit on top of him, and with my heartbeat in my throat, I kiss him. He sits up straighter and I feel his hands on my shoulders. His fingers slip down my spine and a shiver follows them down to the small of my back. He unzips my jacket a few inches, and I press my hands to my legs to stop them from shaking. I should not be nervous. This is Tobias.

Cold air slips across my bare skin. He pulls away and looks carefully at the tattoos just above my collarbone. His fingers brush over them, and he smiles.

"Birds," he says. "Are they crows? I keep forgetting to ask."

I try to return his smile. "Ravens. One for each member of my family," I say. "You like them?"

He doesn't answer. He tugs me closer, pressing his lips to each bird in turn. I close my eyes. His touch is light, sensitive. A heavy, warm feeling, like spilling honey, fills my body, slowing my thoughts. He touches my cheek.

"I hate to say this," he says, "but we have to get up now."

I nod and open my eyes. We both stand, and he tugs me with him to the open door of the train car. The wind is not as strong now that the train has slowed. It's past midnight, so all the street lights are dark, and the buildings look like mammoths as they rise from the darkness and then sink into it again. Tobias lifts a hand and points at a cluster of buildings, so far away they are the size of a fingernail. They are the only bright spot in the dark sea around us. Erudite headquarters again.

"Apparently the city ordinances don't mean anything to them," he says, "because their lights will be on all night."

"No one else has noticed?" I say, frowning.

"I'm sure they have, but they haven't done anything to stop it. It may be because they don't want to cause a problem over something so small." Tobias shrugs, but the tension in his features worries me. "But it made me wonder what the Erudite are doing that requires night light."

He turns toward me, leaning against the wall.

"Two things you should know about me. The first is that I am deeply suspicious of people in general," he says. "It is my nature to expect the worst of them. And the second is that I am unexpectedly good with computers."

I nod. He said his other job was working with computers, but I still have trouble picturing him sitting in front of a screen all day.

"A few weeks ago, before training started, I was at work and I found a way into the Dauntless secure files. Apparently we are not as skilled as the Erudite are at security," he says, "and what I discovered was what looked like war plans. Thinly veiled commands, supply lists, maps. Things like that. And those files were sent by Erudite."

"War?" I brush my hair away from my face. Listening to my father insult Erudite all my life has made me wary of them, and my experiences in the Dauntless compound make me wary of authority and human beings in general, so I'm not shocked to hear that a faction could be planning a war.

And what Caleb said earlier. *Something big is happening, Beatrice.* I look up at Tobias.

"War on Abnegation?"

He takes my hands, lacing his fingers with mine, and says, "The faction that controls the government. Yes."

My stomach sinks.

"All those reports are supposed to stir up dissension against Abnegation," he says, his eyes focused on the city beyond the train car. "Evidently the Erudite now want to speed up the process. I have no idea what to do about it . . . or what could even be done."

"But," I say, "why would Erudite team up with Dauntless?"

And then something occurs to me, something that hits me in the gut and gnaws at my insides. Erudite doesn't have weapons, and they don't know how to fight—but the Dauntless do.

I stare wide-eyed at Tobias.

"They're going to use us," I say.

"I wonder," he says, "how they plan to get us to fight."

I told Caleb that the Erudite know how to manipulate people. They could coerce some of us into fighting with misinformation, or by appealing to greed—any number of ways. But the Erudite are as meticulous as they are manipulative, so they wouldn't leave it up to chance. They would need to make sure that all their weaknesses are shored up. But how?

The wind blows my hair across my face, cutting my vision into strips, and I leave it there.

"I don't know," I say.

CHAPTER TWENTY-NINE

I HAVE ATTENDED Abnegation's initiation ceremony every year except this one. It is a quiet affair. The initiates, who spend thirty days performing community service before they can become full members, sit side by side on a bench. One of the older members reads the Abnegation manifesto, which is a short paragraph about forgetting the self and the dangers of self-involvement. Then all the older members wash the initiates' feet. Then they all share a meal, each person serving food to the person on his left.

The Dauntless don't do that.

Initiation day plunges the Dauntless compound into insanity and chaos. There are people everywhere, and most of them are inebriated by noon. I fight my way through them to get a plate of food at lunch and carry it back to the dormitory with me. On the way I see someone fall off the path on the Pit wall and, judging by his screams and the way he grabs at his leg, he broke something.

The dormitory, at least, is quiet. I stare at my plate of food. I just grabbed what looked good to me at the time, and now that I take a closer look, I realize that I chose a plain chicken breast, a scoop of peas, and a piece of brown bread. Abnegation food.

I sigh. Abnegation is what I am. It is what I am when I'm not thinking about what I'm doing. It is what I am when I am put to the test. It is what I am even when I appear to be brave. Am I in the wrong faction?

The thought of my former faction sends a tremor through my hands. I have to warn my family about the war the Erudite are planning, but I don't know how. I will find a way, but not today. Today I have to focus on what awaits me. One thing at a time.

I eat like a robot, rotating from chicken to peas to bread and back again. It doesn't matter what faction I really belong in. In two hours I will walk to the fear landscape room with the other initiates, go through my fear landscape, and become Dauntless. It's too late to turn back.

When I finish, I bury my face in my pillow. I don't mean to fall asleep, but after a while, I do, and I wake up to Christina shaking my shoulder.

"Time to go," she says. She looks ashen.

I rub my eyes to press the sleep from them. I have my shoes on already. The other initiates are in the dormitory, tying shoelaces and buttoning jackets and throwing smiles around like they don't mean it. I pull my hair into a bun and put on my black jacket, zipping it up to my throat. The torture will be over soon, but can we forget the simulations? Will we ever sleep soundly again, with the memories of our fears in our heads? Or will we finally forget our fears today, like we're supposed to?

We walk to the Pit and up the path that leads to the glass building. I look up at the glass ceiling. I can't see daylight because the soles of shoes cover every inch of glass above us. For a second I think I hear the glass creak, but it is my imagination. I walk up the stairs with Christina, and the crowd chokes me.

I am too short to see above anyone's head, so I stare at Will's back and walk in his wake. The heat of so many bodies around me makes it difficult to breathe. Beads of sweat gather on my forehead. A break in the crowd reveals what they are all clustered around: a series of screens on the wall to my left.

I hear a cheer and stop to look at the screens. The screen on the left shows a black-clothed girl in the fear landscape room—Marlene. I watch her move, her eyes wide, but I can't tell what obstacle she's facing. Thank God no one out here will see my fears either—just my reactions to them.

The middle screen shows her heart rate. It picks up for a second and then decreases. When it reaches a normal rate, the screen flashes green and the Dauntless cheer. The screen on the right shows her time.

I tear my eyes from the screen and jog to catch up to Christina and Will. Tobias stands just inside a door on the left side of the room that I barely noticed the last time I was here. It is next to the fear landscape room. I walk past him without looking at him.

The room is large and contains another screen, similar to the one outside. A line of people sit in chairs in front of it. Eric is one of them, and so is Max. The others are also older. Judging by the wires connected to their heads, and their blank eyes, they are observing the simulation.

Behind them is another line of chairs, all occupied now. I am the last to enter, so I don't get one.

"Hey, Tris!" Uriah calls out from across the room. He sits with the other Dauntless-born initiates. Only four of them are left; the rest have gone through their fear landscapes already. He pats his leg. "You can sit on my lap, if you want."

"Tempting," I call back, grinning. "It's fine. I like to stand."

I also don't want Tobias to see me sitting on someone else's lap.

The lights lift in the fear landscape room, revealing Marlene in a crouch, her face streaked with tears. Max, Eric, and a few others shake off the simulation daze and walk out. A few seconds later I see them on the screen, congratulating her for finishing.

"Transfers, the order in which you go through the final test was taken from your rankings as they now stand," Tobias says. "So Drew will go first, and Tris will go last."

That means five people will go before I do.

I stand in the back of the room, a few feet away from Tobias. He and I exchange glances when Eric sticks Drew with the needle and sends him into the fear landscape room. By the time it's my turn, I will know how well the others did, and how well I will have to do to beat them.

The fear landscapes are not interesting to watch from the outside. I can see that Drew is moving, but I don't know what he is reacting to. After a few minutes, I close my eyes instead of watching and try to think of nothing. Speculating about which fears I will have to face, and how many there will be, is useless at this point. I just have to remember that I have the power to manipulate the simulations, and that I have practiced it before.

Molly goes next. It takes her half as long as it takes Drew, but even Molly has trouble. She spends too much time breathing heavily, trying to control her panic. At one point she even screams at the top of her lungs.

It amazes me how easy it is to tune out everything else—thoughts of war on Abnegation, Tobias, Caleb, my parents, my friends, my new faction fade away. All I can do now is get past this obstacle.

Christina is next. Then Will. Then Peter. I don't watch them. I know only how much time it takes them: twelve minutes, ten minutes, fifteen minutes. And then my name.

"Tris."

I open my eyes and walk to the front of the observation room, where Eric stands with a syringe full of orange liquid. I barely feel the needle as it plunges into my neck, barely see Eric's pierced face as he presses the plunger down. I imagine that the serum is liquid adrenaline rushing through my veins, making me strong.

"Ready?" he asks.

CHAPTER
THIRTY

I AM READY. I step into the room, armed not with a gun or a knife, but with the plan I made the night before. Tobias said that stage three is about mental preparation—coming up with strategies to overcome my fears.

I wish I knew what order the fears will come in. I bounce on the balls of my feet as I wait for the first fear to appear. I am already short of breath.

The ground beneath me changes. Grass rises from the concrete and sways in a wind I cannot feel. A green sky replaces the exposed pipes above me. I listen for the birds and feel my fear as a distant thing, a hammering heart and a squeezed chest, but not something that exists in my mind. Tobias told me to figure out what this simulation means. He was right; it isn't about the birds. It's about control.

Wings flap next to my ear, and the crow's talons dig into my shoulder.

This time, I do not hit the bird as hard as I can. I crouch, listening to the thunder of wings behind me, and run my hand through the grass, just above the ground. What combats powerlessness? Power. And the first time I felt powerful in the Dauntless compound was when I was holding a gun.

A lump forms in my throat and I want the talons *off*. The bird squawks and my stomach clenches, but then I feel something hard and metal in the grass. My gun.

I point the gun at the bird on my shoulder, and it detaches from my shirt in an explosion of blood and feathers. I spin on my heel, aiming the gun at the sky, and see the cloud of dark feathers descending. I squeeze the trigger, firing again and again into the sea of birds above me, watching their dark bodies drop to the grass.

As I aim and shoot, I feel the same rush of power I felt the first time I held a gun. My heart stops racing and the field, gun, and birds fade away. I stand in the dark again.

I shift my weight, and something squeaks beneath my foot. I crouch down and slide my hand along a cold, smooth panel—glass. I press my hands to glass on either side of my body. The tank again. I am not afraid of drowning. This is not about the water; it is about my inability to escape the tank. It is about weakness. I just have to convince myself that I am strong enough to break the glass.

The blue lights come on, and water slips over the floor, but I don't let the simulation get that far. I slam my palm against the wall in front of me, expecting the pane to break.

My hand bounces off, causing no damage.

My heartbeat speeds up. What if what worked in the first simulation doesn't work here? What if I can't break the glass unless I'm under duress? The water laps over my ankles, flowing faster by the second. I have to calm down. Calm down and focus. I lean against the wall behind me and kick as hard as I can. And again. My toes throb, but nothing happens.

I have another option. I can wait for water to fill the tank—and it's already at my knees—and try to calm down as I drown. I brace myself against the wall, shaking my head. No. I can't let myself drown. I can't.

I ball my hands up into fists and pound on the wall. I am stronger than the glass. The glass is as thin as newly frozen ice. My mind will make it so. I close my eyes. The glass is ice. The glass is ice. The glass is—

The glass shatters under my hand, and water spills onto the floor. And then the dark returns.

I shake out my hands. That should have been an easy obstacle to overcome. I've faced it before in simulations. I can't afford to lose time like that again.

What feels like a solid wall hits me from the side, forcing the air from my lungs, and I fall hard, gasping. I can't swim; I've only seen bodies of water this large, this powerful, in pictures. Beneath me is a rock with a jagged edge, slick with water. The water pulls at my legs, and I cling to the rock, tasting salt on my lips. Out of the corner of my eye, I see a dark sky and a blood-red moon.

Another wave hits, slamming against my back. I hit my chin against the stone and wince. The sea is cold, but my blood is hot, running down my neck. I stretch my arm and find the edge of the rock. The water pulls at my legs with irresistible force. I cling as hard as I can, but I am not strong enough—the water pulls me and the wave throws my body back. It flings my legs over my head and my arms to each side, and I collide with the stone, my back pressed against it, water gushing over my face. My lungs scream for air. I twist and grab the edge of the rock, pulling myself above the water. I gasp, and another wave hits me, this one harder than the first, but I have a better hold.

I must not really be afraid of the water. I must be afraid of being out of control. To face it, I have to regain control.

With a scream of frustration, I throw my hand forward and find a hole in the rock. My arms shake violently as I drag myself forward, and I pull my feet up under me before the wave can take me with it. Once my feet are free, I get up and throw my body into a run, into a sprint, my feet quick on the stone, the red moon in front of me, the ocean gone.

Then everything is gone, and my body is still. Too still.

I try to move my arms, but they are bound tightly to my sides. I look down and see rope wrapped around my chest, my arms, my legs. A stack of logs rises around my feet, and I see a pole behind me. I am high above the ground.

People creep out of the shadows, and their faces are familiar. They are the initiates, carrying torches, and Peter is at the front of the pack. His eyes look like black pits, and he wears a smirk that spreads too wide across his face, forcing wrinkles into his cheeks. A laugh starts somewhere in the center of the crowd and rises as voice after voice joins it. Cackling is all I hear.

As the cackling grows louder, Peter lowers his torch to the wood, and flames leap up near the ground. They flicker at the edges of each log and then creep over the bark. I don't struggle against the ropes, as I did the first time I faced this fear. Instead I close my eyes and gulp as much air as I can. This is a simulation. It can't hurt me. The heat from the flames rises around me. I shake my head.

"Smell that, Stiff?" Peter says, his voice louder than even the cackling.

"No," I say. The flames are getting higher.

He sniffs. "That's the smell of your burning flesh."

When I open my eyes, my vision is blurry with tears.

"Know what I smell?" My voice strains to be louder than the laughter all around me, the laughter that oppresses me as much as the heat. My arms twitch, and I want to fight against the ropes, but I won't, I won't struggle pointlessly, I won't panic.

I stare through the flames at Peter, the heat bringing blood to the surface of my skin, flowing through me, melting the toes of my shoes.

"I smell rain," I say.

Thunder roars above my head, and I scream as a flame touches my fingertips and pain shrieks over my skin. I tilt my head back and focus on the clouds gathering above my head, heavy with rain, dark with rain. A line of lightning sprawls over the sky and I feel the first drop on my forehead. *Faster, faster!* The drop rolls down the side of my nose, and the second drop hits my shoulder, so big it feels like it's made of ice or rock instead of water.

Sheets of rain fall around me, and I hear sizzling over the laughter. I smile, relieved, as the rain puts out the fire and soothes the burns on my hands. The ropes fall away, and I push my hands through my hair.

I wish I was like Tobias and had only four fears to face, but I am not that fearless.

I smooth my shirt down, and when I look up, I stand in my bedroom in the Abnegation sector of the city. I have never faced this fear before. The lights are off, but the room is lit by the moonlight coming through the windows. One of my walls is covered with mirrors. I turn toward it, confused. That isn't right. I am not allowed to have mirrors.

I look at the reflection in the mirror: my wide eyes, the bed with the gray sheets pulled taut, the dresser that holds my clothes, the bookcase, the bare walls. My eyes skip to the window behind me.

And to the man standing just outside.

Cold drops down my spine like a bead of sweat, and my body goes rigid. I recognize him. He is the man with the scarred face from the aptitude test. He wears black and he stands still as a statue. I blink, and two men appear at his left and right, just as still as he is, but their faces are featureless—skin-covered skulls.

I whip my body around, and they stand in my room. I press my shoulders to the mirror.

For a moment, the room is silent, and then fists pound against my window, not just two or four or six, but dozens of fists with dozens of fingers, slamming into the glass. The noise vibrates in my rib cage, it is so loud, and then the scarred man and his two companions begin to walk with slow, careful movements toward me.

They are here to take me, like Peter and Drew and Al; to kill me. I know it.

Simulation. This is a simulation. My heart hammering in my chest, I press my palm to the glass behind me and slide it to the left. It is not a mirror but a closet door. I tell myself where the weapon will be. It will be hanging against the right wall, just inches away from my hand. I don't shift my eyes from the scarred man, but I find the gun with my fingertips and wrap my hand around the handle.

I bite my lip and fire at the scarred man. I don't wait to see if the bullet hits him—I aim at each featureless man in turn, as fast as I can. My lip aches from biting it so hard. The pounding on the window stops, but a screeching sound replaces it, and the fists turn into hands with bent fin-

gers, scratching at the glass, fighting to get in. The glass creaks under the
pressure of their hands, and then cracks, and then shatters.

I scream.

I don't have enough bullets in my gun.

Pale bodies—human bodies, but mangled, arms bent at odd angles,
too-wide mouths with needle teeth, empty eye sockets—topple into my
bedroom, one after the other, and scramble to their feet, scramble toward me. I pull back into the closet and shut the door in front of me. A
solution. I need a solution. I sink into a crouch and press the side of the
gun to my head. I can't fight them off. I can't fight them off, so I have to
calm down. The fear landscape will register my slowing heartbeat and
my even breath and it will move on to the next obstacle.

I sit down on the floor of the closet. The wall behind me creaks. I
hear pounding—the fists are at it again, hitting the closet door—but I
turn and peer through the dark at the panel behind me. It is not a wall but
another door. I fumble to push it aside and reveal the upstairs hallway.
Smiling, I crawl through the hole and stand. I smell something baking. I
am at home.

Taking a deep breath, I watch my house fade. I forgot, for a second,
that I was in Dauntless headquarters.

And then Tobias is standing in front of me.

But I'm not afraid of Tobias. I look over my shoulder. Maybe there's
something behind me that I'm supposed to focus on. But no—behind me
is just a four-poster bed.

A bed?

Tobias walks toward me, slowly.

What's going on?

I stare up at him, paralyzed. He smiles down at me. That smile looks
kind. Familiar.

He presses his mouth to mine, and my lips part. I thought it would be
impossible to forget I was in a simulation. I was wrong; he makes everything else disintegrate.

His fingers find my jacket zipper and pull it down in one slow swipe
until the zipper detaches. He tugs the jacket from my shoulders.

Oh, is all I can think, as he kisses me again. *Oh*.

My fear is being with him. I have been wary of affection all my life,
but I didn't know how deep that wariness went.

But this obstacle doesn't feel the same as the others. It is a different
kind of fear—nervous panic rather than blind terror.

He slides his hands down my arms and then squeezes my hips, his
fingers sliding over the skin just above my belt, and I shiver.

I gently push him back and press my hands to my forehead. I have been attacked by crows and men with grotesque faces; I have been set on fire by the boy who almost threw me off a ledge; I have almost drowned—*twice*—and *this* is what I can't cope with? *This* is the fear I have no solutions for—a boy I like, who wants to . . . have sex with me?

Simulation Tobias kisses my neck.

I try to think. I have to face the fear. I have to take control of the situation and find a way to make it less frightening.

I look Simulation Tobias in the eye and say sternly, "I am *not* going to sleep with you in a hallucination. Okay?"

Then I grab him by his shoulders and turn us around, pushing him against the bedpost. I feel something other than fear—a prickle in my stomach, a bubble of laughter. I press against him and kiss him, my hands wrapping around his arms. He feels strong. He feels . . . good.

And he's gone.

I laugh into my hand until my face gets hot. I must be the only initiate with this fear.

A trigger clicks in my ear.

I almost forgot about this one. I feel the heft of a gun in my hand and curl my fingers around it, slipping my index finger over the trigger. A spotlight shines from the ceiling, its source unknown, and standing in the center of its circle of light are my mother, my father, and my brother.

"Do it," hisses a voice next to me. It is female, but harsh, like it's cluttered with rocks and broken glass. It sounds like Jeanine.

The barrel of a gun presses to my temple, a cold circle against my skin. The cold travels across my body, making the hair on the back of my neck stand on end. I wipe my sweaty palm on my pants and look at the woman through the corner of my eye. It is Jeanine. Her glasses are askew, and her eyes are empty of feeling.

My worst fear: that my family will die, and that I will be responsible.

"Do it," she says again, more insistent this time. "Do it or I'll kill you."

I stare at Caleb. He nods, his eyebrows tugged in, sympathetic. "Go ahead, Tris," he says softly. "I understand. It's okay."

My eyes burn. "No," I say, my throat so tight it aches. I shake my head.

"I'll give you ten seconds!" the woman shouts. "Ten! Nine!"

My eyes skip from my brother to my father. The last time I saw him, he gave me a look of contempt, but now his eyes are wide and soft. I have never seen him wear that expression in real life.

"Tris," he says. "You have no other option."

"Eight!"

"Tris," my mother says. She smiles. She has a sweet smile. "We love you."

"Seven!"

"Shut up!" I shout, holding up the gun. I can do it. I can shoot them. They understand. They're asking me to. They wouldn't want me to sacrifice myself for them. They aren't even real. This is all a simulation.

"Six!"

It isn't real. It doesn't mean anything. My brother's kind eyes feel like two drills boring a hole in my head. My sweat makes the gun slippery.

"Five!"

I have no other option. I close my eyes. Think. I have to think. The urgency making my heart race depends on one thing, and one thing only: the threat to my life.

"Four! Three!"

What did Tobias tell me? *Selflessness and bravery aren't that different.*

"Two!"

I release the trigger of my gun and drop it. Before I can lose my nerve, I turn and press my forehead to the barrel of the gun behind me.

Shoot me instead.

"One!"

I hear a click, and a bang.

CHAPTER
THIRTY-ONE

THE LIGHTS COME ON. I stand alone in the empty room with the concrete walls, shaking. I sink to my knees, wrapping my arms around my chest. It wasn't cold when I walked in, but it feels cold now. I rub my arms to get rid of the goose bumps.

I have never felt relief like this before. Every muscle in my body relaxes at once and I breathe freely again. I can't imagine going through my fear landscape in my spare time, like Tobias does. It seemed like bravery to me before, but now it seems more like masochism.

The door opens, and I stand. Max, Eric, Tobias, and a few people I don't know walk into the room in a line, standing in a small crowd in front of me. Tobias smiles at me.

"Congratulations, Tris," says Eric. "You have successfully completed your final evaluation."

I try to smile. It doesn't work. I can't shake the memory of the gun against my head. I can still feel the barrel between my eyebrows.

"Thanks," I say.

"There is one more thing before you can go and get ready for the welcoming banquet," he says. He beckons to one of the unfamiliar people behind him. A woman with blue hair hands him a small black case. He opens it and takes out a syringe and a long needle.

I tense up at the sight of it. The orange-brown liquid in the syringe reminds me of what they inject us with before simulations. And I am supposed to be finished with those.

"At least you aren't afraid of needles," he says. "This will inject you with a tracking device that will be activated only if you are reported missing. Just a precaution."

"How often do people go missing?" I ask, frowning.

"Not often." Eric smirks. "This is a new development, courtesy of the Erudite. We have been injecting every Dauntless throughout the day, and I assume all other factions will comply as soon as possible."

My stomach twists. I can't let him inject me with anything, especially not anything developed by Erudite—maybe even by Jeanine. But I also can't refuse. I can't refuse or he will doubt my loyalty again.

"All right," I say, my throat tight.

Eric approaches me with the needle and syringe in hand. I pull my hair away from my neck and tilt my head to the side. I look away as Eric wipes my neck with an antiseptic wipe and eases the needle into my skin. The deep ache spreads through my neck, painful but brief. He puts the needle back in its case and sticks an adhesive bandage on the injection site.

"The banquet is in two hours," he says. "Your ranking among the other initiates, Dauntless-born included, will be announced then. Good luck."

The small crowd files out of the room, but Tobias lingers. He pauses by the door and beckons for me to follow him, so I do. The glass room above the Pit is full of Dauntless, some of them walking the ropes above our heads, some talking and laughing in groups. He smiles at me. He must not have been watching.

"I heard a rumor that you only had seven obstacles to face," he says. "Practically unheard of."

"You . . . you weren't watching the simulation?"

"Only on the screens. The Dauntless leaders are the only ones who see the whole thing," he says. "They seemed impressed."

"Well, seven fears isn't as impressive as four," I reply, "but it will suffice."

"I would be surprised if you weren't ranked first," he says.

We walk into the glass room. The crowd is still there, but it is thinner now that the last person—me—has gone.

People notice me after a few seconds. I stay close to Tobias's side as they point, but I can't walk fast enough to avoid some cheers, some claps on the shoulder, some congratulations. As I look at the people around me, I realize how strange they would look to my father and brother, and how normal they seem to me, despite all the metal rings in their faces and the tattoos on their arms and throats and chests. I smile back at them.

We descend the steps into the Pit and I say, "I have a question." I bite my lip. "How much did they tell you about my fear landscape?"

"Nothing, really. Why?" he says.

"No reason." I kick a pebble to the side of the path.

"Do you have to go back to the dormitory?" he asks. "Because if you want peace and quiet, you can stay with me until the banquet."

My stomach twists.

"What is it?" he asks.

I don't want to go back to the dormitory, and I don't want to be afraid of him.

"Let's go," I say.

+ + +

He closes the door behind us and slips off his shoes.

"Want some water?" he says.

"No thanks." I hold my hands in front of me.

"You okay?" he says, touching my cheek. His hand cradles the side of my head, his long fingers slipping through my hair. He smiles and holds my head in place as he kisses me. Heat spreads through me slowly. And fear, buzzing like an alarm in my chest.

His lips still on mine, he pushes the jacket from my shoulders. I flinch when I hear it drop, and push him back, my eyes burning. I don't know why I feel this way. I didn't feel like this when he kissed me on the train. I press my palms to my face, covering my eyes.

"What? What's wrong?"

I shake my head.

"Don't tell me it's nothing." His voice is cold. He grabs my arm. "Hey. Look at me."

I take my hands from my face and lift my eyes to his. The hurt in his eyes and the anger in his clenched jaw surprise me.

"Sometimes I wonder," I say, as calmly as I can, "what's in it for you. This . . . whatever it is."

"What's in it for me," he repeats. He steps back, shaking his head. "You're an idiot, Tris."

"I am *not* an idiot," I say. "Which is why I know that it's a little weird that, of all the girls you could have chosen, you chose me. So if you're just looking for . . . um, you know . . . *that* . . ."

"What? Sex?" He scowls at me. "You know, if that was all I wanted, you probably wouldn't be the first person I would go to."

I feel like he just punched me in the stomach. Of course I'm not the first person he would go to—not the first, not the prettiest, not desirable. I press my hands to my abdomen and look away, fighting off tears. I am not the crying type. Nor am I the yelling type. I blink a few times, lower my hands, and stare up at him.

"I'm going to leave now," I say quietly. And I turn toward the door.

"No, Tris." He grabs my wrist and wrenches me back. I push him away, hard, but he grabs my other wrist, holding our crossed arms between us.

"I'm sorry I said that," he says. "What I *meant* was that you aren't like that. Which I knew when I met you."

"You were an obstacle in my fear landscape." My lower lip wobbles. "Did you know that?"

"What?" He releases my wrists, and the hurt look is back. "You're *afraid* of me?"

"Not you," I say. I bite my lip to keep it still. "Being with you . . . with anyone. I've never been involved with someone before, and . . . you're older, and I don't know what your expectations are, and . . ."

"Tris," he says sternly, "I don't know what delusion you're operating under, but this is all new to me, too."

"Delusion?" I repeat. "You mean you haven't . . ." I raise my eyebrows. "Oh. *Oh.* I just assumed . . ." That because I am so absorbed by him, everyone else must be too. "Um. You know."

"Well, you assumed wrong." He looks away. His cheeks are bright, like he's embarrassed. "You can tell me anything, you know," he says. He takes my face in his hands, his fingertips cold and his palms warm. "I am kinder than I seemed in training. I promise."

I believe him. But this has nothing to do with his kindness.

He kisses me between the eyebrows, and on the tip of my nose, and then carefully fits his mouth to mine. I am on edge. I have electricity coursing through my veins instead of blood. I want him to kiss me, I want him to; I am afraid of where it might go.

His hands shift to my shoulders, and his fingers brush over the edge of my bandage. He pulls back with a puckered brow.

"Are you hurt?" he asks.

"No. It's another tattoo. It's healed, I just . . . wanted to keep it covered up."

"Can I see?"

I nod, my throat tight. I pull my sleeve down and slip my shoulder out of it. He stares down at my shoulder for a second, and then runs his fingers over it. They rise and fall with my bones, which stick out farther than I'd like. When he touches me, I feel like everywhere his skin meets mine is changed by the connection. It sends a thrill through my stomach. Not just fear. Something else, too. A wanting.

He peels the corner of the bandage away. His eyes roam over the symbol of Abnegation, and he smiles.

"I have the same one," he says, laughing. "On my back."

"Really? Can I see it?"

He presses the bandage over the tattoo and pulls my shirt back over my shoulder.

"Are you asking me to undress, Tris?"

A nervous laugh gurgles from my throat. "Only . . . partially."

He nods, his smile suddenly fading. He lifts his eyes to mine and unzips his sweatshirt. It slides from his shoulders, and he tosses it onto the desk chair. I don't feel like laughing now. All I can do is stare at him.

His eyebrows pull to the center of his forehead, and he grabs the hem of his T-shirt. In one swift motion, he pulls it over his head.

A patch of Dauntless flames covers his right side, but other than that, his chest is unmarked. He averts his eyes.

"What is it?" I ask, frowning. He looks . . . uncomfortable.

"I don't invite many people to look at me," he says. "Any people, actually."

"I can't imagine why," I say softly. "I mean, look at you."

I walk slowly around him. On his back is more ink than skin. The symbols of each faction are drawn there—Dauntless at the top of his spine, Abnegation just below it, and the other three, smaller, beneath them. For a few seconds I look at the scales that represent Candor, the eye that stands for Erudite, and the tree that symbolizes Amity. It makes sense that he would tattoo himself with the symbol of Dauntless, his refuge, and even the symbol of Abnegation, his place of origin, like I did. But the other three?

"I think we've made a mistake," he says softly. "We've all started to put down the virtues of the other factions in the process of bolstering our own. I don't want to do that. I want to be brave, and selfless, *and* smart, *and* kind, *and* honest." He clears his throat. "I continually struggle with kindness."

"No one's perfect," I whisper. "It doesn't work that way. One bad thing goes away, and another bad thing replaces it."

I traded cowardice for cruelty; I traded weakness for ferocity.

I brush over Abnegation's symbol with my fingertips. "We have to warn them, you know. Soon."

"I know," he says. "We will."

He turns toward me. I want to touch him, but I'm afraid of his bareness; afraid that he will make me bare too.

"Is this scaring you, Tris?"

"No," I croak. I clear my throat. "Not really. I'm only . . . afraid of what I want."

"What do you want?" Then his face tightens. "Me?"

Slowly I nod.

He nods too, and takes my hands in his gently. He guides my palms to his stomach. His eyes lowered, he pushes my hands up, over his abdomen and over his chest, and holds them against his neck. My palms tingle with the feel of his skin, smooth, warm. My face is hot, but I shiver anyway. He looks at me.

"Someday," he says, "if you still want me, we can . . ." He pauses, clears his throat. "We can . . ."

I smile a little and wrap my arms around him before he finishes, pressing the side of my face to his chest. I feel his heartbeat against my cheek, as fast as my own.

"Are you afraid of me, too, Tobias?"

"Terrified," he replies with a smile.

I turn my head and kiss the hollow beneath his throat.

"Maybe you won't be in my fear landscape anymore," I murmur.

He bends his head and kisses me slowly.

"Then everyone can call you Six."

"Four and Six," I say.

We kiss again, and this time, it feels familiar. I know exactly how we fit together, his arm around my waist, my hands on his chest, the pressure of his lips on mine. We have each other memorized.

CHAPTER
THIRTY-TWO

I WATCH TOBIAS's face carefully as we walk to the dining hall, searching for any sign of disappointment. We spent the two hours lying on his bed, talking and kissing and eventually dozing until we heard shouts in the hallway—people on their way to the banquet.

If anything, he seems lighter now than he was before. He smiles more, anyway.

When we reach the entrance, we separate. I go in first, and run to the table I share with Will and Christina. He enters second, a minute later, and sits down next to Zeke, who hands him a dark bottle. He waves it away.

"Where did you go?" asks Christina. "Everyone else went back to the dormitory."

"I just wandered around," I say. "I was too nervous to talk to everyone else about it."

"You have no reason to be nervous," Christina says, shaking her head. "I turned around to talk to Will for one second, and you were already done."

I detect a note of jealousy in her voice, and again, I wish I could explain that I was well prepared for the simulation, because of what I am. Instead I just shrug.

"What job are you going to pick?" I ask her.

"I'm thinking I might want a job like Four's. Training initiates," she says. "Scaring the living daylights out of them. You know, fun stuff. What about you?"

I was so focused on getting through initiation that I barely thought about it. I could work for the Dauntless leaders—but they would kill me if they discover what I am. What else is there?

"I guess . . . I could be an ambassador to the other factions," I say. "I think being a transfer would help me."

"I was so hoping you would say Dauntless-leader-in-training," sighs Christina. "Because that's what Peter wants. He couldn't shut up about it in the dorm earlier."

"And it's what I want," adds Will. "Hopefully I ranked higher than him . . . oh, and all the Dauntless-born initiates. Forgot about them." He groans. "Oh God. This is going to be impossible."

"No, it isn't," she says. Christina reaches for his hand and laces her fingers with his, like it's the most natural thing in the world. Will squeezes her hand.

"Question," says Christina, leaning forward. "The leaders who were watching your fear landscape . . . they were laughing about something."

"Oh?" I bite my lip hard. "I'm glad my terror amuses them."

"Any idea which obstacle it was?" she asks.

"No."

"You're *lying*," she says. "You always bite the inside of your cheek when you lie. It's your tell."

I stop biting the inside of my cheek.

"Will's is pinching his lips together, if it makes you feel better," she adds.

Will covers his mouth immediately.

"Okay, fine. I was afraid of . . . intimacy," I say.

"Intimacy," repeats Christina. "Like . . . sex?"

I tense up. And force myself to nod. Even if it was just Christina, and no one else was around, I would still want to strangle her right now. I go over a few ways to inflict maximum injury with minimum force in my head. I try to throw flames from my eyes.

Will laughs.

"What was *that* like?" she says. "I mean, did someone just . . . try to do it with you? Who was it?"

"Oh, you know. Faceless . . . unidentifiable male," I say. "How were your moths?"

"You promised you would never tell!" cries Christina, smacking my arm.

"Moths," repeats Will. "You're afraid of moths?"

"Not just a cloud of moths," she says, "like . . . a *swarm* of them. Everywhere. All those wings and legs and . . ." She shudders and shakes her head.

"Terrifying," Will says with mock seriousness. "That's my girl. Tough as cotton balls."

"Oh, shut up."

A microphone squeals somewhere, so loud I clap my hands over my ears. I look across the room at Eric, who stands on one of the tables with the microphone in hand, tapping it with his fingertips. After the tapping is done and the crowd of Dauntless is quiet, Eric clears his throat and begins.

"We aren't big on speeches here. Eloquence is for Erudite," he says. The crowd laughs. I wonder if they know that he was an Erudite once; that under all the pretense of Dauntless recklessness and even brutality, he is more like an Erudite than anything else. If they did, I doubt they would laugh at him. "So I'm going to keep this short. It's a new year, and we have a new pack of initiates. And a slightly smaller pack of new members. We offer them our congratulations."

At the word "congratulations" the room erupts, not into applause, but into the pounding of fists on tabletops. The noise vibrates in my chest, and I grin.

"We believe in bravery. We believe in taking action. We believe in freedom from fear and in acquiring the skills to force the bad out of our world so that the good can prosper and thrive. If you also believe in those things, we welcome you."

Even though I know Eric probably doesn't believe in any of those things, I find myself smiling, because I believe in them. No matter how badly the leaders have warped the Dauntless ideals, those ideals can still belong to me.

More pounding fists, this time accompanied by whoops.

"Tomorrow, in their first act as members, our top ten initiates will choose their professions, in the order of how they are ranked," Eric says. "The rankings, I know, are what everyone is really waiting for. They are determined by a combination of three scores—the first, from the combat stage of training; the second, from the simulation stage; and the third, from the final examination, the fear landscape. The rankings will appear on the screen behind me."

As soon as the word "me" leaves his mouth, the names appear on the screen, which is almost as large as the wall itself. Next to the number one is my picture, and the name "Tris."

A weight in my chest lifts. I didn't realize it was there until it was gone, and I didn't have to feel it anymore. I smile, and a tingling spreads through me. First. Divergent or not, this faction is where I belong.

I forget about war; I forget about death. Will's arms wrap around me and he gives me a bear hug. I hear cheering and laughing and shouting. Christina points at the screen, her eyes wide and filled with tears.

1. Tris
2. Uriah
3. Lynn
4. Marlene
5. Peter

Peter stays. I suppress a sigh. But then I read the rest of the names.

6. Will
7. Christina

I smile, and Christina reaches across the table to hug me. I am too distracted to protest against the affection. She laughs in my ear.

Someone grabs me from behind and shouts in my ear. It's Uriah. I can't turn around, so I reach back and squeeze his shoulder.

"Congratulations!" I shout.

"You beat them!" he shouts back. He releases me, laughing, and runs into a crowd of Dauntless-born initiates.

I crane my neck to look at the screen again. I follow the list down.

Eight, nine, and ten are Dauntless-borns whose names I barely recognize.

Eleven and twelve are Molly and Drew.

Molly and Drew are cut. Drew, who tried to run away while Peter held me by the throat over the chasm, and Molly, who fed the Erudite lies about my father, are factionless.

It isn't quite the victory I wanted, but it's a victory nonetheless.

Will and Christina kiss, a little too sloppily for my taste. All around me is the pounding of Dauntless fists. Then I feel a tap on my shoulder and turn to see Tobias standing behind me. I get up, beaming.

"You think giving you a hug would give away too much?" he says.

"You know," I say, "I really don't care."

I stand on my tiptoes and press my lips to his.

It is the best moment of my life.

A moment later, Tobias's thumb brushes over the injection site in my neck, and a few things come together at once. I don't know how I didn't figure this out before.

One: Colored serum contains transmitters.

Two: Transmitters connect the mind to a simulation program.

Three: Erudite developed the serum.

Four: Eric and Max are working with the Erudite.

I break away from the kiss and stare wide-eyed at Tobias.

"Tris?" he says, confused.

I shake my head. "Not now." I meant to say *not here.* Not with Will and Christina standing a foot away from me—staring with open mouths, probably because I just kissed Tobias—and the clamor of the Dauntless surrounding us. But he has to know how important it is.

"Later," I say. "Okay?"

He nods. I don't even know how I'll explain it later. I don't even know how to think straight.

But I do know how Erudite will get us to fight.

CHAPTER
THIRTY-THREE

I TRY TO get Tobias alone after the rankings are announced, but the crowd of initiates and members is too thick, and the force of their congratulations pulls him away from me. I decide to sneak out of the dormitory after everyone is asleep and find him, but the fear landscape exhausted me more than I realized, so soon enough, I drift off too.

I wake to squeaking mattresses and shuffling feet. It's too dark for me to see clearly, but as my eyes adjust, I see that Christina is tying her shoelaces. I open my mouth to ask her what she's doing, but then I notice that across from me, Will is putting on a shirt. Everyone is awake, but everyone is silent.

"Christina," I hiss. She doesn't look at me, so I grab her shoulder and shake it. "Christina!"

She just keeps tying her shoelaces.

My stomach squeezes when I see her face. Her eyes are open, but blank, and her facial muscles are slack. She moves without looking at what she's doing, her mouth half-open, not awake but seeming awake. And everyone else looks just like her.

"Will?" I ask, crossing the room. All the initiates fall into a line when they finish dressing. They start to file silently out of the dormitory. I grab Will's arm to keep him from leaving, but he moves forward with irrepressible force. I grit my teeth and hold on as hard as I can, digging my heels into the ground. He just drags me along with him.

They are sleepwalkers.

I fumble for my shoes. I can't stay here alone. I tie my shoes in a hurry, pull on a jacket, and sprint out of the room, catching up to the line of initiates quickly, conforming my pace to theirs. It takes me a few seconds to realize that they move in unison, the same foot forward as the same arm swings back. I mimic them as best I can, but the rhythm feels strange to me.

We march toward the Pit, but when we reach the entrance, the front of the line turns left. Max stands in the hallway, watching us. My heart hammers in my chest and I stare as vacantly as possible ahead of me, focusing on the rhythm of my feet. I tense as I pass him. He'll notice. He'll notice I'm not brain-dead like the rest of them and something bad will happen to me, I just know it.

Max's dark eyes pass right over me.

We climb a flight of stairs and travel at the same rhythm down four corridors. Then the hallway opens up to a huge cavern. Inside it is a crowd of Dauntless.

There are rows of tables with mounds of black on them. I can't see what the piles are until I am a foot away from them. Guns.

Of course. Eric said every Dauntless was injected yesterday. So now the entire faction is brain-dead, obedient, and trained to kill. Perfect soldiers.

I pick up a gun and a holster and a belt, copying Will, who is directly in front of me. I try to match his movements, but I can't predict what he's going to do, so I end up fumbling more than I'd like to. I grit my teeth. I just have to trust that no one is watching me.

Once I'm armed, I follow Will and the other initiates toward the exit.

I can't wage war against Abnegation, against my family. I would rather die. My fear landscape proved that. My list of options narrows, and I see the path I must take. I will pretend long enough to get to the Abnegation sector of the city. I will save my family. And whatever happens after that doesn't matter. A blanket of calm settles over me.

The line of initiates passes into a dark hallway. I can't see Will ahead of me, or anything ahead of him. My foot hits something hard, and I stumble, my hands outstretched. My knee hits something else—a step. I straighten, so tense my teeth are almost chattering. They didn't see that. It's too dark. Please let it be too dark.

As the staircase turns, light flows into the cavern, until I can finally see Will's shoulders in front of me again. I focus on matching my rhythm to his as I reach the top of the stairs, passing another Dauntless leader. Now I know who the Dauntless leaders are, because they are the only people who are awake.

Well, not the only people. I must be awake because I am Divergent. And if I am awake, that means Tobias is too, unless I am wrong about him.

I have to find him.

I stand next to the train tracks in a group that stretches as far as I can see with my peripheral vision. The train is stopped in front of us, every car open. One by one, my fellow initiates climb into the train car in front of us.

I can't turn my head to scan the crowd for Tobias, but I let my eyes skirt to the side. The faces on my left are unfamiliar, but I see a tall boy with short hair a few yards to my right. It might not be him, and I can't make sure, but it's the best chance I have. I don't know how to get to him without attracting attention. I have to get to him.

The car in front of me fills up, and Will turns toward the next one. I take my cues from him, but instead of stopping where he stops, I slip a few feet to the right. The people around me are all taller than I am; they will shield me. I step to the right again, clenching my teeth. Too much movement. They will catch me. *Please don't catch me.*

A blank-faced Dauntless in the next car offers a hand to the boy in front of me, and he takes it, his movements robotic. I take the next hand without looking at it, and climb as gracefully as I can into the car.

I stand facing the person who helped me. My eyes twitch up, just for a second, to see his face. Tobias, as blank-faced as the rest of them. Was I wrong? Is he not Divergent? Tears spark behind my eyes, and I blink them back as I turn away from him.

People crowd into the car around me, so we stand in four rows, shoulder-to-shoulder. And then something peculiar happens: fingers lace with mine, and a palm presses to my palm. Tobias, holding my hand.

My entire body is alive with energy. I squeeze his hand, and he squeezes back. He is awake. I was right.

I want to look at him, but I force myself to stand still and keep my eyes forward as the train starts to move. He moves his thumb in a slow circle over the back of my hand. It is meant to comfort me, but it frustrates me instead. I need to talk to him. I need to look at him.

I can't see where the train is going because the girl in front of me is so tall, so I stare at the back of her head and focus on Tobias's hand in mine until the rails squeal. I don't know how long I've been standing there, but my back aches, so it must have been a long time. The train screeches to a stop, and my heart pounds so hard it's difficult to breathe.

Right before we jump down from the car, I see Tobias turn his head in my periphery, and I glance back at him. His dark eyes are insistent as he says, "Run."

"My family," I say.

I look straight ahead again, and jump down from the train car when it's my turn. Tobias walks in front of me. I should focus on the back of his head, but the streets I walk now are familiar, and the line of Dauntless I follow fades from my attention. I pass the place I went every six months with my mother to pick up new clothes for our family; the bus stop where

I once waited in the morning to get to school; the strip of sidewalk so cracked Caleb and I played a hopping, jumping game to get across it.

They are all different now. The buildings are dark and empty. The roads are packed with Dauntless soldiers, all marching at the same rhythm except the officers, who stand every few hundred yards, watching us walk by, or gathering in clusters to discuss something. No one seems to be doing anything. Are we really here for war?

I walk a half mile before I get an answer to that question.

I start to hear popping sounds. I can't look around to see where they're coming from, but the farther I walk, the louder and sharper they get, until I recognize them as gunshots. I clench my jaw. I must keep walking; I have to stare straight ahead.

Far ahead of us, I see a Dauntless soldier push a gray-clothed man to his knees. I recognize the man—he is a council member. The soldier takes her gun out of her holster and, with sightless eyes, fires a bullet into the back of the council member's skull.

The soldier has a gray streak in her hair. It's Tori. My steps almost falter.

Keep walking. My eyes burn. *Keep walking.*

We march past Tori and the fallen council member. When I step over his hand, I almost burst into tears.

Then the soldiers in front of me stop walking, and so do I. I stand as still as I can, but all I want to do is find Jeanine and Eric and Max and shoot them all. My hands are shaking and I can't do anything to stop it. I breathe quickly through my nose.

Another gunshot. From the corner of my left eye, I see a gray blur collapse to the pavement. All the Abnegation will die if this continues.

The Dauntless soldiers carry out unspoken orders without hesitation and without question. Some adult members of Abnegation are herded toward one of the nearby buildings, along with the Abnegation children. A sea of black-clothed soldiers guard the doors. The only people I do not see are the Abnegation leaders. Maybe they are already dead.

One by one, the Dauntless soldiers in front of me step away to perform one task or another. Soon the leaders will notice that whatever signals everyone else is getting, I'm not getting them. What will I do when that happens?

"This is insane," coos a male voice on my right. I see a lock of long, greasy hair, and a silver earring. Eric. He pokes my cheek with his index finger, and I struggle against the impulse to slap his hand away.

"They really can't see us? Or hear us?" a female voice asks.

"Oh, they can see and hear. They just aren't processing what they see and hear the same way," says Eric. "They receive commands from our computers in the transmitters we injected them with . . ." At this, he presses his fingers to the injection site to show the woman where it is. *Stay still*, I tell myself. *Still, still, still.* ". . . and carry them out seamlessly."

Eric shifts a step to the side and leans close to Tobias's face, grinning.

"Now, this is a happy sight," he says. "The legendary Four. No one's going to remember that I came in second now, are they? No one's going to ask me, 'What was it like to train with the guy who has only *four fears*?'" He draws his gun and points it at Tobias's right temple. My heart pounds so hard I feel it in my skull. He can't shoot; he wouldn't. Eric tilts his head. "Think anyone would notice if he accidentally got shot?"

"Go ahead," the woman says, sounding bored. She must be a Dauntless leader if she can give Eric permission. "He's nothing now."

"Too bad you didn't just take Max up on his offer, Four. Well, too bad for *you*, anyway," says Eric quietly, as he clicks the bullet into its chamber.

My lungs burn; I haven't breathed in almost a minute. I see Tobias's hand twitch in the corner of my eye, but my hand is already on my gun. I press the barrel to Eric's forehead. His eyes widen, and his face goes slack, and for a second he looks like another sleeping Dauntless soldier.

My index finger hovers over the trigger.

"Get your gun away from his head," I say.

"You won't shoot me," Eric replies.

"Interesting theory," I say. But I can't murder him; I can't. I grit my teeth and shift my arm down, firing at Eric's foot. He screams and grabs his foot with both hands. The moment his gun is no longer pointed at Tobias's head, Tobias draws his gun and fires at Eric's friend's leg. I don't wait to see if the bullet hits her. I grab Tobias's arm and sprint.

If we can make it to the alley, we can disappear into the buildings and they won't find us. There are two hundred yards to go. I hear footsteps behind us, but I don't look back. Tobias grabs my hand and squeezes, pulling me forward, faster than I have ever run, faster than I can run. I stumble behind him. I hear a gunshot.

The pain is sharp and sudden, beginning in my shoulder and spreading outward with electric fingers. A scream stops in my throat, and I fall, my cheek scraping the pavement. I lift my head to see Tobias's knees by my face, and yell, "Run!"

His voice is calm and quiet as he replies, "No."

In seconds we are surrounded. Tobias helps me up, supporting my weight. I have trouble focusing through the pain. Dauntless soldiers surround us and point their guns.

"Divergent rebels," Eric says, standing on one foot. His face is a sickly white. "Surrender your weapons."

CHAPTER THIRTY-FOUR

I LEAN HEAVILY on Tobias. A gun barrel pressed to my spine urges me forward, through the front doors of Abnegation headquarters, a plain gray building, two stories high. Blood trickles down my side. I'm not afraid of what's coming; I'm in too much pain to think about it.

The gun barrel pushes me toward a door guarded by two Dauntless soldiers. Tobias and I walk through it and enter a plain office that contains just a desk, a computer, and two empty chairs. Jeanine sits behind the desk, a phone against her ear.

"Well, send some of them *back* on the train, then," she says. "It needs to be well guarded, it's the most important part—I'm not talk—I have to go." She snaps the phone shut and focuses her gray eyes on me. They remind me of melted steel.

"Divergent rebels," one of the Dauntless says. He must be a Dauntless leader—or maybe a recruit who was removed from the simulation.

"Yes, I can see that." She takes her glasses off, folds them, and sets them on the desk. She probably wears the glasses out of vanity rather than necessity, because she thinks they make her look smarter—my father said so.

"*You*," she says, pointing at me, "I expected. All the trouble with your aptitude test results made me suspicious from the beginning. But *you* . . ."

She shakes her head as she shifts her eyes to Tobias.

"You, Tobias—or should I call you Four?—managed to elude me," she says quietly. "Everything about you checked out: test results, initiation simulations, everything. But here you are nonetheless." She folds her hands and sets her chin on top of them. "Perhaps you could explain to me how that is?"

"You're the genius," he says coolly. "Why don't you tell me?"

Her mouth curls into a smile. "My theory is that you really do belong in Abnegation. That your Divergence is weaker."

She smiles wider. Like she's amused. I grit my teeth and consider lunging across the table and strangling her. If I didn't have a bullet in my shoulder, I might.

"Your powers of deductive reasoning are stunning," spits Tobias. "Consider me awed."

I look sideways at him. I had almost forgotten about this side of him—the part that is more likely to explode than to lie down and die.

"Now that your intelligence has been verified, you might want to get on with killing us." Tobias closes his eyes. "You have a lot of Abnegation leaders to murder, after all."

If Tobias's comments bother Jeanine, she doesn't let on. She keeps smiling and stands smoothly. She wears a blue dress that hugs her body from shoulder to knee, revealing a layer of pudge around her middle. The room spins as I try to focus on her face, and I slump against Tobias for support. He slides his arm around me, supporting me from the waist.

"Don't be silly. There is no rush," she says lightly. "You are both here for an extremely important purpose. You see, it perplexed me that the Divergent were immune to the serum that I developed, so I have been working to remedy that. I thought I might have, with the last batch, but as you know, I was wrong. Luckily I have another batch to test."

"Why bother?" She and the Dauntless leaders had no problem killing the Divergent in the past. Why would it be any different now?

She smirks at me.

"I have had a question since I began the Dauntless project, and it is this." She sidesteps her desk, skimming the surface with her finger. "Why are most of the Divergent weak-willed, God-fearing nobodies from *Abnegation*, of all factions?"

I didn't know that most of the Divergent came from Abnegation, and I don't know why that would be. And I probably won't live long enough to figure it out.

"Weak-willed," Tobias scoffs. "It requires a *strong* will to manipulate a simulation, last time I checked. Weak-willed is mind-controlling an army because it's too hard for you to train one yourself."

"I am not a fool," says Jeanine. "A faction of intellectuals is no army. We are tired of being dominated by a bunch of self-righteous idiots who reject wealth and advancement, but we couldn't do this on our own. And your Dauntless leaders were all too happy to oblige me if I guaranteed them a place in our new, improved government."

"Improved," Tobias says, snorting.

"Yes, improved," Jeanine says. "Improved, and working toward a world in which people will live in wealth, comfort, and prosperity."

"At whose expense?" I ask, my voice thick and sluggish. "All that wealth . . . doesn't come from nowhere."

"Currently, the factionless are a drain on our resources," Jeanine replies. "As is Abnegation. I am sure that once the remains of your old faction are absorbed into the Dauntless army, Candor will cooperate and we will finally be able to get on with things."

Absorbed into the Dauntless army. I know what that means—she wants to control them, too. She wants everyone to be pliable and easy to control.

"Get on with things," Tobias repeats bitterly. He raises his voice. "Make no mistake. You will be dead before the day is out, you—"

"Perhaps if you could control your temper," Jeanine says, her words cutting cleanly across Tobias's, "you would not be in this situation to begin with, Tobias."

"I'm in this situation because you put me here," he snaps. "The second you orchestrated an attack against innocent people."

"Innocent people." Jeanine laughs. "I find that a little funny, coming from you. I would expect Marcus's son to understand that not all those people are innocent." She perches on the edge of the desk, her skirt pulling away from her knees, which are crossed with stretch marks. "Can you tell me honestly that you wouldn't be happy to discover that your father was killed in the attack?"

"No," says Tobias through gritted teeth. "But at least his evil didn't involve the widespread manipulation of an entire faction and the systematic murder of every political leader we have."

They stare at each other for a few seconds, long enough to make me feel tense to my core, and then Jeanine clears her throat.

"What I was going to say," she says, "is that soon, dozens of the Abnegation and their young children will be my responsibility to keep in order, and it does not bode well for me that a large number of them may be Divergent like yourselves, incapable of being controlled by the simulations."

She stands and walks a few steps to the left, her hands clasped in front of her. Her nail beds, like mine, are bitten raw.

"Therefore, it was necessary that I develop a new form of simulation to which they are not immune. I have been forced to reassess my own assumptions. That is where you come in." She paces a few steps to the right. "You are correct to say that you are strong-willed. I cannot control your will. But there are a few things I can control."

She stops and turns to face us. I lean my temple into Tobias's shoulder. Blood trails down my back. The pain has been so constant for the past few minutes that I have gotten used to it, like a person gets used to a siren's wail if it remains consistent.

She presses her palms together. I see no vicious glee in her eyes, and not a hint of the sadism I expect. She is more machine than maniac. She sees problems and forms solutions based on the data she collects. Abnegation stood in the way of her desire for power, so she found a way to eliminate it. She didn't have an army, so she found one in Dauntless. She knew that she would need to control large groups of people in order to stay secure, so she developed a way to do it with serums and transmitters. Divergence is just another problem for her to solve, and that is what makes her so terrifying—because she is smart enough to solve anything, even the problem of our existence.

"I can control what you see and hear," she says. "So I created a new serum that will adjust your surroundings to manipulate your will. Those who refuse to accept our leadership must be closely monitored."

Monitored—or robbed of free will. She has a gift with words.

"You will be the first test subject, Tobias. Beatrice, however . . ." She smiles. "You are too injured to be of much use to me, so your execution will occur at the conclusion of this meeting."

I try to hide the shudder that goes through me at the word "execution," my shoulder screaming with pain, and look up at Tobias. It's hard to blink the tears back when I see the terror in Tobias's wide, dark eyes.

"No," says Tobias. His voice trembles, but his look is stern as he shakes his head. "I would rather die."

"I'm afraid you don't have much of a choice in the matter," replies Jeanine lightly.

Tobias takes my face in his hands roughly and kisses me, the pressure of his lips pushing mine apart. I forget my pain and the terror of approaching death and for a moment, I am grateful that the memory of that kiss will be fresh in my mind as I meet my end.

Then he releases me and I have to lean against the wall for support. With no more warning than the tightening of his muscles, Tobias lunges across the desk and wraps his hands around Jeanine's throat. Dauntless guards by the door leap at him, their guns held ready, and I scream.

It takes two Dauntless soldiers to pull Tobias away from Jeanine and shove him to the ground. One of the soldiers pins him, his knees on Tobias's shoulders and his hands on Tobias's head, pressing his face to the carpet. I lunge toward them, but another guard slams his hands against my shoulders, forcing me against the wall. I am weak from blood loss and too small.

Jeanine braces herself against the desk, spluttering and gasping. She rubs her throat, which is bright red with Tobias's fingerprints. No matter how mechanical she seems, she's still human; there are tears in her eyes as she takes a box from her desk drawer and opens it, revealing a needle and syringe.

Still breathing heavily, she carries it toward Tobias. Tobias grits his teeth and elbows one of the guards in the face. The guard slams the heel of his gun into the side of Tobias's head, and Jeanine sticks the needle into Tobias's neck. He goes limp.

A sound escapes my mouth, not a sob or a scream, but a croaking, scraping moan that sounds detached, like it is coming from someone else.

"Let him up," says Jeanine, her voice scratchy.

The guard gets up, and so does Tobias. He does not look like the sleepwalking Dauntless soldiers; his eyes are alert. He looks around for a few seconds as if confused by what he sees.

"Tobias," I say. "Tobias!"

"He doesn't know you," says Jeanine.

Tobias looks over his shoulder. His eyes narrow and he starts toward me, fast. Before the guards can stop him, he closes a hand around my throat, squeezing my trachea with his fingertips. I choke, my face hot with blood.

"The simulation manipulates him," says Jeanine. I can barely hear her over the pounding in my ears. "By altering what he sees—making him confuse enemy with friend."

One of the guards pulls Tobias off me. I gasp, drawing a rattling breath into my lungs.

He is gone. Controlled by the simulation, he will now murder the people he called innocent not three minutes ago. Jeanine killing him would have hurt less than this.

"The advantage to this version of the simulation," she says, her eyes alight, "is that he can act independently, and is therefore far more effective than a mindless soldier." She looks at the guards who hold Tobias back. He struggles against them, his muscles taut, his eyes focused on me, but not seeing me, not seeing me the way they used to. "Send him to the control room. We'll want a sentient being there to monitor things and, as I understand it, he used to work there."

Jeanine presses her palms together in front of her. "And take *her* to room B13," she says. She flaps her hand to dismiss me. That flapping hand commands my execution, but to her it is just crossing off an item from a list of tasks, the only logical progression of the particular path that she is on. She surveys me without feeling as two Dauntless soldiers pull me out of the room.

They drag me down the hallway. I feel numb inside, but outside I am a screaming, thrashing force of will. I bite a hand that belongs to the Dauntless man on my right and smile as I taste blood. Then he hits me, and there is nothing.

CHAPTER
THIRTY-FIVE

I WAKE IN the dark, wedged in a hard corner. The floor beneath me is smooth and cold. I touch my throbbing head and liquid slips across my fingertips. Red—blood. When I bring my hand back down, my elbow hits a wall. Where am I?

A light flickers above me. The bulb is blue and dim when it's lit. I see the walls of a tank around me, and my shadowed reflection across from me. The room is small, with concrete walls and no windows, and I am alone in it. Well, almost—a small video camera is attached to one of the concrete walls.

I see a small opening near my feet. Connected to it is a tube, and connected to the tube, in the corner of the room, is a huge tank.

The trembling starts in my fingertips and spreads up my arms, and soon my body is shuddering.

I'm not in a simulation this time.

My right arm is numb. When I push myself out of the corner, I see a pool of blood where I was sitting. I can't panic now. I stand, leaning against a wall, and breathe. The worst thing that can happen to me now is that I drown in this tank. I press my forehead to the glass and laugh. That is the worst thing I can imagine. My laugh turns into a sob.

If I refuse to give up now, it will look brave to whoever watches me with that camera, but sometimes it isn't fighting that's brave, it's facing the death you know is coming. I sob into the glass. I'm not afraid of dying, but I want to die a different way, any other way.

It is better to scream than cry, so I scream and slam my heel into the wall behind me. My foot bounces off, and I kick again, so hard my heel throbs. I kick again and again and again, then pull back and throw my left shoulder into the wall. The impact makes the wound in my right shoulder burn like it got stuck with a hot poker.

Water trickles into the bottom of the tank.

The video camera means they're watching me—no, studying me, as only the Erudite would. To see if my reaction in reality matches my reaction in the simulation. To prove that I'm a coward.

I uncurl my fists and drop my hands. I am not a coward. I lift my head and stare at the camera across from me. If I focus on breathing, I can forget that I'm about to die. I stare at the camera until my vision narrows and it is all I see. Water tickles my ankles, then my calves, then my thighs. It rises over my fingertips. I breathe in; I breathe out. The water is soft and feels like silk.

I breathe in. The water will wash my wounds clean. I breathe out. My mother submerged me in water when I was a baby, to give me to God. It has been a long time since I thought about God, but I think about him now. It is only natural. I am glad, suddenly, that I shot Eric in the foot instead of the head.

My body rises with the water. Instead of kicking my feet to stay abreast of it, I push all the air from my lungs and sink to the bottom. The water muffles my ears. I feel its movement over my face. I think about snorting the water into my lungs so it kills me faster, but I can't bring myself to do it. I blow bubbles from my mouth.

Relax. I close my eyes. My lungs burn.

I let my hands float up to the top of the tank. I let the water fold me in its silken arms.

When I was young, my father used to hold me over his head and run with me so I felt like I was flying. I remember how the air felt, gliding over my body, and I am not afraid. I open my eyes.

A dark figure stands in front of me. I must be close to death if I'm seeing things. Pain stabs my lungs. Suffocating is painful. A palm presses to the glass in front of my face, and for a moment as I stare through the water, I think I see my mother's blurry face.

I hear a bang, and the glass cracks. Water sprays out a hole near the top of the tank, and the pane cracks in half. I turn away as the glass shatters, and the force of the water throws my body at the ground. I gasp, swallowing water as well as air, and cough, and gasp again, and hands close around my arms, and I hear her voice.

"Beatrice," she says. "Beatrice, we have to run."

She pulls my arm across her shoulders and hauls me to my feet. She is dressed like my mother and she looks like my mother, but she is holding a gun, and the determined look in her eyes is unfamiliar to me. I stumble beside her over broken glass and through water and out an open doorway. Dauntless guards lie dead next to the door.

My feet slip and slide on the tile as we walk down the hallway, as fast as my weak legs can muster. When we turn the corner, she fires at the two guards standing by the door at the end. The bullets hit them both in the head, and they slump to the floor. She pushes me against the wall and takes off her gray jacket.

She wears a sleeveless shirt. When she lifts her arm, I see the corner of a tattoo under her armpit. No wonder she never changed clothes in front of me.

"Mom," I say, my voice strained. "You were Dauntless."

"Yes," she says, smiling. She makes her jacket into a sling for my arm, tying the sleeves around my neck. "And it has served me well today. Your father and Caleb and some others are hiding in a basement at the intersection of North and Fairfield. We have to go get them."

I stare at her. I sat next to her at the kitchen table, twice a day, for sixteen years, and never once did I consider the possibility that she could have been anything but Abnegation-born. How well did I actually know my mother?

"There will be time for questions," she says. She lifts her shirt and slips a gun from under the waistband of her pants, offering it to me. Then she touches my cheek. "Now we must go."

She runs to the end of the hallway, and I run after her.

We are in the basement of Abnegation headquarters. My mother has worked there for as long as I can remember, so I'm not surprised when she leads me down a few dark hallways, up a dank staircase, and into daylight again without interference. How many Dauntless guards did she shoot before she found me?

"How did you know to find me?" I say.

"I've been watching the trains since the attacks started," she replies, glancing over her shoulder at me. "I didn't know what I would do when I found you. But it was always my intention to save you."

My throat feels tight. "But I betrayed you. I left you."

"You're my daughter. I don't care about the factions." She shakes her head. "Look where they got us. Human beings as a whole cannot be good for long before the bad creeps back in and poisons us again."

She stops where the alley intersects with the road.

I know now isn't the time for conversation. But there is something I need to know.

"Mom, how do you know about Divergence?" I ask. "What is it? Why . . ."

She pushes the bullet chamber open and peers inside. Seeing how many bullets she has left. Then takes a few out of her pocket and reloads. I recognize her expression as the one she wears when she threads a needle.

"I know about them because I am one," she says as she shoves a bullet in place. "I was only safe because my mother was a Dauntless leader. On Choosing Day, she told me to leave my faction and find a safer one. I chose Abnegation." She puts an extra bullet in her pocket and stands up straighter. "But I wanted you to make the choice on your own."

"I don't understand why we're such a threat to the leaders."

"Every faction conditions its members to think and act a certain way. And most people do it. For most people, it's not hard to learn, to find a pattern of thought that works and stay that way." She touches my uninjured shoulder and smiles. "But our minds move in a dozen different directions. We can't be confined to one way of thinking, and that terrifies our leaders. It means we can't be controlled. And it means that no matter what they do, we will always cause trouble for them."

I feel like someone breathed new air into my lungs. I am not Abnegation. I am not Dauntless.

I am Divergent.

And I can't be controlled.

"Here they come," she says, looking around the corner. I peek over her shoulder and see a few Dauntless with guns, moving to the same beat, heading toward us. My mother looks back. Far behind us, another group of Dauntless run down the alley, toward us, moving in time with one another.

She grabs my hands and looks me in the eyes. I watch her long eyelashes move as she blinks. I wish I had something of hers in my small, plain face. But at least I have something of hers in my brain.

"Go to your father and brother. The alley on the right, down to the basement. Knock twice, then three times, then six times." She cups my cheeks. Her hands are cold; her palms are rough. "I'm going to distract them. You have to run as fast as you can."

"No." I shake my head. "I'm not going anywhere without you."

She smiles. "Be brave, Beatrice. I love you."

I feel her lips on my forehead and then she runs into the middle of the street. She holds her gun above her head and fires three times into the air. The Dauntless start running.

I sprint across the street and into the alley. As I run, I look over my shoulder to see if any Dauntless follow me. But my mother fires into the crowd of guards, and they are too focused on her to notice me.

I whip my head over my shoulder when I hear them fire back. My feet falter and stop.

My mother stiffens, her back arching. Blood surges from a wound in her abdomen, dyeing her shirt crimson. A patch of blood spreads over her shoulder. I blink, and the violent red stains the inside of my eyelids. I blink again, and I see her smile as she sweeps my hair trimmings into a pile.

She falls, first to her knees, her hands limp at her sides, and then to the pavement, slumped to the side like a rag doll. She is motionless and without breath.

I clamp my hand over my mouth and scream into my palm. My cheeks are hot and wet with tears I didn't feel beginning. My blood cries out that it belongs to her, and struggles to return to her, and I hear her words in my mind as I run, telling me to be brave.

Pain stabs through me as everything I am made of collapses, my entire world dismantled in a moment. The pavement scrapes my knees. If I lie down now, this can all be done. Maybe Eric was right, and choosing death is like exploring an unknown, uncertain place.

I feel Tobias brushing my hair back before the first simulation. I hear him telling me to be brave. I hear my mother telling me to be brave.

The Dauntless soldiers turn as if moved by the same mind. Somehow I get up and start running.

I am brave.

CHAPTER
THIRTY-SIX

THREE DAUNTLESS SOLDIERS pursue me. They run in unison, their foot-steps echoing in the alley. One of them fires, and I dive, scraping my palms on the ground. The bullet hits the brick wall to my right, and pieces of brick spray everywhere. I throw myself around the corner and click a bullet into the chamber of my gun.

They killed my mother. I point the gun into the alley and fire blindly. It wasn't really them, but it doesn't matter—can't matter, and just like death itself, can't be real right now.

Just one set of footsteps now. I hold the gun out with both hands and stand at the end of the alley, pointing at the Dauntless soldier. My finger squeezes the trigger, but not hard enough to fire. The man running to-ward me is not a man, he is a boy. A shaggy-haired boy with a crease be-tween his eyebrows.

Will. Dull-eyed and mindless, but still Will. He stops running and mirrors me, his feet planted and his gun up. In an instant, I see his fin-ger poised over the trigger and hear the bullet slide into the chamber, and I fire. My eyes squeezed shut. Can't breathe.

The bullet hit him in the head. I know because that's where I aimed it.

I turn around without opening my eyes and stumble away from the alley. North and Fairfield. I have to look at the street sign to see where I am, but I can't read it; my vision is blurred. I blink a few times. I stand just yards away from the building that contains what's left of my family.

I kneel next to the door. Tobias would call me unwise to make any noise. Noise might attract Dauntless soldiers.

I press my forehead to the wall and scream. After a few seconds I clamp my hand over my mouth to muffle the sound and scream again, a scream that turns into a sob. The gun clatters to the ground. I still see Will.

He smiles in my memory. A curled lip. Straight teeth. Light in his eyes. Laughing, teasing, more alive in memory than I am in reality. It was him or me. I chose me. But I feel dead too.

+ + +

I pound on the door—twice, then three times, then six times, as my mother told me to.

I wipe the tears from my face. This is the first time I will see my father since I left him, and I don't want him to see me half-collapsed and sobbing.

The door opens, and Caleb stands in the doorway. The sight of him stuns me. He stares at me for a few seconds and then throws his arms around me, his hand pressing to the wound in my shoulder. I bite my lip to keep from crying out, but a groan escapes me anyway, and Caleb yanks back.

"Beatrice. Oh God, are you shot?"

"Let's go inside," I say weakly.

He drags his thumb under his eyes, catching the moisture. The door falls shut behind us.

The room is dimly lit, but I see familiar faces, former neighbors and classmates and my father's coworkers. My father, who stares at me like I've grown a second head. Marcus. The sight of him makes me ache—Tobias . . .

No. I will not do that; I will not think of him.

"How did you know about this place?" Caleb says. "Did Mom find you?"

I nod. I don't want to think about Mom, either.

"My shoulder," I say.

Now that I am safe, the adrenaline that propelled me here is fading, and the pain is getting worse. I sink to my knees. Water drips from my clothes onto the cement floor. A sob rises within me, desperate for release, and I choke it back.

A woman named Tessa who lived down the street from us rolls out a pallet. She was married to a council member, but I don't see him here. He is probably dead.

Someone else carries a lamp from one corner to the other so we have light. Caleb produces a first-aid kit, and Susan brings me a bottle of water. There is no better place to need help than a room full of members of Abnegation. I glance at Caleb. He's wearing gray again. Seeing him in the Erudite compound feels like a dream now.

My father comes to me, lifts my arm across his shoulders, and helps me across the room.

"Why are you wet?" Caleb says.

"They tried to drown me," I say. "Why are you here?"

"I did what you said—what Mom said. I researched the simulation serum and found out that Jeanine was working to develop long-range transmitters for the serum so its signal could stretch farther, which led me to information about Erudite and Dauntless . . . anyway, I dropped out of initiation when I figured out what was happening. I would have warned you, but it was too late," he says. "I'm factionless now."

"No, you aren't," my father says sternly. "You're with us."

I kneel on the pallet and Caleb cuts a piece of my shirt away from my shoulder with a pair of medical scissors. Caleb peels the square of fabric away, revealing first the Abnegation tattoo on my right shoulder and second, the three birds on my collarbone. Caleb and my father stare at both tattoos with the same look of fascination and shock but say nothing about them.

I lie on my stomach. Caleb squeezes my palm as my father gets the antiseptic from the first aid kit.

"Have you ever taken a bullet out of someone before?" I ask, a shaky laugh in my voice.

"The things I know how to do might surprise you," he replies.

A lot of things about my parents might surprise me. I think of Mom's tattoo and bite my lip.

"This will hurt," he says.

I don't see the knife go in, but I feel it. Pain spreads through my body and I scream through gritted teeth, crushing Caleb's hand. Over the screaming, I hear my father ask me to relax my back. Tears run from the corners of my eyes and I do as he tells me. The pain starts again, and I feel the knife moving under my skin, and I am still screaming.

"Got it," he says. He drops something on the floor with a *ding*.

Caleb looks at my father and then at me, and then he laughs. I haven't heard him laugh in so long that the sound makes me cry.

"What's so funny?" I say, sniffling.

"I never thought I would see us together again," he says.

My father cleans the skin around my wound with something cold. "Stitching time," he says.

I nod. He threads the needle like he's done it a thousand times.

"One," he says, "two . . . *three.*"

I clench my jaw and stay quiet this time. Of all the pain I have suffered today—the pain of getting shot and almost drowning and taking the bullet out again, the pain of finding and losing my mother and Tobias, this is the easiest to bear.

My father finishes stitching my wound, ties off the thread, and covers the stitches with a bandage. Caleb helps me sit up and separates the hems of his two shirts, pulling the long-sleeved one over his head and offering it to me.

My father helps me guide my right arm through the shirt sleeve, and I pull the rest over my head. It is baggy and smells fresh, smells like Caleb.

"So," my father says quietly. "Where is your mother?"

I look down. I don't want to deliver this news. I don't want to have this news to begin with.

"She's gone," I say. "She saved me."

Caleb closes his eyes and takes a deep breath.

My father looks momentarily stricken and then recovers himself, averting his glistening eyes and nodding.

"That is good," he says, sounding strained. "A good death."

If I speak right now, I will break down, and I can't afford to do that. So I just nod.

Eric called Al's suicide brave, and he was wrong. My mother's death was brave. I remember how calm she was, how determined. It isn't just brave that she died for me; it is brave that she did it without announcing it, without hesitation, and without appearing to consider another option.

He helps me to my feet. Time to face the rest of the room. My mother told me to save them. Because of that, and because I am Dauntless, it's my duty to lead now. I have no idea how to bear that burden.

Marcus gets up. A vision of him whipping my arm with a belt rushes into my mind when I see him, and my chest squeezes.

"We are only safe here for so long," Marcus says eventually. "We need to get out of the city. Our best option is to go to the Amity compound in the hope that they'll take us in. Do you know anything about the Dauntless strategy, Beatrice? Will they stop fighting at night?"

"It's not Dauntless strategy," I say. "This whole thing is masterminded by the Erudite. And it's not like they're giving orders."

"Not giving orders," my father says. "What do you mean?"

"I mean," I say, "ninety percent of the Dauntless are sleepwalking right now. They're in a simulation and they don't know what they're doing. The only reason I'm not just like them is that I'm . . ." I hesitate on the word. "The mind control doesn't affect me."

"Mind control? So they don't know that they're killing people right now?" my father asks me, his eyes wide.

"No."

"That's . . . awful." Marcus shakes his head. His sympathetic tone sounds manufactured to me. "Waking up and realizing what you've done . . ."

The room goes quiet, probably as all the Abnegation imagine themselves in the place of the Dauntless soldiers, and that's when it occurs to me.

"We have to wake them up," I say.

"What?" Marcus says.

"If we wake the Dauntless up, they will probably revolt when they realize what's going on," I explain. "The Erudite won't have an army. The Abnegation will stop dying. This will be over."

"It won't be that simple," my father says. "Even without the Dauntless helping them, the Erudite will find another way to—"

"And how are we supposed to wake them up?" Marcus says.

"We find the computers that control the simulation and destroy the data," I say. "The program. Everything."

"Easier said than done," Caleb says. "It could be anywhere. We can't just appear at the Erudite compound and start poking around."

"It's . . ." I frown. Jeanine. Jeanine was talking about something important when Tobias and I came into her office, important enough to hang up on someone. *You can't just leave it undefended.* And then, when she was sending Tobias away: *Send him to the control room.* The control room where Tobias used to work. With the Dauntless security monitors. And the Dauntless computers.

"It's at Dauntless headquarters," I say. "It makes sense. That's where all the data about the Dauntless is stored, so why not control them from there?"

I faintly register that I said *them.* As of yesterday, I technically became Dauntless, but I don't feel like one. And I am not Abnegation, either.

I guess I am what I've always been. Not Dauntless, not Abnegation, not factionless. Divergent.

"Are you sure?" my father asks.

"It's an informed guess," I say, "and it's the best theory I have."

"Then we'll have to decide who goes and who continues on to Amity," he says. "What kind of help do you need, Beatrice?"

The question stuns me, as does the expression he wears. He looks at me like I'm a peer. He speaks to me like I'm a peer. Either he has accepted that I am an adult now, or he has accepted that I am no longer his daughter. The latter is more likely, and more painful.

"Anyone who can and will fire a gun," I say, "and isn't afraid of heights."

CHAPTER
THIRTY-SEVEN

ERUDITE AND DAUNTLESS forces are concentrated in the Abnegation sector of the city, so as long as we run away from the Abnegation sector, we are less likely to encounter difficulty.

I didn't get to decide who is coming with me. Caleb was the obvious choice, since he knows the most about the Erudite plan. Marcus insisted that he go, despite my protests, because he is good with computers. And my father acted like his place was assumed from the beginning.

I watch the others run in the opposite direction—toward safety, toward Amity—for a few seconds, and then I turn away, toward the city, toward the war. We stand next to the railroad tracks, which will carry us into danger.

"What time is it?" I ask Caleb.

He checks his watch. "Three twelve."

"Should be here any second," I say.

"Will it stop?" he asks.

I shake my head. "It goes slowly through the city. We'll run next to the car for a few feet and then climb inside."

Jumping on trains seems easy to me now, natural. It won't be as easy for the rest of them, but we can't stop now. I look over my left shoulder and see the headlights burning gold against the gray buildings and roads. I bounce on the balls of my feet as the lights grow larger and larger, and then the front of the train glides past me, and I start jogging. When I see an open car, I pick up my pace to keep stride with it and grab the handle on the left, swinging myself inside.

Caleb jumps, landing hard and rolling on his side to get in, and he helps Marcus. My father lands on his stomach, pulling his legs in behind him. They move away from the doorway, but I stand on the edge with one hand on a handle, watching the city pass.

If I were Jeanine, I would send the majority of Dauntless soldiers to the Dauntless entrance above the Pit, outside the glass building. It would be smarter to go in the back entrance, the one that requires jumping off a building.

"I assume you now regret choosing Dauntless," Marcus says.

I am surprised my father didn't ask that question, but he, like me, is watching the city. The train passes the Erudite compound, which is dark now. It looks peaceful from a distance, and inside those walls, it probably is peaceful. Far removed from the conflict and the reality of what they have done.

I shake my head.

"Not even after your faction's leaders decided to join in a plot to overthrow the government?" Marcus spits.

"There were some things I needed to learn."

"How to be brave?" my father says quietly.

"How to be selfless," I say. "Often they're the same thing."

"Is that why you got Abnegation's symbol tattooed on your shoulder?" Caleb asks. I am almost sure that I see a smile in my father's eyes.

I smile faintly back and nod. "And Dauntless on the other."

+ + +

The glass building above the Pit reflects sunlight into my eyes. I stand, holding the handle next to the door for balance. Almost there.

"When I tell you to jump," I say, "you jump, as far as you can."

"Jump?" Caleb asks. "We're seven stories up, Tris."

"Onto a roof," I add. Seeing the stunned look on his face, I say, "That's why they call it a test of bravery."

Half of bravery is perspective. The first time I did this, it was one of the hardest things I had ever done. Now, preparing to jump off a moving train is nothing, because I have done more difficult things in the past few weeks than most people will in a lifetime. And yet none of it compares to what I am about to do in the Dauntless compound. If I survive, I will undoubtedly go on to do far more difficult things than even that, like live without a faction, something I never imagined possible.

"Dad, you go," I say, stepping back so he can stand by the edge. If he and Marcus go first, I can time it so they have to jump the shortest distance. Hopefully Caleb and I can jump far enough to make it, because we're younger. It's a chance I have to take.

The train tracks curve, and when they line up with the edge of the roof, I shout, "Jump!"

My father bends his knees and launches himself forward. I don't wait to see if he makes it. I shove Marcus forward and shout, "Jump!"

My father lands on the roof, so close to the edge that I gasp. He sits down on the gravel, and I push Caleb in front of me. He stands at the edge of the train car and jumps without me having to tell him to. I take a few steps back to give myself a running start and leap out of the car just as the train reaches the end of the roof.

For an instant I am suspended in nothingness, and then my feet slam into cement and I stumble to the side, away from the roof's edge. My knees ache, and the impact shudders through my body, making my shoulder throb. I sit down, breathing hard, and look across the rooftop. Caleb and my father stand at the edge of the roof, their hands around Marcus's arms. He didn't make it, but he hasn't fallen yet.

Somewhere inside me, a vicious voice chants: *fall, fall, fall.*

But he doesn't. My father and Caleb haul him onto the roof. I stand up, brushing gravel off my pants. The thought of what comes next has me preoccupied. It is one thing to ask people to jump off a train, but a roof?

"This next part is why I asked about fear of heights," I say, walking to the edge of the roof. I hear their shuffling footsteps behind me and step onto the ledge. Wind rushes up the side of the building and lifts my shirt from my skin. I stare down at the hole in the ground, seven stories below me, and then close my eyes as the air blows over my face.

"There's a net at the bottom," I say, looking over my shoulder. They look confused. They haven't figured out what I am asking them to do yet.

"Don't think," I say. "Just jump."

I turn, and as I turn, I lean back, compromising my balance. I drop like a stone, my eyes closed, one arm outstretched to feel the wind. I relax my muscles as much as I can before I hit the net, which feels like a slab of cement hitting my shoulder. I grit my teeth and roll to the edge, grabbing the pole that supports the net, and swing my leg over the side. I land on my knees on the platform, my eyes blurry with tears.

Caleb yelps as the net curls around his body and then straightens. I stand with some difficulty.

"Caleb!" I hiss. "Over here!"

Breathing heavily, Caleb crawls to the side of the net and drops over the edge, hitting the platform hard. Wincing, he pushes himself to his feet and stares at me, his mouth open.

"How many times . . . have you . . . done that?" he asks between breaths.

"Twice now," I say.

He shakes his head.

When my father hits the net, Caleb helps him across. When he stands on the platform, he leans and vomits over the side. I descend the stairs, and when I get to the bottom, I hear Marcus hit the net with a groan.

The cavern is empty and the hallways stretch into darkness.

Jeanine made it sound like there was no one left in the Dauntless compound except the soldiers she sent back to guard the computers. If we can find Dauntless soldiers, we can find the computers. I look over my shoulder. Marcus stands on the platform, white as a sheet but unharmed.

"So this is the Dauntless compound," says Marcus.

"Yes," I say. "And?"

"And I never thought I would get to see it," he replies, his hand skimming a wall. "No need to be so defensive, Beatrice."

I never noticed how cold his eyes were before.

"Do you have a plan, Beatrice?" my father says.

"Yes." And it's true. I do, though I'm not sure when I developed it.

I'm also not sure it will work. I can count on a few things: There aren't many Dauntless in the compound, the Dauntless aren't known for their subtlety, and I'll do anything to stop them.

We walk down the hallway that leads to the Pit, which is striped with light every ten feet. When we walk into the first patch of light, I hear a gunshot and drop to the ground. Someone must have seen us. I crawl into the next dark patch. The spark from the gun flashed across the room by the door that leads to the Pit.

"Everyone okay?" I ask.

"Yes," my father says.

"Stay here, then."

I run to the side of the room. The lights protrude from the wall, so directly beneath each one is a slit of shadow. I am small enough to hide in it, if I turn to the side. I can creep along the edge of the room and surprise whatever guard is shooting at us before he gets the chance to fire a bullet into my brain. Maybe.

One of the things I thank Dauntless for is the preparedness that eliminates my fear.

"Whoever's there," a voice shouts, "surrender your weapons and put your hands up!"

I turn to the side and press my back to the stone wall. I shuffle quickly sideways, one foot crossing over the other, squinting to see through the semidarkness. Another gunshot fires into silence. I reach the last light and stand for a moment in shadow, letting my eyes adjust.

I can't win a fight, but if I can move fast enough, I won't have to fight. My footsteps light, I walk toward the guard who stands by the door. A few yards away, I realize that I *know* that dark hair that always gleams, even in relative darkness, and that long nose with a narrow bridge.

It's Peter.

Cold slips over my skin and around my heart and into the pit of my stomach.

His face is tense—he isn't a sleepwalker. He looks around, but his eyes search the air above me and beyond me. Judging by his silence, he does not intend to negotiate with us; he will kill us without question.

I lick my lips, sprint the last few steps, and thrust the heel of my hand up. The blow connects with his nose, and he shouts, bringing both hands up to cover his face. My body jolts with nervous energy and as his eyes squint, I kick him in the groin. He drops to his knees, his gun clattering to the ground. I grab it and press the barrel to the top of his head.

"How are you awake?" I demand.

He lifts his head, and I click the bullet into its chamber, raising an eyebrow at him.

"The Dauntless leaders . . . they evaluated my records and removed me from the simulation," he says.

"Because they figured out that you already have murderous tendencies and wouldn't mind killing a few hundred people while conscious," I say. "Makes sense."

"I'm not . . . murderous!"

"I never knew a Candor who was such a liar." I tap the gun against his skull. "Where are the computers that control the simulation, Peter?"

"You won't shoot me."

"People tend to overestimate my character," I say quietly. "They think that because I'm small, or a girl, or a Stiff, I can't possibly be cruel. But they're wrong."

I shift the gun three inches to the left and fire at his arm.

His screams fill the hallway. Blood spurts from the wound, and he screams again, pressing his forehead to the ground. I shift the gun back to his head, ignoring the pang of guilt in my chest.

"Now that you realize your mistake," I say, "I will give you another chance to tell me what I need to know before I shoot you somewhere worse."

Another thing I can count on: Peter is not selfless.

He turns his head and focuses a bright eye on me. His teeth close over his lower lip, and his breaths shake on the way out. And on the way in. And on the way out again.

"They're listening," he spits. "If you don't kill me, they will. The only way I'll tell you is if you get me out of here."

"What?"

"Take me . . . *ahh* . . . with you," he says, wincing.

"You want me to take *you*," I say, "the person who tried to kill me . . . *with* me?"

"I do," he groans. "If you expect to find out what you need to know."

It feels like a choice, but it isn't. Every minute that I waste staring at Peter, thinking about how he haunts my nightmares and the damage he did to me, another dozen Abnegation members die at the hands of the brain-dead Dauntless army.

"Fine," I say, almost choking on the word. "Fine."

I hear footsteps behind me. Holding the gun steady, I look over my shoulder. My father and the others walk toward us.

My father takes off his long-sleeved shirt. He wears a gray T-shirt beneath it. He crouches next to Peter and loops the fabric around his arm, tying it tightly. As he presses the fabric to the blood running down Peter's arm, he looks up at me and says, "Was it really necessary to shoot him?"

I don't answer.

"Sometimes pain is for the greater good," says Marcus calmly.

In my head, I see him standing before Tobias with a belt in hand and hear his voice echo. *This is for your own good.* I look at him for a few seconds. Does he really believe that? It sounds like something the Dauntless would say.

"Let's go," I say. "Get up, Peter."

"You want him to *walk*?" Caleb demands. "Are you insane?"

"Did I shoot him in the leg?" I say. "No. He walks. Where do we go, Peter?"

Caleb helps Peter to his feet.

"The glass building," he says, wincing. "Eighth floor."

He leads the way through the door.

I walk into the roar of the river and the blue glow of the Pit, which is emptier now than I have ever seen it before. I scan the walls, searching for signs of life, but I see no movement and no figures standing in darkness. I keep my gun in hand and start toward the path that leads to the glass ceiling. The emptiness makes me shiver. It reminds me of the endless field in my crow nightmares.

"What makes you think you have the right to shoot someone?" my father says as he follows me up the path. We pass the tattoo place. Where is Tori now? And Christina?

"Now isn't the time for debates about ethics," I say.

"Now is the perfect time," he says, "because you will soon get the opportunity to shoot someone again, and if you don't realize—"

"Realize what?" I say without turning around. "That every second I waste means another Abnegation dead and another Dauntless made into a murderer? I've realized that. Now it's your turn."

"There is a right way to do things."

"What makes you so sure that you know what it is?" I say.

"Please stop fighting," Caleb interrupts, his voice chiding. "We have more important things to do right now."

I keep climbing, my cheeks hot. A few months ago I would not have dared to snap at my father. A few hours ago I might not have done it either. But something changed when they shot my mother. When they took Tobias.

I hear my father huff and puff over the sound of rushing water. I forgot that he is older than I am, that his frame can no longer tolerate the weight of his body.

Before I ascend the metal stairs that will carry me above the glass ceiling, I wait in darkness and watch the light cast on the Pit walls by the sun. I watch until a shadow shifts over the sunlit wall and count until the next shadow appears. The guards make their rounds every minute and a half, stand for twenty seconds, and then move on.

"There are men with guns up there. When they see me, they will kill me, if they can," I tell my father quietly. I search his eyes. "Should I let them?"

He stares at me for a few seconds.

"Go," he says, "and God help you."

I climb the stairs carefully, stopping just before my head emerges. I wait, watching the shadows move, and when one of them stops, I step up, point my gun, and shoot.

The bullet does not hit the guard. It shatters the window behind him. I fire again and duck as bullets hit the floor around me with a ding. Thank God the glass ceiling is bulletproof, or the glass would break and I would fall to my death.

One guard down. I breathe deeply and put just my hand over the ceiling, looking through the glass to see my target. I tilt the gun back and fire at the guard running toward me. The bullet hits him in the arm. Luckily it is his shooting arm, because he drops his gun and it skids across the floor.

My body shaking, I launch myself through the hole in the ceiling and snatch the fallen gun before he can get to it. A bullet whizzes past my head, so close to hitting me that it moves my hair. Eyes wide, I fling my right arm over my shoulder, forcing a searing pain through my body, and fire three times behind me. By some miracle, one of the bullets hits a guard, and my eyes water uncontrollably from the pain in my shoulder. I just ripped my stitches. I'm sure of it.

Another guard stands across from me. I lie flat on my stomach and point both guns at him, my arms resting on the floor. I stare into the black pinprick that is his gun barrel.

Then something surprising happens. He jerks his chin to the side. Telling me to go.

He must be Divergent.

"All clear!" I shout.

The guard ducks into the fear landscape room, and he's gone.

Slowly I get to my feet, holding my right arm against my chest. I have tunnel vision. I am running along this path and I will not be able to stop, will not be able to think of anything, until I reach the end.

I hand one gun to Caleb and slide the other one under my belt.

"I think you and Marcus should stay here with *him*," I say, jerking my head toward Peter. "He'll just slow us down. Make sure no one comes after us."

I hope he doesn't understand what I'm doing—keeping him here so he stays safe, even though he would gladly give his life for this. If I go up into the building, I probably won't come back down. The best I can hope for is to destroy the simulation before someone kills me. When did I decide on this suicide mission? Why wasn't it more difficult?

"I can't stay here while you go up there and risk your life," says Caleb.

"I need you to," I say.

Peter sinks to his knees. His face glistens with sweat. For a second I almost feel bad for him, but then I remember Edward, and the itch of fabric over my eyes as my attackers blindfolded me, and my sympathy is lost to hatred. Caleb eventually nods.

I approach one of the fallen guards and take his gun, keeping my eyes away from the injury that killed him. My head pounds. I haven't eaten; I haven't slept; I haven't sobbed or screamed or even paused for a moment. I bite my lip and push myself toward the elevators on the right side of the room. Level eight.

Once the elevator doors close, I lean the side of my head against the glass and listen to the beeps.

I glance at my father.

"Thank you. For protecting Caleb," my father says. "Beatrice, I—"

The elevator reaches the eighth floor and the doors open. Two guards stand ready with guns in hand, their faces blank. My eyes widen, and I drop to my belly on the ground as the shots go off. I hear bullets strike glass. The guards slump to the ground, one alive and groaning, the other fading fast. My father stands above them, his gun still held out from his body.

I stumble to my feet. Guards run down the hallway on the left. Judging by the synchronicity of their footsteps, they are controlled by the simulation. I could run down the right hallway, but if the guards came from the left hallway, that's where the computers are. I drop to the ground between the guards my father just shot and lie as still as I can.

My father jumps out of the elevator and sprints down the right hallway, drawing the Dauntless guards after him. I clap my hand over my mouth to keep from screaming at him. That hallway will end.

I try to bury my head so I don't see it, but I can't. I peer over the fallen guard's back. My father fires over his shoulder at the guards pursuing him, but he is not fast enough. One of them fires at his stomach, and he groans so loud I can almost feel it in my chest.

He clutches his gut, his shoulders hitting the wall, and fires again. And again. The guards are under the simulation; they keep moving even when the bullets hit them, keep moving until their hearts stop, but they don't reach my father. Blood spills over his hand and the color drains from his face. Another shot and the last guard is down.

"Dad," I say. I mean for it to be a shout, but it is just a wheeze.

He slumps to the ground. Our eyes meet like the yards between us are nothing.

His mouth opens like he's about to say something, but then his chin drops to his chest and his body relaxes.

My eyes burn and I am too weak to rise; the scent of sweat and blood makes me feel sick. I want to rest my head on the ground and let that be the end of it. I want to sleep now and never wake.

But what I said to my father before was right—for every second that I waste, another Abnegation member dies. There is only one thing left for me in the world now, and it is to destroy the simulation.

I push myself up and run down the hallway, turning right at the end. There is only one door ahead. I open it.

The opposite wall is made up entirely of screens, each a foot tall and a foot wide. There are dozens of them, each one showing a different part of the city. The fence. The Hub. The streets in the Abnegation sector, now crawling with Dauntless soldiers. The ground level of the building below us, where Caleb, Marcus, and Peter wait for me to return. It is a wall of everything I have ever seen, everything I have ever known.

One of the screens has a line of code on it instead of an image. It breezes past faster than I can read. It is the simulation, the code already compiled, a complicated list of commands that anticipate and address a thousand different outcomes.

In front of the screen is a chair and a desk. Sitting in the chair is a Dauntless soldier.

"Tobias," I say.

CHAPTER
THIRTY-EIGHT

TOBIAS'S HEAD TURNS, and his dark eyes shift to me. His eyebrows draw in. He stands. He looks confused. He raises his gun.

"Drop your weapon," he says.

"Tobias," I say, "you're in a simulation."

"Drop your weapon," he repeats. "Or I'll fire."

Jeanine said he didn't know me. Jeanine also said that the simulation made Tobias's friends into enemies. He will shoot me if he has to.

I set my gun down at my feet.

"Drop your weapon!" shouts Tobias.

"I did," I say. A little voice in my head sings that he can't hear me, he can't see me, he doesn't know me. Tongues of flame press behind my eyes. I can't just stand here and let him shoot me.

I run at him, grabbing his wrist. I feel his muscles shift as he pinches the trigger and duck my head just in time. The bullet hits the wall behind me. Gasping, I kick him in the ribs and twist his wrist to the side as hard as I can. He drops the gun.

I can't beat Tobias in a fight. I know that already. But I have to destroy the computer. I dive for the gun, but before I can touch it, he grabs me and wrenches me to the side.

I stare into his dark, conflicted eyes for an instant before he punches me in the jaw. My head jerks to the side and I cringe away from him, flinging my hands up to protect my face. I can't fall; I can't fall or he'll kick me, and that will be worse, that will be much worse. I kick the gun back with my heel so he can't grab it and, ignoring the throbbing in my jaw, kick him in the stomach.

He catches my foot and pulls me down so I fall on my shoulder. The pain makes my vision go black at the edges. I stare up at him. He pulls his foot back like he's about to kick me, and I roll onto my knees, stretching my arm out for the gun. I don't know what I'll do with it. I can't shoot him, I can't shoot him, I can't. He is in there somewhere.

He grabs me by my hair and yanks me to the side. I reach back and grab his wrist, but he's too strong and my forehead smacks into the wall.

He is in there somewhere.

"Tobias," I say.

Did his grip falter? I twist and kick back, my heel hitting him in the leg. When my hair slips through his fingers, I dive at the gun and my fingertips close around the cool metal. I flip over onto my back and point the gun at him.

"Tobias," I say. "I know you're in there somewhere."

But if he was, he probably wouldn't start toward me like he's about to kill me for certain this time.

My head throbs. I stand.

"Tobias, please." I am begging. I am pathetic. Tears make my face hot. "Please. See me." He walks toward me, his movements dangerous, fast, powerful. The gun shakes in my hands. "Please see me, Tobias, please!"

Even when he scowls, his eyes look thoughtful, and I remember how his mouth curled when he smiled.

I can't kill him. I am not sure if I love him; not sure if that's why. But I am sure of what he would do if our positions were reversed. I am sure that nothing is worth killing him for.

I have done this before—in my fear landscape, with the gun in my hand, a voice shouting at me to fire at the people I love. I volunteered to die instead, that time, but I can't imagine how that would help me now. But I just know, I *know* what the right thing to do is.

My father says—used to say—that there is power in self-sacrifice.

I turn the gun in my hands and press it into Tobias's palm.

He pushes the barrel into my forehead. My tears have stopped and the air feels cold as it touches my cheeks. I reach out and rest my hand on his chest so I can feel his heartbeat. At least his heartbeat is still him.

The bullet clicks into the chamber. Maybe it will be as easy to let him shoot me as it was in the fear landscape, as it is in my dreams. Maybe it will just be a bang, and the lights will lift, and I will find myself in another world. I stand still and wait.

Can I be forgiven for all I've done to get here?

I don't know. I don't know.

Please.

CHAPTER
THIRTY-NINE

THE SHOT DOESN'T COME. He stares at me with the same ferocity but doesn't move. Why doesn't he shoot me? His heart pounds against my palm, and my own heart lifts. He is Divergent. He can fight this simulation. Any simulation.

"Tobias," I say. "It's me."

I step forward and wrap my arms around him. His body is stiff. His heart beats faster. I can feel it against my cheek. A thud against my cheek. A thud as the gun hits the floor. He grabs my shoulders—too hard, his fingers digging into my skin where the bullet was. I cry out as he pulls me back. Maybe he means to kill me in some crueler way.

"Tris," he says, and it's him again. His mouth collides with mine.

His arm wraps around me and he lifts me up, holding me against him, his hands clutching at my back. His face and the back of his neck are slick with sweat, his body is shaking, and my shoulder blazes with pain, but I don't care, I don't care, I don't care.

He sets me down and stares at me, his fingers brushing over my forehead, my eyebrows, my cheeks, my lips.

Something like a sob and a sigh and a moan escapes him, and he kisses me again. His eyes are bright with tears. I never thought I would see Tobias cry. It makes me hurt.

I pull myself to his chest and cry into his shirt. All the throbbing in my head comes back, and the ache in my shoulder, and I feel like my body weight doubles. I lean against him, and he supports me.

"How did you do it?" I say.

"I don't know," he says. "I just heard your voice."

+ + +

After a few seconds, I remember why I'm here. I pull back and wipe my cheeks with the heels of my hands and turn toward the screens again. I see one that overlooks the drinking fountain. Tobias was so paranoid when I was railing against Dauntless there. He kept looking at the wall above the fountain. Now I know why.

Tobias and I stand there for a while, and I think I know what he's thinking, because I'm thinking it too: How can something so small control so many people?

"Was *I* running the simulation?" he says.

"I don't know if you were running it so much as monitoring it," I say. "It's already complete. I have no idea how, but Jeanine made it so it could work on its own."

He shakes his head. "It's . . . incredible. Terrible, evil . . . but incredible."

I see movement on one of the screens and see my brother, Marcus, and Peter standing on the first floor of the building. Surrounding them are Dauntless soldiers, all in black, all carrying weapons.

"Tobias," I say tersely. "Now!"

He runs to the computer screen and taps it a few times with his finger. I can't look at what he's doing. All I can see is my brother. He holds the gun I gave him straight out from his body, like he's ready to use it. I bite my lip. *Don't shoot.* Tobias presses the screen a few more times, typing in letters that make no sense to me. *Don't shoot.*

I see a flash of light—a spark, from one of the guns—and gasp. My brother and Marcus and Peter crouch on the ground with their arms over their heads. After a moment they all stir, so I know they're still alive, and the Dauntless soldiers advance. A cluster of black around my brother.

"Tobias," I say.

He presses the screen again, and everyone on the first floor goes still.

Their arms drop to their sides.

And then the Dauntless move. Their heads turn from side to side, and they drop their guns, and their mouths move like they're shouting, and they shove each other, and some of them sink to their knees, holding their heads and rocking back and forth, back and forth.

All the tension in my chest unravels, and I sit down, heaving a sigh.

Tobias crouches next to the computer and pulls the side of the case off. "I have to get the data," he says, "or they'll just start the simulation again."

I watch the frenzy on the screen. It is the same frenzy that must be happening on the streets. I scan the screens, one by one, looking for one that shows the Abnegation sector of the city. There is only one—it's at the far end of the room, on the bottom. The Dauntless on that screen are firing at one another, shoving one another, screaming—chaos. Black-clothed men and women drop to the ground. People sprint in every direction.

"Got it," says Tobias, holding up the computer's hard drive. It is a piece of metal about the size of his palm. He offers it to me, and I shove it in my back pocket.

"We have to leave," I say, getting to my feet. I point at the screen on the right.

"Yes, we do." He wraps his arm across my shoulders. "Come on."

We walk together down the hallway and around the corner. The elevator reminds me of my father. I can't stop myself from looking for his body.

It is on the floor next to the elevator, surrounded by the bodies of several guards. A strangled scream escapes me. I turn away. Bile leaps into my throat and I throw up against the wall.

For a second I feel like everything inside me is breaking, and I crouch by a body, breathing through my mouth so I don't smell the blood. I clamp my hand over my mouth to contain a sob. Five more seconds. Five seconds of weakness and then I get up. One, two. Three, four.

Five.

+ + +

I am not really aware of my surroundings. There is an elevator and a glass room and a rush of cold air. There is a shouting crowd of Dauntless soldiers dressed in black. I search for Caleb's face, but it is nowhere, nowhere until we leave the glass building and step out into sunlight.

Caleb runs to me when I walk through the doors, and I fall against him. He holds me tightly.

"Dad?" he says.

I just shake my head.

"Well," he says, almost choking on the word, "he would have wanted it that way."

Over Caleb's shoulder, I see Tobias stop in the middle of a footstep. His entire body goes rigid as his eyes focus on Marcus. In the rush to destroy the simulation, I forgot to warn him.

Marcus walks up to Tobias and wraps his arms around his son. Tobias stays frozen, his arms at his sides and his face blank. I watch his Adam's apple bob up and down and his eyes lift to the ceiling.

"Son," sighs Marcus.

Tobias winces.

"Hey," I say, pulling away from Caleb. I remember the belt stinging on my wrist in Tobias's fear landscape and slip into the space between them, pushing Marcus back. "Hey. Get away from him."

I feel Tobias's breaths against my neck; they come in sharp bursts.

"Stay away," I hiss.

"Beatrice, what are you doing?" asks Caleb.

"Tris," Tobias says.

Marcus gives me a scandalized look that seems false to me—his eyes are too wide and his mouth is too open. If I could find a way to smack that look off his face, I would.

"Not all those Erudite articles were full of lies," I say, narrowing my eyes at Marcus.

"What are you talking about?" Marcus says quietly. "I don't know what you've been told, Beatrice, but—"

"The only reason I haven't shot you yet is because he's the one who should get to do it," I say. "Stay away from him or I'll decide I no longer care."

Tobias's hands slip around my arms and squeeze. Marcus's eyes stay on mine for a few seconds, and I can't help but see them as black pits, like they were in Tobias's fear landscape. Then he looks away.

"We have to go," Tobias says unsteadily. "The train should be here any second."

We walk over unyielding ground toward the train tracks. Tobias's jaw is clenched and he stares straight ahead. I feel a twinge of regret. Maybe I should have let him deal with his father on his own.

"Sorry," I mutter.

"You have nothing to be sorry for," he replies, taking my hand. His fingers are still shaking.

"If we take the train in the opposite direction, out of the city instead of in, we can get to Amity headquarters," I say. "That's where the others went."

"What about Candor?" my brother asks. "What do you think they'll do?"

I don't know how Candor will respond to the attack. They wouldn't side with the Erudite—they would never do something that underhanded. But they may not fight the Erudite either.

We stand next to the tracks for a few minutes before the train comes. Eventually Tobias picks me up, because I am dead on my feet, and I lean my head into his shoulder, taking deep breaths of his skin. Since he saved me from the attack, I have associated his smell with safety, so as long as I focus on it, I feel safe now.

The truth is, I will not feel safe as long as Peter and Marcus are with us. I try not to look at them, but I feel their presence like I would feel a blanket over my face. The cruelty of fate is that I must travel with the people I hate when the people I love are dead behind me.

Dead, or waking as murderers. Where are Christina and Tori now? Wandering the streets, plagued with guilt for what they've done? Or turning guns on the people who forced them to do it? Or are they already dead too? I wish I knew.

At the same time, I hope I never find out. If she is still alive, Christina will find Will's body. And if she sees me again, her Candor-trained eyes will see that I am the one who killed him, I know it. I know it and the guilt strangles me and crushes me, so I have to forget it. I make myself forget it.

The train comes, and Tobias sets me down so I can jump on. I jog a few steps next to the car and then throw my body to the side, landing on my left arm. I wiggle my body inside and sit against the wall. Caleb sits across from me, and Tobias sits next to me, forming a barrier between my body and Marcus and Peter. My enemies. His enemies.

The train turns, and I see the city behind us. It will get smaller and smaller until we see where the tracks end, the forests and fields I last saw when I was too young to appreciate them. The kindness of Amity will comfort us for a while, though we can't stay there forever. Soon the Erudite and the corrupt Dauntless leaders will look for us, and we will have to move on.

Tobias pulls me against him. We bend our knees and our heads so that we are enclosed together in a room of our own making, unable to see those who trouble us, our breath mixing on the way in and on the way out.

"My parents," I say. "They died today."

Even though I said it, and even though I know it's true, it doesn't feel real.

"They died for *me*," I say. That feels important.

"They loved you," he replies. "To them there was no better way to show you."

I nod, and my eyes follow the line of his jaw.

"You nearly died today," he says. "I almost shot you. Why didn't you shoot me, Tris?"

"I couldn't do that," I say. "It would have been like shooting myself."

He looks pained and leans closer to me, so his lips brush mine when he speaks.

"I have something to tell you," he says.

I run my fingers along the tendons in his hand and look back at him.

"I might be in love with you." He smiles a little. "I'm waiting until I'm sure to tell you, though."

"That's sensible of you," I say, smiling too. "We should find some paper so you can make a list or a chart or something."

I feel his laughter against my side, his nose sliding along my jaw, his lips pressing behind my ear.

"Maybe I'm already sure," he says, "and I just don't want to frighten you."

I laugh a little. "Then you should know better."

"Fine," he says. "Then I love you."

I kiss him as the train slides into unlit, uncertain land. I kiss him for as long as I want, for longer than I should, given that my brother sits three feet away from me.

I reach into my pocket and take out the hard drive that contains the simulation data. I turn it in my hands, letting it catch the fading light and reflect it. Marcus's eyes cling greedily to the movement. *Not safe*, I think. *Not quite.*

I clutch the hard drive to my chest, lean my head on Tobias's shoulder, and try to sleep.

+ + +

Abnegation and Dauntless are both broken, their members scattered. We are like the factionless now. I do not know what life will be like, separated from a faction—it feels disengaged, like a leaf divided from the tree that gives it sustenance. We are creatures of loss; we have left everything behind. I have no home, no path, and no certainty. I am no longer Tris, the selfless, or Tris, the brave.

I suppose that now, I must become more than either.

ACKNOWLEDGMENTS

Thank you, God, for your Son and for blessing me beyond comprehension.

Thanks also to: Joanna Stampfel-Volpe, my badass agent, who works harder than anyone I know—your kindness and generosity continue to amaze me. Molly O'Neill, also known as the Editor of Wonder—I don't know how you manage to have a sharp editorial eye and a huge heart at the same time, but you do. I am so fortunate to have two people like you and Joanna on my side.

Katherine Tegen, who runs an amazing imprint. Barb Fitzsimmons, Amy Ryan, and Joel Tippie, who designed a beautiful and powerful cover. Brenna Franzitta, Amy Vinchesi, and Jennifer Strada, my production editor, copy editor, and proofreader (respectively), also known as grammar/punctuation/formatting ninjas—your work is so important. Fantastic marketing and publicity directors Suzanne Daghlian, Patty Rosati, Colleen O'Connell, and Sandee Roston; Allison Verost, my publicist; and everyone else in the marketing and publicity departments.

Jean McGinley, Alpha Wong, and the rest of the subrights team, who have made it possible for my book to be read in more languages than I will ever be able to read, and thanks to all the amazing foreign publishers who have given my book a home. The production team and the HarperMedia audio and e-book team, for all their hard work. The brilliant people over in sales, who have done so much for my book, and who, I've heard, have almost as much love for Four as I do. And everyone else at HarperCollins who has supported my book—it takes a village, and I'm so happy to live in yours.

Nancy Coffey, literary agent legend, for believing in my book and for giving me such a warm welcome. Pouya Shahbazian, for being a filmrights whiz and for supporting my *Top Chef* addiction. Shauna Seliy, Brian Bouldrey, and Averill Curdy, my professors, for helping me to drastically improve my writing. Jennifer Wood, my writing buddy, for her expert brainstorming skills. Sumayyah Daud, Veronique Pettingill, Kathy Bradey, Debra Driza, Lara Erlich, and Abigail Schmidt, my beta readers, for all their notes and enthusiasm. Nelson Fitch, for taking my pictures and being so supportive.

My friends, who stick with me even when I'm moody and reclusive. Mike, for teaching me a lot about life. Ingrid and Karl, my sister and brother, for their unfailing love and enthusiasm, and Frank, for talking me through the hard stuff—your support means more to me than you know. And Barbara, my mother, who always encouraged me to write, even before any of us knew that it would come to anything.

INSURGENT

To Nelson,

who was worth every risk

Like a wild animal, the truth is too powerful to remain caged.
—From the Candor faction manifesto

CHAPTER
ONE

I WAKE WITH his name in my mouth.

Will.

Before I open my eyes, I watch him crumple to the pavement again. Dead.

My doing.

Tobias crouches in front of me, his hand on my left shoulder. The train car bumps over the rails, and Marcus, Peter, and Caleb stand by the doorway. I take a deep breath and hold it in an attempt to relieve some of the pressure that is building in my chest.

An hour ago, nothing that happened felt real to me. Now it does.

I breathe out, and the pressure is still there.

"Tris, come on," Tobias says, his eyes searching mine. "We have to jump."

It is too dark to see where we are, but if we are getting off, we are probably close to the fence. Tobias helps me to my feet and guides me toward the doorway.

The others jump off one by one: Peter first, then Marcus, then Caleb. I take Tobias's hand. The wind picks up as we stand at the edge of the car opening, like a hand pushing me back, toward safety.

But we launch ourselves into darkness and land hard on the ground. The impact hurts the bullet wound in my shoulder. I bite my lip to keep from crying out, and search for my brother.

"Okay?" I say when I see him sitting in the grass a few feet away, rubbing his knee.

He nods. I hear him sniff like he's fending off tears, and I have to turn away.

We landed in the grass near the fence, several yards away from the worn path that the Amity trucks travel to deliver food to the city, and the gate that lets them out—the gate that is currently shut, locking us in. The fence towers over us, too high and flexible to climb over, too sturdy to knock'down.

"There are supposed to be Dauntless guards here," says Marcus. "Where are they?"

"They were probably under the simulation," Tobias says, "and are now . . ." He pauses. "Who knows where, doing who knows what."

We stopped the simulation—the weight of the hard drive in my back pocket reminds me—but we didn't pause to see the aftermath. What happened to our friends, our peers, our leaders, our factions? There is no way to know.

Tobias approaches a small metal box on the right side of the gate and opens it, revealing a keypad.

"Let's hope the Erudite didn't think to change this combination," he says as he types in a series of numbers. He stops at the eighth one, and the gate clicks open.

"How did you know that?" says Caleb. His voice sounds thick with emotion, so thick I am surprised it does not choke him on the way out.

"I worked in the Dauntless control room, monitoring the security system. We only change the codes twice a year," Tobias says.

"How lucky," says Caleb. He gives Tobias a wary look.

"Luck has nothing to do with it," Tobias says. "I only worked there because I wanted to make sure I could get out."

I shiver. The way he talks about getting out—it's like he thinks we're trapped. I never thought about it that way before, and now that seems foolish.

We walk in a small pack, Peter cradling his bloody arm to his chest— the arm that I shot—and Marcus with his hand on Peter's shoulder, keeping him stable. Caleb wipes his cheeks every few seconds, and I know he's crying but I don't know how to comfort him, or why I am not crying myself.

Instead I take the lead, Tobias silent at my side, and though he does not touch me, he steadies me.

+ + +

Pinpricks of light are the first sign that we are nearing Amity headquarters. Then squares of light that turn into glowing windows. A cluster of wooden and glass buildings.

Before we can reach them, we have to walk through an orchard. My feet sink into the ground, and above me, the branches grow into one another, forming a kind of tunnel. Dark fruit hangs among the leaves, ready to drop. The sharp, sweet smell of rotting apples mixes with the scent of wet earth in my nose.

When we get close, Marcus leaves Peter's side and walks in front. "I know where to go," he says.

He leads us past the first building to the second one on the left. All the buildings except the greenhouses are made of the same dark wood, unpainted, rough. I hear laughter through an open window. The contrast between the laughter and the stone stillness within me is jarring.

Marcus opens one of the doors. I would be shocked by the lack of security if we were not at Amity headquarters. They often straddle the line between trust and stupidity.

In this building the only sound is of our squeaking shoes. I don't hear Caleb crying anymore, but then, he was quiet about it before.

Marcus stops before an open room, where Johanna Reyes, representative of Amity, sits, staring out the window. I recognize her because it is hard to forget Johanna's face, whether you've seen her once or a thousand times. A scar stretches in a thick line from just above her right eyebrow to her lip, rendering her blind in one eye and giving her a lisp when she talks. I have only heard her speak once, but I remember. She would have been a beautiful woman if not for that scar.

"Oh, thank God," she says when she sees Marcus. She walks toward him with her arms open. Instead of embracing him, she just touches his shoulders, like she remembers the Abnegation's distaste for casual physical contact.

"The other members of your party got here a few hours ago, but they weren't sure if you had made it," she says. She is referring to the group of Abnegation who were with my father and Marcus in the safe house. I didn't even think to worry about them.

She looks over Marcus's shoulder, first at Tobias and Caleb, then at me, then at Peter.

"Oh my," she says, her eyes lingering on the blood soaking Peter's shirt. "I'll send for a doctor. I can grant you all permission to stay the night, but tomorrow, our community must decide together. And"—she eyes Tobias and me—"they will likely not be enthusiastic about a Dauntless presence in our compound. I of course ask you to turn over any weapons you might have."

I wonder, suddenly, how she knows that I am Dauntless. I am still wearing a gray shirt. My father's shirt.

At that moment, his smell, which is an even mixture of soap and sweat, wafts upward, and it fills my nose, fills my entire head with him. I clench my hands so hard into fists that my fingernails cut into my skin. *Not here. Not here.*

Tobias hands over his gun, but when I reach behind me to take out my own concealed weapon, he grabs my hand, guiding it away from my back. Then he laces his fingers with mine to cover up what he just did.

I know it's smart to keep one of our guns. But it would have been a relief to hand it over.

"My name is Johanna Reyes," she says, extending her hand to me, and then Tobias. A Dauntless greeting. I am impressed by her awareness of the customs of other factions. I always forget how considerate the Amity are until I see it for myself.

"This is T—" Marcus starts, but Tobias interrupts him.

"My name is Four," he says. "This is Tris, Caleb, and Peter."

A few days ago, "Tobias" was a name only I knew, among the Dauntless; it was the piece of himself that he gave me. Outside Dauntless headquarters, I remember why he hid that name from the world. It binds him to Marcus.

"Welcome to the Amity compound." Johanna's eyes fix on my face, and she smiles crookedly. "Let us take care of you."

+ + +

We do let them. An Amity nurse gives me a salve—developed by Erudite to speed healing—to put on my shoulder, and then escorts Peter to the hospital ward to mend his arm. Johanna takes us to the cafeteria, where we find some of the Abnegation who were in the safe house with Caleb and my father. Susan is there, and some of our old neighbors, and rows of wooden tables as long as the room itself. They greet us—especially Marcus—with held-in tears and suppressed smiles.

I cling to Tobias's arm. I sag under the weight of the members of my parents' faction, their lives, their tears.

One of the Abnegation puts a cup of steaming liquid under my nose and says, "Drink this. It will help you sleep as it helped some of the others sleep. No dreams."

The liquid is pink-red, like strawberries. I grab the cup and drink it fast. For a few seconds the heat from the liquid makes me feel like I am full of something again. And as I drain the last drops from the cup, I feel myself relaxing. Someone leads me down the hallway, to a room with a bed in it. That is all.

CHAPTER
TWO

I OPEN MY eyes, terrified, my hands clutching at the sheets. But I am not running through the streets of the city or the corridors of Dauntless headquarters. I am in a bed in Amity headquarters, and the smell of sawdust is in the air.

I shift, and wince as something digs into my back. I reach behind me, and my fingers wrap around the gun.

For a moment I see Will standing before me, both our guns between us—*his hand, I could have shot his hand, why didn't I, why?*—and I almost scream his name.

Then he's gone.

I get out of bed and lift the mattress with one hand, propping it up on my knee. Then I shove the gun beneath it and let the mattress bury it. Once it is out of sight and no longer pressed to my skin, my head feels clearer.

Now that the adrenaline rush of yesterday is gone, and whatever made me sleep has worn off, the deep ache and shooting pains of my shoulder are intense. I am wearing the same clothes I wore last night. The corner of the hard drive peeks out from under my pillow, where I shoved it right before I fell asleep. On it is the simulation data that controlled the Dauntless, and the record of what the Erudite did. It feels too important for me to even touch, but I can't leave it here, so I grab it and wedge it between the dresser and the wall. Part of me thinks it would be a good idea to destroy it, but I know it contains the only record of my parents' deaths, so I'll settle for keeping it hidden.

Someone knocks on my door. I sit on the edge of the bed and try to smooth my hair down.

"Come in," I say.

The door opens, and Tobias steps halfway in, the door dividing his body in half. He wears the same jeans as yesterday, but a dark red T-shirt instead of his black one, probably borrowed from one of the Amity. It's a strange color on him, too bright, but when he leans his head back against the doorframe, I see that it makes the blue in his eyes lighter.

"The Amity are meeting in a half hour." He quirks his eyebrows and adds, with a touch of melodrama, *"To decide our fate."*

I shake my head. "Never thought my fate would be in the hands of a bunch of Amity."

"Me either. Oh, I brought you something." He unscrews the cap of a small bottle and holds out a dropper filled with clear liquid. "Pain medicine. Take a dropperful every six hours."

"Thanks." I squeeze the dropper into the back of my throat. The medicine tastes like old lemon.

He hooks a thumb in one of his belt loops and says, "How are you, Beatrice?"

"Did you just call me *Beatrice*?"

"Thought I would give it a try." He smiles. "Not good?"

"Maybe on special occasions only. Initiation days, Choosing Days . . ." I pause. I was about to rattle off a few more holidays, but only the Abnegation celebrate them. The Dauntless have holidays of their own, I assume, but I don't know what they are. And anyway, the idea that we would celebrate anything right now is so ludicrous I don't continue.

"It's a deal." His smile fades. "How are you, Tris?"

It's not a strange question, after what we've been through, but I tense up when he asks it, worried that he'll somehow see into my mind. I haven't told him about Will yet. I want to, but I don't know how. Just the thought of saying the words out loud makes me feel so heavy I could break through the floorboards.

"I'm . . ." I shake my head a few times. "I don't know, Four. I'm awake. I . . ." I am still shaking my head. He slides his hand over my cheek, one finger anchored behind my ear. Then he tilts his head down and kisses me, sending a warm ache through my body. I wrap my hands around his arm, holding him there as long as I can. When he touches me, the hollowed-out feeling in my chest and stomach is not as noticeable.

I don't have to tell him. I can just try to forget—he can help me forget.

"I know," he says. "Sorry. I shouldn't have asked."

For a moment all I can think is, *How could you* possibly *know?* But something about his expression reminds me that he does know something about loss. He lost his mother when he was young. I don't remember how she died, just that we attended her funeral.

Suddenly I remember him clutching the curtains in his living room, about nine years old, wearing gray, his dark eyes shut. The image is fleeting, and it could be my imagination, not a memory.

He releases me. "I'll let you get ready."

+ + +

The women's bathroom is two doors down. The floor is dark brown tile, and each shower stall has wooden walls and a plastic curtain separating it from the central aisle. A sign on the back wall says REMEMBER: TO CONSERVE RESOURCES, SHOWERS RUN FOR ONLY FIVE MINUTES.

The stream of water is cold, so I wouldn't want the extra minutes even if I could have them. I wash quickly with my left hand, leaving my right hand hanging at my side. The pain medicine Tobias gave me worked fast—the pain in my shoulder has already faded to a dull throb.

When I get out of the shower, a stack of clothes waits on my bed. It contains some yellow and red, from the Amity, and some gray, from the Abnegation, colors I rarely see side by side. If I had to guess, I would say that one of the Abnegation put the stack there for me. It's something they would think to do.

I pull on a pair of dark red pants made of denim—so long I have to roll them up three times—and a gray Abnegation shirt that is too big for me. The sleeves come down to my fingertips, and I roll them up too. It hurts to move my right hand, so I keep the movements small and slow.

Someone knocks on the door. "Beatrice?" The soft voice is Susan's.

I open the door for her. She carries a tray of food, which she sets down on the bed. I search her face for a sign of what she has lost—her father, an Abnegation leader, didn't survive the attack—but I see only the placid determination characteristic of my old faction.

"I'm sorry the clothes don't fit," she says. "I'm sure we can find some better ones for you if the Amity allow us to stay."

"They're fine," I say. "Thank you."

"I heard you were shot. Do you need my help with your hair? Or your shoes?"

I am about to refuse, but I really do need help.

"Yes, thank you."

I sit down on a stool in front of the mirror, and she stands behind me, her eyes dutifully trained on the task at hand rather than her reflection. They do not lift, not even for an instant, as she runs a comb through my hair. And she doesn't ask about my shoulder, how I was shot, what happened when I left the Abnegation safe house to stop the simulation. I get the sense that if I were to whittle her down to her core, she would be Abnegation all the way through.

"Have you seen Robert yet?" I say. Her brother, Robert, chose Amity when I chose Dauntless, so he is somewhere in this compound. I wonder if their reunion will be anything like Caleb's and mine.

"Briefly, last night," she says. "I left him to grieve with his faction as I grieve with mine. It is nice to see him again, though."

I hear a finality in her tone that tells me the subject is closed.

"It's a shame this happened when it did," Susan says. "Our leaders were about to do something wonderful."

"Really? What?"

"I don't know." Susan blushes. "I just knew that something was happening. I didn't mean to be curious; I just noticed things."

"I wouldn't blame you for being curious even if you had been."

She nods and keeps combing. I wonder what the Abnegation leaders—including my father—were doing. And I can't help but marvel at Susan's assumption that whatever they were doing was wonderful. I wish I could believe that of people again.

If I ever did.

"The Dauntless wear their hair down, right?" she says.

"Sometimes," I say. "Do you know how to braid?"

So her deft fingers tuck pieces of my hair into one braid that tickles the middle of my spine. I stare hard at my reflection until she finishes. I thank her when she's done, and she leaves with a small smile, closing the door behind her.

I keep staring, but I don't see myself. I can still feel her fingers brushing the back of my neck, so much like my mother's fingers, the last morning I spent with her. My eyes wet with tears, I rock back and forth on the stool, trying to push the memory from my mind. I am afraid that if I start to sob, I will never stop until I shrivel up like a raisin.

I see a sewing kit on the dresser. In it are two colors of thread, red and yellow, and a pair of scissors.

I feel calm as I undo the braid in my hair and comb it again. I part my hair down the middle and make sure that it is straight and flat. I close the scissors over the hair by my chin.

How can I look the same, when she's gone and everything is different? I can't.

I cut in as straight a line as I can, using my jaw as a guide. The tricky part is the back, which I can't see very well, so I do the best I can by touch instead of sight. Locks of blond hair surround me on the floor in a semicircle.

I leave the room without looking at my reflection again.

+ + +

When Tobias and Caleb come to get me later, they stare at me like I am not the person they knew yesterday.

"You cut your hair," says Caleb, his eyebrows high. Grabbing hold of facts in the midst of shock is very Erudite of him. His hair sticks up on one side from where he slept on it, and his eyes are bloodshot.

"Yeah," I say. "It's . . . too hot for long hair."

"Fair enough."

We walk down the hallway together. The floorboards creak beneath our feet. I miss the way my footsteps echoed in the Dauntless compound; I miss the cool underground air. But mostly I miss the fears of the past few weeks, rendered small by my fears now.

We exit the building. The outside air presses around me like a pillow meant to suffocate me. It smells green, the way a leaf does when you tear it in half.

"Does everyone know you're Marcus's son?" Caleb says. "The Abnegation, I mean?"

"Not to my knowledge," says Tobias, glancing at Caleb. "And I would appreciate it if you didn't mention it."

"I don't need to mention it. Anyone with eyes can see it for themselves." Caleb frowns at him. "How old are you, anyway?"

"Eighteen."

"And you don't think you're too old to be with my little sister?"

Tobias lets out a short laugh. "She isn't *your little* anything."

"Stop it. Both of you," I say. A crowd of people in yellow walks ahead of us, toward a wide, squat building made entirely of glass. The sunlight reflecting off the panes feels like a pinch to my eyes. I shield my face with my hand and keep walking.

The doors to the building are wide open. Around the edge of the circular greenhouse, plants and trees grow in troughs of water or small pools. Dozens of fans positioned around the room serve only to blow the hot air around, so I am already sweating. But that fades from my mind when the crowd before me thins and I see the rest of the room.

In its center grows a huge tree. Its branches are spread over most of the greenhouse, and its roots bubble up from the ground, forming a dense web of bark. In the spaces between the roots, I see not dirt but water, and metal rods holding the roots in place. I should not be surprised—the Amity spend their lives accomplishing feats of agriculture like this one, with the help of Erudite technology.

Standing on a cluster of roots is Johanna Reyes, her hair falling over the scarred half of her face. I learned in Faction History that the Amity recognize no official leader—they vote on everything, and the result is usually close to unanimous. They are like many parts of a single mind, and Johanna is their mouthpiece.

The Amity sit on the floor, most with their legs crossed, in knots and clusters that vaguely resemble the tree roots to me. The Abnegation sit in tight rows a few yards to my left. My eyes search the crowd for a few seconds before I realize what I'm looking for: my parents.

I swallow hard, and try to forget. Tobias touches the small of my back, guiding me to the edge of the meeting space, behind the Abnegation. Before we sit down, he puts his mouth next to my ear and says, "I like your hair that way."

I find a small smile to give him, and lean into him when I sit down, my arm against his.

Johanna lifts her hands and bows her head. All conversation in the room ceases before I can draw my next breath. All around me the Amity sit in silence, some with their eyes closed, some with their lips mouthing words I can't hear, some staring at a point far away.

Every second chafes. By the time Johanna lifts her head I am worn to the bone.

"We have before us today an urgent question," she says, "which is: How will we conduct ourselves in this time of conflict as people who pursue peace?"

Every Amity in the room turns to the person next to him or her and starts talking.

"How do they get anything done?" I say, as the minutes of chatter wear on.

"They don't care about efficiency," Tobias says. "They care about agreement. Watch."

Two women in yellow dresses a few feet away rise and join a trio of men. A young man shifts so that his small circle becomes a large one with the group next to him. All around the room, the smaller crowds grow and expand, and fewer and fewer voices fill the room, until there are only three or four. I can only hear pieces of what they say: "Peace—Dauntless—Erudite—safe house—involvement—"

"This is bizarre," I say.

"I think it's beautiful," he says.

I give him a look.

"What?" He laughs a little. "They each have an equal role in government; they each feel equally responsible. And it makes them care; it makes them kind. I think that's beautiful."

"I think it's unsustainable," I say. "Sure, it works for the Amity. But what happens when not everyone wants to strum banjos and grow crops? What happens when someone does something terrible and talking about it can't solve the problem?"

He shrugs. "I guess we'll find out."

Eventually someone from each of the big groups stands and approaches Johanna, picking their way carefully over the roots of the big tree. I expect them to address the rest of us, but instead they stand in a circle with Johanna and the other spokespeople and talk quietly. I begin to get the feeling that I will never know what they're saying.

"They're not going to let us argue with them, are they," I say.

"I doubt it," he says.

We are done for.

When everyone has said his or her piece, they sit down again, leaving Johanna alone in the center of the room. She angles her body toward us and folds her hands in front of her. Where will we go when they tell us to leave? Back into the city, where nothing is safe?

"Our faction has had a close relationship with Erudite for as long as any of us can remember. We need each other to survive, and we have always cooperated with each other," says Johanna. "But we have also had a strong relationship with Abnegation in the past, and we do not think it is right to revoke the hand of friendship when it has for so long been extended."

Her voice is honey-sweet, and moves like honey too, slow and careful. I wipe the sweat from my hairline with the back of my hand.

"We feel that the only way to preserve our relationships with both factions is to remain impartial and uninvolved," she continues. "Your presence here, though welcome, complicates that."

Here it comes, I think.

"We have arrived at the conclusion that we will establish our faction headquarters as a safe house for members of all factions," she says, "under a set of conditions. The first is that no weaponry of any kind is allowed on the compound. The second is that if any serious conflict arises, whether verbal or physical, all involved parties will be asked to leave. The third is that the conflict may not be discussed, even privately, within the confines of this compound. And the fourth is that everyone who stays here must contribute to the welfare of this environment by working. We will report this to Erudite, Candor, and Dauntless as soon as we can."

Her stare drifts to Tobias and me, and stays there.

"You are welcome to stay here if and only if you can abide by our rules," she says. "That is our decision."

I think of the gun I hid under my mattress, and the tension between me and Peter, and Tobias and Marcus, and my mouth feels dry. I am not good at avoiding conflict.

"We won't be able to stay long," I say to Tobias under my breath.

A moment ago, he was still faintly smiling. Now the corners of his mouth have disappeared into a frown. "No, we won't."

CHAPTER
THREE

THAT EVENING I return to my room and slide my hand beneath my mattress to make sure the gun is still there. My fingers brush over the trigger, and my throat tightens like I am having an allergic reaction. I withdraw my hand and kneel on the edge of the bed, taking hard swallows of air until the feeling subsides.

What is wrong with you? I shake my head. *Pull it together.*

And that is what it feels like: pulling the different parts of me up and in like a shoelace. I feel suffocated, but at least I feel strong.

I see a flicker of movement in my periphery, and look out the window that faces the apple orchard. Johanna Reyes and Marcus Eaton walk side by side, pausing at the herb garden to pluck mint leaves from their stems. I am out of my room before I can evaluate why I want to follow them.

I sprint through the building so that I don't lose them. Once I am outside, I have to be more careful. I walk around the far side of the greenhouse and, after I see Johanna and Marcus disappear into one row of trees, I creep down the next row, hoping the branches will hide me if either of them looks back.

". . . been confused about is the timing of the attack," says Johanna. "Is it just that Jeanine finally finished planning it, and acted, or was there an inciting incident of some kind?"

I see Marcus's face through a divided tree trunk. He presses his lips together and says, "Hmm."

"I suppose we'll never know." Johanna raises her good eyebrow. "Will we?"

"No, perhaps not."

Johanna places her hand on his arm and turns toward him. I stiffen, afraid for a moment that she will see me, but she looks only at Marcus. I sink into a crouch and crawl toward one of the trees so that the trunk will hide me. The bark itches my spine, but I don't move.

"But you *do* know," she says. "You know why she attacked when she did. I may not be Candor anymore, but I can still tell when someone is keeping the truth from me."

"Inquisitiveness is self-serving, Johanna."

If I were Johanna, I would snap at him for a comment like that, but she says kindly, "My faction depends on me to advise them, and if you know information this crucial, it is important that I know it also so that I can share it with them. I'm sure you can understand that, Marcus."

"There is a reason you don't know all the things I know. Along time ago, the Abnegation were entrusted with some sensitive information," says Marcus. "Jeanine attacked us to steal it. And if I am not careful, she will destroy it, so that is all I can tell you."

"But surely—"

"No," Marcus cuts her off. "This information is far more important than you can imagine. Most of the leaders of this city risked their lives to protect it from Jeanine and died, and I will not jeopardize it now for the sake of sating your selfish curiosity."

Johanna is quiet for a few seconds. It's so dark now I can barely see my own hands. The air smells like dirt and apples, and I try not to breathe it too loudly.

"I'm sorry," says Johanna. "I must have done something to make you believe I am not trustworthy."

"The last time I trusted a faction representative with this information, all my friends were murdered," he replies. "I don't trust anyone anymore."

I can't help it—I lean forward so that I can see around the trunk of the tree. Both Marcus and Johanna are too preoccupied to notice the movement. They are close together, but not touching, and I've never seen Marcus look so tired or Johanna so angry. But her face softens, and she touches Marcus's arm again, this time with a light caress.

"In order to have peace, we must first have trust," says Johanna. "So I hope you change your mind. Remember that I have always been your friend, Marcus, even when you did not have many to speak of."

She leans in and kisses his cheek, then walks to the end of the orchard. Marcus stands for a few seconds, apparently stunned, and starts toward the compound.

The revelations of the past half hour buzz in my mind. I thought Jeanine attacked the Abnegation to seize power, but she attacked them to steal information—information only they knew.

Then the buzzing stops as I remember something else Marcus said:

Most of the leaders of this city risked their lives for it. Was one of those leaders my father?

I have to know. I have to find out what could possibly be important enough for the Abnegation to die for—and the Erudite to kill for.

+ + +

I pause before knocking on Tobias's door, and listen to what's going on inside.

"No, not like *that*," Tobias says through laughter.

"What do you mean, 'not like that'? I imitated you perfectly." The second voice belongs to Caleb.

"You did not."

"Well, do it again, then."

I push open the door just as Tobias, who is sitting on the floor with one leg stretched out, hurls a butter knife at the opposite wall. It sticks, handle out, from a large hunk of cheese they positioned on top of the dresser. Caleb, standing beside him, stares in disbelief, first at the cheese and then at me.

"Tell me he's some kind of Dauntless prodigy," says Caleb. "Can you do this too?"

He looks better than he did earlier—his eyes aren't red anymore and some of the old spark of curiosity is in them, like he is interested in the world again. His brown hair is tousled, his shirt buttons in the wrong buttonholes. He is handsome in a careless way, my brother, like he has no idea what he looks like most of the time.

"With my right hand, maybe," I say. "But yes, *Four* is some kind of Dauntless prodigy. Can I ask *why* you're throwing knives at cheese?"

Tobias's eyes catch mine on the word "Four." Caleb doesn't know that Tobias wears his excellence all the time in his own nickname.

"Caleb came by to discuss something," Tobias says, leaning his head against the wall as he looks at me. "And knife-throwing just came up somehow."

"As it so often does," I say, a small smile inching its way across my face.

He looks so relaxed, his head back, his arm slung over his knee. We stare at each other for a few more seconds than is socially acceptable. Caleb clears his throat.

"Anyway, I should be getting back to my room," Caleb says, looking from Tobias to me and back again. "I'm reading this book about the water-filtration systems. The kid who gave it to me looked at me like I was crazy for wanting to read it. I think it's supposed to be a repair manual, but it's fascinating." He pauses. "Sorry. You probably think I'm crazy too."

"Not at all," Tobias says with mock sincerity. "Maybe *you* should read that repair manual too, Tris. It sounds like something you might like."

"I can loan it to you," Caleb says.

"Maybe later," I say. When Caleb closes the door behind him, I give Tobias a dirty look.

"Thanks for that," I say. "Now he's going to talk my ear off about water filtration and how it works. Though I guess I might prefer that to what he wants to talk to me about."

"Oh? And what's that?" Tobias quirks his eyebrows. "Aquaponics?"

"Aqua-what?"

"It's one of the ways they grow food here. You don't want to know."

"You're right, I don't," I say. "What did he come to talk to you about?"

"You," he says. "I think it was the big-brother talk. 'Don't mess around with my sister' and all that."

He gets up.

"What did you tell him?"

He comes toward me.

"I told him how we got together—that's how knife-throwing came up," he says, "and I told him I wasn't messing around."

I feel warm everywhere. He wraps his hands around my hips and presses me gently against the door. His lips find mine.

I don't remember why I came here in the first place.

And I don't care.

I wrap my uninjured arm around him, pulling him against me. My fingers find the hem of his T-shirt, and slide beneath it, spreading wide over the small of his back. He feels so strong.

He kisses me again, more insistent this time, his hands squeezing my waist. His breaths, my breaths, his body, my body, we are so close there is no difference.

He pulls back, just a few centimeters. I almost don't let him get that far.

"This isn't what you came here for," he says.

"No."

"What did you come for, then?"

"Who cares?"

I push my fingers through his hair, and draw his mouth to mine again. He doesn't resist, but after a few seconds, he mumbles, "Tris," against my cheek.

"Okay, okay." I close my eyes. I did come here for something important: to tell him the conversation I overheard.

We sit side by side on Tobias's bed, and I start from the beginning. I tell him how I followed Marcus and Johanna into the orchard. I tell him Johanna's question about the timing of the simulation attack, and

Marcus's response, and the argument that followed. As I do, I watch his expression. He does not look shocked or curious. Instead, his mouth works its way into the bitter pucker that accompanies any mention of Marcus.

"Well, what do you think?" I say once I finish.

"I think," he says carefully, "that it's Marcus trying to feel more important than he is."

That was not the response I was expecting.

"So . . . what? You think he's just talking nonsense?"

"I think there probably is some information the Abnegation knew that Jeanine wanted to know, but I think he's exaggerating its importance. Trying to build up his own ego by making Johanna think he's got something she wants and he won't give it to her."

"I don't . . ." I frown. "I don't think you're right. He didn't sound like he was lying."

"You don't know him like I do. He is an excellent liar."

He is right—I don't know Marcus, and certainly not as well as he does. But my instinct was to believe Marcus, and I usually trust my instincts.

"Maybe you're right," I say, "but shouldn't we find out what's going on? Just to be sure?"

"I think it's more important that we deal with the situation at hand," says Tobias. "Go back to the city. Find out what's going on there. Find a way to take Erudite down. Then maybe we can find out what Marcus was talking about, after this is all resolved. Okay?"

I nod. It sounds like a good plan—a smart plan. But I don't believe him—I don't believe it's more important to move forward than to find out the truth. When I found out that I was Divergent . . . when I found out that Erudite would attack Abnegation . . . those revelations changed everything. The truth has a way of changing a person's plans.

But it is difficult to persuade Tobias to do something he doesn't want to do, and even more difficult to justify my feelings with no evidence except my intuition.

So I agree. But I do not change my mind.

CHAPTER FOUR

"Biotechnology has been around for a long time, but it wasn't always very effective," Caleb says. He starts on the crust of his toast—he ate the middle first, just like he used to when we were little.

He sits across from me in the cafeteria, at the table closest to the windows. Carved into the wood along the table's edge are the letters "D" and "T" linked together by a heart, so small I almost didn't see them. I run my fingers over the carving as Caleb speaks.

"But Erudite scientists developed this highly effective mineral solution a while back. It was better for the plants than dirt," he says. "It's an earlier version of that salve they put on your shoulder—it accelerates the growth of new cells."

His eyes are wild with new information. Not all the Erudite are power hungry and devoid of conscience, like their leader, Jeanine Matthews. Some of them are like Caleb: fascinated by everything, dissatisfied until they find out how it works.

I rest my chin on my hand and smile a little at him. He seems upbeat this morning. I am glad he has found something to distract him from his grief.

"So Erudite and Amity work together, then?" I say.

"More closely than Erudite and any other faction," he says. "Don't you remember from our Faction History book? It called them the 'essential factions'—without them, we would be incapable of survival. Some of the Erudite texts called them the 'enriching factions.' And one of Erudite's missions as a faction was to become both—essential and enriching."

It doesn't sit well with me, how much our society needs Erudite to function. But they *are* essential—without them, there would be inefficient farming, insufficient medical treatments, and no technological advance.

I bite my apple.

"You aren't going to eat your toast?" he says.

"The bread tastes strange," I say. "You can have it if you want."

"I'm amazed by how they live here," he says as he takes the toast from my plate. "They're completely self-sustaining. They have their own source of power, their own water pumps, their own water filtration, their own food sources. . . . They're independent."

"Independent," I say, "and uninvolved. Must be nice."

It *is* nice, from what I can tell. The large windows beside our table let in so much sunlight I feel like I'm sitting outside. Clusters of Amity sit at the other tables, their clothes bright against their tanned skin. On me the yellow looks dull.

"So I take it Amity wasn't one of the factions you had an aptitude for," he says, grinning.

"No." The group of Amity a few seats away from us bursts into laughter. They haven't even glanced in our direction since we sat down to eat. "Keep it down, all right? It's not something I want to broadcast."

"Sorry," he says, leaning over the table so that he can talk quieter. "So what were they?"

I feel myself tensing, straightening. "Why do you want to know?"

"Tris," he says, "I'm your brother. You can tell me anything."

His green eyes never waver. He's abandoned the useless spectacles he wore as a member of Erudite in favor of an Abnegation gray shirt and their trademark short haircut. He looks just as he did a few months ago, when we were living across the hall from each other, both of us considering switching factions but not brave enough to tell one another. Not trusting him enough to tell him was a mistake I do not want to make again.

"Abnegation, Dauntless," I say, "and Erudite."

"*Three* factions?" His eyebrows lift.

"Yes. Why?"

"It just seems like a lot," he says. "We each had to choose a research focus in Erudite initiation, and mine was the aptitude test simulation, so I know a lot about the way it's designed. It's really difficult for a person to get two results—the program actually doesn't allow it. But to get *three* . . . I'm not even sure how that's possible."

"Well, the test administrator had to alter the test," I say. "She forced it to go to that situation on the bus so that she could rule out Erudite—except Erudite wasn't ruled out."

Caleb props his chin on a fist. "A program override," he says. "I wonder how your test administrator knew how to do that. It's not something they're taught."

I frown. Tori was a tattoo artist and an aptitude test volunteer—how *did* she know how to alter the aptitude test program? If she was good with computers, it was only as a hobby, and I doubt that a computer hobby would enable someone to fiddle with an Erudite simulation.

Then something from one of my conversations with her surfaces. *My brother and I both transferred from Erudite.*

"She was Erudite," I say. "A faction transfer. Maybe that's how."

"Maybe," he says, tapping his fingers—from left to right—against his cheek. Our breakfasts sit, almost forgotten, between us. "What does this mean about your brain chemistry? Or anatomy?"

I laugh a little. "I don't know. All I know is that I'm always aware during simulations, and sometimes I can wake myself up from them. Sometimes they don't even work. Like the attack simulation."

"How do you wake yourself up from them? What do you do?"

"I . . ." I try to remember. I feel like it has been a long time since I was in one, though it was only a few weeks. "It's hard to say, because the Dauntless simulations were supposed to end when we had calmed down. But in one of mine . . . the one where Tobias figured out what I was . . . I just did something impossible. I broke glass just by putting my hand on it."

Caleb's expression becomes distant, like he is looking into faraway places. Nothing like what I just described ever happened to him in the aptitude test simulation, I know. So maybe he is wondering what it felt like, or how it's possible. My cheeks grow warmer—he is analyzing my brain like he would analyze a computer or a machine.

"Hey," I say. "Come back."

"Sorry," he says, focusing on me again. "It's just . . ."

"Fascinating. Yeah, I know. You always look like someone's sucked the life right out of you when something fascinates you."

He laughs.

"Can we talk about something else, though?" I say. "There may not be any Erudite or Dauntless traitors around, but it still feels weird, talking about it in public like this."

"All right."

Before he can go on, the cafeteria doors open, and a group of Abnegation come in. They wear Amity clothes, like me, but also like me, it's obvious what faction they are really in. They are silent, but not somber—they smile at the Amity they pass, inclining their heads, a few of them stopping to exchange pleasantries.

Susan sits down next to Caleb with a small smile. Her hair is pulled

back in its usual knot, but her blond hair shines like gold. She and Caleb
sit just slightly closer than friends would, though they do not touch. She
bobs her head to greet me.

"I'm sorry," she says. "Did I interrupt?"

"No," says Caleb. "How are you?"

"I'm well. How are you?"

I am just about to flee the dining hall rather than participate in careful, polite Abnegation conversation when Tobias comes in, looking ha-
rassed. He must have been working in the kitchen this morning, as part
of our agreement with the Amity. I have to work in the laundry rooms
tomorrow.

"What happened?" I say as he sits down next to me.

"In their enthusiasm for conflict resolution, the Amity have apparently forgotten that meddling creates *more* conflict," says Tobias. "If we
stay here much longer, I am going to punch someone, and it's not going to
be pretty."

Caleb and Susan both raise their eyebrows at him. A few of the Amity
at the table next to ours stop talking to stare.

"You heard me," Tobias says to them. They all look away.

"As I said," I say, covering my mouth to hide my smile, "what happened?"

"I'll tell you later."

It must have to do with Marcus. Tobias doesn't like the dubious looks
the Abnegation give him when he refers to Marcus's cruelty, and Susan is
sitting right across from him. I clasp my hands in my lap.

The Abnegation sit at our table, but not right next to us—a respectful
distance of two seats away, though most of them still nod at us. They were
my family's friends and neighbors and coworkers, and before, their
presence would have encouraged me to be quiet and self-effacing. Now it
makes me want to talk louder, to be as far from that old identity and the
pain that accompanies it as possible.

Tobias goes completely still when a hand falls on my right shoulder,
sending prickles of pain down my right arm. I clench my teeth to keep
from groaning.

"She got shot in that shoulder," Tobias says without looking at the
man behind me.

"My apologies." Marcus lifts his hand and sits down on my left.
"Hello."

"What do *you* want?" I say.

"Beatrice," Susan says quietly. "There's no need to—"

"Susan, please," says Caleb quietly. She presses her lips into a line
and looks away.

I frown at Marcus. "I asked you a question."

"I would like to discuss something with you," says Marcus. His expression is calm, but he's angry—the terseness in his voice betrays him. "The other Abnegation and myself have discussed it and decided that we should not stay here. We believe that, given the inevitability of further conflict in our city, it would be selfish of us to stay here while what remains of our faction is inside that fence. We would like to request that you escort us."

I did not expect that. Why does Marcus want to return to the city? Is it really just an Abnegation decision, or does he intend to do something there—something that has to do with whatever information the Abnegation have?

I stare at him for a few seconds and then look at Tobias. He has relaxed a little, but he keeps his eyes focused on the table. I don't know why he acts this way around his father. No one, not even Jeanine, makes Tobias cower.

"What do you think?" I say.

"I think we should leave the day after tomorrow," Tobias says.

"Okay. Thank you," says Marcus. He gets up and sits at the other end of the table with the rest of the Abnegation.

I inch closer to Tobias, not sure how to comfort him without making things worse. I pick up my apple with my left hand, and grab his hand under the table with my right.

But I can't keep my eyes away from Marcus. I want to know more about what he said to Johanna. And sometimes, if you want the truth, you have to demand it.

CHAPTER
FIVE

AFTER BREAKFAST, I tell Tobias I'm going for a walk, but instead I follow
Marcus. I expect him to walk to the guests' dormitory, but he crosses the
field behind the dining hall and walks into the water-filtration building.
I hesitate on the bottom step. Do I really want to do this?

I walk up the steps and through the door that Marcus just closed behind him.

The filtration building is small, just one room with a few huge machines in it. As far as I can tell, some of the machines take in dirty water
from the rest of the compound, a few of them purify it, others test it, and
the last set pumps clean water back out to the compound. The piping systems are all buried except one, which runs along the ground to send water to the power plant, near the fence. The plant provides power to the
entire city, using a combination of wind, water, and solar energy.

Marcus stands near the machines that filter the water. There the
pipes are transparent. I can see brown-tinged water rushing through
one pipe, disappearing into the machine, and emerging clear. Both of us
watch the purification happen, and I wonder if he is thinking what I am:
that it would be nice if life worked this way, stripping the dirt from our
lives and sending us out into the world clean. But some dirt is destined to
linger.

I stare at the back of Marcus's head. I have to do this now.

Now.

"I heard you, the other day," I blurt out.

Marcus whips his head around. "What are you doing, Beatrice?"

"I followed you here." I fold my arms over my chest. "I heard
you talking to Johanna about what motivated Jeanine's attack on Abnegation."

"Did the Dauntless teach you that it's all right to invade another person's privacy, or did you teach yourself?"

"I'm a naturally curious person. Don't change the subject."

Marcus's forehead is creased, especially between the eyebrows, and there are deep lines next to his mouth. He looks like a man who has spent most of his life frowning. He might have been handsome when he was younger—perhaps he still is, to women his age, like Johanna—but all I see when I look at him are the black-pit eyes from Tobias's fear landscape.

"If you heard me talking to Johanna, then you know that I didn't even tell *her* about this. So what makes you think that I would share the information with *you*?"

I don't have an answer at first. But then it comes to me.

"My father," I say. "My father is dead." It's the first time I've said it since I told Tobias, on the train ride over, that my parents died for me. "Died" was just a fact to me then, detached from emotion. But "dead," mingling with the churning and bubbling noises in this room, strikes a blow like a hammer to my chest, and the monster of grief awakens, clawing at my eyes and throat.

I force myself to continue.

"He may not have actually died for whatever information you were referring to," I say. "But I want to know if it was something he risked his life for."

Marcus's mouth twitches.

"Yes," he says. "It was."

My eyes fill with tears. I blink them away.

"Well," I say, almost choking, "then what on earth was it? Was it something you were trying to protect? Or steal? Or what?"

"It was . . ." Marcus shakes his head. "I'm not going to tell you that."

I step toward him. "But you want it back. And Jeanine has it."

Marcus *is* a good liar—or at least, someone who is skilled at hiding secrets. He does not react. I wish I could see like Johanna sees, like the Candor see—I wish I could read his expression. He could be close to telling me the truth. If I press just hard enough, maybe he'll crack.

"I could help you," I say.

Marcus's upper lip curls. "You have no idea how ridiculous that sounds." He spits the words at me. "You may have succeeded in shutting down the attack simulation, girl, but it was by luck alone, not skill. I would die of shock if you managed to do anything useful again for a long time."

This is the Marcus that Tobias knows. The one who knows right where to hit to cause the most damage.

My body shudders with anger. "Tobias is right about you," I say. "You're nothing but an arrogant, lying piece of garbage."

"He said that, did he?" Marcus raises his eyebrows.

"No," I say. "He doesn't mention you enough to say anything like that. I figured it out all on my own." I clench my teeth. "You're almost nothing to him, you know. And as time goes on, you become less and less."

Marcus doesn't answer me. He turns back to the water purifier. I stand for a moment in my triumph, the sound of rushing water combining with the heartbeat in my ears. Then I leave the building, and it isn't until I'm halfway across the field that I realize I didn't win. Marcus did.

Whatever the truth is, I'll have to get it from somewhere else, because I won't be asking him again.

+ + +

That night I dream that I am in a field, and I encounter a flock of crows clustered on the ground. When I swat a few of them away, I realize that they are perched on top of a man, pecking at his clothes, which are Abnegation gray. Without warning, they take flight, and I realize that the man is Will.

Then I wake up.

I turn my face into the pillow and release, instead of his name, a sob that throws my body against the mattress. I feel the monster of grief again, writhing in the empty space where my heart and stomach used to be.

I gasp, pressing both palms to my chest. Now the monstrous thing has its claws around my throat, squeezing my airway. I twist and put my head between my knees, breathing until the strangled feeling leaves me.

Even though the air is warm, I shiver. I get out of bed and creep down the hallway toward Tobias's room. My bare legs almost glow in the dark. His door creaks when I pull it open, loud enough to wake him. He stares at me for a second.

"C'mere," he says, sluggish from sleep. He shifts back on the bed to leave space for me.

I should have thought this through. I sleep in a long T-shirt one of the Amity lent me. It comes down just past my butt, and I didn't think to put on a pair of shorts before I came here. Tobias's eyes skim my bare legs, making my face warm. I lie down, facing him.

"Bad dream?" he says.

I nod.

"What happened?"

I shake my head. I can't tell him that I'm having nightmares about Will, or I would have to explain why. What would he think of me, if he knew what I had done? How would he look at me?

He keeps his hand on my cheek, moving his thumb over my cheek-bone idly.

"We're all right, you know," he says. "You and me. Okay?"

My chest aches, and I nod.

"Nothing else is all right." His whisper tickles my cheek. "But we are."

"Tobias," I say. But whatever I was about to say gets lost in my head, and I press my mouth to his, because I know that kissing him will distract me from everything.

He kisses me back. His hand starts on my cheek, and then brushes over my side, fitting to the bend in my waist, curving over my hip, sliding to my bare leg, making me shiver. I press closer to him and wrap my leg around him. My head buzzes with nervousness, but the rest of me seems to know exactly what it's doing, because it all pulses to the same rhythm, all wants the same thing: to escape itself and become a part of him instead.

His mouth moves against mine, and his hand slips under the hem of the T-shirt, and I don't stop him, though I know I should. Instead a faint sigh escapes me, and heat rushes into my cheeks, embarrassment. Either he didn't hear me or he didn't care, because he presses his palm to my lower back, presses me closer. His fingers move slowly up my back, tracing my spine. My shirt creeps up my body, and I don't pull it down, even when I feel cool air on my stomach.

He kisses my neck, and I grab his shoulder to steady myself, gathering his shirt into my fist. His hand reaches the top of my back and curls around my neck. My shirt is twisted around his arm, and our kisses become desperate. I know my hands are shaking from all the nervous energy inside me, so I tighten my grip on his shoulder so he won't notice.

Then his fingers brush the bandage on my shoulder, and a dart of pain goes through me. It didn't hurt much, but it brings me back to reality. I can't be with him in *that* way if one of my reasons for wanting it is to distract myself from grief.

I lean back and carefully pull the hem of my shirt down so it covers me again. For a second we just lie there, our heavy breaths mixing. I don't mean to cry—now is not a good time to cry; no, it has to stop—but I can't get the tears out of my eyes, no matter how many times I blink.

"Sorry," I say.

He says almost sternly, "Don't apologize." He brushes the tears from my cheeks.

I know that I am birdlike, made narrow and small as if for taking flight, built straight-waisted and fragile. But when he touches me like he can't bear to take his hand away, I don't wish I was any different.

"I don't mean to be such a mess," I say, my voice cracking. "I just feel so . . ." I shake my head.

"It's wrong," he says. "It doesn't matter if your parents are in a better place—they aren't here with you, and that's *wrong*, Tris. It shouldn't have happened. It shouldn't have happened to you. And anyone who tells you it's okay is a liar."

A sob racks my body again, and he wraps his arms around me so tightly I find it difficult to breathe, but it doesn't matter. My dignified weeping gives way to full-on ugliness, my mouth open and my face contorted and sounds like a dying animal coming from my throat. If this continues I will break apart, and maybe that would be better, maybe it would be better to shatter and bear nothing.

He doesn't speak for a long time, until I am quiet again.

"Sleep," he says. "I'll fight the bad dreams off if they come to get you."

"With what?"

"My bare hands, obviously."

I wrap my arm around his waist and take a deep breath of his shoulder. He smells like sweat and fresh air and mint, from the salve he sometimes uses to relax his sore muscles. He smells safe, too, like sunlit walks in the orchard and silent breakfasts in the dining hall. And in the moments before I drift off to sleep, I almost forget about our war-torn city and all the conflict that will come to find us soon, if we don't find it first.

In the moments before I drift off to sleep, I hear him whisper, "I love you, Tris."

And maybe I would say it back, but I am too far gone.

CHAPTER
SIX

THAT MORNING I wake up to the buzz of an electric razor. Tobias stands in front of the mirror, his head tilted so he can see the corner of his jaw.

I hug my knees, covered by the sheet, and watch him.

"Good morning," he says. "How did you sleep?"

"Okay." I get up, and as he tilts his head back to address his chin with the razor, I wrap my arms around him, pressing my forehead to his back where the Dauntless tattoo peeks out from beneath his shirt.

He sets the razor down and folds his hands over mine. Neither of us breaks the silence. I listen to him breathe, and he strokes my fingers idly, the task at hand forgotten.

"I should go get ready," I say after a while. I am reluctant to leave, but I am supposed to work in the laundry rooms, and I don't want the Amity to say I'm not fulfilling my part of the deal they offered us.

"I'll get you something to wear," he says.

I walk barefoot down the hallway a few minutes later, wearing the shirt I slept in and a pair of shorts Tobias borrowed from the Amity. When I get back to my bedroom, Peter is standing next to my bed.

Instinct makes me straighten up and search the room for a blunt object.

"Get out," I say as steadily as I can. But it's hard to keep my voice from shaking. I can't help but remember the look in his eyes as he held me over the chasm by my throat or slammed me against the wall in the Dauntless compound.

He turns to look at me. Lately when he looks at me it's without his usual malice—instead he just seems exhausted, his posture slouched, his wounded arm in a sling. But I am not fooled.

"What are you doing in my room?"

He walks closer to me. "What are you doing stalking Marcus? I saw you after breakfast yesterday."

I match his stare with my own. "That's none of your business. Get out."

"I'm here because I don't know why *you* get to keep track of that hard drive," he says. "It's not like you're particularly stable these days."

"*I'm* unstable?" I laugh. "I find that a little funny, coming from you."

Peter pinches his lips together and says nothing.

I narrow my eyes. "Why are you so interested in the hard drive anyway?"

"I'm not stupid," he says. "I know it contains more than the simulation data."

"No, you aren't stupid, are you?" I say. "You think if you deliver it to the Erudite, they'll forgive your indiscretion and let you back in their good graces."

"I don't want to be back in their good graces," he says, stepping forward again. "If I had, I wouldn't have helped you in the Dauntless compound."

I jab his sternum with my index finger, digging in my fingernail. "You helped me because you didn't want me to shoot you again."

"I may not be an Abnegation-loving faction traitor." He seizes my finger. "But no one gets to control me, especially not the Erudite."

I yank my hand back, twisting so that he won't be able to hold on. My hands are sweaty.

"I don't expect you to understand." I wipe my hands on the hem of my shirt as I inch toward the dresser. "I'm sure if it had been Candor and not Abnegation that got attacked, you would have just let your family get shot between the eyes without protest. But I'm not like that."

"Careful what you say about my family, Stiff." He moves with me, toward the dresser, but I carefully shift so that I stand between him and the drawers. I'm not going to reveal the hard drive's location by getting it out while he's in here, but I don't want to leave the path to it clear, either.

His eyes shift to the dresser behind me, to the left side, where the hard drive is hidden. I frown at him, and then notice something I didn't before: a rectangular bulge in one of his pockets.

"Give it to me," I say. "Now."

"No."

"Give it to me, or so help me, I will kill you in your sleep."

He smirks. "If only you could see how ridiculous you look when you threaten people. Like a little girl telling me she's going to strangle me with her jump rope."

I start toward him, and he shifts back, into the hallway.

"Don't call me 'little girl.' "

"I'll call you whatever I want."

I jerk into action, aiming my left fist where I know it will hurt the worst: at the bullet wound in his arm. He dodges the punch, but instead of trying again, I seize his arm as hard as I can and wrench it to the side. Peter screams at the top of his lungs, and while he's distracted by the pain, I kick him hard in the knee, and he falls to the ground.

People rush into the hallway, wearing gray and black and yellow and red. Peter surges toward me in a half crouch, and punches me in the stomach. I hunch over, but the pain doesn't stop me—I let out something between a groan and a scream, and launch myself at him, my left elbow pulled back near my mouth so that I can slam it into his face.

One of the Amity grabs me by the arms and half lifts, half pulls me away from Peter. The wound in my shoulder throbs, but I hardly feel it through the pulse of adrenaline. I strain toward him and try to ignore the stunned faces of the Amity and the Abnegation—and Tobias—around me, and the woman kneels next to Peter, whispering words in a soothing tone of voice. I try to ignore his groans of pain and the guilt stabbing at my stomach. I hate him. I don't care. I hate him.

"Tris, calm down!" Tobias says.

"He has the hard drive!" I yell. "He stole it from me! He has it!"

Tobias walks over to Peter, ignoring the woman crouched beside him, and presses his foot into Peter's rib cage to keep him in place. He then reaches into Peter's pocket and takes out the hard drive.

Tobias says to him—very quietly—"We won't be in a safe house forever, and this wasn't very smart of you." Then he turns toward me and adds, "Not very smart of you, either. Do you want to get us kicked out?"

I scowl. The Amity man with his hand on my arm starts to pull me down the hallway. I try to wrench my body out of his grasp.

"What do you think you're doing? Let go of me!"

"You violated the terms of our peace agreement," he says gently. "We must follow protocol."

"Just go," says Tobias. "You need to cool down."

I search the faces of the crowd that has gathered. No one argues with Tobias. Their eyes skirt mine. So I allow two Amity men to escort me down the hallway.

"Watch your step," one of them says. "The floorboards are uneven here."

My head pounds, a sign that I am calming down. The graying Amity man opens a door on the left. A label on the door says CONFLICT ROOM.

"Are you putting me in time-out or something?" I scowl. That is something the Amity would do: put me in time-out, and then teach me to do cleansing breaths or think positive thoughts.

The room is so bright I have to squint to see. The opposite wall has large windows that look out over the orchard. Despite this, the room feels small, probably because the ceiling, like the walls and floor, is also covered with wooden boards.

"Please sit," the older man says, gesturing toward the stool in the middle of the room. It, like all other furniture in the Amity compound, is made of unpolished wood, and looks sturdy, like it is still attached to the earth. I do not sit.

"The fight is over," I say. "I won't do it again. Not here."

"We have to follow protocol," the younger man says. "Please sit, and we'll discuss what happened, and then we'll let you go."

All their voices are so soft. Not hushed, like the Abnegation speak, always treading holy ground and trying not to disturb. Soft, soothing, low—I wonder, then, if that is something they teach their initiates here. How best to speak, move, smile, to encourage peace.

I don't want to sit down, but I do, perched on the edge of the chair so I can get up fast, if necessary. The younger man stands in front of me. Hinges creak behind me. I look over my shoulder—the older man is fumbling with something on a counter behind me.

"What are you doing?"

"I am making tea," he says.

"I don't think tea is really the solution to this."

"Then tell us," the younger man says, drawing my attention back to the windows. He smiles at me. "What do you believe is the solution?"

"Throwing Peter out of this compound."

"It seems to me," the man says gently, "that you are the one who attacked him—indeed, that you are the one who shot him in the arm."

"You have no idea what he did to deserve those things." My cheeks get hot again and mimic my heartbeat. "He tried to kill me. And someone else—he stabbed someone else in the eye . . . with a *butter* knife. He is evil. I had every *right* to—"

I feel a sharp pain in my neck. Dark spots cover the man in front of me, obscuring my view of his face.

"I'm sorry, dear," he says. "We are just following protocol."

The older man is holding a syringe. A few drops of whatever he injected me with are still in it. They are bright green, the color of grass. I blink rapidly, and the dark spots disappear, but the world still swims before me, like I am tilting forward and back in a rocking chair.

"How do you feel?" the younger man says.

"I feel . . ." *Angry,* I was about to say. Angry with Peter, angry with the Amity. *But that's not true, is it?* I smile. "I feel good. I feel a little like . . . like I'm floating. Or swaying. How do *you* feel?"

"Dizziness is a side effect of the serum. You may want to rest this afternoon. And I'm feeling well. Thank you for asking," he says. "You may leave now, if you would like."

"Can you tell me where to find Tobias?" I say. When I imagine his face, affection for him bubbles up inside me, and all I want to do is kiss him. "Four, I mean. He's handsome, isn't he? I don't really know why he likes me so much. I'm not very nice, am I?"

"Not most of the time, no," the man says. "But I think you could be, if you tried."

"Thank you," I say. "That's nice of you to say."

"I think you'll find him in the orchard," he says. "I saw him go outside after the fight."

I laugh a little. "The fight. What a silly thing . . ."

And it does seem like a silly thing, slamming your fist into someone else's body. Like a caress, but too hard. A caress is much nicer. Maybe I should have run my hand along Peter's arm instead. That would have felt better to both of us. My knuckles wouldn't ache right now.

I get up and steer myself toward the door. I have to lean against the wall for balance, but it's sturdy, so I don't mind. I stumble down the hallway, giggling at my inability to balance. I'm clumsy again, just like I was when I was younger. My mother used to smile at me and say, "Be careful where you put your feet, Beatrice. I don't want you to hurt yourself."

I walk outside and the green on the trees seems greener, so potent I can almost taste it. Maybe I *can* taste it, and it is like the grass I decided to chew when I was a child just to see what it was like. I almost fall down the stairs because of the swaying and burst into laughter when the grass tickles my bare feet. I wander toward the orchard.

"Four!" I call out. Why am I calling out a number? Oh yes. Because that's his name. I call out again, "Four! Where are you?"

"Tris?" says a voice from the trees on my right. It almost sounds like the tree is talking to me. I giggle, but of course it's just Tobias, ducking under a branch.

I run toward him, and the ground lurches to the side, so I almost fall. His hand touches my waist, steadies me. The touch sends a shock through my body, and all my insides burn like his fingers ignited them. I pull closer to him, pressing my body against his, and lift my head to kiss him.

"What did they—" he starts, but I stop him with my lips. He kisses me back, but too quickly, so I sigh heavily.

"That was lame," I say. "Okay, no it wasn't, but . . ."

I stand on my tiptoes to kiss him again, and he presses his finger to my lips to stop me.

"Tris," he says. "What did they do to you? You're acting like a lunatic."

"That's not very nice of you to say," I say. "They put me in a good mood, that's all. And now I really want to kiss you, so if you could just *relax—*"

"I'm not going to kiss you. I'm going to figure out what's going on," he says.

I pout my lower lip for a second, but then I grin as the pieces come together in my mind.

"*That's* why you like me!" I exclaim. "Because you're not very nice either! It makes so much more sense now."

"Come on," he says. "We're going to see Johanna."

"I like you, too."

"That's encouraging," he replies flatly. "Come *on.* Oh, for God's sake. I'll just carry you."

He swings me into his arms, one arm under my knees and the other around my back. I wrap my arms around his neck and plant a kiss on his cheek. Then I discover that the air feels nice on my feet when I kick them, so I move my feet up and down as he walks us toward the building where Johanna works.

When we reach her office, she is sitting behind a desk with a stack of paper in front of her, chewing on a pencil eraser. She looks up at us, and her mouth drifts open slightly. A hunk of dark hair covers the left side of her face.

"You really shouldn't cover up your scar," I say. "You look prettier with your hair out of your face."

Tobias sets me down too heavily. The impact is jarring and hurts my shoulder a little, but I like the sound my feet made when they hit the floor. I laugh, but neither Johanna nor Tobias laughs with me. Strange.

"What did you do to her?" Tobias says, terse. "What in God's name did you do?"

"I . . ." Johanna frowns at me. "They must have given her too much. She's very small; they probably didn't take her height and weight into account."

"They must have given her too much of *what*?" he says.

"You have a nice voice," I say.

"Tris," he says, "please be quiet."

"The peace serum," Johanna says. "In small doses, it has a mild, calming effect and improves the mood. The only side effect is some slight dizziness. We administer it to members of our community who have trouble keeping the peace."

Tobias snorts. "I'm not an idiot. *Every* member of your community has trouble keeping the peace, because they're all human. You probably dump it into the water supply."

Johanna does not respond for a few seconds. She folds her hands in front of her.

"Clearly you know that is not the case, or this conflict would not have occurred," she says. "But whatever we agree to do here, we do together, as a faction. If I could give the serum to everyone in this city, I would. You would certainly not be in the situation you are in now if I had."

"Oh, definitely," he says. "Drugging the entire population is the best solution to our problem. Great plan."

"Sarcasm is not kind, Four," she says gently. "Now, I am sorry about the mistake in giving too much to Tris, I really am. But she violated the terms of our agreement, and I'm afraid that you might not be able to stay here much longer as a result. The conflict between her and the boy—Peter—is not something we can forget."

"Don't worry," says Tobias. "We intend to leave as soon as humanly possible."

"Good," she says with a small smile. "Peace between Amity and Dauntless can only happen when we maintain our distance from each other."

"That explains a lot."

"Excuse me?" she says. "What are you insinuating?"

"It explains," he says, gritting his teeth, "why, under a pretense of *neutrality*—as if such a thing is possible!—you have left us to die at the hands of the Erudite."

Johanna sighs quietly and looks out the window. Beyond it is a small courtyard with vines growing in it. The vines creep onto the window's corners, like they are trying to come in and join the conversation.

"The Amity wouldn't do something like that," I say. "That's *mean*."

"It is for the sake of peace that we remain uninvolved—" Johanna begins.

"Peace." Tobias almost spits the word. "Yes, I'm sure it will be very peaceful when we are all either dead or cowering in submission under the threat of mind control or stuck in an endless simulation."

Johanna's face contorts, and I mimic her, to see what it feels like to have my face that way. It doesn't feel very good. I'm not sure why she did it to begin with.

She says slowly, "The decision was not mine to make. If it was, perhaps we would be having a different conversation right now."

"Are you saying you disagree with them?"

"I am saying," she says, "that it isn't my place to disagree with my faction publicly, but I might, in the privacy of my own heart."

"Tris and I will be gone in two days," says Tobias. "I hope your faction doesn't change their decision to make this compound a safe house."

"Our decisions are not easily unmade. What about Peter?"

"You'll have to deal with him separately," he says. "Because he won't be coming with us."

Tobias takes my hand, and his skin feels nice against mine, though it's not smooth or soft. I smile apologetically at Johanna, and her expression remains unchanged.

"Four," she says. "If you and your friends would like to remain . . . untouched by our serum, you may want to avoid the bread."

Tobias says thank you over his shoulder as we make our way down the hallway together, me skipping every other step.

CHAPTER
SEVEN

THE SERUM WEARS off five hours later, when the sun is just beginning to set. Tobias shut me in my room for the rest of the day, checking on me every hour. This time when he comes in, I am sitting on the bed, glaring at the wall.

"Thank God," he says, pressing his forehead to the door. "I was beginning to think it would never wear off and I would have to leave you here to . . . smell flowers, or whatever you wanted to do while you were on that stuff."

"I'll kill them," I say. "I will *kill* them."

"Don't bother. We're leaving soon anyway," he says, closing the door behind him. He takes the hard drive from his back pocket. "I thought we could hide this behind your dresser."

"That's where it was before."

"Yeah, and that's why Peter won't look for it here again." Tobias pulls the dresser away from the wall with one hand and wedges the hard drive behind it with the other.

"Why couldn't I fight the peace serum?" I say. "If my brain is weird enough to resist the simulation serum, why not this one?"

"I don't know, really," he says. He drops down next to me on the bed, jostling the mattress. "Maybe in order to fight off a serum, you have to *want* to."

"Well, obviously I *wanted* to," I say, frustrated, but without conviction. Did I want to? Or was it nice to forget about anger, forget about pain, forget about everything for a few hours?

"Sometimes," he says, sliding his arm across my shoulders, "people just want to be happy, even if it's not real."

He's right. Even now, this peace between us comes from not talking about things—about Will, or my parents, or me almost shooting him in the head, or Marcus. But I do not dare to disturb it with the truth, because I am too busy clinging to it for support.

"You might be right," I say quietly.

"Are you *conceding*?" he says, his mouth falling open with mock surprise. "Seems like that serum did you some good after all. . . ."

I shove him as hard as I can. "Take that back. Take it back *now*."

"Okay, okay!" He puts up his hands. "It's just . . . I'm not very nice either, you know. That's why I like you so—"

"Out!" I shout, pointing at the door.

Laughing to himself, Tobias kisses my cheek and leaves the room.

+ + +

That evening, I am too embarrassed by what happened to go to dinner, so I spend the time in the branches of an apple tree at the far end of the orchard, picking ripe apples. I climb as high as I dare to get them, muscles burning. I have discovered that sitting still leaves little spaces for the grief to get in, so I stay busy.

I am wiping my forehead with the hem of my shirt, standing on a branch, when I hear the sound. It is faint, at first, joining the buzz of cicadas. I stand still to listen, and after a moment, I realize what it is: cars.

The Amity own about a dozen trucks that they use for transporting goods, but they only do that on weekends. The back of my neck tingles. If it isn't the Amity, it's probably the Erudite. But I have to be sure.

I grab the branch above me with both hands, but pull myself up with only my left arm. I'm surprised I'm still able to do that. I stand hunched, twigs and leaves tangled in my hair. A few apples fall to the ground when I shift my weight. Apple trees aren't very tall; I may not be able to see far enough.

I use the nearby branches as steps, with my hands to steady me, twisting and leaning around the tree's maze. I remember climbing the Ferris wheel on the pier, my muscles shaking, my hands throbbing. I am wounded now, but stronger, and the climbing feels easier.

The branches get thinner, weaker. I lick my lips and look at the next one. I need to climb as high as possible, but the branch I'm aiming for is short and looks pliable. I put my foot on it, testing its strength. It bends, but holds. I start to lift myself up, to put the other foot down, and the branch snaps.

I gasp as I fall back, seizing the tree trunk at the last second. This will have to be high enough. I stand on my tiptoes and squint in the direction of the sound.

At first I see nothing but a stretch of farmland, a strip of empty ground, the fence, and the fields and beginnings of buildings that lie beyond it. But approaching the gate are a few moving specks—silver, when the light catches them. Cars with black roofs—solar panels, which means only one thing. Erudite.

A breath hisses between my teeth. I don't allow myself to think; I just put one foot down, then the other, so fast that bark peels off the branches and drifts toward the ground. As soon as my feet touch the earth, I run.

I count the rows of trees as I pass them. *Seven, eight.* The branches dip low, and I pass just beneath them. *Nine, ten.* I hold my right arm against my chest as I sprint faster, the bullet wound in my shoulder throbbing with each footstep. *Eleven, twelve.*

When I reach the thirteenth row, I throw my body to the right, down one of the aisles. The trees are close together in the thirteenth row. Their branches grow into one another, creating a maze of leaves and twigs and apples.

My lungs sting from a lack of oxygen, but I am not far from the end of the orchard. Sweat runs into my eyebrows. I reach the dining hall and throw open the door, shoving my way through a group of Amity men, and he is there; Tobias sits at one end of the cafeteria with Peter and Caleb and Susan. I can barely see them between the spots on my vision, but Tobias touches my shoulder.

"Erudite," is all I manage to say.

"Coming here?" he says.

I nod.

"Do we have time to run?"

I am not sure about that.

By now, the Abnegation at the other end of the table are paying attention. They gather around us.

"Why do we need to run?" says Susan. "The Amity established this place as a safe house. No conflict allowed."

"The Amity will have trouble enforcing that policy," says Marcus. "How do you stop conflict without conflict?"

Susan nods.

"But we can't leave," Peter says. "We don't have time. They'll see us."

"Tris has a gun," Tobias says. "We can try to fight our way out."

He starts toward the dormitory.

"Wait," I say. "I have an idea." I scan the crowd of Abnegation. "Disguises. The Erudite don't know for sure that we're still here. We can pretend to be Amity."

"Those of us who aren't dressed like the Amity should go to the dormitories, then," Marcus says. "The rest of you, put your hair down; try to mimic their behavior."

The Abnegation who are dressed in gray leave the dining hall in a pack and cross the courtyard to the guests' dormitory. Once inside, I run to my bedroom, get on my hands and knees, and reach under the mattress for the gun.

I feel around for a few seconds before I find it, and when I do, my throat pinches, and I can't swallow. I don't want to touch the gun. I don't want to touch it again.

Come on, Tris. I shove the gun under the waistband of my red pants. It is lucky they are so baggy. I notice the vials of healing salve and pain medicine on the bedside table and shove them in my pocket, just in case we do manage to escape.

Then I reach behind the dresser for the hard drive.

If the Erudite catch us—which is likely—they will search us, and I don't want to just hand over the attack simulation again. But this hard drive also contains the surveillance footage from the attack. The record of our losses. Of my parents' deaths. The only piece of them I have left. And because the Abnegation don't take photographs, the only documentation I have of how they looked.

Years from now, when my memories begin to fade, what will I have to remind me of what they looked like? Their faces will change in my mind. I will never see them again.

Don't be stupid. It's not important.

I squeeze the hard drive so tightly it hurts.

Then why does it feel *so important?*

"Don't be stupid," I say aloud. I grit my teeth and grab the lamp from my bedside table. I yank the plug from the socket, throw the lampshade onto the bed, and crouch over the hard drive. Blinking tears from my eyes, I slam the base of the lamp into it, creating a dent.

I bring the lamp down again, and again, and again, until the hard drive cracks and pieces of it spread across the floor. Then I kick the shards under the dresser, put the lamp back, and walk into the hallway, wiping my eyes with the back of my hand.

A few minutes later, a small crowd of gray-clad men and women—and Peter—stand in the hallway, sorting through stacks of clothes.

"Tris," says Caleb. "You're still wearing gray."

I pinch my father's shirt, and hesitate.

"It's Dad's," I say. If I change out of it, I will have to leave it behind. I bite my lip so that the pain will steady me. I have to get rid of it. It's just a shirt. That's all it is.

"I'll put it on under mine," Caleb says. "They'll never see it."

I nod and grab a red shirt from the dwindling pile of clothes. It is large enough to conceal the bulge of the gun. I duck into a nearby room to

change, and hand off the gray shirt to Caleb when I get to the hallway.
The door is open, and through it I see Tobias stuffing Abnegation clothes
into the trash bin.

"Do you think the Amity will lie for us?" I ask him, leaning out the
open doorway.

"To prevent conflict?" Tobias nods. "Absolutely."

He wears a red collared shirt and a pair of jeans that are fraying at
the knee. The combination looks ridiculous on him.

"Nice shirt," I say.

He wrinkles his nose at me. "It was the only thing that covered up the
neck tattoo, okay?"

I smile nervously. I forgot about my tattoos, but the shirt hides them
well enough.

The Erudite cars pull up to the compound. There are five of them, all
silver with black roofs. Their engines seem to purr as the wheels bump
over uneven ground. I slip just inside the building, leaving the door open
behind me, and Tobias busies himself with the latch on the trash bin.

The cars all pull to a stop, and the doors pop open, revealing at least
five men and women in Erudite blue.

And about fifteen in Dauntless black.

When the Dauntless come closer, I see strips of blue fabric wrapped
around their arms that can only signify their allegiance to Erudite. The
faction that enslaved their minds.

Tobias takes my hand and leads me into the dormitory.

"I didn't think our faction would be that stupid," he says. "You have
the gun, right?"

"Yes," I say. "But there's no guarantee I can fire it with any accuracy
with my left hand."

"You should work on that," he says. Always an instructor.

"I will," I say. I shake a little as I add, "If we live."

His hands skim my bare arms. "Just bounce a little when you walk,"
he says, kissing my forehead, "and pretend you're afraid of their guns"—
another kiss between my eyebrows—"and act like the shrinking violet
you could never be"—a kiss on my cheek—"and you'll be fine."

"Okay," I say. My hands tremble as I grip his shirt collar. I pull his
mouth down to mine.

A bell sounds, once, twice, three times. It is a summons to the dining hall, where the Amity gather for less formal occasions than the meeting we attended. We join the crowd of Abnegation-turned-Amity.

I pull pins from Susan's hair—the hairstyle is too severe for Amity.
She gives me a small, grateful smile as her hair falls on her shoulders,
the first time I have ever seen it that way. It softens her square jaw.

I am supposed to be braver than the Abnegation, but they don't seem as worried as I am. They offer each other smiles and walk in silence—in too much silence. I wedge my way between them and jab one of the older women in the shoulder.

"Tell the kids to play tag," I say to her.

"Tag?" she says.

"They're acting respectful and . . . Stiff," I say, cringing as I say the word that was my nickname in Dauntless. "And Amity kids would be causing a ruckus. Just do it, okay?"

The woman touches one Abnegation child on the shoulder and whispers something to him, and a few seconds later a small group of children run down the hallway, dodging Amity feet and yelling, "I touched you! You're *it*!" "No, that was my sleeve!"

Caleb catches on, jabbing Susan in the ribs so she shrieks with laughter. I try to relax, injecting a bounce into my step as Tobias suggested, letting my arms swing as I turn corners. It is amazing how pretending to be in a different faction changes everything—even the way I walk. That must be why it's so strange that I could easily belong in three of them.

We catch up to the Amity in front of us as we cross the courtyard to the dining hall and disperse among them. I keep Tobias in my peripheral vision, not wanting to stray too far from him. The Amity don't ask questions; they just let us dissolve into their faction.

A pair of Dauntless traitors stand by the door to the dining hall, their guns in hand, and I stiffen. It feels real to me, suddenly, that I am unarmed and being herded into a building surrounded by Erudite and Dauntless, and if they discover me, there will be nowhere to run. They will shoot me on the spot.

I consider making a break for it. But where would I go that they could not catch me? I try to breathe normally. I am almost past them—*don't look, don't look.* A few steps away—*eyes away, away.*

Susan loops her arm through mine.

"I'm telling you a joke," she says, "that you find very funny."

I cover my hand with my mouth and force a giggle that sounds high-pitched and foreign, but judging by the smile she gives me, it was believable. We hang on each other the way Amity girls do, glancing at the Dauntless and then giggling again. I am amazed by how I manage to do it, with the leaden feeling inside me.

"Thank you," I mutter once we're inside.

"You're welcome," she replies.

Tobias sits across from me at one of the long tables, and Susan sits

next to me. The rest of the Abnegation spread throughout the room, and
Caleb and Peter are a few seats down from me.

I tap my fingers on my knees as we wait for something to happen. For
a long time we just sit there, and I pretend to be listening to an Amity girl
telling a story on my left. But every so often I look at Tobias, and he looks
back at me, like we're passing fear back and forth between us.

Finally Johanna walks in with an Erudite woman. Her bright blue
shirt seems to glow against her skin, which is dark brown. She searches
the room as she speaks to Johanna. I hold my breath as her eyes find me—
and then let it out when she moves on without a moment's hesitation. She
did not recognize me.

At least, not yet.

Someone bangs on a tabletop, and the room goes quiet. This is it.
This is the moment she either hands us over, or doesn't.

"Our Erudite and Dauntless friends are looking for some people,"
Johanna says. "Several members of Abnegation, three members of
Dauntless, and a former Erudite initiate." She smiles. "In the interest of
full cooperation, I told them that the people they were looking for were,
in fact, here, but have since moved on. They would like permission to
search the premises, which means we have to vote. Does anyone object to
a search?"

The tension in her voice suggests that if anyone does object, they
should keep their mouth shut. I don't know if the Amity pick up on that
kind of thing, but no one says anything. Johanna nods to the Erudite
woman.

"Three of you stick around," the woman says to the Dauntless guards
clustered by the entrance. "The rest of you, search all the buildings and
report back if you find anything. Go."

There is so much they could find. The pieces of the hard drive.
Clothes I forgot to throw out. A suspicious lack of trinkets and decorations in our living spaces. I feel my pulse behind my eyes as the three
Dauntless soldiers who stayed behind pace up and down the rows of
tables.

The back of my neck tingles as one of them walks behind me, his
footsteps loud and heavy. Not for the first time in my life, I'm glad that
I'm small and plain. I don't draw people's eyes to me.

But Tobias does. He wears his pride in his posture, in the way his
eyes claim everything they land on. That is not an Amity trait. It can only
be a Dauntless one.

The Dauntless woman walking toward him looks at him right away.
Her eyes narrow as she walks closer, and then stops directly behind him.

I wish the collar of his shirt were higher. I wish he didn't have so many tattoos. I wish . . .

"Your hair is pretty short for an Amity," she says.

. . . he did not cut his hair like the Abnegation.

"It's hot," he says.

The excuse might work if he knew how to deliver it, but he says it with a snap.

She stretches out her hand and, with her index finger, pulls back the collar of his shirt to see his tattoo.

And Tobias moves.

He grabs the woman's wrist, yanking her forward so she loses her balance. She hits her head against the edge of the table and falls. Across the room, a gun goes off, someone screams, and everyone dives under the tables or crouches next to the benches.

Everyone except me. I sit where I was before the gunshot sounded, clutching the edge of the table. I know that's where I am, but I don't see the cafeteria anymore. I see the alley I escaped down after my mother died. I stare at the gun in my hands, at the smooth skin between Will's eyebrows.

A small sound gurgles in my throat. It would have been a scream if my teeth had not been clamped shut. The flash of memory fades, but I still can't move.

Tobias grabs the Dauntless woman by the back of her neck and wrenches her to her feet. He has her gun in his hand. He uses her to shield him as he fires over her right shoulder at the Dauntless soldier across the room.

"Tris!" he shouts. "A little help here?"

I pull my shirt up just far enough to reach the handle of the gun, and my fingers meet metal. It feels so cold that it hurts my fingertips, but that can't be; it's so hot in here. A Dauntless man at the end of the aisle aims his own revolver at me. The black spot at the end of the barrel grows around me, and I can hear my heart but nothing else.

Caleb lunges forward and grabs my gun. He holds it in both hands and fires at the knees of the Dauntless man who stands just feet away from him.

The Dauntless man screams and collapses, his hands clutching his leg, which gives Tobias the opportunity to shoot him in the head. His pain is momentary.

My entire body is trembling and I can't stop it. Tobias still has the Dauntless woman by the throat, but this time, he aims his gun at the Erudite woman.

"Say another word," says Tobias, "and I'll shoot."

The Erudite woman's mouth is open, but she doesn't speak.

"Whoever's with us should start running," Tobias says, his voice filling the room.

All at once, the Abnegation rise from their places under tables and benches, and start toward the door. Caleb pulls me up from the bench. I start toward the door.

Then I see something. A twitch, a flicker of movement. The Erudite woman lifts a small gun, points it at a man in a yellow shirt in front of me. Instinct, not presence of mind, pushes me into a dive. My hands collide with the man, and the bullet hits the wall instead of him, instead of me.

"Put the gun down," says Tobias, pointing his revolver at the Erudite woman. "I have *very* good aim, and I'm betting that you don't."

I blink a few times to get the blurriness out of my eyes. Peter stares back at me. I just saved his life. He does not thank me, and I don't acknowledge him.

The Erudite woman drops her gun. Together Peter and I walk toward the door. Tobias follows us, walking backward so he can keep his gun on the Erudite woman. At the last second before he passes through the threshold, he slams the door between him and her.

And we all run.

We sprint down the center aisle of the orchard in a breathless pack. The night air is heavy as a blanket and smells like rain. Shouts follow us. Car doors slam. I run faster than I can possibly run, like I'm breathing adrenaline instead of air. The purr of engines chases me into the trees. Tobias's hand closes around mine.

We run through a cornfield in a long line. By then, the cars have caught up to us. The headlights creep through the tall stalks, illuminating a leaf here, an ear of corn there.

"Split up!" someone yells, and it sounds like Marcus.

We divide and spread through the field like spilling water. I grab Caleb's arm. I hear Susan gasping behind Caleb.

We crash over cornstalks. The heavy leaves cut my cheeks and arms. I stare between Tobias's shoulder blades as we run. I hear a heavy thump and a scream. There are screams everywhere, to my left, to my right. Gunshots. The Abnegation are dying again, dying like they were when I pretended to be under the simulation. And all I'm doing is running.

Finally we reach the fence. Tobias runs along it, pushing it until he finds a hole. He holds the chain links back so Caleb, Susan, and I can crawl through. Before we start running again, I stop and look back at the cornfield we just left. I see headlights distantly glowing. But I don't hear anything.

"Where are the others?" whispers Susan.

I say, "Gone."

Susan sobs. Tobias pulls me to his side roughly, and starts forward. My face burns with shallow cuts from the corn leaves, but my eyes are dry. The Abnegation deaths are just another weight I am unable to set down.

We stay away from the dirt road the Erudite and Dauntless took to get to the Amity compound, following the train tracks toward the city. There is nowhere to hide out here, no trees or buildings that can shield us, but it doesn't matter. The Erudite can't drive through the fence anyway, and it will take them a while to reach the gate.

"I have to . . . stop . . ." says Susan from somewhere in the darkness behind me.

We stop. Susan collapses to the ground, crying, and Caleb crouches next to her. Tobias and I look toward the city, which is still illuminated, because it's not midnight yet. I want to feel something. Fear, anger, grief. But I don't. All I feel is the need to keep moving.

Tobias turns toward me.

"What was that, Tris?" he says.

"What?" I say, and I am ashamed of how weak my voice sounds. I don't know whether he's talking about Peter or what came before or something else.

"You froze! Someone was about to kill you and you just *sat* there!" He is yelling now. "I thought I could rely on you at least to save your own life!"

"Hey!" says Caleb. "Give her a break, all right?"

"No," says Tobias, staring at me. "She doesn't need a break." His voice softens. "What happened?"

He still believes that I am strong. Strong enough that I don't need his sympathy. I used to think he was right, but now I am not sure. I clear my throat.

"I panicked," I say. "It won't happen again."

He raises an eyebrow.

"It won't," I say again, louder this time.

"Okay." He looks unconvinced. "We have to get somewhere safe. They'll regroup and start looking for us."

"You think they care that much about us?" I say.

"Us, yes," he says. "We were probably the only ones they were really after, apart from Marcus, who is most likely dead."

I don't know how I expected him to say it—with relief, maybe, because Marcus, his father and the menace of his life, is finally gone. Or with pain and sadness, because his father might have been killed, and sometimes grief doesn't make much sense. But he says it like it's just a fact, like the direction we're moving or the time of day.

"Tobias . . ." I start to say, but then I realize I don't know what comes after it.

"Time to go," Tobias says over his shoulder.

Caleb coaxes Susan to her feet. She moves only with the help of his arm across her back, pressing her forward.

I didn't realize until that moment that Dauntless initiation had taught me an important lesson: how to keep going.

CHAPTER
EIGHT

WE DECIDE TO follow the railroad tracks to the city, because none of us is good at navigation. I walk from tie to tie, Tobias balances on the rail, wobbling only occasionally, and Caleb and Susan shuffle behind us. I twitch at every unidentified noise, tensing until I realize it is just the wind, or the squeak of Tobias's shoes on the rail. I wish we could keep running, but it's a feat that my legs are even moving at this point.

Then I hear a low groan from the rails.

I bend down and press my palms to the rail, closing my eyes to focus on the feeling of the metal beneath my hands. The vibration feels like a sigh going through my body. I stare between Susan's knees down the tracks and see no train light, but that doesn't mean anything. The train could be running with no horns and no lamps to announce its arrival.

I see the gleam of a small train car, far away now but approaching fast.

"It's coming," I say. It is an effort to get to my feet when all I want to do is sit down, but I do, brushing my hands on my jeans. "I think we should get on."

"Even if it's run by the Erudite?" says Caleb.

"If the Erudite were running the train, they would have taken it to the Amity compound to look for us," Tobias says. "I think it's worth the risk. We'll be able to hide in the city. Here we're just waiting for them to find us."

We all get off the tracks. Caleb gives Susan step-by-step instructions for getting on a moving train, the way only a former Erudite can. I watch the first car approach; listen to the rhythmic bump of the car over the ties, the whisper of metal wheel against metal rail.

As the first car passes me, I start to run. I ignore the burning in my legs. Caleb helps Susan into a middle car first, then jumps in himself. I take a quick breath and throw my body to the right, slamming into the floor of the car with my legs dangling over the edge. Caleb grabs my left arm and pulls me in the rest of the way. Tobias uses the handle to swing himself in after me.

I look up, and stop breathing.

Eyes glitter in the darkness. Dark shapes sit in the car, more numerous than we are.

The factionless.

+ + +

The wind whistles through the car. Everyone is on their feet and armed—except Susan and me, who have no weapons. A factionless man with an eye patch has a gun pointed at Tobias. I wonder how he got it.

Next to him, an older factionless woman holds a knife—the kind I used to cut bread with. Behind him, someone else holds a large plank of wood with a nail sticking out of it.

"I've never seen the Amity armed before," the factionless woman with the knife says.

The factionless man with the gun looks familiar. He wears tattered clothes in different colors—a black T-shirt with a torn Abnegation jacket over it, blue jeans mended with red thread, brown boots. All faction clothing is represented in the group before me: black Candor pants paired with black Dauntless shirts, yellow dresses with blue sweatshirts over them. Most items are torn or smudged in some way, but some are not. Freshly stolen, I imagine.

"They aren't Amity," the man with the gun says. "They're Dauntless."

Then I recognize him: he is Edward, a fellow initiate who left Dauntless after Peter attacked him with a butter knife. That is why he wears an eye patch.

I remember steadying his head as he lay screaming on the floor, and cleaning the blood he left behind.

"Hello, Edward," I say.

He inclines his head to me, but doesn't lower his gun. "Tris."

"Whatever you are," the woman says, "you'll have to get off this train if you want to stay alive."

"Please," says Susan, her lip wobbling. Her eyes fill with tears. "We've been running . . . and the rest of them are dead and I don't . . ." She starts to sob again. "I don't think I can keep going, I . . ."

I get the strange urge to hit my head against the wall. Other people's sobs make me uncomfortable. It's selfish of me, maybe.

"We're running from the Erudite," says Caleb. "If we get off, it will be easier for them to find us. So we would appreciate it if you let us ride into the city with you."

"Yeah?" Edward tilts his head. "What have you ever done for us?"

"I helped you when no one else would," I say. "Remember?"

"You, maybe. But the others?" says Edward. "Not so much."

Tobias steps forward, so Edward's gun is almost against his throat.

"My name is Tobias Eaton," Tobias says. "I don't think you want to push me off this train."

The effect of the name on the people in the car is immediate and bewildering: they lower their weapons. They exchange meaningful looks.

"Eaton? Really?" Edward says, eyebrows raised. "I have to admit, I did not see that coming." He clears his throat. "Fine, you can come. But when we get to the city, you've got to come with us."

Then he smiles a little. "We know someone who's been looking for you, Tobias Eaton."

+ + +

Tobias and I sit on the edge of the car with our legs dangling over the edge.

"Do you know who it is?"

Tobias nods.

"Who, then?"

"It's hard to explain," he says. "I have a lot to tell you."

I lean against him.

"Yeah," I say. "So do I."

+ + +

I don't know how much time passes before they tell us to get off. But when they do, we are in the part of the city where the factionless live, about a mile from where I grew up. I recognize each building we pass as one I walked by every time I missed the bus home from school. The one with the broken bricks. The one with a fallen streetlight leaning against it.

We stand in the doorway of the train car, all four of us in a line. Susan whimpers.

"What if we get hurt?" she says.

I grab her hand. "We'll jump together. You and me. I've done this a dozen times and never got hurt."

She nods and squeezes my fingers so hard they hurt.

"On three. One," I say, "Two. *Three.*"

I jump, and pull her with me. My feet slam into the ground and continue forward, but Susan just falls to the pavement and rolls onto her side. Aside from a scraped knee, though, she seems to be all right. The others jump off without difficulty—even Caleb, who has only jumped from a train once before, as far as I know.

I'm not sure who could know Tobias among the factionless. It could be Drew or Molly, who failed Dauntless initiation—but they didn't even know Tobias's real name, and besides, Edward probably would have killed them by now, judging by how ready he was to shoot us. It must be someone from Abnegation, or from school.

Susan seems to have calmed down. She walks on her own now, next to Caleb, and her cheeks are drying with no new tears to wet them.

Tobias walks beside me, touching my shoulder lightly.

"It's been a while since I checked that shoulder," he says. "How is it?"

"Okay. I brought the pain medicine, luckily," I say. I'm glad to talk about something light—as light as a wound can be, anyway. "I don't think I'm letting it heal very well. I keep using my arm or landing on it."

"There will be plenty of time for healing once all this is over."

"Yeah." *Or it won't matter if I heal,* I add silently, *because I'll be dead.*

"Here," he says, taking a small knife from his back pocket and handing it to me. "Just in case."

I put it in my own pocket. I feel even more nervous now.

The factionless lead us down the street and left into a grimy alleyway that stinks of garbage. Rats scatter in front of us with squeaks of terror, and I see only their tails, slipping between mounds of waste, empty trash cans, soggy cardboard boxes. I breathe through my mouth so I don't throw up.

Edward stops next to one of the crumbling brick buildings and forces a steel door open. I wince, half expecting the entire building to fall down if he pulls too hard. The windows are so thick with grime that almost no light penetrates them. We follow Edward into a dank room. In the flickering glow of a lantern, I see . . . people.

People sitting next to rolls of bedding. People prying open cans of food. People sipping bottles of water. And children, weaving between the groups of adults, not confined to a particular color of clothing—factionless children.

We are in a factionless storehouse, and the factionless, who are supposed to be scattered, isolated, and without community . . . are together inside it. Are together, like a *faction.*

I don't know what I expected of them, but I am surprised by how normal they seem. They don't fight one another or avoid one another. Some of them tell jokes, others speak to each other quietly. Gradually, though, they all seem to realize that we aren't supposed to be there.

"Come on," Edward says, bending his finger to beckon us toward him. "She's back here."

Stares and silence greet us as we follow Edward deeper into the building that is supposed to be abandoned. Finally I can't contain my questions any longer.

"What's going on here? Why are you all together like this?"

"You thought they—we—were all split up," Edward says over his shoulder. "Well, they were, for a while. Too hungry to do much of anything except look for food. But then the Stiffs started giving them food, clothes, tools, everything. And they got stronger, and waited. They were like that when I found them, and they welcomed me."

We walk into a dark hallway. I feel at home, in the dark and the quiet that are like the tunnels in Dauntless headquarters. Tobias, however, winds a loose thread from his shirt around his finger, backward and forward, over and over. He knows who we're meeting, but I still have no idea. How is it I know this little about the boy who says he loves me—the boy whose real name is powerful enough to keep us alive in a train car full of enemies?

Edward stops at a metal door and pounds on it with his fist.

"Wait, you said they were waiting?" says Caleb. "What were they waiting *for*, exactly?"

"For the world to fall apart," Edward says. "And now it has."

The door opens, and a severe-looking woman with a lazy eye stands in the doorway. Her steady eye scans the four of us.

"Strays?" she says.

"Not hardly, Therese." He jabs his thumb over his shoulder, at Tobias. "This one's Tobias Eaton."

Therese stares at Tobias for a few seconds, then nods. "He certainly is. Hold on."

She shuts the door again. Tobias swallows hard, his Adam's apple bobbing.

"You know who she's going to get, don't you," says Caleb to Tobias.

"Caleb," Tobias says. "Please shut up."

To my surprise, my brother suppresses his Erudite curiosity.

The door opens again, and Therese steps back to let us in. We walk into an old boiler room with machinery that emerges from the darkness so suddenly I hit it with my knees and elbows. Therese leads us through the maze of metal to the back of the room, where several bulbs dangle from the ceiling over a table.

A middle-aged woman stands behind the table. She has curly black hair and olive skin. Her features are stern, so angular they almost make her unattractive, but not quite.

Tobias clutches my hand. At that moment I realize that he and the woman have the same nose—hooked, a little too big on her face but the right size on his. They also have the same strong jaw, distinct chin, spare upper lip, stick-out ears. Only her eyes are different—instead of blue, they are so dark they look black.

"Evelyn," he says, his voice shaking a little.

Evelyn was the name of Marcus's wife and Tobias's mother. My grip on Tobias's hand loosens. Just days ago I was remembering her funeral. Her *funeral*. And now she stands in front of me, her eyes colder than the eyes of any Abnegation woman I've ever seen.

"Hello." She walks around the table, surveying him. "You look older."

"Yes, well. The passage of time tends to do that to a person."

He already knew she was alive. How long ago did he find out?

She smiles. "So you've finally come—"

"Not for the reason you think," he interrupts her. "We were running from Erudite, and the only chance of escape we had required me to tell your poorly armed lackeys my name."

She must have made him angry somehow. But I can't help but think that if I discovered my mother was alive after thinking she was dead for so long, I would never speak to her the way Tobias speaks to his mother now, no matter what she had done.

The truth of that thought makes me ache. I push it aside and focus instead on what's in front of me. On the table behind Evelyn is a large map with markers all over it. A map of the city, obviously, but I'm not sure what the markers mean. On the wall behind her is a chalkboard with a chart on it. I can't decipher the information in the chart; it's written in shorthand I don't know.

"I see." Evelyn's smile remains, but without its former touch of amusement. "Introduce me to your fellow refugees, then."

Her eyes drift down to our joined hands. Tobias's fingers spring apart. He gestures to me first. "This is Tris Prior. Her brother, Caleb. And their friend Susan Black."

"Prior," she says. "I know of several Priors, but none of them are named Tris. Beatrice, however . . ."

"Well," I say, "I know of several living Eatons, but none of them are named Evelyn."

"Evelyn Johnson is the name I prefer. Particularly among a pack of Abnegation."

"Tris is the name *I* prefer," I reply. "And we're not Abnegation. Not all of us, anyway."

Evelyn gives Tobias a look. "Interesting friends you've made."

"Those are population counts?" says Caleb from behind me. He

walks forward, his mouth open. "And . . . what? Factionless safe
houses?" He points to the first line on the chart, which reads 7. . . . .
Grn Hse. "I mean, these places, on the map? They're safe houses, like this
one, right?"

"That's a lot of questions," says Evelyn, arching an eyebrow. I recognize the expression. It belongs to Tobias—as does her distaste for questions. "For security purposes, I will not answer any of them. Anyway, it is
time for dinner."

She gestures toward the door. Susan and Caleb start toward it, followed by me, and Tobias and his mother are last. We work our way through
the maze of machinery again.

"I'm not stupid," she says in a low voice. "I know you want nothing to
do with me—though I still don't quite understand why—"

Tobias snorts.

"But," she says, "I will extend my invitation again. We could use your
help here, and I know you are like-minded about the faction system—"

"Evelyn," Tobias says. "I chose Dauntless."

"Choices can be made again."

"What makes you think I'm interested in spending time anywhere
near you?" he demands. I hear his footsteps stop, and slow down so I can
hear how she responds.

"Because I'm your mother," she says, and her voice almost breaks
over the words, uncharacteristically vulnerable. "Because you're my son."

"You really don't get it," he says. "You don't have the vaguest concep-
tion of what you've done to me." He sounds breathless. "I don't want to
join up with your little band of factionless. I want to get out of here as
quickly as possible."

"My *little* band of factionless is twice the size of Dauntless," says Evelyn. "You would do well to take it seriously. Its actions may determine
the future of this city."

With that, she walks ahead of him, and ahead of me. Her words echo
in my mind: *Twice the size of Dauntless.* When did they become so large?

Tobias looks at me, eyebrows lowered.

"How long have you known?" I say.

"About a year." He slumps against the wall and closes his eyes. "She
sent a coded message to me in Dauntless, telling me to meet her at the
train yard. I did, because I was curious, and there she was. Alive. It wasn't
a happy reunion, as you can probably guess."

"Why did she leave Abnegation?"

"She had an affair." He shakes his head. "And no wonder, since my
father . . ." He shakes his head again. "Well, let's just say Marcus wasn't
any nicer to her than he was to me."

"Is . . . that why you're angry with her? Because she was unfaithful to him?"

"No," he says too sternly, his eyes opening. "No, that's not why I'm angry."

I walk toward him as if approaching a wild animal, each footstep careful on the cement floor. "Then why?"

"She had to leave my father, I get that," he says. "But did she think of taking me with her?"

I purse my lips. "Oh. She left you with *him*."

She left him alone with his worst nightmare. No wonder he hates her.

"Yeah." He kicks at the floor. "She did."

My fingers find his, fumbling, and he guides them into the spaces between his own. I know that's enough questions, for now, so I let the silence linger between us until he decides to break it.

"It seems to me," he says, "that the factionless are better friends than enemies."

"Maybe. But what would the cost of that friendship be?" I say.

He shakes his head. "I don't know. But we may not have any other option."

CHAPTER
NINE

ONE OF THE factionless started a fire so we could heat up our food. Those who want to eat sit in a circle around the large metal bowl that contains the fire, first heating the cans, then passing out spoons and forks, then passing cans around so everyone can have a bite of everything. I try not to think about how many diseases could spread this way as I dip my spoon into a can of soup.

Edward drops to the ground next to me and takes the can of soup from my hands.

"So you were all Abnegation, huh?" He shovels several noodles and a piece of carrot into his mouth, and passes the can to the woman on his left.

"We were," I say. "But obviously Tobias and I transferred, and . . ." Suddenly it occurs to me that I shouldn't tell anyone Caleb joined Erudite. "Caleb and Susan are still Abnegation."

"And he's your brother. Caleb," he says. "You ditched your family to become Dauntless?"

"You sound like the Candor," I say irritably. "Mind keeping your judgments to yourself?"

Therese leans over. "He was Erudite first, actually. Not Candor."

"Yeah, I know," I say, "I—"

She interrupts me. "So was I. Had to leave, though."

"What happened?"

"I wasn't smart enough." She shrugs and takes a can of beans from Edward, plunging her spoon into it. "I didn't get a high enough score on my initiation intelligence test. So they said, 'Spend your entire life cleaning up the research labs, or leave.' And I left."

She looks down and licks her spoon clean. I take the beans from her and pass them along to Tobias, who is staring at the fire.

"Are many of you from Erudite?" I say.

Therese shakes her head. "Most are from Dauntless, actually." She jerks her head toward Edward, who scowls. "Then Erudite, then Candor, then a handful of Amity. No one fails Abnegation initiation, though, so we have very few of those, except for a bunch who survived the simulation attack and came to us for refuge."

"I guess I shouldn't be surprised about Dauntless," I say.

"Well, yeah. You've got one of the worst initiations, and there's that whole old-age thing."

"Old-age thing?" I say. I glance at Tobias. He is listening now, and he looks almost normal again, his eyes thoughtful and dark in the firelight.

"Once the Dauntless reach a certain level of physical deterioration," he says, "they are asked to leave. In one way or another."

"What's the other way?" My heart pounds, like it already knows an answer I can't face without prompting.

"Let's just say," says Tobias, "that for some, death is preferable to factionlessness."

"Those people are idiots," says Edward. "I'd rather be factionless than Dauntless."

"How fortunate that you ended up where you did, then," says Tobias coldly.

"Fortunate?" Edward snorts. "Yeah. I'm so fortunate, with my one eye and all."

"I seem to recall hearing rumors that you provoked that attack," says Tobias.

"What are you talking about?" I say. "He was winning, that's all, and Peter was jealous, so he just . . ."

I see the smirk on Edward's face and stop talking. Maybe I don't know everything about what happened during initiation.

"There was an inciting incident," says Edward. "In which Peter did not come out the victor. But it certainly didn't warrant a butter knife to the eye."

"No arguments here," says Tobias. "If it makes you feel any better, he got shot in the arm from a foot away during the simulation attack."

And it does seem to make Edward feel better, because his smirk carves a deeper line into his face.

"Who did that?" he says. "You?"

Tobias shakes his head. "Tris did."

"Well done," Edward says.

I nod, but I feel a little sick to be congratulated for that. Well, not *that* sick. It was Peter, after all.

I stare at the flames wrapping around the fragments of wood that fuel them. They move and shift, like my thoughts. I remember the first time I realized I had never seen an elderly Dauntless. And when I realized my father was too old to climb the paths of the Pit. Now I understand more about that than I'd like to.

"Do you know much about how things are right now?" Tobias asks Edward. "Did all the Dauntless side with Erudite? Has Candor done anything?"

"Dauntless is split in half," Edward says, talking around the food in his mouth. "Half at Erudite headquarters, half at Candor headquarters. What's left of Abnegation is with us. Nothing much has happened yet. Except for whatever happened to you, I guess."

Tobias nods. I feel a little relieved to know that half of the Dauntless, at least, are not traitors.

I eat spoonful after spoonful until my stomach is full. Then Tobias gets us sleeping pallets and blankets, and I find an empty corner for us to lie down in. When he bends over to untie his shoes, I see the symbol of Amity on the small of his back, the branches curling over his spine. When he straightens, I step across the blankets and put my arms around him, brushing the tattoo with my fingers.

Tobias closes his eyes. I trust the dwindling fire to disguise us as I run my hand up his back, touching each tattoo without seeing it. I imagine Erudite's staring eye, Candor's unbalanced scales, Abnegation's clasped hands, and the Dauntless flames. With my other hand I find the patch of fire tattooed over his rib cage. I feel his heavy breaths against my cheek.

"I wish we were alone," he says.

"I almost always wish that," I say.

+ + +

I drift off to sleep, carried by the sound of distant conversations. These days it's easier for me to fall asleep when there is noise around me. I can focus on the sound instead of whatever thoughts would crawl into my head in silence. Noise and activity are the refuges of the bereaved and the guilty.

I wake when the fire is just a glow, and only a few of the factionless are still up. It takes me a few seconds to figure out why I woke up: I heard Evelyn's and Tobias's voices, a few feet away from me. I stay still and hope they don't discover that I'm awake.

"You'll have to tell me what's going on here if you expect me to consider helping you," he says. "Though I'm still not sure why you need me at all."

I see Evelyn's shadow on the wall, flickering with the fire. She is lean and strong, just like Tobias. Her fingers twist into her hair as she speaks.

"What would you like to know, exactly?"

"Tell me about the chart. And the map."

"Your friend was correct in thinking that the map and the chart listed all of our safe houses," she says. "He was wrong about the population counts . . . sort of. The numbers don't document all the factionless—only certain ones. And I'll bet you can guess which ones those are."

"I'm not in the mood for guessing."

She sighs. "The Divergent. We're documenting the Divergent."

"How do you know who they are?"

"Before the simulation attack, part of the Abnegation aid effort involved testing the factionless for a certain genetic anomaly," she says. "Sometimes that testing involved re-administering the aptitude test. Sometimes it was more complicated than that. But they explained to us that they suspected we might have the highest Divergent population of any group in the city."

"I don't understand. Why—"

"Why would the factionless have a high Divergent population?" It sounds like she's smirking. "Obviously those who can't confine themselves to a particular way of thinking would be most likely to leave a faction or fail its initiation, right?"

"That's not what I was going to ask," he says. "I want to know why *you* care how many Divergent there are."

"The Erudite are looking for manpower. They found it temporarily in Dauntless. Now they'll be looking for more, and we're the obvious place, unless they figure out that we've got more Divergent than any other group. Just in case they don't, I want to know how many people we've got who are resistant to simulations."

"Fair enough," he says, "but why were the Abnegation so concerned with finding the Divergent? It wasn't to help Jeanine, was it?"

"Of course not," she says. "But I'm afraid I don't know. The Abnegation were reluctant to provide information that only serves to relieve curiosity. They told us as much as they believed we should know."

"Strange," he mumbles.

"Perhaps you should ask your father about it," she says. "He was the one who told me about you."

"About me," says Tobias. "What about me?"

"That he suspected you were Divergent," she says. "He was always watching you. Noting your behavior. He was very attentive to you. That's why . . . that's why I thought you would be safe with him. Safer with him than with me."

Tobias says nothing.

"I see now that I must have been wrong."

He still says nothing.

"I wish—" she starts.

"Don't you dare try to apologize." His voice shakes. "This is not something you can bandage with a word or two and some hugging, or something."

"Okay," she says. "Okay. I won't."

"For what purpose are the factionless uniting?" he says. "What do you intend to do?"

"We want to usurp Erudite," she says. "Once we get rid of them, there's not much stopping us from controlling the government ourselves."

"That's what you expect me to help you with. Overthrowing one corrupt government and instating some kind of factionless tyranny." He snorts. "Not a chance."

"We don't want to be tyrants," she says. "We want to establish a new society. One without factions."

My mouth goes dry. No factions? A world in which no one knows who they are or where they fit? I can't even fathom it. I imagine only chaos and isolation.

Tobias lets out a laugh. "Right. So how are you going to usurp Erudite?"

"Sometimes drastic change requires drastic measures." Evelyn's shadow lifts a shoulder. "I imagine it will involve a high level of destruction."

I shiver at the word "destruction." Somewhere in the darker parts of me, I crave destruction, as long as it is Erudite being destroyed. But the word carries new meaning for me, now that I have seen what it can look like: gray-clothed bodies slung across curbs and over sidewalks, Abnegation leaders shot on their front lawns, next to their mailboxes. I press my face into the pallet I'm sleeping on, so hard it hurts my forehead, just to force the memory out, out, *out.*

"As for why we need you," Evelyn says. "In order to do this, we will need Dauntless's help. They have the weapons and the combat experience. You could bridge the gap between us and them."

"Do you think I'm important to the Dauntless? Because I'm not. I'm just someone who isn't afraid of much."

"What I am suggesting," she says, "is that you *become* important." She stands, her shadow stretching from ceiling to floor. "I am sure you can find a way, if you want to. Think about it."

She pulls back her curly hair and ties it in a knot. "The door is always open."

A few minutes later he lies next to me again. I don't want to admit that I was eavesdropping, but I want to tell him I don't trust Evelyn, or the factionless, or anyone who speaks so casually about demolishing an entire faction.

Before I can muster the courage to speak, his breaths become even, and he falls asleep.

CHAPTER
TEN

I RUN MY hand over the back of my neck to lift the hair that sticks there. My entire body aches, especially my legs, which burn with lactic acid even when I am not moving. And I don't smell very good. I need to shower.

I wander down the hall and into the bathroom. I am not the only person with bathing in mind—a group of women stand at the sinks, half of them naked, the other half completely unfazed by it. I find a free sink in the corner and stick my head under the faucet, letting cold water spill over my ears.

"Hello," Susan says. I turn my head to the side. Water courses down my cheek and into my nose. She is carrying two towels: one white, one gray, both frayed at the edges.

"Hi," I say.

"I have an idea," she says. She turns her back to me and holds up a towel, blocking my view of the rest of the bathroom. I sigh with relief. Privacy. Or as much of it as possible.

I strip quickly and grab the bar of soap next to the sink.

"How are you?" she says.

"I'm fine." I know she's only asking because faction rules dictate that she does. I wish she would just speak to me freely. "How are you, Susan?"

"Better. Therese told me there is a large group of Abnegation refugees in one of the factionless safe houses," says Susan as I lather soap into my hair.

"Oh?" I say. I shove my head under the faucet again, this time massaging my scalp with my left hand to get the soap out. "Are you going to go?"

"Yes," says Susan. "Unless you need my help."

"Thanks for the offer, but I think your faction needs you more," I say, turning off the faucet. I wish I didn't have to get dressed. It's too hot for denim pants. But I grab the other towel from the floor and dry myself in a hurry.

I put on the red shirt I was wearing before. I don't want to put on something that dirty again, but I have no other choice.

"I suspect some of the factionless women have spare clothes," says Susan.

"You're probably right. Okay, your turn."

I stand with the towel as Susan washes up. My arms start to ache after a while, but she ignored the pain for me, so I'll do the same for her. Water splashes on my ankles when she washes her hair.

"This is a situation I never thought we would be in together," I say after a while. "Bathing from the sink of an abandoned building, on the run from the Erudite."

"I thought we would live near each other," says Susan. "Go to social events together. Have our kids walk to the bus stop together."

I bite my lip at that. It is my fault, of course, that that was never a possibility, because I chose another faction.

"I'm sorry, I didn't mean to bring it up," she says. "I just regret that I didn't pay more attention. If I had, maybe I would have known what you were going through. I acted selfishly."

I laugh a little. "Susan, there's nothing wrong with the way you acted."

"I'm done," she says. "Can you hand me that towel?"

I close my eyes and turn so she can grab the towel from my hands. When Therese walks into the bathroom, smoothing her hair into a braid, Susan asks her for spare clothes.

By the time we leave the bathroom, I wear jeans and a black shirt that is so loose up top that it slips off my shoulders, and Susan wears baggy jeans and a white Candor shirt with a collar. She buttons it up to her throat. The Abnegation are modest to the point of discomfort.

When I enter the large room again, some of the factionless are walking out with buckets of paint and paintbrushes. I watch them until the door closes behind them.

"They're going to write a message to the other safe houses," says Evelyn from behind me. "On one of the billboards. Codes formed out of personal information—so-and-so's favorite color, someone else's childhood pet."

I am not sure why she would choose to tell me something about the factionless codes until I turn around. I see a familiar look in her eyes—it is the same as the one Jeanine wore when she told Tobias she had developed a serum that could control him: pride.

"Clever," I say. "Your idea?"

"It was, actually." She shrugs, but I am not fooled. She is anything but nonchalant. "I was Erudite before I was Abnegation."

"Oh," I say. "Guess you couldn't keep up with a life of academia, then?"

She doesn't take the bait. "Something like that, yes." She pauses. "I imagine your father left for the same reason."

I almost turn away to end the conversation, but her words create a kind of pressure inside my mind, like she is squeezing my brain between her hands. I stare.

"You didn't know?" She frowns. "I'm sorry; I forgot that faction members rarely discuss their old factions."

"What?" I say, my voice cracking.

"Your father was born in Erudite," she says. "His parents were friends with Jeanine Matthews's parents, before they died. Your father and Jeanine used to play together as children. I used to watch them pass books back and forth at school."

I imagine my father, a grown man, sitting next to Jeanine, a grown woman, at a lunch table in my old cafeteria, a book between them. The idea is so ridiculous to me that I half snort, half laugh. It can't be true.

Except.

Except: He never talked about his family or his childhood.

Except: He did not have the quiet demeanor of someone who grew up in Abnegation.

Except: His hatred of Erudite was so vehement it must have been *personal.*

"I'm sorry, Beatrice," Evelyn says. "I didn't mean to reopen closing wounds."

I frown. "Yes, you did."

"What do you mean—"

"Listen carefully," I say, lowering my voice. I check over her shoulder for Tobias, to make sure he isn't listening in. All I see is Caleb and Susan on the ground in the corner, passing a jar of peanut butter back and forth. No Tobias.

"I'm not stupid," I say. "I can see that you're trying to use him. And I'll tell him so, if he hasn't figured it out already."

"My dear girl," she says. "I am his family. I am permanent. You are only temporary."

"Yeah," I say. "His mom abandoned him, and his dad beat him up. How could his loyalty *not* be with his blood, with a family like that?"

I walk away, my hands shaking, and sit down next to Caleb on the floor. Susan is now across the room, helping one of the factionless clean up. He passes me the jar of peanut butter. I remember the rows of peanut plants in the Amity greenhouses. They grow peanuts because they are high in protein and fat, which is important for the factionless in particular. I scoop some of the peanut butter out with my fingers and eat it.

Should I tell him what Evelyn just told me? I don't want to make him think that he has Erudite in his blood. I don't want to give him any reason to return to them.

I decide to keep it to myself for now.

"I wanted to talk to you about something," says Caleb.

I nod, still working the peanut butter off the roof of my mouth.

"Susan wants to go see the Abnegation," he says. "And so do I. I also want to make sure she's all right. But I don't want to leave you."

"It's okay," I say.

"Why don't you come with us?" he asks. "Abnegation would welcome you back; I'm sure of it."

So am I—the Abnegation don't hold grudges. But I am teetering on the edge of grief's mouth, and if I returned to my parents' old faction, it would swallow me.

I shake my head. "I have to go to Candor headquarters and find out what's going on," I say. "I'm going crazy, not knowing." I force a smile. "But you should go. Susan needs you. She seems better, but she still needs you."

"Okay." Caleb nods. "Well, I'll try to join you soon. Be careful, though."

"Aren't I always?"

"No, I think the word for how you usually are is 'reckless.'"

Caleb squeezes my good shoulder lightly. I eat another fingertip's worth of peanut butter.

Tobias emerges from the men's bathroom a few minutes later, his red Amity shirt replaced by a black T-shirt, and his short hair glistening with water. Our eyes meet across the room, and I know it's time to leave.

+ + +

Candor headquarters is large enough to contain an entire world. Or so it seems to me.

It is a wide cement building that overlooks what was once the river. The sign says MERC   IS MART—it used to read "Merchandise Mart," but most people refer to it as the Merciless Mart, because the Candor are merciless, but honest. They seem to have embraced the nickname.

I don't know what to expect, because I have never been inside. Tobias and I pause outside the doors and look at each other.

"Here we go," he says.

I can't see anything beyond my reflection in the glass doors. I look tired and dirty. For the first time, it occurs to me that we don't have to do anything. We could hole up with the factionless and let the rest of them sort through this mess. We could be nobodies, safe, together.

He still hasn't told me about the conversation he had with his mother last night, and I don't think he's going to. He seemed so determined to get to Candor headquarters that I wonder if he's planning something without me.

I don't know why I walk through the doors. Maybe I decide that we've come this far, we might as well see what's going on. But I suspect it's more that I know what's true and what's not. I am Divergent, so I am not no-body, there's no such thing as "safe," and I have other things on my mind than playing house with Tobias. And so, apparently, does he.

The lobby is large and well-lit, with black marble floors that stretch back to an elevator bank. A ring of white marble tiles in the center of the room form the symbol of Candor: a set of unbalanced scales, meant to symbolize the weighing of truth against lies. The room is crawling with armed Dauntless.

A Dauntless soldier with an arm in a sling approaches us, gun held ready, barrel fixed on Tobias.

"Identify yourselves," she says. She is young, but not young enough to know Tobias.

The others gather behind her. Some of them eye us with suspicion, the rest with curiosity, but far stranger than both is the light I see in some of their eyes. Recognition. They might know Tobias, but how could they possibly recognize me?

"Four," he says. He nods toward me. "And this is Tris. Both Dauntless."

The Dauntless soldier's eyes widen, but she does not lower her gun.

"Some help here?" she asks. Some of the Dauntless step forward, but they do it cautiously, like we're dangerous.

"Is there a problem?" Tobias says.

"Are you armed?"

"Of course I'm armed. I'm Dauntless, aren't I?"

"Stand with your hands behind your head." She says it wildly, like she expects us to refuse. I glance at Tobias. Why is everyone acting like we're about to attack them?

"We walked through the front door," I say slowly. "You think we would have done that if we were here to hurt you?"

Tobias doesn't look back at me. He just touches his fingertips to the back of his head. After a moment, I do the same. Dauntless soldiers crowd around us. One of them pats down Tobias's legs while the other takes the gun tucked under his waistband. Another one, a round-faced boy with pink cheeks, looks at me apologetically.

"I have a knife in my back pocket." I say. "Put your hands on me, and I will make you regret it."

He mumbles some kind of apology. His fingers pinch the knife handle, careful not to touch me.

"What's going on?" asks Tobias.

The first soldier exchanges looks with some of the others.

"I'm sorry," she says. "But we were instructed to arrest you upon your arrival."

CHAPTER
ELEVEN

THEY SURROUND US, but don't handcuff us, and walk us to the elevator bank. No matter how many times I ask why we are under arrest, no one says anything or even looks in my direction. Eventually I give up and stay silent, like Tobias.

We go to the third level, where they take us to a small room with a white marble floor instead of a black one. There's no furniture except for a bench along the back wall. Every faction is supposed to have holding rooms for those who make trouble, but I've never been in one before.

The door closes behind us, and locks, and we're alone again.

Tobias sits down on the bench, his brow furrowed. I pace back and forth in front of him. If he had any idea why we were in here, he would tell me, so I don't ask. I walk five steps forward and five steps back, five steps forward and five steps back, at the same rhythm, hoping it will help me figure something out.

If Erudite didn't take over Candor—and Edward told us they didn't—why would the Candor arrest us? What could we have done to them?

If Erudite *didn't* take over, the only real crime left is siding with them. Did I do anything that could have been interpreted as siding with Erudite? My teeth dig into my lower lip so hard I wince. Yes, I did. I shot Will. I shot a number of other Dauntless. They were under the simulation, but maybe Candor doesn't know that or doesn't think it's a good enough reason.

"Can you please calm down?" Tobias says. "You're making me nervous."

"This is me calming down."

He leans forward, resting his elbows on his knees, and stares between his sneakers. "The wound in your lip begs to differ."

I sit next to him and hug my knees to my chest with one arm, my right arm hanging at my side. For a long time, he says nothing, and my arm wraps tighter and tighter around my legs. I feel like, the smaller I become, the safer I am.

"Sometimes," he says, "I worry that you don't trust me."

"I trust you," I say. "Of course I trust you. Why would you think otherwise?"

"Just seems like there's something you're not telling me. I told *you* things. . . ." He shakes his head. "I would never have told anyone else. Something's been going on with you, though, and you haven't told me yet."

"There's been a lot going on. You know that," I say. "And anyway, what about you? I could say the same thing to you."

He touches my cheek, his fingers pushing into my hair. Ignoring my question just like I ignored his.

"If it's just about your parents," he says softly, "tell me and I'll believe you."

His eyes should be wild with apprehension, given where we are, but they are still and dark. They transport me to familiar places. Safe places, where confessing that I shot one of my best friends would be easy, where I would not be afraid of the way that Tobias will look at me when he finds out what I did.

I cover his hand with mine. "That's all it is," I say weakly.

"Okay," he says. He touches his mouth to mine. Guilt clutches at my stomach.

The door opens. A few people file in—two Candor with guns; a dark-skinned, older Candor man; a Dauntless woman I don't recognize. And then: Jack Kang, representative of Candor.

By most faction standards, he is a young leader—only thirty-nine years old. But by Dauntless standards, that's nothing. Eric became a Dauntless leader at seventeen. But that's probably one of the reasons the other factions don't take our opinions or decisions seriously.

Jack is handsome, too, with short black hair and warm, slanted eyes, like Tori's, and high cheekbones. Despite his good looks, he isn't known for being charming, probably because he's Candor, and they see charm as deceptive. I do trust him to tell us what's going on without wasting time on pleasantries. That is something.

"They told me you seemed confused about why you were arrested," he says. His voice is deep, but strangely flat, like it could not create an echo even at the bottom of an empty cavern. "To me that means either you're falsely accused or good at pretending. The only—"

"What are we accused of?" I interrupt him.

"*He* is accused of crimes against humanity. *You* are accused of being his accomplice."

"Crimes against humanity?" Tobias finally sounds angry. He gives Jack a disgusted look. "What?"

"We saw video footage of the attack. You were *running* the attack simulation," says Jack.

"How could you have seen footage? We took the data," says Tobias.

"You took one copy of the data. All the footage of the Dauntless compound recorded during the attack was also sent to other computers throughout the city," says Jack. "All we saw was you running the simulation and *her* nearly getting punched to death before she gave up. Then you stopped, had a rather abrupt lovers' reconciliation, and stole the hard drive together. One possible reason is because the simulation was over and you didn't want us to get our hands on it."

I almost laugh. My great act of heroism, the only important thing I have ever done, and they think I was working for the Erudite when I did it.

"The simulation didn't end," I say. "We *stopped* it, you—"

Jack holds up his hand. "I am not interested in what you have to say right now. The truth will come out when you are both interrogated under the influence of truth serum."

Christina told me about truth serum once. She said the most difficult part of Candor initiation was being given truth serum and answering personal questions in front of everyone in the faction. I don't need to search myself for my deepest, darkest secrets to know that truth serum is the last thing I want in my body.

"Truth serum?" I shake my head. "No. No way."

"There's something you have to hide?" Jack says, lifting both eyebrows.

I want to tell him that anyone with an ounce of dignity wants to keep some things to herself, but I don't want to arouse his suspicions. So I shake my head.

"All right, then." He checks his watch. "It is now noon. The interrogation will be at seven. Don't bother preparing for it. You can't withhold information while under the influence of truth serum."

He turns on his heel and walks out of the room.

"What a pleasant man," says Tobias.

+ + +

A group of armed Dauntless escort me to the bathroom in the early afternoon. I take my time, letting my hands turn red in the hot-faucet water and staring at my reflection. When I was in Abnegation and wasn't allowed to look into mirrors, I used to think that a lot could change in a person's appearance in three months. But it only took a few days to change me this time.

I look older. Maybe it's the short hair or maybe it's just that I wear all that has happened like a mask. Either way, I always thought I would be happy when I stopped looking like a child. But all I feel is a lump in my throat. I am no longer the daughter my parents knew. They will never know me as I am now.

I turn away from the mirror and shove the door to the hallway open with the heels of my hands.

When the Dauntless drop me off at the holding room, I linger by the door. Tobias looks like he did when I first met him—black T-shirt, short hair, stern expression. The sight of him used to fill me with nervous excitement. I remember when I grabbed his hand outside the training room, just for a few seconds, and when we sat together on the rocks next to the chasm, and I feel a pang of longing for how things used to be.

"Hungry?" he says. He offers me a sandwich from the plate next to him.

I take it and sit down, leaning my head on his shoulder. All that's left for us to do is wait, so that's what we do. We eat until the food is gone. We sit until we get uncomfortable. Then we lie down next to each other on the floor, shoulders touching, staring at the same patch of white ceiling.

"What are you afraid of saying?" he says.

"Any of it. All of it. I don't want to relive anything."

He nods. I close my eyes and pretend to sleep. There's no clock in the room, so I can't count down the minutes until the interrogation. Time might as well not exist in this place, except I feel it pressing against me as seven o'clock inevitably draws closer, pushing me into the floor tiles.

Maybe time would not feel as heavy if I didn't have this guilt—the guilt of knowing the truth and stuffing it down where no one can see it, not even Tobias. Maybe I should not be so afraid of saying anything, because honesty will make me feel lighter.

I must fall asleep eventually, because I jerk awake at the sound of the door opening. A few Dauntless walk in as we get to our feet, and one of them says my name. Christina shoves her way past the others and throws her arms around me. Her fingers dig into the wound in my shoulder, and I cry out.

"Got shot," I say. "Shoulder. Ow."

"Oh God!" She releases me. "Sorry, Tris."

She doesn't look like the Christina I remember. Her hair is shorter, like a boy's, and her skin is grayish instead of a warm brown. She smiles at me, but the smile doesn't travel to her eyes, which still look tired. I try to smile back, but I'm too nervous. Christina will be there at my interrogation. She will hear what I did to Will. She will never forgive me.

Unless I fight the serum, swallow the truth—if I can.

But is that really what I want? To let it fester inside me forever?

"You okay? I heard you were here so I asked to escort you," she says as we leave the holding room. "I know you didn't do it. You're not a traitor."

"I'm fine," I say. "And thank you. How are you?"

"Oh, I'm . . ." Her voice trails off, and she bites her lip. "Did anyone tell you . . . I mean, maybe now isn't the time, but . . ."

"What? What is it?"

"Um . . . Will died in the attack," she says.

She gives me a worried look, and an expectant one. Expecting what?

Oh. I am not supposed to know that Will is dead. I could pretend to be emotional, but I probably wouldn't do it convincingly. It's best to admit that I already knew. But I don't know how to explain that without telling her everything.

I feel suddenly sick. Am I really evaluating how best to deceive my friend?

"I know," I say. "I saw him on the monitors when I was in the control room. I'm sorry, Christina."

"Oh." She nods. "Well, I'm . . . glad you already knew. I really didn't want to break the news to you in a hallway."

A short laugh. A flash of a smile. Neither of them like they used to be.

We file into an elevator. I can feel Tobias staring at me—he knows I didn't see Will in the monitors, and he didn't know that Will was dead. I stare straight ahead and pretend his eyes aren't setting me on fire.

"Don't worry about the truth serum," she says. "It's easy. You barely know what's happening when you're under. It's only when you resurface that you even know what you said. I went under when I was a kid. It's pretty commonplace in Candor."

The other Dauntless in the elevator give each other looks. In normal circumstances, someone would probably reprimand her for discussing her old faction, but these are not normal circumstances. At no other time in Christina's life will she escort her best friend, now a suspected traitor, to a public interrogation.

"Is everyone else all right?" I say. "Uriah, Lynn, Marlene?"

"All here," she says. "Except Uriah's brother, Zeke, who is with the other Dauntless."

"What?" Zeke, who secured my straps on the zip line, a traitor?

The elevator stops on the top floor, and the others file out.

"I know," she says. "No one saw it coming."

She takes my arm and tugs me toward the doors. We walk down a black-marble hallway—it must be easy to get lost in Candor headquarters, since everything looks the same. We walk down another hallway and through a set of double doors.

From the outside, the Merciless Mart is a squat block with a narrow raised portion in its center. From the inside, that raised portion is a hollow three-story room with empty spaces in the walls instead of windows. I see the darkening sky above me, starless.

Here the marble floors are white, with a black Candor symbol in the center of the room, and the walls are lit with rows of dim yellow lights, so the whole room glows. Every voice echoes.

Most of Candor and the remnants of Dauntless are already gathered. Some of them sit on the tiered benches that wrap around the edge of the room, but there isn't enough space for everyone, so the rest are crowded around the Candor symbol. In the center of the symbol, between the unbalanced scales, are two empty chairs.

Tobias reaches for my hand. I lace my fingers in his.

Our Dauntless guards lead us to the center of the room, where we are greeted with, at best, murmurs, and at worst, jeers. I spot Jack Kang in the front row of the tiered benches.

An old, dark-skinned man steps forward, a black box in his hands.

"My name is Niles," he says. "I will be your questioner. You—" He points at Tobias. "You will be going first. So if you will please step forward . . ."

Tobias squeezes my hand, and then releases it, and I stand with Christina at the edge of the Candor symbol. The air in the room is warm—moist, summer air, sunset air—but I feel cold.

Niles opens the black box. It contains two needles, one for Tobias and one for me. He also takes an antiseptic wipe from his pocket and offers it to Tobias. We didn't bother with that kind of thing in Dauntless.

"The injection site is in your neck," Niles says.

All I hear, as Tobias applies antiseptic to his skin, is the wind. Niles steps forward and plunges the needle into Tobias's neck, squeezing the cloudy, bluish liquid into his veins. The last time I saw someone inject Tobias with something, it was Jeanine, putting him under a new simulation, one that was effective even on the Divergent—or so she believed. I thought, then, that he was lost to me forever.

I shudder.

CHAPTER
TWELVE

"I will ask you a series of simple questions so that you can grow accustomed to the serum as it takes full effect," says Niles. "Now. What is your name?"

Tobias sits with slouched shoulders and a lowered head, like his body is too heavy for him. He scowls and squirms in the chair, and through gritted teeth says, "Four."

Maybe it isn't possible to lie under the truth serum, but to select which version of the truth to tell: Four is his name, but it is not his name.

"That is a nickname," Niles says. "What is your real name?"

"Tobias," he says.

Christina elbows me. "Did you know that?"

I nod.

"What are the names of your parents, Tobias?"

Tobias opens his mouth to answer, and then clenches his jaw as if to stop the words from spilling out.

"Why is this relevant?" Tobias asks.

The Candor around me mutter to each other, some of them scowling. I raise my eyebrow at Christina.

"It's extremely difficult not to immediately answer questions while under the truth serum," she says. "It means he has a seriously strong will. And something to hide."

"Maybe it wasn't relevant before, Tobias," Niles says, "but it is now that you've resisted answering the question. The names of your parents, please."

Tobias closes his eyes. "Evelyn and Marcus Eaton."

Surnames are just an additional means of identification, useful only to prevent confusion in official records. When we marry, one spouse has to take the other's surname, or both have to take a new one. Still, while we may carry our names from family to faction, we rarely mention them.

But everyone recognizes Marcus's surname. I can tell by the clamor that rises in the room after Tobias speaks. The Candor all know Marcus is the most influential government official, and some of them must have read the article Jeanine released about his cruelty toward his son. It was one of the only things she said that was true. And now everyone knows that Tobias is that son.

Tobias Eaton is a powerful name.

Niles waits for silence, then continues. "So you are a faction transfer, are you not?"

"Yes."

"You transferred from Abnegation to Dauntless?"

"*Yes*," snaps Tobias. "Isn't that obvious?"

I bite my lip. He should calm down; he is giving away too much. The more reluctant he is to answer a question, the more determined Niles will be to hear the answer.

"One of the purposes of this interrogation is to determine your loyalties," says Niles, "so I must ask: Why did you transfer?"

Tobias glares at Niles, and keeps his mouth shut. Seconds pass in complete silence. The longer he tries to resist the serum, the harder it seems to be for him: color fills his cheeks, and he breathes faster, heavier. My chest aches for him. The details of his childhood should stay inside him, if that's where he wants them to be. Candor is cruel for forcing them from him, for taking away his freedom.

"This is horrible," I say hotly to Christina. "Wrong."

"What?" she says. "It's a simple question."

I shake my head. "You don't understand."

Christina smiles a little at me. "You really care about him."

I am too busy watching Tobias to respond.

Niles says, "I'll ask again. It is important that we understand the extent of your loyalty to your chosen faction. So why did you transfer to Dauntless, Tobias?"

"To protect myself," says Tobias. "I transferred to protect myself."

"Protect yourself from what?"

"From my father."

All the conversations in the room stop, and the silence they leave in their wake is worse than the muttering was. I expect Niles to keep probing, but he doesn't.

"Thank you for your honesty," Niles says. The Candor repeat the phrase under their breath. All around me are the words "Thank you for your honesty" at different volumes and pitches, and my anger begins to dissolve. The whispered words seem to welcome Tobias, to embrace and then discard his darkest secret.

It's not cruelty, maybe, but a desire to understand, that motivates them. That doesn't make me any less afraid of going under truth serum.

"Is your allegiance with your current faction, Tobias?" Niles says.

"My allegiance lies with anyone who does not support the attack on Abnegation," he says.

"Speaking of which," Niles says, "I think we should focus on what happened that day. What do you remember about being under the simulation?"

"I was not under the simulation, at first," says Tobias. "It didn't work."

Niles laughs a little. "What do you mean, it didn't *work*?"

"One of the defining characteristics of the Divergent is that their minds are resistant to simulations," says Tobias. "And I am Divergent. So no, it didn't work."

More mutters. Christina nudges me with her elbow.

"Are you too?" she says, close to my ear so she can stay quiet. "Is that why you were awake?"

I look at her. I have spent the past few months afraid of the word "Divergent," terrified that anyone would discover what I am. But I won't be able to hide it anymore. I nod.

It's like her eyes swell to fill their sockets; that's how big they get. I have trouble identifying her expression. Is it shock? Fear? Awe?

"Do you know what it means?" I say.

"I heard about it when I was young," she says in a reverent whisper.

Definitely awe.

"Like it was a fantasy story," she says. " 'There are people with special powers among us!' Like that."

"Well, it's not a fantasy, and it's not that big a deal," I say. "It's like the fear landscape simulation—you were aware while you were in it, and you could manipulate it. Except for me, it's like that in every simulation."

"But Tris," she says, setting her hand on my elbow. "That's *impossible*."

In the center of the room, Niles has his hands up and is trying to silence the crowd, but there are too many whispers—some hostile, some terrified, and some awed, like Christina's. Finally Niles stands and yells, "If you don't quiet down, you will be asked to leave!"

At last everyone quiets down. Niles sits.

"Now," he says. "When you say 'resistant to simulations,' what do you mean?"

"Usually, it means we're aware during simulations," says Tobias. He seems to have an easier time with the truth serum when he answers factual questions instead of emotional ones. He doesn't sound like he's under the truth serum at all now, though his slumped posture and wandering eyes indicate otherwise. "But the attack simulation was different, using a different kind of simulation serum, one with long-range transmitters. Evidently the long-range transmitters didn't work on the Divergent at all, because I awoke in my own mind that morning."

"You say you weren't under the simulation *at first*. Can you explain what you mean by that?"

"I mean that I was discovered and brought to Jeanine, and she injected a version of the simulation serum that specifically targeted the Divergent. I was aware during *that* simulation, but it didn't do much good."

"The video footage from the Dauntless headquarters shows you *running* the simulation," Niles says darkly. "How, exactly, do you explain that?"

"When a simulation is running, your eyes still see and process the actual world, but your brain no longer comprehends them. On some level, though, your brain still knows what you're seeing and where you are. The nature of this new simulation was that it recorded my emotional responses to outside stimuli," Tobias says, closing his eyes for a few seconds, "and responded by altering the appearance of that stimuli. The simulation made my enemies into friends, my friends into enemies. I thought I was shutting the simulation down. Really I was receiving instructions about how to keep it running."

Christina nods along to his words. I feel calmer when I see that most of the crowd is doing the same thing. This is the benefit of the truth serum, I realize. Tobias's testimony is irrefutable this way.

"We have seen footage of what ultimately happened to you in the control room," says Niles, "but it is confusing. Please describe it to us."

"Someone entered the room, and I thought it was a Dauntless soldier, trying to stop me from destroying the simulation. I was fighting her, and . . ." Tobias scowls, struggling. ". . . and then she stopped, and I got confused. Even if I had been awake, I would have been confused. Why would she surrender? Why didn't she just kill me?"

His eyes search the crowd until they find my face. My heartbeat lives in my throat; lives in my cheeks.

"I still don't understand," he says softly, "how she knew that it would work."

Lives in my fingertips.

"I think my conflicted emotions confused the simulation," he says. "And then I heard her voice. Somehow, that enabled me to fight the simulation."

My eyes burn. I have tried not to think of that moment, when I thought he was lost to me and that I would soon be dead, when all I wanted was to feel his heartbeat. I try not to think of it now; I blink the tears from my eyes.

"I recognized her, finally," he says. "We went back into the control room and stopped the simulation."

"What is the name of this person?"

"Tris," he says. "Beatrice Prior, I mean."

"Did you know her before this happened?"

"Yes."

"How did you know her?"

"I was her instructor," he says. "Now we're together."

"I have a final question," Niles says. "Among the Candor, before a person is accepted into our community, they have to completely expose themselves. Given the dire circumstances we are in, we require the same of you. So, Tobias Eaton: what are your deepest regrets?"

I look him over, from his beat-up sneakers to his long fingers to his straight eyebrows.

"I regret . . ." Tobias tilts his head, and sighs. "I regret my choice."

"What choice?"

"Dauntless," he says. "I was born for Abnegation. I was planning on leaving Dauntless, and becoming factionless. But then I met *her*, and . . . I felt like maybe I could make something more of my decision."

Her.

For a moment, it's like I'm looking at a different person, sitting in Tobias's skin, one whose life is not as simple as I thought. He wanted to leave Dauntless, but he stayed because of me. He never told me that.

"Choosing Dauntless in order to escape my father was an act of cowardice," he says. "I regret that cowardice. It means I am not worthy of my faction. I will always regret it."

I expect the Dauntless to let out indignant shouts, maybe to charge the chair and beat him to a pulp. They are capable of far more erratic things than that. But they don't. They stand in stony silence, with stony faces, staring at the young man who did not betray them, but never truly felt that he belonged to them.

For a moment we are all silent. I don't know who starts the whisper; it seems to originate from nothing, to come from no one. But someone whispers, "Thank you for your honesty," and the rest of the room repeats it.

"Thank you for your honesty," they whisper.

I don't join in.

I am the only thing that kept him in the faction he wanted to leave. I am not worth that.

Maybe he deserves to know.

+ + +

Niles stands in the center of the room with a needle in hand. The lights above him make it shine. All around me, the Dauntless and the Candor wait for me to step forward and spill my entire life before them.

The thought occurs to me again: *Maybe I can fight the serum.* But I don't know if I should try. It might be better for the people I love if I come clean.

I walk stiffly to the center of the room as Tobias leaves it. As we pass each other, he takes my hand and squeezes my fingers. Then he's gone, and it's just me and Niles and the needle. I wipe the side of my neck with the antiseptic, but when he reaches out with the needle, I pull back.

"I would rather do it myself," I say, holding out my hand. I will never let someone else inject me again, not after letting Eric inject me with attack simulation serum after my final test. I can't change the contents of the syringe just by doing it myself, but at least this way, I am the instrument of my own destruction.

"Do you know how?" he says, raising a bushy eyebrow.

"Yes."

Niles offers me the syringe. I position it over the vein in my neck, insert the needle, and press the plunger. I barely feel the pinch. I am too charged with adrenaline.

Someone comes forward with a trash can, and I toss the needle in. I feel the effects of the serum immediately afterward. It makes my blood feel like lead in my veins. I almost collapse on my way to the chair—Niles has to grab my arm and guide me toward it.

Seconds later my brain goes silent. *What was I thinking about?* It doesn't seem to matter. Nothing matters except the chair beneath me and the man sitting across from me.

"What is your name?" he says.

The second he asks the question, the answer pops out of my mouth. "Beatrice Prior."

"But you go by Tris?"

"I do."

"What are the names of your parents, Tris?"

"Andrew and Natalie Prior."

"You are also a faction transfer, are you not?"

"Yes," I say, but a new thought whispers at the back of my mind. *Also?*

Also refers to someone else, and in this case, someone else is Tobias. I frown as I try to picture Tobias, but it is difficult to force the image of him into my mind. Not so difficult that I can't do it, though. I see him, and then I see a flash of him sitting in the same chair I'm sitting in.

"You came from Abnegation? And chose Dauntless?"

"Yes," I say again, but this time, the word sounds terse. I don't know why, exactly.

"Why did you transfer?"

That question is more complicated, but I still know the answer. *I was not good enough for Abnegation* is on the tip of my tongue, but another phrase replaces it: *I wanted to be free.* They are both true. I want to say them both. I squeeze the armrests as I try to remember where I am, what I'm doing. I see people all around me, but I don't know why they're there.

I strain, the way I used to strain when I could almost remember the answer to a test question but couldn't call it to mind. I used to close my eyes and picture the textbook page the answer was on. I struggle for a few seconds, but I can't do it; I can't remember.

"I wasn't good enough for Abnegation," I say, "and I wanted to be free. So I chose Dauntless."

"Why weren't you good enough?"

"Because I was selfish," I say.

"You *were* selfish? You aren't anymore?"

"Of course I am. My mother said that everyone is selfish," I say, "but I became less selfish in Dauntless. I discovered there were people I would fight for. Die for, even."

The answer surprises me—but why? I pinch my lips together for a moment. Because it's true. If I say it here, it must be true.

That thought gives me the missing link in the chain of thought I was trying to find. I am here for a lie-detector test. Everything I say is true. I feel a bead of sweat roll down the back of my neck.

Lie-detector test. Truth serum. I have to remind myself. It is too easy to get lost in honesty.

"Tris, would you please tell us what happened the day of the attack?"

"I woke up," I say, "and everyone was under the simulation. So I played along until I found Tobias."

"What happened after you and Tobias were separated?"

"Jeanine tried to have me killed, but my mother saved me. She used to be Dauntless, so she knew how to use a gun." My body feels even heavier now, but no longer cold. I feel something stir in my chest, something worse than sadness, worse than regret.

I know what comes next. My mother died and then I killed Will; I shot him; I killed him.

"She distracted the Dauntless soldiers so I could get away, and they killed her," I say.

Some of them ran after me, and I killed them. But there are Dauntless in the crowd around me, Dauntless, I killed some of the Dauntless, I shouldn't talk about it here.

"I kept running," I say, "And . . ." *And Will ran after me. And I killed him.* No, no. I feel sweat near my hairline.

"And I found my brother and father," I say, my voice strained. "We formed a plan to destroy the simulation."

The edge of the armrest digs into my palm. I withheld some of the truth. Surely that counts as deception.

I fought the serum. And in that short moment, I won.

I should feel triumphant. Instead I feel the weight of what I did crush me again.

"We infiltrated the Dauntless compound, and my father and I went up to the control room. He fought off Dauntless soldiers at the expense of his life," I say. "I made it to the control room, and Tobias was there."

"Tobias said you fought him, but then stopped. Why did you do that?"

"Because I realized that one of us would have to kill the other," I say, "and I didn't want to kill him."

"You gave up?"

"No!" I snap. I shake my head. "No, not exactly. I remembered something I had done in my fear landscape in Dauntless initiation . . . in a simulation, a woman demanded that I kill my family, and I let her shoot me instead. It worked then. I thought . . ." I pinch the bridge of my nose. My head is starting to ache and my control is gone and my thoughts run into words. "I was so frantic, but all I could think was that there was something to it; there was a strength in it. And I couldn't kill him, so I had to try."

I blink tears from my eyes.

"So you were never under the simulation?"

"No." I press the heel of my hands to my eyes, pushing the tears out of them so they don't fall on my cheeks where everyone can see them.

"No," I say again. "No, I am Divergent."

"Just to clarify," says Niles. "Are you telling me that you were almost murdered by the Erudite . . . and then fought your way into the Dauntless compound . . . and destroyed the simulation?"

"Yes," I say.

"I think I speak for everyone," he says, "when I say that you have earned the title of Dauntless."

Shouts rise up from the left side of the room, and I see blurs of fists pressing into the dark air. My faction, calling to me.

But no, they're wrong, I'm not brave, I'm not brave, I shot Will and I can't admit it, I can't even admit it. . . .

"Beatrice Prior," says Niles, "what are your deepest regrets?"

What do I regret? I do not regret choosing Dauntless or leaving Abnegation. I do not even regret shooting the guards outside the control room, because it was so important that I get past them.

"I regret . . ."

My eyes leave Niles's face and drift over the room, and land on Tobias. He is expressionless, his mouth in a firm line, his stare blank. His hands, crossed over his chest, clasp his arms so hard his knuckles are white. Next to him stands Christina. My chest squeezes, and I can't breathe.

I have to tell them. I have to tell the truth.

"Will," I say. It sounds like a gasp, like it was pulled straight from my stomach. Now there is no turning back.

"I shot Will," I say, "while he was under the simulation. I killed him. He was going to kill me, but I killed him. My friend."

Will, with the crease between his eyebrows, with green eyes like celery and the ability to quote the Dauntless manifesto from memory. I feel pain in my stomach so intense that I almost groan. It hurts to remember him. It hurts every part of me.

And there is something else, something worse that I didn't realize before. I was willing to die rather than kill Tobias, but the thought never occurred to me when it came to Will. I decided to kill Will in a fraction of a second.

I feel bare. I didn't realize that I wore my secrets as armor until they were gone, and now everyone sees me as I really am.

"Thank you for your honesty," they say.

But Christina and Tobias say nothing.

CHAPTER
THIRTEEN

I RISE FROM the chair. I don't feel as dizzy as I did a moment ago; the serum is already wearing off. The crowd tilts, and I search for a door. I don't usually run away from things, but I would run from this.

Everyone starts to file out of the room except for Christina. She stands where I left her, her hands in fists that are in the process of uncurling. Her eyes meet mine and yet they do not. Tears swim in her eyes and yet she is not crying.

"Christina," I say, but the only words I can think of—*I'm sorry*—sound more like an insult than an apology. Sorry is what you are when you bump someone with your elbow, what you are when you interrupt someone. I am more than sorry.

"He had a gun," I say. "He was about to shoot me. He was under the simulation."

"You killed him," she says. Her words sound bigger than words usually do, like they expanded in her mouth before she spoke them. She looks at me as if she doesn't recognize me for a few seconds, then turns away.

A younger girl with the same skin color and the same height takes her hand—Christina's younger sister. I saw her on Visiting Day, a thousand years ago. The truth serum makes the sight of them swim before me, or that could be the tears gathering in my eyes.

"You okay?" says Uriah, emerging from the crowd to touch my shoulder. I haven't seen him since before the simulation attack, but I can't find it in me to greet him.

"Yeah."

"Hey." He squeezes my shoulder. "You did what you had to do, right?"

To save us from being Erudite slaves. She'll see that eventually. When the grief fades."

I can't even find it in me to nod. Uriah smiles at me and walks away. Some Dauntless brush against me and they murmur words that sound like gratitude, or compliments, or reassurance. Others give me a wide berth, look at me with narrowed, suspicious eyes.

The black-clothed bodies smear together in front of me. I am empty. Everything has spilled out of me.

Tobias stands next to me. I brace myself for his reaction.

"I got our weapons back," he says, offering me my knife.

I shove it in my back pocket without meeting his eyes.

"We can talk about it tomorrow," he says. Quietly. Quiet is dangerous, with Tobias.

"Okay."

He slides his arm across my shoulders. My hand finds his hip, and I pull him against me.

I hold on tight as we walk toward the elevators together.

+ + +

He finds us two cots at the end of a hallway somewhere. We lie with our heads inches apart, not speaking.

When I'm sure he's asleep, I slip out from beneath the blankets and walk down the hallway, past a dozen sleeping Dauntless. I find the door that leads to the stairs.

As I climb step after step, and my muscles begin to burn, and my lungs fight for air, I feel the first moments of relief I've experienced in days.

I may be good at running on flat ground, but walking up stairs is another matter. I massage a spasm from my hamstring as I march past the twelfth floor, and try to recover some of my lost air. I grin at the fierce burn in my legs, in my chest. Using pain to relieve pain. It doesn't make much sense.

By the time I reach the eighteenth floor, my legs feel like they have turned to liquid. I shuffle toward the room where I was interrogated. It's empty now, but the amphitheater benches are still there, as is the chair I sat in. The moon glows behind a haze of clouds.

I set my hands on the back of the chair. It's plain: wooden, a little creaky. How strange that something so simple could have been instrumental in my decision to ruin one of my most important relationships, and damage another.

It's bad enough that I killed Will, that I didn't think fast enough to come up with another solution. Now I have to live with everyone else's judgment as well as my own, and the fact that nothing—not even me—will ever be the same again.

The Candor sing the praises of the truth, but they never tell you how much it costs.

The edge of the chair bites into my palms. I was squeezing it harder than I thought. I stare down at it for a second and then lift it, balancing it legs-up on my good shoulder. I search the edge of the room for a ladder or a staircase that will help me climb. All I see are the amphitheater benches, rising high above the floor.

I walk up to the highest bench, and lift the chair above my head. It just barely touches the ledge beneath one of the window spaces. I jump, shoving the chair forward, and it slides onto the ledge. My shoulder aches—I shouldn't really be using my arm—but I have other things on my mind.

I jump, grab the ledge, and pull myself up, my arms shaking. I swing my leg up and drag the rest of my body onto the ledge. When I'm up, I lie there for a moment, sucking in air and heaving it back out again.

I stand on the ledge, under the arch of what used to be a window, and stare out at the city. The dead river curls around the building and disappears. The bridge, its red paint peeling, stretches over the muck. Across it are buildings, most of them empty. It is hard to believe there were ever enough people in the city to fill them.

For a second, I allow myself to reenter the memory of the interrogation. Tobias's lack of expression; his anger afterward, suppressed for the sake of my sanity. Christina's empty look. The whispers, "Thank you for your honesty." Easy to say that when what I did doesn't affect them.

I grab the chair and hurl it over the ledge. A faint cry escapes me. It grows into a yell, which transforms into a scream, and then I'm standing on the ledge of the Merciless Mart, screaming as the chair sails toward the ground, screaming until my throat burns. Then the chair hits the ground, shattering like a brittle skeleton. I sit down on the ledge, leaning into the side of the window frame, and close my eyes.

And then I think of Al.

I wonder how long Al stood at the ledge before he pitched himself over it, into the Dauntless Pit.

He must have stood there for a long time, making a list of all the terrible things he had done—almost killing me was one of those things—and another list of all the good, heroic, brave things he had not done, and then decided that he was tired. Tired, not just of living, but of existing. Tired of being Al.

I open my eyes, and stare at the pieces of chair I can faintly see on the pavement below. For the first time I feel like I understand Al. I am tired of being Tris. I have done bad things. I can't take them back, and they are part of who I am. Most of the time, they seem like the only thing I am.

I lean forward, into the air, holding on to the side of the window with one hand. Another few inches and my weight would pull me to the ground. I would not be able to stop it.

But I can't do it. My parents lost their lives out of love for me. Losing mine for no good reason would be a terrible way to repay them for that sacrifice, no matter what I've done.

"Let the guilt teach you how to behave next time," my father would say.

"I love you. No matter what," my mother would say.

Part of me wishes I could burn them from my mind, so I would never have to mourn for them. But the rest of me is afraid of who I would be without them.

My eyes blurry with tears, I lower myself back into the interrogation room.

+ + +

I return to my cot early that morning, and Tobias is already awake. He turns and walks toward the elevators, and I follow him, because I know that's what he wants. We stand in the elevator, side by side. I hear ringing in my ears.

The elevator sinks to the second floor, and I start to shake. It starts with my hands, but travels to my arms and my chest, until little shudders go through my entire body and I have no way to stop them. We stand between the elevators, right above another Candor symbol, the uneven scales. The symbol that is also drawn on the middle of his spine.

He doesn't look at me for a long time. He stands with his arms crossed and his head down until I can't stand it anymore, until I feel like I might scream. I should say something, but I don't know what to say. I can't apologize, because I only told the truth, and I can't change the truth into a lie. I can't give excuses.

"You didn't tell me," he says. "Why not?"

"Because I didn't . . ." I shake my head. "I didn't know how to."

He scowls. "It's pretty *easy*, Tris—"

"Oh yeah," I say, nodding. "It's *so* easy. All I have to do is go up to you and say, 'By the way, I shot Will, and now guilt is ripping me to shreds, but what's for breakfast?' Right? *Right?*" Suddenly it is too much, too much to contain. Tears fill my eyes, and I yell, "Why don't *you* try killing one of your best friends and then dealing with the consequences?"

I cover my face with my hands. I don't want him to see me sobbing again. He touches my shoulder.

"Tris," he says, gently this time. "I'm sorry. I shouldn't pretend that I understand. I just meant that . . ." He struggles for a moment. "I wish you trusted me enough to tell me things like that."

I do trust you, is what I want to say. But it isn't true—I didn't trust him to love me despite the terrible things I had done. I don't trust anyone to do that, but that isn't his problem; it's mine.

"I mean," he says, "I had to find out that you almost drowned in a water tank from *Caleb.* Doesn't that seem a little strange to you?"

Just when I was about to apologize.

I wipe my cheeks hard with my fingertips and stare at him.

"Other things seem stranger," I say, trying to make my voice light. "Like finding out that your boyfriend's supposedly dead mother is still alive by *seeing her in person.* Or overhearing his plans to ally with the factionless, but he never tells you about it. That seems a little strange to me."

He takes his hand from my shoulder.

"Don't pretend this is only my problem," I say. "If I don't trust you, you don't trust me either."

"I thought we would get to those things eventually," he says. "Do I have to tell you everything right away?"

I feel so frustrated I can't even speak for a few seconds. Heat fills my cheeks.

"God, *Four!*" I snap. "You don't want to have to tell me everything right away, but I have to tell *you* everything right away? Can't you see how stupid that is?"

"First of all, don't use that name like a weapon against me," he says, pointing at me. "Second, I was not making plans to ally with the faction-less; I was just thinking it over. If I had made a decision, I would have said something to you. And third, it would be different if you had actu-ally intended to tell me about Will at some point, but it's obvious that you didn't."

"I *did* tell you about Will!" I say. "That wasn't truth serum; it was me. *I* said it because I chose to."

"What are you talking about?"

"I was aware. Under the serum. I could have lied; I could have kept it from you. But I didn't, because I thought you deserved to know the truth."

"What a way to tell me!" he says, scowling. "In front of over a hun-dred people! How intimate!"

"Oh, so it's not enough that I told you; it has to be in the right set-ting?" I raise my eyebrows. "Next time should I brew some tea and make sure the lighting is right, too?"

Tobias lets out a frustrated sound and turns away from me, pacing a few steps. When he turns back, his cheeks are splotchy. I can't remember ever seeing his face change color before.

"Sometimes," he says quietly, "it isn't easy to be with you, Tris." He looks away.

I want to tell him that I know it's not easy, but I wouldn't have made it through the past week without him. But I just stare at him, my heart pounding in my ears.

I can't tell him I need him. I can't need him, period—or really, we can't need each other, because who knows how long either of us will last in this war?

"I'm sorry," I say, all my anger gone. "I should have been honest with you."

"That's it? That's all you have to say?" He frowns.

"What else do you want me to say?"

He just shakes his head. "Nothing, Tris. Nothing."

I watch him walk away. I feel like a space has opened up within me, expanding so rapidly it will break me apart.

CHAPTER
FOURTEEN

"OKAY, WHAT THE hell are you doing here?" a voice demands.

I sit on a mattress in one of the hallways. I came here to do something, but I lost my train of thought when I arrived, so I just sat down instead. I look up. Lynn—who I first met when she stomped on my toes in a Hancock building elevator—stands over me with raised eyebrows. Her hair is growing out—it's still short, but I can't see her skull anymore.

"I'm sitting," I say. "Why?"

"You're ridiculous, is what you are." She sighs. "Get your stuff together. You're Dauntless, and it's time you acted like it. You're giving us a bad reputation among the Candor."

"How exactly am I doing that?"

"By acting like you don't know us."

"I'm just doing Christina a favor."

"Christina." Lynn snorts. "She's a lovesick puppy. People die. That's what happens in war. She'll figure it out eventually."

"Yeah, people die, but it's not always your good friend who kills them."

"Whatever." Lynn sighs impatiently. "Come on."

I don't see a reason to refuse. I get up and follow her down a series of hallways. She moves at a brisk pace, and it's difficult to keep up with her.

"Where's your scary boyfriend?" she says.

My lips pucker like I just tasted something sour. "He's not scary."

"Sure he's not." She smirks.

"I don't know where he is."

She shrugs. "Well, you can grab him a bunk, too. We're trying to forget those Dauntless-Erudite bastard children. Pull together again."

I laugh. "Dauntless-Erudite bastard children, huh."

She pushes a door open, and we stand in a large, open room that reminds me of the building's lobby. Unsurprisingly, the floors are black with a huge white symbol in the center of the room, but most of it has been covered up with bunk beds. Dauntless men, women, and children are everywhere, and there isn't a single Candor in sight.

Lynn leads me to the left side of the room and between the rows of bunks. She looks at the boy sitting on one of the bottom bunks—he is a few years younger than we are, and he's trying to undo a knot in his shoelaces.

"Hec," she says, "you're going to have to find another bunk."

"What? No way," he says without looking up. "I'm not relocating *again* just because you want to have late-night pillow chats with one of your stupid friends."

"She is not my friend," snaps Lynn. I almost laugh. "Hec, this is Tris. Tris, this is my little brother, Hector."

At the sound of my name, his head jerks up, and he stares at me, openmouthed.

"Nice to meet you," I say.

"You're *Divergent*," he says. "My mom said to stay away from you because you might be dangerous."

"Yeah. She's a big scary Divergent, and she's going to make your head explode with only the power of her brain," says Lynn, jabbing him between the eyes with her index finger. "Don't tell me you actually *believe* all that kid stuff about the Divergent."

He turns bright red and snatches some of his things from a pile next to the bed. I feel bad for making him move until I see him toss his things down a few bunks over. He doesn't have to go far.

"I could have done that," I say. "Slept over there, I mean."

"Yeah, I know." Lynn grins. "He deserves it. He called Zeke a traitor right to Uriah's face. It's not like it's not true, but that's no reason to be a jerk about it. I think Candor is rubbing off on him. He feels like he can just say whatever he wants. Hey, Mar!"

Marlene pokes her head around one of the bunks and smiles toothily at me.

"Hey, Tris!" says Marlene. "Welcome. What's up, Lynn?"

"Can you get some of the smaller girls to give up a few pieces of clothing each?" Lynn says, "Not all shirts, though. Jeans, underwear, maybe a spare pair of shoes?"

"Sure," says Marlene.

I put my knife down next to the bottom bunk.

"What 'kid stuff' were you referring to?" I say.

"*The Divergent*. People with special brainpowers? Come on." She shrugs. "I know you believe in it, but I don't."

"So how do you explain me being awake during simulations?" I say. "Or resisting one entirely?"

"I think the leaders choose people at random and change the simulations for them."

"Why would they do that?"

She waves her hand in my face. "Distraction. You're so busy worrying about the Divergent—like my mom—that you forget to worry about what the leaders are doing. It's just a different kind of mind control."

Her eyes skirt mine, and she kicks at the marble floor with the toe of her shoe. I wonder if she's remembering the last time she was on mind control. During the attack simulation.

I have been so focused on what happened to Abnegation that I almost forgot what happened to Dauntless. Hundreds of Dauntless woke to discover the black mark of murder on them, and they didn't even choose it for themselves.

I decide not to argue with her. If she wants to believe in a government conspiracy, I don't think I can dissuade her. She would have to experience it for herself.

"I come bearing clothes," says Marlene, stepping in front of our bunk. She holds a stack of black clothes the size of her torso, which she offers to me with a proud look on her face. "I even guilt-tripped your sister into handing over a dress, Lynn. She brought three."

"You have a sister?" I ask Lynn.

"Yeah," she says, "she's eighteen. She was in Four's initiate class."

"What's her name?"

"Shauna," she says. She looks at Marlene. "I *told* her none of us would need dresses anytime soon, but she didn't listen, as usual."

I remember Shauna. She was one of the people who caught me after zip lining.

"I think it would be easier to fight in a dress," says Marlene, tapping her chin. "It would give your legs freer movement. And who really cares if you flash people your underwear, as long as you're kicking the crap out of them?"

Lynn goes silent, like she recognizes that as a spark of brilliance but can't bring herself to admit it.

"What's this about flashing underwear?" says Uriah, sidestepping a bunk. "Whatever it is, I'm in."

Marlene punches him in the arm.

"Some of us are going to the Hancock building tonight," says Uriah. "You should all come. We're leaving at ten."

"Zip lining?" says Lynn.

"No. Surveillance. We've heard the Erudite keep their lights on all night, which will make it easier to look through their windows. See what they're doing."

"I'll go," I say.

"Me too," says Lynn.

"What? Oh. Me too," Marlene says, smiling at Uriah. "I'm going to get food. Want to come?"

"Sure," he says.

Marlene waves as they walk away. She used to walk with a lift in her step, like she was skipping. Now her steps are smoother—more elegant, maybe, but lacking the childish joy I associate with her. I wonder what she did when she was under the simulation.

Lynn's mouth puckers.

"What?" I say.

"Nothing," she snaps. She shakes her head. "They've just been hanging out alone all the time lately."

"He needs all the friends he can get, it sounds like," I say. "What with Zeke and all."

"Yeah. What a nightmare that was. One day he was here, and the next . . ." She sighs. "No matter how long you train someone to be brave, you never know if they are or not until something real happens."

Her eyes fix on mine. I never noticed before how strange they are, a golden brown. And now that her hair has grown in somewhat, and her baldness isn't the first thing I see, I also notice her delicate nose, her full lips—she is striking without trying to be. I am envious of her for a moment, and then I think she must hate it, and that's why she shaved her head.

"*You* are brave," she says. "You don't need me to say it, because you already know it. But I want you to know that I know."

She is complimenting me, but I still feel like she smacked me with something.

Then she adds, "Don't mess it up."

+ + +

A few hours later, after I've eaten lunch and taken a nap, I sit down on the edge of my bed to change the bandage on my shoulder. I take off my T-shirt, leaving my tank top on—there are a lot of Dauntless around, gathering between the bunks, laughing at one another's jokes. I have just finished applying more healing salve when I hear a shriek of laughter. Uriah charges down the aisle between the bunks with Marlene thrown over his shoulder. She waves at me as they pass, her face red.

Lynn, who is sitting on the next bunk, snorts. "I don't see how he can be *flirty*, with everything that's going on."

"He's supposed to shuffle around, scowling all the time?" I say, reaching over my shoulder to press the bandage to my skin. "Maybe you can learn something from him."

"You're one to talk," she says. "You're always moping. We should start calling you Beatrice Prior, Queen of Tragedy."

I stand and punch her arm, harder than if I was kidding, softer than if I was serious. "Shut up."

Without looking at me, she shoves my shoulder into the bunk. "I don't take orders from Stiffs."

I notice a slight curl in her lip and suppress a grin myself.

"Ready to go?" Lynn says.

"Where are you going?" Tobias says, slipping between his bunk and mine to stand in the aisle with us. My mouth feels dry. I haven't spoken to him all day, and I'm not sure what to expect. Will it be awkward, or will we go back to normal?

"Top of the Hancock building to spy on Erudite," Lynn says. "Want to come?"

Tobias gives me a look. "No, I've got a few things to take care of here. But be careful."

I nod. I know why he doesn't want to come—Tobias tries to avoid heights, if at all possible. He touches my arm, holding me back for just a moment. I tense up—he hasn't touched me since before our fight—and he releases me.

"I'll see you later," he mutters. "Don't do anything stupid."

"Thanks for that vote of confidence," I say, frowning.

"I didn't mean that," he says. "I meant don't let anyone else do anything stupid. They'll listen to you."

He leans toward me like he's going to kiss me, then seems to think better of it and leans back, biting his lip. It's a small act, but it still feels like rejection. I avoid his eyes and run after Lynn.

Lynn and I walk down the hallway toward the elevator bank. Some of the Dauntless have started to mark the walls with colored squares. Candor headquarters is like a maze to them, and they want to learn to navigate it. I know only how to get to the most basic places: the sleeping area, the cafeteria, the lobby, the interrogation room.

"Why did everyone leave Dauntless headquarters?" I say. "The traitors aren't there, are they?"

"No, they're at Erudite headquarters. We left because Dauntless headquarters has the most surveillance cameras of any area in the city," Lynn says. "We knew the Erudite could probably access all the footage, and that it would take forever to find all the cameras, so we thought it was best to just leave."

"Smart."

"We have our moments."

Lynn jabs her finger into the button for the first floor. I stare at our reflections in the doors. She's taller than I am by just a few inches, and though her baggy shirt and pants try to obscure it, I can tell that her body bends and curves like it's supposed to.

"What?" she says, scowling at me.

"Why did you shave your head?"

"Initiation," she says. "I love Dauntless, but Dauntless guys don't see Dauntless girls as a threat during initiation. I got sick of it. So I figured, if I don't look so much like a girl, maybe they won't look at me that way."

"I think you could have used being underestimated to your advantage."

"Yeah, and what? Acted all faint every time something scary came around?" Lynn rolls her eyes. "Do you think I have zero dignity or something?"

"I think a mistake the Dauntless make is refusing to be cunning," I say. "You don't always have to smack people in the face with how strong you are."

"Maybe you should dress in blue from now on," she says, "if you're going to act like such an Erudite. Plus, you do the same thing, but without the head shaving."

I slip out of the elevator before I say something I'll regret. Lynn is quick to forgive, but quick to ignite, like most Dauntless. Like me, except for the "quick to forgive" part.

As usual, a few Dauntless with large guns cross back and forth in front of the doors, watching for intruders. Just in front of them stands a small group of younger Dauntless, including Uriah; Marlene; Lynn's sister, Shauna; and Lauren, who taught the Dauntless-born initiates as Four taught the faction transfers during initiation. Her ear gleams when she moves her head—it is pierced from top to bottom.

Lynn stops short, and I step on her heel. She swears.

"What a charmer you are," says Shauna, smiling at Lynn. They don't look much alike, except for their hair color, which is a medium brown, but Shauna's is chin length, like mine.

"Yes, that's my goal. To be charming," Lynn replies.

Shauna drapes an arm across Lynn's shoulders. It's strange to see Lynn with a sister—to see Lynn with a connection to someone at all. Shauna glances at me, her smile disappearing. She looks wary.

"Hi," I say, because there's nothing else to say.

"Hello," she says.

"Oh God, Mom's gotten to you, too, hasn't she." Lynn covers her face with one hand. "Shauna—"

"Lynn. Keep your mouth shut for once," says Shauna, her eyes still on me. She seems tense, like she thinks I might attack her at any moment. With my special brainpowers.

"Oh!" says Uriah, rescuing me. "Tris, do you know Lauren?"

"Yeah," Lauren says, before I can answer. Her voice is sharp and clear, like she's scolding him, except it seems to be the way she naturally sounds. "She went through my fear landscape for practice during initiation. So she knows me better than she should, probably."

"Really? I thought the transfers would go through Four's landscape," says Uriah.

"Like he would let anyone do that," she says, snorting.

Something inside me gets warm and soft. He let *me* go through it.

I see a flicker of blue over Lauren's shoulder, and peer around her to get a better look.

Then the guns go off.

The glass doors explode into fragments. Dauntless soldiers with blue armbands stand on the sidewalk outside, carrying guns I've never seen before, guns with narrow, blue beams of light streaming from above their barrels.

"Traitors!" someone screams.

The Dauntless draw their guns, almost in unison. I do not have one to draw, so I duck behind the wall of loyal Dauntless in front of me, my shoes crunching pieces of glass beneath their soles, and pull my knife out of my back pocket.

All around me, people drop to the ground. My fellow faction members. My closest friends. All of them falling—they must be dead, or dying—as the earsplitting bang of bullets filling my ears.

Then I freeze. One of the blue beams is fixed on my chest. I dive sideways to get out of the line of fire, but I don't move fast enough.

The gun goes off. I fall.

CHAPTER
FIFTEEN

THE PAIN SUBSIDES to a dull ache. I slide my hand under my jacket and feel for the wound.

I'm not bleeding. But the force of the gunshot knocked me down, so I had to have been hit with something. I run my fingers over my shoulder, and feel a hard bump where the skin used to be smooth.

I hear a crack against the floor next to my face, and a metal cylinder about the size of my hand rolls to a stop against my head. Before I can move it, white smoke sprays out of both ends. I cough, and throw it away from me, deeper into the lobby. It isn't the only cylinder, though—they are everywhere, filling the room with smoke that does not burn or sting. In fact, it only obscures my view for a few seconds before evaporating completely.

What was the point of that?

Lying on the floor all around me are Dauntless soldiers with their eyes closed. I frown as I look Uriah up and down—he doesn't seem to be bleeding. I see no wound near his vital organs, which means he isn't dead. So what knocked him unconscious? I look over my left shoulder, where Lynn fell in a strange, half-curled position. She's also unconscious.

The Dauntless traitors walk into the lobby, their guns held up. I decide to do what I always do when I'm not sure what's going on: I act like everyone else. I let my head drop and close my eyes. My heart pounds as the Dauntless's footsteps come closer, and closer, squeaking on the marble floors. I bite my tongue to suppress a cry of pain as one of them steps on my hand.

"Not sure why we can't just shoot them all in the head," one of them says. "If there's no army, we win."

"Now, Bob, we can't just kill *everyone*," a cold voice says.

The hair on the back of my neck stands up. I would know that voice anywhere. It belongs to Eric, leader of the Dauntless.

"No people means no one left to create prosperous conditions," Eric continues. "Anyway, it's not your job to ask questions." He raises his voice. "Half in the elevators, half in the stairwells, left and right! Go!"

There's a gun a few feet to my left. If I opened my eyes, I could grab it and fire at him before he knew what hit him. But there's no guarantee I would be able to touch it without panicking again.

I wait until I hear the last footstep disappear behind an elevator door or into a stairwell before opening my eyes. Everyone in the lobby appears to be unconscious. Whatever they gassed us with, it had to be simulation-inducing or I wouldn't be the only one awake. It doesn't make any sense—it doesn't follow the simulation rules I'm familiar with—but I don't have time to think it through.

I grab my knife and get up, trying to ignore the ache in my shoulder. I run over to one of the dead Dauntless traitors near the doorway. She was middle-aged; there are hints of gray in her dark hair. I try not to look at the bullet wound in her head, but the dim light glows on what looks like bone, and I gag.

Think. I don't care who she was, or what her name was, or how old she was. I care only about the blue armband she wears. I have to focus on that. I try to hook my finger around the fabric, but it doesn't come loose. It appears to be attached to her black jacket. I will have to take that, too.

I unzip my jacket and toss it over her face so I don't have to look at her. Then I unzip her jacket and pull it, first from her left arm, and then from her right arm, gritting my teeth as I slide it from beneath her heavy body.

"Tris!" someone says. I turn around, jacket in one hand, knife in the other. I put the knife away—the invading Dauntless weren't carrying them, and I don't want to be conspicuous.

Uriah stands behind me.

"Divergent?" I ask him. There is no time to be shocked.

"Yeah," he says.

"Get a jacket," I say.

He crouches next to one of the other Dauntless traitors, this one young, not even old enough to be a Dauntless member. I flinch at the sight of his death-pale face. Someone so young shouldn't be dead; shouldn't even have been here in the first place.

My face hot with anger, I shrug the woman's jacket on. Uriah pulls his own jacket on, his mouth pinched.

"*They're* the only ones who are dead," he says quietly. "Something about that seem wrong to you?"

"They must have known we would shoot at them, but they came anyway," I say. "Questions later. We have to get up there."

"Up there? Why?" he says. "We should get out of here."

"You want to run away before you know what's going on?" I scowl at him. "Before the Dauntless upstairs know what hit them?"

"What if someone recognizes us?"

I shrug. "We just have to hope they won't."

I sprint toward the stairwell, and he follows me. As soon as my foot touches the first stair, I wonder what on earth I intend to do. There are bound to be more of the Divergent in this building, but will they know what they are? Will they know to hide? And what do I expect to gain from submerging myself in an army of Dauntless traitors?

Deep inside me I know the answer: I am being reckless. I will probably gain nothing. I will probably die.

And more disturbing still: I don't really care.

"They'll work their way upward," I say between breaths. "So you should . . . go to the third floor. Tell them to . . . evacuate. Quietly."

"Where are *you* going, then?"

"Floor two," I say. I shove my shoulder into the second-floor door. I know what to do on the second floor: look for the Divergent.

+ + +

As I walk down the hallway, stepping over unconscious people dressed in black and white, I think of a verse of the song Candor children used to sing when they thought no one could hear them:

Dauntless is the cruelest of the five
They tear each other to pieces. . . .

It has never seemed truer to me than now, watching Dauntless traitors induce a sleeping simulation that is not so different from the one that forced them to kill members of Abnegation not a month ago.

We are the only faction that could divide like this. Amity would not allow a schism; no one in Abnegation would be so selfish; Candor would argue until they found a common solution; and even Erudite would never do something so illogical. We really are the cruelest faction.

I step over a draped arm and a woman with her mouth hanging open, and hum the beginning of the next verse of the song under my breath.

Erudite is the coldest of the five
Knowledge is a costly thing. . . .

I wonder when Jeanine realized that Erudite and Dauntless would make a deadly combination. Ruthlessness and cold logic, it seems, can accomplish almost anything, including putting one and a half factions to sleep.

I scan faces and bodies as I walk, searching for irregular breaths, flickering eyelids, anything to suggest that the people lying on the ground are just pretending to be unconscious. So far, all the breathing is even and all the eyelids are still. Maybe none of the Candor are Divergent.

"Eric!" I hear someone shout from down the hall. I hold my breath as he walks right toward me. I try not to move. If I move, he'll look at me, and he'll recognize me, I know it. I look down, and tense so hard I tremble. *Don't look at me don't look at me don't look at me . . .*

Eric strides past me and down the hallway to my left. I should continue my search as quickly as possible, but curiosity urges me forward, toward whoever called for Eric. The shout sounded urgent.

When I lift my eyes, I see a Dauntless soldier standing over a kneeling woman. She wears a white blouse and a black skirt, and has her hands behind her head. Eric's smile looks greedy even in profile.

"Divergent," he says. "Well done. Bring her to the elevator bank. We'll decide which ones to kill and which ones to bring back later."

The Dauntless soldier grabs the woman by the ponytail and starts toward the elevator bank, dragging her behind him. She shrieks, and then scrambles to her feet, bent over. I try to swallow but it feels like I have a wad of cotton balls in my throat.

Eric continues down the hallway, away from me, and I try not to stare as the Candor woman stumbles past me, her hair still trapped in the fist of the Dauntless soldier. By now I know how terror works: I let it control me for a few seconds, and then force myself to act.

One . . . two . . . three . . .

I start forward with a new sense of purpose. Watching each person to see if they're awake is taking too much time. The next unconscious person I come across, I step hard on their pinkie finger. No response, not even a twitch. I step over them and find the next person's finger, pressing hard with the toe of my shoe. No response there either.

I hear someone else shout, "Got one!" from a distant hallway and start to feel frantic. I hop over fallen man after fallen woman, over children and teenagers and the elderly, stepping on fingers or stomachs or ankles, searching for signs of pain. I barely see their faces after a while, but still I get no response. I am playing hide-and-seek with the Divergent, but I'm not the only person who's "it."

And then it happens. I step on a Candor girl's pinkie, and her face twitches. Just a little—an impressive attempt at concealing the pain—but enough to catch my attention.

I look over my shoulder to see if anyone is near me, but they've all moved on from this central hallway. I check for the nearest stairwell—

there's one just ten feet away, down a side hallway to my right. I crouch next to the girl's head.

"Hey, kid," I say as quietly as I can. "It's okay. I'm not one of them."

Her eyes open, just a little.

"There's a staircase about three yards away," I say. "I'll tell you when no one is watching, and then you have to run, understand?"

She nods.

I stand and turn in a slow circle. A Dauntless traitor to my left is looking away, nudging a limp Dauntless with her foot. Two Dauntless traitors behind me are laughing about something. One in front of me is spacing out in my direction, but then he lifts his head and starts down the hallway again, away from me.

"Now," I say.

The girl gets up and sprints toward the door to the stairwell. I watch her until the door clicks shut, and see my reflection in one of the windows. But I'm not standing alone in a hallway of sleeping people, like I thought. Eric is standing right behind me.

+ + +

I look at his reflection, and he looks back at me. I could make a break for it. If I move fast enough, he might not have the presence of mind to grab me. But I know, even as the idea occurs to me, that I won't be able to outrun him. And I won't be able to shoot him, because I didn't take a gun.

I spin around, bringing my elbow up as I do, and thrust it toward Eric's face. It catches the end of his chin, but not hard enough to do any damage. He grabs my left arm with one hand and presses a gun barrel to my forehead with the other, smiling down at me.

"I don't understand," he says, "how you could possibly be stupid enough to come up here with no gun."

"Well, I'm smart enough to do this," I say. I stomp hard on his foot, which I fired a bullet into less than a month ago. He screams, his face contorting, and drives the heel of the gun into my jaw. I clench my teeth to suppress a groan. Blood trickles down my neck—he broke the skin.

Through all that, his grip on my arm does not loosen once. But the fact that he didn't just shoot me in the head tells me something: He's not allowed to kill me yet.

"I was surprised to discover you were still alive," he says. "Considering I'm the one who told Jeanine to construct that water tank just for you."

I try to figure out what I can do that will be painful enough for him to release me. I've just decided on a hard kick to the groin when he slips behind me and grabs me by both arms, pressing against me so I can barely move my feet. His fingernails dig into my skin, and I grit my teeth, both from the pain and from the sickening feeling of his chest on my back.

"She thought studying one of the Divergent's reaction to a real-life version of a simulation would be fascinating," he says, and he presses me forward so I have to walk. His breath tickles my hair. "And I agreed. You see, ingenuity—one of the qualities we most value in Erudite—requires creativity."

He twists his hands so the calluses scrape against my arms. I shift my body slightly to the left as I walk, trying to position one of my feet between his advancing feet. I notice with fierce pleasure that he's limping.

"Sometimes creativity seems wasteful, illogical . . . unless it's done for a greater purpose. In this case, the accumulation of knowledge."

I stop walking just long enough to bring my heel up, hard, between his legs. A high-pitched cry hitches in his throat, stopped before it really began, and his hands go limp for just a moment. In that moment, I twist my body as hard as I can and break free. I don't know where I will run, but I have to run, I have to—

He grabs my elbow, yanking me back, and pushes his thumb into the wound in my shoulder, twisting until pain makes my vision go black at the edges, and I scream at the top of my lungs.

"I *thought* I recalled from the footage of you in that water tank that you got shot in that shoulder," he says. "It seems I was right."

My knees crumple beneath me, and he grabs my collar almost carelessly, dragging me toward the elevator bank. The fabric digs into my throat, choking me, and I stumble after him. My body throbs with lingering pain.

When we reach the elevator bank, he forces me to my knees next to the Candor woman I saw earlier. She and four others sit between the two rows of elevators, kept in place by Dauntless with guns.

"I want one gun on her at all times," says Eric. "Not just aimed at her. *On* her."

A Dauntless man pushes a gun barrel into the back of my neck. It forms a cold circle on my skin. I lift my eyes to Eric. His face is red, his eyes watering.

"What's the matter, Eric?" I say, raising my eyebrows. "Afraid of a little girl?"

"I'm not stupid," he says, pushing his hands through his hair. "That little-girl act may have worked on me before, but it won't work again. You're the best attack dog they've got." He leans closer to me. "Which is why I'm sure you'll be put down soon enough."

One of the elevator doors opens, and a Dauntless soldier shoves

Uriah—whose lips are stained with blood—toward the short row of the Divergent. Uriah glances at me, but I can't read his expression well enough to know if he succeeded or failed. If he's here, he probably failed. Now they'll find all the Divergent in the building, and most of us will die.

I should probably be afraid. But instead a hysterical laugh bubbles inside me, because I just remembered something:

Maybe I can't hold a gun. But I have a knife in my back pocket.

CHAPTER
SIXTEEN

I SHIFT MY hand back, centimeter by centimeter, so the soldier pointing a gun at me doesn't notice. The elevator doors open again, bringing more of the Divergent with more Dauntless traitors. The Candor woman on my right whimpers. Strands of her hair are stuck to her lips, which are wet with spit, or tears, I can't tell.

My hand reaches the corner of my back pocket. I keep it steady, my fingers shaking with anticipation. I have to wait for the right moment, when Eric is close.

I focus on the mechanics of my breathing, imagining air filling every part of my lungs as I inhale, then remembering as I exhale how all my blood, oxygenated and unoxygenated, travels to and from the same heart.

It's easier to think of biology than the line of the Divergent sitting between the elevators. A Candor boy who can't be older than eleven sits to my left. He's braver than the woman to my right—he stares at the Dauntless soldier in front of him, unflinching.

Air in, air out. Blood pushed all the way to my extremities—the heart is a powerful muscle, the strongest muscle in the body in terms of longevity. More Dauntless arrive, reporting successful sweeps of specific floors of the Merciless Mart. Hundreds of people unconscious on the floor, shot with something other than bullets, and I have no idea why.

But I am thinking of the heart. Not of my heart anymore, but of Eric's, and how empty his chest will sound when his heart is no longer beating. Despite how much I hate him, I don't really want to kill him, at least not with a knife, up close where I can see the life leave him. But I have one chance left to do something useful, and if I want to hit the Erudite where it hurts, I have to take one of their leaders from them.

I notice that no one ever brought the Candor girl I warned to the elevator bank, which means she must have gotten away. Good.

Eric clasps his hands behind his back and begins to pace, back and forth, before the line of Divergent.

"My orders are to take only two of you back to Erudite headquarters for testing," says Eric. "The rest of you are to be executed. There are several ways to determine who among you will be least useful to us."

His footsteps slow when he approaches me. I tense my fingers, about to grab the knife handle, but he doesn't come close enough. He keeps walking and stops in front of the boy to my left.

"The brain finishes developing at age twenty-five," says Eric. "Therefore your Divergence is not completely developed."

He lifts his gun and fires.

A strangled scream leaps out of my body as the boy slumps to the ground, and I squeeze my eyes shut. Every muscle in my body strains toward him, but I hold myself back. *Wait, wait, wait.* I can't think of the boy. *Wait.* I force my eyes open and blink tears from them.

My scream accomplished one thing: now Eric stands in front of me, smiling. I caught his attention.

"You are also rather young," he says. "Nowhere near finished developing."

He steps toward me. My fingertips inch closer to the knife handle.

"Most of the Divergent get two results in the aptitude test. Some only get one. No one has ever gotten three, not because of aptitude, but simply because in order to get that result, you have to refuse to choose something," he says, moving closer still. I tilt my head back to look at him, at all the metal gleaming in his face, at his empty eyes.

"My superiors suspect that you got two, Tris," he says. "They don't think you're that complex—just an even blend of Abnegation and Dauntless—selfless to the point of idiocy. Or is that brave to the point of idiocy?"

I close my hand around the knife handle and squeeze. He leans closer.

"Just between you and me . . . *I* think you might have gotten three, because you're the kind of bullheaded person who would refuse to make a simple choice just because she was told to," he says. "Care to enlighten me?"

I lurch forward, pulling my hand out of my pocket. I close my eyes as I thrust the blade up and toward him. I don't want to see his blood.

I feel the knife go in and then pull it out again. My entire body throbs to the rhythm of my heart. The back of my neck is sticky with sweat. I open my eyes as Eric slumps to the ground, and then—chaos.

The Dauntless traitors aren't holding lethal guns, only ones that shoot whatever it is they shot at us before, so they all scramble for their real guns. As they do, Uriah launches himself at one of them and punches him hard in the jaw. The life goes out of the soldier's eyes and he falls, knocked out. Uriah takes the soldier's gun and starts shooting at the Dauntless closest to us.

I reach for Eric's gun, so panicked I can barely see, and when I look up, I swear the amount of Dauntless in the room has doubled. Gunshots fill my ears, and I drop to the ground as everyone starts running. My fingers brush the gun barrel, and I shudder. My hands are too weak to grasp it.

A heavy arm wraps around my shoulders and shoves me toward the wall. My right shoulder burns, and I see the Dauntless symbol tattooed on the back of a neck. Tobias turns, crouched around me to shield me from the gunfire, and shoots.

"Tell me if anyone's behind me!" he says.

I peer over his shoulder, curling my hands into fists around his shirt.

There *are* more Dauntless in the room, Dauntless without blue armbands—loyal Dauntless. My faction. My faction has come to save us. How are they awake?

The Dauntless traitors sprint away from the elevator bank. They were not prepared for an attack, not from all sides. Some of them fight back, but most run for the stairs. Tobias fires over and over again, until his gun runs out of bullets, and the trigger makes a clicking sound instead. My vision is too blurry with tears and my hands too useless to fire a gun. I scream into gritted teeth, frustrated. I can't help. I am worthless.

On the floor, Eric moans. Still alive, for now.

The gunshots gradually stop. My hand is wet. One glimpse of red tells me it's covered in blood—Eric's. I wipe it off on my pants and try to blink the tears away. My ears ring.

"Tris," Tobias says. "You can put the knife down now."

CHAPTER
SEVENTEEN

TOBIAS TELLS ME this story:

When the Erudite reached the lobby stairwell, one of them didn't go up to the second floor. Instead, she ran up to one of the highest levels of the building. There she evacuated a group of loyal Dauntless—including Tobias—to a fire escape the Dauntless traitors had not sealed off. Those loyal Dauntless gathered in the lobby and split into four groups that stormed the stairwells simultaneously, surrounding the Dauntless traitors, who had clustered around the elevator banks.

The Dauntless traitors were not prepared for that much resistance. They thought everyone but the Divergent was unconscious, so they ran.

The Erudite woman was Cara. Will's older sister.

+ + +

Heaving a sigh, I let the jacket slide from my arms and examine my shoulder. A metal disc about the size of my pinkie fingernail is pressed against my skin. Surrounding it is a patch of blue strands, like someone injected blue dye into the tiny veins just beneath the surface of my skin. Frowning, I try to peel the metal disc away from my arm, and feel a sharp pain.

Gritting my teeth, I wedge the flat of my knife blade under the disc and force it up. I scream into my teeth as the pain races through me, making everything go black for a moment. But I keep pushing, as hard as I can, until the disc lifts from my skin enough for me to get my fingers around it. Attached to the bottom of the disc is a needle.

I gag, grasp the disc in my fingertips, and pull one last time. This time, the needle comes free. It's as long as my littlest finger and smeared with my blood. I ignore the blood running down my arm and hold the disc and the needle up to the light above the sink.

Judging by the blue dye in my arm and the needle, they must have injected us with something. But what? Poison? An explosive?

I shake my head. If they had wanted to kill us, most of us were unconscious already, so they could have just shot us all. Whatever they injected us with isn't meant to kill us.

Someone knocks on the door. I don't know why—I'm in a public restroom, after all.

"Tris, you in there?" Uriah's muffled voice asks.

"Yeah," I call back.

Uriah looks better than he did an hour ago—he washed the blood from his mouth, and some of the color has returned to his face. I'm struck, suddenly, by how handsome he is—all his features are proportionate, his eyes dark and lively, his skin bronze-brown. And he has probably always been that handsome. Only boys who have been handsome from a young age have that arrogance in their smile.

Not like Tobias, who is almost shy when he smiles, like he is surprised you bothered to look at him in the first place.

My throat aches. I put the needle and disc on the edge of the sink.

Uriah looks from me to the needle in my hand to the line of blood running from my shoulder to my wrist.

"Gross," he says.

"Wasn't paying attention," I say. I set the needle down and grab a paper towel, mopping up the blood on my arm. "How are the others?"

"Marlene's cracking jokes, as usual." Uriah's smile grows, putting a dimple in his cheek. "Lynn's grumbling. Wait, you yanked that out of your own arm?" He points to the needle. "God, Tris. Do you have no nerve endings or something?"

"I think I need a bandage."

"You think?" Uriah shakes his head. "You should get some ice for your face, too. So, everyone's waking up now. It's a madhouse out there."

I touch my jaw. It is tender where Eric's gun struck me—I will have to put healing salve on it so it doesn't bruise.

"Is Eric dead?" I don't know which answer I'm hoping for, yes or no.

"No. Some of the Candor decided to give him medical treatment." Uriah scowls at the sink. "Something about honorable treatment of prisoners. Kang's interrogating him in private right now. Doesn't want us there, disturbing the peace or whatever."

I snort.

"Yeah. Anyway, no one gets it," he says, perching on the edge of the sink next to mine. "Why storm in here and fire those things at us and then knock us all out? Why not just kill us?"

"No idea," I say. "The only use I see for it is that it helped them figure out who's Divergent and who's not. But that can't be the only reason they did it."

"I don't get why they have it out for us. I mean, when they were trying to mind control themselves an army, sure, but now? Seems useless."

I frown as I press a clean paper towel to my shoulder, to stop the bleeding. He's right. Jeanine already has an army. So why kill the Divergent now?

"Jeanine doesn't want to kill everyone," I say slowly. "She knows that would be illogical. Without each faction, society doesn't function, because each faction trains its members for particular jobs. What she wants is *control*."

I glance up at my reflection. My jaw is swollen, and fingernail marks are still on my arms. Disgusting.

"She must be planning another simulation," I say. "Same thing as before, but this time, she wants to make sure that everyone is either under its influence or dead."

"But the simulation only lasts for a certain period of time," he says. "It's not useful unless you're trying to accomplish something specific."

"Right." I sigh. "I don't know. I don't get it." I pick up the needle. "I don't get what this thing is either. If it was like the other simulation-inducing injections, it was just meant for one use. So why shoot these things at us just to put us unconscious? It doesn't make any sense."

"I dunno, Tris, but right now we've got a huge building full of panicked people to deal with. Let's go get you a bandage." He pauses and then says, "Can you do me a favor?"

"What is it?"

"Don't tell anyone I'm Divergent." He bites his lip. "Shauna's my friend, and I don't want her to suddenly become afraid of me."

"Sure," I say, forcing a smile. "I'll keep it to myself."

+ + +

I am awake all night removing needles from people's arms. After a few hours I stop trying to be gentle. I just pull as hard as I can.

I find out that the Candor boy Eric shot in the head was named Bobby, and that Eric is in stable condition, and that of the hundreds of people in the Merciless Mart, only eighty don't have needles buried in their flesh, seventy of whom are Dauntless, one of whom is Christina. All night I puzzle over needles and serums and simulations, trying to inhabit the minds of my enemies.

In the morning, I run out of needles to remove and go to the cafeteria, rubbing my eyes. Jack Kang announced that we would have a meeting at noon, so maybe I can fit in a long nap after I eat.

When I walk into the cafeteria, though, I see Caleb.

Caleb runs up to me and folds me carefully into his arms. I breathe a sigh of relief. I thought I had gotten to the point where I didn't need my brother anymore, but I don't think such a point actually exists. I relax against him for a moment, and catch Tobias's eye over Caleb's shoulder.

"Are you all right?" Caleb says, pulling back. "Your jaw . . ."

"It's nothing," I say. "Just swollen."

"I heard they got a bunch of the Divergent and started shooting them. Thank God they didn't find you."

"Actually, they did. But they only killed one," I say. I pinch the bridge of my nose to relieve some of the pressure in my head. "But I'm all right. When did you get here?"

"About ten minutes ago. I came with Marcus," he says. "As our only legal political leader, he felt it was his duty to be here—we didn't hear about the attack until an hour ago. One of the factionless saw the Dauntless storming into the building, and news takes a while to travel among the factionless."

"Marcus is *alive*?" I say. We never actually saw him die when we escaped the Amity compound, but I just assumed he had—I'm not sure how I feel. Disappointed, maybe, because I hate him for how he treated Tobias? Or relieved, because the last Abnegation leader is still alive? Is it possible to feel both?

"He and Peter escaped, and walked back to the city," says Caleb.

I am not at all relieved to find out that Peter is still alive. "Where's Peter, then?"

"He is where you would expect him to be," Caleb replies.

"Erudite," I say. I shake my head. "What a—"

I can't even think of a word strong enough to describe him. Apparently I need to expand my vocabulary.

Caleb's face twists for a moment, then he nods and touches my shoulder. "Are you hungry? Want me to get you something?"

"Yes, please," I say. "I'll be back in a little while, okay? I have to talk to Tobias."

"All right." Caleb squeezes my arm and walks off, probably to get in the miles-long cafeteria line. Tobias and I stand yards away from each other for a few seconds.

He approaches me slowly.

"You okay?" he says.

"I might throw up if I have to answer that one more time," I say. "I don't have a bullet in my head, do I? So I'm good."

"Your jaw is so swollen you look like you have a wad of food in your cheek, and you just stabbed Eric," he says, frowning. "I'm not allowed to ask if you're okay?"

I sigh. I should tell him about Marcus, but I don't want to do it here, with so many people around. "Yeah. I'm okay."

His arm jerks like he was thinking of touching me but decided against it. Then he reconsiders and slides his arm around me, pulling me to him.

Suddenly I think maybe I'll let someone else take all the risks, maybe I'll just start acting selfishly so that I can stay close to Tobias without hurting him. All I want is to bury my face in his neck and forget anything else exists.

"I'm sorry it took me so long to come get you," he whispers into my hair.

I sigh and touch his back with just my fingertips. I could stand here until I go unconscious from exhaustion, but I shouldn't; I can't. I pull back and say, "I need to talk to you. Can we go somewhere quiet?"

He nods, and we leave the cafeteria. One of the Dauntless we pass yells, "Oh, look! It's *Tobias Eaton!*"

I had almost forgotten about the interrogation, and the name it revealed to all of Dauntless.

Another one yells, "I saw your daddy here earlier, Eaton! Are you gonna go hide?"

Tobias straightens and stiffens, like someone is training a gun at his chest instead of jeering at him.

"Yeah, are you gonna hide, coward?"

A few people around us laugh. I grab Tobias's arm and steer him toward the elevators before he can react. He looked like he was about to punch someone. Or worse.

"I was going to tell you—he came with Caleb," I say. "He and Peter escaped Amity—"

"What were you waiting for, then?" he says, but not harshly. His voice sounds somehow detached from him, like it is floating between us.

"It's not the kind of news you deliver in a cafeteria," I say.

"Fair enough," he says.

We wait in silence for the elevator, Tobias chewing on his lip and staring into space. He does that all the way to the eighteenth floor, which is empty. There, the silence wraps around me like Caleb's embrace did, calming me. I sit down on one of the benches on the edge of the interrogation room, and Tobias pulls Niles's chair over to sit in front of me.

"Didn't there used to be two of these?" he says, frowning at the chair.

"Yeah," I say. "I, uh . . . it got thrown out the window."

"Strange," he says. He sits. "So what did you want to talk about? Or was that about Marcus?"

"No, that wasn't it. Are you . . . all right?" I say cautiously.

"I don't have a bullet in my head, do I?" he says, staring at his hands. "So I'm fine. I'd like to talk about something else."

"I want to talk about simulations," I say. "But first, something else—your mother thought Jeanine would go after the factionless next. Obviously she was wrong—and I'm not sure why. It's not like the Candor are battle ready or anything—"

"Well, think about it," he says. "Think it through, like the Erudite." I give him a look.

"What?" he says. "If you can't, the rest of us have no hope."

"Fine," I say. "Um . . . it had to be because Dauntless and Candor were the most logical targets. Because . . . the factionless are in multiple places, whereas we're all in the same place."

"Right," he says. "Also, when Jeanine attacked Abnegation, she got all the Abnegation data. My mother told me that the Abnegation had documented the factionless Divergent populations, which means that after the attack, Jeanine must have found out that the proportion of Divergent among the factionless is higher than among the Candor. That makes them an illogical target."

"All right. Then tell me about the serum again," I say. "It has a few parts, right?"

"Two," he says, nodding. "The transmitter and the liquid that induces the simulation. The transmitter communicates information to the brain from the computer, and vice versa, and the liquid alters the brain to put it in a simulation state."

I nod. "And the transmitter only works for one simulation, right? What happens to it after that?"

"It dissolves," he says. "As far as I know, the Erudite haven't been able to develop a transmitter that lasts for more than one simulation, although the attack simulation lasted far longer than any simulation I've seen before."

The words "as far as I know" stick in my mind. Jeanine has spent most of her adult life developing the serums. If she's still hunting down the Divergent, she's probably still obsessed with creating more advanced versions of the technology.

"What's this about, Tris?" he says.

"Have you seen this yet?" I say, pointing at the bandage covering my shoulder.

"Not up close," he says. "Uriah and I were hauling wounded Erudite up to the fourth floor all morning."

I peel away the edge of the bandage, revealing the puncture wound—no longer bleeding, thankfully—and the patch of blue dye that doesn't seem to be fading. Then I reach into my pocket and take out the needle that was buried in my arm.

"When they attacked, they weren't trying to kill us. They were shooting us with these," I say.

His hand touches the dyed skin around the puncture wound. I didn't notice it before because it was happening right in front of me, but he looks different than he used to, during initiation. He's let his facial hair grow in a little, and his hair is longer than I've ever seen it—dense enough to show me that it is brown, not black.

He takes the needle from me and taps the metal disc at the end of it. "This is probably hollow. It must have contained whatever that blue stuff in your arm is. What happened after you were shot?"

"They tossed these gas-spewing cylinders into the room, and everyone went unconscious. That is, everyone but Uriah and me and the other Divergent."

Tobias doesn't seem surprised. I narrow my eyes.

"Did you know that Uriah was Divergent?"

He shrugs. "Of course. I ran his simulations, too."

"And you never told me?"

"Privileged information," he says. "Dangerous information."

I feel a flare of anger—how many things is he going to keep from me?—and try to stifle it. Of course he couldn't tell me Uriah was Divergent. He was just respecting Uriah's privacy. It makes sense.

I clear my throat. "You saved our lives, you know," I say. "Eric was trying to hunt us down."

"I think we're past keeping track of who has saved whose life." He looks at me for a few long seconds.

"Anyway," I say to break the silence. "After we figured out that everyone was asleep, Uriah ran upstairs to warn the people who were up there, and I went to the second floor to figure out what was going on. Eric had all the Divergent by the elevators, and he was trying to figure out which of us he was going to take back with him. He said he was allowed to take two. I don't know why he was going to take any."

"Odd," he says.

"Any ideas?"

"My guess is that the needle injected you with a transmitter," he says, "and the gas was an aerosol version of the liquid that alters the brain. But why . . ." A crease appears between his eyebrows. "Oh. She put everyone to sleep to find out who the Divergent were."

"You think that's the only reason for shooting us with transmitters?"

He shakes his head, and his eyes lock on mine. Their blue is so dark and familiar that I feel like it could swallow me whole. For a moment I wish it would, so that I could escape this place and all that has happened.

"I think you've already figured it out," he says, "but you want me to contradict you. And I'm not going to."

"They've developed a long-lasting transmitter," I say.

He nods.

"So now we're all wired for multiple simulations," I add. "As many as Jeanine wants, maybe."

He nods again.

My next breath shakes on the way out of my mouth. "This is really bad, Tobias."

+ + +

In the hallway outside the interrogation room, he stops, leaning against the wall.

"So you attacked Eric," he says. "Was that during the invasion? Or when you were by the elevators?"

"By the elevators," I say.

"One thing I don't understand," he says. "You were downstairs. You could have just run away. But instead, you decided to dive into a crowd of armed Dauntless all by yourself. And I'm willing to bet you weren't carrying a gun."

I press my lips together.

"Is that true?" he demands.

"What makes you think I didn't have a gun?" I scowl.

"You haven't been able to touch a gun since the attack," he says. "I understand why, with the whole Will thing, but—"

"That has nothing to do with it."

"No?" He lifts his eyebrows.

"I did what I had to do."

"Yeah. But now you should be done," he says, pulling away from the wall to face me. Candor hallways are wide, wide enough for all the space I want to keep between us. "You should have stayed with the Amity. You should have stayed far away from all of this."

"No, I shouldn't have," I say. "You think you know what's best for me? You have no idea. I was going crazy with the Amity. Here I finally feel . . . sane again."

"Which is odd, considering you are acting like a psychopath," he says. "It's not brave, choosing the position you were in yesterday. It's beyond stupid—it's suicidal. Don't you have any regard for your own life?"

"Of course I do!" I retort. "I was trying to do something useful!"

For a few seconds he just stares at me.

"You're more than Dauntless," he says in a low voice. "But if you want to be just like them, hurling yourself into ridiculous situations for no reason and retaliating against your enemies without any regard for what's ethical, go right ahead. I thought you were better than that, but maybe I was wrong!"

I clench my hands, my jaw.

"You shouldn't insult the Dauntless," I say. "They took you in when you had nowhere else to go. Trusted you with a good job. Gave you all your friends."

I lean against the wall, my eyes on the floor. The tiles in the Merciless Mart are always black and white, and here they are in a checkered pattern. If I unfocus my eyes, I see exactly what the Candor don't believe in—gray. Maybe Tobias and I don't believe in it either. Not really.

I weigh too much, more than my frame can support, so much I should fall right through the floor.

"Tris."

I keep staring.

"*Tris.*"

I finally look at him.

"I just don't want to lose you."

We stand there for a few minutes. I don't say what I'm thinking, which is that he might be right. There is a part of me that wants to be lost, that struggles to join my parents and Will so that I don't have to ache for them anymore. A part of me that wants to see whatever comes next.

+ + +

"So you're her brother?" says Lynn. "I guess we know who got the good genes."

I laugh at the expression on Caleb's face, his mouth drawn into a slight pucker and his eyes wide.

"When do you have to get back?" I say, nudging him with my elbow.

I bite into the sandwich Caleb got me from the cafeteria line. I am nervous to have him here, mixing the sad remains of my family life with the sad remains of my Dauntless life. What will he think of my friends, my faction? What will my faction think of him?

"Soon," he says. "I don't want anyone to worry."

"I didn't realize Susan had changed her name to 'Anyone,' " I say, raising an eyebrow.

"Ha-ha," he says, making a face at me.

Teasing between siblings should feel familiar, but it doesn't for us. Abnegation discouraged anything that might make someone feel uncomfortable, and teasing was included.

I can feel how cautious we are with each other, now that we're discovering a different way to relate in light of our new factions and our parents' deaths. Every time I look at him, I realize that he's the only family I have left and I feel desperate, desperate to keep him around, desperate to narrow the gap between us.

"Is Susan another Erudite defector?" says Lynn, stabbing a string bean with her fork. Uriah and Tobias are still in the lunch line, waiting behind two dozen Candor who are too busy bickering to get their food.

"No, she was our neighbor when we were kids. She's Abnegation," I say.

"And you're involved with her?" she asks Caleb. "Don't you think that's kind of a stupid move? I mean, when all this is over, you'll be in different factions, living in completely different places. . . ."

"Lynn," Marlene says, touching her shoulder, "shut up, will you?"

Across the room, something blue catches my attention. Cara just walked in. I put down my sandwich, my appetite gone, and look up at her with my head lowered. She walks to the far corner of the cafeteria, where a few tables of Erudite refugees sit. Most of them have abandoned their blue clothes in favor of black-and-white ones, but they still wear their glasses. I try to focus on Caleb instead—but Caleb is watching the Erudite, too.

"I can't go back to Erudite any more than *they* can," says Caleb. "When this is over, I won't have a faction."

For the first time I notice how sad he looks when he talks about the Erudite. I didn't realize how difficult the decision to leave them must have been for him.

"You could go sit with them," I say, nodding toward the Erudite refugees.

"I don't know them." He shrugs. "I was only there for a month, remember?"

Uriah drops his tray on the table, scowling. "I overheard someone talking about Eric's interrogation in the lunch line. Apparently he knew almost *nothing* about Jeanine's plan."

"What?" Lynn slaps her fork on the table. "How is that even possible?"

Uriah shrugs, and sits.

"I'm not surprised," Caleb says.

Everyone stares at him.

"What?" He flushes. "It would be stupid to confide your entire plan to one person. It's infinitely smarter to give little pieces of it to each person working with you. That way, if someone betrays you, the loss isn't too great."

"Oh," says Uriah.

Lynn picks up her fork and starts eating again.

"I heard the Candor made ice cream," says Marlene, twisting her head around to see the lunch line. "You know, as a kind of 'it sucks we got attacked, but at least there are desserts' thing."

"I feel better already," says Lynn dryly.

"It probably won't be as good as Dauntless cake," says Marlene mournfully. She sighs, and a strand of mousy brown hair falls in her eyes.

"We had good cake," I tell Caleb.

"We had fizzy drinks," he says.

"Ah, but did you have a ledge overlooking an underground river?" says Marlene, waggling her eyebrows. "Or a room where you faced all your nightmares at once?"

"No," says Caleb, "and to be honest, I'm kind of okay with that."

"*Si-ssy*," sings Marlene.

"*All* your nightmares?" says Caleb, his eyes lighting up. "How does that work? I mean, are the nightmares produced by the computer or by your brain?"

"Oh God." Lynn drops her head into her hands. "Here we go."

Marlene launches into a description of the simulations, and I let her voice, and Caleb's voice, wash over me as I finish my sandwich. Then, despite the clatter of forks and the roar of hundreds of conversations all around me, I rest my head on the table and fall asleep.

CHAPTER
EIGHTEEN

"QUIET DOWN, EVERYONE!"

Jack Kang lifts his hands, and the crowd goes silent. That is a talent.

I stand among the crowd of Dauntless who got here late, when there were no seats left. A flash of light catches my eye—lightning. It's not the best time to be meeting in a room with holes in the walls instead of windows, but this is the biggest room they have.

"I know many of you are confused and shaken by what happened yesterday," Jack says. "I have heard many reports from a variety of perspectives, and have gotten a sense for what is straightforward and what requires more investigation."

I tuck my wet hair behind my ears. I woke up ten minutes before the meeting was supposed to start and ran to the showers. Though I'm still exhausted, I feel more alert now.

"What seems to me to require more investigation," Jack says, "is the Divergent."

He looks tired—he has dark circles under his eyes, and his short hair sticks out at random, like he's been pulling it all night. Despite the stifling heat of the room, he wears a long-sleeved shirt that buttons at the wrists—he must have been distracted when he dressed this morning.

"If you are one of the Divergent, please step forward so that we can hear from you."

I look sideways at Uriah. This feels dangerous. My Divergence is something I am supposed to hide. Admitting it is supposed to mean death. But there is no sense in hiding it now—they already know about me.

Tobias is the first to move. He starts into the crowd, at first turning his body to wedge his way between people, and then, when they step back for him, moving straight toward Jack Kang with his shoulders back.

I move, too, muttering "Excuse me" to the people in front of me. They draw back like I just threatened to spit poison at them. A few others step forward, in Candor black and white, but not many. One of them is the girl I helped.

Despite the notoriety Tobias now has among the Dauntless, and my new title as That Girl Who Stabbed Eric, we are not the real focus of everyone's attention. Marcus is.

"You, Marcus?" says Jack when Marcus reaches the middle of the room and stands on top of the lower scale in the floor.

"Yes," Marcus says. "I understand that you are concerned—that you all are concerned. You had never heard of the Divergent a week ago, and now all that you know is that they are immune to something to which you are susceptible, and that is a frightening thing. But I can assure you that there is nothing to be afraid of, as far as we are concerned."

As he speaks, his head tilts and his eyebrows lift in sympathy, and I understand at once why some people like him. He makes you feel that if you just placed everything in his hands, he would take care of it.

"It seems clear to me," says Jack, "that we were attacked so that the Erudite could find the Divergent. Do you know why that is?"

"No, I do not," says Marcus. "Perhaps their intention was merely to identify us. It seems like useful information to have, if they intend to use their simulations again."

"That was *not* their intention." The words are past my lips before I decide to speak them. My voice sounds high and weak compared to Marcus's and Jack's, but it's too late to stop. "They wanted to kill us. They've been killing us since before any of this happened."

Jack's eyebrows draw together. I hear hundreds of tiny sounds, raindrops hitting the roof. The room darkens, as if under the gloom of what I just said.

"That sounds very much like a conspiracy theory," Jack says. "What reason would the Erudite have to kill you?"

My mother said people feared the Divergent because we couldn't be controlled. That may be true, but fear of the uncontrollable is not a concrete enough reason to give Jack Kang for the Erudite wanting us dead. My heart races as I realize that I can't answer his question.

"I . . ." I start. Tobias interrupts me.

"Obviously we don't know," he says, "but there are nearly a dozen mysterious deaths recorded among the Dauntless from the past six years, and there is a correlation between those people and irregular aptitude test results or initiation simulation results."

Lightning strikes, making the room glow. Jack shakes his head. "While that is intriguing, correlation does not constitute evidence."

"A Dauntless leader shot a Candor child in the *head*," I snap. "Did you get a report of *that*? Did it seem 'worthy of investigation'?"

"In fact I did," he says. "And shooting a child in cold blood is a terrible crime that cannot go unpunished. Fortunately, we have the perpetrator in custody and will be able to put him on trial. *However,* we must keep in mind that the Dauntless soldiers did not give any evidence of wanting to harm the majority of us, or they would have killed us while we were unconscious."

I hear irritated murmurs all around me.

"Their peaceful invasion suggests to me that it may be possible to negotiate a peace treaty with the Erudite and the other Dauntless," he continues. "So I will arrange a meeting with Jeanine Matthews to discuss that possibility as soon as possible."

"Their invasion wasn't *peaceful*," I say. I can see the corner of Tobias's mouth from where I stand, and he is smiling. I take a deep breath and begin again. "Just because they didn't shoot you all in the head doesn't mean their intentions were somehow honorable. Why do you think they came here? Just to run through your hallways, knock you unconscious, and leave?"

"I assume they came here for people like you," says Jack. "And while I am concerned for your safety, I don't think we can attack them just because they wanted to kill a fraction of our population."

"Killing you is not the worst thing they can do to you," I say. "Controlling you is."

Jack's lips curl with amusement. *Amusement.* "Oh? And how will they manage that?"

"They shot you with needles," Tobias says. "Needles full of simulation transmitters. Simulations control you. That's how."

"We know how simulations work," says Jack. "The transmitter is not a permanent implant. If they intended to control us, they would have done it right away."

"But—" I begin.

He interrupts me. "I know you have been under a lot of stress, Tris," he says quietly, "and that you have done a great service to your faction and to Abnegation. But I think your traumatic experience may have compromised your ability to be completely objective. I can't launch an attack based on a little girl's speculations."

I stand statue-still, unable to believe that he could be so stupid. My face burning. *Little girl,* he called me. A little girl who is stressed out to the point of paranoia. That is not me, but now, it's who the Candor think I am.

"*You* don't make our decisions for us, Kang," says Tobias.

All around me, the Dauntless shout their assent. Someone else yells, "You are not the leader of our faction!"

Jack waits for their shouts to die down and then says, "That is true. If you want to, you can feel free to storm the Erudite compound by yourselves. But you will do so without our support, and may I remind you, you are greatly outnumbered and unprepared."

He's right. We can't attack Dauntless traitors and Erudite without Candor's numbers. It would be a bloodbath if we tried. Jack Kang has all the power. And now we all know it.

"I thought so," he says smugly. "Very well. I will contact Jeanine Matthews, and see if we can negotiate a peace. Any objections?"

We can't attack without Candor, I think, *unless we have the factionless.*

CHAPTER
NINETEEN

THAT AFTERNOON I join a group of Candor and Dauntless cleaning up the broken windows in the lobby. I focus on the path of the broom, keeping my eyes on the dust that collects between glass fragments. My muscles remember the movement before the rest of me does, but when I look down, instead of dark marble I see plain white tile and the bottom of a light gray wall; I see strands of blond hair that my mother trimmed, and the mirror safely tucked behind its wall panel.

My body goes weak, and I lean into the broom handle for support.

A hand touches my shoulder, and I twitch away from it. But it's just a Candor girl—a child. She looks up at me, wide-eyed.

"Are you all right?" she says, her voice high and indistinct.

"I'm fine," I say. Too sharply. I hurry to amend it. "Just tired. Thank you."

"I think you're lying," she says.

I notice a bandage peeking out from the end of her sleeve, probably covering the needle puncture. The idea of this little girl under a simulation nauseates me. I can't even look at her. I turn away.

And I see them: outside, a traitor Dauntless man, propping up a woman with a bleeding leg. I see the gray streaks in the woman's hair and the end of the man's hooked nose and the blue armband of a Dauntless traitor just beneath their shoulders, and recognize them both. Tori and Zeke.

Tori is trying to walk, but one of her legs drags behind her, useless. A wet, dark patch covers most of her thigh.

The Candor stop sweeping and stare at them. The Dauntless guards standing near the elevators rush toward the entrance with their guns lifted. My fellow sweepers back up to get out of the way, but I stay where I am, heat rushing through me as Zeke and Tori approach.

"Are they even armed?" someone says.

Tori and Zeke reach what used to be the doors, and he puts up one of his hands when he sees the row of Dauntless with guns. The other he keeps wrapped around Tori's waist.

"She needs medical attention," says Zeke. "Right now."

"Why should we give a traitor medical attention?" a Dauntless man with wispy blond hair and a double-pierced lip asks over his gun. A patch of blue dye marks his forearm.

Tori moans, and I slip between two Dauntless to reach for her. She puts her hand, which is sticky with blood, in mine. Zeke lowers her to the ground with a grunt.

"Tris," she says, sounding dazed.

"Better step back, girl," the blond Dauntless man says.

"No," I say. "Put your gun down."

"Told you the Divergent were crazy," one of the other armed Dauntless mutters to the woman next to him.

"I don't care if you bring her upstairs and tie her to a bed to keep her from going on a shooting spree!" says Zeke, scowling. "Don't let her bleed to death in the lobby of Candor headquarters!"

Finally, a few Dauntless come forward and lift Tori up.

"Where should we . . . take her?" one of them asks.

"Find Helena," Zeke says. "Dauntless nurse."

The men nod and carry her toward the elevators. Zeke and I meet eyes.

"What happened?" I ask him.

"The traitor Dauntless found out we were collecting information from them," he says. "Tori tried to get away, but they shot her as she was running. I helped her get here."

"That's a nice story," says the blond Dauntless man. "Want to tell it again under truth serum?"

Zeke shrugs. "All right." He puts his wrists together in front of him dramatically. "Haul me away, if you're so desperate to."

Then his eyes focus on something over my shoulder, and he starts walking. I turn to see Uriah jogging from the elevator bank. He is grinning.

"Heard a rumor you were a dirty traitor," Uriah says.

"Yeah, whatever," says Zeke.

They collide in an embrace that looks almost painful to me, slapping each other's backs and laughing with their fists clasped between them.

+ + +

"I can't believe you didn't tell us," says Lynn, shaking her head. She sits across from me at the table, her arms crossed and one of her legs propped up.

"Oh, don't get all huffy about it," says Zeke. "I wasn't even supposed to tell Shauna and Uriah. And it sort of defeats the purpose of being a spy if you tell everyone that's what you are."

We sit in a room in Candor headquarters called the Gathering Place, which the Dauntless have taken to saying in a mocking way whenever they can. It is large and open, with black-and-white cloth draped on every wall, and a circle of podiums in the center of the room. Large round tables surround the podiums. Lynn told me they host monthly debates here, for entertainment, and also hold religious services here once a week. But even when no events are scheduled, the room is usually full.

Zeke was cleared by the Candor an hour ago, in a short interrogation on the eighteenth floor. It was not as somber an occasion as Tobias's and my interrogation, partly because there was no suspicious video footage implicating Zeke, and partly because Zeke is funny even when under truth serum. Maybe especially so. In any case, we came to the Gathering Place "for a 'Hey, you're not a dirty traitor!' celebration," as Uriah put it.

"Yeah, but we've been insulting you since the simulation attack," Lynn says. "And now I feel like a jerk about it."

Zeke puts his arm around Shauna. "You *are* a jerk, Lynn. It's part of your charm."

Lynn launches a plastic cup at him, which he deflects. Water sprays over the table, hitting him in the eye.

"Anyway, as I was saying," says Zeke, rubbing his eye, "I was mostly working on getting Erudite defectors out safely. That's why there's a big group of them here, and a small group at Amity headquarters. But Tori . . . I have no idea what she was doing. She kept sneaking away for hours at a time, and whenever she was around, it was like she was about to explode. It's no wonder she gave us away."

"How'd *you* get the job?" says Lynn. "You're not that special."

"It was more because of where I was after the simulation attack. Smack-dab in a pack of Dauntless traitors. I decided to go with it," he says. "Not sure about Tori, though."

"She transferred from Erudite," I say.

What I don't say, because I'm sure she wouldn't want everyone to know, is that Tori probably seemed explosive in Erudite headquarters because they murdered her brother for being Divergent.

She told me once that she was waiting for an opportunity to get revenge.

"Oh," says Zeke. "How do you know that?"

"Well, all the faction transfers have a secret club," I say, leaning back in my chair. "We meet every third Thursday."

Zeke snorts.

"Where's Four?" says Uriah, checking his watch. "Should we start without him?"

"We can't," says Zeke. "He's getting The Info."

Uriah nods like that means something. Then he pauses and says, "What info, again?"

"The info about Kang's little peacemaking meeting with Jeanine," says Zeke. "Obviously."

Across the room, I see Christina sitting at a table with her sister. They are both reading something.

My entire body tenses. Cara, Will's older sister, is walking across the room toward Christina's table. I duck my head.

"What?" Uriah says, looking over his shoulder. I want to punch him.

"Stop it!" I say. "Could you be any more obvious?" I lean forward, folding my arms on the table. "Will's sister is over there."

"Yeah, I talked to her about getting out of Erudite once, while I was there," says Zeke. "Said she saw an Abnegation woman get killed while she was on a mission for Jeanine and couldn't stomach it anymore."

"Are we sure she's not just an Erudite spy?" Lynn says.

"Lynn, she saved half our faction from *this* stuff," says Marlene, tapping the bandage on her arm from where the Dauntless traitors shot her.

"Well, half of half of our faction."

"In some circles they call that a quarter, Mar," Lynn says.

"Anyway, who cares if she is a traitor?" Zeke says. "We're not planning anything that she can inform them about. And we certainly wouldn't include her if we were."

"There is plenty of information for her to gather here," Lynn says. "How many of us there are, for example, or how many of us aren't wired for simulations."

"You didn't see her when she was telling me why she left," says Zeke. "I believe her."

Cara and Christina have gotten up, and are walking out of the room.

"I'll be right back," I say. "I have to go to the bathroom."

I wait until Cara and Christina have gone through the doors, then half walk, half jog in that direction. I open one of the doors slowly, so it doesn't make any noise, and then close it slowly behind me. I am in a dim hallway that smells like garbage—this must be where the Candor trash chute is.

I hear two female voices around the corner and creep toward the end of the hallway to hear better.

". . . just can't handle her being here," one of them sobs. Christina. "I can't stop picturing it . . . what she did. . . . I don't understand how she could have done that!"

Christina's sobs make me feel like I am about to crack open.

Cara takes her time responding.

"Well, I do," she says.

"What?" Christina says with a hiccup.

"You have to understand; we're trained to see things as logically as possible," says Cara. "So don't think that I'm callous. But that girl was probably scared out of her mind, certainly not capable of assessing situations cleverly at the time, if she was ever able to do so."

My eyes fly open. *What a—* I run through a short list of insults in my mind before listening to her continue.

"And the simulation made her incapable of reasoning with him, so when he threatened her life, she reacted as she had been trained by the Dauntless to react: Shoot to kill."

"So what are you saying?" says Christina bitterly. "We should just forget about it, because it makes perfect sense?"

"Of course not," says Cara. Her voice wobbles, just a little, and she repeats herself, quietly this time. "Of *course* not."

She clears her throat. "It's just that you have to be around her, and I want to make it easier for you. You don't have to forgive her. Actually, I'm not sure why you were friends with her in the first place; she always seemed a bit erratic to me."

I tense up as I wait for Christina to agree with her, but to my surprise—and relief—she doesn't.

Cara continues. "Anyway. You don't have to forgive her, but you should try to understand that what she did was not out of malice; it was out of panic. That way, you can look at her without wanting to punch her in her exceptionally long nose."

My hand moves automatically to my nose. Christina laughs a little, which feels like a hard poke to the stomach. I back up through the door to the Gathering Place.

Even though Cara was rude—and the nose comment was a low blow—I am grateful for what she said.

+ + +

Tobias emerges from a door hidden behind a length of white cloth. He flicks the cloth out of the way irritably before coming toward us and sitting beside me at the table in the Gathering Place.

"Kang is going to meet with a representative of Jeanine Matthews at seven in the morning," he says.

"A representative?" Zeke says. "She's not going herself?"

"Yeah, and stand out in the open where a bunch of angry people with guns can take aim?" Uriah smirks a little. "I'd like to see her try. No, really, I would."

"Is Kang the Brilliant taking a Dauntless escort, at least?" Lynn says.

"Yes," Tobias says. "Some of the older members volunteered. Bud said he would keep his ears open and report back."

I frown at him. How does he know all this information? And why, after two years of avoiding becoming a Dauntless leader at all costs, is he suddenly acting like one?

"So I guess the real question is," says Zeke, folding his hands on the table, "if you were Erudite, what would *you* say at this meeting?"

They all look at me. Expectantly.

"What?" I say.

"You're Divergent," Zeke replies.

"So is Tobias."

"Yeah, but he doesn't have aptitude for Erudite."

"And how do you know I do?"

Zeke lifts his shoulder. "Seems likely. Doesn't it seem likely?"

Uriah and Lynn nod. Tobias's mouth twitches, as if in a smile, but if that's what it was, he suppresses it. I feel like a stone just dropped into my stomach.

"You all have functional brains, last time I checked," I say. "You can think like the Erudite, too."

"But we don't have special *Divergent* brains!" says Marlene. She touches her fingertips to my scalp and squeezes lightly. "Come on, do your magic."

"There's no such thing as Divergent magic, Mar," says Lynn.

"And if there is, we shouldn't be consulting it," says Shauna. It's the first thing she's said since we sat down. She doesn't even look at me when she says it; she just scowls at her younger sister.

"Shauna—" Zeke starts.

"Don't 'Shauna' me!" she says, focusing her scowl on him instead. "Don't you think someone with the aptitude for multiple factions might have a loyalty problem? If she's got aptitude for Erudite, how can we be sure she's not *working* for Erudite?"

"Don't be ridiculous," says Tobias, his voice low.

"I am not being ridiculous." She smacks the table. "I know I belong in Dauntless because everything I did in that aptitude test told me so. I'm loyal to my faction for that reason—because there's nowhere else I could possibly be. But her? And you?" She shakes her head. "I have no idea who you're loyal to. And I'm not going to pretend like everything's okay."

She gets up, and when Zeke reaches for her, she throws his hand aside, marching toward one of the doors. I watch her until the door closes behind her and the black fabric that hangs in front of it settles.

I feel wound up, like I might scream, only Shauna isn't here for me to scream at.

"It's not *magic*," I say hotly. "You just have to ask yourself what the most logical response to a particular situation is."

I am greeted with blank stares.

"Seriously," I say. "If I were in this situation, staring at a group of Dauntless guards and Jack Kang, I probably wouldn't resort to violence, right?"

"Well, you might, if you had your own Dauntless guards. And then all it takes is one shot—bam, he's dead, and Erudite's better off," says Zeke.

"Whoever they send to talk to Jack Kang isn't going to be some random Erudite kid; it's going to be someone important," I say. "It would be a stupid move to fire on Jack Kang and risk losing whoever they send as Jeanine's representative."

"See? This is why we need you to analyze the situation," Zeke says. "If it was me, I would kill him; it would be worth the risk."

I pinch the bridge of my nose. I already have a headache. "Fine."

I try to put myself in Jeanine Matthews's place. I already know she won't negotiate with Jack Kang. Why would she need to? He has nothing to offer her. She will use the situation to her advantage.

"I think," I say, "that Jeanine Matthews will manipulate him. And that he will do anything to protect his faction, even if it means sacrificing the Divergent." I pause for a moment, remembering how he held his faction's influence over our heads at the meeting. "Or sacrificing the Dauntless. So we *need* to hear what they say in that meeting."

Uriah and Zeke exchange a look. Lynn smiles, but it isn't her usual smile. It doesn't spread to her eyes, which look more like gold than ever, with that coldness in them.

"So let's listen in," she says.

CHAPTER TWENTY

I CHECK MY watch. It is seven o'clock in the evening. Just twelve hours until we can hear what Jeanine has to say to Jack Kang. I have checked my watch at least a dozen times in the past hour, as if that will make the time go faster. I am itching to do something—*anything* except sit in the cafeteria with Lynn, Tobias, and Lauren, picking at my dinner and sneaking looks at Christina, who sits with her Candor family at one of the other tables.

"I wonder if we'll be able to return to the old way after all this is over," says Lauren. She and Tobias have been talking about Dauntless initiate training methods for at least five minutes already. It's probably the only thing they have in common.

"If there's a faction *left* after all this is over," Lynn says, piling her mashed potatoes onto a roll.

"Don't tell me you're going to eat a mashed-potato sandwich," I say to her.

"So what if I am?"

A group of Dauntless walk between our table and the one next to us. They are older than Tobias, but not by much. One of the girls has five different colors in her hair, and her arms are covered with tattoos so that I can't see even an inch of bare skin. One of the boys leans close to Tobias, whose back is to them, and whispers, "Coward," as he passes.

A few of the others do the same thing, hissing "coward" into Tobias's ears and then continuing on their way. He pauses with his knife against a piece of bread, a glob of butter waiting to be spread, and stares at the table.

I wait, tense, for him to explode.

"What idiots," says Lauren. "And the Candor, for making you spill your life story for everyone to see . . . they're idiots too."

Tobias doesn't answer. He puts down his knife and the piece of bread, and pushes back from the table. His eyes lift and focus on something across the room.

"This needs to stop," he says distantly, and starts toward whatever it is he's looking at before I figure out what it is. This can't be good.

He slips between the tables and the people like he's more liquid than solid, and I stumble after him, muttering apologies as I push people aside.

And then I see exactly who Tobias is headed toward. Marcus. He is sitting with a few of the older Candor.

Tobias reaches him and grabs him by the back of the neck, wrestling him from his seat. Marcus opens his mouth to say something, and that is a mistake, because Tobias punches him hard in the teeth. Someone shouts, but no one rushes to Marcus's aid. We are in a room full of Dauntless, after all.

Tobias shoves Marcus toward the middle of the room, where there is a space between the tables to reveal the symbol of Candor. Marcus stumbles over one of the scales, his hands covering his face so I can't see the damage Tobias did.

Tobias shoves Marcus to the ground and presses the heel of his shoe to his father's throat. Marcus smacks at Tobias's leg, blood streaming past his lips, but even if he was at his strongest, he still wouldn't be as strong as his son. Tobias undoes his belt buckle and slides it from its loops.

He lifts his foot from Marcus's throat and draws the belt back.

"This is for your own good," he says.

That, I remember, is what Marcus, and his many manifestations, always says to Tobias in his fear landscape.

Then the belt flies through the air and hits Marcus in the arm. Marcus's face is bright red, and he covers his head as the next blow falls, this one hitting his back. All around me is laughter, coming from the Dauntless tables, but I am not laughing, I cannot possibly laugh at this.

Finally I come to my senses. I run forward and grab Tobias's shoulder. "Stop!" I say. "Tobias, stop *right now!*"

I expect to see a wild look in his eyes, but when he looks at me, I do not. His face is not flushed and his breaths are steady. This was not an act performed in the heat of passion.

It was a calculated act.

He drops the belt and reaches into his pocket. From it he takes a silver chain with a ring dangling from it. Marcus is on his side, gasping. Tobias drops the ring onto the ground next to his father's face. It is made of tarnished, dull metal, an Abnegation wedding band.

"My mother," says Tobias, "says hello."

Tobias walks away, and it takes a few seconds for me to breathe again. When I do, I leave Marcus cringing on the floor and run after him. It takes me until I reach the hallway to catch up to him.

"What *was* that?" I demand.

Tobias presses the down button for the elevator and doesn't look at me.

"It was necessary," he says.

"Necessary for what?" I say.

"What, you're feeling sorry for *him* now?" Tobias says, turning toward me with a scowl. "Do you know how many times he did that to me? How do you think I learned the moves?"

I feel brittle, like I might break. It did seem rehearsed, like Tobias had gone over the steps in his mind, recited the words in front of a mirror. He knew it by heart; he was just playing the other part this time.

"No," I say quietly. "No, I don't feel sorry for him, not at all."

"Then *what*, Tris?" His voice is rough; it could be the thing that breaks me. "You haven't cared about what I do or say for the past week; what's so different about this?"

I am almost afraid of him. I don't know what to say or do around the erratic part of him, and it is here, bubbling just beneath the surface of what he does, just like the cruel part of me. We both have war inside of us. Sometimes it keeps us alive. Sometimes it threatens to destroy us.

"Nothing," I say.

The elevator beeps as it arrives. He gets on, and presses the CLOSE button so the doors shut between us. I stare at the brushed metal and try to think through the last ten minutes.

"This needs to stop," he said. "This" was the ridicule, which was a result of the interrogation, where he admitted that he joined Dauntless to escape his father. And then he beat up Marcus—publicly, where all the Dauntless could see it.

Why? To salvage his pride? It can't be. It was far too intentional for that.

+ + +

On my way back to the cafeteria, I see a Candor man walk Marcus toward the bathroom. He walks slowly, but he isn't hunched over, which makes me think Tobias didn't do him any serious damage. I watch the door close behind him.

I had all but forgotten about what I heard in the Amity compound, about the information my father risked his life for. *Supposedly,* I remind myself. It may not be wise to trust Marcus. And I promised myself I wouldn't ask him about this again.

I dawdle outside the bathroom until the Candor man walks out, and then walk in before the door has a chance to shut properly. Marcus is sitting on the floor by the sink with a wad of paper towel pressed to his mouth. He doesn't look happy to see me.

"What, here to gloat?" he says. "Get out."

"No," I say.

Why am I here, exactly?

He looks at me expectantly. "Well?"

"I thought you could use a reminder," I say. "Whatever it is you want to get from Jeanine, you won't be able to do it alone, and you won't be able to do it with only the Abnegation to help you."

"I thought we went over this." His voice is muffled by the paper towels. "The idea that *you* could help—"

"I don't know where you get this delusion that I'm useless, but that's what it is," I snap. "And I'm not interested in hearing about it. All I want to say is that when you stop being delusional and start feeling desperate because you're too inept to figure this out on your own, you know who to come to."

I leave the bathroom just as the Candor man comes back with an ice pack.

CHAPTER
TWENTY-ONE

I STAND BEFORE the sinks in the women's bathroom on the newly claimed Dauntless floor, a gun resting on my palm. Lynn put it there a few minutes ago; she seemed confused that I did not wrap my hand around it and put it somewhere, in a holster or under the waistband of my jeans. I just let it stay there, and walked to the bathroom before I started to panic.

Don't be an idiot. I can't set out to do what I'm doing without a gun. It would be crazy. So I will have to solve this problem I've been having in the next five minutes.

I curl my pinkie around the handle first, then my second finger, then the others. The weight is familiar. My index finger slips around the trigger. I release a breath.

I start to lift it, bringing my left hand to meet my right to steady it. I hold the gun out from my body, my arms straight, just as Four taught me, when that was his only name. I used a gun like this to defend my father and brother from simulation-bound Dauntless. I used it to stop Eric from shooting Tobias in the head. It is not inherently evil. It is just a tool.

I see a flicker of movement in the mirror, and before I can stop myself, I stare at my reflection. *This is how I looked to him*, I think. *This is how I looked when I shot him.*

Moaning like a wounded animal, I let the gun fall from my hands and wrap my arms around my stomach. I want to sob because I know it will make me feel better, but I can't force the tears to come. I just crouch in the bathroom, staring at the white tiles. I can't do it. I can't take the gun with me.

I shouldn't even go; I am still going to.

"Tris?" Someone knocks. I stand and uncross my arms as the door squeaks open a few inches. Tobias steps into the room.

"Zeke and Uriah told me you were going to eavesdrop on Jack," he says.

"Oh."

"Are you?"

"Why should I tell you? You don't tell me about *your* plans."

His straight eyebrows furrow. "What are you talking about?"

"I'm talking about beating Marcus to a pulp in front of all the Dauntless for no apparent reason." I step toward him. "But there is a reason, isn't there? Because it's not like you lost control; it's not like he did something to provoke you, so there has to be a reason!"

"I needed to prove to the Dauntless that I am not a coward," he says. "That's all. That's all it was."

"Why would you need to . . ." I start.

Why would Tobias need to prove himself to the Dauntless? Only if he wanted them to hold him in high regard. Only if he wants to become a Dauntless leader. I remember Evelyn's voice, speaking in the shadows in the factionless safe house: "What I am suggesting is that you *become* important."

He wants the Dauntless to ally with the factionless, and he knows the only way he can make that happen is to do it himself.

Why he didn't feel the need to share this plan with me is another mystery entirely. Before I can ask, he says, "So are you going to eavesdrop or not?"

"What does it matter?"

"You're throwing yourself into danger for no reason again," he says. "Just like when you stormed up to fight the Erudite with only a . . . a *pocket knife* to protect yourself."

"There is a reason. A good one. We won't know what's going on unless we eavesdrop, and we need to know what's going on."

He crosses his arms. He is not bulky, the way some Dauntless boys are. And some girls might focus on the way his ears stick out, or the way his nose hooks at the end, but to me . . .

I swallow the rest of that thought. He's here to yell at me. He's been keeping things from me. Whatever we are now, I can't indulge thoughts about how attractive he is. It will just make it harder for me to do what needs to be done. And right now, that is going to listen to what Jack Kang has to say to the Erudite.

"You're not cutting your hair like the Abnegation anymore," I say. "That because you want to look more Dauntless?"

"Don't change the subject," he says. "There are four people going to eavesdrop already. You don't need to be there."

"Why are you so insistent on me staying home?" My voice gets louder.

"I am not the kind of person who just sits back and lets other people take all the risks!"

"As long as you are someone who doesn't seem to value her own life . . . someone who can't even pick up and fire a *gun* . . ." He leans toward me. "You should sit back and let other people take the risks."

His quiet voice pulses around me like a second heartbeat. I hear the words "doesn't seem to value her own life" again and again.

"What are you going to do?" I say. "Lock me in the bathroom? Because that's the only way you'll be able to keep me from going."

He touches his forehead and lets his hand drag down the side of his face. I have never seen his face sag that way before.

"I don't want to stop you. I want you to stop yourself," he says. "But if you're going to be reckless, you can't prevent me from coming along."

+ + +

It is still dark, but just barely, when we reach the bridge, which is two-tiered, with stone pillars at each corner. We descend the stairs next to one of the stone pillars and creep with silent feet at river level. Large puddles of standing water gleam as the light of day hits them. The sun is rising; we have to get into position.

Uriah and Zeke are in the buildings on either side of the bridge so they can get a better view and cover us from a distance. They have better aim than Lynn or Shauna, who came because Lynn asked her to, despite her outburst in the Gathering Place.

Lynn goes first, her back pressed to the stone as she inches along the lower lip of the bridge supports. I follow her, with Shauna and Tobias behind me. The bridge is supported by four curved metal structures that secure it to the stone wall, and by a maze of narrow girders beneath its lower tier. Lynn wedges herself under one of the metal structures and climbs quickly, keeping the narrow girders beneath her as she works her way to the middle of the bridge.

I let Shauna go in front of me because I can't climb as well. My left arm shakes as I try to balance on top of the metal structure. I feel Tobias's cool hand on my waist, steadying me.

I crouch low to fit in the space between the bottom of the bridge and the girders beneath me. I don't make it very far before I have to stop, my feet on one girder and my left arm on another. And I will have to stay that way for a long time.

Tobias slides along one of the girders and puts his leg under me. It is long enough to stretch beneath me and onto a second girder. I breathe out and smile at him as a kind of thank-you. It's the first time we have acknowledged each other since we left the Merciless Mart.

He smiles back, but grimly.

We bide our time in silence. I breathe through my mouth and try to control the shaking of my arms and legs. Shauna and Lynn seem to communicate without speaking. They make faces at each other that I can't read, and nod and smile at each other when they reach an understanding. I have never thought about what it would be like to have a sister. Would Caleb and I be closer if he were a girl?

The city is so quiet in the morning that the footsteps echo as they approach the bridge. The sound comes from behind me, which must mean it's Jack and his Dauntless escort, not the Erudite, who have arrived. The Dauntless know that we are here, though Jack Kang himself does not. If he stares down for more than a few seconds, he might see us through the metal mesh beneath his feet. I try to breathe as quietly as possible.

Tobias checks his watch, and then holds his arm out to me to show me the time. Seven o'clock exactly.

I glance up and peer through the steel web above me. Feet pass over my head. And then I hear him.

"Hello, Jack," he says.

It's Max, who appointed Eric to Dauntless leadership at Jeanine's demand, who implemented policies of cruelty and brutality in Dauntless initiation. I have never spoken to him directly, but the sound of his voice makes me shiver.

"Max," Jack says. "Where's Jeanine? I thought she would at least have the courtesy to show up herself."

"Jeanine and I divide our responsibilities according to our strengths," he says. "That means I make all military decisions. I believe that includes what we are doing today."

I frown. I haven't heard Max speak much, but something about the words he's using, and their rhythm, sounds . . . *off*.

"Fine," says Jack. "I came to—"

"I should inform you that this will not be a negotiation," Max says. "In order to negotiate, you have to be on even footing, and you, Jack, are not."

"What do you mean?"

"I mean that you are the only disposable faction. Candor does not provide us with protection, sustenance, or technological innovation. Therefore you are expendable to us. And you have not done much to win the favor of your Dauntless guests," says Max, "so you are completely vulnerable and completely useless. I recommend, therefore, that you do exactly as I say."

"You piece of scum," says Jack through gritted teeth. "How *dare*—"

"Now let's not get testy," Max says.

I chew on my lip. I should trust my instincts, and my instincts tell me that something is wrong here. No self-respecting Dauntless man would say the word "testy." Nor would he react so calmly to an insult. He's speaking like someone else. He's speaking like Jeanine.

The back of my neck prickles. It makes perfect sense. Jeanine would not trust anyone, particularly not a volatile Dauntless, to speak on her behalf. The best solution to that problem is to give Max an earpiece. And the signal from an earpiece can stretch only a quarter of a mile at most.

I catch Tobias's eye, and slowly move my hand to point at my ear. Then I point above me, at my best approximation of where Max stands.

Tobias frowns for a moment, then nods, but I'm not sure he understands me.

"I have three requirements," says Max. "First, that you return the Dauntless leader you currently hold in captivity unharmed. Second, that you allow your compound to be searched by our soldiers so that we can extract the Divergent; and third, that you provide us with the names of those who were not injected with the simulation serum."

"Why?" Jack says bitterly. "What are you searching for? And why do you need those names? What do you intend to do with them?"

"The purpose of our search would be to locate and remove any of the Divergent from the premises. And as for the names, that is none of your concern."

"None of my concern!" I hear footsteps squeak above me and stare up through the mesh. From what I can see, Jack has the collar of Max's shirt wrapped around his fist.

"Release me," says Max. "Or I will order my guards to fire."

I frown. If Jeanine is speaking through Max, she had to be able to see him in order to know that he was grabbed. I lean forward to look at the buildings on the other side of the bridge. On my left, the river bends, and a squat glass building stands at the edge. That must be where she is.

I start to climb backward, toward the metal structure that supports the bridge, toward the staircase that will lead me to Wacker Drive. Tobias follows me immediately, and Shauna taps Lynn on the shoulder. But Lynn is doing something else.

I was too busy thinking about Jeanine. I failed to notice that Lynn took out her gun and started to climb toward the edge of the bridge. Shauna's mouth opens and her eyes go wide as Lynn swings herself forward, grabbing the lip of the bridge, and shoves her arm over it. Her finger squeezes the trigger.

Max gasps, his hand clapping over his chest, and stumbles back. When he pulls his hand away, it is dark with blood.

I don't bother to climb anymore. I drop into the mud, closely followed by Tobias, Lynn, and Shauna. My legs sink into the mire, and my feet make sucking noises as I pull them free. My shoes slip off but I keep going until I reach the concrete. Guns fire and bullets stick in the mud next to me. I throw myself against the wall under the bridge so they can't aim at me.

Tobias presses into the wall behind me, so close to me that his chin floats over my head and I can feel his chest against my shoulders. Shielding me.

I can run back to Candor headquarters, and to temporary safety. Or I can find Jeanine in what is probably the most vulnerable state she will ever be in.

It's not even a choice.

"Come on!" I say. I sprint up the stairs, the others on my heels. On the lower tier of the bridge, our Dauntless shoot at the Dauntless traitors. Jack is safe, bent over with a Dauntless arm slung across his back. I run faster. I run across the bridge and don't look behind me. I can already hear Tobias's footsteps. He is the only one who can keep up with me.

The glass building is in my sights. And then I hear more footsteps, more gunshots. I weave as I run, to make it more difficult for the Dauntless traitors to hit me.

I am close to the glass building. I am yards away. I grit my teeth and push myself harder. My legs are numb; I barely feel the ground beneath me. But before I reach the doors, I see movement in the alley to my right. I swerve and follow it with my feet.

Three figures run down the alley. One is blond. One is tall. And one is Peter.

I stumble, and almost fall.

"Peter!" I shout. He lifts his gun, and behind me, Tobias lifts his own, and we stand just yards away from each other, at a standstill. Behind him, the blond woman—Jeanine, probably—and the tall Dauntless traitor turn the corner. Though I don't have a weapon, and I don't have a plan, I want to run after them, and maybe I would if Tobias did not clamp his hand over my shoulder and hold me in place.

"You traitor," I say to Peter. "I knew it. I *knew* it."

A scream pierces the air. It is anguished and female.

"Sounds like your friends need you," Peter says with the flash of a smile—or bared teeth, I can't tell. He keeps his gun steady. "So you have a choice. You can let us go, and help them, or you can die trying to follow us."

I almost scream. We both know what I'm going to do.

"I hope you die," I say.

I back up into Tobias, who backs up with me, until we reach the end of the alley, and then turn and run.

CHAPTER
TWENTY-TWO

SHAUNA LIES ON the ground, facedown, blood pooling on her shirt. Lynn crouches at her side. Staring. Doing nothing.

"It's my fault," Lynn mumbles. "I shouldn't have shot him. I shouldn't have . . ."

I stare at the patch of blood. A bullet hit her in the back. I can't tell if she's breathing or not. Tobias places two fingers on the side of her neck, and nods.

"We've got to get out of here," he says. "Lynn. Look at me. I'm going to carry her, and it's going to hurt her a lot, but it's our only option."

Lynn nods. Tobias crouches next to Shauna and puts his hands under her arms. He lifts her, and she moans. I rush forward to help him pull her limp body over his shoulder. My throat tightens, and I cough to relieve the pressure.

Tobias stands with a grunt of effort, and together we walk toward the Merciless Mart—Lynn in front, with her gun, and me in the back. I walk backward to watch behind us, but I don't see anyone. I think the Dauntless traitors retreated. But I have to make sure.

"Hey!" someone shouts. It's Uriah, jogging toward us. "Zeke had to help them get Jack . . . oh no." He stops. "Oh no. Shauna?"

"Now's not the time," says Tobias sharply. "Run back to the Merciless Mart and get a doctor."

But Uriah just stares.

"Uriah! Go, *now!*" The shout rings with nothing on the street to soften the sound of it. Uriah finally turns and sprints in the direction of the Merciless Mart.

It's only half a mile back, but with Tobias's grunts and Lynn's uneven breathing and the knowledge that Shauna is bleeding to death, it feels endless. I watch the muscles in Tobias's back expanding and contracting with each labored breath, and I don't hear our footsteps; I hear only my heartbeat. When we finally reach the doors, I feel like I might throw up, or faint, or scream at the top of my lungs.

Uriah, an Erudite man with a comb-over, and Cara meet us just inside the entrance. They set up a sheet for Shauna to lie on. Tobias lowers her onto it, and the doctor gets to work immediately, cutting the shirt away from Shauna's back. I turn away. I don't want to see the bullet wound.

Tobias stands in front of me, his face red with exertion. I want him to fold me into his arms again, like he did after the last attack, but he doesn't, and I know better than to initiate it.

"I'm not going to pretend to know what's going on with you," he says. "But if you senselessly risk your life again—"

"I am not senselessly risking my life. I am trying to make *sacrifices*, like my parents would have, like—"

"You are *not* your parents. You are a sixteen-year-old girl—"

I grit my teeth. "How *dare* you—"

"—who doesn't understand that the value of a sacrifice lies in its *necessity*, not in throwing your life away! And if you do that again, you and I are done."

I wasn't expecting him to say that.

"You're giving me an ultimatum?" I try to keep my voice down so the others can't hear.

He shakes his head. "No, I'm telling you a fact." His lips are just a line. "If you throw yourself into danger for no reason again, you will have become nothing more than a Dauntless adrenaline junkie looking for a hit, and I'm not going to help you do it." He spits the words out bitterly. "I love Tris the Divergent, who makes decisions apart from faction loyalty, who isn't some faction archetype. But the Tris who's trying as hard as she can to destroy herself . . . I can't love her."

I want to scream. But not because I'm angry, because I'm afraid he's right. My hands shake and I grab the hem of my shirt to steady them.

He touches his forehead to mine and closes his eyes. "I believe you're still in there," he says against my mouth. "Come back."

He kisses me lightly, and I am too shocked to stop him.

He walks back to Shauna's side, and I stand over one of the Candor scales in the lobby, at a loss.

+ + +

"It's been a while."

I sink down on the bed across from Tori. She is sitting up, her leg propped on a stack of pillows.

"Yes, it has," I say. "How are you feeling?"

"Like I got shot." A smile plays over her lips. "I hear you're familiar with the feeling."

"Yeah. It's great, right?" All I can think of is the bullet in Shauna's back. At least Tori and I will recover from our wounds.

"Did you discover anything interesting at Jack's meeting?" she says.

"A few things. Do you know how we might go about calling a Dauntless meeting?"

"I can make it happen. One thing about being a tattoo artist in Dauntless is . . . you know pretty much everyone."

"Right," I say. "You also have the prestige of being a former spy."

Tori's mouth twists. "I had almost forgotten."

"Did *you* discover anything interesting? As a spy, I mean."

"My mission was primarily focused on Jeanine Matthews." She glares at her hands. "How she spends her days. And, more importantly, *where* she spends them."

"Not in her office, then?"

Tori doesn't answer at first.

"I guess I can trust you, Divergent." She looks at me from the corner of her eye. "She has a private laboratory on the top level. Insane security measures protecting it. I was trying to get up there when they figured out what I was."

"You were trying to get up there," I say. Her eyes flit away from mine. "Not to spy, I take it."

"I thought it would be more . . . *expedient* if Jeanine Matthews didn't survive much longer."

I see a kind of thirst in her expression, the same one I saw when she told me about her brother in the back room of the tattoo parlor. Before the attack simulation I might have called it a thirst for justice, or even revenge, but now I am able to identify it as a thirst for blood. And even as it frightens me, I understand it.

Which should probably frighten me even more.

Tori says, "I'll work on calling that meeting."

+ + +

The Dauntless are gathered in the space between the rows of bunk beds and the doors, which are held shut by a tightly wrapped bedsheet, the best lock the Dauntless could muster. I have no doubt that Jack Kang will agree to Jeanine's demands. We aren't safe here anymore.

"What were the terms?" Tori says. She sits in a chair between a few of the bunks, her wounded leg stuck out in front of her. She asks Tobias, but he doesn't seem to be paying attention. He is leaning against one of the bunks, his arms crossed, staring at the floor.

I clear my throat. "There were three. Return Eric to the Erudite. Report the names of all people who did not get shot with needles last time. And deliver the Divergent to Erudite headquarters."

I look at Marlene. She smiles back at me a little sadly. She is probably worried about Shauna, who is still with the Erudite doctor. Lynn, Hector, their parents, and Zeke are with her.

"If Jack Kang is making deals with the Erudite, we can't stay here," says Tori. "So where can we go?"

I think of the blood on Shauna's shirt, and long for the Amity orchards, the sound of the wind in the leaves, the feeling of bark beneath my hands. I never thought I would crave that place. I didn't think it was in me.

I close my eyes briefly, and when I open them I am in reality, and Amity is a dream.

"Home," Tobias says, lifting his head at last. Everyone is listening. "We should take back what's ours. We can break the security cameras in Dauntless headquarters so the Erudite can't see us. We should go home."

Someone assents with a shout, and someone else joins in. That is how things in Dauntless are decided: with nods and yells. In these moments we don't seem like individuals anymore. We are all a part of the same mind.

"But before we do that," says Bud, who once worked with Tori in the tattoo parlor and who now stands with his hand on the back of Tori's chair, "we need to decide what to do about Eric. To let him stay here with the Erudite, or to execute him."

"Eric is Dauntless," Lauren says, turning the ring in her lip with her fingertips. "That means we decide what happens to him. Not Candor."

This time a yell tears from my body of its own volition, joining with the others in agreement.

"According to Dauntless law, only Dauntless leaders can perform an execution. All five of our former leaders are Dauntless traitors," says Tori. "So I think it's time we pick new ones. The law says we need more than one, and we need an odd number. If you've got suggestions, you should shout them out now, and we'll vote if we need to."

"You!" someone calls out.

"Okay," says Tori. "Anyone else?"

Marlene cups her hands around her mouth and calls out, "Tris!"

My heart pounds. But to my surprise, no one mutters in dissent and no one laughs. Instead, a few people nod, just like they did when

Tori's name was mentioned. I scan the crowd and find Christina. She stands with her arms crossed, and does not seem to react at all to my nomination.

I wonder how I seem to them. They must see someone I don't see. Someone capable and strong. Someone I can't be; someone I can be.

Tori acknowledges Marlene with a nod and scans the crowd for another recommendation.

"Harrison," someone says. I don't know who Harrison is until someone slaps a middle-aged man with a blond ponytail on the shoulder, and he grins. I recognize him—he's the Dauntless man who called me "girl" when Zeke and Tori came back from Erudite headquarters.

The Dauntless are quiet for a moment.

"I'm going to nominate Four," says Tori.

Apart from a few angry murmurs in the back of the room, no one disagrees. No one is calling him a coward anymore, not after he beat up Marcus in the cafeteria. I wonder how they would react if they knew how calculated that move was.

Now he could get exactly what he intended to get. Unless I stand in his way.

"We only need three leaders," Tori says. "We'll have to vote."

They would never have considered me if I had not stopped the attack simulation. And maybe they wouldn't have considered me if I hadn't stabbed Eric by those elevators, or put myself under that bridge. The more reckless I get, the more popular I am with the Dauntless.

Tobias looks at me. I can't be popular with the Dauntless, because Tobias is right—I'm not Dauntless; I'm Divergent. I am whatever I choose to be. And I can't choose to be *this*. I have to stay separate from them.

"No," I say. I clear my throat and say it louder. "No, you don't have to vote. I refuse my nomination."

Tori raises her eyebrows at me. "Are you sure, Tris?"

"Yes," I say. "I don't want it. I'm sure."

And then, without argument and without ceremony, Tobias is elected to be a leader of Dauntless. And I am not.

CHAPTER
TWENTY-THREE

NOT TEN SECONDS after we choose our new leaders, something rings—one long pulse, two short ones. I move toward the sound, my right ear toward the wall, and find a speaker suspended from the ceiling. There is another one across the room.

Then Jack Kang's voice speaks all around us.

"Attention all occupants of Candor headquarters. A few hours ago I met with a representative of Jeanine Matthews. He reminded me that we Candor are in a weak position, dependent on Erudite for our survival, and told me that if I intend to keep my faction free, I will have to meet a few demands."

I stare up at the speaker, stunned. I shouldn't be surprised that the leader of Candor is this forthright, but I wasn't expecting a public announcement.

"In order to comply with these demands, I ask that everyone make their way to the Gathering Place to report whether you have an implant or not," he says. "The Erudite have also ordered all Divergent to be turned over to Erudite. I do not know for what purpose."

He sounds listless. Defeated. *Well, he is defeated,* I think. *Because he was too weak to fight back.*

One thing Dauntless knows that Candor does not is how to fight even when fighting seems useless.

Sometimes I feel like I am collecting the lessons each faction has to teach me, and storing them in my mind like a guidebook for moving through the world. There is always something to learn, always something that is important to understand.

Jack Kang's announcement ends with the same three rings it started with. The Dauntless rush through the room, throwing their things into bags. A few young Dauntless men cut the sheet away from the door, screaming something about Eric. Someone's elbow presses me to a wall, and I just stand and watch the pandemonium intensify.

On the other hand, one thing Candor knows that Dauntless does not is how not to get carried away.

+ + +

The Dauntless stand in a semicircle around the interrogation chair, where Eric now sits. He looks more dead than alive. He is slumped in the chair, sweat shining on his pale forehead. He stares at Tobias with his head tilted down, so his eyelashes blend into his eyebrows. I try to keep my eyes on him, but his smile—how the piercings pull wide when his lips spread—is almost too awful to take.

"Would you like me to tell you your crimes?" says Tori. "Or would you like to list them yourself?"

Rain sprays against the side of the building and streams down the walls. We stand in the interrogation room, on the top floor of the Merciless Mart. The afternoon storm is louder here. Every crack of thunder and flash of lightning makes the back of my neck prickle, as if electricity is dancing over my skin.

I like the smell of wet pavement. It is faint here, but once this is done, all the Dauntless will storm down the stairs and leave the Merciless Mart behind, and wet pavement will be the only thing I smell.

We have our bags with us. Mine is a sack made of a sheet and some rope. It contains my clothes and a spare pair of shoes. I wear the jacket I stole from the Dauntless traitor—I want Eric to see it if he looks at me.

Eric scans the crowd for a few seconds, and then his eyes settle on me. He laces his fingers and sets them—gingerly—on his stomach. "I'd like *her* to list them. Since she's the one who stabbed me, clearly she is familiar with them."

I don't know what game he's playing, or what the point of rattling me is, especially now, before his execution. He seems arrogant, but I notice that his fingers tremble when he moves them. Even Eric must be afraid of death.

"Leave her out of this," says Tobias.

"Why? Because you're doing her?" Eric smirks. "Oh wait, I forgot. Stiffs don't *do* that sort of thing. They just tie each other's shoes and cut each other's hair."

Tobias's expression does not change. I think I understand: Eric doesn't really care about me. But he knows exactly where to hit Tobias, and how hard. And one of the places to hit Tobias the hardest is to hit me.

This is what I wanted most to avoid: for my rises and falls to become

Tobias's rises and falls. That's why I can't let him step in to defend me now.

"I want her to list them," repeats Eric.

I say, as evenly as possible:

"You conspired with Erudite. You are responsible for the deaths of hundreds of Abnegation." As I go on, I can't keep my voice steady anymore; I start to spit out the words like venom. "You betrayed Dauntless. You shot a child in the head. You are a ridiculous plaything of Jeanine Matthews."

His smile fades.

"Do I deserve to die?" he says.

Tobias opens his mouth to interrupt. But I respond before he can.

"Yes."

"Fair enough." His dark eyes are empty, like pits, like starless nights. "But do you have the right to decide that, Beatrice Prior? Like you decided the fate of that other boy—what was his name? Will?"

I don't answer. I hear my father asking me, "What makes you think you have the right to shoot someone?" as we fought our way to the control room in Dauntless headquarters. He told me there is a right way to do something, and I needed to figure it out. I feel something in my throat, like a ball of wax, so thick I can barely swallow, barely breathe.

"You have committed every crime that warrants execution among the Dauntless," says Tobias. "We have the right to execute you, under the laws of Dauntless."

He crouches by the three guns on the floor near Eric's feet. One by one, he empties the chambers of bullets. They almost jingle as they hit the floor, and then roll, coming to rest against the toes of Tobias's shoes. He picks up the middle gun and puts a bullet into the first slot.

Then he moves the three guns on the floor, around and around, until my eyes can't follow the middle gun anymore. I lose track of which one holds the bullet. He picks up the guns and offers one to Tori, and another one to Harrison.

I try to think of the attack simulation, and what it did to the Abnegation. All the gray-clothed innocents lying dead on the street. There weren't even enough Abnegation left to take care of the bodies, so most of them are probably still there. And that would not have been possible without Eric.

I think of the Candor boy, shot without a second's hesitation, how stiff he was as he hit the ground next to me.

Maybe we are not the ones deciding if Eric lives or dies. Maybe he is the one who decided that, when he did all those terrible things.

But it's still hard to breathe.

I look at him without malice, without hatred, and without fear. The rings in his face shine, and a lock of dirty hair falls into his eyes.

"Wait," he says. "I have a request."

"We don't take requests from criminals," says Tori. She's standing on one leg, and has been for the past few minutes. She sounds tired—she probably wants to get this over with so she can sit down again. To her this execution is just an inconvenience.

"I am a leader of Dauntless," he says. "And all I want is for Four to be the one who fires that bullet."

"*Why?*" Tobias says.

"So you can live with the guilt," Eric replies. "Of knowing that you usurped me and then shot me in the head."

I think I understand. He wants to see people break—has always wanted to, ever since he set up the camera in my execution room when I nearly drowned, and probably long before then. And he believes that if Tobias has to kill him, he will see that before he dies.

Sick.

"There won't be any guilt," says Tobias.

"Then you'll have no problem doing it." Eric smiles again.

Tobias picks up one of the bullets.

"Tell me," says Eric quietly, "because I've always wondered. Is it your daddy who shows up in every fear landscape you've ever gone through?"

Tobias puts the bullet into an empty chamber without looking up.

"You didn't like that question?" Eric says. "What, afraid the Dauntless are going to change their minds about you? Realize that even though you've only got four fears, you're still a coward?"

He straightens in the chair and puts his hands on the armrests.

Tobias holds his gun out from his left shoulder.

"Eric," he says, "be brave."

He squeezes the trigger.

I shut my eyes.

CHAPTER
TWENTY-FOUR

BLOOD IS A strange color. It's darker than you expect it to be.

I stare down at Marlene's hand, which is wrapped around my arm. Her fingernails are short and jagged—she bites them. She pushes me forward, and I must be walking, because I can feel myself moving, but in my mind I stand before Eric and he is still alive.

He died just like Will did. Slumped just like Will did.

I thought the swollen feeling in my throat would go away once he was dead, but it didn't. I have to take deep, hard breaths to get enough air. Good thing the crowd around me is so loud that no one can hear me. We march toward the doors. At the front of the pack is Harrison, carrying Tori on his back like a child. She laughs, her arms wrapped around his neck.

Tobias sets his hand on my back. I know because I see him come up behind me and do it, not because I feel it. I don't feel anything at all.

The doors open from the outside. We stop short of stampeding Jack Kang and the group of Candor that followed him here.

"What have you done?" he says. "I was just told that Eric is missing from his holding cell."

"He was under our jurisdiction," says Tori. "We gave him a trial and executed him. You should be thanking us."

"Why . . ." Jack's face turns red. Blood is darker than blush, even though one consists of the other. "Why should I be thanking you?"

"Because you wanted him to be executed, too, right? Since he murdered one of your children?" Tori tilts her head, her eyes wide, innocent. "Well, we took care of it for you. And now, if you'll excuse us, we're leaving."

"Wha—*Leaving?*" Jack splutters.

If we leave, he will be incapable of fulfilling two of the three demands Max had of him. The thought terrifies him, and it is all over his face.

"I can't let you do that," he says.

"You don't *let* us do anything," says Tobias. "If you don't step aside, we will be forced to walk over you instead of past you."

"Didn't you come here to find allies?" Jack scowls. "If you do this, we will side with Erudite, I promise you, and you will never find an ally in us again, you—"

"We don't need you as an ally," says Tori. "We're Dauntless."

Everyone shouts, and somehow their screams pierce the haze in my mind. The entire crowd presses forward at once. The Candor in the corridor yelp and dive out of the way as we spill into the hallway like a burst pipe, Dauntless water spreading to fill the empty space.

Marlene's grip on my arm breaks. I run down the stairs, chasing the heels of the Dauntless in front of me, ignoring the jostle of elbows and all the shouts around me. I feel like I am an initiate again, storming the stairs of the Hub right after the Choosing Ceremony. My legs burn, but that is all right.

We reach the lobby. A group of Candor and Erudite are waiting there, including the blond Divergent woman who got dragged to the elevators by her hair, the girl I helped escape, and Cara. They watch the Dauntless stream past them with helpless looks on their faces.

Cara spots me and grabs my arm, wrenching me back. "Where are you all going?"

"Dauntless headquarters." I try to pull my arm free, but she won't let go. I don't look at her face. I can't look at her right now.

"Go to Amity," I say. "They promised safety to anyone who wants it. You won't be safe here."

She releases me, almost pushing me away from her in the process.

Outside, the ground feels slick beneath my sneakers, and my sack of clothes thumps against my back as I slow to a jog. Rain sprinkles my head and my back. My feet splash through puddles, soaking my pant legs.

I smell wet pavement, and pretend that this is all there is.

+ + +

I stand at the railing overlooking the chasm. Water hits the wall beneath me, but it doesn't come high enough to splash my shoes.

A hundred yards away, Bud passes out paintball guns. Someone else passes out paintballs. Soon the hidden corners of Dauntless headquarters will be coated in multicolored paint, blocking the lenses of the surveillance cameras.

"Hey, Tris," Zeke says, joining me at the railing. His eyes are red and swollen, but his mouth is curled into a small smile.

"Hey. You made it."

"Yeah. We waited until Shauna was stable and then took her here." He rubs one of his eyes with his thumb. "I didn't want to move her, but . . . wasn't safe with Candor anymore. Obviously."

"How is she?"

"Dunno. She's gonna survive it, but the nurse thinks she might be paralyzed from the waist down. And that wouldn't bother me, but . . ." He lifts a shoulder. "How can she be Dauntless if she can't walk?"

I stare across the Pit, where some Dauntless children chase each other up the path, hurling paintballs at the walls. One of them breaks and splatters the stone with yellow.

I think of what Tobias told me when we spent the night with the factionless, about the older Dauntless leaving the faction because they were no longer physically capable of staying in it. I think of Candor's rhyming song, which calls us the cruelest faction.

"She can," I say.

"Tris. She won't even be able to move around."

"Sure she will." I look up at him. "She can get a wheelchair, and someone can push her up the paths in the Pit, and there's an elevator in the building up *there*." I point above our heads. "She doesn't need to be able to walk to slide down the zip line or fire a gun."

"She won't want me to push her." His voice cracks a little. "She won't want me to lift her, or carry her."

"She'll have to get over it, then. Are you going to let her drop out of Dauntless for a stupid reason like not being able to walk?"

Zeke is quiet for a few seconds. His eyes shift over my face, and he squints, as if weighing and measuring me.

Then he turns and bends and wraps his arms around me. It's been so long since someone hugged me that I stiffen. Then I relax, and let the gesture force warmth into my body, which is chilled by damp clothing.

"I'm gonna go shoot things," he says as he pulls away. "Want to come?"

I shrug and chase him across the Pit floor. Bud hands each of us a paintball gun, and I load mine. Its weight, shape, and material are so different from a revolver that I have no trouble holding it.

"We've mostly got the Pit and the underground covered," Bud says. "But you should tackle the Pire."

"The Pire?"

Bud points up at the glass building above us. The sight pierces me like a needle. The last time I stood in this spot and stared up at this ceiling, I was on a mission to destroy the simulation. I was with my father.

Zeke is already on his way up the path. I force myself to follow him, one foot and then the other. It's difficult to walk because it's difficult to breathe, but somehow I manage. By the time I reach the stairs, the pressure on my chest is almost gone.

Once we're in the Pire, Zeke lifts up his gun and aims at one of the cameras near the ceiling. He fires, and green paint sprays across one of the windows, missing the camera lens.

"Ooh," I say, wincing. "Ouch."

"Yeah? I'd like to see you do it perfectly the first time."

"Would you?" I lift my own gun, propping it up on my left shoulder instead of my right. The gun feels unfamiliar in my left hand, but I can't bear its weight with my right yet. Through the scope I find the camera, and then squint to stare at the lens. A voice whispers in my head. *Inhale. Aim. Exhale. Fire.* It takes me a few seconds to realize it's Tobias's voice, because he's the one who taught me to shoot. I squeeze the trigger and the paintball hits the camera, spraying blue paint across the lens. "There. Now you have. With the wrong hand, too."

Zeke mutters something under his breath that doesn't sound pleasant.

"Hey!" shouts a cheerful voice. Marlene pokes her head above the glass floor. Paint is smeared across her forehead, giving her a purple eyebrow. With a wicked smile, she aims at Zeke, hitting his leg, and then at me. The paintball hits my arm, stinging.

Marlene laughs and ducks under the glass. Zeke and I look at each other, and then run after Marlene. She laughs as she sprints down the path, weaving through a crowd of kids. I shoot at her, and hit the wall instead. Marlene fires at a boy near the railing—Hector, Lynn's little brother. He looks shocked at first, but then fires back, hitting the person next to Marlene.

Popping sounds fill the air as everyone in the Pit starts to fire at one another, young and old, the cameras momentarily forgotten. I charge down the path, surrounded by laughter and shouting. We cluster together to form teams, and then turn against one another.

By the time the fight dies down, my clothes are more paint-colored than black. I decide to keep the shirt to remind me why I chose Dauntless in the first place: not because they are perfect, but because they are alive. Because they are free.

CHAPTER
TWENTY-FIVE

SOMEONE RAIDS THE Dauntless kitchens and heats up the imperishables kept there, so we have a warm dinner that night. I sit at the same table I used to claim with Christina, Al, and Will. From the moment I sit down, I feel a lump in my throat. How is it that only half of us are left?

I feel responsible for that. My forgiveness could have saved Al, but I withheld it. My clearheadedness could have spared Will, but I could not summon it.

Before I can sink too far into my guilt, Uriah drops his tray next to me. It is loaded with beef stew and chocolate cake. I stare at the cake pile.

"There was cake?" I say, looking at my own plate, which is more sensibly stocked than Uriah's.

"Yeah, someone just brought it out. Found a couple boxes of the mix in the back and baked it," he says. "You can have a few bites of mine."

"A *few* bites? So you're planning on eating that mountain of cake by yourself?"

"Yes." He looks confused. "Why?"

"Never mind."

Christina sits across the table, as far away from me as she can get. Zeke puts his tray down next to her. We are soon joined by Lynn, Hector, and Marlene. I see a flash of movement under the table, and see Marlene's hand meet Uriah's over his knee. Their fingers twist together. They are both clearly trying to look casual, but they sneak looks at each other.

To Marlene's left, Lynn looks like she just tasted something sour. She shovels food into her mouth.

"Where's the fire?" Uriah asks her. "You're going to hurl if you keep eating that fast."

Lynn scowls at him. "I'm going to hurl anyway, with you two making eyes at each other all the time."

Uriah's ears turn red. "What are you talking about?"

"I am not an idiot, and neither is anyone else. So why don't you just make out with her and get it over with?"

Uriah looks stunned. Marlene, however, glares at Lynn, leans over, and kisses Uriah firmly on the mouth, her fingers sliding around his neck, under the collar of his shirt. I notice that all the peas have fallen off my fork, which was on its way to my mouth.

Lynn grabs her tray and storms away from the table.

"What was that all about?" says Zeke.

"Don't ask me," says Hector. "She's always angry about something. I've stopped trying to keep track."

Uriah's and Marlene's faces are still close together. And they are still smiling.

I force myself to stare at my plate. It is so strange to see two people you have known separately join together, though I have watched it happen before. I hear a squeak as Christina scratches her plate with her fork idly.

"Four!" Zeke calls out, beckoning. He looks relieved. "C'mere, there's room."

Tobias rests his hand on my good shoulder. A few of his knuckles are split, and the blood looks fresh. "Sorry, I can't stay."

He leans down and says, "Can I borrow you for a while?"

I get up, waving a good-bye to everyone at the table who is paying attention—which is just Zeke, really, because Christina and Hector are staring at their plates, and Uriah and Marlene are talking quietly. Tobias and I walk out of the cafeteria.

"Where are we going?"

"The train," he says. "I have a meeting, and I want you there to help me read the situation."

We walk up one of the paths that lines the Pit walls, toward the stairs that lead us to the Pire.

"Why do you need *me* to—"

"Because you're better at it than I am."

I don't have a response to that. We ascend the stairs and cross the glass floor. On our way out, we walk through the dank room in which I faced my fear landscape. Judging by the syringe on the floor, someone has been there recently.

"Did you go through your fear landscape today?" I say.

"What makes you say that?" His dark eyes skirt mine. He pushes the front door open, and the summer air swims around me. There is no wind.

"Your knuckles are cut up and someone's been using that room."

"This is exactly what I mean. You're far more perceptive than most." He checks his watch. "They told me to catch the one leaving at 8:05. Come on."

I feel a surge of hope. Maybe we won't argue this time. Maybe things will finally get better between us.

We walk to the tracks. The last time we did this, he wanted to show me that the lights were on in the Erudite compound, wanted to tell me that Erudite was planning an attack on Abnegation. Now I get the sense we are about to meet with the factionless.

"Perceptive enough to know you're evading the question," I say.

He sighs. "Yes, I went through my fear landscape. I wanted to see if it had changed."

"And it has. Hasn't it?"

He brushes a stray hair away from his face and avoids my eyes. I didn't know his hair was so thick—it was hard to tell when it was buzzed short, Abnegation hair, but now it's two inches long and almost hangs over his forehead. It makes him look less threatening, more like the person I've come to know in private.

"Yes," he says. "But the number is still the same."

I hear the train horn blasting to my left, but the light fixed to the first car is not on. Instead it slides over the rails like some hidden, creeping thing.

"Fifth car back!" he shouts.

We both break into a sprint. I find the fifth car and grab the handle on the side with my left hand, pulling as hard as I can. I try to swing my legs inside, but they don't quite make it; they are dangerously close to the wheels—I shriek, and scrape my knee against the floor as I yank myself inside.

Tobias gets in after me and crouches by my side. I clutch my knee and grit my teeth.

"Here, let me see," he says. He pushes my jeans up my leg and over my knee. His fingers leave streaks of cold on my skin, invisible to the eye, and I think about wrapping his shirt around my fist and pulling him in to kiss me; I think about pressing myself against him, but I can't, because all our secrets would keep a space between us.

My knee is red with blood. "It's shallow. It'll heal quickly," he says.

I nod. The pain is already subsiding. He rolls my jeans so they will stay up. I lie back, staring at the ceiling.

"So is *he* still in your fear landscape?" I say.

It looks like someone lit a match behind his eyes. "Yes. But not in the same way."

He told me, once, that his fear landscape hadn't changed since he first went through it, during his initiation. So if it has, even in a small way, that's something.

"You're in it, though." He frowns at his hands. "Instead of having to shoot that woman, like I used to, I have to watch you die. And there's nothing I can do to stop it."

His hands shake. I try to think of something helpful to say. *I'm not going to die*—but I don't know that. We live in a dangerous world, and I am not so attached to life that I will do anything to survive. I can't reassure him.

He checks his watch. "They'll be here any minute."

I get up, and see Evelyn and Edward standing next to the tracks. They run before the train passes them, and jump in with almost as little trouble as Tobias. They must have been practicing.

Edward smirks at me. Today his eye patch has a big blue "X" stitched over it.

"Hello," Evelyn says. She looks only at Tobias as she says it, like I'm not even there.

"Nice meeting location," says Tobias. It is almost dark now, so I see only shadows of buildings against a dark blue sky, and a few glowing lights near the lake that must belong to Erudite headquarters.

The train takes a turn it doesn't usually take—left, away from the glow of Erudite and into the abandoned part of the city. I can tell by the growing quiet in the car that it is slowing down.

"It seemed safest," says Evelyn. "So you wanted to meet."

"Yes. I'd like to discuss an alliance."

"An alliance," repeats Edward. "And who gave you the authority to do that?"

"He's a Dauntless leader," I say. "He has the authority."

Edward raises his eyebrows, looking impressed. Evelyn's eyes finally shift to me, but only for a second before she smiles at Tobias again.

"Interesting," she says. "And is *she* also a Dauntless leader?"

"No," he says. "She's here to help me decide whether or not to trust you."

Evelyn purses her lips. Part of me wants to thumb my nose at her and say, "Ha!" But I settle for a small smile.

"We will, of course, agree to an alliance . . . under a certain set of conditions," Evelyn says. "A guaranteed—and equal—place in whatever government forms after Erudite is destroyed, and full control over Erudite data after the attack. Clearly—"

"What are you going to do with the Erudite data?" I interrupt her.

"Obviously we will destroy it. The only way to deprive the Erudite of power is to deprive them of knowledge."

My first instinct is to tell her she's a fool. But something stops me. Without the simulation technology, without the data they had about all the other factions, without their focus on technological advancement, the attack on Abnegation would not have happened. My parents would be alive.

Even if we manage to kill Jeanine, could the Erudite be trusted not to attack and control us again? I am not sure.

"What would we receive in return, under those terms?" Tobias says.

"Our much-needed manpower, in order to take Erudite headquarters, and an equal place in government, with us."

"I am sure that Tori would also request the right to rid the world of Jeanine Matthews," he says in a low voice.

I raise my eyebrows. I didn't know that Tori's hatred of Jeanine was common knowledge—or maybe it isn't. He must know things about her that others don't, now that he and Tori are leaders.

"I'm sure that could be arranged," Evelyn replies. "I don't care who kills her; I just want her dead."

Tobias glances at me. I wish I could tell him why I feel so conflicted . . . explain to him why I, of all people, have reservations about burning Erudite to the ground, so to speak. But I would not know how to say it even if I had the time to. He turns toward Evelyn.

"Then we are agreed," he says.

He extends his hand, and she shakes it.

"We should convene in a week's time," she says. "In neutral territory. Most of the Abnegation have graciously agreed to let us stay in their sector of the city to plan as they clean up the aftermath of the attack."

"Most of them," he says.

Evelyn's expression turns flat. "I'm afraid your father still commands the loyalty of many of them, and he advised them to avoid us when he came to visit a few days ago." She smiles bitterly. "And they agreed, just as they did when he persuaded them to exile me."

"They exiled you?" says Tobias. "I thought you *left*."

"No, the Abnegation were inclined toward forgiveness and reconciliation, as you might expect. But your father has a lot of influence over the Abnegation, and he always has. I decided to leave rather than face the indignity of public exile."

Tobias looks stunned.

Edward, who has been leaning out the side of the car for a few seconds, says, "It's time!"

"See you in a week," Evelyn says.

As the train dips down to street level, Edward leaps. A few seconds later, Evelyn follows. Tobias and I remain on the train, listening to it hiss against the rails, without speaking.

"Why did you even bring me along, if you were just going to make an alliance anyway?" I say flatly.

"You didn't stop me."

"What was I supposed to do, wave my hands in the air?" I scowl at him. "I don't like it."

"It has to be done."

"I don't think it does," I say. "There has to be another way—"

"What other way?" he says, folding his arms. "You just don't like her. You haven't since you first met her."

"Obviously I don't like her! She abandoned you!"

"They *exiled* her. And if I decide to forgive her, you had better try to do it too! I'm the one who got left behind, not you."

"This is about more than that. I don't trust her. I think she's trying to use you."

"Well, it isn't for you to decide."

"Why did you bring me, again?" I say, mirroring him by folding my arms. "Oh yeah—so that I could read the situation for you. Well, I read it, and just because you don't like what I decided doesn't mean—"

"I forgot about how your biases cloud your judgment. If I had re-membered, I might not have brought you."

"*My* biases. What about *your* biases? What about thinking everyone who hates your father as much as you do is an ally?"

"This is not about him!"

"Of course it is! He knows things, Tobias. And we should be trying to find out what they are."

"This again? I thought we resolved this. He is a *liar*, Tris."

"Yeah?" I raise my eyebrows. "Well, so is your mother. You think the Abnegation would really exile someone? Because I don't."

"Don't talk about my mother that way."

I see light up ahead. It belongs to the Pire.

"Fine." I walk to the edge of the car door. "I won't."

I jump out, running a few steps to keep my balance. Tobias jumps out after me, but I don't give him a chance to catch up—I walk straight into the building, down the stairs, and back into the Pit to find a place to sleep.

CHAPTER
TWENTY-SIX

SOMETHING SHAKES ME awake.

"Tris! Get up!"

A shout. I don't question it. I throw my legs over the edge of the bed and let a hand pull me toward the door. My feet are bare, and the ground is uneven here. It scrapes at my toes and the edges of my heels. I squint ahead of me to figure out who's dragging me. Christina. She's almost pulling my left arm from its socket.

"What happened?" I say. "What's going on?"

"Shut up and run!"

We run to the Pit, and the roar of the river follows me up the paths. The last time Christina pulled me out of bed, it was to see Al's body lifted out of the chasm. I grit my teeth and try not to think about that. It can't have happened again. It can't.

I gasp—she runs faster than I do—as we sprint across the glass floor of the Pire. Christina slams her palm into an elevator button and slips inside before the doors are fully open, dragging me behind her. She jabs the DOOR CLOSE button, and then the button for the top floor.

"Simulation," she says. "There's a simulation. It's not everyone, it's just . . . just a few."

She puts her hands on her knees and takes deep breaths.

"One of them said something about the Divergent," she says.

"Said that?" I say. "While under a simulation?"

She nods. "Marlene. Didn't sound like her, though. Too . . . monotone."

The doors open, and I follow her down the hallway to the door marked ROOF ACCESS.

"Christina," I say, "why are we going to the roof?"

She doesn't answer me. The stairs to the roof smell like old paint. Dauntless graffiti is scrawled on the cement-block walls in black paint. The symbol of Dauntless. Initials paired together with plus signs: RG + NT, BR + FH. Couples who are probably old now, maybe broken up. I touch my chest to feel my heartbeat. It's so fast, it's a wonder I'm still breathing at all.

The night air is cool; it gives me goose bumps on my arms. My eyes have adjusted to the darkness by now, and across the roof I see three figures standing on the ledge, facing me. One is Marlene. One is Hector. One is someone I don't recognize—a young Dauntless, barely eight years old, with a green streak in her hair.

They stand still on the ledge, though the wind is blowing hard, tossing their hair over their foreheads, into their eyes, into their mouths. Their clothes snap in the wind, but still they stand motionless.

"Just come down off the ledge now," Christina says. "Don't do anything stupid. Come on, now . . ."

"They can't hear you," I say quietly as I walk toward them. "Or see you."

"We should all jump at them at once. I'll take Hec, you—"

"We'll risk shoving them off the roof if we do that. Stand by the girl, just in case."

She is too young for this, I think, but I don't have the heart to say it, because it means Marlene is old enough.

I stare at Marlene, whose eyes are blank like painted stones, like spheres of glass. I feel as if those stones are slipping down my throat and settling in my stomach, pulling me toward the ground. There is no way to get her off that ledge.

Finally she opens her mouth and speaks.

"I have a message for the Divergent." Her voice sounds flat. The simulation is using her vocal cords, but robs them of the natural fluctuations of human emotion.

I look from Marlene to Hector. Hector, who was so afraid of what I am because his mother told him to be. Lynn is probably still at Shauna's bedside, hoping Shauna can move her legs when she wakes up again. Lynn can't lose Hector.

I step forward to receive the message.

"This is not a negotiation. It is a warning," says the simulation through Marlene, moving her lips and vibrating in her throat. "Every two days until one of you delivers yourself to Erudite headquarters, this will happen again."

This.

Marlene steps back, and I throw myself forward, but not at her. Not at Marlene, who once let Uriah shoot a muffin off her head on a dare. Who gathered a stack of clothing for me to wear. Who always, always greeted me with a smile. No, not at Marlene.

As Marlene and the other Dauntless girl step off the edge of the roof, I dive at Hector.

I grab whatever my hands can find. An arm. A fistful of shirt. The rough rooftop scrapes my knees as his weight drags me forward. I am not strong enough to lift him. I whisper, "Help," because I can't speak any louder than that.

Christina is already at my shoulder. She helps me haul Hector's limp body onto the roof. His arm flops to the side, lifeless. A few feet away, the little girl lies on her back on the rooftop.

Then the simulation ends. Hector opens his eyes, and they are no longer empty.

"Ow," he says. "What's going on?"

The little girl whimpers, and Christina walks over to her, mumbling something in a reassuring voice.

I stand, my entire body shaking. I inch toward the edge of the roof and stare at the ground. The street below isn't lit very well, but I can see Marlene's faint outline on the pavement.

Breathing—who cares about breathing?

I turn from the sight, listening to my heart beat in my ears. Christina's mouth moves. I ignore her, and walk to the door and down the stairs and down the hallway and into the elevator.

The doors close and as I drop to the earth, just as Marlene did after I decided not to save her, I scream, my hands tearing at my clothes. My throat is raw after just a few seconds, and there are scratches on my arms where I missed the fabric, but I keep screaming.

The elevator stops with a *ding*. The doors open.

I straighten my shirt, smooth my hair down, and walk out.

+ + +

I have a message for the Divergent.
I am Divergent.
This is not a negotiation.
No, it is not.
It is a warning.
I understand.
Every two days until one of you delivers yourself to Erudite headquarters . . .
I will.
. . . this will happen again.
It will never happen again.

CHAPTER
TWENTY-SEVEN

I WEAVE THROUGH the crowd next to the chasm. It's loud in the Pit, and not just because of the river's roar. I want to find some silence, so I escape into the hallway that leads to the dormitories. I don't want to hear the speech Tori will make on Marlene's behalf or be around for the toasting and the shouting as the Dauntless celebrate her life and her bravery.

This morning Lauren reported that we missed some of the cameras in the initiate dormitories, where Christina, Zeke, Lauren, Marlene, Hector, and Kee, the girl with the green hair, were sleeping. That's how Jeanine figured out who the simulation was controlling. I do not doubt that Jeanine chose young Dauntless because she knew their deaths would affect us more.

I stop in an unfamiliar hallway and press my forehead to the wall. The stone feels rough and cool on my skin. I can hear the Dauntless shouting behind me, their voices muffled by layers of rock.

I hear someone approaching, and look to the side. Christina, still wearing the same clothes she wore last night, stands a few feet away.

"Hey," she says.

"I'm not really in the mood to feel more guilt right now. So go away, please."

"I just want to say one thing, and then I will."

Her eyes are puffy and her voice sounds a little sleepy, which is either due to exhaustion or a little alcohol, or both. But her stare is direct enough that she must know what she's saying. I pull away from the wall.

"I'd never seen that kind of simulation before. You know, from the outside. But yesterday . . ." She shakes her head. "You were right. They couldn't hear you, couldn't see you. Just like Will . . ."

She chokes on his name. Stops, takes a breath, swallows hard. Blinks a few times. Then looks at me again.

"You told me you had to do it, or he would have shot you, and I didn't believe you. I believe you now, and . . . I'm going to try to forgive you. That's . . . all I wanted to say."

There's a part of me that feels relief. She believes me, she's trying to forgive me, even though it won't be easy.

But a larger part of me feels anger. What did she think, before now? That I *wanted* to shoot Will, one of my best friends? She should have trusted me from the beginning, should have *known* that I wouldn't have done it if I had been able to see another option at the time.

"How fortunate for me that you finally got *proof* that I'm not a cold-blooded murderer. You know, other than my word. I mean, what reason would you have to trust that?" I force a laugh, trying to stay nonchalant. She opens her mouth, but I keep talking, unable to stop myself. "You'd better hurry on that forgiving-me thing, because there isn't much time—"

My voice cracks, and I can't hold myself together anymore. I start sobbing. I lean against the wall for support and feel myself sliding down as my legs get weak.

My eyes are too blurry to see her, but I feel her when she wraps her arms around me and squeezes so hard it hurts. She smells like coconut oil and she feels strong, exactly like she was during initiation into Dauntless, when she hung over the chasm by her fingertips. Back then—which was not so long ago—she made me feel weak, but now her strength makes me feel like I could be stronger too.

We kneel together on the stone floor, and I clutch her as tightly as she clutches me.

"It's already done," she says. "That's what I meant to say. That the forgiving was already done."

+ + +

All the Dauntless go quiet when I walk into the cafeteria that night. I don't blame them. As one of the Divergent, I have the power to let Jeanine kill one of them. Most of them probably want me to sacrifice myself. Or they are terrified that I won't.

If this were Abnegation, no Divergent would be sitting here right now.

For a moment I don't know where to go or how to get there. But then Zeke waves me over to his table, looking grim, and I guide my feet in that direction. But before I make it there, Lynn approaches me.

She is a different Lynn from the one I have always known. She doesn't have a fierce look in her eyes. Instead she is pale and biting her lip to hide its wobble.

"Um . . ." she says. She looks to the left, to the right, anywhere but at my face. "I really . . . I miss Marlene. I've known her for a long time, and I . . ." She shakes her head. "The point is, don't think that my saying this means *anything* about Marlene," she says, like she's scolding me, "but . . . thank you for saving Hec."

Lynn shifts her weight from one foot to the other, her eyes flicking around the room. Then she hugs me with one arm, her hand gripping my shirt. Pain shoots through my shoulder. I don't say anything about it.

She lets go, sniffs, and walks back to her table like nothing happened. I stare at her retreating back for a few seconds, and then sit down.

Zeke and Uriah sit side by side at the otherwise empty table. Uriah's face is slack, like he's not completely awake. He has a dark brown bottle in front of him that he sips from every few seconds.

I feel cautious around him. I saved Hec—which means I failed to save Marlene. But Uriah doesn't look at me. I pull out the chair across from him and sit on the edge of it.

"Where's Shauna?" I say. "Still in the hospital?"

"No, she's over there," says Zeke, nodding to the table Lynn walked back to. I see her there, so pale she might as well be translucent, sitting in a wheelchair. "Shauna shouldn't be up, but Lynn's pretty messed up, so she's keeping her company."

"But if you're wondering why they're all the way over there . . . Shauna found out I'm Divergent," says Uriah sluggishly. "And she doesn't want to catch it."

"Oh."

"She got all weird with me, too," says Zeke, sighing. " 'How do you know your brother isn't working against us? Have you been watching him?' What I wouldn't give to punch whoever poisoned her mind."

"You don't have to give anything," says Uriah. "Her mother's sitting right there. Go ahead and hit her."

I follow his gaze to a middle-aged woman with blue streaks in her hair and earrings all the way down her earlobe. She is pretty, just like Lynn.

Tobias enters the room a moment later, followed by Tori and Harrison. I have been avoiding him. I haven't spoken to him since that fight we had, before Marlene . . .

"Hello, Tris," Tobias says when I'm close enough to hear him. His voice is low, rough. It transports me to quiet places.

"Hi," I say in a tight little voice that does not belong to me.

He sits next to me and puts his arm on the back of my chair, leaning close. I don't stare back—I *refuse* to stare back.

I stare back.

Dark eyes—a peculiar shade of blue, somehow capable of shutting the rest of the cafeteria out, of comforting me and also of reminding me that we are farther away from each other than I want us to be.

"Aren't you going to ask me if I'm all right?" I say.

"No, I'm pretty sure you're not all right." He shakes his head. "I'm going to ask you not to make any decisions until we've talked about it."

It's too late, I think. *The decision's made.*

"Until we've all talked about it, you mean, since it involves all of us," says Uriah. "I don't think anyone should turn themselves in."

"No one?" I say.

"No!" Uriah scowls. "I think we should attack back."

"Yeah," I say hollowly, "let's provoke the woman who can force half of this compound to kill themselves. That sounds like a great idea."

I was too harsh. Uriah tips the contents of his bottle down his throat. He brings the bottle down on the table so hard I'm afraid it will shatter.

"Don't talk about it like that," he says in a growl.

"I'm sorry," I say. "But you know I'm right. The best way to ensure that half our faction doesn't die is to sacrifice one life."

I don't know what I expected. Maybe that Uriah, who knows too well what will happen if one of us does not go, would volunteer himself. But he looks down. Unwilling.

"Tori and Harrison and I decided to increase security. Hopefully if everyone is more aware of these attacks, we will be able to stop them," Tobias says. "If it doesn't work, then we will think of another solution. End of discussion. But no one is going to do anything yet. Okay?"

He looks at me when he asks and raises his eyebrows.

"Okay," I say, not quite meeting his eyes.

+ + +

After dinner, I try to go back to the dormitory where I've been sleeping, but I can't quite walk through the door. Instead I walk through the corridors, brushing the stone walls with my fingers, listening to the echoes of my footsteps.

Without meaning to, I pass the water fountain where Peter, Drew, and Al attacked me. I knew it was Al by the way he smelled—I can still call the scent of lemongrass to mind. Now I associate it not with my friend but with the powerlessness I felt as they dragged me to the chasm.

I walk faster, keeping my eyes wide open so it will be harder to picture the attack in my mind. I have to get away from here, far from the places where my friend attacked me, where Peter stabbed Edward, where a sightless army of my friends began its march toward the Abnegation sector and all this insanity began.

I go straight toward the last place where I felt safe: Tobias's small apartment. The second I reach the door, I feel calmer.

The door is not completely closed. I nudge it open with my foot. He isn't there, but I don't leave. I sit on his bed and gather the quilt in my arms, burying my face in the fabric and taking deep breaths of it through my nose. The smell it used to have is almost gone, it's been so long since he slept on it.

The door opens and Tobias slips in. My arms go limp, and the quilt falls into my lap. How will I explain my presence here? I'm supposed to be angry with him.

He doesn't scowl, but his mouth is so tense that I know he's angry with *me*.

"Don't be an idiot," he says.

"An idiot?"

"You were lying. You said you wouldn't go to Erudite, and you were lying, and going to Erudite would make you an idiot. So don't."

I set the blanket down and get up.

"Don't try to make this simple," I say. "It's not. You know as well as I do that this is the right thing to do."

"You choose *this* moment to act like the Abnegation?" His voice fills the room and makes fear prickle in my chest. His anger seems too sudden. Too strange. "All that time you spent insisting that you were too selfish for them, and now, when your *life* is on the line, you've got to be a hero? What's wrong with you?"

"What's wrong with *you*? People died. They walked right off the edge of a building! And I can stop it from happening again!"

"You're too important to just . . . die." He shakes his head. He won't even look at me—his eyes keep shifting across my face, to the wall behind me or the ceiling above me, to everything but me. I am too stunned to be angry.

"I'm not important. Everyone will do just fine without me," I say.

"Who cares about everyone? What about *me*?"

He lowers his head into his hand, covering his eyes. His fingers are trembling.

Then he crosses the room in two long strides and touches his lips to mine. Their gentle pressure erases the past few months, and I am the girl who sat on the rocks next to the chasm, with river spray on her ankles, and kissed him for the first time. I am the girl who grabbed his hand in the hallway just because I wanted to.

I pull back, my hand on his chest to keep him away. The problem is, I am also the girl who shot Will and lied about it, and chose between Hector and Marlene, and now a thousand other things besides. And I can't erase those things.

"You *would* be fine." I don't look at him. I stare at his T-shirt between my fingers and the black ink curling around his neck, but I don't look at his face. "Not at first. But you would move on, and do what you have to."

He wraps an arm around my waist and pulls me against him. "That's a *lie*," he says, before he kisses me again.

This is wrong. It's wrong to forget who I have become, and to let him kiss me when I know what I'm about to do.

But I want to. Oh, I want to.

I stand on my tiptoes and wrap my arms around him. I press one hand between his shoulder blades and curl the other one around the back of his neck. I can feel his breaths against my palm, his body expanding and contracting, and I know he's strong, steady, unstoppable. All things I need to be, but I am not, I am not.

He walks backward, pulling me with him so I stumble. I stumble right out of my shoes. He sits on the edge of the bed and I stand in front of him, and we're finally eye to eye.

He touches my face, covering my cheeks with his hands, sliding his fingertips down my neck, fitting his fingers to the slight curve of my hips.

I can't stop.

I fit my mouth to his, and he tastes like water and smells like fresh air. I drag my hand from his neck to the small of his back, and put it under his shirt. He kisses me harder.

I knew he was strong; I didn't know how strong until I felt it myself, the muscles in his back tightening beneath my fingers.

Stop, I tell myself.

Suddenly it's as if we're in a hurry, his fingertips brushing my side under my shirt, my hands clutching at him, struggling closer but there is no closer. I have never longed for someone this way, or this much.

He pulls back just enough to look into my eyes, his eyelids lowered.

"Promise me," he whispers, "that you won't go. For me. Do this one thing for me."

Could I do that? Could I stay here, fix things with him, let someone else die in my place? Looking up at him, I believe for a moment that I could. And then I see Will. The crease between his eyebrows. The empty, simulation-bound eyes. The slumped body.

Do this one thing for me. Tobias's dark eyes plead with me.

But if I don't go to Erudite, who will? Tobias? It's the kind of thing he would do.

I feel a stab of pain in my chest as I lie to him. "Okay."

"Promise," he says, frowning.

The pain becomes an ache, spreads everywhere—all mixed together, guilt and terror and longing. "I promise."

CHAPTER
TWENTY-EIGHT

When he starts to fall asleep, he keeps his arms around me fiercely, a life-preserving prison. But I wait, kept awake by the thought of bodies hitting pavement, until his grip loosens and his breathing steadies.

I will not let Tobias go to Erudite when it happens again, when someone else dies. I will not.

I slip out of his arms. I shrug on one of his sweatshirts so I can carry the smell of him with me. I slip my feet into my shoes. I don't take any weapons or keepsakes.

I pause by the doorway and look at him, half buried under the quilt, peaceful and strong.

"I love you," I say quietly, trying out the words. I let the door close behind me.

It's time to put everything in order.

I walk to the dormitory where the Dauntless-born initiates once slept. The room looks just like the one I slept in when I was an initiate: it is long and narrow, with bunk beds on either side and a chalkboard on one wall. I see by a blue light in the corner that no one bothered to erase the rankings that are written there—Uriah's name is still at the top.

Christina sleeps in the bottom bunk, beneath Lynn. I don't want to startle her, but there's no way to wake her otherwise, so I cover her mouth with my hand. She wakes with a start, her eyes wide until they find me. I touch my finger to my lips and beckon for her to follow me.

I walk to the end of the hallway and turn a corner. The corridor is lit by a paint-spattered emergency lamp that hangs over one of the exits. Christina isn't wearing shoes; she curls her toes under to protect them from the cold.

"What is it?" she says. "Are you going somewhere?"

"Yeah, I'm . . ." I have to lie, or she'll try to stop me. "I'm going to see my brother. He's with the Abnegation, remember?"

She narrows her eyes.

"I'm sorry to wake you," I say. "But there's something I need you to do. It's really important."

"Okay. Tris, you're acting really strange. Are you sure you're not—"

"I'm not. Listen to me. The timing of the simulation attack wasn't random. The reason it happened when it did is because the Abnegation were about to do something—I don't know what it was, but it had to do with some important information, and now Jeanine *has* that information. . . ."

"What?" She frowns. "You don't know what they were about to do? Do you know what the information is?"

"No." I must sound crazy. "The thing is, I haven't been able to find out very much about this, because Marcus Eaton is the only person who knows everything, and he won't tell me. I just . . . it's the reason for the attack. It's the *reason*. And we need to know it."

I don't know what else to say. But Christina is already nodding.

"The reason Jeanine forced us to attack innocent people," she says bitterly. "Yeah. We need to know it."

I had almost forgotten—*she* was under the simulation. How many Abnegation did she kill, guided by the simulation? How did she feel when she awoke from that dream a murderer? I have never asked, and I never will.

"I want your help, and soon. I need someone to persuade Marcus to cooperate, and I think you can do it."

She tilts her head and stares at me for a few seconds.

"Tris. Don't do anything stupid."

I force a smile. "Why do people keep saying that to me?"

She grabs my arm. "I'm not kidding around."

"I told you, I'm going to visit Caleb. I'll be back in a few days, and we can make a strategy then. I just thought it would be better if someone else knew about all this before I left. Just in case. Okay?"

She holds my arm for a few seconds, and then releases me. "Okay," she says.

I walk toward the exit. I hold myself together until I'm through the door, and then I feel the tears come.

The last conversation I'll ever have with her, and it was full of lies.

+ + +

Once I'm outside, I put up the hood of Tobias's sweatshirt. When I reach the end of the street, I glance up and down, searching for signs of life. There is nothing.

The cool air prickles in my lungs on the way in, and on the way out unfurls in a cloud of vapor. Winter will be here soon. I wonder if Erudite and Dauntless will still be at a standstill then, waiting for one group to obliterate the other. I'm glad I won't have to see it.

Before I chose Dauntless, thoughts like that never occurred to me. I felt assured of my long lifespan, if nothing else. Now there are no reassurances, except that where I go, I go because I choose to.

I walk in the shadows of buildings, hoping my footsteps won't attract any attention. None of the city lights are on in this area, but the moon is bright enough that I can walk by it without too much trouble.

I walk beneath the elevated tracks. They shudder with the movement of an oncoming train. I have to walk fast if I want to get there before anyone notices that I'm gone. I sidestep a large crack in the street, and jump over a fallen streetlight.

I didn't think about how far I would have to walk when I set out. It isn't long before my body warms with the exertion of walking and checking over my shoulder and dodging hazards in the road. I pick up the pace, half walking and half jogging.

Soon I reach a part of the city that I recognize. The streets are better kept here, swept clean, with few holes. Far away I see the glow of Erudite headquarters, their lights violating our energy conservation laws. I don't know what I will do when I get there. Demand to see Jeanine? Or just stand there until someone notices me?

My fingertips skim a window in the building beside me. Not long now. Tremors go through my body now that I am close, making it difficult to walk. Breathing is tricky too; I stop trying to be quiet, and let air wheeze in and out of my lungs. What will they do with me when I get there? What plans do they have for me before I outlive my usefulness, and they kill me? I don't doubt that they will kill me eventually. I concentrate on forward motion, on moving my legs even though they seem to be unwilling to support my weight.

And then I'm standing in front of Erudite headquarters.

Inside, crowds of blue-shirted people sit around tables, typing on computers or bent over books or passing sheets of paper back and forth. Some of them are decent people who do not understand what their faction has done, but if their entire building collapsed in on them before my eyes, I might not find it in myself to care.

This is the last moment I will be able to turn back. The cold air stings my cheeks and my hands as I hesitate. I can walk away now. Take refuge in the Dauntless compound. Hope and pray and wish that no one else dies because of my selfishness.

But I can't walk away, or the guilt, the weight of Will's life, and my parents' lives, and now Marlene's life, will break my bones, will make it impossible to breathe.

I slowly walk toward the building and push open the doors.

This is the only way to keep from suffocating.

+ + +

For a second after my feet touch the wood floors, and I stand before the giant portrait of Jeanine Matthews hung on the opposite wall, no one notices me, not even the two Dauntless traitor guards milling around near the entryway. I walk up to the front desk, where a middle-aged man with a bald patch on the crown of his head sits, sorting through a stack of paper. I set my hands on the desk.

"Excuse me," I say.

"Give me a moment," he says without looking up.

"No."

At *that* he looks up, his glasses askew, scowling like he's about to chastise me. Whatever words he was about to use seem to stick in his throat. He stares at me with an open mouth, his eyes skipping from my face to the black sweatshirt I wear.

In my terror, his expression seems amusing. I smile a little and conceal my hands, which are trembling.

"I believe Jeanine Matthews wanted to see me," I say. "So I would appreciate it if you would contact her."

He signals to the Dauntless traitors by the door, but there is no need. The guards have finally caught on. Dauntless soldiers from the other parts of the room have also started forward, and they all surround me, but don't touch me, and don't speak to me. I scan their faces, trying to look as placid as possible.

"Divergent?" one of them finally asks as the man behind the desk picks up the receiver of the building's communication system.

If I close my hands into fists, I can stop them from shaking. I nod.

My eyes shift to the Dauntless coming out of the elevator on the left side of the room, and the muscles in my face go slack. Peter is coming toward us.

A thousand potential reactions, ranging from launching myself at Peter's throat to crying to making some kind of joke, rush through my mind at once. I can't decide on one. So I stand still and watch him. Jeanine must have known that I would come, she must have chosen Peter on purpose to collect me, she must have.

"We've been instructed to take you upstairs," says Peter.

I mean to say something sharp, or nonchalant, but the only sound

that escapes me is an assenting noise, squeezed tight by my swollen
throat. Peter starts toward the elevators, and I follow him.

We walk down a series of sleek corridors. Despite the fact that we
climb a few flights of stairs, I still feel like I am plunging into the earth.

I expect them to take me to Jeanine, but they don't. They stop walking in a short hallway with a series of metal doors on each side. Peter
types in a code to open one of the doors, and the traitor Dauntless surround me, shoulder to shoulder, forming a narrow tunnel for me to pass
through on my way into the room.

The room is small, maybe six feet long by six feet wide. The floor, the
walls, and the ceiling are all made of the same light panels, dim now, that
glowed in the aptitude test room. In each corner is a tiny black camera.

I finally let myself panic.

I look from corner to corner, at the cameras, and fight the scream
building in my stomach, chest, and throat, the scream that fills every
part of me. Again I feel guilt and grief clawing inside me, warring with
each other for dominance, but terror is stronger than both. I breathe in,
and don't breathe out. My father once told me it was a cure for hiccups. I
asked him if I could die from holding my breath.

"No," he said. "Your body's instincts will take over, and force you to
breathe."

A shame, really. I could use a way out. The thought makes me want to
laugh. And then scream.

I curl up so I can press my face to my knees. I have to make a plan. If
I can make a plan, I won't be so afraid.

But there is no plan. No escape from deep in Erudite headquarters,
no escape from Jeanine, and no other escape from what I've done.

CHAPTER
TWENTY-NINE

I FORGOT MY watch.

Minutes or hours later, when the panic subsides, that is what I most regret. Not coming here in the first place—that seemed like an obvious choice—but my bare wrist, which makes it impossible for me to know how long I have been sitting in this room. My back aches, which is some indication, but it is not definite enough.

After a while I get up and pace, stretching my arms above my head. I hesitate to do anything while the cameras are there, but they can't learn anything by watching me touch my toes.

The thought makes my hands tremble, but I don't try to push it from my mind. Instead I tell myself that I am Dauntless and I am no stranger to fear. I will die in this place. Perhaps soon. Those are the facts.

But there are other ways to think of it. Soon I will honor my parents by dying as they died. And if all they believed about death was true, soon I will join them in whatever comes next.

I shake my hands as I pace. They're still trembling. I want to know what time it is. I arrived a little after midnight. It must be early in the morning by now, maybe 4:00, or 5:00. Or maybe it hasn't been that long, and only seems that way because I haven't been doing anything.

The door opens, and at last I stand face-to-face with my enemy and her Dauntless guards.

"Hello, Beatrice," Jeanine says. She wears Erudite blue and Erudite spectacles and an Erudite look of superiority that I was taught by my father to hate. "I thought you might be the one who came."

But I don't feel hate when I look at her. I don't feel anything at all, even though I know she's responsible for countless deaths, including

Marlene's. The deaths exist in my mind as a string of meaningless equations, and I stand frozen, unable to solve them.

"Hello, Jeanine," I say, because it is the only thing that comes to mind.

I look from Jeanine's watery gray eyes to the Dauntless who flank her. Peter stands at her right shoulder, and a woman with lines on either side of her mouth stands at her left. Behind her is a bald man with sharp planes in his skull. I frown.

How does Peter find himself in such a prestigious position, as Jeanine Matthews's bodyguard? Where is the logic in that?

"I'd like to know what time it is," I say.

"Would you," she says. "That's interesting."

I should have known she wouldn't tell me. Every piece of information she receives factors into her strategy, and she won't tell me what time it is unless she decides that providing the information is more useful than withholding it.

"I'm sure my Dauntless companions are disappointed," she says, "that you have not tried to claw my eyes out yet."

"That would be stupid."

"True. But in keeping with your 'act first, think second' behavioral trend."

"I'm sixteen." I purse my lips. "I change."

"How refreshing." She has a way of flattening even those phrases that should have inflection built into them. "Let's go on a little tour, shall we?"

She steps back and gestures toward the doorway. The last thing I want to do is walk out of this room and toward an uncertain destination, but I don't hesitate. I walk out, the severe-looking Dauntless woman in front of me. Peter follows me soon afterward.

The hallway is long and pale. We turn a corner and walk down a second one exactly like the first.

Two more hallways follow. I am so disoriented I could never find my way back. But then my surroundings change—the white tunnel opens to a large room where Erudite men and women in long blue jackets stand behind tables, some holding tools, some mixing multicolored liquids, some staring at computer screens. If I had to guess, I would say they are mixing simulation serum, but I hesitate to confine Erudite's work to simulations alone.

Most of them stop to watch us as we walk down the center aisle. Or rather, they watch *me*. Some of them whisper, but most remain silent. It is so quiet here.

I follow the Dauntless traitor woman through a doorway, and stop so abruptly Peter runs into me.

This room is just as large as the last one, but there is only one thing in it: a large metal table with a machine next to it. A machine I vaguely recognize as a heart monitor. And dangling above it, a camera. I shudder without meaning to. Because I know what this is.

"I am very pleased that *you*, in particular, are here," says Jeanine. She walks past me and perches on the table, her fingers curled around the edge.

"I am pleased, of course, because of your aptitude test results." Her blond hair, pulled tight to her skull, reflects the light, catches my attention.

"Even among the Divergent, you are somewhat of an oddity, because you have aptitude for three factions. Abnegation, Dauntless, and Erudite."

"How . . ." My voice croaks. I push the question out. "How do you know that?"

"All in good time," she says. "From your results I have determined that you are one of the strongest Divergent, which I say not to compliment you but to explain my purpose. If I am to develop a simulation that cannot be thwarted by the Divergent mind, I must study the strongest Divergent mind in order to shore up all weaknesses in the technology. Understand?"

I don't respond. I am still staring at the heart monitor next to the table.

"Therefore, for as long as possible, my fellow scientists and I will be studying you." She smiles a little. "And then, at the conclusion of my study, you will be executed."

I knew that. I knew it, so why do my knees feel weak, why is my stomach writhing, why?

"That execution will take place here." She runs her fingertips over the table beneath her. "On this table. I thought it would be interesting to show it to you."

She wants to study my response. I barely breathe. I used to think that cruelty required malice, but that is not true. Jeanine has no reason to act out of malice. But she is cruel because she doesn't care what she does, as long as it fascinates her. I may as well be a puzzle or a broken machine she wants to fix. She will break open my skull just to see the inner workings of my brain; I will die here, and that will be the merciful thing.

"I knew what would happen when I came here," I say. "It's just a table. And I'd like to go back to my room now."

+ + +

I don't really comprehend time's passing, at least not in the way that I used to, when time was available to me. So when the door opens again and Peter walks into my cell, I don't know how much time has gone by, only that I am exhausted.

"Let's go, Stiff," he says.

"I'm not Abnegation." I stretch my arms above my head so they brush against the wall. "And now that you're an Erudite lackey, you can't call me 'Stiff.' It's inaccurate."

"I said, let's go."

"What, no snide comments?" I look up at him with mock surprise. "No 'You're an idiot for coming here; your brain must be deficient as well as Divergent'?"

"That really goes without saying, doesn't it?" he says. "You can either get up or I can drag you down the hallway. Your choice."

I feel calmer. Peter is always mean to me; this is familiar.

I stand and walk out of the room. I notice as I walk that Peter's arm, the one I shot, is no longer in a sling.

"Did they fix up your bullet wound?"

"Yeah," he says. "Now you'll need to find a different weakness to exploit. Too bad I'm fresh out of them." He grabs my good arm and walks faster, pulling me along beside him. "We're late."

Despite the length and emptiness of the hallway, our footsteps don't echo much. I feel like someone put their hands over my ears and I only just noticed it. I try to keep track of the hallways we walk down, but I lose count after a while. We reach the end of one and turn left, into a dim room that reminds me of an aquarium. One of the walls is made of one-way glass—reflective on my side, but I'm sure it's transparent on the other side.

A large machine stands on the other side, with a man-sized tray coming out of it. I recognize it from my Faction History textbook, the unit on Erudite and medicine. An MRI machine. It will take pictures of my brain.

Something sparks inside me. It's been so long since I felt it that I barely recognize it at first. Curiosity.

A voice—Jeanine's voice—speaks over an intercom.

"Lie down, Beatrice."

I look at the man-sized tray that will slide me into the machine.

"No."

She sighs. "If you don't do it yourself, we have ways of making you."

Peter is standing behind me. Even with an injured arm, he was stronger than me. I imagine his hands on me, wrestling me toward the tray, shoving me against the metal, pulling the straps that dangle from the tray across my body, too tightly.

"Let's make a deal," I say. "If I cooperate, I get to see the scan."

"You will cooperate whether you want to or not."

I hold up a finger. "That's not true."

I look at the mirror. It's not so difficult to pretend that I'm speaking to Jeanine when I speak to my own reflection. My hair is blond like hers; we are both pale and stern-looking. The thought is so disturbing to me that I lose my train of thought for a few seconds, and instead stand with my finger in the air in silence.

I am pale-skinned, pale-haired, and cold. I am curious about the pictures of my brain. I am like Jeanine. And I can either despise it, attack it, eradicate it . . . or I can use it.

"That's not true," I repeat. "No matter how many restraints you use, you can't keep me as still as I need to be for the pictures to be clear." I clear my throat. "I want to see the scans. You're going to kill me anyway, so does it really matter how much I know about my own brain before you do?"

Silence.

"Why do you want to see them so badly?" she says.

"Surely you, of all people, understand. I have equal aptitude for Erudite as I do for Dauntless and Abnegation, after all."

"All right. You can see them. Lie down."

I walk over to the tray and lie down. The metal feels like ice. The tray slides back, and I am inside the machine. I stare up at whiteness. When I was young, I thought that was what heaven would be like, all white light and nothing else. Now I know that can't be true, because white light is menacing.

I hear thumping, and I close my eyes as I remember one of the obstacles in my fear landscape, the fists pounding against my windows and the sightless men trying to kidnap me. I pretend the pounding is a heartbeat, a drumbeat. The river crashing against the walls of the chasm in the Dauntless compound. Feet stamping at the end-of-initiation ceremony. Feet pounding on the staircase after the Choosing Ceremony.

I don't know how much time has passed when the thumping stops and the tray slides back. I sit up and rub my neck with my fingertips.

The door opens, revealing Peter in the hallway. He beckons to me. "Come on. You can go see the scans now."

I hop down from the tray and walk toward him. When we're in the hallway, he shakes his head at me.

"What?"

"I don't know how you manage to always get what you want."

"Yeah, because I wanted to get myself into a cell in Erudite head-quarters. I wanted to be executed."

I sound cavalier, like executions are something I face on a regular basis. But forming my lips around the word "executed" makes me shudder. I pretend I'm cold, squeezing my arms with my hands.

"Didn't you, though?" he says. "I mean, you did come here of your own free will. That's not what I call a good survival instinct."

He types in a series of numbers on a keypad outside the next door, and it opens. I enter the room on the other side of the mirror. It's full of screens and light, reflecting off the glass in the Erudites' spectacles. Across the room, another door clicks shut. There is an empty chair behind one of the screens, still turning. Someone just left.

Peter stands too close behind me—ready to grab me if I decide to attack anyone. But I won't attack anyone. How far could I get if I did? Down one hallway, or two? And then I would be lost. I couldn't get out of here even if there weren't guards stopping me from leaving.

"Put them up there," says Jeanine, pointing toward the large screen on the left wall. One of the Erudite scientists taps his own computer screen, and an image appears on the left wall. An image of my brain.

I don't know what I'm looking at, exactly. I know what a brain looks like, and generally what each region of it does, but I don't know how mine compares to others. Jeanine taps her chin and stares for what feels like a long time.

Finally she says, "Someone instruct Ms. Prior as to what the prefrontal cortex does."

"It's the region of the brain behind the forehead, so to speak," one of the scientists says. She doesn't look much older than I am, and wears large round glasses that make her eyes look bigger. "It's responsible for organizing your thoughts and actions to attain your goals."

"Correct," Jeanine says. "Now someone tell me what they observe about Ms. Prior's lateral prefrontal cortex."

"It's large," another scientist—this one a man with thinning hair—says.

"Specificity," says Jeanine. Like she's chastising him.

I am in a classroom, I realize, because every room with more than one Erudite in it is a classroom. And among them, Jeanine is their most valued teacher. They all stare at her with wide eyes and eager, open mouths, waiting to impress her.

"It's much larger than average," the man with thinning hair corrects himself.

"Better." Jeanine tilts her head. "In fact, it is one of the largest lateral prefrontal cortexes I've ever seen. Yet the orbitofrontal cortex is remarkably small. What do these two facts indicate?"

"The orbitofrontal cortex is the reward center of the brain. Those who exhibit reward-seeking behavior have a large orbitofrontal cortex," someone says. "That means that Ms. Prior engages in very little reward-seeking behavior."

"Not just that." Jeanine smiles a little. Blue light from the screens makes her cheekbones and forehead brighter but casts shadows in her eye sockets. "It does not merely indicate something about her behavior, but about her desires. She is not reward motivated. Yet she is extremely good at directing her thoughts and actions toward her goals. This explains both her tendency toward harmful-but-selfless behavior and, perhaps, her ability to wriggle out of simulations. How does this change our approach to the new simulation serum?"

"It should suppress some, but not all, of the activity in the prefrontal cortex," the scientist with the round glasses says.

"Precisely," says Jeanine. She finally looks at me, her eyes gleaming with delight. "Then that is how we will proceed. Did this satisfy my end of our agreement, Ms. Prior?"

My mouth is dry, so it's difficult to swallow.

And what happens if they suppress the activity in my prefrontal cortex—if they damage my ability to make decisions? What if this serum works, and I become a slave to the simulations like everyone else? What if I forget reality entirely?

I did not know that my entire personality, my entire being, could be discarded as the byproduct of my anatomy. What if I really am just someone with a large prefrontal cortex . . . and nothing more?

"Yes," I say. "It did."

+ + +

In silence Peter and I make our way back to my room. We turn left, and a group of people stands at the other end of the hallway. It is the longest of the corridors we will travel through, but that distance shrinks when I see him.

Held at either arm by a Dauntless traitor, a gun aimed at the back of his skull.

Tobias, blood trailing down the side of his face and marking his white shirt with red; Tobias, fellow Divergent, standing in the mouth of this furnace in which I will burn.

Peter's hands clamp around my shoulders, holding me in place.

"Tobias," I say, and it sounds like a gasp.

The Dauntless traitor with the gun presses Tobias toward me. Peter tries to push me forward too, but my feet remain planted. I came here so that no one else would die. I came here to protect as many people as I could. And I care more about Tobias's safety than anyone else's. So why am I here, if he's here? What's the point?

"What did you do?" I mumble. He is just a few feet away from me now, but not close enough to hear me. As he passes me he stretches out his hand. He wraps it around my palm and squeezes. Squeezes, then lets go. His eyes are bloodshot; he is pale.

"What did you do?" This time the question tears from my throat like a growl.

I throw myself toward him, struggling against Peter's grip, though his hands chafe.

"What did you do?" I scream.

"You die, I die too." Tobias looks over his shoulder at me. "I asked you not to do this. You made your decision. These are the repercussions."

He disappears around the corner. The last I see of him and the Dauntless traitors leading him is the gleam of the gun barrel and blood on the back of his earlobe from an injury I didn't see before.

All the life goes out of me as soon as he's gone. I stop struggling and let Peter's hands push me toward my cell. I slump to the ground as soon as I walk in, waiting for the door to slide shut to signify Peter's departure, but it doesn't.

"Why did he come here?" Peter says.

I glance at him.

"Because he's an idiot."

"Well, yeah."

I rest my head against the wall.

"Did he think he could rescue you?" Peter snorts a little. "Sounds like a Stiff-born thing to do."

"I don't think so," I say. If Tobias intended to rescue me, he would have thought it through; he would have brought others. He would not have burst into Erudite headquarters alone.

Tears well up in my eyes, and I don't try to blink them away. Instead I stare through them and watch my surroundings smear together. A few days ago I would never have cried in front of Peter, but I don't care anymore. He is the least of all my enemies.

"I think he came to die with me," I say. I clamp my hand over my mouth to stifle a sob. If I can keep breathing, I can stop crying. I didn't need or want him to die with me. I wanted to keep him safe. *What an idiot,* I think, but my heart isn't in it.

"That's ridiculous," he says. "That doesn't make any sense. He's eighteen; he'll find another girlfriend once you're dead. And he's stupid if he doesn't know that."

Tears run down my cheeks, hot at first and then cold. I close my eyes. "If you think that's what it's about . . ." I swallow another sob. ". . . you're the stupid one."

"Yeah. Whatever."

His shoes squeak as he turns away. About to leave.

"Wait!" I look up at his blurry silhouette, unable to make out his face. "What will they do to him? The same thing they're doing to me?"

"I don't know."

"Can you find out?" I wipe my cheeks with the heels of my hands, frustrated. "Can you at least find out if he's all right?"

He says, "Why would I do that? Why would I do anything for you?"

A moment later I hear the door slide shut.

CHAPTER
THIRTY

I READ SOMEWHERE, once, that crying defies scientific explanation. Tears are only meant to lubricate the eyes. There is no real reason for tear glands to overproduce tears at the behest of emotion.

I think we cry to release the animal parts of us without losing our humanity. Because inside me is a beast that snarls, and growls, and strains toward freedom, toward Tobias, and, above all, toward life. And as hard as I try, I cannot kill it.

So I sob into my hands instead.

+ + +

Left, right, right. Left, right, left. Right, right. Our turns, in order, from our point of origin—my cell—to our destination.

It is a new room. In it is a partially reclined chair, like a dentist's chair. In one corner is a screen and a desk. Jeanine sits at the desk.

"Where is he?" I say.

I have been waiting for hours to ask that question. I fell asleep and dreamed that I was chasing Tobias through Dauntless headquarters. No matter how fast I ran he was always just far enough ahead of me that I watched him disappear around corners, catching sight of a sleeve or the heel of a shoe.

Jeanine gives me a puzzled look. But she is not puzzled. She is playing with me.

"Tobias," I say anyway. My hands shake, but not from fear this time— from anger. "Where is he? What are you doing to him?"

"I see no reason to provide that information," says Jeanine. "And since you are all out of leverage, I see no way for you to give me a reason, unless you would like to change the terms of our agreement."

I want to scream at her that of course, of *course* I would rather know about Tobias than about my Divergence, but I don't. I can't make hasty decisions. She will do what she intends to do to Tobias whether I know about it or not. It is more important that I fully understand what is happening to me.

I breathe in through my nose, and out through my nose. I shake my hands. I sit down in the chair.

"Interesting," she says.

"Aren't you supposed to be running a faction and planning a war?" I say. "What are you doing here, running tests on a sixteen-year-old girl?"

"You choose different ways of referring to yourself depending on what is convenient," she says, leaning back in her chair. "Sometimes you insist that you are not a little girl, and sometimes you insist that you are. What I am curious to know is: How do you really view yourself? As one or the other? As both? As neither?"

I make my voice flat and factual, like hers. "I see no reason to provide that information."

I hear a faint snort. Peter is covering his mouth. Jeanine glares at him, and his laughter effortlessly transforms into a coughing fit.

"Mockery is childish, Beatrice," she says. "It does not become you."

"*Mockery is childish, Beatrice,*" I repeat in my best imitation of her voice. "*It does not become you.*"

"The serum," Jeanine says, eyeing Peter. He steps forward and fumbles with a black box on the desk, taking out a syringe with a needle already attached to it.

Peter starts toward me, and I hold out my hand.

"Allow me," I say.

He looks at Jeanine for permission, and she says, "All right, then." He hands me the syringe and I shove the needle into the side of my neck, pressing down on the plunger. Jeanine jabs one of the buttons with her finger, and everything goes dark.

+ + +

My mother stands in the aisle with her arm stretched above her head so she can hold the bar. Her face is turned, not toward the people sitting around me, but toward the city we pass as the bus lurches forward. I see wrinkles in her forehead and around her mouth when she frowns.

"What is it?" I ask her.

"There is so much to be done," she says with a small gesture toward the bus windows. "And so few of us left to do it."

It is clear what she's referring to. Beyond the bus is rubble as far as I can see. Across the street, a building lies in ruins. Fragments of glass litter the alleyways. I wonder what caused so much destruction.

"Where are we going?" I say.

She smiles at me, and I see different wrinkles than before, at the corners of her eyes. "We're going to Erudite headquarters."

I frown. Most of my life has been spent avoiding Erudite headquarters. My father used to say that he didn't even like to breathe the air in there. "Why are we going there?"

"They're going to help us."

Why do I feel a pang in my stomach when I think of my father? I picture his face, weathered by a lifetime of frustration with the world around him, and his hair, kept short by Abnegation standard practice, and feel the same kind of pain in my stomach that I get when I have not eaten in too long—a hollow pain.

"Did something happen to Dad?" I say.

She shakes her head. "Why would you ask that?"

"I don't know."

I don't feel the pain when I look at my mother. But I do feel like every second we spend standing these inches apart is one that I must impress upon my mind until my entire memory conforms to its shape. But if she is not permanent, what is she?

The bus stops, and the doors creak open. My mother starts down the aisle, and I follow her. She is taller than I am, so I stare between her shoulders, at the top of her spine. She looks fragile, but she is not.

I step down onto the pavement. Pieces of glass crinkle beneath my feet. They are blue and, judging by the holes in the building to my right, used to be windows.

"What happened?"

"War," my mother says. "This is what we've been trying so hard to avoid."

"And the Erudite will help us . . . by doing what?"

"I worry that all your father's blustering about Erudite has been to your detriment," she says gently. "They've made mistakes, of course, but they, like everyone else, are a blend of good and bad, not one or the other. What would we do without our doctors, our scientists, our teachers?"

She smooths down my hair.

"Take care to remember that, Beatrice."

"I will," I promise.

We keep walking. But something about what she said bothers me. Is it what she said about my father? No—my father is always complaining about Erudite. Is it what she said about Erudite? I hop over a large shard of glass. No, that can't be it. She was right about Erudite. All my teachers were Erudite, and so was the doctor who set my mother's arm when she broke it several years ago.

It's the last part. "Take care to remember." As if she won't have the opportunity to remind me later.

I feel something shift in my mind, like something that was closed has just opened.

"Mom?" I say.

She looks back at me. A lock of blond hair falls from its knot and touches her cheek.

"I love you."

I point at a window to my left, and it explodes. Particles of glass rain over us.

I don't want to wake up in a room in Erudite headquarters, so I don't open my eyes right away, not even when the simulation fades. I try to preserve the image of my mother and the hair sticking to her cheekbone for as long as I can. But when all I see is the redness of my own eyelids, I open them.

"You'll have to do better than that," I say to Jeanine.

She says, "That was only the beginning."

CHAPTER
THIRTY-ONE

THAT NIGHT I dream, not of Tobias, and not of Will, but of my mother. We stand in the Amity orchards, where the apples are ripe and dangle just inches above our heads. Leaf shadows pattern her face, and she wears black, though I never saw her in black when she was alive. She is teaching me to braid hair, demonstrating on a lock of her own, laughing when my fingers fumble.

I wake wondering how I did not notice, every day I sat across from her at the breakfast table, that she was full to bursting with Dauntless energy. Was it because she hid it well? Or was it because I wasn't looking?

I bury my face in the thin mattress I slept on. I will never know her. But at least she will never know what I did to Will, either. At this point I don't think I could bear it if she did.

I am still blinking the haze of sleep from my eyes when I follow Peter down the corridor, seconds or minutes later, I can't tell.

"Peter." My throat aches; I must have screamed while I slept. "What time is it?"

He wears a watch, but the face is covered, so I can't see it. He doesn't even bother to look at it.

"Why are you constantly escorting me places?" I say. "Isn't there a depraved activity you're supposed to be taking part in? Kicking puppies or spying on girls while they change, or something?"

"I know what you did to Will, you know. Don't pretend that you're better than I am, because you and I, we're exactly the same."

The only thing that distinguishes one hallway from another, here, is their length. I decide to label them according to how many steps I take before I turn. Ten. Forty-seven. Twenty-nine.

"You're wrong," I say. "We may both be bad, but there's a huge difference between us—I'm not content with being this way."

Peter snorts a little, and we walk between the Erudite lab tables. That's when I realize where I am, and where we're going: back to the room Jeanine showed me. The room where I will be executed. I shudder so hard my teeth chatter, and it's difficult to keep walking, hard to keep my thoughts straight. *It's just a room,* I tell myself. *Just a room like any other room.*

I am such a liar.

This time the execution chamber is not empty. Four Dauntless traitors mill around in one corner, and two of the Erudite, one a dark-skinned woman, one an older man, both wearing lab coats, stand with Jeanine near the metal table in the center. Several machines are set up around it, and there are wires everywhere.

I don't know what most of those machines do, but among them is a heart monitor. What does Jeanine plan to do that requires a heart monitor?

"Get her on the table," says Jeanine, sounding bored. I stare for a second at the sheet of steel that awaits me. What if she changed her mind about waiting to execute me? What if this is when I die? Peter's hands clamp around my arms and I writhe, throwing all my strength into the struggle.

But he just lifts me up, dodging my kicking feet, and slams me down on the metal slab, knocking the wind out of me. I gasp, and fling a fist out at whatever I can hit, which just happens to be Peter's wrist. He winces, but by now the other Dauntless traitors have come forward to help.

One of them holds down my ankles, and the other holds down my shoulders as Peter pulls black straps across my body to keep me pinned. I flinch at the pain in my wounded shoulder and stop struggling.

"What the hell is going on?" I demand, craning my neck to look at Jeanine. "We agreed—cooperation in exchange for results! We *agreed*—"

"This is entirely separate from our agreement," says Jeanine, glancing at her watch. "This is not about you, Beatrice."

The door opens again.

Tobias walks in—*limps* in—flanked by Dauntless traitors. His face is bruised and there's a cut above his eyebrow. He does not move with his usual care; he's holding himself perfectly straight. He must be injured. I try not to think about how he got that way.

"What is this?" he says, his voice rough and creaky.

From screaming, probably.

My throat feels swollen.

"Tris," he says, and he lurches toward me, but the Dauntless traitors are too quick. They grab him before he can move more than a few steps. "Tris, are you okay?"

"Yeah," I say. "Are you?"

He nods. I don't believe him.

"Rather than waste any more time, Mr. Eaton, I thought I would take the most logical approach. Truth serum would be preferable, of course, but it would take days to coerce Jack Kang into handing some over, as it is jealously guarded by the Candor, and I'd rather not waste a few days." She steps forward, a syringe in hand. This serum is tinted gray. It could be a new version of the simulation serum, but I doubt it.

I wonder what it does. It can't be good, if she looks this pleased with herself.

"In a few seconds, I will inject Tris with this liquid. At that point, I trust, your selfless instincts will take over and you will tell me exactly what I need to know."

"What does she need to know?" I say, interrupting her.

"Information about the factionless safe houses," he replies without looking at me.

My eyes widen. The factionless are the last hope any of us has, now that half the loyal Dauntless and all the Candor are simulation-ready, and half the Abnegation are dead.

"Don't give it to her. I'm going to die anyway. Don't give her anything."

"Remind me, Mr. Eaton," says Jeanine. "What do Dauntless simulations do?"

"This isn't a classroom," he replies through gritted teeth. "Tell me what you're going to do."

"I will if you answer my very simple question."

"Fine." Tobias's eyes shift to me. "The simulations stimulate the amygdala, which is responsible for processing fear, induce a hallucination based on that fear, and then transmit the data to a computer to be processed and observed."

It sounds like he's had that memorized for a long time. Maybe he has—he did spend a lot of time running simulations.

"Very good," she says. "When I was developing the Dauntless simulations, years ago, we discovered that certain levels of potency overwhelmed the brain and made it too insensible with terror to invent new surroundings, which was when we diluted the solution so that the simulations would be more instructive. But I still remember how to make it."

She taps the syringe with her fingernail.

"Fear," she says, "is more powerful than pain. So is there anything you'd like to say, before I inject Ms. Prior?"

Tobias presses his lips together.

And Jeanine inserts the needle.

+ + +

It begins quietly, with the pounding of a heart. I am not sure, at first, whose heartbeat I'm hearing, because it's far too loud to be my own. But then I realize that it is my own, and it's getting faster and faster.

Sweat collects in my palms and behind my knees.

And then I have to gasp in order to breathe.

That's when the screaming starts

And I

Can't

Think.

+ + +

Tobias is fighting the Dauntless traitors by the door.

I hear what sounds like a child's scream beside me, and wrench my head around to see where it's coming from, but there is only a heart monitor. Above me the lines between the ceiling tiles warp and twist into monstrous creatures. The scent of rotting flesh fills the air and I gag. The monstrous creatures take on a more definite shape—they are birds, crows, with beaks as long as my forearm and wings so dark they seem to swallow all the light.

"Tris," says Tobias. I look away from the crows.

He stands by the door, where he was before I was injected, but now he has a knife. He holds it out from his body and turns it so the blade points in, at his stomach. Then he brings it toward himself, touching the tip of the blade to his stomach.

"What are you doing? Stop!"

He smiles a little and says, "I'm doing this for you."

He pushes the knife in farther, slow, and blood stains the hem of his shirt. I gag, and throw myself against the bonds holding me to the table. "No, stop!" I thrash and in a simulation I would have pulled free by now so this must mean that this is real, it's real. I scream and he sticks the knife in to the handle. He collapses to the floor and his blood spills fast and surrounds him. The shadow-birds turn their beady eyes on him and swarm in a tornado of wings and talons, pecking at his skin. I see his eyes through the whirling feathers and he is still awake.

A bird lands on the fingers that hold the knife. He draws it out again and it clatters to the ground and I should hope that he is dead but I'm selfish so I can't. My back lifts from the table and all my muscles clench and my throat aches from this scream that no longer shapes itself into words and will not stop.

+ + +

"Sedative," a stern voice commands.

Another needle in my neck, and my heart begins to slow down. I sob with relief. For seconds all I can do is sob with relief.

That was not fear. That was something else; an emotion that should not exist.

"Let me go," Tobias says, and he sounds scratchier than before. I blink fast so I can see him through my tears. There are red marks on his arms from where the Dauntless traitors held him back, but he is not dying; he is all right. "That's the only way I'll tell you, is if you let me go."

Jeanine nods, and he runs to me. He wraps one hand around mine and touches my hair with the other. His fingertips come away wet with tears. He doesn't wipe them off. He leans over and presses his forehead to mine.

"The factionless safe houses," he says dully, right against my cheek. "Get me a map and I'll mark them for you."

His forehead feels cool and dry against mine. My muscles ache, probably from being clenched for however long Jeanine left me with that serum pulsing through me.

He pulls back, his fingers wrapped around my fingers for as long as they can be until the Dauntless traitors pull him from my grasp to escort him elsewhere. My hand falls heavy on the table. I don't want to struggle against the restraints anymore. All I want to do is sleep.

"While you're here . . ." Jeanine says once Tobias and his escorts are gone. She looks up and focuses her watery eyes on one of the Erudite. "Get him and bring him in here. It's time."

She looks back down at me.

"While you sleep, we will be performing a short procedure to observe a few things about your brain. It will not be invasive. But before that . . . I promised you full transparency with these procedures. So I feel it's only fair that you know exactly who has been assisting me in my endeavors." She smiles a little. "Who told me what three factions you had an aptitude for, and what our best chance was to get you to come here, and to put your mother in the last simulation to make it more effective."

She looks toward the doorway as the sedative sets in, making everything blur at the edges. I look over my shoulder, and through the haze of drugs I see him.

Caleb.

CHAPTER
THIRTY-TWO

I WAKE TO a headache. I try to go back to sleep—at least when I'm asleep, I'm calm—but the image of Caleb standing in the doorway runs through my mind over and over again, accompanied by the sound of squawking crows.

Why did I never wonder how Eric and Jeanine knew that I had aptitude for three factions?

Why did it never occur to me that only three people in the world knew that particular fact: Tori, Caleb, and Tobias?

My head pounds. I can't make sense of it. I don't know why Caleb would betray me. I wonder when it happened—after the attack simulation? After the escape from Amity? Or was it earlier than that—was it back when my father was still alive? Caleb told us he left Erudite when he found out what they were planning—was he lying?

He must have been. I press the heel of my hand to my forehead. My brother chose faction over blood. There has to be a reason. She must have threatened him. Or coerced him in some way.

The door opens. I don't lift my head or open my eyes.

"Stiff." It's Peter. Of course.

"Yes." When I let my hand fall from my face, a lock of hair falls with it. I look at it from the corner of my eye. My hair has never been this greasy before.

Peter sets a bottle of water next to the bed, and a sandwich. The thought of eating it nauseates me.

"You brain-dead?" he asks.

"Don't think so."

"Don't be so sure."

"Ha-ha," I say. "How long have I been asleep?"

"About a day. I'm supposed to escort you to the showers."

"If you say something about how badly I need one," I say tiredly, "I *will* poke you in the eye."

The room spins when I lift my head, but I manage to put my legs over the edge of the bed and stand. Peter and I start down the hallway. When we turn the corner to get to the bathroom, though, there are people at the end of the hallway.

One of them is Tobias. I can see where our paths will intersect, between where I stand now and my cell door. I stare, not at him but at where he will be when he reaches for my hand, as he did the last time we passed each other. My skin tingles with anticipation. For just a moment, I will touch him again.

Six steps until we pass each other. Five steps.

At four steps, though, Tobias stops. His entire body goes limp, catching his Dauntless traitor escort off guard. The guard loses his grip on him for just a second, and Tobias crumples to the floor.

Then he twists around. Lurches forward. And grabs a gun from the shorter Dauntless traitor's holster.

The gun goes off. Peter dives to the right, dragging me with him. My head skims the wall. The Dauntless guard's mouth is open—he must be screaming. I can't hear him.

Tobias kicks him hard in the stomach. The Dauntless in me admires his form—perfect—and his speed—incredible. Then he turns, training the gun on Peter. But Peter has already released me.

Tobias reaches for my left arm, helps me to my feet, and starts running. I stumble after him. Each time my foot hits the ground, pain slices into my head, but I can't stop. I blink tears from my eyes. *Run,* I tell myself, as if that will make it easier. Tobias's hand is rough and strong. I let it guide me around a corner.

"Tobias," I wheeze.

He stops, and looks back at me. "Oh no," he says, brushing my cheek with his fingers. "Come on. On my back."

He bends, and I put my arms around his neck, burying my face between his shoulder blades. He lifts me without difficulty and holds on to my leg with his left hand. His right hand still holds the gun.

He runs, and even with my weight, he is fast. Idly I think, *How could he ever have been Abnegation?* He seems designed specifically for speed and deadly accuracy. But not strength, not particularly—he is smart, but not strong. Only strong enough to carry me.

The hallways are empty now, but not for long. Soon every Dauntless in the building will rush toward us from every angle, and we will be trapped in this pale maze. I wonder how Tobias plans to get past them.

I lift my head long enough to see that he just ran past an exit.

"Tobias, you missed it."

"Missed . . . what?" he says between breaths.

"An exit."

"Not trying to escape. We'd get shot if we did," he says. "Trying to . . . find something."

I would suspect that I'm dreaming if the pain in my head wasn't so intense. Usually only my dreams make this little sense. Why, if he was not trying to escape, did he take me with him? And what is he doing, if not escaping?

He stops abruptly, almost dropping me, as he reaches a wide hallway with panes of glass on either side, revealing offices. The Erudite sit frozen at their desks, staring at us. Tobias pays no attention to them; his eyes, as far as I can tell, are fixed on the door at the end of the corridor. A sign outside the door says CONTROL-A.

Tobias searches every corner of the room, and then shoots at the camera attached to the ceiling on our right. The camera drops. He shoots at the camera attached to the ceiling on our left. Its lens shatters.

"Time to get down," he says. "No more running, I promise."

I slide off his back and take his hand instead. He walks toward a closed door that we passed already, and into a supply closet. He shuts the door and wedges a busted chair under the doorknob. I face him, a shelf stacked with paper at my back. Above us, the blue light flickers. His eyes roam over my face almost hungrily.

"I don't have much time, so I'm going to be direct," he says.

I nod.

"I didn't come here on some suicide mission," he says. "I came for two reasons. The first was to find Erudite's two central control rooms so that when we invade, we'll know what to destroy first to get rid of all the simulation data, so she can't activate the Dauntless's transmitters."

That explains the running without escaping. And we found a control room, at the end of that hallway.

I stare at him, still dazed from the past few minutes.

"The second," he says, clearing his throat, "is to make sure you hold on, because we have a plan."

"What plan?"

"According to one of our insiders, your execution is tentatively scheduled for two weeks from today," he says. "At least, that's Jeanine's target date for the new, Divergent-proof simulation. So fourteen days from now, the factionless, the loyal Dauntless, and the Abnegation who are willing to fight will storm the Erudite compound and take out their best weapon—their computer system. That means we'll outnumber the traitor Dauntless, and therefore the Erudite."

"But you told Jeanine where the factionless safe houses were."

"Yeah." He frowns a little. "That is problematic. But as you and I know, a lot of the factionless are Divergent, and many of them were already moving toward the Abnegation sector when I left, so only some of the safe houses will be affected. So they will still have a huge population to contribute to the invasion."

Two weeks. Will I be able to make it through two weeks of this? I am already so tired I'm finding it difficult to stand on my own. Even the rescue that Tobias is proposing barely appeals to me. I don't want freedom. I want sleep. I want this to end.

"I don't . . ." I choke on the words and start to cry. "I can't . . . make it . . . that long."

"Tris," he says sternly. He never coddles me. I wish that, just this once, he would coddle me. "You have to. You have to survive this."

"Why?" The question forms in my stomach and launches from my throat like a moan. I feel like thumping my fists against his chest, like a child throwing a tantrum. Tears cover my cheeks, and I know I'm acting ridiculous but I can't stop. "Why do I have to? Why can't someone else do something for once? What if I don't want to do this anymore?"

And what *this* is, I realize, is life. I don't want it. I want my parents and I have for weeks. I've been trying to claw my way back to them, and now I am so close and he is telling me not to.

"I know." I have never heard his voice sound so soft. "I know it's hard. The hardest thing you've had to do."

I shake my head.

"I can't force you. I can't make you want to survive this." He pulls me against him and runs his hand over my hair, tucking it behind my ear. His fingers trail down my neck and over my shoulder, and he says, "But you will do it. It doesn't matter if you believe you can or not. You will, because that's who you are."

I pull back and fit my mouth to his, not gently, not hesitantly. I kiss him like I used to, when I felt sure of us, and run my hands over his back, down his arms, like I used to.

I don't want to tell him the truth: that he is wrong, and I do not want to survive this.

The door opens. Dauntless traitors crowd into the supply closet. Tobias steps back, turns the gun in his hand, and offers it, handle first, to the nearest Dauntless traitor.

CHAPTER
THIRTY-THREE

"BEATRICE."

I jerk awake. The room I am in now—for whatever experiment they want to run on me—is large, with screens along the back wall and blue lights glowing just above the floor and rows of padded benches across the middle. I'm sitting on the farthest bench back with Peter at my left shoulder, my head leaning against the wall. I still can't seem to get enough sleep.

Now I wish I hadn't woken up. Caleb stands a few feet away, his weight on one foot, an uncertain posture.

"Did you *ever* leave Erudite?" I say.

"It's not that simple," he starts. "I—"

"It is that simple." I want to yell, but instead my voice comes out flat. "At what point did you betray our family? Before our parents died, or after?"

"I did what I had to do. You think you understand this, Beatrice, but you don't. This whole situation . . . it's much bigger than you think it is." His eyes plead with me to understand, but I recognize his tone—it's the one he employed when we were younger, to scold me. It is condescending.

Arrogance is one of the flaws in the Erudite heart—I know. It is often in mine.

But greed is the other. And I do not have that. So I am halfway in and halfway out, as always.

I push myself to my feet. "You still haven't answered my question."

Caleb steps back.

"This isn't about Erudite; it's about everyone. All the factions," he says, "and the city. And what's outside the fence."

"I don't care," I say, but that isn't true. The phrase "outside the fence" prickles in my brain. Outside? How could any of this have to do with what's outside?

Something itches at the back of my mind. Marcus said that information the Abnegation possessed motivated Jeanine's attack on Abnegation. Does that information have to do with what's outside, too?

I push the thought away for the time being.

"I thought you were all about facts. About freedom of information? Well, how about *this* fact, Caleb? When—" My voice quakes. "*When* did you betray our parents?"

"I have always been Erudite," he says softly. "Even when I was supposed to be Abnegation."

"If you're with Jeanine, then I hate you. Just like our father would have."

"Our father." Caleb snorts a little. "Our father *was* Erudite, Beatrice. Jeanine told me—he was in her year at school."

"He wasn't Erudite," I say after a few seconds. "He chose to leave them. He chose a different identity, just like you, and became something else. Only you chose this . . . this *evil.*"

"Spoken like a true Dauntless," says Caleb sharply. "It's either one way or the other way. No nuances. The world doesn't *work* like that, Beatrice. Evil depends on where you're standing."

"No matter where I stand, I'll still think mind controlling an entire city of people is evil." I feel my lip wobble. "I'll still think delivering your sister to be prodded and executed is evil!"

He is my brother, but I want to tear him to pieces.

Instead of trying to, though, I find myself sitting down again. I could never hurt him enough to make his betrayal stop hurting. And it *hurts*, in every part of my body. I press my fingers to my chest to massage some of the smarting tension away.

Jeanine and her army of Erudite scientists and Dauntless traitors walk in just as I wipe tears from my cheeks. I blink rapidly so she won't see. She barely even gives me a glance.

"Let us view the results, shall we?" she announces. Caleb, now standing by the screens, presses something at the front of the room, and the screens turn on. Words and numbers I don't understand fill them.

"We discovered something extremely interesting, Ms. Prior." I have never seen her so cheerful before. She almost smiles—but not quite. "You have an abundance of a particular kind of neuron, called, quite simply, a mirror neuron. Would someone like to explain to Ms. Prior exactly what mirror neurons do?"

The Erudite scientists raise their hands in unison. She points to an older woman in the front.

"Mirror neurons fire both when one performs an action and when one sees another person performing that action. They allow us to imitate behavior."

"What else are they responsible for?" Jeanine scans her "class" the same way my teachers did in Upper Levels. Another Erudite raises his hand.

"Learning language, understanding other people's intentions based on their behavior, um . . ." He frowns. "And empathy."

"More specifically," Jeanine says, and this time she does smile at me, broadly, forcing creases into her cheeks, "someone with many, strong mirror neurons could have a flexible personality—capable of mimicking others as the situation calls for it rather than remaining constant."

I understand why she smiles. I feel like my mind is cracked open, its secrets spilling over the floor for me to finally see.

"A flexible personality," she says, "would probably have aptitude for more than one faction, don't you agree, Ms. Prior?"

"Probably," I say. "Now if only you could get a simulation to suppress that particular ability, we could be done with this."

"One thing at a time." She pauses. "I must admit, it confuses me that you are so eager for your own execution."

"No, it doesn't." I close my eyes. "It doesn't confuse you at all." I sigh. "Can I go back to my cell now?"

I must seem nonchalant, but I'm not. I want to go back to my room so that I can cry in peace. But I don't want her to know that.

"Don't get too comfortable," she chirps. "We'll have a simulation serum to try out soon."

"Yeah," I say. "Whatever."

+ + +

Someone shakes my shoulder. I jerk awake, my eyes wide and searching, and I see Tobias kneeling over me. He wears a Dauntless traitor jacket, and one side of his head is coated with blood. The blood streams from a wound on his ear—the top of his ear is gone. I wince.

"What happened?" I say.

"Get up. We have to run."

"It's too soon. It hasn't been two weeks."

"I don't have time to explain. Come on."

"Oh God. Tobias."

I sit up and wrap my arms around him, pressing my face into his neck. His arms tighten around me and squeeze. Warmth courses through me, and comfort. If he is here, that means I'm safe. My tears make his skin slippery.

He stands and pulls me to my feet, which makes my wounded shoulder throb.

"Reinforcements will be here soon. Come on."

I let him lead me out of the room. We make it down the first hallway without difficulty, but in the second hallway, we encounter two Dauntless guards, one a young man and one a middle-aged woman. Tobias fires twice in a matter of seconds, both hits, one in the head and one in the chest. The woman, who was hit in the chest, slumps against the wall but doesn't die.

We keep moving. One hallway, then another, all of them look the same. Tobias's grip on my hand never falters. I know that if he can throw a knife so that it hits just the tip of my ear, he can fire accurately at the Dauntless soldiers who ambush us. We step over fallen bodies—the people Tobias killed on the way in, probably—and finally reach a fire exit.

Tobias lets go of my hand to open the door, and the fire alarm screeches in my ears, but we keep running. I am gasping for air but I don't care, not when I'm finally escaping, not when this nightmare is finally over. My vision starts to go black at the edges, so I grab Tobias's arm and hold on tight, trusting him to lead me safely to the bottom of the stairs.

I run out of steps to run down, and I open my eyes. Tobias is about to open the exit door, but I hold him back. "Got to . . . catch my breath. . . ."

He pauses, and I put my hands on my knees, leaning over. My shoulder still throbs. I frown, and look up at him.

"Come on, let's get out of here," he says insistently.

My stomach sinks. I stare into his eyes. They are dark blue, with a patch of light blue on his right iris.

I take his chin in hand and pull his lips down to mine, kissing him slowly, sighing as I pull back.

"We can't get out of here," I say. "Because this is a simulation."

He pulled me to my feet with my right hand. The real Tobias would have remembered the wound in my shoulder.

"What?" He scowls at me. "Don't you think I would know if I was under a simulation?"

"You aren't under a simulation. You *are* the simulation." I look up and say in a loud voice, "You'll have to do better than that, Jeanine."

All I have to do now is wake up, and I know how—I have done it before, in my fear landscape, when I broke a glass tank just by touching my palm to it, or when I made a gun appear in the grass to shoot descending birds. I take a knife from my pocket—a knife that wasn't there a moment ago—and will my leg to be hard as diamond.

I thrust the knife toward my thigh, and the blade bends.

+ + +

I wake with tears in my eyes. I wake to Jeanine's scream of frustration.

"What is it?" She grabs Peter's gun out of his hand and stalks across the room, pressing the barrel to my forehead. My body stiffens, goes cold. She won't shoot me. I am a problem she can't solve. She won't shoot me.

"What is it that clues you in? Tell me. Tell me or I will kill you."

I slowly push myself up from the chair, coming to my feet, pushing my skin harder into the cold barrel.

"You think I'm going to tell you?" I say. "You think I believe that you would kill me without figuring out the answer to this question?"

"You stupid girl," she says. "You think this is about you, and your abnormal brain? This is not about you. It is not about me. It is about keeping this city safe from the people who intend to plunge it into hell!"

I summon the last of my strength and launch myself at her, clawing at whatever skin my fingernails find, digging in as hard as I can. She screams at the top of her lungs, a sound that turns my blood into fire. I punch her hard in the face.

A pair of arms wrap around me, pulling me off her, and a fist meets my side. I groan, and lunge toward her, held at bay by Peter.

"Pain can't make me tell you. Truth serum can't make me tell you. Simulations can't make me tell you. I'm immune to all three."

Her nose is bleeding, and I see lines of fingernail scrapes in her cheeks, on the side of her throat, turning red with blossoming blood. She glares at me, pinching her nose closed, her hair disheveled, her free hand trembling.

"You have *failed*. You can't control me!" I scream, so loud it hurts my throat. I stop struggling and sag against Peter's chest. "You will *never* be able to control me."

I laugh, mirthless, a mad laugh. I savor the scowl on her face, the hate in her eyes. She was like a machine; she was cold and emotionless, bound by logic alone. And I broke her.

I broke her.

CHAPTER
THIRTY-FOUR

ONCE I'M IN the hallway, I stop struggling toward Jeanine. My side throbs from where Peter punched me, but it's nothing compared to the pulse of triumph in my cheeks.

Peter walks me back to my cell without a word. I stand in the middle of the room for a long time, staring at the camera in the back-left corner. Who is watching me all the time? Is it Dauntless traitors, guarding me, or the Erudite, observing me?

Once the heat leaves my face and my side stops hurting, I lie down.

A picture of my parents floats into my head the moment I close my eyes. Once, when I was about eleven, I stopped at the doorway to my parents' bedroom to watch them make the bed together. My father smiled at my mother as they pulled the sheets back and smoothed them down in perfect synchronicity. I knew by the way he looked at her that he held her in a higher regard than he held even himself.

No selfishness or insecurity kept him from seeing the full extent of her goodness, as it so often does with the rest of us. That kind of love may only be possible in Abnegation. I do not know.

My father: Erudite-born, Abnegation-grown. He often found it difficult to live up to the demands of his chosen faction, just as I did. But he tried, and he knew true selflessness when he saw it.

I clutch my pillow to my chest and bury my face in it. I don't cry. I just ache.

Grief is not as heavy as guilt, but it takes more away from you.

+ + +

"Stiff."

I wake with a start, my hands still clutching the pillow. There is a wet patch on the mattress under my face. I sit up, wiping my eyes with my fingertips.

Peter's eyebrows, which usually turn up in the middle, are furrowed.

"What happened?" Whatever it is, it can't be good.

"Your execution has been scheduled for tomorrow morning at eight o'clock."

"My execution? But she . . . she hasn't developed the right simulation yet; she couldn't *possibly* . . ."

"She said that she will continue the experiments on Tobias instead of you," he says.

All I can say is: "Oh."

I clutch the mattress and rock forward and back, forward and back. Tomorrow my life will be over. Tobias may survive long enough to escape in the factionless invasion. The Dauntless will elect a new leader. All the loose ends I will leave will be easily tied up.

I nod. No family left, no loose ends, no great loss.

"I could have forgiven you, you know," I say. "For trying to kill me during initiation. I probably could have."

We are both quiet for a while. I don't know why I told him that. Maybe just because it's true, and tonight, of all nights, is the time for honesty. Tonight I will be honest, and selfless, and brave. Divergent.

"I never asked you to," he says, and turns to leave. But then he stops at the door frame and says, "It's 9:24."

Telling me the time is a small act of betrayal—and therefore an ordinary act of bravery. It is maybe the first time I've seen Peter be truly Dauntless.

+ + +

I'm going to die tomorrow. It has been a long time since I felt certainty about anything, so this feels like a gift. Tonight, nothing. Tomorrow, whatever comes after life. And Jeanine still doesn't know how to control the Divergent.

When I start to cry, I clutch the pillow to my chest and let it happen. I cry hard, like a child cries, until my face is hot and I feel like I might be sick. I can pretend to be brave, but I'm not.

I suppose that now would be the time to ask for forgiveness for all the things I've done, but I'm sure my list would never be complete. I also don't believe that whatever comes after life depends on my correctly reciting a list of my transgressions—that sounds too much like an Erudite afterlife to me, all accuracy and no feeling. I don't believe that what comes after depends on anything I do at all.

I am better off doing as Abnegation taught me: turning away from myself, projecting always outward, and hoping that in whatever is next, I will be better than I am now.

I smile a little. I wish I could tell my parents that I will die like the Abnegation. They would be proud, I think.

CHAPTER
THIRTY-FIVE

THIS MORNING I put on the clean clothes I am given: black pants—too loose, but who cares?—and a long-sleeved black shirt. No shoes.

It is not time yet. I find myself lacing my fingers together and bowing my head. Sometimes my father did this in the morning before sitting down at the breakfast table, but I never asked him what he was doing. Still, I would like to feel like I belong to my father again before I . . . well, before it's over.

A few silent moments later, Peter tells me it's time to go. He barely looks at me, scowls at the back wall instead. I suppose it would have been too much to ask, to see a friendly face this morning. I stand, and together we walk down the hallway.

My toes are cold. My feet stick to the tiles. We turn a corner, and I hear muffled shouts. At first I can't tell what the voice is saying, but as we draw closer, it takes shape.

"I want to . . . her!" Tobias. "I . . . *see* her!"

I glance at Peter. "I can't speak to him one last time, can I?"

Peter shakes his head. "There's a window, though. Maybe if he sees you he'll finally shut up."

He takes me down a dead-end corridor that's only six feet long. At the end is a door, and Peter is right, there's a small window near the top, about a foot above my head.

"Tris!" Tobias's voice is even clearer here. "I want to see her!"

I reach up and press my palm to the glass. The shouts stop, and his face appears behind the glass. His eyes are red; his face, blotchy. Handsome. He stares down at me for a few seconds and then presses his hand to the glass so it lines up with mine. I pretend I can feel the warmth of it through the window.

He leans his forehead against the door and squeezes his eyes shut.

I take my hand down and turn away before he can open his eyes. I feel pain in my chest, worse than when I got shot in the shoulder. I clutch the front of my shirt, blink away tears, and rejoin Peter in the main hallway.

"Thank you," I say quietly. I meant to say it louder.

"Whatever." Peter scowls again. "Let's just go."

I hear rumbling somewhere ahead of us—the sound of a crowd. The next hallway is packed with Dauntless traitors, tall and short, young and old, armed and unarmed. They all wear the blue armband of betrayal.

"Hey!" Peter shouts. "Clear a path!"

The Dauntless traitors closest to us hear him, and press against the walls to make way for us. The other Dauntless traitors follow suit soon after, and everyone is quiet. Peter steps back to let me go ahead of him. I know the way from here.

I don't know where the pounding starts, but someone drums their fists against the wall, and someone else joins in, and I walk down the aisle between solemn-but-raucous Dauntless traitors, their hands in motion at their sides. The pounding is so fast my heart races to keep up with it.

Some of the Dauntless traitors incline their heads to me—I'm not sure why. It doesn't matter.

I reach the end of the hallway and open the door to my execution chamber.

I open it.

Dauntless traitors crowded the hallway; the Erudite crowd the execution room, but there, they have made a path for me already. Silently they study me as I walk to the metal table in the center of the room. Jeanine stands a few steps away. The scratches on her face show through hastily applied makeup. She doesn't look at me.

Four cameras dangle from the ceiling, one at each corner of the table. I sit down first, wipe my hands off on my pants, and then lie down.

The table is cold. Frigid, seeping into my skin, into my bones. Appropriate, perhaps, because that is what will happen to my body when all the life leaves it; it will become cold and heavy, heavier than I have ever been. As for the rest of me, I am not sure. Some people believe that I will go nowhere, and maybe they're right, but maybe they're not. Such speculations are no longer useful to me anyway.

Peter slips an electrode beneath the collar of my shirt and presses it to my chest, right over my heart. He then attaches a wire to the electrode and switches on the heart monitor. I hear my heartbeat, fast and strong. Soon, where that steady rhythm was, there will be nothing.

And then rising from within me is a single thought:

I don't want to die.

All those times Tobias scolded me for risking my life, I never took him seriously. I believed that I wanted to be with my parents and for all of this to be over. I was sure I wanted to emulate their self-sacrifice. But no. No, no.

Burning and boiling inside me is the desire to live.

I don't want to die I don't want to die I don't want to!

Jeanine steps forward with a syringe full of purple serum. Her glasses reflect the fluorescent light above us, so I can barely see her eyes.

Every part of my body chants it in unison. *Live, live, live.* I thought that in order to give my life in exchange for Will's, in exchange for my parents', that I needed to die, but I was wrong; I need to live my life in the light of their deaths. I need to live.

Jeanine holds my head steady with one hand and inserts the needle into my neck with the other.

I'm not done! I shout in my head, and not at Jeanine. *I am not done here!*

She presses the plunger down. Peter leans forward and looks into my eyes.

"The serum will go into effect in one minute," he says. "Be brave, Tris."

The words startle me, because that is exactly what Tobias said when he put me under my first simulation.

My heart begins to race.

Why would Peter tell me to be brave? Why would he offer any kind words at all?

All the muscles in my body relax at once. A heavy, liquid feeling fills my limbs. If this is death, it isn't so bad. My eyes stay open, but my head drops to the side. I try to close my eyes, but I can't—I can't move.

Then the heart monitor stops beeping.

CHAPTER
THIRTY-SIX

BUT I'M STILL breathing. Not deeply; not enough to satisfy, but *breathing*. Peter pushes my eyelids over my eyes. Does he know I'm not dead? Does Jeanine? Can she see me breathing?

"Take the body to the lab," Jeanine says. "The autopsy is scheduled for this afternoon."

"All right," Peter replies.

Peter pushes the table forward. I hear mutters all around me as we pass the group of Erudite bystanders. My hand falls off the edge of the table as we turn a corner, and smacks into the wall. I feel a prickle of pain in my fingertips, but I can't move my hand, as hard as I try.

This time, when we go down the hallway of Dauntless traitors, it is silent. Peter walks slowly at first, then turns another corner and picks up the pace. He almost sprints down the next corridor, and stops abruptly. Where am I? I can't be in the lab already. Why did he stop?

Peter's arms slide under my knees and shoulders, and he lifts me. My head falls against his shoulder.

"For someone so small, you're *heavy*, Stiff," he mutters.

He knows I'm awake. He *knows*.

I hear a series of beeps, and a slide—a locked door, opening.

"What do—" Tobias's voice. *Tobias!* "Oh my God. Oh—"

"Spare me your blubbering, okay?" Peter says. "She's not dead; she's just paralyzed. It'll only last for about a minute. Now get ready to run."

I don't understand.

How does Peter know?

"Let me carry her," Tobias says.

"No. You're a better shot than I am. Take my gun. I'll carry her."

I hear the gun slide out of its holster. Tobias brushes a hand over my forehead. They both start running.

At first all I hear is the pounding of their feet, and my head snaps back painfully. I feel tingling in my hands and feet. Peter shouts, "Left!" at Tobias.

Then a shout from down the hallway. "Hey, what—!"

A bang. And nothing.

More running. Peter shouts, "Right!" I hear another bang, and another. "Whoa," he mumbles. "Wait, stop here!"

Tingling down my spine. I open my eyes as Peter opens another door. He charges through it, and just before I smack my head against the door frame, I stick my arm out and stop us.

"Careful!" I say, my voice strained. My throat still feels as tight as it did when he first injected me and I found it difficult to breathe. Peter turns sideways to bring me through the door, then nudges it shut with his heel and drops me on the floor.

The room is almost empty, except for a row of empty trash cans along one wall and a square metal door large enough for one of the cans to fit through it along the other wall.

"Tris," Tobias says, crouching next to me. His face is pale, almost yellow.

There is too much I want to say. The first thing that comes out is, "Beatrice."

He laughs weakly.

"Beatrice," he amends, and touches his lips to mine. I curl my fingers into his shirt.

"Unless you want me to throw up all over you guys, you might want to save it for later."

"Where are we?" I ask.

"This is the trash incinerator," says Peter, slapping the square door. "I turned it off. It'll take us to the alley. And then your aim had better be perfect, Four, if you want to get out of the Erudite sector alive."

"Don't concern yourself with my aim," Tobias retorts. He, like me, is barefoot.

Peter opens the door to the incinerator. "Tris, you first."

The trash chute is about three feet wide and four feet high. I slide one leg down the chute and, with Tobias's help, swing the other leg in. My stomach drops as I slide down a short metal tube. Then a series of rollers pound against my back as I slip over them.

I smell fire and ash, but I am not burned. Then I drop, and my arm smacks into a metal wall, making me groan. I land on a cement floor, hard, and pain from the impact prickles up my shins.

"Ow." I limp away from the opening and shout, "Go ahead!"

My legs have recovered by the time Peter lands, on his side instead of his feet. He groans, and drags himself away from the opening to re-cover.

I look around. We are inside the incinerator, which would be completely dark if not for the lines of light glowing in the shape of a small door on the other side. The floor is solid metal in some places and metal grating in others. Everything smells like rotting garbage and fire.

"Don't say I never took you anywhere nice," Peter says.

"Wouldn't dream of it," I say.

Tobias drops to the floor, landing first on his feet and then tilting forward to his knees, wincing. I pull him to his feet and then draw close to his side. All the smells and sights and feelings of the world feel magnified. I was almost dead, but instead I am alive. Because of Peter.

Of all people.

Peter walks across the grate and opens the small door. Light streams into the incinerator. Tobias walks with me away from the fire smell, away from the metal furnace, into the cement-walled room that contains it.

"Got that gun?" Peter says to Tobias.

"No," says Tobias, "I figured I would shoot the bullets out of my nostrils, so I left it upstairs."

"Oh, shut up."

Peter holds another gun in front of him and leaves the incinerator room. A dank hallway with exposed pipes in the ceiling greets us, but it's only ten feet long. The sign next to the door at the end says EXIT. I am alive, and I am leaving.

+ + +

The stretch of land between Dauntless headquarters and Erudite headquarters does not look the same in reverse. I suppose everything is bound to look different when you aren't on your way to die.

When we reach the end of the alley, Tobias presses his shoulder to one wall and leans forward just enough to see around the corner. His face blank, he puts one arm around the corner, steadying it with the building wall, and fires twice. I shove my fingers in my ears and try not to pay attention to the gunshots and what they make me remember.

"Hurry," Tobias says.

We sprint, Peter first, me second, and Tobias last, down Wabash Avenue. I look over my shoulder to see what Tobias shot at, and see two men on the ground behind Erudite headquarters. One isn't moving, and the other is clutching his arm and running toward the door. They will send others after us.

My head feels muddled, probably from exhaustion, but the adrenaline keeps me running.

"Take the least logical route!" shouts Tobias.

"What?" Peter says.

"The least logical route," Tobias says. "So they won't find us!"

Peter swerves to the left, down another alley, this one full of cardboard boxes that contain frayed blankets and stained pillows—old factionless dwellings, I assume. He jumps over a box that I go crashing through, kicking it behind me.

At the end of the alley he turns left, toward the marsh. We are back on Michigan Avenue. In plain sight of Erudite headquarters, if anyone cares to glance down the street.

"Bad idea!" I shout.

Peter takes the next right. At least all the streets here are clear—no fallen street signs to dodge or holes to jump over. My lungs burn like I inhaled poison. My legs, which ached at first, are now numb, which is better. Somewhere far away, I hear shouts.

Then it occurs to me: The least logical thing to do is stop running.

I grab Peter's sleeve and drag him toward the nearest building. It is six stories high, with wide windows arranged into a grid, divided by pillars of brick. The first door I try is locked, but Tobias fires at the window next to it until it breaks, and unlocks the door from the inside.

The building is completely empty. Not a single chair or table. And there are too many windows. We walk toward the emergency stairwell, and I crawl beneath the first flight so that we are hidden by the staircase. Tobias sits next to me, and Peter across from us both, his knees drawn to his chest.

I try to catch my breath and calm myself down, but it isn't easy. I was dead. I was *dead*, and then I wasn't, and why? Because of Peter? *Peter?*

I stare at him. He still looks so innocent, despite all that he has done to prove that he is not. His hair lies smooth against his head, shiny and dark, like we didn't just run for a mile at full speed. His round eyes scan the stairwell and then rest on my face.

"What?" he says. "Why are you looking at me like that?"

"How did you do it?" I say.

"It wasn't that hard," he says. "I dyed a paralytic serum purple and switched it out with the death serum. Replaced the wire that was supposed to read your heartbeat with a dead one. The bit with the heart monitor was harder; I had to get some Erudite help with a remote and stuff—you wouldn't understand it if I explained it to you."

"*Why* did you do it?" I say. "You *want* me dead. You were willing to do it yourself! What changed?"

He presses his lips together and doesn't look away, not for a long time. Then he opens his mouth, hesitates, and finally says, "I can't be in anyone's debt. Okay? The idea that I owed you something made me sick. I would wake up in the middle of the night feeling like I was going to vomit. Indebted to a Stiff? It's ridiculous. Absolutely ridiculous. And I couldn't have it."

"What are you talking about? You owed me something?"

He rolls his eyes. "The Amity compound. Someone shot me—the bullet was at head level; it would have hit me right between the eyes. And you shoved me out of the way. We were even before that—I almost killed you during initiation, you almost killed me during the attack simulation; we're square, right? But after that . . ."

"You're insane," says Tobias. "That's not the way the world works . . . with everyone keeping score."

"It's not?" Peter raises his eyebrows. "I don't know what world *you* live in, but in mine, people only do things for you for one of two reasons. The first is if they want something in return. And the second is if they feel like they owe you something."

"Those aren't the only reasons people do things for you," I say. "Sometimes they do them because they love you. Well, maybe not *you*, but . . ."

Peter snorts. "That's exactly the kind of garbage I expect a delusional Stiff to say."

"I guess we just have to make sure you owe us," says Tobias. "Or you'll go running to whoever offers you the best deal."

"Yeah," Peter says. "That's pretty much how it is."

I shake my head. I can't imagine living the way he does—always keeping track of who gave me what and what I should give them in return, incapable of love or loyalty or forgiveness, a one-eyed man with a knife in hand, looking for someone else's eye to poke out. That isn't life. It's some paler version of life. I wonder where he learned it from.

"So when can we get out of here, you think?" Peter says.

"Couple hours," says Tobias. "We should go to the Abnegation sector. That's where the factionless and the Dauntless who aren't wired for simulations will be by now."

"Fantastic," says Peter.

Tobias puts his arm around me. I press my cheek into his shoulder, and close my eyes so I don't have to look at Peter. I know there is a lot to say, though I'm not sure exactly what it is, but we can't say it here, or now.

+ + +

As we walk the streets I once called home, conversations sputter and die, and eyes cling to my face and body. As far as they knew—and I'm sure they knew, because Jeanine knows how to spread news—I died less than six hours ago. I notice that some of the factionless I pass are marked with patches of blue dye. They are simulation-ready.

Now that we're here, and safe, I realize that there are cuts all over the bottoms of my feet from running over rough pavement and bits of glass from broken windows. Every step stings. I focus on that instead of all the stares.

"Tris?" someone calls out ahead of us. I lift my head, and see Uriah and Christina on the sidewalk, comparing revolvers. Uriah drops his gun in the grass and sprints toward me. Christina follows him, but at a slower pace.

Uriah reaches for me, but Tobias sets a hand on his shoulder to stop him. I feel a surge of gratitude. I don't think I can handle Uriah's embrace, or his questions, or his surprise, right now.

"She's been through a lot," Tobias says. "She just needs to sleep. She'll be down the street—number thirty-seven. Come visit tomorrow."

Uriah frowns at me. The Dauntless don't usually understand restraint, and Uriah has only ever known the Dauntless. But he must respect Tobias's assessment of me, because he nods and says, "Okay. Tomorrow."

Christina reaches out as I pass her and squeezes my shoulder lightly. I try to stand up straighter, but my muscles feel like a cage, holding my shoulders hunched. The eyes follow me down the street, pinching the back of my neck. I am relieved when Tobias leads us up the front walk of the gray house that belonged to Marcus Eaton.

I don't know by what strength Tobias marches through the doorway. For him this house must contain echoes of screaming parents and belt snaps and hours spent in small, dark closets, yet he doesn't look troubled as he leads Peter and me into the kitchen. If anything he stands taller. But maybe that is Tobias—when he's supposed to be weak, he's strong.

Tori, Harrison, and Evelyn stand in the kitchen. The sight overwhelms me. I lean my shoulder into the wall and squeeze my eyes shut. The outline of the execution table is printed on my eyelids. I open my eyes. I try to breathe. They are talking but I can't hear what they're saying. Why is Evelyn here, in Marcus's house? Where is Marcus?

Evelyn puts one arm around Tobias and touches his face with the other, pressing her cheek to his. She says something to him. He smiles at her when he pulls away. Mother and son, reconciled. I am not sure it's wise.

Tobias turns me around and, keeping one hand on my arm and one on my waist, to avoid my shoulder wound, presses me toward the staircase. We climb the steps together.

Upstairs are his parents' old bedroom and his old bedroom, with a bathroom between them, and that's it. He takes me into his bedroom, and I stand for a moment, looking around at the room where he spent most of his life.

He keeps his hand on my arm. He has been touching me in some way since we left the stairwell of that building, like he thinks I might break apart if he doesn't hold me together.

"Marcus didn't go into this room after I left, I'm pretty sure," says Tobias. "Because nothing was moved when I came back here."

Members of Abnegation don't own many decorations, since they are viewed as self-indulgent, but what few things we were allowed, he has. A stack of school papers. A small bookshelf. And, strangely, a sculpture made of blue glass on his dresser.

"My mother smuggled that to me when I was young. Told me to hide it," he says. "The day of the ceremony, I put it on my dresser before I left. So he would see it. A small act of defiance."

I nod. It is strange to be in a place that carries one single memory so completely. This room is sixteen-year-old Tobias, about to choose Dauntless to escape his father.

"Let's take care of your feet," he says. But he doesn't move, just shifts his fingers to the inside of my elbow.

"Okay," I say.

We walk into the adjoined bathroom, and I sit on the edge of the tub. He sits next to me, a hand on my knee as he turns on the faucet and plugs the drain. Water spills into the tub, covering my toenails. My blood turns the water pink.

He crouches in the tub and puts my foot in his lap, dabbing at the deeper cuts with a washcloth. I don't feel it. Even when he smears soap lather over them, I don't feel anything. The bathwater turns gray.

I pick up the bar of soap and turn it in my hands until my skin is coated with white lather. I reach for him and run my fingers over his hands, careful to get the lines in his palms and the spaces between his fingers. It feels good to do something, to clean something, and to have my hands on him again.

We get water all over the bathroom floor as we both splash it on ourselves to get the soap off. The water makes me cold, but I shiver and I don't care. He gets a towel and starts to dry my hands.

"I don't . . ." I sound like I am being strangled. "My family is all *dead*, or traitors; how can I . . ."

I am not making any sense. The sobs take over my body, my mind, everything. He gathers me to him, and bathwater soaks my legs. His hold is tight. I listen to his heartbeat and, after a while, find a way to let the rhythm calm me.

"I'll be your family now," he says.

"I love you," I say.

I said that once, before I went to Erudite headquarters, but he was asleep then. I don't know why I didn't say it when he could hear it. Maybe I was afraid to trust him with something so personal as my devotion. Or afraid that I did not know what it was to love someone. But now I think the scary thing was not saying it before it was almost too late. Not saying it before it was almost too late for me.

I am his, and he is mine, and it has been that way all along.

He stares at me. I wait with my hands clutching his arms for stability as he considers his response.

He frowns at me. "Say it again."

"Tobias," I say, "I love you."

His skin is slippery with water and he smells like sweat and my shirt sticks to his arms when he slides them around me. He presses his face to my neck and kisses me right above the collarbone, kisses my cheek, kisses my lips.

"I love you, too," he says.

CHAPTER THIRTY-SEVEN

He lies next to me as I fall sleep. I expect to have nightmares, but I must be too tired, because my mind stays empty. When I open my eyes next, he's gone, but there's a stack of clothes on the bed beside me.

I get up and walk into the bathroom and I feel raw, like my skin was scraped clean and every breath of air stings it a little, but stable. I don't turn on the lights in the bathroom because I know they will be pale and bright, just like the lights in the Erudite compound. I shower in the dark, barely able to tell soap from conditioner, and tell myself that I will emerge new and strong, that the water will heal me.

Before I leave the bathroom, I pinch my cheeks hard to bring blood to the surface of my skin. It's stupid, but I don't want to look weak and exhausted in front of everyone.

When I walk back into Tobias's room, Uriah is sprawled across the bed facedown; Christina is holding the blue sculpture above Tobias's desk, examining it; and Lynn is poised above Uriah with a pillow, a wicked grin creeping across her face.

Lynn smacks Uriah hard in the back of the head, Christina says, "Hey Tris!" and Uriah cries, "Ow! How on earth do you make a *pillow* hurt, Lynn?"

"My exceptional strength," she says. "Did you get smacked, Tris? One of your cheeks is bright red."

I must not have pinched the other one hard enough. "No, it's just . . . my morning glow."

I try the joke out on my tongue like it's a new language. Christina laughs, maybe a little harder than my comment warrants, but I appreciate the effort. Uriah bounces on the bed a few times when he moves to the edge.

"So, the thing we're all not talking about," he says. He gestures to me. "You almost died, a sadistic pansycake saved you, and now we're all waging some serious war with the factionless as allies."

"Pansycake?" says Christina.

"Dauntless slang." Lynn smirks. "Supposed to be a huge insult, only no one uses it anymore."

"Because it's so offensive," says Uriah, nodding.

"No. Because it's so stupid no Dauntless with any sense would speak it, let alone think it. Pansycake. What are you, twelve?"

"And a half," he says.

I get the feeling their banter is for my benefit, so that I don't have to say anything; I can just laugh. And I do, enough to warm the stone that has formed in my stomach.

"There's food downstairs," says Christina. "Tobias made scrambled eggs, which, as it turns out, is a disgusting food."

"Hey," I say. "I *like* scrambled eggs."

"Must be a Stiff breakfast, then." She grabs my arm. "C'mon."

Together we go down the stairs, our footsteps thundering as they never would have been allowed to in my parents' house. My father used to scold me for running down the stairs. "Do not call attention to yourself," he said. "It is not courteous to the people around you."

I hear voices in the living room—a chorus of them, in fact, joined by occasional bursts of laughter and a faint melody plucked on an instrument, a banjo or a guitar. It is not what I expect in an Abnegation house, where everything is always quiet, no matter how many people are gathered within. The voices and the laughter and the music breathe life into the sullen walls. I feel even warmer.

I stand in the doorway to the living room. Five people are crowded onto the three-person couch, playing a card game I recognize from Candor headquarters. A man sits in the armchair with a woman balanced on his lap, and someone else perches on the arm, a can of soup in hand. Tobias sits on the floor, his back against the coffee table. Every part of his posture suggests ease—one leg bent, the other straight, an arm slung across his knee, his head tilted to listen. I have never seen him look so comfortable without a gun. I didn't think it was possible.

I get the same sinking feeling in my stomach that I always get when I know I've been lied to, but I don't know who it was that lied to me this time, or about what, exactly. But this is not what I was taught to expect of factionlessness. I was taught that it was worse than death.

I stand there for just a few seconds before people realize that I'm there. Their conversation peters out. I wipe my palms off on the hem of my shirt. Too many eyes, and too much silence.

Evelyn clears her throat. "Everyone, this is Tris Prior. I believe you may have heard a lot about her yesterday."

"And Christina, Uriah, and Lynn," supplies Tobias. I'm grateful for his attempt to divert everyone's attention from me, but it doesn't work.

I stand glued to the door frame for a few seconds, and then one of the factionless men—older, his wrinkled skin patterned with tattoos— speaks up.

"Aren't you supposed to be dead?"

Some of the others laugh, and I try a smile. It emerges crooked and small.

"Supposed to be," I say.

"We don't like to give Jeanine Matthews what she wants, though," Tobias says. He gets up and hands me a can of peas—but it isn't full of peas; it's full of scrambled eggs. The aluminum warms my fingers.

He sits, so I sit next to him, and scoop some of the eggs into my mouth. I am not hungry, but I know I need to eat, so I chew and swallow anyway. I am familiar with the way the factionless eat, so I pass the eggs to Christina, and take a can of peaches from Tobias.

"Why is everyone camped out in Marcus's house?" I ask him.

"Evelyn kicked him out. Said it was her house, too, and he'd gotten to use it for years, and it was her turn." Tobias grins. "It caused a huge blowup on the front lawn, but eventually Evelyn won."

I glance at Tobias's mother. She is in the far corner of the room, talking to Peter and eating more eggs from another can. My stomach churns. Tobias talks about her almost reverently. But I still remember what she said to me about my transience in Tobias's life.

"There's bread somewhere." He picks up a basket from the coffee table and hands it to me. "Take two pieces. You need it."

As I chew on the bread crust, I look at Peter and Evelyn again.

"I think she's trying to recruit him," Tobias says. "She has a way of making the factionless life sound extraordinarily appealing."

"Anything to get him out of Dauntless. I don't care if he saved my life, I still don't like him."

"Hopefully we won't have to worry about faction distinctions anymore by the time this is over. It'll be nice, I think."

I don't say anything. I don't feel like picking a fight with him here. Or reminding him that it won't be so easy to persuade Dauntless and Candor to join the factionless in their crusade against the faction system. It may take another war.

The front door opens, and Edward enters. Today he wears a patch with a blue eye painted on it, complete with a half-lowered eyelid. The effect of the overlarge eye against his otherwise handsome face is both grotesque and amusing.

"Eddie!" someone calls out in greeting. But Edward's good eye has already fallen on Peter. He starts across the room, nearly kicking a can of food out of someone's hand. Peter presses into the shadow of the door frame like he is trying to disappear into it.

Edward stops inches from Peter's feet, and then jerks toward him like he is about to throw a punch. Peter jolts back so hard he slams his head into the wall. Edward grins, and all around us, the factionless laugh.

"Not so brave in broad daylight," Edward says. And then, to Evelyn, "Make sure you don't give him any utensils. Never know what he might do with them."

As he speaks, he plucks the fork from Peter's hand.

"Give that back," says Peter.

Edward slams his free hand into Peter's throat, and presses the tines of the fork between his fingers, right against Peter's Adam's apple. Peter stiffens, blood rushing into his face.

"Keep your mouth shut around me," he says, his voice low, "or I will do this again, only next time, I'll shove it right through your esophagus."

"That's enough," Evelyn says. Edward drops the fork and releases Peter. Then he walks across the room and sits next to the person who called him "Eddie" a moment before.

"I don't know if you know this," Tobias says, "but Edward is a little unstable."

"I'm getting that," I say.

"That Drew guy, who helped Peter perform that butter-knife maneuver," Tobias says. "Apparently when he got kicked out of Dauntless, he tried to join the same group of factionless Edward was a part of. Notice that you haven't seen Drew anywhere."

"Did Edward kill him?" I say.

"Nearly," Tobias says. "Evidently that's why that other transfer—Myra, I think her name was?—left Edward. Too gentle to bear it."

I feel hollow at the thought of Drew, almost dead at the hands of Edward. Drew attacked me, too.

"I don't want to talk about this," I say.

"Okay," Tobias says. He touches my shoulder. "Is it hard for you to be in an Abnegation house again? I meant to ask before. We can go somewhere else, if it is."

I finish my second piece of bread. All Abnegation houses are the same, so this living room is exactly the same as my own, and it does bring back memories, if I look at it carefully. Light glowing through the blinds every morning, enough for my father to read by. The click of my mother's knitting needles every evening. But I don't feel like I'm choking. It's a start.

"Yes," I say. "But not as hard as you might think."

He raises an eyebrow.

"Really. The simulations in Erudite headquarters . . . helped me, somehow. To hold on, maybe." I frown. "Or maybe not. Maybe they helped me to stop holding on so tightly." That sounds right. "Someday I'll tell you about it." My voice sounds far away.

He touches my cheek and, even though we're in a room full of people, crowded by laughter and conversation, slowly kisses me.

"Whoa there, Tobias," says the man to my left. "Weren't you raised a Stiff? I thought the most you people did was . . . graze hands or something."

"Then how do you explain all the Abnegation children?" Tobias raises his eyebrows.

"They're brought into being by sheer force of will," the woman on the arm of the chair interjects. "Didn't you know that, Tobias?"

"No, I wasn't aware." He grins. "My apologies."

They all laugh. *We* all laugh. And it occurs to me that I might be meeting Tobias's true faction. They are not characterized by a particular virtue. They claim all colors, all activities, all virtues, and all flaws as their own.

I don't know what binds them together. The only common ground they have, as far as I know, is failure. Whatever it is, it seems to be enough.

I feel, as I look at him, that I am finally seeing him as he is, instead of how he is in relation to me. So how well do I really know him, if I have not seen this before?

+ + +

The sun is beginning to set. The Abnegation sector is far from quiet. The Dauntless and factionless wander the streets, some with bottles in their hands, some with guns in their other hands.

Ahead of me, Zeke pushes Shauna in her wheelchair past the house of Alice Brewster, former Abnegation leader. They don't see me.

"Do it again!" she says.

"Are you sure?"

"Yes!"

"Okay . . ." Zeke starts to jog behind the wheelchair. Then, when he's almost too far away for me to see, he pushes himself up with the handles so that his feet aren't touching the ground, and together they fly down the middle of the street, Shauna shrieking, Zeke laughing.

I turn left at the next intersection and start down the cracked side-walk toward the building where Abnegation had its monthly faction-wide meetings. Though it feels like it has been a long time since I last went there, I still remember where it is. One block south, two blocks west.

The sun inches toward the horizon as I walk. The color drains from the surrounding buildings in the evening light, so that they all appear to be gray.

The face of Abnegation headquarters is just a cement rectangle, like all the other buildings in the Abnegation sector. But when I shove the front door open, familiar wood floors and rows of wooden benches ar-ranged in a square greet me. In the center of the room is a skylight that lets in a square of orange sunlight. It is the room's only adornment.

I sit on my family's old bench. I used to sit next to my father, and Ca-leb, next to my mother. Now I feel like the only one left. The last Prior.

"It's nice, isn't it?" Marcus walks in and sits down across from me, his hands folded in his lap. The sunlight is between us.

He has a large bruise on his jaw from where Tobias hit him, and his hair is freshly buzzed.

"It's fine," I say, straightening. "What are you doing here?"

"I saw you come in." He examines his fingernails carefully. "And I want to have a word with you about the information Jeanine Matthews stole."

"What if you're too late? What if I already know what it is?"

Marcus looks up from his fingernails, and his dark eyes narrow. The look is far more poisonous than any Tobias could muster, though he has his father's eyes. "You can't possibly."

"You don't know that."

"I do, actually. Because I have seen what happens to people when they hear the truth. They look like they have forgotten what they were searching for, and are just wandering around trying to remember."

A chill makes its way up my spine and spreads down my arms, giving me goose bumps.

"I know that Jeanine decided to murder half a faction to steal it, so it must be incredibly important," I say. I pause. I know something else, too, but I only just realized it.

Right before I attacked Jeanine, she said, "This is not about you! It's not about me!"

And *this* meant what she was doing to me—trying to find a simulation that worked on me. On the Divergent.

"I know it has something to do with the Divergent," I blurt out. "I know the information is about what's outside the fence."

"That is not the same thing as knowing what's outside the fence."

"Well, are you going to tell me or are you going to dangle it over my head and make me jump for it?"

"I did not come here for self-indulgent arguing. And no, I am not going to tell you, but not because I don't want to. It's because I have no idea how to describe it to you. You have to see it for yourself."

As he speaks, I notice the sunlight turning more orange than yellow, and casting darker shadows over his face.

"I think Tobias might be right," I say. "You *like* to be the only one who knows. You like that I don't know. It makes you feel important. That's why you won't tell me, not because it's indescribable."

"That's not true."

"How am I supposed to know that?"

Marcus stares, and I stare back.

"A week before the simulation attack, the Abnegation leaders decided it was time to reveal the information in the file to everyone. *Everyone*, in the entire city. The day we intended to reveal it was approximately seven days after the simulation attack. Obviously we were unable to do so."

"She didn't want you to reveal what was outside the fence? Why not? How did she even know about it in the first place? I thought you said only the Abnegation leaders knew."

"We are not *from* here, Beatrice. We were all placed here, for a specific purpose. A while ago, the Abnegation were forced to enlist the help of Erudite in order to achieve that purpose, but eventually everything went awry because of Jeanine. Because she doesn't want to do what we are supposed to do. She would rather resort to murder."

Placed here.

My brain feels like it is buzzing with information. I clutch the edge of the bench beneath me.

"What are we supposed to do?" I say, my voice barely more than a whisper.

"I have told you enough to convince you that I am not a liar. As for the rest, I truly find myself unequal to the task of explaining it to you. I only told you as much as I did because the situation has become dire."

Dire. Suddenly I understand the problem. The factionless plan to destroy, not only the important figures in Erudite, but all the data they have. They will level everything.

I have never thought that plan was a good idea, but I knew that we could come back from it, because the Erudite still *know* the relevant information, even if they don't have their data. But this is something even the most intelligent Erudite do not know; something that, if everything is destroyed, we cannot replicate.

"If I help you, I betray Tobias. I will lose him." I swallow hard. "So you have to give me a good reason."

"Aside from the good of everyone in our society?" Marcus wrinkles his nose in disgust. "That isn't enough for you?"

"Our society is in pieces. So no, it's not."

Marcus sighs.

"Your parents died for *you*, it's true. But the reason your mother was in Abnegation headquarters the night you were almost executed was not to save you. She didn't know you were there. She was trying to rescue the file from Jeanine. And when she heard that you were about to die, she rushed to save you, and left the file in Jeanine's hands."

"That's not what she told me," I say hotly.

"She was lying. Because she had to. But Beatrice, the point is . . . the point is, your mother knew she probably would not get out of Abnegation headquarters alive, but she had to try. This file, it was something she was willing to die for. Understand?"

The Abnegation are willing to die for any person, friend or enemy, if the situation calls for it. That is, perhaps, why they find it difficult to survive in life-threatening situations. But there are few *things* they are willing to die for. They don't value many things in the physical world.

So if he's telling me the truth, and my mother really was willing to die for this information to become public . . . I would do just about anything to accomplish the goal she failed to achieve.

"You're trying to manipulate me. Aren't you."

"I suppose," he says as shadows slip into his eye sockets like dark water, "that is something you must decide for yourself."

CHAPTER
THIRTY-EIGHT

I TAKE MY time on my walk back to the Eaton house, and try to remember what my mother told me when she saved me from the tank during the simulation attack. Something about having watched the trains since the attack started. *I didn't know what I would do when I found you. But it was always my intention to save you.*

But when I go over the memory of her voice in my mind, it sounds different. *I didn't know what I would do, when I found you.* Meaning: I didn't know how to save both you and the file. *But it was always my intention to save you.*

I shake my head. Is that how she said it, or am I manipulating my own memory because of what Marcus told me? There is no way to know. All I can do is decide if I trust Marcus or not.

And while he has done cruel, evil things, our society is not divided into "good" and "bad." Cruelty does not make a person dishonest, the same way bravery does not make a person kind. Marcus is not good or bad, but both.

Well, he is probably more bad than good.

But that doesn't mean he's lying.

On the street ahead of me, I see the orange glow of fire. Alarmed, I walk faster, and see that the fire rises from large, man-sized metal bowls set up on the sidewalks. The Dauntless and the factionless have gathered between them, a narrow divide separating one group from the other. And before them stand Evelyn, Harrison, Tori, and Tobias.

I spot Christina, Uriah, Lynn, Zeke, and Shauna on the right side of the cluster of Dauntless, and stand with them.

"Where've you been?" Christina says. "We looked all over for you."

"I went for a walk. What's going on?"

"They're finally going to tell us the attack plan," says Uriah, looking eager.

"Oh," I say.

Evelyn lifts her hands, palms out, and the factionless fall silent. They are better trained than the Dauntless, whose voices take thirty seconds to peter out.

"The past few weeks, we have been developing a plan to fight the Erudite," Evelyn says, her low voice carrying easily. "And now that we have finished, we would like to share it with you."

Evelyn nods at Tori, who takes over. "Our strategy is not pointed, but broad. There is no way to know who among the Erudite supports Jeanine and who does not. It is therefore safer to assume that all those who do not support her have already vacated Erudite headquarters."

"We all know that Erudite's power lies not in its people but in its information," says Evelyn. "As long as they still possess that information, we will never be free of them, especially while large numbers of us are wired for simulations. They have used information to control us and keep us under their thumb for far too long."

A shout, beginning among the factionless and spreading to the Dauntless, rises up from the crowd like we are all parts of one organism, following the commands of a single brain. But I am not sure what I think, or how I feel. There is a part of me that is shouting, too—clamoring for the destruction of every single Erudite and all that they hold dear.

I look at Tobias. His expression is neutral, and he stands behind the glow of firelight, where he is difficult to see. I wonder what he thinks of this.

"I am sorry to tell you that those of you who were shot with simulation transmitters will have to remain here," says Tori, "or you can be activated as a weapon of Erudite at any time."

There are a few cries of protest, but no one seems all that surprised. They know too well what Jeanine can do with simulations, maybe.

Lynn groans and looks at Uriah. "We have to *stay*?"

"*You* have to stay," he says.

"You got shot too," she says. "I saw it."

"Divergent, remember?" he says. Lynn rolls her eyes, and he hurries on, probably to avoid hearing Lynn's Divergent conspiracy theory again. "Anyway, I bet you no one checks, and what are the odds she'll activate you, specifically, if she knows everyone else with simulation transmitters is staying behind?"

Lynn frowns, considering this. But she looks more cheerful—as cheerful as Lynn gets, anyway—as Tori begins speaking again.

"The rest of us will divide into groups of mixed factionless and Dauntless," says Tori. "A single, large group will attempt to penetrate Erudite headquarters and work its way up through the building, cleansing it of Erudite's influence. Several other, smaller groups will proceed immediately to the higher levels of the building to dispense with certain key Erudite officials. You will receive your group assignments later this evening."

"The attack will occur in three days' time," says Evelyn. "Prepare yourselves. This will be dangerous and difficult. But the factionless are familiar with difficulty—"

At this the factionless cheer, and I am reminded that we, the Dauntless, are the same people who, just a few weeks ago, were criticizing Abnegation for giving the factionless food and other necessary items. How was that so easy to forget?

"And the Dauntless are familiar with danger—"

Everyone around me punches the air with their fists and screams. I feel their voices inside my head, and the burn of triumph in my chest that makes me want to join them.

Evelyn's expression is too empty for someone giving an impassioned speech. Her face looks like a mask.

"Down with Erudite!" Tori yells, and everyone repeats her, all voices joining together, regardless of faction. We share a common enemy, but does that make us friends?

I notice that Tobias does not join in the chant, and neither does Christina.

"This doesn't feel right," she says.

"What do you mean?" Lynn says as the voices rise around us. "Don't you remember what they did to us? Put our minds under a simulation and forced us to shoot people without even knowing it? Murdered every single Abnegation leader?"

"Yeah," says Christina. "It's just . . . Invading a faction's headquarters and killing everyone, isn't that what the Erudite just did to Abnegation?"

"This is different. *This* is not an attack out of nowhere, unprovoked," says Lynn, scowling at her.

"Yeah," Christina says. "Yeah, I know."

She looks at me. I don't say anything. She has a point—it doesn't feel right.

I walk toward the Eaton house in search of silence.

I open the front door and climb the stairs. When I reach Tobias's old room, I sit on the bed and look out the window, where factionless and

Dauntless are gathered around the fires, laughing and talking. But they aren't mixed together; there is still an uneasy divide between them, factionless on one side and Dauntless on the other.

I watch Lynn, Uriah, and Christina by one of the fires. Uriah snatches at the flames, too quickly to be burned. His smile looks more like a grimace, twisted as it is by grief.

After a few minutes I hear footsteps on the stairs, and Tobias comes into the room, slipping off his shoes by the doorway.

"What's wrong?" he says.

"Nothing, really," I say. "I was just thinking, I'm surprised the factionless agreed to work with Dauntless so easily. It's not like the Dauntless were ever kind to them."

He stands beside me at the window and leans into the frame.

"It's not a natural alliance, is it," he says. "But we have the same goal."

"Right now. But what happens when the goals change? The factionless want to get rid of factions, and the Dauntless don't."

Tobias presses his mouth into a line. I suddenly remember Marcus and Johanna, walking together through the orchard—Marcus wore the same expression when he was keeping something from her.

Did Tobias get that expression from his father? Or does it mean something different?

"You're in my group," he says. "During the attack. I hope you don't mind. We're supposed to lead the way to the control rooms."

The attack. If I participate in the attack, I can't go after the information Jeanine stole from Abnegation. I have to choose one or the other.

Tobias said that dealing with Erudite was more important than finding out the truth. And if he had not promised the factionless control over all of Erudite's data, he might have been right. But he left me no choice. I have to help Marcus, if there is even a chance that he is telling the truth. I have to work against the people I love best.

And right now, I have to lie.

I twist my fingers together.

"What is it?" he says.

"I still can't fire a gun." I look up at him. "And after what happened in Erudite headquarters . . ." I clear my throat. "Risking my life doesn't seem so appealing anymore."

"Tris." He brushes my cheek with his fingertips. "You don't have to go."

"I don't want to seem like a coward."

"Hey." His fingers fit beneath my jaw. They are cool against my skin. He looks sternly at me. "You have done more for this faction than any other person. You . . ."

He sighs, and touches his forehead to mine.

"You're the bravest person I've ever met. Stay here. Let yourself mend."

He kisses me, and I feel like I am crumbling again, beginning with the deepest parts of me. He thinks I will be here, but I will be working against him, working with the father he despises. This lie—this lie is the worst I have ever told. I will never be able to take it back.

When we part, I am afraid he will hear my breaths shake, so I turn toward the window.

CHAPTER
THIRTY-NINE

"OH YEAH. You totally look like a banjo-strumming softie," says Christina.

"Really?"

"No. Not at all, actually. Just . . . let me fix it, okay?"

She rummages in her bag for a few seconds and pulls out a small box. In it are different-sized tubes and containers that I recognize as makeup, but wouldn't know what to do with.

We are in my parents' house. It was the only place I could think of to go to get ready. Christina has no reservations about poking around—she already discovered two textbooks wedged between the dresser and the wall, evidence of Caleb's Erudite leanings.

"Let me get this straight. So you left the Dauntless compound to get ready for war . . . and took your makeup bag with you?"

"Yep. Figured it would be harder for anyone to shoot me if they saw how devastatingly attractive I was," she says, arching an eyebrow. "Hold still."

She takes the cap off a black tube about the size of one of my fingers, revealing a red stick. Lipstick, obviously. She touches it to my mouth and dabs it until my lips are covered in color. I can see it when I purse them.

"Has anyone ever talked to you about the miracle of eyebrow tweezing?" she says, holding up a pair of tweezers.

"Get those away from me."

"Fine." She sighs. "I would take out the blush, but I'm pretty sure it's not the right color for you."

"Shocking, considering we're so similar in skin tone."

"Ha-ha," she says.

By the time we leave, I have red lips and curled eyelashes, and I'm wearing a bright red dress. And there's a knife strapped to the inside of my knee. This all makes perfect sense.

"Where's Marcus, Destroyer of Lives, going to meet us?" Christina says. She wears Amity yellow instead of red, and it glows against her skin.

I laugh. "Behind Abnegation headquarters."

We walk down the sidewalk in the dark. All the others should be eating dinner now—I made sure of that—but in case we run into someone, we wear black jackets to conceal most of our Amity clothing. I hop over a crack in the cement out of habit.

"Where are you two going?" Peter's voice says. I look over my shoulder. He's standing on the sidewalk behind us. I wonder how long he's been there.

"Why aren't you with your attack group, eating dinner?" I say.

"I don't have one." He taps the arm I shot. "I'm injured."

"Yeah right, you are!" says Christina.

"Well, I don't want to go to battle with a bunch of factionless," he says, his green eyes glinting. "So I'm going to stay here."

"Like a coward," says Christina, her lip curled in disgust. "Let everyone else clean up the mess for you."

"Yep!" he says with a kind of malicious cheer. He claps his hands. "Have fun dying."

He crosses the street, whistling, and walks in the other direction.

"Well, we distracted him," she says. "He didn't ask where we were going again."

"Yeah. Good." I clear my throat. "So, this plan. It's kind of stupid, right?"

"It's not . . . *stupid.*"

"Oh, come on. Trusting Marcus is stupid. Trying to get past the Dauntless at the fence is stupid. Going against the Dauntless and factionless is stupid. All three combined is . . . a different kind of stupid formerly unheard of by humankind."

"Unfortunately it's also the best plan we have," she points out. "If we want everyone to know the truth."

I trusted Christina to take up this mission when I thought I would die, so it seemed stupid not to trust her now. I was worried she wouldn't want to come with me, but I forgot where Christina came from: Candor, where the pursuit of truth is more important than anything else. She may be Dauntless now, but if there's one thing I've learned through all this, it's that we never leave our old factions behind.

"So this is where you grew up. Did you like it here?" She frowns. "I guess you couldn't have, if you wanted to leave."

The sun inches toward the horizon as we walk. I never used to like evening light because it made everything in the Abnegation sector look more monochromatic than it already is, but now I find the unchanging gray comforting.

"I liked some things and hated some things," I say. "And there were some things I didn't know I had until I lost them."

We reach Abnegation headquarters, and its face is just a cement square like everything else in the Abnegation sector. I would love to walk into the meeting room and breathe the smell of old wood, but we don't have time. We slip into the alley next to the building and walk to the back, where Marcus told me he would be waiting.

A powder-blue pickup truck waits there, its engine running. Marcus is behind the wheel. I let Christina walk ahead of me so that she can be the one to slide into the middle. I don't want to sit close to him if I can help it. I feel like hating him while I work with him lessens my betrayal of Tobias somehow.

You have no other choice, I tell myself. *There is no other way.*

With that in mind, I pull the door shut and look for a seat belt to buckle. I find only the frayed end of a seat belt and a broken buckle.

"Where did you find this piece of junk?" says Christina.

"I stole it from the factionless. They fix them up. It wasn't easy to get it to start. Better ditch those jackets, girls."

I ball up our jackets and toss them out the half-open window. Marcus shifts the truck into drive, and it groans. I half expect it to stay still when he presses the gas pedal, but it moves.

From what I remember, it takes about an hour to drive from the Abnegation sector to Amity headquarters, and the trip requires a skilled driver. Marcus pulls onto one of the main thoroughfares and pushes his foot into the gas pedal. We lurch forward, narrowly avoiding a gaping hole in the road. I grab the dashboard to steady myself.

"Relax, Beatrice," says Marcus. "I've driven a car before."

"I've done a lot of things before, but that doesn't mean I'm any good at them!"

Marcus smiles and jerks the truck to the left so that we don't hit a fallen stoplight. Christina whoops as we bump over another piece of debris, like she's having the time of her life.

"A different kind of stupid, right?" she says, her voice loud enough to be heard over the rush of wind through the cab.

I clutch the seat beneath me and try not to think of what I ate for dinner.

+ + +

When we reach the fence, we see the Dauntless standing in our headlight beams, blocking the gate. Their blue armbands stand out against the rest of their clothing. I try to keep my expression pleasant. I will not be able to fool them into thinking I'm Amity with a scowl on my face.

A dark-skinned man with a gun in hand approaches Marcus's window. He shines a flashlight at Marcus first, then Christina, then me. I squint into the beam, and force a smile at the man like I don't mind bright lights in the eyes and guns pointed at my head in the slightest.

The Amity must be deranged if this is how they really think. Or they've been eating too much of that bread.

"So tell me," the man says. "What's an Abnegation member doing in a truck with two Amity?"

"These two girls volunteered to bring provisions to the city," Marcus says, "and I volunteered to escort them so that they would be safe."

"Also, we don't know how to drive," says Christina, grinning. "My dad tried to teach me years ago but I kept confusing the gas pedal for the brake pedal, and you can imagine what a disaster that was! Anyway, it was *really* nice of Joshua to volunteer to take us, because it would have taken us forever otherwise, and the boxes were *so* heavy—"

The Dauntless man holds up his hand. "Okay, I get it."

"Oh, of course. Sorry." Christina giggles. "I just thought I would explain, because you seemed so confused, and no wonder, because how many times do you encounter this—"

"Right," the man says. "And do you intend to return to the city?"

"Not anytime soon," Marcus says.

"All right. Go ahead, then." He nods to the other Dauntless by the gate. One of them types a series of numbers on the keypad, and the gate slides open to admit us. Marcus nods to the guard who let us through and drives over the worn path to Amity headquarters. The truck's headlights catch tire tracks and prairie grass and insects weaving back and forth. In the darkness to my right I see fireflies lighting up to a rhythm that is like a heartbeat.

After a few seconds, Marcus glances at Christina. "What on earth was *that*?"

"There's nothing the Dauntless hate more than cheerful Amity babble," says Christina, lifting a shoulder. "I figured if he got annoyed it would distract him and he would let us through."

I smile with all my teeth. "You are a *genius*."

"I know." She tosses her head like she's throwing her hair over one shoulder, only she doesn't have enough to throw.

"Except," says Marcus, "Joshua is not an Abnegation name."

"Whatever. As if anyone knows the difference."

I see the glow of Amity headquarters ahead, the familiar cluster of wooden buildings with the greenhouse in their center. We drive through the apple orchard. The air smells like warm earth.

Again I remember my mother stretching to pick an apple in this orchard, years ago when we came to help the Amity with the harvest. A pang hurts my chest, but the memory doesn't overwhelm me as it did a few weeks ago. Maybe it's because I am on a mission to honor her. Or maybe I am too apprehensive about what's coming to grieve properly. But something has changed.

Marcus parks the truck behind one of the sleeping cabins. For the first time I notice that there are no keys in the ignition.

"How did you get it to start?" I ask him.

"My father taught me a lot about mechanics and computers," he says. "Knowledge that I passed to my own son. You didn't think he figured it all out on his own, did you?"

"Actually yes, I did." I push the door open and climb out of the truck. Grass brushes my toes and the back of my calves. Christina stands at my right shoulder and tilts her head back.

"It's so different out here," she says. "You could almost forget what's going on in *there*." She points her thumb toward the city.

"And they often do," I say.

"They know what's beyond the city, though, right?" she asks.

"They know about as much as the Dauntless patrols," says Marcus. "Which is that the outside world is unknown and potentially dangerous."

"How do you know what they know?" I say.

"Because that's what we told them," he says, and he walks toward the greenhouse.

I exchange a look with Christina. Then we jog to catch up to him.

"What does *that* mean?"

"When you are entrusted with all the information, you have to decide how much other people should know," says Marcus. "The Abnegation leaders told them what we had to tell them. Now, let's hope Johanna is keeping up her normal habits. She is usually in the greenhouse this early in the evening."

He opens the greenhouse door. The air is just as dense as the last time I was in here, but now it is misty, too. The moisture cools my cheeks.

"Wow," Christina says.

The room is lit by moonlight, so it is hard to distinguish plant from tree from man-made structure. Leaves brush my face as I make my way around the outer edge of the room. And then I see Johanna, crouched beside a bush with a bowl in her hands, picking what appear to be raspberries. Her hair is pulled back, so I can see her scar.

"I didn't think I would see you here again, Ms. Prior," she says.

"Is that because I'm supposed to be dead?" I say.

"I always expect those who live by the gun to die by it. I am often pleasantly surprised." She balances the bowl on her knees and looks up at me. "Although I also know better than to think you came back because you like it here."

"No," I say. "We came for something else."

"All right," she says, standing. "Let's go talk about it, then."

She carries the bowl toward the middle of the room, where the Amity meetings are held. We follow her onto the tree roots, where she sits and offers me the bowl of raspberries. I take a small handful of berries and pass the bowl to Christina.

"Johanna, this is Christina," Marcus says. "Candor-born Dauntless."

"Welcome to Amity headquarters, Christina." Johanna smiles knowingly. It seems so strange, that two people born in Candor could end up in such different places: Dauntless, and Amity.

"Tell me, Marcus," says Johanna. "Why have you come to visit?"

"I think Beatrice should handle that," he says. "I am merely the transportation."

She shifts her focus to me without question, but I can tell by the wary look in her eyes that she would rather talk to Marcus. She would deny it if I asked her, but I am almost certain Johanna Reyes hates me.

"Um . . ." I say. Not my most brilliant opening. I wipe my palms on my skirt. "Things have gotten bad."

The words start to spill out, without finesse or sophistication. I explain that the Dauntless have allied with the factionless, and they plan to destroy all of Erudite, leaving us without one of the two essential factions. I tell her that there is important information in the Erudite compound, in addition to all the knowledge they possess, that especially needs to be recovered. When I finish, I realize I haven't told her why that has anything to do with her or her faction, but I don't know how to say it.

"I'm confused, Beatrice," she says. "What exactly do you want us to do?"

"I didn't come here to ask you for help," I say. "I thought you should know that a lot of people are going to die, very soon. And I know you don't want to stay here doing nothing while that happens, even if some of your faction does."

She looks down, her crooked mouth betraying just how right I am.

"I also wanted to ask you if we can talk to the Erudite you're keeping safe here," I say. "I know they're hidden, but I need access to them."

"And what do you intend to do?" she says.

"Shoot them," I say, rolling my eyes.

"That isn't funny."

I sigh. "Sorry. I need information. That's all."

"Well, you'll have to wait until tomorrow," Johanna says. "You can sleep here."

+ + +

I sleep as soon as my head touches the pillow, but wake earlier than I planned. I can tell by the glow near the horizon that the sun is about to rise.

Across the narrow aisle between two beds is Christina, her face pressed to the mattress with her pillow over her head. A dresser with a lamp on top of it stands between us. The wooden floorboards creak no matter where you step on them. And on the left wall is a mirror, casually placed. Everyone but the Abnegation takes mirrors for granted. I still feel a prickle of shock whenever I see one in the open.

I get dressed, not bothering to be quiet—five hundred stomping Dauntless can't wake Christina when she's deeply asleep, though an Erudite whisper might be able to. She is odd that way.

I walk outside as the sun peeks through the tree branches, and see a small group of Amity gathered near the orchard. I move closer to see what they are doing.

They stand in a circle, hands clasped. Half of them are in their early teens, and the other half are adults. The oldest one, a woman with braided gray hair, speaks.

"We believe in a God who gives peace and cherishes it," she says. "So we give peace to each other, and cherish it."

I would not hear that as a cue, but the Amity seem to. They all begin to move at once, finding someone across the circle and clasping hands with them. When everyone is paired off, they stand for several seconds, looking at each other. Some of them mutter a phrase, some smile, some remain silent and still. Then they break apart and move to someone else, performing the same series of actions again.

I have never seen an Amity religious ceremony before. I am only familiar with the religion of my parents' faction, which part of me still holds to and the other rejects as foolishness—the prayers before dinner, the weekly meetings, the acts of service, the poems about a selfless God. This is something different, something mysterious.

"Come and join us," the gray-haired woman says. It takes me a few seconds to realize she's talking to me. She beckons to me, smiling.

"Oh no," I say. "I'm just—"

"Come," she says again, and I feel like I have no choice but to walk forward and stand among them.

She approaches me first, clasping my hand. Her fingers are dry and rough and her eyes seek mine, persistent, though I feel strange meeting her gaze.

Once I do, the effect is immediate and peculiar. I stand still, and every part of me is still, like it weighs more than it used to, only the weight is not unpleasant. Her eyes are brown, the same shade throughout, and unmoving.

"May the peace of God be with you," she says, her voice low, "even in the midst of trouble."

"Why would it?" I say softly, so no one else can hear. "After all I've done . . ."

"It isn't about you," she says. "It is a gift. You cannot earn it, or it ceases to be a gift."

She releases me and moves to someone else, but I stand with my hand outstretched, alone. Someone moves to take my hand, but I withdraw from the group, first at a walk, and then at a run.

I sprint into the trees as fast as I can, and only when my lungs feel like they are on fire do I stop.

I press my forehead to the nearest tree trunk, though it scrapes my skin, and fight off tears.

+ + +

Later that morning I walk through light rain to the main greenhouse. Johanna has called an emergency meeting.

I stay as hidden as possible at the edge of the room, between two large plants that are suspended in mineral solution. It takes me a few minutes to find Christina, dressed in Amity yellow on the right side of the room, but it is easy to spot Marcus, who stands on the roots of the giant tree with Johanna.

Johanna has her hands clasped in front of her and her hair pulled back. The injury that gave her the scar also damaged her eye—her pupil is so dilated it overwhelms her iris, and her left eye doesn't move with the right one as she scans the Amity in front of her.

But there are not just Amity. There are people with close-cropped hair and tightly twisted buns who must belong to Abnegation, and a few rows of people in glasses who must be Erudite. Cara is among them.

"I have received a message from the city," says Johanna when everyone quiets down. "And I would like to communicate it to you."

She tugs at the hem of her shirt, then clasps her hands in front of her. She seems nervous.

"The Dauntless have allied with the factionless," she says. "They intend to attack Erudite in two days' time. Their battle will be waged not against the Erudite-Dauntless army but against Erudite innocents and the knowledge they have worked so hard to acquire."

She looks down, breathes deeply, and continues: "I know that we recognize no leader, so I have no right to address you as if that is what I am," she says. "But I am hoping that you will forgive me, just this once, for asking if we can reconsider our previous decision to remain uninvolved."

There are murmurs. They are nothing like Dauntless murmurs—they are gentler, like birds launching from branches.

"Our relationship with Erudite notwithstanding, we know better than any faction how essential their role in this society is," she says. "They must be protected from needless slaughter, if not because they are human beings, then because we cannot survive without them. I propose that we enter the city as nonviolent, impartial peacekeepers in order to curb in whatever way possible the extreme violence that will undoubtedly occur. Please discuss this."

Rain dusts the glass panels above our heads. Johanna sits on a tree root to wait, but the Amity do not burst into conversation as they did the last time I was here. Whispers, almost indistinguishable from the rain, turn to normal speech, and I hear some voices lift above others, almost yelling, but not quite.

Every lifted voice sends a jolt through me. I've sat through plenty of arguments in my life, mostly in the last two months, but none of them ever scared me like this. The Amity aren't supposed to argue.

I decide not to wait any longer. I walk along the edge of the meeting area, squeezing past the Amity who are on their feet and hopping over hands and outstretched legs. Some of them stare at me—I may be wearing a red shirt, but the tattoos along my collarbone are clear as ever, even from a distance.

I pause near the row of Erudite. Cara stands when I get close, her arms folded.

"What are you doing here?" she says.

"I came to tell Johanna what was going on," I say. "And to ask you for help."

"Me?" she says. "Why—"

"Not *you*," I say. I try to forget what she said about my nose, but it's hard. "All of you. I have a plan to save some of your faction's data, but I need your help."

"Actually," Christina says, appearing at my left shoulder, "*we* have a plan."

Cara looks from me to Christina and back to me again.

"*You* want to help Erudite?" she says. "I'm confused."

"You wanted to help Dauntless," I say. "You think you're the only one who doesn't just blindly do what your faction tells you to?"

"It is in keeping with your pattern of behavior," says Cara. "Shooting people who get in your way is a Dauntless trait, after all."

I feel a pinch at the back of my throat. She looks so much like her brother, down to the crease between her eyebrows and the dark streaks in her otherwise blond hair.

"Cara," says Christina. "Will you help us, or not?"

Cara sighs. "Obviously I will. I'm sure the others will, too. Meet us in the Erudite dormitory at the end of the meeting, and tell us the plan."

+ + +

The meeting lasts for another hour. By then the rain has stopped, though water still sprinkles the wall and ceiling panels. Christina and I have been sitting against one of the walls, playing a game in which each of us tries to pin down the other's thumb. She always wins.

Finally Johanna and the others who emerged as discussion leaders stand in a line on the tree roots. Johanna's hair now hangs over her lowered face. She is supposed to tell us the outcome of the conversation, but she just stands with her arms folded, her fingers tapping against her elbow.

"What's going on?" Christina says.

Finally Johanna looks up.

"Obviously it was difficult to find agreement," she says. "But the majority of you wish to uphold our policy of uninvolvement."

It does not matter to me whether the Amity decide to go into the city or not. But I had begun to hope they were not all cowards, and to me, this decision sounds very much like cowardice. I sink back against the window.

"It is not my wish to encourage division in this community, which has given so much to me," says Johanna. "But my conscience forces me to go against this decision. Anyone else whose conscience drives them toward the city is welcome to come with me."

At first I, like everyone else, am not sure what she's saying. Johanna tilts her head so that her scar is again visible, and adds, "I understand if this means I can't be a part of Amity anymore." She sniffs. "But please know that if I have to leave you, I leave you with love, rather than malice."

Johanna bows in the general direction of the crowd, tucks her hair behind her ears, and walks toward the exit. A few of the Amity scramble to their feet, then a few more, and soon the entire crowd is on their feet, and some of them—not many, but some—are walking out behind her.

"That," says Christina, "is not what I was expecting."

CHAPTER FORTY

THE ERUDITE DORMITORY is one of the larger sleeping rooms in Amity headquarters. There are twelve beds total: a row of eight crammed together along the far wall, and two pressed together on each side, leaving a huge space in the middle of the room. A large table occupies that space, covered with tools and scraps of metal and gears and old computer parts and wires.

Christina and I just finished explaining our plan, which sounded a lot dumber with more than a dozen Erudite staring us down as we talked.

"Your plan is flawed," Cara says. She is the first to respond.

"That's why we came to you," I say. "So you could tell us how to fix it."

"Well, first of all, this important data you want to rescue," she says. "Putting it on a disc is a ridiculous idea. Discs just end up breaking or in the wrong person's hands, like all other physical objects. I suggest you make use of the data network."

"The . . . what?"

She glances at the other Erudite. One of the others—a brown-skinned young man in glasses—says, "Go on. Tell them. There's no reason to keep secrets anymore."

Cara looks back at me. "Many of the computers in the Erudite compound are set up to access data from the computers in other factions. That's how it was so easy for Jeanine to run the attack simulation from a Dauntless computer instead of an Erudite one."

"What?" says Christina. "You mean you can just take a stroll through every faction's data whenever you want?"

"You can't 'take a stroll' through data," the young man says. "That's illogical."

"It's a metaphor," says Christina. She frowns. "Right?"

"A metaphor, or simply a figure of speech?" he says, also frowning. "Or is a metaphor a definite category beneath the heading of 'figure of speech'?"

"Fernando," says Cara. "Focus."

He nods.

"The fact is," Cara continues, "the data network exists, and that is ethically questionable, but I believe it can work to our advantage here. Just as the computers can access data from other factions, they can *send* data to other factions. If we sent the data you wished to rescue to every other faction, destroying it all would be impossible."

"When you say 'we,' " I say, "are you implying that—"

"That we would be going with you?" she says. "Obviously not all of us would go, but some of us must. How do you expect to navigate Erudite headquarters on your own?"

"You do realize that if you come with us, you might get shot," says Christina. She smiles. "And no hiding behind us because you don't want to break your glasses, or whatever."

Cara removes her glasses and snaps them in half at the bridge.

"We risked our lives by defecting from our faction," says Cara, "and we will risk them again to save our faction from itself."

"Also," pipes up a small voice behind Cara. A girl no older than ten or eleven peers around Cara's elbow. Her black hair is short, like mine, and a halo of frizz surrounds her head. "We have useful gadgets."

Christina and I exchange a look.

I say, "What kinds of gadgets?"

"They're just prototypes," Fernando says, "so there's no need to scrutinize them."

"Scrutiny's not really our thing," says Christina.

"Then how do you make things better?" the little girl asks.

"We don't, really," Christina says, sighing. "They kind of just keep getting worse."

The little girl nods. "Entropy."

"What?"

"Entropy," she chirps. "It's the theory that all matter in the universe is gradually moving toward the same temperature. Also known as 'heat death.' "

"Elia," Cara says, "that is a gross oversimplification."

Elia sticks out her tongue at Cara. I can't help but laugh. I have never seen one of the Erudite stick out her tongue before. But then again, I haven't interacted with many young Erudite. Only Jeanine and the people who work for her. Including my brother.

Fernando crouches next to one of the beds and takes out a box. He digs inside it for a few seconds, then picks up a small, round disc. It is made of a pale metal that I saw often in Erudite headquarters but have never seen anywhere else. He carries it toward me on his palm. When I reach for it, he jerks it away from me.

"Careful!" he says. "I brought this from headquarters. It's not something we invented here. Were you there when they attacked Candor?"

"Yes," I say. "*Right* there."

"Remember when the glass shattered?"

"Were *you* there?" I say, narrowing my eyes.

"No. They recorded it and showed the footage at Erudite headquarters," he says. "Well, it looked like the glass shattered because they shot at it, but that's not really true. One of the Dauntless soldiers tossed one of *these* near the windows. It emits a signal that you can't hear, but that will cause glass to shatter."

"Okay," I say. "And how will that be useful to us?"

"You may find that it's rather distracting for people when all their windows shatter at once," he says with a small smile. "Especially in Erudite headquarters, where there are a lot of windows."

"Right," I say.

"What else have you got?" says Christina.

"The Amity will like this," Cara says. "Where is it? Ah. Here."

She picks up a black box made of plastic, small enough for her to wrap her fingers around it. At the top of the box are two pieces of metal that look like teeth. She flips a switch at the bottom of the box, and a thread of blue light stretches across the gap between the teeth.

"Fernando," says Cara. "Want to demonstrate?"

"Are you joking?" he says, his eyes wide. "I'm never doing that again. You're dangerous with that thing."

Cara grins at him, and explains, "If I touched you with this stunner right now, it would be extremely painful, and then it would disable you. Fernando found that out the hard way yesterday. I made it so that the Amity would have a way of defending themselves without shooting anyone."

"That's . . ." I frown. "Understanding of you."

"Well, technology is supposed to make life better," she says. "No matter what you believe, there's a technology out there for you."

What did my mother say, in that simulation? "I worry that your father's blustering about Erudite has been to your detriment." What if she was right, even if she was just a part of a simulation? My father taught me to see Erudite a particular way. He never taught me that they made no judgments about what people believed, but designed things for them within the confines of those beliefs. He never told me that they could be funny, or that they could critique their own faction from the inside.

Cara lunges toward Fernando with the stunner, laughing when he jumps back.

He never told me that an Erudite could offer to help me even after I killed her brother.

+ + +

The attack will begin in the afternoon, before it is too dark to see the blue armbands that mark some of the Dauntless as traitors. As soon as our plans are finalized, we walk through the orchard to the clearing where the trucks are kept. When I emerge from the trees, I see that Johanna Reyes is perched on the hood of one of the trucks, the keys dangling from her fingers.

Behind her waits a small convoy of vehicles packed with Amity—but not just Amity, because Abnegation, with their severe hairstyles and still mouths, are among them. Robert, Susan's older brother, is with them.

Johanna hops down from the hood. In the back of the truck she was just sitting on is a stack of crates marked APPLES and FLOUR and CORN. It's a good thing we only have to fit two people in the back.

"Hello, Johanna," says Marcus.

"Marcus," she says. "I hope you don't mind if we accompany you to the city."

"Of course not," he says. "Lead the way."

Johanna gives Marcus the keys and climbs into the bed of one of the other trucks. Christina starts toward the truck cab, and I go for the truck bed, with Fernando behind me.

"You don't want to sit up front?" says Christina. "And you call your-self a Dauntless. . . ."

"I went for the part of the truck in which I was least likely to vomit," I say.

"Puking is a part of life."

I am about to ask her exactly how often she intends to throw up in the future when the truck surges forward. I grab the side with both hands so that I don't fall out, but after a few minutes, when I get used to the bump-ing and jostling, I let go. The other trucks trundle along in front of us, behind Johanna's, which leads the way.

I feel calm until we reach the fence. I expect to encounter the same guards who tried to stop us on the way in, but the gate is abandoned, left open. A tremor starts in my chest and spreads to my hands. In the midst of meeting new people and making plans, I forgot that my plan is to walk straight into a battle that could claim my life. Right after I realized that my life was worth living.

The convoy slows down as we pass through the fence, like they expect someone to jump out and stop us. Everything is silent apart from the cicadas in the distant trees and the truck engines.

"Do you think it's already started?" I say to Fernando.

"Perhaps. Perhaps not," he says. "Jeanine has many informants. Someone probably told her that something was going to happen, so she called all the Dauntless forces back to Erudite headquarters."

I nod, but I am really thinking of Caleb. He was one of those informants. I wonder why he believed so strongly that the outside world should be hidden from us that he would betray everyone he supposedly cared about for Jeanine, who cares about no one.

"Did you ever meet someone named Caleb?" I say.

"Caleb," Fernando says. "Yes, there was a Caleb in my initiate class. Brilliant, but he was . . . what's the colloquial term for it? A suck-up." He smirks. "There was a bit of a division between initiates. Those who embraced everything Jeanine said and those who didn't. Obviously I was a member of the latter group. Caleb was a member of the former. Why do you ask?"

"I met him while I was imprisoned," I say, and my voice sounds far away even to me. "I was just curious."

"I wouldn't judge him too harshly," says Fernando. "Jeanine can be extraordinarily persuasive to those who aren't naturally suspicious. I have always been naturally suspicious."

I stare over his left shoulder, at the skyline that gets clearer the closer we get to the city. I search for the two prongs at the top of the Hub, and when I find them, I feel better and worse at the same time—better, because the building is so familiar, and worse, because seeing the prongs means that we are getting closer.

"Yeah," I say. "So have I."

CHAPTER
FORTY-ONE

By the time we reach the city, all conversation has halted in the truck, replaced by pressed lips and pale faces. Marcus steers around potholes the size of a person and parts from broken-down buses. The ride is smoother when we get out of factionless territory and into the clean parts of the city.

Then I hear gunshots. From this distance they sound like popping.

For a moment I am disoriented, and all I can see are the leaders of Abnegation on their knees on the pavement and the slack-faced Dauntless with guns in hand; all I can see is my mother turning to embrace the bullets, and Will dropping to the ground. I bite my fist to keep from crying out, and the pain brings me back to the present.

My mother told me to be brave. But if she had known that her death would make me so afraid, would she have sacrificed herself so willingly?

Breaking away from the convoy of trucks, Marcus turns on Madison Avenue and, when we are just two blocks away from Michigan Avenue, where the fighting is, he pulls the truck into an alley and turns off the engine.

Fernando hops out of the truck bed and offers me his arm.

"Come on, Insurgent," he says with a wink.

"What?" I say. I take his arm and slide down the side of the truck.

He opens the bag he was sitting with. It is full of blue clothes. He sorts through them, tossing garments to Christina and me. I get a bright blue T-shirt and a pair of blue jeans.

"Insurgent," he says. "Noun. A person who acts in opposition to the established authority, who is not necessarily regarded as a belligerent."

"Do you need to give *everything* a name?" says Cara, running her hands over her dull blond hair to tuck the stray pieces back. "We're just doing something and it happens to be in a group. No need for a new title."

"I happen to enjoy categorization," Fernando replies, arching a dark eyebrow.

I look at Fernando. The last time I broke into a faction's headquarters, I did it with a gun in my hand, and I left bodies behind me. I want this time to be different. I *need* this time to be different. "I like it," I say. "Insurgent. It's perfect."

"See?" Fernando says to Cara. "I'm not the only one."

"Congratulations," she says wryly.

I stare at my Erudite clothes while the others strip off their outer layers of clothing.

"No time for modesty, Stiff!" Christina says, giving me a pointed look.

I know she's right, so I pull off the red shirt I was wearing and put on the blue one instead. I glance at Fernando and Marcus to make sure they aren't watching, and change out of my pants too. I have to roll up the jeans four times, and when I belt them, they bunch at the top like the neck of a crushed paper bag.

"Did she just call you 'Stiff'?" Fernando says.

"Yeah," I say. "I transferred into Dauntless from Abnegation."

"Huh." He frowns. "That's quite a shift. That kind of leap in personality between generations is almost genetically impossible these days."

"Sometimes personality has nothing to do with a person's choice of faction," I say, thinking of my mother. She left Dauntless not because she was ill-suited for it but because it was safer to be Divergent in Abnegation. And then there's Tobias, who switched to Dauntless to escape his father. "There are many factors to consider."

To escape the man I have made my ally. I feel a twinge of guilt.

"Keep talking like that and they'll never discover you're not really Erudite," Fernando says.

I run a comb through my hair to smooth it down and then tuck it behind my ears.

"Here," says Cara. She lifts a piece of hair from my face and pins it back with a silver hair clip, the way Erudite girls do.

Christina takes out the guns we brought with us and looks at me.

"Do you want one?" she says. "Or would you rather carry the stunner?"

I stare at the gun in her hand. If I don't take the stunner, I leave myself completely undefended against people who will gladly shoot me. If I do, I admit to weakness in front of Fernando, Cara, and Marcus.

"You know what Will would say?" says Christina.

"What?" I say, my voice breaking.

"He would tell you to get over it," she says. "To stop being so irrational and take the stupid gun."

Will had little patience for the irrational. Christina must be right; she knew him better than I did.

And she—who lost someone dear to her that day, just as I did—was able to forgive me, an act that must have been nearly impossible. It would have been impossible for me, if the situation were reversed. So why is it so difficult for me to forgive myself?

I close my hand around the gun Christina offered me. The metal is warm from where she touched it. I feel the memory of shooting him poking at the back of my mind, and try to stifle it. But it won't be stifled. I let go of the gun.

"The stunner is a perfectly good option," Cara says as she plucks a hair from her shirtsleeve. "If you ask me, the Dauntless are too gun-happy anyway."

Fernando offers me the stunner. I wish I could communicate my gratitude to Cara, but she isn't looking at me.

"How am I going to conceal this thing?" I say.

"Don't bother," Fernando says.

"Right."

"We'd better go," says Marcus, glancing at his watch.

My heart beats so hard it marks each second for me, but the rest of me is numb. I can barely feel the ground. I have never been this afraid before, and considering all that I have seen in simulations, and all that I did during the attack simulation, that doesn't make any sense.

Or maybe it does. Whatever the Abnegation were about to show everyone before the attack, it was enough to make Jeanine take drastic and terrible measures to stop them. And now I am about to finish their work, the work my old faction died for. So much more than my life is at stake now.

Christina and I lead the way. We run down the clean, even sidewalks on Madison Avenue, passing State Street, toward Michigan Avenue.

Half a block from Erudite headquarters, I come to a sudden stop.

Standing in four rows in front of us are a group of people, mostly dressed in black and white, spaced two feet apart, guns held up and ready. I blink and they become simulation-controlled Dauntless in the Abnegation sector, during the simulation attack. *Get a grip! Get a grip get a grip get a grip.* . . . I blink again and they are the Candor again—though some of them, dressed all in black, do look like Dauntless. If I'm not careful I'll lose touch with where, and when, I am.

"Oh my God," Christina says. "My sister, my *parents* . . . what if they . . ."

She looks at me, and I think I know her thoughts, because I have experienced them before. *Where are my parents? I have to find them.* But if her parents are like these Candor, simulation controlled and armed, there is nothing she can do for them.

I wonder if Lynn stands in one of these rows, somewhere else.

"What do we do?" Fernando asks.

I step toward the Candor. Maybe they aren't programmed to shoot. I stare into the glazed eyes of a woman in a white blouse and black slacks. She looks like she just came from work. I take another step.

Bang. By instinct I drop to the ground, covering my head with my arms, and scramble backward, toward Fernando's shoes. He helps me to my feet.

"How about let's not do *that*?" he says.

I lean forward—not too far—and peer into the alley between the building next to us and Erudite headquarters. The Candor are in the alley too. I wouldn't be surprised if there was a dense layer of Candor surrounding the entire complex of Erudite buildings.

"Is there any other way to Erudite headquarters?" I say.

"Not that I know of," says Cara. "Unless you want to jump from one roof to another."

She laughs a little as she says it, like it's a joke. I raise my eyebrows at her.

"Wait," she says. "You aren't considering—"

"The roof?" I say. "No. Windows."

I walk to the left, careful not to advance even an inch toward the Candor. The building on my left overlaps with Erudite headquarters on its far left side. There have to be a few windows that face each other.

Cara mutters something about crazy Dauntless stunts, but runs after me, and Fernando, Marcus, and Christina follow. I try to open the back door of the building, but it's locked.

Christina steps forward and says, "Stand back." She points her gun at the lock. I shield my face with an arm as she fires. We hear a loud bang, and then a high ringing, the aftereffects of firing a gun in such a close space. The lock is broken.

I pull the door open and walk inside. A long hallway with a tile floor greets me, doors on either side, some open, some closed. When I look into the open rooms, I see rows of old desks, and chalkboards on the walls like the ones in Dauntless headquarters. The air smells musty, like the pages of a library book mixed with cleaning solution.

"This used to be a commercial building," says Fernando, "but Erudite converted it into a school, for post-Choosing education. After the major renovations in Erudite headquarters about a decade ago—you know, when all the buildings across from Millennium were connected?—they stopped teaching there. Too old, hard to update."

"Thanks for the history lesson," says Christina.

When I reach the end of the hallway, I walk into one of the classrooms to see where I am. I see the back of Erudite headquarters, but there are no windows across the alley at street level.

Right outside the window, so close I could touch her if I stretched my hand through the window, is a Candor child, a girl, holding a gun that is as long as her forearm. She stands so still I wonder if she is even breathing.

I crane my neck to see the windows above street level. Over my head in the school building there are plenty of windows. At the back of Erudite headquarters, there is only one that lines up. And it's on the third story.

"Good news," I say. "I found a way across."

CHAPTER
FORTY-TWO

EVERYONE SPREADS THROUGHOUT the building in search of janitor's closets, per my instruction to find a ladder. I hear sneakers squeaking on the tile and shouts of "I found one—no, wait, it's just got buckets in it, never mind" and "How long does the ladder have to be? A stepladder won't work, right?"

While they search, I find the third-floor classroom that looks into the Erudite window. It takes me three tries to open the right window.

I lean out, over the alley, and shout, "Hey!" Then I duck as fast as I can. But I don't hear gunshots—*Good*, I think. *They don't respond to noise.*

Christina marches into the classroom with a ladder under her arm, the others behind her. "Got one! I think it'll be long enough once we stretch it out."

She tries to turn too soon, and the ladder smacks into Fernando's shoulder.

"Oh! Sorry, Nando."

The jolt knocked his glasses askew. He smiles at Christina and takes the glasses off, shoving them into his pocket.

"Nando?" I say to him. "I thought the Erudite didn't like nick-names?"

"When a pretty girl calls you by a nickname," he says, "it is only logical to respond to it."

Christina looks away, and at first I think she is bashful, but then I see her face contort like he slapped her instead of complimented her. It is too soon after Will's death for her to be flirted with.

I help her guide the end of the ladder through the classroom window and across the gap between buildings. Marcus helps us steady it. Fernando whoops when the ladder hits the Erudite window across the alley.

"Time to break the glass," I say.

Fernando takes the glass-breaking device from his pocket and offers it to me. "You probably have the best aim."

"I wouldn't count on it," I say. "My right arm is out of commission. I'd have to throw with my left."

"I'll do it," says Christina.

She presses the button on the side of the device and tosses it across the alley, underhand. I clench my hands as I wait for it to land. It bounces onto the windowsill and rolls into the glass. An orange light flashes, and all at once the window—and the windows above, below, and next to it—shatters into hundreds of tiny pebbles that shower over the Candor below.

At the same time, the Candor twist and fire up into the sky. Everyone else drops to the ground, but I stay on my feet, part of me marveling at the perfect synchronicity of it, and the other part disgusted at how Jeanine Matthews has turned yet another faction from human beings into parts of a machine. None of the bullets even hit the classroom windows, let alone penetrate the room.

When the Candor do not fire another round, I peer down at them. They have returned to their original position, half facing Madison Avenue and half facing Washington Street.

"They respond to movement only, so . . . don't fall off the ladder," I say. "Whoever goes first will secure the ladder on the other side."

I notice that Marcus, who is supposed to selflessly offer himself up for every task, does not volunteer.

"Not feeling very Stiff today, Marcus?" says Christina.

"If I were you, I would be careful who you insult," he says. "I am still the only person here who can find what we're looking for."

"Is that a *threat*?"

"I'll go," I say, before Marcus can answer. "I'm part Stiff too, right?"

I shove the stunner under the waistband of my jeans and climb onto a desk to get a better angle on the window. Christina holds the ladder from the side as I clamber on top of it and start forward.

Once I'm through the window, I position my feet on the narrow edges of the ladder and my hands on the rungs. The ladder feels about as solid and stable as an aluminum can. It creaks and sags beneath my weight. I try not to look down at the Candor; try not to think about their guns lifting and firing at me.

Taking quick breaths, I stare at my destination, the Erudite window. Just a few rungs left.

A breeze blows through the alley, pushing me to one side, and I think of scaling the Ferris wheel with Tobias. He kept me steady then. There is no one left to keep me steady now.

I catch a glimpse of the ground, three stories down, the bricks smaller than they should be, the lines of Candor Jeanine enslaved. My arms—especially my right arm—ache as I inch my way across the gap.

The ladder shifts, moving closer to the edge of the window frame on the other side. Christina is holding one side steady, but she can't keep the ladder from slipping off the other windowsill. I grit my teeth and try not to move it too much, but I can't move both legs at the same time. I have to let the ladder sway a little. Just four more rungs to go.

The ladder jerks to the left, and then, as I move my right foot forward, I miss the edge of the rung.

I yell as my body shifts to the side, my arms wrapping around the ladder and my leg dangling in space.

"Are you okay?" Christina calls from behind me.

I don't answer. I bring my leg up and wedge it beneath my body. My fall made the ladder slip even farther off the windowsill. It is now supported by just a millimeter of concrete.

I decide to move fast. I lurch toward the opposite windowsill just as the ladder slips off. My hands catch the sill and concrete scrapes my fingertips as they bear my body weight. Several voices behind me scream.

I grit my teeth as I pull myself up, my right shoulder shrieking with pain. I kick at the brick building, hoping it will give me traction, but it doesn't help. I scream into my teeth as I pull myself up and over the windowsill, half my body in the building and the other half still dangling. Thankfully Christina didn't let the ladder drop too far. None of the Candor shoot me.

I pull myself into the Erudite room across the alley. It is a bathroom. I collapse to the floor on my left shoulder, and try to breathe through the pain. Sweat trickles down my forehead.

An Erudite woman comes out of a stall, and I scramble to my feet, draw the stunner, and point it at her, all without thinking.

She freezes, her arms up, toilet paper stuck to her shoe.

"Don't shoot!" Her eyes bulge from her head.

I remember, then, that I am dressed like the Erudite. I set the stunner on the edge of a sink.

"My apologies," I say. I try to adopt the formal speech common to the Erudite. "I am slightly edgy, with everything that's occurring. We are reentering in order to retrieve some of our test results from . . . Laboratory 4-A."

"Oh," the woman says. "That seems rather unwise."

"The data is of the utmost importance," I say, trying to sound as arrogant as some of the Erudite I've met. "I would rather not leave it to get riddled with bullets."

"It's hardly my place to prevent you from trying to recover it," she says. "Now if you'll excuse me, I'm going to wash my hands and take cover."

"Sounds good," I say. I decide not to tell her she has toilet paper on her shoe.

I turn back to the window. Across the alley, Christina and Fernando are trying to lift the ladder back onto the windowsill. Though my arms and hands ache, I lean out the window and grab the other end of the ladder, lifting it back onto the windowsill. Then I hold it in place as Christina crawls across.

This time the ladder is more stable, and Christina makes it across the gap without trouble. She takes my place holding it as I shove the trash can in front of the door so no one else can come in. I then run my fingers under cool water to soothe them.

"This is pretty smart, Tris," she says.

"You don't have to sound so surprised."

"It's just . . ." She pauses. "You had aptitude for Erudite, didn't you?"

"Does it matter?" I say too sharply. "The factions are destroyed, and it was all stupid to begin with."

I have never said anything like that before. I have never even thought it. But I'm surprised to find that I believe it—surprised to find that I agree with Tobias.

"I wasn't trying to insult you," says Christina. "Having aptitude for Erudite isn't a bad thing. Especially right now."

"Sorry. I'm just . . . tense. That's all."

Marcus comes through the window and drops to the tile floor. Cara is surprisingly nimble—she moves over the rungs like she's plucking banjo strings, touching each one only briefly before she moves to the next one.

Fernando will be last, and he will be in the same position I was in, with the ladder secured from only one side. I move closer to the window so I can tell him to stop if I see the ladder slip.

Fernando, who I didn't think would have trouble, moves more awkwardly than anyone else. He has probably spent his entire life behind a computer or a book. He shuffles forward, his face bright red, and holds the rungs so tightly that his hands turn blotchy and purple.

Halfway across the alley, I see something slip out of his pocket. It is his spectacles.

I scream, "Fernan—"

But I am too late.

The spectacles fall, hit the edge of the ladder, and topple to the pavement.

In a wave, the Candor below twist and fire upward. Fernando yells, and collapses against the ladder. One bullet hit his leg. I didn't see where

the others went, but I know when I see blood drip between the rungs of
the ladder that it was not a good place.

Fernando stares at Christina, his face ashen. Christina surges forward, through the window, about to reach for him.

"Don't be an idiot!" he says, his voice weak. "Leave me."

It is the last thing he says.

CHAPTER
FORTY-THREE

CHRISTINA STEPS BACK into the room. We are all still.

"I don't mean to be insensitive," says Marcus, "but we have to go before the Dauntless and factionless enter this building. If they haven't already."

I hear tapping against the window and jerk my head to the side, for a split second believing that it is Fernando, trying to get in. But it's just rain.

We follow Cara out of the bathroom. She is our leader now. She knows Erudite headquarters best. Christina follows, then Marcus, then me. We leave the bathroom, and we are in an Erudite hallway like every other Erudite hallway: pale, bright, sterile.

But this hallway is more active than I have ever seen it. People in Erudite blue sprint back and forth, in groups and alone, shouting things at each other like, "They're at the front doors! Go as high as you can!" and "They've disabled the elevators! Run for the stairs!" It's only there, in the midst of chaos, that I realize I forgot the stunner in the bathroom. I am unarmed again.

Dauntless traitors also run past us, though they are less frantic than the Erudite. I wonder what Johanna, the Amity, and the Abnegation are doing in this chaos. Are they tending to the wounded? Or are they standing between Dauntless guns and Erudite innocents, taking bullets for the sake of peace?

I shudder. Cara leads us to a back staircase, and we join a group of terrified Erudite as we run up one, two, three flights of stairs. Then Cara shoves her shoulder into a door next to the landing, holding her gun close to her chest.

I recognize this floor.

It is my floor.

My thoughts become sluggish. I almost died here. I craved death here.

I slow down and fall behind. I can't break out of the daze, though people keep rushing past me, and Marcus shouts something at me, but his voice is muffled. Christina doubles back and grabs me, dragging me toward Control-A.

Inside the control room, I see rows of computers but I don't really see them; there is a film covering my eyes. I try to blink it away. Marcus sits at one of the computers, and Cara sits at another. They will send all the data from the Erudite computers to the other faction computers.

Behind me, the door opens.

And I hear Caleb say, "What are you doing here?"

+ + +

His voice wakes me. I turn and stare right at his gun.

His eyes are my mother's eyes—a dull green, almost gray, though his blue shirt makes their color appear more potent.

"Caleb," I say. "What do you think you're doing?"

"I'm here to stop whatever you're doing!" His voice trembles. The gun wavers in his hands.

"We're here to save the Erudite data that the factionless want to destroy," I say. "I don't think you want to stop us."

"That's not true," he says. He jerks his head toward Marcus. "Why would you bring him if you weren't trying to find something else? Something more important to him than all the Erudite data combined?"

"She told *you* about it?" Marcus says. "*You*, a child?"

"She didn't tell me at first," Caleb says. "But she didn't want me to choose a side without knowing the facts!"

"The facts," says Marcus, "are that she is terrified of reality, and the Abnegation were not. Are not. And neither is your sister. To her credit."

I scowl. Even when he is complimenting me, I want to smack him.

"My sister," says Caleb gently, looking at me again, "doesn't know what she's getting into. Doesn't know what it is that you want to show everyone . . . doesn't know it will ruin *everything*!"

"We are here to serve a purpose!" Marcus is almost yelling now. "We have completed our mission, and it is time for us to do what we were sent here to do!"

I don't know the purpose or the mission that Marcus is referring to, but Caleb doesn't look confused.

"*We* were not sent here," Caleb says. "We have no responsibility to anyone but ourselves."

"That kind of self-interested thinking is what I have come to expect from those who have spent too much time with Jeanine Matthews. You are so unwilling to relinquish your comfort that your selfishness drains you of humanity!"

I don't care to hear more. While Caleb stares down Marcus, I turn and kick hard at Caleb's wrist. The impact shocks him, and his gun topples from his hands. I slide it across the floor with my toes.

"You need to trust me, Beatrice," he says, chin wobbling.

"After you helped her torture me? After you let her almost *kill* me?"

"I didn't help her tort—"

"You certainly didn't stop her! You were right there, and you just *watched*—"

"What could I have done? What—"

"You could have *tried*, you coward!" I scream so loud my face gets hot and tears jump into my eyes. "Tried, and failed, because you love me!"

I gasp, just to take in enough air. All I hear is the click of keys as Cara works on the task at hand. Caleb doesn't seem to have a response. His pleading look slowly disappears, replaced by a blank stare.

"You won't find what you're looking for here," he says. "She wouldn't keep such important files on public computers. That would be illogical."

"So she hasn't destroyed it?" Marcus says.

Caleb shakes his head. "She does not believe in the destruction of information. Only its containment."

"Well, thank God for that," says Marcus. "Where is she keeping it?"

"I'm not going to tell you," Caleb says.

"I think I know," I say. Caleb said she wouldn't keep the information on a public computer. So he must mean she is keeping it on a private one: either the one in her office or the one in the laboratory Tori told me about.

Caleb doesn't look at me.

Marcus picks up Caleb's revolver and turns it in his hand so the butt of the gun protrudes from his fist. Then he swings, striking Caleb under the jaw. Caleb's eyes roll back, and he falls to the floor.

I don't want to know how Marcus perfected that maneuver.

"We can't have him running off to tell someone what we're doing," says Marcus. "Let's go. Cara can take care of the rest, right?"

Cara nods without looking up from her computer. A sick feeling in my stomach, I follow Marcus and Christina out of the control room and toward the stairs.

+ + +

The hallway outside is now empty. There are scraps of paper and footprints on the tile. Marcus, Christina, and I jog in a line to the stairwell. I stare at the back of his head, where the shape of his skull shows through his buzzed hair.

All I can see when I look at him is a belt swinging toward Tobias, and the butt of a gun slamming into Caleb's jaw. I don't care that he hurt Caleb—I would have done it, too—but that he is simultaneously a man who knows how to hurt people and a man who parades around as the self-effacing leader of Abnegation, suddenly makes me so angry I can't see straight.

Especially because I chose him. I chose *him* over Tobias.

"Your brother is a traitor," says Marcus as we turn a corner. "He deserved worse. There's no need to look at me that way."

"Shut up!" I shout, shoving him hard into the wall. He is too surprised to push back. "I hate you, you know that! I hate you for what you did to him, and I am *not* talking about Caleb." I lean close to his face and whisper, "And while I may not shoot you myself, I will definitely not help you if someone tries to kill you, so you'd better hope to God we don't get into that situation."

He stares at me, apparently indifferent. I release him and start toward the stairs again, Christina on my heels, Marcus a few steps behind.

"Where are we going?" she says.

"Caleb said what we're looking for won't be on a public computer, so it has to be on a private one. As far as I know, Jeanine only has two private computers, one in her office, and one in her laboratory," I say.

"So which one do we go to?"

"Tori told me there were insane security measures protecting Jeanine's laboratory," I say. "And I've been to her office; it's just another room."

"So . . . laboratory, then."

"Top floor."

We reach the door to the stairwell, and when I throw it open, a group of Erudite, including children, are sprinting down the stairs. I cling to the railing and force my way through them with my elbow, not looking at their faces, like they are not human, just a wall of mass to push aside.

I expect the stream to stop, but more come from the next landing, a steady flow of blue-clad people in dim blue light, the whites of their eyes bright as lamps by contrast to everything else. Their terrified sobs echo in the cement chamber a hundred times, the shrieks of the demons with glowing eyes.

When we reach the seventh-floor landing, the crowd thins, and then disappears. I run my hands along my arms to get rid of the ghosts of hair, sleeves, and skin that brushed against me on the way up. I can see the top of the stairs from where we stand.

I also see the body of a guard, his arm dangling over the edge of a stair, and standing over him, a factionless man with an eye patch. Edward.

+ + +

"Look who it is," Edward says. He stands at the top of a short flight, only seven steps long, and I stand at the bottom. The Dauntless traitor guard lies between us, his eyes glazed, a dark patch on his chest from where someone—Edward, probably—shot him.

"That's a strange outfit for someone who is supposed to despise Erudite," he says. "I thought you were supposed to be at home, waiting for your boyfriend to come back a hero?"

"As you may have gathered," I say, walking up a step, "that was never going to happen."

The blue light casts shadows into the faint hollows beneath Edward's cheekbones. He reaches behind him.

If he is here, that means Tori is already up here. Which means that Jeanine might already be dead.

I feel Christina close behind me; I hear her breaths.

"We are going to get past you," I say, walking up another step.

"I doubt that," he replies. He grabs his gun. I launch myself forward, over the fallen guard. He fires, but my hands are wrapped around his wrist, so he doesn't fire straight.

My ears ring, and my feet scramble for stability on the dead guard's back.

Christina punches over my head. Her knuckles connect with Edward's nose. I can't balance on top of the body; I fall to my knees, digging my fingernails into his wrist. He wrenches me to the side and fires again, hitting Christina in the leg.

Gasping, Christina draws her gun and shoots. The bullet hits him in the side. Edward screams and drops the gun, pitching forward. He falls on top of me, and I smack my head against one of the cement steps. The dead guard's arm is jammed into my spine.

Marcus picks up Edward's gun and trains it on both of us.

"Get up, Tris," he says. And to Edward: "You. Don't move."

My hand searches for the corner of a step, and I squeeze from between Edward and the dead guard. Edward pushes himself to a sitting position on top of the guard—like he's some kind of *cushion*—clutching his side with both hands.

"You okay?" I ask Christina.

Her face contorts. "*Ahh.* Yeah. It hit the side, not the bone."

I reach for her, to help her up.

"Beatrice," Marcus says. "We have to leave her."

"What do you mean *leave*?" I demand. "We can't leave! Something terrible could happen!"

Marcus presses his index finger to my sternum, in the gap between my collarbones, and leans over me.

"Listen to me," he says. "Jeanine Matthews will have retreated to her laboratory at the first sign of attack, because it is the safest room in this building. And at any moment, she will decide that Erudite is lost and it is better to delete the data than risk anyone else finding it, and this mission of ours will be useless."

And I will have lost everyone: my parents, Caleb, and finally, Tobias, who will never forgive me for working with his father, especially if I have no way to prove that it was worthwhile.

"We are going to leave your friend here." His breath smells stale. "And move on, unless you would rather me go on alone."

"He's right," says Christina. "There's no time. I'll stay here and keep Ed from coming after you."

I nod. Marcus removes his finger, leaving an aching circle behind. I rub the pain away and open the door at the top of the landing. I look back before I walk through it, and Christina gives me a pained smile, her hand pressed to her thigh.

CHAPTER
FORTY-FOUR

THE NEXT ROOM is more like a hallway: it is wide, but not deep, with blue tile, blue walls, and a blue ceiling, all the same shade. Everything glows, but I can't tell where the light is coming from.

At first I don't see any doors, but once my eyes adjust to the shock of color, I see a rectangle in the wall to my left, and another one in the wall to my right. Just two doors.

"We have to split up," I say. "We don't have time to try each one together."

"Which one do you want?" Marcus says.

"Right," I say. "Wait, no. Left."

"Fine. I will go right."

"If I'm the one who finds the computer," I say, "what should I look for?"

"If you find the computer, you will find Jeanine. I assume you know a few ways to coerce her into doing what you want. She is not, after all, accustomed to pain," he says.

I nod. We walk at the same pace toward our respective doors. A moment ago I would have said that separating from Marcus would be a relief. But going on alone is its own burden. What if I can't get through the security measures Jeanine undoubtedly has in place to keep out intruders? What if, if I somehow manage to get through them, I can't find the right file?

I put my hand on the door handle. There doesn't seem to be a lock. When Tori said there were insane security measures, I thought she meant eye scanners and passwords and locks, but so far, everything has been open.

Why does that worry me?

I open my door, and Marcus opens his. We share a look. I walk into the next room.

+ + +

The room, like the hallway outside, is blue, though here it is clear where the light is coming from. It glows from the center of every panel, ceiling, floor, and walls.

Once the door closes behind me, I hear a thud like a dead bolt shifting into place. I grab the door handle again and push down as hard as I can, but it doesn't budge. I am trapped.

Small, piercing lights come at me from all angles. My eyelids aren't enough to block them, so I have to press my palms over my eye sockets.

I hear a calm, feminine voice:

"Beatrice Prior, second generation. Faction of origin: Abnegation. Selected faction: Dauntless. Confirmed Divergent."

How does this room know who I am?

And what does "second generation" mean?

"Status: Intruder."

I hear a click, and pull my fingers apart just enough to see if the lights are gone. They aren't, but fixtures in the ceiling spray tinted vapor. Instinctively I clap my hand over my mouth. In seconds I stare through a blue fog. And then I stare at nothing.

I now stand in darkness so complete that when I hold my hand in front of my nose, I can't even see its silhouette. I should walk forward and search for a door on the other side of the room, but I am afraid to move—who knows what would happen to me here if I did?

Then the lights lift, and I stand in the Dauntless training room, in the circle in which we used to spar. I have so many mixed memories of this circle, some triumphant, like beating Molly, and some haunting— Peter punching me until I fell unconscious. I sniff, and the air smells the same, like sweat and dust.

Across the circle is a blue door that doesn't belong there. I frown at it.

"Intruder," the voice says, and now it sounds like Jeanine, but that could be my imagination. "You have five minutes to reach the blue door before the poison will kick in."

"*What?*"

But I know what she said. Poison. Five minutes. I shouldn't be surprised; this is Jeanine's work, just as empty of conscience as she is. My body shudders, and I wonder if that is the poison, if the poison is already shutting down my brain.

Focus. I can't get out; I have to move forward, or . . .

Or nothing. I have to move forward.

I start toward the door, and someone appears in my path. She is short, thin, and blond, with dark circles under her eyes. She is me.

A reflection? I wave at her to see if she will mirror me. She doesn't.

"Hello," I say. She doesn't answer. I didn't really think she would.

What is this? I swallow hard to pop my ears, which feel like they are stuffed with cotton. If Jeanine designed this, it is probably a test of intelligence or logic, which means I will have to think clearly, which means I will have to calm down. I clasp my hands over my chest and press down, hoping the pressure will make me feel safe, like an embrace.

It doesn't.

I step to the right to get a better angle on the door, and my double hops to the side, her shoes scraping the dirt, to block my way again.

I think I know what will happen if I start toward the door, but I have to try. I break into a run, intending to swerve around her, but she is ready for me: she grabs my wounded shoulder and wrenches me to the side. I scream so loud it scrapes my throat; I feel like knives are stabbing deeper and deeper into my right side. As I begin to sink to my knees, she kicks me in the stomach and I sprawl across the floor, inhaling dust.

That, I realize as I clutch my stomach, is exactly what I would have done if I had been in her position. Which means that in order to defeat her, I have to think of a way to defeat myself. And how can I be a better fighter than myself, if she knows the same strategies I know, and is exactly as resourceful and clever as I am?

She starts toward me again, so I scramble to my feet and try to put aside the pain in my shoulder. My heart beats faster. I want to punch her, but she gets there first. I duck at the last second, and her fist hits my ear, knocking me off balance.

I back up a few steps, hoping that she won't pursue me, but she does. She comes at me again, this time seizing my shoulders and pulling me down, toward her bent knee.

I put my hands up, between my stomach and her knee, and push as hard as I can. She was not expecting that; she stumbles back, but doesn't fall.

I run at her, and as the desire to kick her slips into my mind, I realize that it is also *her* desire. I twist away from her foot.

The second I want something, she also wants it. She and I can only be, at best, at a standstill—but I need to *beat* her to get through the door. To survive.

I try to think it through, but she is coming at me again, her forehead tightened into a scowl of concentration. She grabs my arm, and I grab hers, so that we are clutched forearm to forearm.

At the same time, we yank our elbows back and thrust them forward. I lean in at the last second, and my elbow smashes into her teeth.

Both of us cry out. Blood spills over her lip, and runs down my forearm. She grits her teeth and yells, diving at me, stronger than I anticipated.

Her weight knocks me down. She pins me to the floor with her knees and tries to punch my face, but I cross my arms in front of me. Her fists hit my arms instead, each one like a stone striking my skin.

With a heavy exhale, I grab at one of her wrists, and I notice that spots are dancing at the corners of my eyes. *Poison.*

Focus.

As she struggles to free herself, I bring my knee up to my chest. Then I push her back, grunting with effort, until I can press my foot to her stomach. I kick her, my face boiling hot.

The logical puzzle: In a fight between two perfect equals, how can one win?

The answer: One can't.

She pushes herself to her feet and wipes the blood from her lip.

Therefore: we must not be perfectly equal. So what is different about us?

She walks toward me again, but I need more time to think, so for every step she takes forward, I take back. The room sways, and then twists, and I lurch to the side, brushing my fingertips on the ground to steady myself.

What is different about us? We have the same mass, skill level, patterns of thinking . . .

I see the door over her shoulder, and I realize: We have different goals. I *have* to get through that door. She has to protect it. But even in a simulation, there is no way she is as desperate as I am.

I sprint toward the edge of the circle, where there is a table. A moment ago, it was empty, but I know the rules of simulations and how to control them. A gun appears on it as soon as I think it.

I slam into the table, the spots crowding my view of it. I don't even feel pain when I collide with it. I feel my heartbeat in my face, like my heart has detached from its moorings in my chest and begun to migrate to my brain.

Across the room, a gun appears on the ground before my double. We both reach for our weapons.

I feel the weight of the gun, and its smoothness, and I forget about her; I forget about the poison; I forget about everything.

My throat constricts, and I feel like there is a hand around it, tightening. My head throbs from the sudden loss of air, and I feel my heart-beat everywhere, everywhere.

Across the room, it's no longer my double who stands between me and my goal; it's Will. *No, no.* It can't be Will. I force myself to breathe in. The poison is cutting off oxygen to my brain. He is just a hallucination within a simulation. I exhale in a sob.

For a moment I see my double again, holding the gun but visibly shuddering, the weapon as far out from her body as she can possibly hold it. She is as weak as I am. No, not as weak, because she is not going blind and losing air, but almost as weak, almost.

Then Will is back, his eyes simulation-dead, his hair a yellow halo around his head. Brick buildings loom from each side, but behind him is the door, the door that separates me from my father and brother.

No, no, it is the door that separates me from Jeanine and my goal.

I have to get through that door. I *have to.*

I lift the gun, though it hurts my shoulder to do it, and wrap one hand around the other to steady it.

"I . . ." I choke, and tears smear my cheeks, run into my mouth. I taste salt. "I'm sorry."

And I do the one thing my double is unable to do, because she is not desperate enough:

I fire.

CHAPTER
FORTY-FIVE

I DON'T SEE him die again.

I close my eyes at the moment the trigger presses back, and when I open them, it is the other Tris who lies on the ground between the dark patches in my vision; it is me.

I drop the gun and sprint toward the door, almost tripping over her. I throw my body against the door, twist the handle, and fall through. My hands numb, I press it closed behind me, and shake them to regain feeling.

The next room is twice as big as the first one, and it, too, is blue-lit, but paler. A large table stands in the middle, and taped to the walls are photographs, diagrams, and lists.

I take deep breaths, and my vision begins to clear, my heart rate returning to normal. Among the photographs on the walls, I recognize my own face, and Tobias's, and Marcus's, and Uriah's. A long list of what appear to be chemicals is posted on the wall beside our pictures. Each one is crossed out with red marker. This must be where Jeanine develops the simulation serums.

I hear voices somewhere ahead of me, and scold myself. *What are you doing? Hurry!*

"My brother's name," I hear. "I want to hear you say it."

Tori's voice.

How did she get through that simulation? Is she Divergent too?

"I didn't kill him." Jeanine's voice.

"Do you think that exonerates you? Do you think that means you don't deserve to die?"

Tori is not screaming, but wailing, the whole of her grief escaping through her mouth. I start toward the door. Too quickly, though, because my hip slams into the corner of the table in the middle of the room, and I have to stop, wincing.

"The reasons for my actions are beyond your understanding," Jeanine says. "I was willing to make a sacrifice for the greater good, something you have never understood, not even when we were classmates!"

I limp toward the door, which is a pane of frosted glass. It slides back to admit me, and I see Jeanine, pressed against a wall, with Tori standing a few feet away, her gun high.

Behind them is a glass table with a silver box on it—a computer—and a keyboard. The entire far wall is covered with a computer screen.

Jeanine stares at me, but Tori doesn't move an inch; doesn't seem to hear me. Her face is red and tear-streaked, her hand shaking.

I have no confidence that I can find the video file on my own. If Jeanine is here, I can get her to find it for me, but if she's dead . . .

"No!" I scream. "Tori, don't!"

But her finger is already over the trigger. I launch myself at her as hard as I can, my arms slamming into her side. The gun goes off, and I hear a scream.

My head hits the tile. I ignore the stars in my eyes and throw myself across Tori. I shove the gun forward and it slides away from us.

Why didn't you grab it, you idiot?!

Tori's fist connects with the side of my throat. I choke, and she uses the opportunity to throw me off, to crawl toward the gun.

Jeanine is slumped against the wall, blood soaking her leg. *Leg!* I remember, and punch Tori hard near the bullet wound in her thigh. She yells, and I find my feet.

I step toward the fallen weapon, but Tori is too quick. She wraps her arms around my legs and pulls them out from under me. My knees slam into the ground, but I am still above her; I punch down, at her rib cage.

She groans, but it doesn't stop her; as I drag myself toward the gun, she sinks her teeth into my hand. It is a different pain than any blow I've ever received, different even from a bullet wound. I scream louder than I thought possible, tears blurring my vision.

I have not come this far to let Tori shoot Jeanine before I've gotten what I need.

I yank my hand from between her teeth, my vision going black at the edges, and with a lurch, smack my hand around the handle of the gun. I twist, and point it at Tori.

My hand. My hand is covered in blood, and so is Tori's chin. I hide my hand from view so that it's easier to ignore the pain and get up, still pointing the gun at her.

"I didn't take you for a traitor, Tris," she says, and it sounds like a snarl, not a sound any human can make.

"I'm not," I say. I blink the tears down my cheeks so that I can see her better. "I can't explain it right now, but . . . all I'm asking is for you to trust me, please. There's something important, something only she knows the location of—"

"That's right!" says Jeanine. "It is on *that* computer, Beatrice, and only I can locate it. If you don't help me survive this, it will die with me."

"She is a liar," says Tori. "A *liar*, and if you believe her, you are both an idiot and a traitor, Tris!"

"I do believe her," I say. "I believe her because it makes perfect sense! The most sensitive information that exists and it's hidden on *that computer*, Tori!" I take a deep breath, and lower my voice. "Please listen to me. I hate her as much as you do. I have no reason to defend her. I'm telling you the truth. This is important."

Tori is silent. I think, for a moment, that I've won, that I've persuaded her. But then she says, "Nothing is more important than her death."

"If that's what you insist upon believing," I say, "I can't help you. But I'm also not going to let you kill her."

Tori pushes herself to her knees, and wipes my blood from her chin. She looks up into my eyes.

"I am a Dauntless leader," she says. "You don't get to decide what I do."

And before I can think—

Before I can even think about firing the gun I'm holding—

She draws a long knife from the side of her boot, lunges, and stabs Jeanine in the stomach.

I yell. Jeanine releases a horrible sound—a gurgling, screaming, dying sound. I see Tori's gritted teeth, I hear her murmur her brother's name—"George Wu"—and then I watch the knife go in again.

And Jeanine's eyes turn into glass.

CHAPTER
FORTY-SIX

TORI STANDS, A wild look in her eyes, and turns toward me.

I feel numb.

All the risks I took to get here—conspiring with Marcus, asking the Erudite for help, crawling across a ladder three stories up, shooting myself in a simulation—and all the sacrifices I made—my relationship with Tobias, Fernando's life, my standing among the Dauntless—were for nothing.

Nothing.

A moment later, the glass door opens again. Tobias and Uriah storm in as if to fight a battle—Uriah coughing, probably from the poison—but the battle is done. Jeanine is dead, Tori is triumphant, and I am a Dauntless traitor.

Tobias stops in the middle of a step, almost stumbling over his feet, when he sees me. His eyes open wider.

"She is a traitor," says Tori. "She just almost shot me to defend Jeanine."

"What?" says Uriah. "Tris, what's going on? Is she right? Why are you even here?"

But I look only at Tobias. A sliver of hope pierces me, strangely painful, when combined with the guilt I feel for how I deceived him. Tobias is stubborn and proud, but he is mine—maybe he will listen, maybe there's a chance that all I did was not in vain—

"You know why I'm here," I say quietly. "Don't you?"

I hold out Tori's gun. He walks forward, a little unsteady on his feet, and takes it.

"We found Marcus in the next room, caught in a simulation," Tobias says. "You came up here with him."

"Yes, I did," I say, blood from Tori's bite trickling down my arm.

"I trusted you," he says, his body shaking with rage. "I *trusted* you and you abandoned me to work with *him*?"

"No." I shake my head. "He told me something, and everything my brother said, everything Jeanine said while I was in Erudite headquarters, fit perfectly with what he told me. And I wanted—I *needed* to know the truth."

"The truth." He snorts. "You think you learned the *truth* from a liar, a traitor, and a sociopath?"

"The truth?" says Tori. "What are you talking about?"

Tobias and I stare at each other. His blue eyes, usually so thoughtful, are now hard and critical, like they are peeling back layer after layer of me and searching each one.

"I think," I say. I have to pause and take a breath, because I have not convinced him; I have failed, and this is probably the last thing they will let me say before they arrest me.

"I think that *you* are the liar!" I say, my voice quaking. "You tell me you love me, you trust me, you think I'm more perceptive than the average person. And the first second that belief in my perceptiveness, that trust, that *love* is put to the test, it all falls apart." I am crying now, but I am not ashamed of the tears shining on my cheeks or the thickness of my voice. "So you must have lied when you told me all those things . . . you must have, because I can't believe your love is really that feeble."

I step closer to him, so that there are only inches between us, and none of the others can hear me.

"I am still the person who would have died rather than kill you," I say, remembering the attack simulation and the feel of his heartbeat under my hand. "I am exactly who you think I am. And right now, I'm telling you that I know . . . I *know* this information will change everything. Everything we have done, and everything we are about to do."

I stare at him like I can communicate the truth with my eyes, but that is impossible. He looks away, and I'm not sure he even heard what I said.

"Enough of this," says Tori. "Take her downstairs. She will be tried along with all the other war criminals."

Tobias doesn't move. Uriah takes my arm and leads me away from him, through the laboratory, through the room of light, through the blue hallway. Therese of the factionless joins us there, eyeing me curiously.

Once we're in the stairwell, I feel something nudge my side. When I look back, I see a wad of gauze in Uriah's hand. I take it, trying to give him a grateful smile and failing.

As we descend the stairs, I wrap the gauze tightly around my hand, sidestepping bodies without looking at their faces. Uriah takes my elbow to keep me from falling. The gauze wrapping doesn't help with the pain of the bite, but it makes me feel a little better, and so does the fact that Uriah, at least, doesn't seem to hate me.

For the first time the Dauntless's disregard for age does not seem like an opportunity. It seems like the thing that will condemn me. They will not say, *But she's young; she must have been confused.* They will say, *She is an adult, and she made her choice.*

Of course, I agree with them. I did make my choice. I chose my mother and father, and what they fought for.

+ + +

Walking down the stairs is easier than going up. We reach the fifth level before I realize that we're going down to the lobby.

"Give me your gun, Uriah," says Therese. "Someone needs to be able to shoot potential belligerents, and you can't do it if you're keeping her from falling down the stairs."

Uriah surrenders his gun without question. I frown—Therese already *has* a gun, so why did it matter for him to give his? But I don't ask. I am in enough trouble as it is.

We reach the bottom floor and walk past a large meeting room full of people dressed in black and white. I pause for a moment to watch them. Some of them are huddled in small groups, leaning on one another, tears streaking their faces. Others are alone, leaning against walls or sitting in corners, their eyes hollow or staring at something that is far away.

"We had to shoot so many," Uriah mutters, squeezing my arm. "Just to get into the building, we had to."

"I know," I say.

I see Christina's sister and mother clutched together on the right side of the room. And on the left side, a young man with dark hair that gleams in the fluorescent light—Peter. His hand is on the shoulder of a middle-aged woman I recognize as his mother.

"What is he doing here?" I say.

"Little coward came in the aftermath, after all the work was done," Uriah says. "I heard his dad's dead. Looks like his mother's okay, though."

Peter looks over his shoulder, and his gaze meets mine, just for a second. In that second I try to summon some pity for the person who saved my life. But while the hatred I once had for him is gone, I still feel nothing.

"What's the holdup?" demands Therese. "Let's get going."

We walk past the meeting room to the main lobby, where I once embraced Caleb. The giant portrait of Jeanine is in pieces on the floor. The smoke that hovers in the air is condensed around the bookshelves, which are burned to cinders. All the computers are in pieces, strewn across the floor.

Sitting in rows in the center of the room are some of the Erudite who didn't get away, and the Dauntless traitors who survived. I search the faces for anything familiar. I find Caleb near the back, looking dazed. I look away.

"Tris!" I hear. Christina sits near the front, next to Cara, her leg wrapped tightly with fabric. She beckons to me, and I sit down next to her.

"No success?" she says quietly.

I shake my head.

She sighs, and puts her arm around me. The gesture is so comforting I almost start to cry. But Christina and I are not people who cry together; we're people who fight together. So I hold my tears in.

"I saw your mom and your sister in the next room," I say.

"Yeah, me too," she says. "My family is okay."

"Good," I say. "How's your leg?"

"Fine. Cara said it'll be fine; it's not bleeding too much. One of the Erudite nurses stuffed some pain meds and antiseptic and gauze into her pockets before they took her down here, so it doesn't hurt too bad either," she says. Beside her, Cara is examining another Erudite's arm. "Where's Marcus?"

"Dunno," I say. "We had to split up. He should be down here. Unless they killed him or something."

"I wouldn't be that surprised, honestly," she says.

The room is chaotic for a while—people rushing in and rushing out again, our factionless guards trading places, new people in Erudite blue brought to sit among us—but gradually everything gets quieter, and then I see him: Tobias, walking through the stairwell door.

I bite my lip, hard, and try not to think, try not to dwell on the cold feeling that surrounds my chest and the weight that hangs over my head. He hates me. He does not believe me.

Christina clutches me tighter as he walks past us, without even looking at me. I watch him over my shoulder. He stops next to Caleb, grabs his arm, and wrenches him to his feet. Caleb wriggles for a second, but he is not half as strong as Tobias and can't break away.

"What?" Caleb says, panicking. "What do you want?"

"I want you to disarm the security system for Jeanine's laboratory," says Tobias without looking back. "So that the factionless can access her computer."

And destroy it, I think, and if possible, my heart becomes even heavier. Tobias and Caleb disappear into the stairwell again.

Christina slumps against me, and I slump against her, so we hold each other up.

"Jeanine activated all the Dauntless transmitters, you know," Christina says. "One of the factionless groups got ambushed by simulation-controlled Dauntless, coming late from the Abnegation sector about ten minutes ago. I guess the factionless won, though I don't know how you call shooting a bunch of brain-dead people winning."

"Yeah." There isn't much more to say. She seems to realize that.

"What happened after I got shot?" she says.

I describe the blue hallway with two doors, and the simulation that followed, from the moment I recognized the Dauntless training room to the moment I shot myself. I do not tell her about hallucinating Will.

"Wait," she says. "It was a simulation? Without a transmitter?"

I frown. I hadn't bothered to wonder about that. Especially not at the time. "If the laboratory recognizes people, maybe it also knows data about everyone, and can present a corresponding simulated environment depending on your faction."

It doesn't matter, now, to figure out how Jeanine set up the security on her laboratory, of all things. But it feels good to put myself to some use, to think of a new problem to solve now that I have failed to solve the most important one.

Christina sits up straighter. Maybe she feels the same way.

"Or the poison somehow contains a transmitter."

I hadn't thought of that.

"But how did Tori get past it? She's not Divergent."

I tilt my head. "I don't know."

Maybe she is, I think. Her brother was, and after what happened to him, she might never admit it, no matter how accepted it becomes.

People, I have discovered, are layers and layers of secrets. You believe you know them, that you understand them, but their motives are always hidden from you, buried in their own hearts. You will never know them, but sometimes you decide to trust them.

"What do you think they're going to do to us when they find us guilty?" she says after a few minutes of silence have passed.

"Honestly?"

"Does now seem like the time for honesty?"

I look at her from the corner of my eye. "I think they're going to force us to eat lots of cake and then take an unreasonably long nap."

She laughs. I try not to—if I let myself laugh, I'll start to cry, too.

+ + +

I hear a yell, and peer around the crowd to see where it came from.

"Lynn!" The yell came from Uriah. He runs toward the door, where two Dauntless are carrying Lynn in on a makeshift stretcher, made of what looks like a shelf from a bookcase. She is pale—too pale—and her hands are folded over her stomach.

I jump to my feet and start toward her, but a few factionless guns stop me from going much farther. I put up my hands and stand still, watching.

Uriah walks around the crowd of war criminals and points to a severe-looking Erudite woman with gray hair. "You. Come here."

The woman gets to her feet and brushes off her pants. She walks, light-footed, to the edge of the seated crowd and looks expectantly at Uriah.

"You're a doctor, right?" he says.

"I am, yes," she says.

"Then fix her!" He scowls. "She's hurt."

The doctor approaches Lynn and asks the two Dauntless to set her down. They do, and she crouches over the stretcher.

"My dear," she says. "Please remove your hands from your wound."

"I can't," moans Lynn. "It hurts."

"I am aware that it hurts," the doctor says. "But I won't be able to assess your wound if you do not reveal it to me."

Uriah kneels across from the doctor and helps her shift Lynn's hands away from her stomach. The doctor peels Lynn's shirt back from her stomach. The bullet wound itself is just a round, red circle in Lynn's skin, but surrounding it is what looks like a bruise. I have never seen a bruise that dark.

The doctor purses her lips, and I know that Lynn is as good as dead.

"Fix her!" says Uriah. "You can fix her, so do it!"

"On the contrary," the doctor says, looking up at him. "Because you set the hospital floors of this building on fire, I cannot fix her."

"There are other hospitals!" he says, almost shouting. "You can get stuff from there and heal her!"

"Her condition is far too advanced," the doctor says, her voice quiet. "If you had not insisted upon burning everything that came into your path, I could have tried, but as the situation stands, trying would be worthless."

"You shut up!" he says, pointing at the doctor's chest. "I'm not the one who burned your hospital! She's my friend, and I . . . I just . . ."

"Uri," says Lynn. "Shut up. It's too late."

Uriah lets his arms fall to his sides, then reaches for Lynn's hand, his lip quivering.

"I'm her friend too," I say to the factionless pointing guns at me. "Can you at least point guns at me from over there?"

They let me pass, and I run to Lynn's side, holding her free hand, which is sticky with blood. I ignore the gun barrels pointed at my head and focus on Lynn's face, which is now yellowish instead of white.

She doesn't seem to notice me. She focuses on Uriah.

"I'm just glad I didn't die while under the simulation," she says weakly.

"You're not gonna die now," he says.

"Don't be stupid," she says. "Uri, listen. I loved her too. I did."

"You loved who?" he says, his voice breaking.

"Marlene," says Lynn.

"Yeah, we all loved Marlene," he says.

"No, that's not what I mean." She shakes her head. She closes her eyes.

Still, it takes a few minutes before her hand goes limp in mine. I guide it across her stomach, and then take her other hand from Uriah and do the same to it. He wipes his eyes before his tears can fall. Our eyes meet across her body.

"You should tell Shauna," I say. "And Hector."

"Right." He sniffs and presses his palm to Lynn's face. I wonder if her cheek is still warm. I don't want to touch her and find that it's not.

I rise and walk back to Christina.

CHAPTER FORTY-SEVEN

MY MIND KEEPS tugging me toward my memories of Lynn, in an attempt to persuade me that she is actually gone, but I push away the short flashes as they come. Someday I will stop doing that, if I'm not executed as a traitor, or whatever our new leaders have planned. But right now I fight to keep my mind blank, to pretend that this room is all that has ever existed and all that will ever exist. It should not be easy, but it is. I have learned how to fend off grief.

Tori and Harrison come to the lobby after a while, Tori limping toward a chair—I almost forgot about her bullet wound again; she was so nimble when she killed Jeanine—and Harrison following her.

Behind both of them is one of the Dauntless with Jeanine's body slung over his shoulder. He heaves it like a stone on a table in front of the rows of Erudite and Dauntless traitors.

Behind me I hear gasps and mutters, but no sobs. Jeanine was not the kind of leader people cry for.

I stare up at her body, which seems so much smaller in death than it did in life. She is only a few inches taller than I am, her hair only a few shades darker. She looks calm now, almost peaceful. I have trouble connecting this body with the woman I knew, the woman without a conscience.

And even she was more complicated than I thought, keeping a secret that she thought was too terrible to reveal, out of a heinously twisted protective instinct.

Johanna Reyes steps into the lobby, soaked to the bone from all the rain, her red clothes smeared with a darker red. The factionless flank her, but she doesn't appear to notice them or the guns they carry.

"Hello," she says to Harrison and Tori. "What is it that you want?"

"I didn't know the leader of Amity would be so curt," says Tori with a wry smile. "Isn't that against your manifesto?"

"If you were actually familiar with Amity's customs, you would know that they don't have a formal leader," says Johanna, her voice simultaneously gentle and firm. "But I'm not the representative of Amity anymore. I stepped down in order to come here."

"Yeah, I saw you and your little band of peacekeepers, getting in everyone's way," says Tori.

"Yes, that was intentional," Johanna replies. "Since getting in the way meant standing between guns and innocents, and saved a great number of lives."

Color fills her cheeks, and I think it again: that Johanna Reyes might still be beautiful. Except now I think that she isn't just beautiful in spite of the scar, she's somehow beautiful *with* it, like Lynn with her buzzed hair, like Tobias with the memories of his father's cruelty that he wears like armor, like my mother in her plain gray clothing.

"Since you are still so very generous," says Tori, "I wonder if you might carry a message back to the Amity."

"I don't feel comfortable leaving you and your army to dole out justice as you see fit," says Johanna, "but I will certainly send someone else to Amity with a message."

"Fine," says Tori. "Tell them that a new political system will soon be formed that will exclude them from representation. This, we believe, is their just punishment for failing to choose a side in this conflict. They will, of course, be obligated to continue to produce and deliver food to the city, but they will be under supervision by one of the leading factions."

For a second, I think that Johanna might launch herself at Tori and strangle her. But she draws herself up taller and says, "Is that all?"

"Yes."

"Fine," she says. "I'm going to go do something useful. I don't suppose you would allow some of us to come in here and tend to *these* wounded?"

Tori gives her a look.

"I didn't think so," says Johanna. "Do remember, though, that sometimes the people you oppress become mightier than you would like."

She turns and walks out of the lobby.

Something about her words hits me. I am sure she meant them as a threat, and a feeble one, but it rings in my head like it was something more—like she could easily have been talking not about the Amity, but about another oppressed group. The factionless.

And as I look around the room, at every Dauntless soldier and every factionless soldier, I begin to see a pattern.

"Christina," I say. "The factionless have all the guns."

She looks around, and then back at me, frowning.

In my mind I see Therese, taking Uriah's gun when she already had one herself. I see Tobias's mouth pressed into a line when I asked him about the uneasy Dauntless-factionless alliance, holding something back.

Then Evelyn emerges into the lobby, her posture regal, like a queen returning to her kingdom. Tobias does not follow her. *Where is he?*

Evelyn stands behind the table where Jeanine Matthews's body lies. Edward limps into the lobby behind her. Evelyn takes out a gun, points it at the fallen portrait of Jeanine, and fires.

A hush falls over the room. Evelyn drops the gun on the table, next to Jeanine's head.

"Thank you," she says. "I know that you are all wondering what will happen next, so I am here to tell you."

Tori sits up straighter in her chair and leans toward Evelyn, like she wants to say something. But Evelyn pays no attention.

"The faction system that has long supported itself on the backs of discarded human beings will be disbanded at once," says Evelyn. "We know this transition will be difficult for you, but—"

"*We?*" Tori breaks in, looking scandalized. "What are you talking about, disbanded?"

"What I am talking about," says Evelyn, looking at Tori for the first time, "is that your faction, which up until a few weeks ago was clamoring along with the Erudite for the restriction of food and goods to the factionless, a clamor that resulted in the destruction of the Abnegation, will no longer exist."

Evelyn smiles a little.

"And if you decide to take up arms against us," she says, "you will be hard pressed to find any arms to take up."

I watch, then, as each factionless soldier holds up a gun. Factionless are evenly spaced around the edge of the room, and they disappear into one of the stairwells. They have us all surrounded.

It is so elegant, so clever, that I almost laugh.

"I instructed my half of the army to relieve your half of the army of their weapons as soon as their missions were completed," says Evelyn. "I see now that they were successful. I regret the duplicity, but we knew that you have been conditioned to cling to the faction system like it is your own mother, and that we would have to help ease you into this new era."

"*Ease us?*" Tori demands. She pushes herself to her feet and limps toward Evelyn, who calmly takes her gun in hand and points it at Tori.

"I have not been starving for more than a decade just to give in to a Dauntless woman with a leg injury," Evelyn says. "So unless you want me to shoot you, take a seat with your fellow ex-faction members."

I see all the muscles in Evelyn's arm standing at attention, her eyes not cold, not quite like Jeanine's, but calculating, assessing, planning. I don't know how this woman could have ever bent to Marcus's will. She must not have been this woman then, all steel, tested in fire.

Tori stands before Evelyn for a few seconds. She then limps backward, away from the gun and toward the edge of the room.

"Those of you who assisted us in the effort to take down Erudite will be rewarded," says Evelyn. "Those of you who resisted us will be tried and punished according to your crimes." She raises her voice for the last sentence, and I am surprised by how well it carries over the space.

Behind her, the door to the stairwell opens, and Tobias steps out with Marcus and Caleb behind him, almost unnoticed. Almost, except I notice him, because I have trained myself to notice him. I watch his shoes as he comes closer. They are black sneakers with chrome eyelets for the laces. They stop right next to me, and he crouches by my shoulder.

I look at him, expecting to find his eyes cold and unyielding.

But I don't.

Evelyn is still talking, but her voice fades for me.

"You were right," Tobias says quietly, balancing on the balls of his feet. He smiles a little. "I do know who you are. I just needed to be reminded."

I open my mouth, but I don't have anything to say.

Then all the screens in the Erudite lobby—at least those that weren't destroyed in the attack—flicker on, including a projector positioned over the wall where Jeanine's portrait used to be.

Evelyn stops in the middle of whatever sentence she was speaking. Tobias takes my hand and helps me to my feet.

"What is this?" Evelyn demands.

"This," he says, only to me, "is the information that will change everything."

My legs shake with relief and apprehension.

"You did it?" I say.

"*You* did it," he says. "All I did was force Caleb to cooperate."

I throw my arm around his neck, and press my lips to his. He holds my face in both hands and kisses me back. I press into the distance between us until it is gone, crushing the secrets we have kept and the suspicions we have harbored—for good, I hope.

And then I hear a voice.

We pull apart and turn toward the wall, where a woman with short brown hair is projected. She sits at a metal desk with her hands folded, in a location I don't recognize. The background is too dim.

"Hello," she says. "My name is Amanda Ritter. In this file I will tell you only what you need to know. I am the leader of an organization fighting for justice and peace. This fight has become increasingly more important—and consequently, nearly impossible—in the past few decades. That is because of this."

Images flash across the wall, almost too fast for me to see. A man on his knees with a gun pressed to his forehead. The woman pointing it at him, her face emotionless.

From a distance, a small person hanging by the neck from a telephone pole.

A hole in the ground the size of a house, full of bodies.

And there are other images too, but they move faster, so I get only impressions of blood and bone and death and cruelty, empty faces, soulless eyes, terrified eyes.

Just when I have had enough, when I feel like I am going to scream if I see any more, the woman reappears on the screen, behind her desk.

"You do not remember any of that," she says. "But if you are thinking these are the actions of a terrorist group or a tyrannical government regime, you are only partially correct. Half of the people in those pictures, committing those terrible acts, were your neighbors. Your relatives. Your coworkers. The battle we are fighting is not against a particular group. It is against human nature itself—or at least what it has become."

This is what Jeanine was willing to enslave minds and murder people for—to keep us all from knowing. To keep us all ignorant and safe and *inside the fence.*

There is a part of me that understands.

"That is why you are so important," Amanda says. "Our struggle against violence and cruelty is only treating the symptoms of a disease, not curing it. *You* are the cure.

"In order to keep you safe, we devised a way for you to be separated from us. From our water supply. From our technology. From our societal structure. We have formed your society in a particular way in the hope that you will rediscover the moral sense most of us have lost. Over time, we hope that you will begin to change as most of us cannot.

"The reason I am leaving this footage for you is so that you will know when it's time to help us. You will know that it is time when there are many among you whose minds appear to be more flexible than the others. The name you should give those people is Divergent. Once they become abundant among you, your leaders should give the command for

Amity to unlock the gate forever, so that you may emerge from your isolation."

And that is what my parents wanted to do: to take what we had learned and use it to help others. Abnegation to the end.

"The information in this video is to be restricted to those in government only," Amanda says. "You are to be a clean slate. But do not forget us."

She smiles a little.

"I am about to join your number," she says. "Like the rest of you, I will voluntarily forget my name, my family, and my home. I will take on a new identity, with false memories and a false history. But so that you know the information I have provided you with is accurate, I will tell you the name I am about to take as my own."

Her smile broadens, and for a moment, I feel that I recognize her.

"My name will be Edith Prior," she says. "And there is much I am happy to forget."

Prior.

The video stops. The projector glows blue against the wall. I clutch Tobias's hand, and there is a moment of silence like a withheld breath.

Then the shouting begins.

ACKNOWLEDGMENTS

Thank you, God, for keeping your promises.

Thank you:

Nelson, beta reader, tireless supporter, photographer, best friend, and most importantly, husband. . . . I think the Beach Boys said it best: God only knows what I'd be without you.

Joanna Volpe, I could not ask for a better agent or friend. Molly O'Neill, my editor of wonder, for your tireless work on this book in all arenas. Katherine Tegen, for being kind and discerning, and the whole KT Books crew, for your support.

Susan Jeffers, Andrea Curley, and the illustrious Brenna Franzitta, for watching my words; Joel Tippie and Amy Ryan, for making this book so beautiful; and Jean McGinley and Alpha Wong, for extending the reach of these books farther than I ever expected. Jessica Berg, Suzanne Daghlian, Barb Fitzsimmons, Lauren Flower, Kate Jackson, Susan Katz, Alison Lisnow, Casey McIntyre, Diane Naughton, Colleen O'Connell, Aubrey Parks-Fried, Andrea Pappenheimer, Shayna Ramos, Patty Rosati, Sandee Roston, Jenny Sheridan, Megan Sugrue, Molly Thomas, and Allison Verost, as well as everyone in audio, design, finance, international sales, inventory, legal, managing editorial, marketing, online marketing, publicity, production, sales, school and library marketing, special sales, and subrights at HarperCollins, for doing such fantastic work in the world of books as well as *my* world of books.

All the teachers, librarians, and booksellers who have supported my books with so much enthusiasm. Book bloggers, reviewers, and readers of all ages and varieties and countries of origin. I'm probably biased, but I think I have the best readers ever.

Lara Ehrlich, for much writing wisdom. My writer friends—listing all of the people in the writer community who have been kind to me would take multiple pages, but I could not ask for better peers. Alice, Mary Katherine, Mallory, and Danielle—what fantastic friends I have.

Nancy Coffey, for your eyes and your wisdom. Pouya Shahbazian and Steve Younger, my fantastic film team; and Summit Entertainment, Red Wagon, and Evan Daugherty, for wanting to live in this world I made.

My family: My incredible mother-slash-psychologist-slash-cheerleader, Frank Sr., Karl, Ingrid, Frank Jr., Candice, McCall, and Dave. You are incredible people and I am so glad I have you.

Beth and Darby, who have won me more readers than I can possibly count through charm and sheer determination; and Chase-baci and

Sha-neni, who took such good care of us in Romania. Also Roger, Trevor, Tyler, Rachel, Fred, Billie, and Granny, for so effortlessly embracing me as one of you.

Multumesc/Köszönöm to Cluj-Napoca/Kolozsvár, for all the inspiration and the dear friends I left there—but not forever.

ABOUT THE AUTHOR

© Nelson Fitch

Veronica Roth is the *New York Times* bestselling author of **DIVERGENT** and **INSURGENT,** the first two books in a trilogy she began writing while still a college student. Now a full-time writer, Ms. Roth and her husband call the Chicago area home.